END GAMES

The Twelfth Book of the
Imager Portfolio

L. E. MODESITT, JR.

TOR®
fantasy

A TOM DOHERTY ASSOCIATES BOOK
NEW YORK

This is a work of fiction. All of the characters, organizations, and events portrayed in this novel are either products of the author's imagination or are used fictitiously.

ENDGAMES

Copyright © 2019 by Modesitt Family Revocable Living Trust

All rights reserved.

Map by Jon Lansberg

A Tor Book
Published by Tom Doherty Associates
120 Broadway
New York, NY 10271

www.tor-forge.com

Tor® is a registered trademark of Macmillan Publishing Group, LLC.

ISBN 978-1-250-29365-7

Our books may be purchased in bulk for promotional, educational, or business use. Please contact your local bookseller or the Macmillan Corporate and Premium Sales Department at 1-800-221-7945, extension 5442, or by email at MacmillanSpecialMarkets@macmillan.com.

First Edition: February 2019
First Mass Market Edition: February 2020

Printed in the United States of America

0 9 8 7 6 5 4

For Emma, who knows the distances

CHARACTERS

- **REGIAL FAMILY**

CHARYN D'REX   Rex of Solidar

CHELIA D'LORIEN   Charyn's mother, widow of Rex Lorien

BHAYRN D'LORIEN   Brother of Charyn

ALORYANA D'LORIEN   Imager and sister of Charyn

- **HIGH HOLDERS**

ALMEIDA D'ALTE   L'Excelsis

AISHFORD D'ALTE   Nordeau

BASALYT D'ALTE   Bartolan, High Councilor

CALKORAN D'ALTE   Vaestora, High Councilor

CHAELTAR D'ALTE   Estisle, High Councilor

DELCOEUR D'ALTE [FERRAND]   L'Excelsis

FHAEDYRK D'ALTE   Dyrkholm, Head, High Holders' Council

FHERNON D'ALTE   L'Excelsis

GHASPHAR D'ALTE   Nacliano

HAEBYN D'ALTE   Piedryn

KHUNTHAN D'ALTE   Eshtora, High Councilor

LAEVORYN D'ALTE   L'Excelsis

LAASTYN D'ALTE   Charpen

MOERYN D'ALTE   Khelgror

MEINYT D'ALTE   Alkyra

NACRYON D'ALTE   Mantes

NUALT D'ALTE   Barna

OLEFSYRT D'ALTE   Noira

OSKARYN D'ALTE   Cloisonyt

PAELLYT D'ALTE   Sommeil

PLESSAN D'ALTE   L'Excelsis

REGIAL D'ALTE   Montagne, minor son of Ryentar, Charyn's deceased uncle
RUELYR D'ALTE   Ruile
RYEL D'ALTE   Karyel, minor nephew of Chelia, his guardian
SAEFFEN D'ALTE   L'Excelsis
SHENDAEL D'ALTE   L'Excelsis
SOUVEN D'ALTE   Dueraan
STAENDEN D'ALTE   Tacqueville
THYSOR D'ALTE   Extela
THURL D'ALTE   Extela
VAUN D'ALTE   Tilbora
ZAERLYN D'ALTE   Rivages, brother of Maitre Alyna

• IMAGERS

ALASTAR   Maitre D'Image
ALYNA   Maitre D'Image, wife of Alastar
BELSIOR   Maitre D'Structure
CHARLINA   Maitre D'Structure
GAELLEN   Maitre D'Structure, healer
HOWAL   Maitre D'Aspect
KAYLET   Maitre D'Aspect, assistant stablemaster
LHENDYR   Maitre D'Aspect
LYSTARA   Maitre D'Aspect, daughter of Alastar and Alyna
MALYNA   Maitre D'Aspect, niece of Alyna
THELIA   Maitre D'Aspect, Collegium bookkeeper
YULLA   Maitre D'Aspect
ISKHAR   Chorister of the Collegium
ARION   Maitre D'Esprit, Maitre of Westisle Collegium
SELIORA   Maitre D'Structure, Westisle, wife of Arion
LYNZIA   Maitre D'Aspect, Westisle
TAUREK   Maitre D'Structure, Maitre of Estisle Collegium
CELIENA   Maitre D'Structure, Estisle

- **FACTORS**

CUIPRYN D'FACTORIUS Brass/copper

ELTHYRD D'FACTORIUS Timber, lumber, Chief, Factors' Council, L'Excelsis

ESHMAEL D'FACTORIUS Cloth and ceramics

ESTAFEN D'FACTORIUS Banque D'Excelsis, ironworks

HARLL D'FACTORIUS Brick and stone, Factors' Council, Montagne

HISARIO D'FACTORIUS Shipping, Factors' Council, Liantiago

JHALIOST D'FACTORIUS Salt, coal, Factors' Council, Khelghor

KARL D'FACTORIUS Coal, mining

KATHILA D'FACTORIA Spices, scents, and oils

LYTHORYN D'FACTORIUS Mining, custom minting

ROBLEN D'FACTORIUS Woolens and cloth

PAERSYT D'FACTORIUS Custom forging

THALMYN D'FACTORIUS Fishing, Factors' Council, Tilbora

WALLTYL D'FACTORIUS Coaches, carriages, wagons

WEEZYR D'FACTORIUS Banque D'Aluse

- **GUILDERS**

GASSEL Master Stonemason

ARGENTYL Master Silversmith, head of Metalworkers' Guild

- **OTHERS**

VAELLN D'CORPS Marshal of the Army

MAUREK D'CORPS Vice-Marshal

TYNAN D'NAVIA Sea Marshal

CHAALT D'CORPS Commander, Chief of Staff

LUERRYN D'CORPS Subcommander

AEVIDYR D'SOLIDAR Minister of Administration

ALUCAR D'SOLIDAR Minister of Finance

SANAFRYT D'SOLIDAR Minister of Justice

REFAAL D'ANOMEN Chorister, Anomen D'Excelsis

SAERLET D'ANOMEN Chorister, Anomen D'Rex

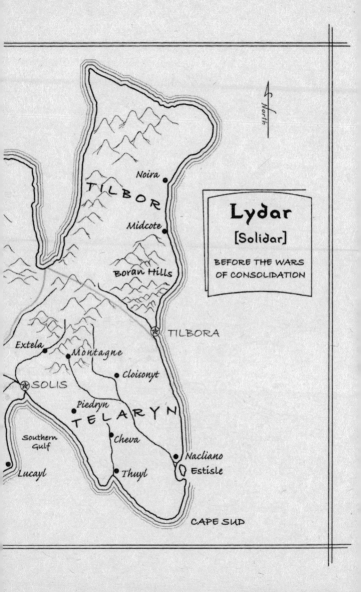

North

Lydar
[Solidar]

BEFORE THE WARS
OF CONSOLIDATION

TILBOR

Noira

Midcote

Boran Hills

Extela

Montagne

⊛ TILBORA

Cloisonyt

⊛ SOLIS

Piedryn

TELARYN

Southern
Gulf

Cheva

Nacliano

Lucayl

Thuyl

Estisle

CAPE SUD

END GAMES

PROLOGUE

At a quint past seventh glass, on the last night of Avryl, Charyn stood at the window and looked out into the twilight sky, his eyes taking in the golden half orb of Artiema nearly overhead, and the nearly full small disc of Erion. *The hunter pursuing the goddess of life and love.*

With a wry smile, he turned and departed the Rex's sitting room, walking along the south corridor and across the landing at the top of the grand staircase and then into the small sitting room that adjoined the grand ballroom. He wore the close-fitting jacket of regial green, trimmed in silver, with silver buckles, a pale green shirt and black cravat, and black trousers. His belt was black and matched his highly polished black dress boots. None of that felt strange. He'd worn the same clothing to balls for years. The difference from what he'd worn to the Year-Turn Ball two months earlier was the addition of the gold-edged deep green formal sash that signified he was the Rex Regis of Solidar.

In less than half a glass *he* would be presiding over the Spring-Turn Ball, rather than his father. He still had trouble at times believing his father was dead, shot by an assassin at the end of the Year-Turn Ball, all the result of a plot by Charyn's own, and now-dead, uncle.

Because Charyn was unmarried, he would escort his mother Chelia into the ball, but that presented a problem for Charyn regarding his younger brother Bhayrn, also unmarried, because Bhayrn had no one to escort, since Charyn and Bhayrn's younger sister Aloryana had turned out to be an imager. Including her under the circumstances of the past few months would have been seen as too great a break with tradition at present, and not having another member of the regial family would have openly revealed how few regials there remained. For that reason, Charyn and Chelia had come up with the alternative of including Charyn's distant cousin Malyna in the family party. Although Malyna was a junior imager maitre, she had been the one to save Charyn and the rest of the regial family from the assassins. Also, since she was an imager, Charyn could not marry her, but as both a heroine and the daughter of a distinguished High Holder, her presence with the diminished regial family would create no rumors about marriage while suggesting that Charyn intended to maintain strong ties with both High Holders and the Collegium Imago.

At least, that's the hope, thought Charyn, as he closed the sitting room door and looked to where his brother stood beside one of the chairs, glowering, and then to his mother, who wore a gown of regial green trimmed in black.

"You look very regial," observed Chelia.

"He should," said Bhayrn sourly, walking to the sideboard that did not contain refreshments. "He's the Rex."

"Bhayrn," said Chelia firmly, but not loudly.

"I know. I know. It's just that I'm not looking forward to being inspected like a bargain bull, the one some High Holder's daughter will settle for if she can't land Charyn."

"Do you think it's going to be any better for Charyn?" asked Chelia. "Any woman in her right mind is going to be wary of marrying into this family—unless she or her family are desperate. Or unless she's truly in love with either of you."

"You make us sound like—"

"Like we are?" replied Chelia. "Aren't we? Just remember. At the last ball you were complaining that no one would pay you any attention at all."

"It's . . . never mind." Bhayrn flushed and looked away.

Charyn decided to say nothing, although he definitely understood Bhayrn's feelings, particularly since he'd had to accept the fact that he, in many ways, was more constrained by his position than was his brother. Were he Bhayrn, Charyn could have married Palenya, although it would have raised eyebrows and caused a minor scandal. Instead, she was now the musician for the Collegium, with a comfortable stipend as well. That had been all that Charyn had been able to do for all she had given him. *Rather . . . all she would accept.*

Charyn shook his head. For the coming two glasses, he would need to dance with eligible High Holders' daughters, as well as a few other women, all of them far older than he, as well as be cheerful, warm, and welcoming to all those at the ball.

Just before half past the glass, the door to the sitting room opened, and Malyna entered, wearing the same gown she had worn at the Year-Turn Ball, high-necked and of a deep teal that fringed on the regial colors, confirming her relationship to the regial line. The imager maitre was barely twenty, almost petite, if too trimly muscular for that, and half a head shorter than Charyn. Her skin was a light almost unnoticeable honeyed brown, a reminder of the Pharsi forebears in both her lineage and Charyn's. Intent black eyes fixed squarely on Charyn as she stopped a yard or so away and offered the slightest of curtseys and said, "Good evening, Rex Charyn, Lady Chelia, Lord Bhayrn."

"Good evening, Malyna," replied Chelia warmly. "It's good to see you again. I hope you can enjoy this ball."

Malyna smiled in return. "I'd like to . . . very much."

With Malyna's entrance, Charyn realized again how much he missed Aloryana. *You need to visit the Collegium before long.*

"How is Aloryana?" asked Chelia.

"She's doing well. I understand she might be a third by fall if she keeps up the way she's been doing, almost certainly by year end. She and Lystara are getting along well." A hint of a grin crossed her lips. "I've enjoyed watching them."

"You mean that Aloryana is acting the way Lystara did toward you when you lived in the Maitre's house?" asked Chelia.

"There are similarities."

Charyn found himself smiling as he listened.

Before all that long, or so it seemed, the chimes sounded eighth glass, and Charyn looked to Chelia. "It's time."

Within moments, Bhayrn led the way into the ballroom, escorting Malyna, while Charyn followed with his mother. Immediately, the players began the "Processional of the Rex."

Ahead of them, Bhayrn and Malyna took a position before the dais on which the musicians were seated, just to the left of the center. Charyn and Chelia took their place to the right. Charyn remembered to gesture, and a brief fanfare followed.

"Maitre Alastar D'Image, Maitre Alyna D'Image," announced the Chateau herald.

Charyn watched as the pair who ruled the Collegium Imago approached him and the small regial group. Alastar's once-silver-gray hair was even more streaked with white. Beside him walked Maitre Alyna, a good head shorter than her husband, an older version of Malyna, unsurprisingly, given that she was the younger maitre's aunt. Both inclined their heads slightly. Charyn responded with an equal nod. Then the two maitres took a position a yard or so to Chelia's left.

Then came the High Councilors, followed by the members of the Factors' Council of Solidar. Once the last of the factor councilors had been announced, the orchestra began to play, and Charyn turned to his mother, took her hand, and began the dance. Behind them, Bhayrn danced with Malyna.

"You know, I never danced with Palenya," said Charyn, to the only person to whom he could safely have said that.

"You miss her, I know, but you'll find someone, and a ball is a good place to start looking. Just don't stop looking until you find someone whose presence and love is strong enough. Give it time. Even if you find the right woman tonight, you won't be ready to commit to her for a very long time . . . and you shouldn't." Chelia smiled. "That's all I'll say about that."

"For now, that is." Charyn gave a warm but sardonic smile.

"Of course."

After the very short first dance ended, Charyn guided his mother to Bhayrn for the younger man's dance with her. Then Charyn turned to Malyna. "Might I have the next dance?"

"You might."

As they moved across the polished floor, he said, "I see that two of your uncles are here. Did Maitre Alastar have anything to do with that? Or your father?"

"Are you asking me to divulge family secrets?"

"Only if you're willing. Besides . . ." Charyn let the words hang.

"You'll assume they did." Malyna finished the thought. "With reason. Father doesn't like to come to L'Excelsis, but he and Maitre Alastar did prevail on Uncle Calkoran to accept the position as High Councilor. I think all that they had to do was ask him if he wanted another member of the Council like your late uncle." Malyna smiled sweetly.

"I have to admit your uncles have a better record than mine—on either side." Charyn didn't even have to mention Ryentar, his father's brother, who had willingly been the figurehead for the last High Holders' revolt. "But then, that's why I've relied on you and your family. What other advice might you have for me?"

"One advises the Rex with great care, I've been told."

"Since you saved my life, you needn't be so careful."

"What if I choose to be?"

"That's a good question, and I won't press you."

"I told you before that if you could not change the times,

you needed to change yourself. You've apparently done some of each. It still might not be enough."

"My late uncle Ryel made me well aware of that. The question is how much do I need to change."

"You'd know more of that than I. And, no, that's not an equivocation or evasion."

"From you . . . I'll accept such an answer. And from my mother, and Aloryana."

"You miss Palenya, don't you?"

That surprised Charyn. In all the time Malyna had stayed at the Chateau, she'd never mentioned Palenya except in Palenya's capacity as Chateau musician. "Why do you say that?"

"Because it's true."

"It's that obvious?"

Malyna shook her head. "I've talked to her. She worries about you."

"She always did."

"Then don't make her worry more. She knows it wouldn't have worked, even if she had been able to have children."

"She told you to say that?" asked Charyn wryly.

"Not in quite those words, but yes."

"It appears that all the women who are family," *or were that close in another way,* "have decided the course of my marital future."

"Who else would care as much for you, and not just because Solidar desperately needs an heir?"

"From you, I especially appreciate that." Since Charyn really didn't want to make small talk, he just enjoyed dancing the last moments of the first melody. Then, he guided Malyna to the dais, where, not totally surprisingly, Ferron D'Fhernon-Alte waited.

The young High Holder heir inclined his head. "Rex Charyn, if I might ask Maitre Malyna for a dance?"

"You need only her permission, Ferron."

"I'd be happy to accept, Ferron," said Malyna.

Charyn did not shake his head, although he had hoped Ferron would not pursue Malyna, since it would lead only to his heartbreak. He turned, looking for another partner, one who would be pleasant, but not emotionally taxing.

Charyn moved away from the dais and his family toward the nearest young woman whose name he knew, stopping short of her father. "Good evening, High Holder Taulyn."

"Good evening, Rex Charyn."

Charyn turned. "Mistress Diasyra, might I have the pleasure of the next dance?"

"I'd be honored, Lord Charyn." Her voice was more assured than it had been at the previous ball.

Charyn inclined his head, then eased Diasyra out onto the dancing area. "Did you enjoy the last ball?"

Her first response was a slightly flustered smile. "I did, but I don't remember that much, except that I danced with you. I hope I wasn't an embarrassment."

"You danced well, better than many. I didn't tell you that, because I feared you might take it as undeserved flattery. Do you remember if your feet were sore?"

"I don't." Her smile was warmer, more assured, and Charyn found it hard to believe that she was only a few years older than Aloryana, given that Diasyra had been very much unsure of herself just two months earlier.

"Your family has a place somewhere near, as I recall, but I don't remember where."

"It's about sixteen milles north of here, on the west side of the Aluse."

"Do you still enjoy riding?"

"I do, especially early in the day . . ."

Charyn just listened, prompting her occasionally and enjoying the dance, as he knew he would.

After that dance ended, Charyn decided to look for Alyncya D'Shendael, wondering what she might be wearing. He hoped it wasn't the crimson she'd worn to the first Year-Turn Ball at which he'd noticed her, but would it be peach like the last ball . . . or green . . . ?

As he made his way along the side of the ballroom, he couldn't help but wonder why he just hadn't kept asking others to dance, rather than seeking out Alyncya so soon. *Because you recall Alyncya so favorably, and you want to test that recollection before you dance with any others.* Diasyra didn't count, because she was too young and far too sweet. That might change in time, but a match with someone that sweet wouldn't be good for either of them.

At that moment, High Holder Fhaedyrk, the head of the High Holders' Council, eased up to Charyn. "Your Grace."

"Good evening."

"I would not trouble you at a ball, not normally, but I've heard a disturbing rumor, and since it will be nearly three weeks before the next Council meeting . . ."

Charyn managed a smile. "And since you would prefer not to announce that you have a concern, especially if it is unfounded, you'd like to bring it to me quietly."

"Of course." Fhaedyrk smiled warmly.

Charyn nodded for the High Holder to continue.

"The councils agreed with your proposal for a modest increase in tariffs. Now, it has been brought to my attention that your Minister of Finance is reviewing all the tariff records, and, in some cases, increasing the assessment and tariff due, which will be effective with those tariffs paid this coming Feuillyt. If true, this would seem, to some, as just another way of increasing tariffs."

"I have directed Minister Alucar to begin a review of all tariff assessments." Charyn held up a hand to forestall any immediate objection. "There has not been such a review in more than a decade, possibly longer. The review works both ways. High Holders whose lands and other holdings have lessened have seen their assessments decrease; those who have increased their holdings will see an increase. Others will see no change. It's a very time-consuming process. So far, we've only reviewed some thirty holdings. Twenty-three have seen no change. Five have seen increases, two decreases."

Fhaedyrk frowned. "That's more than twice as many increases as decreases."

Charyn laughed softly. "There's a good reason for that. When High Holders have to sell lands, they're more likely to report the sale because it reduces their annual tariff. When they buy or otherwise obtain more holdings, they tend to leave it to the Finance Ministry to discover."

"I can see that, Your Grace, but some High Holders will not be pleased."

"I am trying to be fair," Charyn replied. "If tariffs are not adjusted, the High Holders who do not report their gains are paying less in tariffs for each hectare of land than those whose assessments are accurate."

"I cannot gainsay that, Your Grace."

"Also, we are not increasing tariffs without sending a notification of our findings to each High Holder. In one case, for example, the High Holder showed us that he had not held the increased holdings but gifted them to his daughter as dowry. We changed the assessment to reflect that."

"You are notifying everyone who might be affected and telling them why and how it's being done?"

"We are. The process will likely take several years." Charyn smiled wryly. "As a matter of fact, it's likely to be continuous, because by the time we finish reviewing the more than fifteen hundred High Holders, enough time will have passed that it will be time for another review."

"At least you're not rushing through it."

"We are trying to be fair."

"I can accept that, Your Grace. I fear there will be some who do not, but I think most will accept the need and the fact that you are notifying and offering a chance for them to contest anything they believe unfair. That is a welcome change. I will not trouble you more this evening." Fhaedyrk inclined his head.

Charyn managed not to shake his head. He'd known that the reassessment would ruffle some feathers, but it had seemed to him that he and Alucar were being as fair as possible.

With a wry smile, he continued to survey the dancers.

Abruptly, he caught sight of his cousin Ferrand, officially now High Holder Delcoeur. With him was a young woman he didn't recognize, although he was certain it wasn't Ferrand's younger sister. With a smile he moved toward Ferrand. "I'm glad you're here."

"I'm glad to be here." Ferrand half-turned, nodding to the brown-haired, gray-eyed young woman. "Faerlyna, I'd like to present you to my cousin, Rex Charyn. Charyn, Faerlyna D'Kastyl."

"I'm honored, Your Grace." Faerlyna lowered her eyes.

"And I'm pleased that you're here and enjoying the ball with Ferrand. He's my favorite cousin, well, along with his sisters." Charyn smiled warmly. That statement was definitely true, given who his other cousins happened to be. "I won't keep you two."

He turned and moved away, hoping his words would help Ferrand, who definitely needed it, given all the troubles he faced.

The dance was ending when he finally located the sandy-haired and hazel-eyed Alyncya, who was conversing with her father and another man of indeterminate age. Rather than ask her for what was bound to be a short time and knowing that, by custom, asking her for more than two dances implied an interest he definitely did not wish to announce publicly, he waited for the first note played by the orchestra for the next dance before moving forward.

"Again . . . you look lovely," he offered. "Might I have this dance?" After inclining his head to High Holder Shendael, who nodded, if not necessarily enthusiastically, Charyn returned his attention completely to Alyncya.

"You might, Rex Charyn."

As the music rose and he guided her away from her father, he said, "As I told you in Finitas, I prefer you in the peach, rather than the crimson."

Alyncya smiled, with a hint of mischief in the expression. "I remembered that . . . and I didn't have to refresh my memory by studying a list."

"You think I did?" He shook his head. "Not this time."

"That's an admission that you did the last time."

"I did indeed, but I told you so."

"You're still working to turn my head with your diligence."

"You don't think you're worth that diligence?"

"I certainly wouldn't want to be thought a duty of some sort." Her tone was amused. "Duties turn into bothersome chores."

This time Charyn did grin at the way she'd turned his own words on him. "You're even more dangerous than I recalled, Mistress Alyncya."

"And you have become more formidable."

"Formidable? That's truly a terrible word to apply when I'm trying to get to know you better."

"For what purpose, my lord?"

"Any honest answer I give to that question would be misconstrued."

"I can't believe that, as Rex, you haven't given answers of another variety on at least a few occasions."

"So far, I believe I've managed to avoid that variety." His smile turned rueful. "There are some questions I've declined to answer."

"Better to defer than deceive?"

"The problem with that, alas, is that some take deferral as the answer they wish, and that is also deception."

"When so many hope for much from you, some will deceive themselves," she observed. "How could it be otherwise for a Rex?"

"It's the same for anyone with golds or power, is it not?"

"Being a poor and less informed woman . . ."

Charyn laughed. "You, I would judge, are neither. Especially as the heir to your holding."

"You would judge me?"

"As you told me at Year-Turn, we all make judgments. Whether they're wise . . ." He looked into her hazel eyes.

Her eyes locked on his for a long moment before she looked away.

To Charyn it seemed as though time had stopped, and he finally said gently, "I remembered your words. Does that displease you?"

Alyncya looked at him once more. "It frightens me more than I care to say."

And in so saying, you just did. "I'd never wish that." *Never.* A third thought came to mind. *She was definitely shaken. But why?* "I didn't mean my words to upset you."

"It wasn't your words." In a lower voice, she said, "My mother held the holding."

For a moment, her words didn't seem to follow . . . and then they did. She could be the designated heir, and she could wed whom she pleased—but she could not do that and keep the holding in her own name without the permission of the Rex. His permission. Without his permission and a formal announcement, the only way she could keep the holding as her own was to remain unmarried.

She laughed gently, but her voice seemed a trace unsteady as she added, after a moment, "I'm glad you didn't hesitate in replying."

"I said what I felt." Charyn found himself slightly unsettled. He'd never meant to make her afraid. "I . . . don't know what else to say." And he really didn't.

Neither did she, clearly, because she said nothing, except her fingers tightened slightly around his.

As the dance music faded, Charyn guided Alyncya back to her father. There he reluctantly released her hand and managed a smile. "Thank you for the dance."

Her voice was low, but firm, neither encouraging nor discouraging, as she replied, "The dance was my pleasure."

Charyn inclined his head, more deeply, and looked into her eyes.

She looked back, then said, "Others will expect a dance from you, Rex Charyn. I'd rather not be blamed for keeping you."

Charyn *thought* he caught a hint of mischief in her eyes, but as he turned and left, he wondered if he'd imagined it.

1

On Lundi morning, the sixteenth of Juyn, Charyn was up earlier than usual, most likely because the day promised to be particularly hot, a reminder that the first days of spring, heralded by the Spring-Turn Ball, were some three months gone, and there wasn't that much of summer left. Unlike his late father, he was always an early riser, trying to cram in a host of matters before going to his study to begin dealing with the routine daily matters of being Rex. After pulling on exercise clothes, he made his way to the guard post in the alcove off the main entrance to the Chateau.

Guard Captain Maertyl turned. "Good morning, Your Grace."

"Good morning, Guard Captain. Is there anything I should know?"

"Nothing out of the ordinary, sir. As I told you on Samedi, Lead Guard Charseyt is on leave for the week."

"If he needs more time . . ."

"His sister is taking care of the children. She lives within a few blocks." Maertyl smiled sadly. "Knowing Charseyt, being here might be better than having too much time on his hands."

Charyn nodded. He *thought* he understood that.

He and Maertyl walked back through the Chateau and out into the open rear courtyard and then to the enclosed and covered courtyard where all of the Chateau guards were assembling, not in full uniform, but in trousers and worn shirts. Charyn moved to the corner behind Maertyl.

Maertyl stripped off his uniform jacket. "Guards, ready!"

"Ready, Guard Captain!" came the response.

With that, Maertyl began the morning exercise routine.

Charyn had been joining the guards for exercise most weekday mornings for months, and the majority of guards no longer even looked in his direction. While it might have seemed definitely unregial to Charyn's father, after all the assassination attempts Charyn had weathered, joining the guards was the safest way to get exercise, and exercise helped not only to keep him fit, which might also increase his chances of avoiding further attempts, but also, at least in part, to keep his mind from dwelling excessively on both Alyncya and Palenya.

Once he finished exercising, he slipped away and up to his apartments to wash up and dress, before going down to the breakfast room. By the time he'd eaten and made his way to his study, right before seventh glass, it was more than clear that the day was going to be hot and hazy, hardly surprising given that it was midsummer.

Just before he reached the circular back staircase, Norstan appeared. "Your Grace?"

The seneschal looked slightly discomfited.

"What is it, Norstan?"

"Sir . . . Chorister Saerlet has requested an appointment for him and Chorister Refaal to see you, today, if possible."

Charyn frowned. After all that had happened to his family at the Anomen D'Rex, he hadn't attended services there since his father's memorial service. Saerlet had sent at least one note saying that he hoped to see the Rex. And Refaal was the chorister for the largest anomen in the city, the Anomen D'Excelsis. He'd also replaced Chorister Lytaarl, who had been the brother of Factor Elthyrd. "Did he say why?"

"His messenger just said that Chorister Refaal had a matter that would be of interest and import to you."

Interest and import? That could mean anything. Still, his Lundi wasn't that busy, unlike Meredi, when he had the monthly meeting of both councils.

"I'll see them at the first glass of the afternoon."

"Thank you, sir." Norstan inclined his head.

When Charyn reached the study door, he nodded to Mo-encriff, one of the two Chateau guards most often assigned to duty outside the study. "Good morning. It's likely to be quiet today."

"Nothing wrong with quiet, Your Grace."

Once he was seated behind the wide table desk, Charyn reached for the copy of the master ledgers provided by Alu-car, whose entries he had been perusing over the weekend in preparation for the Wednesday Council meeting. Alucar hadn't finished compiling the latest figures on shipbuilding and the new shipyard, because the report from Solis hadn't arrived until late on Vendrei, but Charyn needed a better feel for the other expenditures.

Some four glasses later, he had almost finished jotting down the notes he wanted to review when the chimes struck first glass and Moencriff announced, "Chorister Saerlet and Chorister Refaal, sir."

"Have them come in."

The round-faced Saerlet was sturdy, but not fat, his glis-tening dark black hair slicked back with just traces of white at his temples, and he wore the same dark gray jacket, trousers, and shirt Charyn had seen before when he wasn't conducting services, while around his jacket collar was the black and white chorister's scarf that did not quite reach his belt. He stopped short of the chairs before the desk and in-clined his head.

Refaal looked to be around fifteen years older than Charyn himself. His face was oval, his skin smooth, and his hair was a dark brown. His jacket, shirt, and trousers were all dark green, as was his scarf.

"Good afternoon, Choristers." Charyn gestured to the chairs in front of the table desk, then reseated himself.

"Thank you for seeing us so promptly, Your Grace," of-fered Saerlet, not quite unctuously.

"I appreciate your willingness to convey information that might be of interest to me."

"The information came to Refaal," declared Saerlet, "and I thought you should know."

"It is information both of interest to me and to Chorister Saerlet, but also to you." Refaal paused. "Have you heard of the True Believers?"

True Believers in what? was Charyn's first thought, but he only said, "No, I haven't."

"I fear we both may be hearing more of them in the days, seasons, and years ahead." Refaal continued, "They are a group of former choristers and their followers who claim that the majority of choristers of the Nameless have forgotten both the meaning of the Nameless and the true teachings of Rholan. They claim we are misleading those who worship in our anomens."

"In what way do they claim you're misleading worshippers?"

"They claim that we urge the people to follow the laws of the land, even when those laws are inequitable and unjust, and that when we do we are urging people to seek the favor of the Nameless in a fashion that promotes injustice."

"As I have often discussed with the Minister of Justice," replied Charyn, "the law is not always as just as it could be, and at times there don't seem to be practical ways to improve certain laws, or to use the law to remedy certain ills . . . but I'm not sure how urging people to follow the laws has anything to do with seeking favor with the Nameless or that not following the laws is more likely to please the Nameless. You don't assert that, do you?"

"Neither of us would condone that," interjected Saerlet smoothly.

"We certainly don't," added Refaal. "I offer homilies that suggest we should all do our best to follow the precepts of the Nameless, as did Rholan. There are scores of references to what Rholan said about law—and all of them boil down to the same precepts. Justice is what men should do, while law is what codes and powers require them to do, and that is invariably less than what they should do or what the Nameless requires of them. All good choristers are familiar with those words."

"I'm afraid I don't see the problem. Have I missed something?" asked Charyn.

The two choristers exchanged glances, before Refaal cleared his throat and said, "Two weeks ago, these True Believers stormed the Anomen D'Ruile. Chorister Tharyn had to flee for his life. These . . . fanatics claim that he is the avatar, whatever that means, of the ancient Tharyn Arysyn who barred Rholan from the anomen in Montagne. They shouted that his presence demonstrated the corruption that has overtaken the anomens of the Nameless."

"How did you discover this?"

"He wrote me from a small town near Ruile where he is hiding in fear for his life."

"What about the Civic Patrol?"

"The Patrol Captain there said that since no one was hurt and that the anomen wasn't damaged and that Tharyn couldn't identify any of the True Believers, there wasn't much the Patrol could do."

"He couldn't identify people who threatened his life?"

"I forgot to mention that they wore white gowns with hoods that concealed their faces." Refaal added sardonically, "White for purity, of course."

Charyn had to wonder if Chorister Tharyn just might be . . . less than the measure of probity presented or assumed by Refaal. Certainly, Charyn's limited experience in dealing with Chorister Saerlet had been suggestive that Saerlet was always wanting more, ostensibly for his anomen, not that Charyn was about to allude to that, especially at the moment. "It sounds as though Chorister Tharyn has made some enemies. Would you know how that might have happened?"

"He's a good chorister, and devoted to the Nameless. It's not just about him."

Not just about him? Interesting word choice. "If it's not about him, then what is it about?"

"These True Believers aren't just in Ruile. Other choristers have reported that there are some in Ferravyl, and in Tilbora and Midcote."

Charyn frowned. Ferravyl wasn't that far from Ruile, but Midcote was more than a thousand milles from either. "How long have you known about the True Believers?"

"Chorister Ellkyt in Tilbora wrote me about them two years ago," replied Refaal. "That was when I was chorister in Talyon."

"Why did he write you? Did they threaten him?"

Refaal shook his head. "He lost part of his congregation to them."

And part of their offerings . . . and his income, no doubt.

"There have been threats before, but nothing this violent," added Saerlet.

"You didn't ever mention anything like this," Charyn said mildly. "Is that because reports from other choristers went to Chorister Lytaarl as head of the anomen in L'Excelsis?"

"Oh, no," said Saerlet. "Every anomen is separate. Organizing the anomens, with a head chorister like a High Holder or a Rex . . . that would be a form of Naming. We just correspond with the choristers we know. My family comes from Suemyron, and I know more choristers in Antiago and to the west of L'Excelsis, while Refaal tends to know more in the east."

"Through all of the east of Solidar?" asked Charyn.

"No, Your Grace. I do know a number. I only know Ellkyt by correspondence because he helped a distant cousin many years ago. He sent me copies of letters from other choristers."

Saerlet cleared his throat. "I did hear something about the True Believers from Chorister Baardyn last autumn in Eluthyn, but I thought it was an isolated instance."

"What did Baardyn say?"

"Not all that much. He'd heard of an anomen in Semlem that had been taken over by them . . . that is, before the local High Holder ran them out. High Holder Lenglan, I think it was. The younger, that is. His father . . ." Saerlet shook his head.

Charyn had never heard of Lenglan, although it was clear there was something notorious about Lenglan's father, but with something around fifteen hundred High Holders, he couldn't be expected to know, let alone remember, all of them. "Have either of you heard of anything else?"

The two exchanged glances once more, then both shook their heads.

"If you do," continued Charyn, "I would appreciate your letting me know."

"We will," said Saerlet.

"It's was my duty and pleasure, sir," declared Refaal. "Perhaps at some time you could come and visit the Anomen D'Excelsis. It dates back to the time of the Bovarians, with some improvements, of course."

"And, Your Grace," added Saerlet smoothly, "I know events have weighed heavily upon you, but your presence at the Anomen D'Rex has been sorely missed. I would hope that you might be able to attend services at least now and again. I do believe that it would serve you well if word got around that you were present at services."

And it would likely serve you well, also. "You make an excellent point, Chorister Saerlet. Indeed, you do." He paused. "I cannot make a commitment to be there every Solayi, nor would it be wise for me to inform you or anyone when I might again attend services, but your observation has merit, and I will give it serious consideration." Charyn rose from his chair. "I do thank you both for coming and for letting me know about the True Believers."

"It was our duty as choristers and as loyal subjects," replied Saerlet.

Refaal nodded in agreement, then inclined his head, as did Saerlet, and the two turned and made their way from the study.

Once the door closed, Charyn recalled that Refaal had requested a meeting not long after Charyn's father's assassination, and that Charyn had deferred such a meeting. Was the talk about the True Believers just a ploy to meet Charyn?

Charyn frowned. With two of them and the specifics they had mentioned, there was likely enough to the True Believers to disconcert the two choristers . . . and, self-serving as Saerlet was about Charyn attending services, he was also right. Charyn knew he had withdrawn from public view far too much . . . but . . . he still needed to be very careful.

2

When Charyn reached his study on Meredi morning, it was still only seventh glass, but he knew he had to think out more thoroughly how he was going to handle the joint Council meeting scheduled for the first glass of the afternoon, always held in the study on the eighteenth of the month. As usual, he wore the uniform greens of an army officer, but without any insignia.

The first thing he did upon sitting down at the wide desk was to pick up the copy of *Veritum,* one of the two newssheets circulated in L'Excelsis, and quickly read through it. One of the stories on the first page reported that a Jariolan frigate had attacked the *Diamond Thuyl,* which had retaliated with Antiagon Fire shells that had turned the Jariolan into an inferno. In return, a Jariolan first-rate ship of the line sank the *Diamond Thuyl* using long-range cannon.

Charyn lowered the newssheet. Marshal Vaelln had sent him a similar report on Lundi evening, and that meant that the newssheet had gotten the information almost as soon as Charyn had. It also meant that High Holder Chaeltar, the other new member of the High Holders' Council besides Calkoran, would likely be demanding to know why the navy hadn't prevented the sinking of the *Diamond Thuyl* . . . or something along that line.

The remainder of the newssheet contained nothing of extreme interest except the observation that Juyn had been unseasonably warm and dry and that, if the lack of rainfall continued, the late-summer and early-harvest crop yields would be low, and that without more immediate rainfall some of the maize harvest might be completely lost. Since the heavy spring rains had washed out some crops, especially in low-lying areas along the River Aluse, quite a number of growers could suffer, and grain prices would be high, which meant many more would suffer.

Charyn set aside the newssheet and stood, walking to the study door and stepping out. "Moencriff, I'm going to see Minister Alucar. I hope I won't be too long."

Not that it likely mattered. Bhayrn was the only family member left in the Chateau since their mother had left for Rivages with Karyel and Iryella over a month ago. That was a very mixed blessing, since, even with Chelia's success in instilling more manners and care in her charges—her grandnephew and grandniece—Karyel had gotten on Charyn's nerves more than a few times, especially when he attempted to employ the sincerely warm—and totally false—smile that seemed to run in most of the Ryel line, and Karyel's younger sister always seemed to be concealing some machination, even when she was not.

Alucar's study door was locked. Charyn frowned. Alucar was always punctual, incredibly punctual. He'd never been late or missed a day without letting Charyn know in advance.

Shaking his head, Charyn walked back to his own study, stopping at the door. "Moencriff, will you have someone let me know when Minister Alucar arrives?"

"Yes, sir. I'll pass the word to the duty guard. Do you want the minister to come to your study?"

"No. I'll go to his. It won't take that long."

"Thank you."

Almost a glass passed before Moencriff opened the door. "Minister Alucar just came in. He's in his study."

Charyn immediately stood and walked along the upper corridor until he reached Alucar's study, where he opened the study door and immediately motioned for Alucar to remain seated. "I was a little worried. You always give me notice . . ."

"Your Grace . . . I must apologize. You know old Slaasyrn?"

"Your head clerk?"

"He died last night. It was very sudden. His daughter sent word, and I went there before I came here. I didn't realize how long it might take."

"He's been the head clerk for . . . ?" Charyn knew it had been a long time, possibly since before his father had been Rex.

"At least several years before I became Finance Minister and while Aevidyr was acting Finance Minister."

"I'm sorry to hear that." Charyn seated himself in the straight-backed chair he'd used not all that long ago in studying with the Finance Minister. "Do you know how? As I recall, he was old, but not that old."

"The healer said his heart stopped. Lately, he'd had a few spells where he was light-headed, but he'd seemed fine the last few weeks, and he was very helpful in setting things up for updating the factorages and landholdings of the High Holders. That's why I was surprised to hear it. We'll miss him."

"I'm sorry to hear that. You'll take care of matters, then?"

"I will."

"Thank you." Charyn paused, then said, "Since you already brought it up, how is the updating coming?"

"Very, very slowly. It's going to take longer without Slaasyrn. He was the most familiar with the records. Then we also have to have the regional finance ministers send out people. It's going to take years. I did tell you that."

"I know, but the tariff levies are based largely on either landholdings recorded generations ago or on what they report."

Alucar smiled sardonically. "As I told you before, it's worse than that. Those who've sold or bequeathed lands are quick to report those losses—at least until they get close to the minimum number of hectares to be a High Holder. Those who have expanded their holdings seldom report them. We catch some when they make petitions, but the most successful High Holders are almost all undertariffed, while a few of the least successful are overtariffed. There's one High Holder who has lands scattered all across Solidar, so that we've had to contact all the regional governors." He shook his head. "Some of those lands are on our rolls and not the regional rolls, and some are on their rolls and not ours."

"Are they all like that?"

"That kind of scattering is rare, but the inconsistency in records is more common than I'd like. One in fifteen, so far."

"How can you reconcile that?"

"If the regional governors report different tariff payments from what we received the previous year, we could inquire. Your father wouldn't allow us to reassess. Neither did his father. Slaasyrn told me he almost lost his position over it."

"Did he say why?"

"He said it was better left behind."

Charyn shook his head. With all the ways his father had tried to avoid conflict with individual High Holders, why had he antagonized them as a group? Charyn sometimes wondered how Solidar had survived as long as it had. But the past was past. All he could do was try to make things better.

"Do you have the figures on the shipyard and shipbuilding?"

Alucar smiled and pointed to a single sheet on the corner of the desk. "It's laid out the way you requested." He handed the sheet to Charyn.

"Thank you. Now . . . where do we stand on the repairs to piers and the wall on the west side of the river?"

"The temporary repairs have cost just under six hundred golds. Aevidyr estimates that the permanent repairs will cost at least four thousand golds, but there's no point in starting them until the water levels drop."

Charyn nodded. "What about reserves?"

"You're down to eight thousand golds."

Charyn didn't bother to hide his wince, not that the amount was unexpected, but annual tariff revenues wouldn't start to come in for three months, not until mid-Feuillyt at the earliest, and the unbudgeted and unexpected outlays were continuing. "I may have to draw on those."

"You've mentioned that. It would be better if you could wait."

"We'll see. What about revenues from customs duties?"

"Those in Mayas were about the same as in last Mayas . . ."

When Alucar finished going over the latest budget figures, Charyn made his way to the study of Aevidyr, the Minister of Administration. He could have summoned Aevidyr to his study, but he'd discovered it was far easier to end meetings smoothly with Aevidyr in the minister's study than in the Rex's study.

He opened the study door and immediately motioned for Aevidyr to remain seated. "Do you have any other suggestions for the position of regional governor of Khel?"

"I hoped you might consider Nuaraan D'Nualt as a possible successor to Regional Governor Warheon."

"He's a junior son of High Holder Nualt?"

"Of course."

"To what other High Holders is he related?"

"Ah . . . his wife is a younger sister of High Holder Nacryon."

"The former High Councilor from Khel?" With whom Maitre Alastar had had a certain considerable difficulty, if Charyn recalled correctly.

"Yes, sir."

"To what other High Holder might he be related?"

"Sir, every High Holder's offspring are related to other High Holders."

Charyn managed not to sigh, because Aevidyr was absolutely right, but why did his Minister of Administration keep coming up with names related to High Holders who'd been thorns in either his father's side or Maitre Alastar's side?

"Your Grace," replied Aevidyr, "you've rejected every name I've come up with who is willing to serve."

"That's because every one of them who wants to serve would be no better than Warheon . . . or even worse, Voralch." Charyn didn't like thinking about Voralch, who had absconded with almost two thousand golds and taken a ship to the Abierto Isles, largely because Charyn hadn't acted on his impulse to sack Voralch immediately. *But then, Voralch would have done the same thing, just earlier, and Ryel still would have burned the former regial chateau in Solis.* That said, Voralch wouldn't have been able to make off with all the valuables that he'd taken. "We need to think about a different approach to selecting a regional governor."

"In the past, sir, Rexes have always chosen from recommendations made by High Holders." Aevidyr smiled pleasantly.

"Who largely made recommendations to serve their own interests."

"Everyone has interests, sir."

"Perhaps you could think of a way to harness those interests to benefit Solidar as a whole and not just the High Holder making the recommendation," suggested Charyn. "Or to a few relatives."

Aevidyr frowned, then said, "What about Nuaraan D'Nualt?"

"Given the trouble created by his family, I think not."

"Sir . . . that's the fifth name you've rejected."

That should tell you something. "You're absolutely correct, Aevidyr. Why don't you think about how we can get names that will better serve Solidar?" Charyn smiled politely. "We'll talk later."

As he left Aevidyr's study, he had to ask himself why he'd bothered to keep Aevidyr as minister, but it was far from the first time he'd asked that question and the answer was always the same. *Because you understand Aevidyr and know*

*his weaknesses, and, in the end, he does what is necessary.
If you watch him closely.*

The danger with that way of thinking, he knew, was that
he'd never get a minister any better and that he might come
tacitly around to Aevidyr's views. *Which means you also
need to find a way to get better ministers, at least a better
Minister of Administration.*

Once he was back in his study, he began to read the appeals, largely from the east and mostly from High Holders,
to his change to the law governing water rights, a change
that had made the law the same across all Solidar.

He was still reading when Moencriff rapped on the study
door.

"Lord Bhayrn, sir."

Even before Moencriff finished speaking, Bhayrn was inside the study and walking toward Charyn. He settled into
the chair facing the table and closest to the open window.

"How long do I have to stay in the Chateau?"

"I've told you for months that you don't have to stay. I've
also been willing to show you what I do and why."

"You make it feel like I'm being tutored."

"As I told you before, you could work with any of the
ministers . . ."

"They're worse."

Charyn managed a smile. "If you change your mind . . ."

"I'll let you know." Bhayrn shook his head. "It's not as
bad as when Father had us imprisoned here in the Chateau,
but you work so much that it's not much better."

Charyn momentarily thought about explaining why, but,
instead, just asked, "Where do you want to go?"

"Anywhere . . ."

"Then go. Arrange with Maertyl for two or three guards
to accompany you. I would suggest that both you and the
guards wear army greens."

"Army uniforms? For Chateau guards?"

Charyn nodded. "I told you that I had Maertyl purchase some, including two sets for you and several for me. People see army officers enough that no one pays any attention. Just wear them while you're traveling. That way, any of the few rebels that might still be around won't be tempted to shoot at you." At Bhayrn's appalled expression, Charyn added, "That's if you're traveling for longer distances, say to Rivages to visit Mother."

"I still don't see why you just don't travel as you please. Laamyst and his father think that by using an unmarked coach you're showing you're afraid. They think that might encourage attacks. You just ought to have the guards shoot anyone who causes trouble . . ."

"That would be possible only if the troublemakers were considerate enough to stand out in the open and announce their intentions."

"Most humorous." Bhayrn snorted. "You know what I meant. And why does Mother have to spend so much time in Rivages?"

"As I might have mentioned, she's the guardian for Karyel and Iryella, and someone has to run the High Holding and teach Karyel how to do it properly." *Not to mention instilling at least a rudimentary set of ethics in the self-centered little bastard.* Except, Charyn knew, he had been close to that self-centered, and without the guidance of his mother and Palenya . . .

"You were too kind to Ryel and his offspring."

"Not kind. In our interests."

Bhayrn made a dismissive gesture, then asked, "Do I have to go to Rivages right now? Is that my choice, brother dear?"

Charyn shook his head. "No. You agreed to go later. You might actually enjoy it. It is cooler there in summer and harvest than here. For the present, all I *am* strongly suggesting is that you wear greens if you travel extensively. I'd prefer not to preside over another family memorial service."

"I was thinking more of visiting Laamyst. His father has a summer villa in Talyon."

"High Holder Laastyn seems to have a number of . . . retreats."

"Laamyst's father has never really liked the family hold near Charpen. So he built places he liked better in other locales, including the one in Talyon. I also think there's a hunting lodge north of Asseroiles." Bhayrn grinned. "When Laamyst wants to be away from L'Excelsis, he always picks one where his father isn't."

"I thought they got along well."

"They do, but you did a lot that Father didn't know and wasn't happy when he found out, and that made things harder for me."

Charyn doubted the last half of what his brother said.

"Laamyst doesn't always want to look over his shoulder. Nor do I."

"I understand that. If you want to go to Talyon, be my guest. But work it out with Maertyl, and no more than four guards. Also, let me know when you're leaving and when you'll be back. If you decide to stay longer, send a message."

"I can do that. I'm thinking of leaving on Vendrei and staying a week, maybe ten days."

"And don't get into a costly dalliance."

Bhayrn raised his eyebrows.

"Not a word," said Charyn, trying not to smile. "That was an education, and it took a year and then some. If you can learn as much as I did, I won't complain."

"That's something, anyway." Bhayrn rose from the chair. "I won't be here for dinner. Laamyst asked me there. Rather, his father did. I'll likely have to endure one of Laamyst's cousins."

"Endure away."

After his brother left the study, Charyn permitted himself a smile. Bhayrn's attitude toward young women had changed remarkably over the past half year. Unhappily, some of his other attitudes remained the same.

Sometime before noon, Moencriff rapped on the door. "Sir, I have a letter from Lady Chelia."

Charyn was on his feet even before he replied. "Please bring it in."

After taking the letter from Moencriff, Charyn asked, "Are there any others?"

"No, sir."

Charyn nodded. Except for letters from Aloryana and his mother, there had been few indeed over the last two months. Except largely for water issues, High Holders had made far fewer pleas when it had become obvious that Charyn was holding to the law as laid out in the Codex Legis and not granting exemptions or favors to them, and factors weren't writing him as much as they were writing the members of the Factors' Council. *Which is likely as it should be.*

Once Moencriff had left and closed the door, Charyn immediately slit the letter open, noting, that, as always, the seal his mother used was her own, and not that of the Hold of Ryel, which she was entitled to use, both as Karyel's guardian and as the senior adult member of the family. He began to read.

> *Dear Charyn,*
> *The weather here is still hot and dry. If it continues,*
> *we'll see a marked decrease in the yield from the upland*
> *maize fields. The winter wheat corn harvest was better*
> *than usual, thank the Nameless. As you know, I never*
> *expected that I'd have to be worrying about harvests*
> *again, let alone be teaching someone. Karyel is bright*
> *enough, but . . .*

Charyn shook his head, then continued to read, wondering if his mother could change Karyel enough so that the youth wouldn't end up like his grandsire. He nodded at the next paragraph.

> *As you requested, I've arranged to have five thousand golds transferred to the account of Factor Suyrien at the L'Excelsis Exchange, which is a two-year loan, also as you requested . . .*
>   *. . . know you take after your father in not being terribly social. I worry about that now that I'm at Ryel. I'd like to suggest that you invite your ministers and their wives to dinner or to an end-day afternoon . . . or, if you feel more comfortable, the Marshal and some of the High Command officers and their wives . . .*

You really should . . . Charyn sighed, thinking also about what Chorister Saerlet had said on Lundi, then smiled as he came to another paragraph.

> *. . . Aloryana's letters are frequent and often amusing. She also enjoys your letters, but since Bhayrn has never written, you might remind him that she'd enjoy hearing from him. She did tell me that I should tell you to keep practicing your skills with the clavecin and that they might even help you find someone with the traits you admired in Palenya . . .*

As if that would be easy . . . or even likely.

Nonetheless, he read on and finished the letter, enjoying, or at least appreciating his mother's words.

At a quint before first glass, Maitre Alastar arrived.

"Greetings," offered Charyn, rising from behind the desk and walking toward the long Council table. He did not sit at the head of the table, but in one of the two chairs set to the side near the head of the table.

Alastar took the other one. "Do you have any surprises planned, Charyn?"

"Only if Marshal Vaelln has even more recent news about the Jariolans." Charyn wanted to shake his head when he thought about the Jariolans. They'd started attacking Solidaran shipping months and months before his father's death and then escalated the attacks. "What about you? How are matters at the Collegium?"

"We have a few more new imagers, and Maitre Taurek has sent word that he and Celiena have completed the buildings for the Estisle Collegium."

"How many imagers are there now?"

"Eleven, besides Taurek and Celiena. And Howal. He decided to go there after he came back to the Collegium. They'll need another junior maitre soon, but we're still considering who might be best to send."

"Marshal Vaelln," announced Moencriff.

Both Alastar and Charyn rose as Vaelln entered.

"Rex Charyn, Maitre Alastar." Vaelln inclined his head.

"Is there any more news since your last dispatch?"

"Unfortunately. The Jariolans have announced they will blockade the Abierto Isles, unless the Abiertans deny our ships the right to port and resupply there."

"What might be the reason for that?"

"To divert some of our ships from patrolling the oceans off Jariola and Ferrum, not to mention Otelyrn."

"What do you recommend?"

Vaelln offered a grim smile. "Divert some of the fleet to the Isles. It doesn't matter where we destroy their ships."

"If you do that, it's likely that the shippers and factors will lose more ships trading with the lands of Otelyrn, isn't it?" asked Charyn.

"It is, for several months at least."

"I'd like you to report on both what the Jariolans are doing and what you recommend."

Vaelln nodded.

"The councils, sir," announced Moencriff, opening the study door.

As had become customary before, Elthyrd led the factors. Thalmyn came next, then Harll, Jhaliost, and Hisario. They stood waiting behind their chairs on the left side of the long table. Then the five High Holders entered, led by Chaeltar, followed by Calkoran, Basalyt, and Khunthan, with Fhaedyrk, as head of the High Council, entering last. As head of the Factors' Council, Elthyrd took the chair immediately to the left of Charyn, while Fhaedyrk, as chief High Councilor, took the one to the right, with the other High Holders on the same side.

"Welcome to the Chateau on this all too unpleasantly warm summer day." Charyn motioned everyone to seat themselves, then seated himself. "We'll begin with Marshal Vaelln. He has a report on the shipbuilding situation and recent naval engagements with the Jariolans."

Vaelln rose from the chair beside that of Alastar, nodded to Charyn, and surveyed those at the table before beginning. "Thanks to Rex Charyn and Minister Alucar, we have obtained and cleared the land for the new shipyard. The channels and piers are almost complete, and the necessary buildings will be completed sometime in Erntyn. We expect to lay the keel for the first warship, a frigate, in late Feuillyt."

"Just a frigate?" asked Chaeltar.

"The master shipbuilder felt that it would be best to start with a smaller vessel when working for the first time with new workmen. If all goes well, we'll lay the keel for a first-rate ship of the line in late Finitas or early in Ianus."

"I thought—" began Hisario, whose factoring dealt with ships and trading.

"There is the small matter of paying for these additional ships," Charyn interjected smoothly. "You might recall that the agreement reached by the councils was that the added tariffs to fund the shipyard and ships will not be collected until Feuillyt."

"Surely, you as Rex have some funds," pressed Hisario.

"I do. They are funding the purchase of the land, the building of the piers, the deepening of the channels, and the acquisition of tools and other shipbuilding equipment. The reserve funds in the treasury were also depleted by the need to repair the flood damage to the piers in L'Excelsis and the flooding in Liantiago." Charyn looked to Elthyrd. "Was not the Factors' Council firm in approving those repairs?"

Elthyrd nodded. "Factors *and* many High Holders depend on the piers that the ice and high water destroyed."

"Some of those funds went to Liantiago, also," added Charyn, looking directly at Hisario, "to repair the harbor wall there that collapsed. You were insistent on those repairs, I recall."

"But . . ."

"There aren't enough golds to do everything. I asked the councils, and the councils agreed." Charyn offered a humorous smile. "Not necessarily enthusiastically, I will admit." He turned to Vaelln. "If you would continue, Marshal."

"As most of you have heard, we continue to reduce the number of Jariolan warships and privateers every month. In the majority of engagements of warships of the same rate, our forces have prevailed. From all indications we appear to be producing ships more quickly than the Jariolans. There are still too many instances where Jariolan warships have sunk Solidaran merchanters, the latest being the loss of the *Diamond Thuyl*. Diamond ships are armed, and they use shells containing Antiagon Fire. The *Thuyl* sank a Jariolan frigate that attempted to attack and board her. A first-rate Jariolan sank the *Thuyl*."

"How could the navy let that happen?" asked Chaeltar.

"The only navy vessel was several milles away and couldn't reach the *Thuyl* before the Jariolan departed. Our frigate did rescue some of the crew."

Chaeltar scowled, but didn't say more.

"This has led to two other problems," continued Vaelln.

"Jariolan privateers have turned to out-and-out piracy, not only against our merchanters, but against just about any merchant vessel that they can pursue and overtake. This is spreading our ships thinner than we would like. The second problem will make the first worse. I just received word early this morning that the Jariolans have sent an ultimatum to the Abierto Isles. If the Isles' ports do not refuse all Solidaran shipping and warships, Jariola will blockade the Isles."

Before any of the High Holders or factors could speak, Charyn asked, "What do you recommend?"

"We cannot maintain our current efforts without access to the Abiertan ports. The Isles will suffer greatly if trading with Solidar is cut off, but they only have a score of warships, and none larger than a third-rate ship of the line. They will likely refuse to comply with the ultimatum, and will expect us to help break any blockade. I recommend we divert some ships, as necessary to do that."

"Won't that increase the piracy and attacks on Solidaran ships trading with the lands of Otelyrn?" asked Khunthan. "That will just undo the good done by the flotilla you dispatched there."

"Not doing so will lead to more merchanters being lost, I fear," replied Vaelln. "I also believe that if the Jariolans send more ships to the Isles, we'll end up destroying more of their fleet sooner because to enforce a blockade, their ships have to be fairly close to the Isles, and that will make them easier to find."

"So the merchant shippers have to suffer even more?" protested Chaeltar.

"As the Marshal has explained it," replied Charyn, "merchant ships will suffer even more attacks over the next year if the navy loses access to the Isle, and Solidaran traders who trade with the Isles will be cut off."

"That's not much of a choice," groused Khunthan.

"Blame the Jariolans, not the Marshal," said Elthyrd. "He's just trying to make the best of the situation."

"Now . . . if the Council had been willing to increase tariffs last year," ventured Charyn.

"Tariffs are high enough," snapped Basalyt. "And with your reassessments, some High Holders will be paying more this year."

"All of eleven, so far, and that's because they've been paying far less than they should have been for years."

"Which they believe is too much," replied Basalyt. "Not only that, but it looks like a dry summer. That means a poor harvest. Even higher tariffs on top of a bad harvest? Both the High Holders and the factors will be after all of our heads."

"Deal with it the best you can with the golds you have," added Chaeltar.

"That's what the Marshal proposed," replied Charyn mildly. He had no doubt that the rest of the meeting would likely continue in the same fashion, with the councilors unhappy with the situation, but not willing to agree to more tariffs.

And, in fact, that was exactly what happened, with the exception of the last matter, that of artificer standards, something brought to Charyn's attention by Argentyl, the head of the Craftmasters' Council of L'Excelsis, who had earlier complained to Charyn about factors importing cheaper and shoddy goods that were fraudulently stamped or certified as being of higher quality than they actually were.

"You've all had a chance to look over the petition brought to my attention by the craft guilds of L'Excelsis . . ." Charyn mentally braced himself for what he suspected was about to come.

"The artisans have had everything their way for too long," Chaeltar began. "They're demanding you change the law to allow them to keep prices high."

"If factors can find less expensive goods, that only benefits those who buy them," declared Factor Hisario.

"And those who ship and sell them," added Charyn dryly.

"You aren't suggesting, Your Grace," asked Harll, "that you would actually change the laws to keep prices high?"

"No," replied Charyn. "But there does seem to be a problem with goods being represented as being of quality that they are not."

"People get what they pay for," declared Khunthan. "They shouldn't expect quality for bargain prices."

"Exactly my point," added Chaeltar.

"The craftmasters' petition mentions two problems," said Elthyrd slowly. "The first problem is that shoddy or poor-quality goods are being sold as being of higher quality. The second is that the prices are too high for the quality. To have the Rex set prices strikes me as a very bad idea—"

"Exactly!"

"It's a terrible idea . . ."

". . . ruin both factors and High Holders . . ."

"But," Elthyrd finally said, "do we want to encourage the sale of cheap and shoddy goods? You know high quality, High Holder Khunthan. Can most people tell if a piece of silver is solid, plated, or washed? Or the difference between a thin plate and a thick wash?"

"What might be your point, Chief Factor?" asked High Holder Fhaedyrk.

"I agree with all that has been said about price-setting by the Rex. But I don't like the idea of people being deceived by goods represented as being more than they are. In the past, quality standards were maintained by the guilds. We're moving into a time where that isn't working well. What about a law that makes misrepresenting goods a form of theft?"

"Then every Rytersyn in Solidar would be claiming misrepresentation!" snapped Hisario.

"Craftmaster Argentyl made the point that some goods were stamped as sterling and were only plated or silver-washed," Charyn pointed out.

"If you make that a crime," countered Hisario, "then anyone in trade would be responsible for certifying the quality of everything he sells. That's unworkable."

"Totally unworkable," asserted Khunthan.

Charyn considered asking about the instance where a seller knew he was misrepresenting quality. *But how could anyone prove that . . . and how many patrollers would it require . . . how many hearings before justicers?* He wanted to shake his head. Instead, he just nodded and said, "I think you've made your points very clear. Is there anything else anyone wishes to bring up?"

Charyn surveyed the table, then said, "We'll meet at first glass on the eighteenth of Agostos."

After everyone had left, except Maitre Alastar, Charyn took a deep breath.

Alastar offered an amused smile. "That went as well as could have been expected."

"For now, anyway. At least I'm not getting death threats anymore. There was one question I did have. With all the damage in Liantiago and Westisle . . ."

"You're wondering if the imagers at Westisle could help?" Charyn nodded.

"The Collegium there was also damaged, but I sent word to Maitre Arion to offer help once the Collegium was restored."

"Thank you."

"I appreciate your asking privately."

"That would serve us both better, I thought. How is Aloryana coming?" Charyn didn't want to talk any more about all the problems he faced.

"She's very close to becoming a third. She might master what she needs for that by Erntyn, but it's likely to take her a little longer."

"She and Lystara are still getting along?"

"Like sisters." The Maitre laughed softly. "Some squabbling, but more harmony. It's also required Lystara to be more patient and given her a greater appreciation of Malyna. Aloryana can be very determined."

"It runs in the family." Charyn paused, then said, "I do

have one more question that came up from Chorister Saerlet, along with some information you might find interesting . . ."

"Interesting usually means trouble . . ."

"It might." Charyn went on to explain about the True Believers. ". . . and while there haven't been that many incidents, they've occurred all across Solidar, and that troubles me."

"It could be trouble . . . or it could die out. I'll ask Maitre Arion and Maitre Taurek if they've heard anything about these True Believers." Alastar started to rise.

"There is one other thing . . ."

Alastar offered an amused smile and settled back into his chair.

"It's more personal, but Chorister Saerlet made the point that I haven't been seen at services in months. He was kind enough not to point out that it was six months. I'm a little worried about appearing anywhere where my presence might be anticipated . . ."

"How might the Collegium fit into this?"

"I was thinking about attending services, unannounced and occasionally, at perhaps both the Anomen D'Rex and the Anomen D'Imagisle . . ."

"With your sister, and possibly Lystara?"

"Well . . . yes. When we go to the Anomen D'Rex, I could pick them up in the regial coach. Other times, I could be driven to your house and walk with her. I'd also like to arrange a dinner for what might be called the extended family, you and Alyna, Lystara, Malyna, and Calkoran and his wife . . ."

Alastar nodded. "Aloryana has been at the Collegium long enough that it's reasonable for her to visit close relatives. As a member of the regial family, she needs protection. But it has to be her choice. If she agrees, she can certainly attend with you. I'd prefer her escort to be Malyna or Lystara, but that has to be their choice as well. If they decline, although I doubt they will, the Collegium will provide an escort. I will let you know if Aloryana is willing to join you at the Anomen D'Rex. You are always welcome at the Anomen D'Imagisle."

"Thank you." Charyn rose, as did Alastar.

Once the Maitre left, Charyn made his way to the music room.

There, he seated himself at the clavecin and began to play, beginning with Farray's Nocturne Number Three. After that he got up and went to the music cabinet and took out the music for another Farray piece—"Pavane in a Minor Key." He'd never played it, but Palenya had, and he'd liked the way it had sounded. *That also means it's likely harder than anything you've tried before.*

Then he sat down in front of the keyboard. In moments, he realized that he had a great deal of work to do if he wanted to master that particular Farray piece. *A very great deal of work.*

But then, with the Chateau largely empty, he had more than enough time, and learning music was certainly less stressful than presiding over Council meetings. He also hoped Aloryana would agree to attending services, and not just for Charyn's own sake.

3

By Jeudi morning at seventh glass, Charyn had already exercised, washed, dressed, eaten, checked with Guard Captain Maertyl, gone over the day's schedule with Norstan the seneschal, and written a letter to his mother, and another to Aloryana, explaining both about his wanting to attend services with her and the idea of some sort of "family dinner" that would include her. Having done that, he was pacing back and forth in his study, mulling over the latest petition complaint that he'd received, one that had been forwarded to him because the position of regional governor of Telaryn was currently vacant. High Holder Douvyt, from Cloisonyt, was outraged that one Factor Camarouth had built a textile manufactorage upriver from his flax plantation, because the effluent from the dyeworks so contaminated the river that the water couldn't be used to irrigate the fields in times of drought.

In one sense, it was amusing, because little more than a season earlier, Charyn had rejected a similar petition—except the petitioner had been a factor whose textiles couldn't be washed in the river water tainted by runoff from a High Holder's hog farm.

Finally, he sat down and wrote a brief note to Sanafryt, asking him if it wouldn't be wise to revisit the issue and consider a change in the Codex Legis. He doubted that his Minister of Justice would want to consider that, but then, he might, now that it was a High Holder who was the aggrieved party.

He'd no more than finished the note when Moencriff announced, "Lady Delcoeur is here, sir."

"Have her come in."

Officially Lady Delcoeur D'Priora, the woman who entered the study was half a head shorter than Charyn, muscular rather than petite, her hair a black that was no longer naturally occurring, with a slightly oval face and dark green eyes. She stopped short of the desk and asked, "Do you actually have anything for me to do, Rex Charyn?"

"Charyn in private, Aunt Elacia. And yes, I do. I need you to set up some dinners—"

"Dinners? In midsummer? In L'Excelsis?"

"I'm sure Ferrand would come, with whatever young lady he might prefer."

"He can't invite a marriageable woman by herself, and you can't afford to have him invite one who's not."

"Fine." Charyn sighed. "Can you find out who among young women he'd find acceptable is actually in or near L'Excelsis and would be available for dinner, including her parents, of course, a week from Samedi evening—"

"Two weeks would be preferable."

Charyn nodded to that. "I'd also like to invite Alyncya D'Shendael-Alte and her father for the same evening." At Elacia's quizzical expression, Charyn added, "He's widowed, and she's the heir." He managed not to smile and went on. "Also Ferron D'Fhernon-Alte, Shaelyna D'Baeltyn and her parents, and one other pleasant and intelligent High Holder heir."

"I'd suggest one more young woman."

"Do you have one in mind?"

"No. But there should be an odd number so that it's not obvious who might be invited for whom. Do you plan entertainment?"

"I thought it would be less formal. I will play something on the clavecin and invite anyone else to play."

"That's not usual."

"Good."

Elacia did not quite frown, but said, "You should consider some music in addition to anything you or any of the guests play."

"Let me think about that. I'd also like a dinner a week from Samedi, since that date is now available, for certain High Command officers and their wives, Marshal Vaelln, Vice-Marshal Maurek, Commander Chaalt, and Subcommander Luerryn, those who can attend."

"They will all attend," said Elacia dryly, adding, after a pause, "A subcommander?"

"He was particularly helpful to me, and it's a way I can tell him that without infringing too much on Marshal Vaelln's prerogatives. I'd also like you to attend, standing in for my mother, as it were."

"That's very kind."

Charyn smiled ruefully. "No, I'd like you to be your conversational self and later let me know if you heard anything I should know."

"You know, Charyn, that's even kinder. I'm very much enjoying being helpful here."

"I'm glad you are." He pursed his lips. "There is one other thing. While you're at it, I'd like to set up a very small dinner on Meredi, the eighteenth of Agostos, for High Holder Calkoran, and his wife, if she is in L'Excelsis, which she may not be, Maitre Alastar and Maitre Alyna, and Maitres Malyna and Lystara. And Imager Second Aloryana."

Charyn enjoyed Elacia's second look of surprise, then explained, "Calkoran will be in L'Excelsis because that's the day of the joint Council meeting, and Calkoran and Maitre Alyna are cousins. So it will be a family dinner, or as much of one as I can manage at the moment. Bhayrn is certainly welcome, but he's not obligated to come."

"Is such a dinner wise?"

"Some would say it isn't, but Father kept too much to himself, and I've found myself sinking into that pattern. I'm going to try to be more social and open. I'd like you to think it over and let me know if you have any suggestions for other events. That's all I have for now."

"You will keep me busy," said Elacia, inclining her head before leaving and making her way to the study that had once been Charyn's sitting room before he had moved to the Rex's apartments, and redecorated them, at Palenya's request, after she had left.

Less than a quint later, Charyn was in the unmarked coach, heading down the Boulevard D'Ouest to the Nord Bridge and across the River Aluse into the heart of L'Excelsis . . . and the Banque D'Excelsis, with its exterior barred windows and its interior guards.

Charyn knew that there was some risk in leaving the Chateau, but, so far as he knew, at the moment, very few people, outside of a handful of High Holders and imagers, even knew what he looked like. The driver and the coach guards all wore unmarked brown livery, rather than the regial green, and Charyn wore dark blue trousers and a maroon jacket with a cream shirt and a cravat that matched the jacket. The pin that granted him access to the commodity exchange, and marked him as a factor, was also fastened to his jacket lapel. He carried a concealed pistol at all times, one he could quickly fire. It had helped save him twice, but he hoped it wouldn't be necessary again. *And that may be hope against hope.*

When Charyn walked through the doors of the banque, Estafen immediately moved to meet him, greeting him warmly, "Welcome, Factor Suyrien." Then the banking factor guided Charyn into a small study, quickly closing the door and saying, "You didn't have to come here, sir." He motioned to the circular table with the two chairs, then waited for Charyn to sit before seating himself.

"I won't be able to keep doing this for too long, and everyone will know in days if you come to the Chateau. That's why I'd prefer to come here, now, while I can. Now . . . about the ironworks. Have you thought over my proposal?"

"Might I ask why you're so insistent on purchasing the ironworks?"

"If certain projects I'm interested in work out, I'll need an ironworks. Even if those don't, I'll likely still require control of such a works."

"I have to say that I don't understand why, with all the troubles you've had, you want to add to them by acquiring an ironworks."

"It really is about a project that will require an ironworks."

"If your sire had said that . . . but you . . . so far . . ." Estafen smiled ruefully. "Still, if you purchase it, and that becomes known, more than a few factors and High Holders will be less than pleased with either of us."

"You because you sold it to me, and me because they don't want the Rex competing with them?"

"I'd say that's a fair summary." Estafen absently scratched his neck below the square-cut black beard.

"I'm not interested in using my position to gain an unfair profit. I am interested in obtaining the ironworks not only for the projects I have in mind, but also to prevent others from taking advantage of me as those projects become known. I still worry about the rifleworks at the ironworks. I'd like to know who's buying rifles and why. As Maitre Alastar and my father discovered, the lack of information about that cost thousands of men and quite a few imagers their lives."

Estafen fingered his beard. "Do you think I would withhold that information?"

"No . . . but I'd rather not be dependent on goodwill. You received the ironworks for the settlement of a little over six thousand golds. As I said before, I'll offer the same, six thousand five hundred golds, and allow you to retain a ten percent interest, in terms of net income, with no liability for losses. If you don't find that arrangement satisfactory after a year, I'll pay you another thousand golds for your interest. That's almost a twenty percent gain with no risk and the possibility of additional income."

"If . . . if I agree to this, how will you keep it from others, since that would be to neither of our interests?"

"You'll sell the ironworks to Factor Suyrien D'Chaeryll. You'll be paid in golds drawn from that account at the commodity exchange."

Estafen shook his head. "You thought this out some time ago, didn't you?"

Not as long ago as you think, but some time past. Charyn nodded.

"It will take a week or so to work out the papers and come up with a final bookkeeping statement. I can send you a notice of when those will be ready."

"Excellent. I'll look forward to that."

"It will be interesting to see what use you make of the ironworks."

"One way or the other, it's a bit of a risk, but not so much as not trying it." He paused. "I do have an unrelated question. You're the oldest, but you're not at the factorage."

"That's because Thyrand is far better with timber and people. Father agreed with me, and provided some golds to help me start the banque."

"And that's worked out for the best for both of you, it appears."

"I have to say that it has."

"You made it work, I suspect." Charyn smiled as he stood.

Once outside the banque, he told the driver, "Factor Paersyt's down by the west river piers."

"Yes, sir."

Charyn quickly entered the coach. With the purchase of the ironworks, he'd have the rifleworks under his control and a metalworking factorage that could be expanded for his other projects. *Even if it did require a loan from Uncle's holding.* Then again, that was scarcely any recompense given the evils Ryel had perpetrated. *And it's only a loan.* And a good part of the reason he needed a loan was precisely because Ryel had kept Charyn's father from even assessing a modest increase in tariffs for years, despite the need for warships to protect Solidaran shipping.

A quint or so later, the coach stopped just north of the barge piers. Charyn got out of the coach and walked quickly toward the brown stone building, noting the faint haze rising from the factorage chimney, suggesting that Paersyt was hard at work.

Dhuncan, the guard accompanying Charyn, rapped on the factorage door, then opened it and stepped inside, looking around, then motioning for Charyn to enter.

Several different forges filled the space, which was larger than it appeared from without, but only the main forge appeared to be fired, and that was where the wiry and gray-haired Paersyt stood, between the forge and one of the workbenches, wearing his usual stained brown leathers. As he caught sight of the two inside the door, he turned and walked to meet Charyn.

"Rex Charyn."

"Factor Paersyt. How are you coming on the larger steam engine?"

"It will be ready in a week if matters go as expected. They likely won't. So . . . say two to three weeks."

"How much will it carry?"

"It should be able to propel the craft you provided upstream against the current, provided the total weight is less than two tonnes."

"How fast?"

"I won't know that until we put it in the boat and get it working. I'm also worried about the seals around the screw shaft. If I can't make the seals work, we might have to use a paddle wheel."

"You use seals in the pistons, don't you?"

"It's different. If steam or water leaks a little there, there's more water in the supply tank to replace it. If shaft seals leak much, you could fill the boat with water, and before long you'd have water in the firebox."

Charyn nodded. "Let me know when you're ready to have me see it."

"I certainly will, sir."

"We won't keep you." With a smile, Charyn turned and left the factorage. While he knew it was far better not to linger anywhere, since there was still a possibility of assassins, however small, he wasn't looking forward to what awaited him back in his study, most likely a response from Sanafryt about the water effluents, and who knew what else. And he also was obligated to arrange for Craftmaster Argentyl to visit the Chateau to explain the problems with the petition.

Still . . . in some areas, he was making progress . . . if slowly.

4

On Solayi afternoon, Charyn debated briefly on whether to take the regial coach or the unmarked one, but decided that there was little to be gained by taking the gilded coach. Word would get around that he had been at services, and there was no point in making himself a target, although there hadn't been any more threatening letters since his uncle's death.

Then, while he waited for time to pass before he left to pick up Aloryana and whoever was her imager escort, he sat down at the clavecin and spent almost a glass, mostly working on "Pavane in a Minor Key."

At fifth glass, wearing dress uniform greens, without insignia, he stepped into the unmarked coach in the rear courtyard of the Chateau. The two guards and driver were in army greens. Two quints later, after an uneventful ride, the regial coach rolled to a stop outside the Maitre's two-story stone dwelling, one that looked recently completed, for all that it was some four hundred years old and close to indestructible.

Charyn immediately stepped out and started to walk toward the front door.

"Charyn!"

He couldn't help smiling as Aloryana hurried toward him, wearing the tailored light gray imager jacket and trousers, and with her blond hair cut far shorter than he'd seen before.

She slowed to a more deliberate walk as she neared him. "I should be angry at you." The firmness of her tone gave way to a smile. "And I would have been if you hadn't written that letter."

"I didn't know if Maitre Alastar would agree to the plan of my coming here and your going there, but I did arrange for the family-type dinner at the Chateau whether or not you wanted to attend services."

"Maitre Alastar told me that, too."

Behind Aloryana walked another young woman imager—Lystara, who had the black eyes and brown hair of her mother and the height and broad shoulders of her father. Charyn realized, again, that Lystara was almost as tall as he was.

"Good evening, Maitre Lystara."

Lystara offered an embarrassed smile. "Lystara, Your Grace, please. I'm only seventeen, and for a Rex to call me 'Maitre' . . . that doesn't seem right."

"I won't press the point, Lystara, but you're here on duty, to protect me and Aloryana, and for that you deserve being addressed as 'Maitre.'"

"Charyn's right, you know," said Aloryana.

"Are you two ready?" Charyn said quickly.

"Only if you promise you'll come back for refreshments after services," said Aloryana.

"I promise. I already promised."

"I wanted to make sure."

Lystara took the front seat, so that she could look back to see if anyone happened to be following them, while Aloryana sat beside her brother.

"Bhayrn isn't coming?" asked Aloryana as the coach began to move.

"He's visiting Laamyst in Talyon. Even if he were here, he couldn't. It wouldn't be wise for both of us to go out together. It would also be asking a bit much of Lystara." Charyn knew that Lystara had even stronger shields than Malyna, who'd saved his life, but she was also three years younger, and holding shields to protect two people was more than enough, although from what he'd seen of the young imagers, they were very capable.

"That's right," said Aloryana, her voice thoughtful. "He's your heir. Until you marry and have children."

"That's a way off."

"Malyna said you danced with three women twice at the Spring-Turn Ball."

"Four, actually."

"So no one would guess which one you liked best?"

Charyn just raised his eyebrows.

"Are you learning any new music?"

"I'm working on another Farray piece. What about you?"

"Palenya has me working on a melody by Chaarpan and the short Farray piece you learned first. I'm not as good as you are . . . yet."

"You keep practicing and you'll end up better. What about your imaging?"

"I can do shields now. They're not very good, but they might stop one bullet, Maitre Alastar says. Concealments are easier for me."

Charyn frowned. "I thought . . ."

"For most imagers," said Lystara, not taking her eyes from outside the coach, "they're harder, but for Aloryana, they're easier."

"That's because of what you taught me."

The ride ended too soon, as far as Charyn was concerned, because it seemed like almost no time had passed before the coach turned off the Boulevard D'Rex and rolled to a halt outside the Anomen D'Rex.

"You two go first," declared Lystara as soon as all three were out of the coach. "I'm right behind you, but you're both shielded."

Followed by Lystara, and the two guards, Charyn led the way, along the back corridor, toward the regial enclosure, a space he hadn't stood inside in more than seven months. As they neared the side door out into the nave, Chorister Saerlet appeared.

"Your Grace, it's so good to see you, and you, Lady Aloryana . . . or should I say Imager Aloryana."

"I suppose she's both now," said Charyn. "Please don't mention that we're here. People will see, but an announcement," he grinned, "well, that might be a form of Naming."

"You do have a way with words, Your Grace."

"I'll leave the words to your homily, Chorister."

Saerlet nodded and opened the door.

The five in Charyn's party stepped out into the nave and then into the regial space, set off merely by a green and gold braided rope. Charyn noted that the anomen was perhaps only half full. Given that it was summer and warm, that didn't surprise him. Then he noticed something folded carefully over the braided rope—a simple square of white cloth, but when he picked it off the rope, the square unfolded into a white strip nearly a good yard and a half long. There were no markings on the cloth.

"What's that?" murmured Aloryana.

"I don't know. It's just white cloth." Charyn handed it to his sister.

"It's hemmed. It must be a belt of some sort." Aloryana refolded the cloth and handed it back to her brother.

"Someone must have left it here." Charyn tucked it into his jacket.

For several moments, those standing nearby seemed not even to notice their arrival. Then more worshippers looked quickly in their direction and quickly away.

Shortly, the choir sang the choral invocation while Saerlet stood in the center of the dais, facing the congregation. Then he spoke.

"We are gathered here together this evening in the spirit of the Nameless and in affirmation of the quest for goodness and mercy in all that we do."

Charyn didn't really know the opening hymn—"Forsaking Foolish Pride"—and neither did Aloryana. While it was clear that Lystara did, her words and voice were low.

The confession followed, which Charyn did know, although he spoke barely above a murmur. "We do not name You, for naming is a presumption, and we would not presume upon the creator of all that was, is, and will be. We do not pray to You, nor ask favors or recognition from You, for requesting such asks You to favor us over others who are also your creations. Rather we confess that we always risk the sins of pride and presumption and that the very names we bear symbolize those sins, for we too often strive to arrogate our names and ourselves above others, to insist that our petty plans and arid achievements have meaning beyond those whom we love or over whom we have influence and power. Let us never forget that we are less than nothing against your nameless magnificence and that all that we are is a gift to be cherished and treasured, and that we must also respect and cherish the gifts of others, in celebration of You who cannot be named or known, only respected and worshipped."

"In peace and harmony," was the chorused response, followed by the offertory baskets, which did not enter the regial space.

A moment of silence ensued as Saerlet ascended to the pulpit for his homily, the same pulpit from which Charyn had spoken at his father's memorial service—and where he had received one of the letters threatening his own assassination.

"Good evening."

"Good evening," came the reply.

"And it is a good evening, for under the Nameless all evenings are good. Tonight we gather again to offer thanks for that goodness. Some may feel that this life is not what it could be, and that is so. Because life is not what it could be, some people blame the Nameless, or they blame the Rex, or a chorister like me. Or they blame a people, like the Jariolans or the Pharsis. But what makes life less than it could be? Or for that matter, better than it could be, for there are those times as well. The Nameless created the world, and the greater and the lesser moon, the oceans and the tides. They are neither the cause of evil or the source of joy. They are.

"Rholan the Unnamer once observed that more evil and killing was done in this world in a single year by men who wished to impose their view of what was right upon others by force, than all the deaths in history caused by storms or by lightning or by the shaking of the earth. We cannot change the physical world. What we can change is how we live in that world . . ."

Charyn found his thoughts wandering as Saerlet continued, because he was thinking about what Saerlet had not said, or had avoided saying. Lack of rain did cause crops to fail. So did too much rain, but when people died from starvation, it was usually not because there was no food, but because food had become too dear for them to buy or because it would have cost too much to ship grain or maize from elsewhere. *Or it would take too much time.*

He dragged his thoughts back to the service as Saerlet finished the homily, murmured the closing hymn—"The Path to Joy"—and listened to the final benediction.

Then he smiled at Aloryana. "That wasn't too bad, was it?"

"He speaks well. I think I like what Chorister Iskhar says better."

"Sometimes," murmured Lystara dryly, adding, "Shouldn't we go?"

"We should." Charyn immediately turned toward the side door.

Lystara stepped in front of Charyn, opened the door, and held it.

Just as the door closed behind Aloryana, Chorister Saerlet appeared.

"It's so good to see you and Lady Aloryana," began Saerlet.

"And Maitre Lystara," added Charyn. "Without her, we wouldn't be here."

"Will we be seeing Lord Bhayrn?"

Don't get greedy, Chorister. But Charyn merely said, "Since he's my heir, it's unlikely we'll ever be in the same place outside of the Chateau at the same time."

"Oh . . . do you think it's that dangerous?"

"Possibly not, Chorister, but it's an unnecessary risk. I did find your homily thought-provoking. I'm sure I will find others equally so, but my presence is likely to be unpredictable. Now . . . I did promise to have Aloryana back to the Collegium in a timely fashion. So . . ."

"Oh . . . yes."

"Good evening, Chorister," added Aloryana sweetly.

Lystara led the way to the unmarked coach at a brisk pace with the two guards following Charyn and Aloryana.

Once they were in the coach, and headed back northeast on the Boulevard D'Rex, Aloryana said, "At least it wasn't too long."

"The Collegium must be good for you," teased Charyn. "You used to think his services took forever."

"Maitre Obsolym is the one who talks forever," replied Aloryana. "He's interesting, though."

"The first five times you've heard it," murmured Lystara.

"What did you think of the Anomen D'Rex, Lystara?" asked Charyn.

"It's much bigger than our anomen. Darker, too."

"Charyn," said Aloryana, "you said his homily was thought-provoking. Did that mean you didn't agree?"

"I don't think the Nameless cares what storms do. People can die or starve because of prolonged bad weather, but the weather isn't evil. It just is. It is what it is, and it doesn't have a choice. People usually do have a choice, especially people with golds or power. Evil is, in a way, I think, a judgment on the choices people make." *And that means people can term some of your choices as evil, even when there's no good choice.* Which there wasn't, Charyn knew, in choosing where to send warships to fight the Jariolans . . . and in more than a few other decisions he'd made.

"You mean if a choice you make hurts someone, they'll say it's evil?"

Charyn nodded. "And if it helps someone else, that person will likely say it's good."

"You're talking differently," observed Aloryana.

"I'm little older."

Aloryana frowned, but didn't reply.

Both Alastar and Alyna greeted the coach as soon as it pulled up in front of the Maitre's dwelling.

Alastar looked to Lystara and then Charyn.

"There was no sign of trouble," said Charyn, although he hadn't expected any. Trouble, if there were to be any, would come later, when people learned he was attending services, if less than predictably.

"You will join us for refreshments, I hope," said Aloryana.

"I'd be happy to."

"We'll also send some out to the guards and driver," added Alastar.

As Charyn and the imagers walked toward the covered front porch, Alastar said, "I heard from Aloryana that you're not exactly fond of dark lager. So there's also a decent white wine, if you'd like that."

"I appreciate that."

Before long the five were seated in the parlor, beakers or glasses in hand, and there was a platter of assorted biscuits, crackers, and cheese slices on the low table.

Alyna looked to Aloryana. "How was the service?"

"It was like most services."

"She was glad it was short," added Charyn.

"I assume you know that, by the end of the week, if not sooner, one of the newssheets will report that you attended services," said Alastar.

"That's why I'd thought to come here, if that's agreeable, next Solayi and attend your services."

"You will?" asked Aloryana.

"Yes."

"That might fluster Iskhar, but I'm certain he will manage," observed Alastar.

"He'll rise to the occasion, if you tell him in advance," said Alyna.

"Please . . . I'd really appreciate it if he didn't acknowledge my presence," said Charyn.

"I can do both," said Alastar.

"Isn't the Chateau . . . sort of empty?" asked Aloryana.

"Right now, it is. I told you that Bhayrn is visiting friends. You know Mother is in Rivages. She likely won't be back until the beginning of Erntyn, but I do tend to keep busy . . . and, yes, I am continuing to practice on the clavecin, and I'm trying to learn a new piece or two."

"You'll have to play it for us when we come to see you," declared Aloryana.

"We'll see. And only if you play for me."

"I will."

"Then, I'd better arrange for Palenya to tune the clavecin just before you come." Charyn almost wished he hadn't said those words, but she was by far the best that he knew. He'd just have to keep it a matter of tuning. *And not memories.*

"Has Bhayrn been playing?" asked Aloryana.

"No. Mother's not here, and I'm not about to insist that he pound the keys."

"Then Palenya won't have to do much," declared Aloryana.

Lystara raised her eyebrows.

"He hammers the keys," explained Aloryana.

Almost a glass passed, all too quickly for Charyn, before he sensed it was time for him to leave. He stood. "I really should be going."

Immediately, Aloryana wrapped her arms around him. "Thank you for coming."

"I'll see you next Solayi . . . and keep working on your shields," Charyn added. "You know, I'm jealous that you can do that, and I can't." He smiled broadly.

Aloryana just grinned as she released her brother and stepped back.

As Charyn headed for the door, Alyna joined him.

"I'll walk out with you."

Charyn wondered what she was about to convey, but nodded and said, "I do appreciate Lystara's being our escort."

Alyna did not reply until they were on the front porch and out of earshot of the others. "Actually, I'm glad Lystara wanted to escort you two. It's a way for her to see more that she needs to see. Malyna saw that world growing up, and so did I, but Lystara hasn't had that opportunity. That's another reason why both Alastar and I appreciate the invitation to what you called a family gathering." She paused, then asked, "Might I ask what prompted your decision to host such a gathering?"

Charyn laughed. "I had no coldly reasoned rationale. It just felt like I should. In fact, I felt I'd been remiss in not doing so earlier."

Alyna nodded. "That's a very good reason. We'll see you next Solayi, I trust."

"Unless there's something awful and unforeseen, I'll be here."

As the coach carried him away from the Maitre's dwelling, and then over the bridge to the Boulevard D'Rex, Charyn couldn't help feeling just a little wistful. Somehow, the sight of Erion, a thin crescent just above the western horizon, didn't help, although he couldn't have said why.

5

By the time Charyn rose on Mardi morning, the Chateau truly felt empty. With Bhayrn having left the previous Vendrei, the only people with whom he'd interacted since going to Imagisle on Solayi evening were his ministers, Guard Captain Maertyl, Undercaptain Faelln, and other Chateau staff. Even his Aunt Elacia only came on Mardi, Meredi, and Vendrei—unless Charyn was having some sort of function, and he'd had almost none since his mother had left for Rivages and the Ryel holding.

Something you're working to change . . . something you definitely do need to change.

He was making progress in learning "Pavane in a Minor Key," but then, he should have been, given how few distractions he had.

After finishing his morning routine, Charyn made his way to his study, where he immediately picked up *Veritum*. As he had suspected, there was a small article on the bottom of the front page, the key words of which were definitely pointed.

. . . and after months of apparent moping in the Chateau D'Rex, our beloved Rex Regis, Charyn, finally returned to attending services at the Anomen D'Rex, accompanied by no less than his sister, and now imager, Aloryana. Lord Bhayrn was nowhere to be seen . . .

Charyn shook his head, although it was certainly to be expected, given how reclusive he'd been. It also reminded him of the white cloth belt that rested in his armoire. The only thing it could be connected to, so far as he could determine, might be the True Believers, because he didn't know of anyone else who might wear a plain white cloth belt. It had been left for him, but why? *A notice that the True Believers were watching?* But the last thing he or any Rex wanted to do was to interfere with what a chorister did or said.

Along with that, he pondered what other public appearances he might make in order that such appearances might cease to be newsworthy. *That will take more appearances that you may wish to make.*

Moencriff rapped on the study door. "Lady Delcoeur, sir."

Elacia entered, nodding to Charyn not quite perfunctorily, then stood waiting.

"Is Ferrand joining us for a midday refreshments?"

"He is."

"Excellent. And on Samedi?"

"For dinner on Samedi, there will be Marshal Vaelln and his wife, Sephia, Vice-Marshal Maurek and his wife, Amalie, Commander Chaalt, whose wife is visiting family in Tuuryl and will not be here, and Subcommander Luerryn and his wife, Varcela. Do you wish dinner music?"

"I think not," replied Charyn. "What about the following Samedi?"

"Everyone has accepted. Kayrolya D'Taelmyn and her parents, Marenna D'Almeida and her parents, Zhelyn D'Saeffen-Alte, and Sherrona D'Plessan and her mother, Sherryla. High Holder Plessan is Sherrona's brother. Those are the ones you asked me to fill in. The others you requested by name all accepted."

"Is Ferrand pleased?"

"Most likely, pleasantly so, but not totally."

"Because you picked young women whose parents would be more likely to accept him?"

"Wasn't that part of the reason for the dinner?"

"Just part."

"You've been good to us, far more than other members of the regial family in the past."

Charyn wasn't about to get into that part of family history. "Ferrand's been a good friend, and you've been most helpful since Mother was required to be in Ryel."

"You will need music for the larger dinner."

"Strings, please. No clavecin."

Elacia paused just for a moment before replying. "That's a wise choice."

Charyn wasn't sure about that. Picking another clavecin player over Palenya would have been an insult, but Charyn felt uneasy about having Palenya play for a dinner where he was entertaining eligible women, and Charyn owed Palenya too much ever to do anything to hurt her.

He did wonder when she might finish the nocturne commission, but since he wanted a good composition, he wasn't about to hurry her. "What about the family dinner?" He already knew the answer, but not whether the formal replies had reached Elacia.

"Maitre Alyna replied that they would all attend, and would be pleased to be here."

"I'm glad to hear that."

"If you don't have anything pressing for me, Charyn, I thought I'd go over the menu for Samedi with Hassala."

"Please do."

Once Elacia left, Charyn picked up the draft of the letter from Sanafryt as Minister of Justice to High Holder Douvyt and began to read.

You have requested relief from the Rex in the matter of a textile manufactorage built by one Factor Camarouth, charging that said manufactorage so contaminates the river water that your rights to use that water have been invalidated by the fact that the water is so poisoned that irrigating with it damages your flax plants.

> There is no specific provision in the Codex Legis
> dealing directly with damages caused by substances
> placed in stream or river water, nor does the Codex
> Legis require water users not to contaminate the
> water. Since there is no duty to leave the water
> uncontaminated, there is no firm legal basis for anyone
> to seek damages.

Charyn frowned. Wasn't there an unspoken civic duty not to poison the land and water? Certainly, if someone poisoned someone else . . .

But under law, plants aren't people.

He picked up the draft and walked out of the study and made his way to Sanafryt's study.

The Minister of Justice rose as Charyn stepped into the study. "I see you've been reading my response to High Holder Douvyt."

"I have. Isn't there a civic duty not to poison land or water?"

"There may be a *civic* duty, but there's not a legal obligation not to do it."

"I thought as much." Charyn smiled. "What if I enacted a change to the Codex Legis that stated that users of water have the duty to return that water to the stream or river in the same state as when they removed it from the river?"

"I can see several outcomes from that. Some users would dump the contaminated water elsewhere or put it in ponds to evaporate. Someone would certainly challenge the law on the grounds that there is no way to determine the precise state of water. Some would claim that what they were doing made no difference to the state of the water."

Charyn nodded, then said, "Draft something like that for me."

"Everyone will protest, Your Grace. And how could you possibly enforce such a law?"

"I didn't say I was going to make it law. I want to present

the problem and the language to the joint councils and see what they think, or can come up with."

"Is that wise?"

"We've already had two petitions on the matter. With more manufactorages being built, there will be more. The problem won't go away, and I don't want to be the one everyone complains about. At worst, the councils need to agree to do nothing. At best, we might come up with something."

Sanafryt was the one to frown.

"The High Council, in particular, has the tendency to complain, but not to be helpful in resolving complaints, but they want to be more a part of governing." Charyn grinned. "Let's see what they have to say when they have to think about it."

"They'll favor the High Holder."

"And then what happens when I point out, very gently, that I'll have to revoke High Holder Haebyn's rights by that precedent? Remember, all the factor councilors will be sitting across the table from them."

Sanafryt offered a sickly smile. "Ah . . . that will be interesting."

"If you could have draft language by next Lundi, the thirtieth, I'd appreciate that."

"Yes, Your Grace."

"Now . . . there's one other matter. About the artificers' standard."

"You said that the councils rejected any law as unworkable."

"They did, but isn't there a presumption in law that when a good is stamped as, say, sterling silver, and it's not, that would constitute a form of theft, or at least fraud?"

"Yes . . . but you'd have to prove it, and the cost of proving it would likely be more than the worth of the goods."

"What if the Civic Patrol brought such a case before a justicer?"

"They'd have no standing."

"I'd like you to work on drafting something that would

assert that, in the interests of the people of Solidar, the Civic Patrol has the right not only to bring such a charge, but if the charge is sustained, the seller of goods fraudulently presented is to be assessed a penalty, in addition to the costs of bringing the charge, and that upon a third offense, be sentenced to not less than two months in gaol."

"That will be even less popular than the water proposal."

"To the factors and the High Holders, but don't I have the duty to protect people who aren't either?"

"You have to have the support of the factors and the High Holders, sir."

"Don't they have the responsibility to deal fairly?"

"They would claim they do deal fairly, and they would question whether your involvement is that necessary."

"Think some more about it. We'll talk later." Charyn offered a smile before turning and heading back to his study.

Slightly before noon he was pondering the fact that he hadn't seen the documents promised by Estafen regarding the ironworks when Sturdyn, relieving Moencriff, announced, "High Holder Delcoeur."

"Have him come in." Charyn turned from where he stood by the window, smiling as his cousin approached. "How are matters going?"

"You mean with the holding?" Ferrand offered a resigned smile. "I've managed to pay off what Father owed the Banque D'Excelsis. I still owe the Banque D'Aluse three thousand golds."

"Weezyr's not pressing you, then?"

"Why should he? You were right about that. He wants the golds, and he decided he really didn't want to press the cousin of the Rex. Not as long as I've been paying him regularly. There's more income than I thought." Ferrand shook his head. "Father wasn't entering it all in the ledgers. It must have gone straight to the gaming tables. And with what you're paying Mother . . ."

"It's very little." Little at least for the widow of a High Holder, a "mere" two golds a week.

"It's enough for her personal items, and that makes her feel like she's not reducing my inheritance." Ferrand grinned almost boyishly. "People are talking to me again. Of course, as you pointed out, I'll have to be careful for years, but considering I could easily have lost everything . . ."

Not everything, Charyn knew, but enough that Ferrand would no longer have been a High Holder. "But you didn't."

"Your advice and assistance made it possible."

"I did what I could, seeing as neither of us happened to be in the best of positions." In the end, Charyn had "loaned" Ferrand a thousand golds out of his own personal funds, to be repaid after all other debts on the holding were paid. The thousand had been to provide enough, with what Ferrand had been able to raise, to immediately satisfy Weezyr at the Banque D'Aluse. Which was another reason why he'd had to borrow five thousand from the Ryel estate, instead of four, yet having the High Holding of a close relative and friend of the Rex fail, especially through no fault of Ferrand's, wouldn't have reflected well on Charyn. But taking golds from the treasury wouldn't have reflected well on Charyn, either. "Your mother tells me that everyone has accepted for next Samedi's dinner."

"Who, might I ask? She said that I'd have to find out from you because the list was your prerogative."

"There are five young women, one of whom I'd appreciate your not showing an interest in."

"Who might that one be? Not Maitre Malyna, I trust." Ferrand grinned.

"She's not marriageable for either of us. No . . . Alyncya D'Shendael."

"She's attractive, but not a raving beauty. Who are the other four?"

"Shaelyna D'Baeltyn and her parents, Kayrolya D'Taelmyn

and her parents, Marenna D'Almeida and her parents, and Sherrona D'Plessan and her mother. The other heirs are Zhelyn D'Saeffen-Alte and Ferron D'Fhernon-Alte."

"You didn't invite Cynthalya D'Nacryon? I saw you being rather friendly with her at the Year-Turn Ball, and you danced with her at the Spring-Turn Ball."

"Only once. She's nice enough, but I've learned a few things about High Holder Nacryon, and the last thing I need is more family politics."

"You're sounding more like your father."

"He was right about family politics," Charyn said humorously, not that he felt that way.

"Why did you invite Ferron?"

"Because he wants to marry Malyna, and I took pity on him. Besides, from what little I've seen, he's got courage, judgment, and manners. I'd like to find out more about him."

"Are you going to court some of the High Council?"

"I doubt many of them are in L'Excelis at present, but that's a good idea. You'll note that all those I invited to dinner are from comparatively close by. It is summer." Charyn turned toward the door. "We ought to join your mother for refreshments in the family parlor."

The two took the grand staircase down to the family parlor. Charyn still felt slightly uneasy coming down those wide marble steps. He supposed he would for a while, between what happened on them, or at their base, and the ensuing nightmares.

Elacia was waiting in the parlor, standing beside the small circular table. "I wondered when you two might appear," she said cheerfully.

"I was persuading Charyn to share the invitation list for the dinner a week from Samedi. Was Shaelyna D'Baeltyn your idea?"

"Most of the names came from the Rex," said Elacia, her voice slightly arch, "and you'll have to ask him, which I don't suggest, dear."

Ferrand shook his head. "You two."

"We're just looking out for you," said Charyn, grinning as he seated himself, and then poured himself a cool pale ale from the pitcher. Unlike Bhayrn, he didn't care that much for lager, and preferred ale only on warm days.

Elacia smiled sweetly from where she sat between them, but Charyn saw a glint in her eyes, if but for a moment. Then she asked, "Have you heard much from your mother? She writes every week, I understand."

"She's discovered that Karyel and Iryella don't really know all that they should at their age about running a High Holding. She's also worried about the summer heat and the lack of rain."

"Aren't we all?" replied Ferrand. "The landwarden told me to expect a fair harvest at best, but likely a poor one, if not worse."

"Are you mostly in wheat corn?"

"I don't know. I leave it up to him."

Charyn merely nodded, although Ferrand's attitude bothered him. *Then, two years ago, you were just like that.* He almost smiled at the thought that his impatience with pistols had changed everything.

"Do you know what is planted everywhere?" asked Elacia.

"No. I know fairly closely what's planted on the lands at Chaeryll. That's because they were my only source of funds for the past several years. I've been studying the landwardens' reports from the rest of the lands, and I've made some inquiries and suggestions, but I couldn't spend much time on that this year after everything that's happened. Next year, I'll likely make some changes." *And with more than crops, you hope.*

Elacia nodded, then said, "The early melon and the blueberries are quite good."

Charyn took a sip of the ale, deciding to let the conversation be light and about food and weather. "I wish the early melons lasted longer."

"I tend to prefer the later berries," said Ferrand.

By two quints before second glass Charyn was back in his study, going over the treasury account ledgers.

Just before second glass, Moencriff rapped on the study door. "Craftmaster Argentyl, Your Grace."

"Have him come in."

The smallish black-haired silversmith entered the study, immediately inclining his head to Charyn before moving toward the chairs before the table desk.

Charyn stood. "I appreciate your coming to see me, Craftmaster Argentyl." He gestured to the chairs, then sat down.

"It's my pleasure, Your Grace."

"As I promised you, I have looked into the problem with shoddy goods and the misrepresentation of the quality of goods. I also brought the matter before the joint councils—both the Council of Factors and the High Council. They agreed that times have changed, and that such misrepresentation presents a problem." Charyn paused for a moment. "That part is not the problem. The problem lies in finding a workable solution."

"Your Grace. We offered a solution."

"You did. The problem, according to the factors and High Holders, is that they would have to know how, where, and under what conditions everything they sell was made. They claim that is unworkable. As Rex, I do not have the golds to hire thousands of inspectors to patrol the markets and shops of Solidar. Nor are there enough men, or even women, who would know enough to distinguish between, as you pointed out earlier, silver plate and solid sterling, not without cutting into the metal, anyway, and that is only one of hundreds if not thousands of goods."

"It isn't right, Your Grace. They shouldn't be able to claim their goods are what they're not. They're stealing from us. Some craftmasters have had to let go apprentices, even journeymen. Already, you can hardly find a good weaver anywhere, not with those mills. Nor a good gunsmith, not with that rifleworks south of L'Excelsis. Except for a few that work for rich factors or High Holders."

Charyn didn't know what he could really say. "I'll spend some more time with the Minister of Justice and see if there's another way."

"You could make a law, Your Grace."

"I said that to him, and he asked me how I'd be able to enforce it. Would you want me to tariff you to pay for the inspectors? My father fought two civil wars with the High Holders over tariffs."

"We can't pay what we don't have, sir."

"That's my problem, too, strange as it sounds."

"Do you need to fight with the Jariolans?"

"Do you and the metalworkers need tin? It all comes by ship. Do you like spices for your food? Most of them come from Otelyrn."

Argentyl's shoulders slumped.

"I haven't forgotten you and the guilds, Argentyl, but it's going to take some time to see how this can be done."

"You've listened, Your Grace. That's more than any before you. But it doesn't put bread on the table."

"I know that." Charyn stood. "I knew that before you came, but I told you I'd let you know, and I haven't given up yet." *Even if you don't have the faintest idea of what might work.*

"Might be best if you found a solution before long. There are those who won't stay quiet much longer."

"Who might those be?"

"I don't know. Those who do won't tell me. But you should know." The master crafter stood. "I'd best be going, Your Grace."

Charyn just stood there long after the silversmith had left.

6

On Vendrei morning, Charyn received a visit from Factor Estafen with all the documents pertaining to the transfer of the ironworks, as well as a stack of ledgers and copies of the master ledgers of the ironworks dating back to its founding. After changing into his factoring garb, and wearing his gold exchange pin, he took the unmarked coach and went with Estafen to the exchange, where he transferred six thousand golds to Estafen and the deed for the ironworks was recorded in his name.

The rest of the morning was spent on a tour of the ironworks, where Charyn was introduced as Factor Suyrien and the new owner of the ironworks. Charyn made clear to Engineer Ostraaw, the chief foreman of the ironworks, that while he would inspect the works regularly, all correspondence and documents were to be sent to the Banque D'Excelsis, since sending them to Chaeryll would actually mean it would be longer before Factor Suyrien saw them. Charyn took his time inspecting the entire works and asking questions, including a request to Ostraaw that clearly surprised the engineer.

"I'd like you to consider the best location for a manufactorage that would be capable of forging heavy iron assemblies to exacting tolerances."

"Unless I know how large and how many, sir . . ."

"The size of the assemblies will be a minimum of several hundredweight."

Ostraaw's eyebrows rose.

"It will likely be several months, most likely much longer, but I would appreciate your thinking about it."

"Yes, sir."

Charyn had spent almost a glass talking to Ostraaw, whom Estafen had brought in to handle the day-to-day operation of the ironworks, and had left with a sense of the man's competence. Still, he knew he'd need to spend more time there.

By Samedi morning, after his exercise and other routine morning activities, including a meeting with Guard Captain Maertyl, Charyn was still pondering his purchase. It certainly hadn't been spur of the moment. He'd been trying to accomplish it for over seven months. *And now you're wondering if it will work out.* Except, over time, much as he disliked the idea, he knew the rifleworks would be profitable, especially the longer-range rifles used by the naval marines, since it didn't appear that the undeclared war between Solidar and Jariola was likely to end anytime soon.

His pondering was interrupted by the arrival of a letter from Aloryana, which he immediately opened and began to read.

> . . . *I know I told you this on Solayi, but I was so glad you came for refreshments, and I'm looking forward to the kind of family dinner at the Chateau next month. Malyna and I can show Lystara around. Do you think we could play the duet again?*

Charyn smiled. That was something he'd enjoy doing.

When he finished the letter, he placed it with the others from her in the cabinet behind the desk, then turned his attention to the latest reports from the regional governors in Tilbora and Khel, which, while long and detailed, said very little except that both feared hot and dry summers, except in the far northeast of Tilbora, which had endured heavy winter snows and unseasonal spring rains. Since most of that part of Tilbora was mountainous and heavily forested, and the rivers in that area flowed west into the Northern Ocean, and not into the northeastern croplands, that might mean a good year for the trees, but not for much else.

Much later, after dressing for the dinner, in formal greens, Charyn made his way to the music room, where he seated himself at the clavecin and began to play, starting with Farray's Nocturne Number Three. Then he went through his part of the Farray duet he'd played with Aloryana.

Just as he finished, he noticed that Elacia had entered the music room. Rather than continue immediately, he asked, "Is there a problem of some sort?"

"No. I wondered who was playing so well, because you hadn't asked for entertainment."

"I just play for myself . . . and family."

"You play as well as many professional musicians, Charyn. I had no idea."

"I play certain pieces moderately well, thanks to Musician Palenya. I definitely don't have the repertoire of a professional."

"She's no longer here."

"No. She's become the music master at the Collegium. They didn't have one, and Aloryana and Maitre Malyna, among others, wanted to continue to study and improve."

Elacia nodded. "You're much more . . . quiet than your father. It suits you and Solidar." After a pause, she said, "I'm going to make sure that the sideboards in the reception room are properly set up. I do hope you'll play a little more."

"I will. The next piece won't sound as good. I need to work on it."

"I'm sure it will be fine." Elacia turned and left the music room.

Charyn doubted that, since the next piece he wanted to work on was "Pavane in a Minor Key," which was far harder. He spent more than two quints just working on the first two pages, then played the far simpler Farray piece that had been the first one he'd learned under Palenya's tutelage. He would have liked to have played more, but fifth glass was nearing.

So he stood, put away the music for the pavane, and then made his way from the music room, closing the door behind himself. Since the dinner with the selected officers of the High Command was to be comparatively less formal and he didn't have to be announced, he entered the reception room adjoining the formal dining room half a quint before fifth glass, nodding to the servers and making his way to the sideboard.

"The Tacqueville white, please."

"Yes, sir."

Charyn took a slow swallow of the slightly buttery pale golden vintage, then another, waiting as Elacia appeared and joined him.

"Everything is set, and the first carriage is at the steps."

"Thank you."

The first couples to enter the reception room were Marshal Vaelln and his wife Sephia, followed by Vice-Marshal Maurek and his wife Amalie.

"Good evening, Rex Charyn," offered Vaelln.

"The same to you, Marshal, Lady. I'd like you to meet my aunt, Lady Delcoeur, who has been kind enough to take over my mother's obligations in her absence . . ."

After those introductions, the other three arrived, and Charyn met and introduced to Elacia Commander Chaalt, who was Vaelln's chief of staff, and Subcommander Luerryn and his wife Varcela, who was trying very hard not to seem wide-eyed. Then Charyn turned to Varcela and said almost in a murmur, as he offered a mischievous smile, "It's only a very large chateau that often keeps me imprisoned here."

For a moment, Varcela, who had to be at least ten years younger than the grizzled Luerryn, looked almost scandalized, then smiled in return. "I never thought of it that way."

Luerryn turned. "Your Grace?"

"I was only telling your wife that the Chateau was often a very large prison for a very new Rex."

The subcommander paused, then nodded. "I can see that, sir."

"I might add," Charyn said, looking back to Varcela, "that your husband was the one who gave me my first tour of High Command headquarters as well as provided a great deal of basic information that proved very useful in the weeks after the assassination. There was a great deal I didn't know." Charyn laughed softly. "There's still a great deal I don't know, but I've made some inroads on that ignorance. Now . . . you have your choice of ale or lager, red or white wine. The white wine is a Tacqueville and my personal favorite, but the red is good, and it's one my brother prefers. It comes from near Tuuryl." He eased the two toward the nearer sideboard. "Where, might I ask, did you two meet?"

"At a dinner at Commander Chaalt's quarters some five years ago," replied Varcela with an amused smile.

"Varcela is a cousin of the commander. She really wasn't at the dinner, but she was reading to their daughter, and I liked the sound of her voice."

"He was curious."

"Snooping," admitted Luerryn. "I'm not sure the commander has ever forgiven me, totally."

"You obviously knew what you wanted," observed Charyn.

"He always has."

"Sometimes that's good, like with Varcela. Other times . . ." Luerryn shook his head.

Charyn waited until Varcela took a goblet of the red, as did Luerryn, before asking, conversationally, "When you briefed me last Finitas, what would you have liked to tell me, but didn't?"

The subcommander's eyes widened for a moment. Then he smiled. "That I wished your father had taken even half the time you did learning about the army."

Charyn winced. He didn't even try to hide it. "I doubt I've spent the time I should, but there's been so much to learn in the last six months. As a military officer, what do you worry about the most? That is, threats that might face Solidar?"

"The Jariolans first, but you and the Marshal seem to have that in hand, as much in hand as possible, that is."

"And?"

"There's no other military threat that I can see, sir."

"What about the High Holders?"

Luerryn shook his head. "Between you, the Collegium Maitre, and the Marshal, they're not that great a threat."

"The factors are growing more powerful."

"Yes, sir."

". . . and the guilds and the crafters are getting poorer," murmured Varcela.

Luerryn stiffened, but didn't say anything.

"I've thought that, myself," said Charyn, "but I'm rather isolated." He nodded to her. "Thank you." Then he looked to Luerryn. "Do you worry about that?"

"We're getting more who want to be troopers these days. We can pick and choose the best. It hasn't always been like that."

"Some of that is likely because of poor harvests," replied Charyn, "but I have the feeling that it's not the only reason." *More than just a feeling, based on what Argentyl had said.* He managed a smile. "If you will excuse me . . ." He eased away and moved toward Vaelln, who was conversing with Elacia.

". . . can remember when there were thousands and thousands of troopers posted at High Command," Elacia was saying.

"That wasn't where they were needed," replied Vaelln. "Even then we should have had more naval marines and more warships. One of the last things Marshal Wilkorn said to me was that he'd been too worried about the mistakes he'd made in the last battles and not enough about the wars to come. Foreseeing the future is so much harder than repeating the past and hoping it won't change."

"Except," interjected Charyn, "sometimes the past does repeat itself, and sometimes it doesn't, and I'm finding it hard to discern which is when."

"Aren't we all?" Vaelln laughed ruefully.

As he did Elacia slipped away, moving toward Luerryn and his wife.

Charyn accepted a goblet of the Tacqueville white presented by one of the servers, took a sip, and said, conversationally, "Along those lines, I was talking to Chorister Refaal the other day, and he mentioned a group that calls itself the True Believers. They've caused a certain amount of trouble at anomens in various places in Solidar. Have you run across them . . . or any mention of them?"

Vaelln frowned, tilting his head slightly, then nodded. "There was an incident in Tilbora about a year ago at the governor's chateau, the old palace of the Khanarate, you know. Someone broke into the anomen and took all the chorister's vestments and strung them up along the walls. They painted some words on the stones about how the offerings to the Nameless were going for vestments grander than what Rex Regis wore, and that the chorister was a Namer, and that it was time to return to the true beliefs." Vaelln smiled wryly. "The chorister wanted your father to repay him for the vestments. Your father told the governor to pay the chorister one gold and not a copper more."

Charyn nodded. That definitely sounded like his father. "Did the governor discover any more about it?"

"All he could find out was a rumor that it was the work of the True Believers, some sort of throwback cult misconstruing the words of Rholan. He didn't seem to think it was all that serious. None of the army or navy commanders supporting the regional governors have reported anything else like that."

"There haven't been any reports from any of the port cities, either," added Maurek.

"It seems a bit strange. Refaal also reported that a chorister in Ruile had been chased from his anomen, and that High Holder Lenglan had been forced to use his personal guards to drive True Believers from an anomen in Semlem."

"There have always been prophets and charlatans claiming to be the true voice of the Nameless," suggested Amalie.

Maurek looked askance at his wife.

"Grandfather Yussyl was a chorister in Cheva. He always said that there was a lot about Rholan that wasn't in the sayings because people would misinterpret them."

"Such as?"

"He'd never say . . . not exactly. He said people misquoted Rholan to be nasty to Pharsis. The only saying I recall that he said wasn't in the books was that Rholan said that faith was just the beginning. That's what Grandfather said. I asked him what he meant, and he just smiled."

"You never mentioned that," said Maurek.

"You never asked."

"How do you like the wine?" asked Charyn, to whoever might answer.

"It's excellent," offered Vaelln.

Maurek nodded, as did Chaalt.

Fearing he might have been too direct, Charyn vowed to be more charming and less the interrogator for the rest of the evening. He also couldn't help but think about the white belt.

7

On Solayi, Charyn slept late, spent some time in the covered courtyard practicing with his pistol, especially working on shooting quickly and accurately with either hand. Then he went riding in the hunting park, read more of Solidaran history, and spent three glasses, in one-glass increments, working on learning "Pavane in a Minor Key." In addition to that, he studied the shipbuilding plans for the new class of frigates that were to be built in the Solis shipyard, in addition to the first-rate ships of the line. It had taken a certain amount of persuasion to obtain those plans, especially since Charyn wasn't about to offer the entire explanation for why he wanted them.

That evening, at a quint past fifth glass, he got into the unmarked coach and rode to Imagisle, joining Aloryana and the Maitre and his family at the Maitre's dwelling. From there they walked to the Collegium anomen, a building, Charyn recalled from his tour nearly a half year earlier, that predated the Collegium, although it had been rebuilt and refurbished by the first imager of the Collegium.

Charyn stood at one side of the anomen, with Aloryana and the others, and listened to the service, not all that different from the ones conducted by Saerlet. He did concentrate on a part of the homily, and especially the way in which Chorister Iskhar presented it.

". . . the Nameless does not require blind faith and mindless obedience. What the Nameless requires is not only your faith, but your thought. Do not believe blindly all that you hear and read. See if it makes sense, or if you can prove it or disprove it in another fashion. The ancients believed that

Erion was a god, not just a moon, and that the son of Erion would come to the aid of those who were in need. The records of the first Maitre even have a passage that notes that the blade of Erion saved the first Maitre. Do moons forge blades? No . . . a literal reading of that passage makes little sense, but there was very likely a sword called the blade of Erion, and somehow it helped that Maitre . . ."

The Nameless does not require blind faith and mindless obedience . . . That phrase kept repeating itself in Charyn's thoughts throughout the remainder of the homily and service. Somehow, he couldn't imagine Chorister Saerlet offering those words.

After the service, he walked back to the Maitre's dwelling and once more had refreshments and enjoyed being with Aloryana and the Maitre's family, even including Malyna, who had joined them on the walk back from the anomen.

Lundi came early, but Charyn didn't mind. While he expected Bhayrn would have returned late on Solayi, Bhayrn didn't actually arrive at the Chateau D'Rex until mid-afternoon on Lundi, but that was scarcely surprising. Nor was the fact that he immediately went to bed, and Charyn didn't see him until Bhayrn appeared in the breakfast room on Mardi morning just as Charyn was finishing his second mug of tea.

"How was your time at Talyon?"

"It's too early for shooting, or any decent hunting, except boar hunting, but High Holder Laastyn sent word that we were to leave the boars alone because too many had been killed last year."

"Were any of Laamyst's sisters around? Or cousins? You said one of them—"

"No. They decided not to come. One of the serving girls was nice-looking, but Laamyst warned me that she was a favorite of his father's."

That might have been for the best. "I hope that didn't spoil things too much."

"It was better than staying here." Bhayrn sat down across the table from Charyn, then looked to the server. "A lager, Therosa, and anything that has ham and eggs in it."

"Yes, Lord Bhayrn."

Bhayrn turned to Charyn again. "You never told me about the Council meeting."

Charyn wasn't about to tell Bhayrn that might have been because his brother was never around, not if he could help it. "They complained some that we aren't building ships fast enough . . . The Jariolans apparently realized that they're losing. They've threatened to blockade the Abierto Isles unless the Isles refuse their ports to our ships. We'll have to break the blockade, of course, and some of the councilors don't like that, either, because it will take warships away from patrolling the shipping lanes to Otelyrn, as if they wouldn't suffer more from a blockade. And Basalyt complained about the tariff reassessment."

"Tariff reassessment? You're increasing tariffs? You promised not to do that."

"I'm not increasing them. The tariff rolls haven't been updated in at least ten years. That means some High Holders aren't paying enough and some are paying too much. When Alucar finds out that parts of some holdings aren't being tariffed, he sends a notice of inquiry . . ." Charyn went on to explain.

"That still sounds like a tariff increase," said Bhayrn. "The High Holders who have to pay more will think it is."

"I'm sure they will. But it's not fair for one High Holder to be tariffed, say, one silver a hectare, and another a silver and two."

"Most High Holders pay more than enough. That's what Laamyst's father claims."

Charyn doubted that, but he merely replied, "We've found, so far, that the tariffs of the vast majority don't need to be changed."

"Well . . . if you're not raising the levies on most of them . . . Still . . ."

Before Bhayrn could continue in that vein, Charyn went on, "Oh, I had a dinner on Samedi with the officers of the High Command and their wives, and I'll be entertaining again this Samedi. I'm also having a sort of family dinner on the eighteenth of Agostos, with Maitre Alastar and his family, Malyna, Aloryana, as well as High Holder Calkoran, who is Maitre Alyna's cousin. You're most welcome to attend, but you don't have to."

"What about this Samedi?"

"It's partly for Ferrand, a number of marriageable young women and their parents, two other High Holder heirs, Ferrand, and me."

"And one potential young lady for you?" asked Bhayrn dryly.

"I didn't wish to miss the opportunity to learn more about several of them in a way that doesn't make public my inclinations."

"Always so cautious . . . until it's too late for those you wish to ensnare." Bhayrn's laugh was harsh. "I will attend the family dinner. I might watch the other from a distance, at least to satisfy my prurient curiosity."

"As you wish. Let Aunt Elacia know if there's any special meal you'd like for any evening that you'll be here. Oh . . . and you might think about writing Aloryana. She does enjoy getting letters from family."

Bhayrn nodded as Therosa returned with his lager. He took a long swallow, then asked, "Have you heard much from Mother? Besides asking you to nag me to write Aloryana?"

"I promised her I'd suggest it."

"And you always keep your promises." Bhayrn's tone was almost scornfully amused.

"She did say that she expected you would keep your word

and spend the last two weeks of Agostos and part of the first week of Erntyn with her at Ryel."

"I promised, didn't I?"

"You could go earlier, if you find life here boring," suggested Charyn.

"Three weeks at Ryel will be quite enough, thank you, especially with all the travel."

"Mother did write that she's amazed at how little Karyel and Iryella know about running a High Holding. The weather there has been as hot as here . . ." Charyn did his best to summarize what Chelia had written, then asked, "Have you thought about spending some time with any of the ministers?"

"I'm not interested. Maybe later." After a brief pause, Bhayrn asked, "Do you have any more surprises planned?"

"You know about the shipyard in Solis. Some of the High Holders were surprised that the first warship to be built there will be a frigate, rather than a first-rater. That's to work out any problems with the shipyard."

"That makes sense to me. Then, you always try to make sense. That might be your undoing. Some people don't want sense. They just want what they want."

"I've seen some of that." Charyn stood as Therosa returned with Bhayrn's breakfast.

"You'll see more."

"I don't doubt it." Charyn smiled, then stood and made his way up to the study, where he stood looking out the window at the rear courtyard, worrying about Bhayrn and his almost aimless life. *What can you do?* More to the point, what could he do that Bhayrn would want to do . . . and could?

After mulling that over, he picked up the folder with Sanafryt's draft of the proposed language for not unduly contaminating the rivers and streams of Solidar. He'd read it the afternoon before, then laid it aside. He read it again, his eyes concentrating on the heart of the proposed language:

. . . seeing that the waters of Solidar benefit not only immediate users and those all along any watercourse, any use of those waters that renders the water unfit for normal uses by those farther downstream thereby limits the rights of subsequent users. Likewise, excessive removal of water also limits such rights. Under the laws of Solidar, therefore, there is an obligation to use water wisely and to return any waters diverted from the watercourse back into that watercourse in a condition that does not infringe the rights of subsequent users. Those who are injured by the failure of a prior user may seek damages from such a prior user, such damages not to exceed twice the amount of proven losses and the costs of seeking redress before a justicer . . .

It's not perfect, but it won't require the Rex to create an army of water patrollers.

He had barely set that aside when Elacia arrived.

As soon as she entered the study and the door was firmly closed, Charyn motioned to the chairs in front of the table desk, then seated himself behind it. "I'd like to hear what you thought of Samedi evening."

"And what I might have heard?"

Charyn smiled. "Of course."

"Commander Chaalt was most attentive. His wife is visiting her parents. She visits a great deal. I doubt that he is pleased with that. He was also surprised that you had included Subcommander Luerryn. Varcela was reserved, but Subcommander Luerryn was somewhat less taciturn. Did you know that he was essentially under the command of Maitre Alastar at the Lake Shaelyt battle that ended the High Holder rebellion?"

"I didn't. He said he was at the battle."

"Amalie wanted to know if it was true that Maitre Malyna had been staying here and impersonating a High Holder's daughter. I did tell her that both Maitre Alyna and Maitre

Malyna were both High Holders' daughters. She seemed disappointed. She also asked if you'd actually shot someone trying to kill you, but Marshal Vaelln said that you'd personally shot two would-be assassins." Elacia raised her eyebrows. "Is that true?"

"Unhappily, yes." Charyn wasn't sure whether he'd killed Guard Captain Churwyl or the blast had, but he'd certainly wounded Churwyl fatally before the blast.

"Ferrand never mentioned that."

"What else?" prompted Charyn.

"They were talking about the weather, and Maurek said that they'd had to ship supplies from Solis to Westisle for the ships and garrisons there because the early rains had washed out the crops in the west of Antiago and then the heat had baked the fields, and the peasants and tenant growers were starving. Vaelln added something about the fishing fleet out of Tilbora having had a bad year so far as well."

Charyn frowned. While he'd known about the rains in Antiago, the governor hadn't sent any word about the heat and people starving, and he'd certainly heard nothing about the fishing fleet. "That was all?"

"Mostly, except speculation about how soon you'd get married and to whom."

"Thank you, both for the information and for being charming."

Elacia inclined her head.

"I'd appreciate it if you would think about a dinner in late Agosts for some of the local High Holders, those likely to feel less appreciated or those who may feel I've not been duly attentive . . ."

"I'll start on that immediately."

Once Elacia left the study, Charyn returned to considering what to do with Bhayrn, but that didn't last long because Sturdyn announced Minister Aevidyr.

"I've received two more suggestions for the regional governor of Telaryn," said Aevidyr, even before he reached the chairs to which Charyn had gestured.

Charyn thought for a long moment about which High Holders had created the most trouble, waiting until Aevidyr had seated himself. "Would one of them be a close relative to any late High Holders, such as Cransyr or Guerdyn, or even High Holder Haebyn?"

"Your Grace . . . as I have pointed out . . ."

"I know. I understand that. Now . . . is either of them related to any of those three names?"

"Ah . . . Saeblen D'Thurl, he's the younger brother of High Holder Thurl. He's married to High Holder Haebyn's sister."

"Forget him," said Charyn. "Who's the other?"

"Rikkard D'Niasaen."

"What about him?"

"He's the junior son of High Holder Niasaen. That's a smaller High Holding near Cloisonyt. I don't recall exactly where, except it's not far from High Holder Douvyt, I understand."

"Did Douvyt recommend him? To whom is he married?"

"Douvyt wasn't the one. Rikkard's married to a woman named Lylana, from Rhodyn. That's another hold I don't recall."

"Keep that name as a possibility."

Aevidyr raised his eyebrows. "But we don't know anything, really, about him, except that High Holder Thysor recommended him."

"Aevidyr, so far everyone that you've mentioned that we do know anything about isn't someone I'd feel could be trusted as a regional governor. What do you know about Thysor?"

"He's from an old family near Extela. The holding has extensive timberlands, and he ships large quantities of timber to Solis. That's about all I know."

"Keep this Rikkard D'Niasaen as a possibility." *He's likely the best we've received so far.* That also wasn't saying much, Charyn knew. Before Aevidyr could protest, Charyn asked, "How did you come to be Minister of Administration besides the fact that Father picked you?"

"I was fortunate to be the regional minister of administration in Liantiago, Your Grace."

Charyn nodded. "That explains your wealth of experience."

"I would hope so, Your Grace."

Aevidyr had no sooner departed than Sturdyn opened the door slightly and announced, "A missive from High Holder Chaeltar, sir."

Charyn walked to the door and took the sealed missive, knowing that he wasn't going to like what was inside. After slitting the envelope and extracting the contents, he began to read.

> *Your Grace—*
> *A matter of some import has just come to my attention. At the last meeting, Marshal Vaelln reported to the High Council that the* Diamond Thuyl *sank a Jariolan frigate before being sunk by a rated Jariolan warship. Because the Diamond ships are armed and carry cannon that fire shells containing Antiagon Fire, they have been most helpful in dealing with Jariolan warships and privateers . . .*

Charyn wondered how long it would take Chaeltar to get to the point, but he kept reading.

> *. . . despite the significant losses suffered by High Holder Ghasphar at the hands of the brigandish Jariolans. As you may know, Antiagon Fire cannot be made except by an imager. For generations, some imagers of Telaryn have served the High Holder in this capacity. With the untimely death of his imager armsmaster, however, High*

*Holder Ghasphar finds himself unable to adequately
arm his ships. This is because all the young imagers
in Telaryn are now being gathered into the Imager
Collegium at Westisle, and none wish to pursue the
honorable craft of their predecessors . . .*

*Untimely death? Possibly due to the dangers of making
Antiagon Fire?* Charyn turned his eyes back to the letter.

*. . . High Holder Ghasphar has brought this problem
to the attention of Maitre Taurek, who heads the
Collegium at Estisle. Maitre Taurek has declined to
supply any imagers to assist High Holder Ghasphar,
and, as of this writing, Maitre Alastar has not responded
to my inquiries . . .*

*Meaning that you wrote him at the same time you wrote
me, but you're wording it that way so that you can get me
to act sooner.*

Charyn finished the letter and laid it on the desk. At that
moment, he definitely wished he'd searched more diligently
for a private secretary, but after the difficulties with his uncle had been resolved, it seemed as though he had little need
of one.

Leaving the letter on the desk, knowing he shouldn't do
anything until he had more time to think it over, he left and
made his way to Alucar's study.

"Your Grace?" The Finance Minister stood as Charyn
entered.

"Alucar? Do you have any figures on how much it costs to
support the four regional governors?"

"Not immediately at hand. If you want such figures, it
will take a few days because some of the costs are paid by
the High Command."

"You mean, the battalions assigned to each regional governor? Their supplies and the like?"

"That, and the portion of import tariffs that go to the regional governors."

Charyn stiffened. "You never mentioned that."

"I'm sorry. I thought you knew."

"There's still a great deal I don't know. Father never mentioned that, and neither did you. At least, I don't think you did." Charyn paused and added ruefully, "Unless it was more than a year ago. I wasn't listening as well as I should have been back then."

"If you're thinking about doing away with them, who will collect import tariffs and the like?"

"What about the Vice-Marshal of the Navy? Three of the regional governors are located where we have warships and installations."

"Would you save that much? You'd still need the clerks and others who collect the tariffs and keep the records."

"That's true, but I think I'd trust the navy's record-keeping more than that of the regional governors." Charyn paused. "That reminds me. Have you ever heard of a High Holder Thysor? Supposedly, he ships timber from Extela down the river to Solis."

"Thysor?" Alucar nodded. "Yes, he does. While the ship hulls will be live oak from the edge of the Sud Swamp, he was recommended for supplying timbers for the masts and spars. Very trustworthy from all reports. Why? Have you heard otherwise?"

"No. He just recommended someone to be considered for the regional governor of Telaryn, and I didn't know anything about him, and neither does Aevidyr. The man he recommended is Rikkard D'Niasaen."

"I've never heard of him, either."

Charyn wanted to shake his head. The names most High Holders forwarded were names of people he didn't trust, and the only other one was someone who seemed unknown. Except Thysor had at least some people who thought him trustworthy, and most people who were trustworthy in one area tended to be trustworthy in other areas. *But that's a very slender reed.* "I'd still appreciate those numbers sometime in the next week or so."

"Yes, sir."

As Charyn started back to his study, his thoughts went back to Chaeltar's letter.

He knew he had to write a letter to Alastar about the Antiagon Fire. It just galled him because that was exactly what Chaeltar wanted him to do, but there was no help for it.

At that moment, Bhayrn hurried toward the grand staircase.

"Where are you going?"

"Laamyst is coming to pick me up. I thought it would be safer in his coach than in one of the regial coaches, even the unmarked ones."

"I'll walk down with you. It will do me good to get away from the study." Besides, Charyn hadn't actually seen Laamyst in a while, and Bhayrn was spending a fair amount of time with him. As Charyn recalled, Laamyst was about a year older than Bhayrn, but the two had become closer after the assassination of Charyn and Bhayrn's father.

"Suit yourself," replied Bhayrn amiably.

"Where are you going?"

"Just to his father's river mansion north of here, not the town place on the east side of the river . . ."

As Bhayrn continued speaking, Charyn couldn't help wondering just how many houses, mansions, lodges, and villas that High Holder Laastyn actually had.

". . . I'll be there for dinner, and for plaques after that. Gherard will bring me back."

"Gherard?"

"Gherard D'Ghaermyn."

"Is he the heir?"

"He is. Why do you ask?"

"I just wondered. You haven't mentioned him before."

"That's because I got to know him better through Laamyst."

"That's thoughtful of someone you haven't known well for long."

"Isn't that what friends do?"

"If you're fortunate, and you appear to be."

The two waited quietly in the shade at the top of the steps until Bhayrn said, "That's his coach."

Charyn followed his brother down to the lowest step, which functioned as a mounting block, and waited until the coach came to a stop and the footman opened the door.

Laamyst looked to be taller than Bhayrn by several digits, with reddish-blond hair, a fair skin, a pug nose, and a sprinkling of freckles on his face. His hazel eyes smiled with the rest of his face as he saw Charyn. "Your Grace . . . it's been a while. It's good to see you again."

"It's good to see you. You and your family have been very kind to Bhayrn, particularly given all that's happened."

"It's been our pleasure. Mine, especially, since I'd be spending too much time with my sisters otherwise, or, worse, with my female cousins."

Bhayrn eased past Charyn and into the maroon coach trimmed with traces of silver. "I likely won't see you until tomorrow."

"Don't wager too much."

"We don't play for golds, or even coppers," replied Laamyst. "That's too good a way to lose friends."

Charyn stepped back and let the footman close the coach door. As the coach turned away, he headed back up the long white stone steps to the main entry, wondering, not for the first time, why the Chateau had been built with so many steps in the front, but also knowing that trying to change it would have been impossible, if not incredibly expensive, given how it had been restored by imaging.

8

On Vendrei, Charyn was up early, despite having worked late in his study the night before, as he had for several nights, reviewing all of the properties that belonged to the Rex—not really to him personally, but to whoever held the title. In the end, one property seemed far better for his purposes than any other.

After exercising, meeting with Undercaptain Faelln, since Maertyl had Vendrei off, then washing up and dressing in his greens for the day, Charyn made his way to the breakfast room to enjoy a mug of tea while waiting for Bhayrn. He had a second mug before his brother appeared.

"Good morning," offered Charyn.

"Aren't you the cheerful one?"

"It's a pleasant morning, if a touch warm."

"Hot is more like it." Bhayrn looked to Therosa. "A lager, please . . . and whatever the Rex is having. He has good taste." He looked to Charyn. "Don't you, Brother?"

"I tend to be more interested in breakfast than you are."

"You haven't eaten yet?"

"I was waiting for you."

"How thoughtful of you. You're now being more thoughtful to all of us. I even told Laamyst that you've started returning to Solayi services. He was surprised. He didn't think you were that strong a believer in the Nameless."

"Part of that, as you must know, is that it's a way of seeing Aloryana when she's free to see me. She wasn't for a while."

"I said you were being thoughtful."

"I hope so. Sometimes thinking does lead to kinder or more productive ideas."

Therosa returned with a beaker and a pitcher of lager.

Bhayrn filled the beaker, then took a healthy swallow before speaking again. "Since you've been thinking and waiting for me, one of those ideas must have something to do with me. Something you've calculated."

Charyn ignored the barb. "Of course. You're not only my brother, but my heir."

"Only for a while. I'll never be Rex. You're too careful."

"Then . . . if that's what you believe, don't you think you should spend some time learning about how a holding works?"

"That's what landwardens are for." Bhayrn paused. "Since you're Rex, are you going to gift me the Chaeryll lands?"

"No. I've been managing them for the last three years, and that's why they earn more than they used to. But I have spent late glasses for the last week going over the regial properties looking for those that might be the most suitable for you." Charyn paused while Therosa set a platter before him and then one before Bhayrn. In addition to the ham strips and the cheesed eggs, each of the brothers also had a small warm loaf of dark bread.

Rather than say anything immediately, which he might regret, and also because he was hungry, Charyn ate several bites of the ham and eggs before continuing. "I'd thought of Lauckan, the High Holding north of Laaryn. You'd be High Holder Delauck. You could, of course, change the holding name, which most High Holders can't."

"That's even farther from L'Excelsis than Rivages!"

"There's nothing to prevent you from having a mansion in L'Excelsis, since you've made it clear that you don't want to be too deeply involved in running the holding."

"I suppose it's a beggared holding you'd like to pass off."

Charyn shook his head. "It's been in the family for hundreds of years. Rex Clayar stripped it from the High Holder's heirs after the High Holder refused to pay tariffs and attacked the regional governor. It took imagers to extract and execute him, but they also rebuilt and strengthened it, and more lands were added. Its revenues are more than adequate—they're greater than those of the Chaeryll lands by a fair amount—provided you don't totally run it down."

"You're giving it to me now?"

"No. Not until you turn eighteen. That's the customary age of assumption, and that's if Mother says you know enough to take care of it."

"You're a bastard, Charyn." Bhayrn snorted. "You've made your point. I'll leave for Rivages tomorrow. I don't need to watch your lovely little dinner party . . . or be a hanger-on at your so-called family gathering."

Charyn looked coldly at his brother. "You've been moping and hinting for more than a season. I'm giving you a very good High Holding, one of the best . . ."

"You're giving it on your terms, not mine. You want me out of L'Excelsis. I'm not like Uncle Ryentar."

"No, you're not. I just said that I'm not exiling you. It's a fine High Holding, and you can live all year round in L'Excelsis, if that's what you want."

"That's what you say now."

"You couldn't legally have it until then anyway," Charyn pointed out. "I just don't want you to end up like our late uncle Delcoeur."

"I so appreciate your concern."

Rather than say something he was certain to regret, Charyn took several more mouthfuls of breakfast, and then a swallow of tea, before finally saying, "If there's another holding you'd prefer—one that I can gift and has enough revenue—I'd be happy to consider it."

"How would I even know?"

"I have the records in the study. Any time you want to look at them, you can come in while I'm there and look them over."

"I just might."

"It's up to you." Charyn stood, managing, somehow, a pleasant smile. "I need to get to work."

"What great and mighty problem besets you now?"

"No great and mighty problems, just a number of smaller, but not insignificant ones, and none of them seem particularly amenable to solutions."

"I'm sure you'll find or calculate some perfect solution that no one thought of. You always will, until you can't."

As he walked up the small circular staircase to the second level, Charyn wondered if he was being too hard on Bhayrn. *Three years ago, you weren't exactly a paragon of virtue.* After several moments, he added, *You still aren't.*

Once in his study, he immediately read the latest editions of both *Veritum* and *Tableta*.

One of the articles in *Veritum* complained that the Rex should have raised tariffs on the High Holders immediately in order to build more ships and to rebuild the west river piers that had been damaged by the spring floods. As if the High Holders or factors would have paid the additional tariffs. *Not without starting another revolt, anyway.* Besides which, there wasn't any way he could have built that many more ships anyway, given that he needed the new shipyard to do so. As for the piers, rebuilding them would be less expensive in late harvest when the river levels were near their seasonal low. *Costs . . . always costs.*

He set the newssheets aside and walked to the open window, where only the faintest hint of a breeze moved past him. For a moment, Charyn absently thought about the dinner party. In a way it was fitting, because the season would change from summer to harvest at midnight on Samedi, but because of the summer heat, there was no Harvest-Turn Ball, just as there was no Summer-Turn Ball.

"There's a letter from the Collegium on your desk, sir," said Moencriff, opening the study. "It just arrived."

"Thank you." Charyn turned and walked to the door, taking the envelope from the guard before returning to stand at the end of the desk closest to the open window. He opened the letter and began to read.

Rex Charyn—
Like you, I have received a missive from High Councilor
Chaeltar about the needs of High Holder Ghasphar
in regard to the ability of his shipyards to formulate
Antiagon Fire and his request for assistance from the
Collegium Imago.

The Collegium Imago was chartered by the first Rex
Regis to educate, train, and safeguard the imagers of
Solidar, as well as to support the Rex and serve the
people of Solidar. One of the reasons why the Collegium
opened another part of the Collegium in Estisle was
because it had become increasingly clear that imagers
in Telaryn were not receiving that education and
safeguarding.

The creation of Antiagon Fire is a delicate and
complicated process, even for a trained imager, and many
imagers have died in trying to make or making Antiagon
Fire. Nonetheless, when Maitre Taurek was sent to Estisle,
he was given explicit orders not to induce any adult
imagers he might find to join the Collegium. I personally
wrote High Holder Ghasphar to tell him that the Collegium
would only be training young imagers, and would only
accept adult imagers who, of their own free will, wished to
join and abide by the rules of the Collegium.

For this reason, Maitre Taurek is allowed to accept
only those adult imagers who wish to join, who are
suited, and who come to him freely. He is forbidden to
offer, induce, or invite any adult imager. At present,
there is only one adult imager who has joined the
Collegium. There are more than a half score of student
imagers, children largely under the age of fourteen.

In the past, even the fairly recent past, one of the few
occupations open to imagers in old Telaryn, as imagers,
was at the Diamond shipyards, making Antiagon Fire,
where over half of them died. Times have now changed,
and most parents prefer their children come to the

*Collegium. With the recent death of the senior imager
at the shipyard, this has left High Holder Ghasphar
without an imager capable of formulating Antiagon
Fire. While I understand his concern, I cannot in good
conscience force any young imager into working at his
shipyards, not when it is more than likely to result in
their early and painful death. Since there are only three
imagers at the Estisle Collegium with the possible skills
to deal with Antiagon Fire, and since they are required
to educate and safeguard the young imagers, I find it
inadvisable for them to assist High Holder Ghasphar.
Therefore, I fully support Maitre Taurek in his decision.*

*If you have additional questions or concerns about
this, I will be more than happy to meet with you to
discuss the matter.*

Charyn set the letter on the desk. He really hadn't expected any other answer, but that reply and the Maitre's
clear stance weren't going to make the next Council meeting
any easier.

Should you reply immediately to Chaeltar?

Charyn decided to reply, but only to tell Chaeltar that he
was considering the matter. Alastar's letter did remind him
that he needed to send a note to Alastar saying that he would
again be joining them at the Anomen D'Imagisle on Solayi.

9

True to his word, Bhayrn left early Samedi morning for Rivages. He avoided Charyn totally, as he had ever since breakfast on Vendrei morning. The note he left was curt.

> *Charyn—*
> *I'm leaving for Rivages. I won't need to see all the*
> *other holdings. You couldn't live with your most highly*
> *honorable self if you weren't fair in the matter.*

Charyn had known Bhayrn was leaving because Faelln had asked him about the guards and supplies to accompany Bhayrn on the long ride to Rivages, but, if Bhayrn wanted to play the petulant child, that was his choice. Sooner or later, he'd have to grow up. In the meantime, Charyn could only hope that his brother would listen to their mother. Bhayrn had certainly been more likely to listen to her than to either Charyn or their father.

As he settled behind the table desk in the study, Charyn couldn't help but feel slightly guilty at inadvertently pushing Bhayrn off to Rivages, but Bhayrn had shown no interest at all in learning about anything, either from him or from anyone else in the Chateau who could teach him. And that didn't leave many options.

He took a piece of stationery from the cabinet and began to write. It took him three drafts before he had something that was acceptable. Then he read it over.

Mother—

*By the time you receive this, Bhayrn may already have
arrived at Ryel. If not, he should soon arrive. He may
not be in the most receptive of moods.*

*For the past month, especially, I have endeavored
to interest him in learning about matters that would
prove helpful and useful to him in the future as a High
Holder. At present, he appears to be indifferent to such,
as was I at his age. In an effort to encourage him to
think about his future, we discussed what holdings might
be suitable for him, and I suggested Lauckan, the High
Holding north of Laaryn, or any other of comparable
worth. I did point out that he needed to know more
about the business of managing a High Holding. He was
dismissive. I was less than politic and told him that he
could have Lauckan or another comparable holding
after he turned eighteen and after you were satisfied that
he knew enough not to end up like Uncle Delcoeur. He
was not amused and did not speak to me thereafter. He
left a note saying he was heading to Rivages and that
Lauckan was more than satisfactory, or words to that
effect.*

*I regret thrusting him on you in Rivages, but you
appear to be the only one from whom he will take advice.
I will support whatever measures and encouragement
you feel will help him, as your efforts on my behalf were
more than effective . . .*

From there, Charyn went on to offer his weekly update on
what had happened in the Chateau and in L'Excelsis since
he had last written. When he finished, he signed and sealed
the missive and had Sturdyn arrange for its transmittal to
Ryel by army courier.

Then he read through Marshal Vaelln's latest report on
the undeclared naval war between Solidar and Jariola. As
usual, Solidar had lost slightly fewer ships than had Jariola.

With the newer ships being completed, the losses were not as crippling as they might have been. So far, though, Vaelln still had no word on the likely arrival of a Jariolan fleet to blockade the ports of the Abierto Isles.

Various other matters, such as petitions, and two more suggestions from High Holders on possible names for regional governors, required thought and responses.

By the third glass of the afternoon, Elacia and Ferrand had arrived. Elacia immediately headed for the kitchen and to talk to Norstan about what she expected of the seneschal and his staff, leaving Ferrand and Charyn in the study.

"Is Bhayrn here?" asked Ferrand.

"No. He's on his way to Rivages, and the Ryel holding, to spend the first part of harvest, and perhaps longer, with Mother. I'm hoping he'll learn something about running a holding, since he'll have one sooner or later. How did you learn?"

"I didn't. I'm learning now. Mother really ran the holding, but she couldn't stop Father from spending. She still runs the holding, but I'm watching closely and asking a lot of questions. That suits us both. Was that how it was with you?"

"I started learning, really learning, a bit over a year ago. The social side was what I didn't learn." Charyn offered a wry grin. "That's why your mother's here . . . and why I'll be leaning on her or Mother for a while."

"Or until you marry."

"That might be a while."

"Then why this dinner?"

"For you, of course, and because I have to start somewhere."

"Any High Holder's daughter would accept you."

"That's exactly the problem," replied Charyn. "You don't have that particular difficulty. If a good-looking and personable young woman is interested in you, there's a good chance she's really interested in *you*."

"I'd rather have your problem."

Charyn laughed softly. "You only think you would." He motioned. "Come with me. I need to change into something a little more formal."

A glass later, the two young men walked down the grand staircase to the entry foyer of the Chateau. Charyn still carried his small double-barreled pistol, concealed in his regial green dress uniform jacket, which had been tailored specifically for that, as had many of his jackets.

The players of the string quintet appeared just after fifth glass and set up in the music room, where they could be heard through the wide arch into the anteroom, which was large enough to serve as a small reception room . . . and often had, although the last time had been when Charyn, Bhayrn, Aloryana, and Malyna had performed together. For Charyn, that recital seemed even more distant than the more than six months past it had actually been.

While Charyn's father had seldom been in a chamber when the first guests arrived, except for High Command officers or his ministers or family, Charyn wanted to be there in order to meet each party as they arrived. The string quintet began to play just before sixth glass, and the first guests to arrive in the smaller reception room, besides Ferrand, were Zhelyn D'Saeffen-Alte and Ferron D'Fhernon-Alte, slightly past the glass. Ferron immediately glanced around the reception room.

Charyn smiled and said gently, "You two are the first to arrive, but I'm afraid you'll be disappointed, Ferron."

"A man can always hope, Your Grace."

"I understand that." *Indeed, I do.* But there was realistic hope and unrealistic hope, and the line between the two was thin, Charyn knew, but it also cut more deeply than the finest blade. "But do be kind to the young women who will be here. Some of them may have hopes as well."

"Then, might I ask why you invited me?" asked Zhelyn, an amused tone in his voice.

"Because you're an heir who was recommended, and I

trust those who made the recommendation. I understand you also dance well. Who knows? You might find someone to your liking. If not, I trust you'll still enjoy the evening."

Zhelyn couldn't quite contain an expression of puzzlement as Charyn turned toward the next set of arrivals, who happened to be Sherrona D'Plessan, and her mother. "Welcome to the Chateau D'Rex."

"It's an unexpected honor, Your Grace," replied Lady D'Plessan, "but one to which we both have looked forward."

"Your Grace," was all that Sherrona offered, her eyes slightly downcast.

"Sherrona, have you met my cousin, Ferrand, now High Holder Delcoeur?"

The young woman looked to Ferrand, then smiled shyly. "Only at the Spring-Turn Ball."

"Then you should." Charyn gestured toward Ferrand, then slipped away to meet the next arrivals, High Holder and Lady D'Almeida, and their daughter Marenna.

"I appreciate your courtesy in inviting us to accompany Marenna, Rex Charyn." Those words came not from the High Holder, but from his wife.

Charyn offered what he hoped was a slightly abashed smile. "My mother and my aunt would both have been most disappointed in my behavior had I not."

"Are they here?" asked the High Holder.

"My aunt, Lady Delcoeur D'Priora, is here. My mother is also guardian for the grandchildren of the late High Holder Ryel and is with them at Ryel at present."

Lady D'Almeida glanced around, then said, "I take it this is a small gathering?"

"It is. Five young women and their parents, four young men, and my aunt. Besides myself and my cousin Ferrand, High Holder Delcoeur, the other young men are Ferron D'Fhernon-Alte and Zhelyn D'Saeffen-Alte. It's a group that's not too intimate and not too large, at least for me. I've found that while the dancing at balls is enjoyable, I seldom have much time to talk to people because I need to say a few words to as many as possible." Charyn paused for an instant and added, "And I always fail to talk to someone."

"You can't please everyone," replied High Holder Almeida.

"That's true, and most people understand that. But none of us likes feeling ignored." Charyn gestured toward the sideboards. "Please enjoy yourselves." He inclined his head to Marenna. "You, especially."

Then he moved toward Kayrolya D'Taelmyn and her parents, fully aware that Alyncya and her father had not yet arrived. He'd suspected that they would be the last.

Kayrolya was blond and willowy, with an effusive warmth communicated by a broad smile as Charyn stepped up to her and her parents. "Thank you so much for including us, Your Grace."

"With a smile like yours, how could I not? You didn't smile like that at the Spring Ball."

"I felt lost amid so many people."

"You won't feel that way here, I hope. Almost everyone's here." Charyn half-turned and gestured. "You see the tall blond young man in blue and gray. That's my cousin Ferrand, High Holder Delcoeur. There are three other women your age, with one to come, and two other High Holder heirs, in addition to the parents of the other young women."

As Kayrolya eased away from Charyn, her father moved closer and said, "Your Grace, I appreciate the careful way in which you have chaperoned this evening."

"I could do nothing less, that is, if I wanted the young women and their families to be at ease, which is my goal."

As Taelmyn followed his wife and daughter, Charyn moved toward Shaelyna D'Baeltyn and her parents. The daughter offered a poised and polite smile. "Good evening, Your Grace."

"Good evening and welcome to the Chateau. I hope you'll enjoy yourselves." Charyn nodded to Baeltyn. "High Hold-

ers Taelmyn and Almeida are already here, as are Lady Delcoeur D'Priora and Lady Plessan D'Priora."

After exchanging a few more pleasantries, Charyn turned
toward the last arrivals, High Holder Shendael and Alyncya.
"I'm very glad to see you both."

"We could scarcely refuse such an invitation," replied
High Holder Shendael, with an amused smile, some of
which amusement, Charyn suspected, was comprised partly
of rue.

"Nor did we wish to," said Alyncya, adding, "for it does
give us the opportunity to see more of the Chateau." There
was a slightly different kind of amusement in her eyes.

Charyn inclined his head. "And it gives me the opportunity to continue a conversation with you that will not be
interrupted by the end of a dance and the obligation to keep
moving in order to talk to everyone possible." He gestured
toward the sideboard. "Might I guide you both to some
refreshments?"

"You don't have others to greet?" asked Shendael.

"You two are the last. So I'm now at liberty to enjoy
the company of my guests." As they neared the sideboard,
Charyn went on. "There's a very good Tacqueville white,
although some prefer the Tuuryl red. There's also a golden
pale ale or a dark lager." He looked to Alyncya. "What
would you like?"

"The white."

"Two of the white," Charyn said, adding to Alyncya,
"That's my preference as well."

"I'll have the red," declared Shendael. "Always felt that
suited a man more."

Charyn handed the first goblet of white to Alyncya, and
took the second for himself. "I've always thought each
man—or woman—should determine for themselves what
suited them. It's amusing, in a way, how so many people
want to choose for others but resist letting others choose for
them."

"As Rex, you choose for others," countered Shendael.

"Yes, there is that, but any Rex who can't determine what suits most of the High Holders and factors isn't likely to remain Rex all that long. Not these days. You might have an interesting discussion about that with High Holder Taelmyn, there." Charyn inclined his head in the direction of where Taelmyn and Almeida stood talking, then guided Alyncya away from her father.

"Are you going to keep me to yourself, Your Grace?" asked Alyncya, her voice gently inquiring.

"For a moment or three. Then we will join some of the others closer to our age. I apologize for separating you from your father more abruptly than I might have wished, but it appears that he is less than enthusiastic about being here or having you here, most likely both."

"Did you not suspect that would be so?"

"I did. I just didn't expect him to be quite so direct so quickly."

"I fear I share that trait, Your Grace."

"Do you wish not to be here?" Charyn looked directly into her hazel eyes. "I had hoped you might at least have wished to continue our last, and slightly interrupted, conversation."

"I had hoped we might continue it as well, perhaps at the Autumn-Turn Ball."

"Another six months between conversations would have been excessive, I fear."

"I would not wish to become too familiar too quickly. They say that such familiarity breeds contempt."

"Only if those involved share few of the same beliefs and concerns. Holding back from learning about another seems a form of fear, fear either of being disappointed or of being far too greatly attracted."

"There's a great danger to finding the Rex disappointed in one. Had you not thought of that?"

"I have." Charyn had, and he understood her fear that if she were not interested in him that he might force her either never to marry in order to hold on to her holding or to marry someone else and have to give it as dower. "But in matters between women and men, disappointment is always a risk. One must accept that disappointment, should it happen, lies in false expectations on the part of the one disappointed . . . and not hold that disappointment against another. You cannot be other than you are, nor should you be. Nor should I."

"Are hearts really that cold and logical, Your Grace?" An amused but slightly sardonic tone colored her words.

"Alas, no," returned Charyn as melodramatically as he dared.

A gentle laugh replied to his words and tone.

"Do you play the clavecin, Alyncya?"

"Does not every High Holder's daughter?"

"Do you enjoy playing, even when no one is listening?"

"That's when I enjoy it the most."

Charyn nodded.

"And your nod signifies what, Your Grace?"

"That I share that feeling."

Alyncya frowned, if but slightly. "I had not heard that the men of the Chateau played."

"Perhaps we should adjourn through the archway into the music room . . ."

"Your Grace . . . is that not . . ."

"I did not mean that in the way I fear you took it. First, there are five string players there. Second, there is a clavecin there. Third, I was going to suggest that I might play a short piece for you, or just a part of it, and you could decide for yourself whether this man of the Chateau can play well enough for your taste. You have always struck me as a lady—"

"I'm scarcely that old."

"No, but you are the heir, and that reminds me. Last Finitas, when we danced, you said that you were 'a High Holder's unwed and older younger daughter trying to hold to her wits when every word must count for everything and commit one to nothing.' I didn't catch that at the time, but later I realized that could not possibly be true, not with you as the heir."

For an instant, Alyncya froze before replying. "You flatter me with your memory. I am the younger daughter, or I was. My sister died of the flux a year ago, and I was so surprised when you began to talk to me that I said what I had often said, before . . . that is, except I mixed up the words. I should have said unwed surviving younger daughter."

"I'm so sorry. I had no idea."

"You had no reason to know that. She was never in the best of health and had never attended a ball. How could you have known?"

"I can still be sorry for your loss."

"I was going to ask how you could know about such a loss . . . and that would have been thoughtless and stupid . . . after what happened at the Year-Turn Ball." After a pause, she added, "If you still would like to play . . ."

"I would, but just for you . . . and the musicians."

The two eased into the music room, and toward the clavecin. Charyn looked back. No one had followed . . . so far. Or they had studiously ignored the pair, which was far more likely.

The lead violinist looked to Charyn, questioningly.

"You can take a break for a few moments." Charyn wasn't about to try "Pavane in a Minor Key," not when he still had difficulty with parts of it. He settled before the keyboard and began Farray's Nocturne Number Three. He was almost afraid to look at Alyncya as he played. So he didn't.

When he finished and looked up, he discovered that not only had Alyncya been listening, but Ferrand was there, along with Kayrolya D'Taelmyn, as was Zhelyn, accompanied by Sherrona D'Plessan.

Ferrand stepped forward, shaking his head. "I never knew you played . . . or were that good."

"Thank you. I've had some good teachers." Charyn stood and looked to Alyncya. "Would anyone else like to play?"

"I'll play," replied Alyncya, with a smile.

Charyn surrendered the clavecin to her.

As Charyn watched and listened, he realized almost immediately that Alyncya was far better than anyone he'd heard—except Palenya—and that she clearly felt what she played. He just listened. When she finished, Charyn wanted to applaud, but didn't, even as a broad smile crossed his face. "That was excellent. I don't recognize the piece, but it sounded a little like Farray."

"It was. Farray's 'Pavane for a Forgotten Dancer.'"

By now, most everyone was in the music room. Charyn looked around. "Would anyone else like to play?"

No one spoke . . . except Alyncya. "Some of the others didn't hear you. Perhaps you should play another piece."

"Only if you'll agree to play another one after I do."

She raised her eyebrows, then nodded, standing and moving away from the clavecin.

Charyn seated himself and played the less tariffing Farray piece he'd learned before the nocturne, then rose and surrendered the clavecin to Alyncya.

She played another work, shorter, one that was likely by Covaelyt, but her fingering, timing, and musicianship seemed faultless to him.

"Covaelyt?" he asked when she finished.

She nodded. "Variations on a Khellan Melody."

"I've never heard it before. I've never even heard of it."

"Most people haven't."

"I did enjoy it." Charyn extended a hand, not that she needed it, but she took it and rose from the clavecin.

"It's not every day that we get a recital by a lady-heir and the Rex," said Ferron. "You both were impressive."

"Alyncya's better than I am," said Charyn. "And I'm not being charitable."

"But you're both better than most players I've heard," said Shaelyna.

"Lady-heir Alyncya is much the better. I'm just happy I

didn't disgrace myself playing at the same time she did."
Charyn turned to Alyncya. "More wine, perhaps?"

"A little would be nice."

The others moved aside as they made their way back
to the reception room and the sideboard. Behind then, the
string quintet resumed playing.

"I never would have guessed," Alyncya said in a low
voice.

"Nor I," he replied.

"All daughters play."

"Not the way you do. You're better than all but the very,
very best professional musicians."

"I appreciate the compliment, and the honesty."

"I don't think anything else would be right with you."

Two goblets of Tacqueville white were waiting for them,
and Charyn handed one to Alyncya, then took the second,
lifting it slightly. "To your performance."

"And to yours."

"I think you made me look better than I am. I only know a
handful or so of difficult works. I imagine you know a score
or more."

"Those I know well . . . barely a score."

"And you're still learning more, I'd wager."

"You still frighten me, Your Grace," she murmured.

"Me? Or because I'm Rex."

"Your being Rex, mostly. Your recall of everything I've
said, or so it seems, is flattering, but also . . ." Her eyes
dropped for an instant. "You don't play at anything, I think."

"I used to."

"What changed you? I don't mean being Rex. You were
already changing at the Year-Turn Ball."

Charyn laughed, but not harshly. "That I couldn't aim a
pistol well enough, and my desire to blame it on the pistol."

Almost instantly, she smiled softly. "And?"

"I confronted the pistol-maker, and he told me that no pistol in the world could correct for bad technique." It had been

far more complex than that, but that was the gist of what had set Charyn on revisiting his life's aims.

"And you didn't shoot him?"

"I likely couldn't have hit him. Besides, he was right. So I listened to him, and that changed everything. Eventually, I even got to be a better shot, but that mattered less by then." *Although it did save your life . . . twice.*

She shook her head. "If only . . ."

"If only what?"

"'If only's' don't matter. We all must deal with what is. I scarcely have to tell you that."

"No . . . but I enjoy hearing you say that."

Charyn would have liked to have heard more, but at that moment, High Holder and Lady Almeida appeared, escorted by Elacia, who smiled brightly and said, "Your Grace, they wished to say a few words, but did not wish to intrude."

Charyn unhappily understood what Elacia wasn't saying. "You certainly aren't intruding."

"Your Grace, Lady-heir D'Shendael," began Lady Almeida, "we just wanted to tell you how much we appreciated your playing . . . and the example it set. So many of the young people . . . they don't appreciate the beauty of the arts."

"That is true," replied Charyn, offering a sheepish grin. "And until the past year or so I was one of them. While I was trained to play, I really didn't appreciate it, not until I heard someone who truly did play with the skill of the sort Lady-heir Alyncya just demonstrated."

"That is so good to hear. You know, while she wouldn't say so, Marenna was most impressed with the way you both played."

Elacia glanced at Charyn.

In turn, he smiled once more at Lady Almeida and said, "Apparently, my presence is required elsewhere, but, if you would," he nodded to Alyncya, "you might tell them just how long it took you to master the Covaelyt piece you played so beautifully."

"You're too kind, Your Grace."

"Too honest, I fear. Now . . . if you will excuse me . . ."

As Elacia guided Charyn toward a group that held Zhelyn, Ferron, Marenna, and Sherrona, she murmured, "Nicely done, if rather later than desirable. You'll need to spend a long time here."

Charyn understood that as well, but smiled once more as he looked to Marenna D'Almeida. "I just had a delightful talk with your parents . . . about the arts." Then he grinned. "I suspect you've heard it before. And no, you don't have to look appalled. I've heard similar talk for years."

"Your Grace . . . I am so sorry . . ."

Charyn laughed. "For what? Parents being parents? At this moment, my younger brother is on his way to Rivages, dreading, no doubt, the lessons and quiet instruction he is going to receive from our mother. I still remember the glasses I spent poring over legal tomes in the study of the Minister of Justice . . . and him offering profound statements."

"Do you even remember any of them?" asked Ferron.

Charyn squared his shoulders and intoned solemnly, "When you are Rex, do not make a law you cannot enforce because that will do more damage than no law at all." While Ferron was still smiling, Charyn added, "The problem is, I discovered, that he was right." He added humorously, he hoped, "It's a terrible thing to discover that so many of the boring bromides you're fed growing up often have a great deal of truth behind them, especially when you become Rex suddenly and so much younger than you ever thought possible."

He looked to Marenna and grinned. "Have I removed the awful embarrassment of your parents declaiming on the importance of the arts?"

He received a nod in return . . . and the hint of a smile.

He just hoped he could maintain a certain amount of wit and lightheartedness until they adjourned to the large and seldom-used dining hall.

By the time the soft chimes announced dinner, Charyn

had managed to converse with everyone, including parents, although he trod very carefully with High Holder Shendael.

The seating arrangements were not exactly by precedence, but roughly so, with two alterations. Elacia was seated at the far end of the long table, with the parents of the young women seated from her in precedence, while Charyn sat at the head of the table with Alyncya to his right and Marenna D'Almeida to his left. Ferrand was seated beside Marenna, and to his left was Kayrolya. Beyond that younger adults alternated between young heirs and young women. Each diner's place was noted by a place card in a silver holder.

As Alyncya eased into her chair, her eyes went to Charyn.

They held each other's gaze for just a moment longer than proper before she smiled and said, "Not exactly by precedence."

"Your father is seated precisely by precedence. If those of us who are younger were seated precisely that way, it would be so much less enjoyable." He looked at Marenna, and then Ferrand. "Wouldn't you say so?"

"Absolutely." Ferrand grinned.

Once the wine goblets were filled, Charyn raised his. "Since tonight is Harvest-Turn Eve, here's to a good harvest, with appreciation to all of you for sharing your evening with me."

"To a good harvest," came the uneven reply.

Then the staff began to serve a chilled strawberry cream soup, more cool than chilled, Charyn knew as he looked first to Marenna. "What might you be doing for the first part of Agostos?"

"Tomorrow, we'll be returning to the summer villa on the west side of the Aluse, just a little north of Talyon. It's one of my favorite places."

Charyn turned to Alyncya. "And you?"

"Father and I will be visiting friends in Vaestora."

"High Holder Calkoran?"

"His daughter has been a friend for years. We don't see each other as much now."

"You should ask her to accompany her father when he comes to L'Excelsis."

"I hadn't thought of that, but it's kind of you to suggest it, now that he will be traveling here more often."

Charyn caught the puzzled looks on the faces of both Marenna and Sherrona, seated on Ferrand's left, while Ferron, on Alyncya's left, nodded just slightly. "What are your harvest plans, Ferron?"

"Accompanying the landwardens to learn better how to manage harvests."

Charyn nodded. "And then what?"

Ferron grinned. "Explaining it well enough to my sire that he'll find something even more exacting for me to learn."

Conversation over the next four courses was in much the same tenor, much as Charyn would have liked to have spent the time conversing only with Alyncya.

Except for Ferrand and Elacia, High Holder Shendael and Alyncya were the last to say their farewells, beginning with the High Holder.

"You do play the clavecin admirably, Your Grace. Not many High Holders do, and no Rexes that I've known. You also keep your temper well. I imagine we'll see each other more often, at least occasionally. Good evening and thank you." Shendael stepped back, leaving Alyncya with Charyn.

"Those words are the closest you'll ever hear to approval," she murmured.

Charyn took her hand, bent slightly and kissed it, if gently, lowering her hand, but not releasing it. "I did enjoy conversing with you and listening to you play."

"I enjoyed the same, Your Grace." She squeezed his fingers gently, then eased her hand away.

"Until later," he said, just standing there and watching as she crossed the last yard or so of the grand foyer and headed out into the night.

Then he turned, to find Ferrand almost at his elbow.

"Do I detect a certain interest, Charyn?"

"Do you have to ask?" A moment passed. "Did she say anything interesting to you?"

"She's quite witty, but gently barbed when someone says something foolish."

"Such as?"

"Sherrona D'Plessan said that it was surprising that you played so well, and Alyncya said it would have been more surprising if you had played badly."

"She's very bright, and very cautious, I think."

"With your interest in her, Charyn, she'd be an idiot not to be cautious, and she's not that at all."

No . . . she's not. Charyn laughed. "You and your mother need to head home, unless you want to stay here tonight."

"We'll go home. If we don't, I'll spend all day tomorrow answering questions from my sisters. They'll be waiting anyway, and worrying if we don't come home."

"Give them my best."

Once Ferrand had left, Charyn walked back to the empty music room, where he took out the music for "Pavane in a Minor Key."

10

The air was colder than Charyn thought it should be for summer when he walked down the grand staircase on the way to the breakfast room. He usually took the circular staircase, but for some reason he found himself walking down the center of the polished marble risers, his boots echoing with each step, an echo that seemed to reverberate through the entire Chateau, as if foreshadowing something ominous. Why that would be he had no idea. Nor did he have any idea why his breath steamed so much in the chill air. Had there been another unseasonable storm, one with hail that had chilled the air?

As he neared the polished marble tiles of the main foyer, he saw that neither of the two guards posted there moved, but stood motionless, like the painted statues of the ancient Naedarans. He could see his breath in the cold air, but not theirs. He tried to stop, to understand why he kept walking toward the statue-like guards, but his legs failed to obey, carrying him downward until he was on the last riser, and then on the polished white marble tiles of the foyer, even with the pair of guards.

The guard on the right turned, unbelievably swiftly.

Charyn gaped, because above the guard's formal greens, there was no face, just a blank expanse of skin. Before Charyn could speak or move, the faceless guard raised a pistol that Charyn had not seen and aimed it right at Charyn's forehead.

With a soundless yell that froze in his throat, Charyn tried to throw himself to the side, to twist out of the way, but his entire body felt as though it had turned to stone, his legs

rooted to the marble tiles, his mouth frozen open. His eyes
fixed on the grayish-black bullet that oozed through the silent air toward him as he fought to move his stone-like arms,
legs, and body. The bullet moved inexorably closer . . .

"No!"

His own voice echoed in his ears, and suddenly, he was
thrashing against the single sheet, which felt like a shroud
around him.

"NO, no, noooooo . . ."

Then, he could move, although his legs were tangled in
the sheet, and sweat poured from him, and he was shivering,
despite the warmth of the harvest air.

The same frigging dream . . .

It had been months since he'd last had that dream.

"Why now?"

Abruptly, he realized he'd spoken aloud, although there
was certainly no one else in the bedchamber. As he thought
that, he looked around, but even the dim light before dawn
was enough for him to see that he was alone.

He couldn't help shuddering.

11

~~~~~~

After the awakening nightmare on Solayi, the remainder of the day was thankfully uneventful, although Charyn endured Chorister Iskhar's less than scintillating homily that evening. But he definitely enjoyed the time spent with Aloryana, Alastar, and the others after services. Lundi and Mardi were also less than distinguished, filled with routine activities, and Charyn did finish reading through several petitions and working out replies with Sanafryt.

On Meredi morning, the first thing Charyn did after entering his study was to pick up the newssheets that lay on the desk and begin to read them.

The first article of more than passing interest was in *Veritum* and referred to the break-in on Lundi night at a small factorage dealing with porcelainware. Nothing had been taken, but much of the porcelain had been broken and left strewn across the floor. Yet no one reported hearing anything.

"Why would anyone break in and just smash porcelain . . . unless they had a grudge against the factor?" Charyn didn't have an answer to his own question.

Then there was another story, this time in *Tableta,* about Charyn, saying that he had been rumored to have visited Imagisle several times, including on Solayi, and ended by asking the question, "Is our beloved Rex more comfortable attending services among imagers, or might it be brotherly devotion to his sister Aloryana, who is an imager?"

Both newssheets had stories on the rumored Jariolan blockade of the Abierto Isles, and both newssheets declared that the Rex needed to take stronger actions against the Jariolans.

That's all well and good for you to say, but you'll all scream if I raise tariffs enough to do immediately what you want. Not that he could anyway without more shipbuilding.

Charyn set aside the newssheets and looked glumly toward the window, open to the still and warm outside air that blanketed L'Excelsis. He couldn't ever recall the Chateau being so quiet or empty.

That's because it never has been, not in your memory.

"Minister Sanafryt, sir," announced Moencriff, opening the door and ushering the older man into the study.

Sanafryt carried a folder and conveyed an attitude of concern as he neared Charyn and the table desk.

"You look worried," observed Charyn.

"I've just received these documents from the regional justicer in Solis. He's sent them to you for your review, requesting that the case be heard by the High Justicer."

"Why didn't he just refer it?"

"Because, without your approval, he'd have to hear the case, and I doubt that he wants to. I'd rather not say more until you read through the referral documents." Sanafryt extended the folder.

"Then I should read them." As he took the folder, Charyn didn't bother to conceal his resignation to what seemed inevitable . . . and was likely something that could turn nasty. Otherwise, Sanafryt would have drafted something for his approval, modification, or rejection.

Once the Minister of Justice had left the study, Charyn opened the folder. He read the précis once, then read it again, shaking his head, before he went on to the rest of the supporting documents. When he finished, he wanted to shake his head even more.

From the material before him, the facts were clear enough. High Holder Cayloren had offered his older daughter

Hylenia in marriage to a local factor of Lucayl. Hylenia was barely eighteen. Factor Lubarun was fifty-two and recently widowed. Hylenia had attempted to leave her father's holding to avoid the marriage, but had been caught and confined to quarters in a chateau tower. She had escaped by creating a long makeshift rope out of hangings and bed linens, taken a horse, and ridden fifteen milles to Karkas, the High Holding of Karkastyr, where she hurriedly wed Taartyl, the youngest son of High Holder Karkastyr. Being eighteen, she didn't legally require her father's approval.

But it's very unusual for one High Holder to flout the wishes of another in a purely family matter. And it's even more unusual for a High Holder to prefer that his daughter marry a factor, rather than the son of a High Holder, even a junior son.

High Holder Cayloren arrived just after the wedding and through some subterfuge not outlined in the documents reached his daughter and shot her and the groom. Hylenia died, but Taartyl lived. Cayloren was immediately imprisoned by High Holder Karkastyr. Factor Lubarun laid claim to Cayloren's holding and assets, asserting that Hylenia had been promised to him in return for Lubarun's forgiving of thirty thousand golds Cayloran owed to Lubarun.

And you thought Ferrand's father's debts of some nine thousand golds were excessive? And what was Lubarun factoring that he could come up with thirty thousand golds?

Charyn swallowed at the next section—that Cayloren's son shot and killed Lubarun, and had been shot and killed in turn by the factor's bodyguard. On a separate sheet, the regional justicer noted that Lubarun's late wife had died in her sleep a year earlier, after an illness, while Lubarun had been in Solis, but that the healer who had tended her had been paid by Cayloren and had later disappeared. All the assets and property of the High Holding were being claimed as damages by Lubarun's daughter. Cayloren's only surviving heir was a fifteen-year-old daughter, Hypenya.

Charyn shook his head. No wonder the regional justicer hadn't wanted to touch the matter, but there was no sense in forcing him to do so. The High Justicer would have to hear the case, and hopefully sentence Cayloren to death. Then there would be a squabble over the High Holding, and no matter how that turned out, neither factors nor High Holders would be happy.

And, if the High Justicer didn't find Cayloren guilty of assault and murder, there would be an even greater outcry, and that would require Charyn to remove the High Justicer.

Charyn could see the wisdom in granting the request and drafted a letter to the regional justicer agreeing to the request, then had Moencriff take the draft to Sanafryt for his review. He was pondering the case when Sturdyn brought in the latest letter from Rivages, several other letters, and a report from Marshal Vaelln.

Deciding that Vaelln's likely less than encouraging news could wait a quint longer, Charyn immediately opened his mother's letter and began to read.

Dear Charyn—
You're kind to keep me informed on all that is happening in L'Excelsis. I look forward to hearing how your small dinner turned out. I thought Bhayrn might be able to tell me something when he arrived late last evening. He said he was too tired to talk, but that he'd left before the dinner, and he'd tell me what he knew today. That will be a while, since he's still sleeping.

Listen to Elacia, but make your own decisions in terms of entertaining, and, no matter how galling it may be, stick to strict propriety in dealing with women from this point on. I cannot tell you how much failure to maintain such propriety has cost our families over the years . . .

That was clearly an allusion to Charyn's grandmother's dalliance and affair with Chelia's grandfather, which had resulted in the birth of Ryentar, whose actual parentage had not been revealed until the end of the first High Holders' revolt . . . and which had secretly precipitated it.

> . . . Your father, unlike every other man in the families before you, was most proper, perhaps somewhat too proper with me, but that is why matters were the way they were last year. Be proper until you find the right woman and then be proper with all others, and, only after wedding, enjoy each other as you can, for life is more uncertain than any of us can predict.

That message wasn't even between the lines. Charyn smiled briefly.

> Karyel does work at learning, but when he finds matters boring, or difficult, he smiles the family smile and attempts to charm his way out of working or studying. That is too like his grandfather. Iryella pouts, but we're working that through. At times, I feel too old for this, but I remind myself that, for better or worse, I only have a few years before it will be out of my hands and into yours.

The Nameless help me when Karyel becomes High Holder. Charyn continued reading for the next few pages. There were only a few lines on the last page, uncharacteristically, since Chelia tended to fill every sheet.

> I've been worried about the lack of rain, as I wrote earlier, but there are dark clouds to the north, and, with luck, we'll get enough rain so that the maize doesn't suffer too much.
>   Do write me about the dinner, when you can. I'll close now so that I can dispatch this before the rain.

Charyn stood and walked to the window. He looked to the north. He thought he saw a line of clouds on the horizon, but he couldn't be certain. But then, the army couriers usually outpaced the weather, if only by a day or so.

He glanced toward the desk and the dispatch from Vaelln. He slipped his mother's letter into the cabinet and then went through the other letters, one from each person invited to the dinner on Samedi evening, except for Alyncya, whose missive had arrived late on Mardi.

Those from the other young women were formal, flowery, and properly polite. The one from Zhelan was formal and thoughtfully polite.

Charyn smiled at the lines in Ferron's letter that went beyond the formal requirements:

> . . . *your thoughtfulness at the state of my feelings is greatly appreciated, but I trust you understand that after beholding a jewel of perfection any other seems lacking . . .*

Then he read Ferrand's letter, picking out certain phrases . . .

> . . . *as always, you have done more than anyone could expect, even from a close relative . . .*
> . . . *may be interested to know that I've been invited to a soiree by High Holder and Lady D'Almeida . . . but how you guessed that Marenna might be interested in me . . .*

Charyn couldn't have explained that, either, but he didn't have to.

He set aside the thank-you letters and opened the Marshal's dispatch—less than two pages, which revealed that a Jariolan fleet had been sighted in mid-ocean apparently headed toward the Abierto Isles. In the previous weeks, there had been no naval engagements and no ships lost or damaged. At the end was a note that the commander in charge of the navy shipyard at Estisle had reported that an anomen in Nacliano had been burned by a mob wearing all-white garments and hoods that concealed their faces and chanting words about "returning to Rholan" and "purifying the faith of the Nameless." According to Vaelln, the chorister had also perished, but the commander had looked into the matter and discovered that many felt that the deceased chorister had used most of the offerings in ways that increased the splendor of the anomen and the raiment and vestments of the chorister.

Charyn finally placed the letter in the chest that held all of the Marshal's reports.

There are too many incidents involving the anomens and what must be the True Believers.

But then, Charyn himself had felt that too many choristers of the Nameless had been doing too well for themselves and less for those who needed help. *But you can't tell choristers how to conduct themselves, not as Rex.* He frowned. He supposed he could, but was it a good idea? And would they even listen?

He took a deep breath and sat down at the table desk, taking out from the cabinet behind him the other short letter he had received on Mardi, and reread it . . . again.

> *Your Grace—*
> *My father and I both thank you for inviting us to the lovely summer dinner you hosted on Harvest-Turn evening. As you suggested, there is a much better chance for meaningful conversation when smaller numbers of diners are present, although other obligations impose limits, as well you understand.*
>
> *Because you enjoyed Covaelyt's "Variations on a Khellan Melody" and had never heard of it before, I am*

enclosing a copy for your use and enjoyment. Although I am not a professional music engraver, I believe the transcription is accurate, and I look forward to the time when I might be able to hear you play it. This is partly selfish on my part, because I haven't heard anyone else play it in years, not since Heldryk did when I was barely more than a child.

The signature was "Alyncya D'Shendael-Alte."

Charyn couldn't quite believe what she had sent—eight pages of music. *Eight pages that she had copied.* To personally copy that much music would have taken a professional musician like Palenya more than a glass a page. Eight to twelve glasses of perfect copy in two days? That showed more than great talent in musicianship and engraving. *Much more.*

He shook his head, not for the first time.

He'd already taken her copy to the music room and made a first, and very ragged, attempt at sight-reading his way through the "Variations," a piece he judged to be about as difficult as Nocturne Number Three, which meant that he ought to be able to master it in time, but her thoughtfulness, as well as the hints he'd seen of an independent mind, raised another, and disturbing, question.

Do you find her more attractive just because she reminds you of Palenya?

He knew he'd need to answer that question, and honestly, for both their sakes, but he also knew it was too soon to even attempt it.

In everything, timing mattered so much, as he'd learned, not always easily.

Still, he smiled as he looked over the letter and the strong, readable, but not quite perfect penmanship. Then he took out a sheet of paper and began to write.

More than a glass later, and after discarding several different openings and rewriting two drafts, he read over what lay before him.

Lady-heir Alyncya—

I cannot adequately express in ink the joy you have given me in providing a copy of "Variations on a Khellan Melody," especially a copy created by your own hand. The care taken in the transcription is more than evident, as well as the effort and concentration it took. I have already sight-read my way through the music, and it is more than clear that it will take me some time, and a great deal of practice, before I can come anywhere close to matching the skill with which you played it last Samedi evening. Even so, I will endeavor to provide you with my best effort at a future date, hoping that I will do enough justice to Covaelyt's genius that you will be able to enjoy listening to my playing.

In keeping with your intimated preference for conversation between us not to be initially too frequent, nor too intense, I will attempt to be as close to a model of propriety as is possible. That being the case, I trust you will allow me the privilege of corresponding with you and sharing thoughts on matters that might be of mutual interest between a man and a woman of education.

On a recent Solayi, I was listening to a chorister offer his homily, and he declared that Rholan the Unnamer once observed that more evil and killing was done in this world in a single year by men who wished to impose their view of what was right upon others by force than all the deaths in history caused by storms or by lightning or by the shaking of the earth. The more I have thought about his words, the more that they bothered me. That might be because he compared what happened in nature with what men do by intent. So far as I have been able to discern in my admittedly short life, nature does what nature does. There is no intent present. That men and women often suffer from the ravages of nature is not in dispute, but I see no malign intent. Men and women, on

the other hand, have intent, and because we have intent,
we are judged, as we should be. Those, at least, are my
thoughts on the matter, and I would be most interested
in yours.

With my best wishes.

He simply signed it "Charyn," then sealed it.

He did not immediately turn to the short stack of documents on the corner of the desk.

12

Vendrei morning, Charyn woke to the sound of heavy rain beating against the windows of the Chateau D'Rex. Not only that, but the rain and clouds were so heavy that for several moments he thought it was far earlier than it actually was.

Two glasses later, after going through his morning routine, Charyn looked out through the closed study window. The rain hadn't lessened in intensity. His first thought was that the growers should be happy. His second was a worry that, if the rain continued too long, the river would rise enough to weaken the west pier river walls, possibly enough to destroy the piers and flood the lower-lying parts of L'Excelsis on the west side of the river. His next thought was that perhaps the rain that his mother had written about might already have dropped enough water to the north that the river was already beginning to rise.

So he left the study and walked down to the main level to look for Maertyl, whom he eventually found in the armory, after getting soaked crossing the open rear courtyard.

"Sir . . . you could have sent for me."

"A little rain won't hurt. But one of your guards is going to get much wetter. You may recall that the spring floods damaged the west river piers."

"Yes, sir." Maertyl frowned momentarily. "But we've scarcely had any rain since then."

"I know, but Lady Chelia wrote me that they were expecting heavy rains in Rivages." That was an exaggeration, but not one Charyn was likely to be called on. "This storm came in from the north. If it has been raining this heavily all the way south from Rivages, we might see some more flooding. I'd like you to send someone to the river walls where the

Boulevard D'Rex ends at the West River Road, around the north bridge to Imagisle. I need to know how high the river is, and for now, I want you to keep sending men every glass or so and keep me informed whether the river is rising."

Maertyl nodded. "Yes, sir."

"Thank you."

As Charyn hurried back through the heavy rain to the rear door of the Chateau, he doubted that there was much he could really do if the river did flood. There was no way to shore up the damaged river walls, not given the structure, which was why the additional repairs weren't scheduled until the times of low water. *Maybe the rain will end before the river rises too much.*

Once back in his study, he looked out the window again, but the downpour continued and showed no signs of slowing or stopping. *But who would have thought we'd get a rain this heavy in the middle of a drought?*

At that moment, there was a knock on the study door.

"Yes?"

"Undercaptain Faelln, sir."

"Have him come in."

Faelln entered carrying a small package of some sort. "I'm sorry to bother you, sir, but a public courier delivered a package addressed to you. There was no name on the package. He didn't know the person who sent it, but they paid him a silver to deliver it, and told him they'd know if he didn't bring it here. Fairly shaking the boy was. So we thought it best to open it . . . after . . . what happened last winter."

"No one was hurt?"

Faelln shook his head. "There was nothing in it—just the cloth around it and . . . this."

Amid the cloth was another white cloth belt.

Charyn wanted to shiver. Once could have been happenstance. The second time was anything but.

"I don't pretend to understand this, Your Grace, except it must be some sort of message."

"I understand what it's supposed to be from," replied
Charyn, "but I don't have the faintest idea what it means."
At Faelln's puzzled look, he went on. "It has to be something
dealing with the True Believers. They're the only people
who wear white. A belt like this was left for me to find at
the Anomen D'Rex. Am I supposed to be concerned about
them? I already am. Or are they saying that I need to listen
to them?" He smiled wryly. "They have my attention . . . if I
only knew what it meant."

"We'll keep an eye out, ser."

"Thank you. That's all you can. You can take that, but
keep it safe, just in case."

"Yes, ser."

After Faelln left, Charyn just looked at the window, trying to puzzle out what it might mean.

Finally, he turned his attention back to the desk. He still
needed to write a quick note to Maitre Alastar. Less than a
quint later, he read the words.

> *Maitre Alastar—*
> *If it meets with your approval, I would like to attend*
> *services at the Anomen D'Imagisle this Solayi with*
> *Aloryana, as well as on the fifteenth. On the twenty-*
> *second, I would propose taking her to services at the*
> *Anomen D'Rex, which would, of course, require an*
> *imager escort.*
>
> *This seemingly irregular schedule will, I hope, make*
> *it more difficult for those who might wish me harm*
> *to ascertain where I might be. In this regard, I would*
> *appreciate any suggestions you might offer.*

After signing and sealing it, he gave it to Moencriff to arrange for dispatch to Imagisle.

He walked back to the window and studied the rain, but
it continued to fall as heavily as before, and the clouds from
which it fell seemed even darker.

Another quint passed before Moencriff rapped on the door and announced, "Factor Councilor Elthyrd is here to see you, sir."

For a moment, Charyn didn't say a word, because Elthyrd hadn't asked to see him. *But if he's here without an appointment, it can't be good, especially in this rain.* "Please have him come in." Charyn stood.

The gray-haired factor entered the study. Charyn noted that neither his trousers nor his jacket were damp, suggesting that he had come by coach and left a waterproof at the Chateau entry.

"Thank you for seeing me."

"You have seen me more than a few times when I arrived unannounced. Your arrival in this weather suggests a matter of urgency or import." Charyn gestured toward the chairs and seated himself.

"It may not seem of import, but I fear it may be." Elthyrd coughed several times, immediately covering his mouth with a large handkerchief, then went on. "Did you hear about the incident where Factor Belliark had much of the porcelain in his shop destroyed?"

"I read the story in the newssheet. There is more I should know?"

"Indeed." Elthyrd coughed again. "Belliark imports porcelain from the Abierto Isles. It is of good quality, and even with the costs of shipping, is considerably less expensive than wares fired here in Solidar. Every piece of imported porcelain was smashed or damaged. The Solidaran wares were not."

Charyn nodded and waited.

"This is not the first incident of this nature. It is not the second. Since the twenty-fifth of Juyn there have been three other incidents where shops were broken into and imported wares destroyed. Bronzework in one instance, woolens in the others."

"Was anything else taken?"

"Not a thing. Even the doors were closed after the damage was done. It has to be someone connected to the guilds. I just don't understand why it began on the twenty-fifth. If they were unhappy with what the councils decided . . . why did they wait an entire week?"

Charyn knew, unfortunately. "Because I asked Craftmaster Argentyl to see me. He came on the twenty-fourth. I told him what happened at the Council meeting because I promised I would. He asked what I intended to do. I told him that the councils, based on the advice of Minister Sanafryt, had felt that imposing legal penalties based on the artificers' standard was unworkable. I also said that I was still looking for a way to deal with the problem. He said that crafters were having to let go apprentices and that waiting for a solution wouldn't put bread on the table."

"Did he make any threats?"

"No. He asked why I had to spend so many golds fighting with the Jariolans when crafters and artisans were being hurt. I told him that the artisans wouldn't have any tin or spices if we didn't because those came by ship. I said I'd try to find another solution. He said he appreciated my listening, but listening alone didn't help. He said there might be those who wouldn't wait for such a solution, but the people who told him that wouldn't say who the others were. Then he left."

"Did he seem angry?"

Charyn shook his head. "He seemed sad, unhappy, almost defeated."

"Then it's more likely to be someone he told."

"Or someone he told that told someone else," said Charyn dryly. "There are more than a few handfuls of crafters."

"It can't be just one person. In each instance, whoever did it knew exactly what was imported and what was not."

"Has the Civic Patrol found anyone?"

Elthyrd gave Charyn a sour look. "Your Grace, most of the civic patrollers come from the families of crafters or those who work for crafters. They aren't looking that strenuously."

"What do you expect of me?" Charyn was honestly curious. The civic patrollers worked for the factors, and they paid for the Patrol.

"The Factors' Council just wanted you to be aware that these events happened. We fear that there may be more to come."

"Are there that many factors importing cheaper goods?" asked Charyn.

"It's not just about imported goods, Your Grace. It's also about cloth made by the new manufactorages, and less expensive metalwork stamped or formed by machines."

"Argentyl didn't mention that." *Cloth? Both belts were cloth. Did they even come from the True Believers?* Charyn wanted to shake his head at the ambiguity of the belts.

"Why would he? It's much more favorable to portray the problem in the guise of shoddy goods being passed off as better than they are. The new goods allow common people to have wares they couldn't afford before." After the slightest pause, Elthyrd said, conversationally, "I understand that Factor Suyrien has purchased the ironworks. That includes a rifleworks. Those rifles are far cheaper than those made by a gunsmith. It makes golds for the works, but the rifles are also cheaper for your troopers. That means you don't have to raise tariffs or that you can spend more golds on repairing the river walls . . . which may need some more urgent work if this rain doesn't stop."

"I have men watching the river."

"You should. It doesn't look good." Another fit of coughing came over the timber and lumber factor, coughs that he again suppressed with the larger handkerchief.

"Are you all right?"

"A touch of temporary consumption, that's all. I'm sure it will pass." After another cough, Elthyrd said, "That's all I had to convey."

Charyn rose. "Then I won't keep you. I appreciate your letting me know, and please take care not to get chilled on the ride back to your factorage."

Elthyrd stood. "Thank you for your time and your concern, Your Grace."

His carriage was erect and determined as he left the study, but Charyn still worried. Despite Elthyrd's factoring bias, he was far easier to work with than many others, and he was anything but a young man. If he became too sick to continue, it would make Charyn's dealings with the councils even more difficult.

Charyn glanced to the window. The rain continued. Then he sat down and just looked at the empty conference table, not really seeing it.

So far, there had been no reply from Alyncya. *She did say they were traveling to Vaestora, but she didn't say when.* Still, he couldn't help but hope she'd reply before too long. *But she had made that comment about not wanting another conversation until the Autumn-Turn Ball.*

13

On Solayi morning, rather than exercise, Charyn decided to make an informal inspection of the stables, since it had been several weeks since he'd last done so. He doubted he'd ever find anything out of place. He did wonder whether the roof might be leaking, although the rain had lightened overnight from a downpour into a lighter but continuous fall. As he hurried across the rear courtyard to the stables, Charyn just hoped that the rain would end soon. Already, some crops were doubtless ruined, and some fields likely had standing water that would not soon drain . . . including some of his own at Chaeryll.

Once inside the stable, Charyn studied the beams around the closed main doors, but they didn't look damp, and he didn't see any puddles of water on the floor. At the sound of steps he looked up and watched as the stablemaster approached him.

"Your Grace . . . can we do anything for you?"

"No, Aedryt. I was just worrying about the rain. It appears that everything here is tight and dry."

"Yes, sir, for the most part. Yesterday, when it was coming down real hard, and the wind picked up, some water came in under the main doors so heavy that the slop gutters couldn't carry it away fast enough, but the boys took care of that."

"You couldn't tell that now. How are you coming with the trees in the hunting park?"

"We'll have everything trimmed and the deadwood all removed by the end of Agostos, even if we lose some limbs to the rain. We likely won't need as much wood to be shipped in for the Chateau this winter."

"Unless winter is colder."

"I can't speak to that, sir," replied the stablemaster with a smile.

"Is there anything that you need?"

"No, sir. Norstan and I have got things worked out."

Charyn knew what that meant, and he just nodded. "I will be needing a coach around fifth glass."

"Yes, sir. Undercaptain Faelln let me know."

"Thank you."

Once Charyn returned to the Chateau, he headed for the music room, where he settled himself at the clavecin, beginning with Nocturne Number Three before turning his attention to "Pavane in a Minor Key." After close to a glass working on that, he turned to the opening of "Variations on a Khellan Melody."

Then there was a knock on the music room door, and Guard Undercaptain Faelln appeared.

Charyn immediately rose from the clavecin, fearing what Faelln might say.

"I'm sorry to bother you, sir, but I thought you should know. The Civic Patrol sent a messenger, sir. The west river walls south of the piers have given way, and that part of the city immediately west and south of there is flooded."

South of the piers? Not at the piers? Was that because the temporary repairs made in late spring had held, and the river walls south of there had been weaker than anyone had known? Or had been willing to tell Charyn?

He took a deep breath. "I'll need to ride down there and look at the damage."

"Is there anything you can do, sir?"

"I doubt it, but that doesn't matter. If I'm not seen to be there, everyone from High Holders to the lowest crafter will think I don't care. First, I do care. Second, seeming not to care will make working with the factors and crafters even harder."

"I'll tell the stablemaster to have a mount for you. It's

likely to be a quint before I'll have guards ready to ride out with you."

"I'll be ready then."

Charyn put away the music for his "new" pieces, then headed up to his quarters to get an oilskin riding jacket and a plain green visor cap.

Lead Guard Reynalt stood waiting for Charyn, just inside the door to the rear courtyard of the Chateau. "The guard detachment is drawn up just inside the stables, sir."

"Thank you. We'll head out immediately."

Faelln was waiting with the four guards in the stable. "L'Avenue D'Commercia is above water and will take you to the river north of the flooded area. I trust you'll stay out of deep water, Your Grace."

Charyn understood Faelln's unspoken point that few of the mounts were water-trained. "I'll do my best. I hope we won't be too long, but I'll need to see the extent of the flooding myself."

"Yes, sir."

Faelln's tone also told Charyn that the guard undercaptain was anything but pleased with Charyn's decision to ride out to see the damage.

"It's far safer for me to ride out now than it would be tomorrow. It's Solayi and still raining." Charyn led the chestnut gelding out of the stables and mounted.

The four guards—and Reynalt—all wore dark green oilskins, as did Charyn, and were all armed with rifles in holders, as well as sabres. The only weapon Charyn carried was his pistol, although he was decent, but not outstanding, with a rifle.

Two of the guards rode down the back drive to the Ring Road, followed by Reynalt and Charyn, with two guards in the rear. The rain didn't seem as bad as Charyn had thought as they rode to the southeast side of the Ring Road and turned onto L'Avenue D'Commercia. The six of them were the only ones Charyn saw on the avenue for the first mille.

Then he saw several carts and handcarts, some filled with bundles, moving away from the river.

Those working with the carts scarcely looked through the light rain at the riders, except to make sure that they avoided the horses.

More than a quint later, Charyn and the guards reined up at the top of a slight decline in the avenue, less than a hundred yards from the spreading water. Charyn had expected to see something like a torrent of water raging through a break in the stone of the river walls, but what he saw was quite different. From what he could tell, the top courses of stone had been swept away or pushed back and some of the river flowed over the remaining stone walls, almost as if over a spillway of sorts, creating a shallow lake that covered the West River Road. Upstream of the lake, to Charyn's left, the tops of the piers were above water, if barely, and the buildings behind them, including Paersyt's factorage, looked to stand in perhaps a third of a yard of water. The buildings farther south along the river were inundated by a least a yard of brownish water, each building rising like an island out of the slowly swirling brown water that extended at least several hundred yards to the west, until it reached a point where the ground was higher.

Charyn gestured. "We'll take the next street to the right. I need to see just how far the water extends."

For the next glass, Charyn and the guards rode south, flanking the river and the water that covered the lower ground for almost a mille, until the land farther south rose just enough to contain the overflow from the river. Even so, there had to be hundreds if not a thousand or more dwellings and other structures along that strip of land several hundred yards wide and almost a mille long suffering some degree of flooding, although it appeared that in no place was the water deeper than a yard or so.

Just deep enough to ruin almost everything.

When he turned the chestnut back, Charyn was both dismayed at the extent of the flooding and relieved that it hadn't been worse. *Not that it's not going to cause many people to suffer.*

At least a handful of people had likely recognized the guards, even in green oilskins, as Chateau guards, and in time, some might guess that Charyn had been with them. *So long as it's in time, and not immediate.*

Even as he thought that, he wondered if he was getting to be too worried about being killed. The previous attempts had all been targeted at him because Ryel had wanted to wipe out the family, but Ryel and all his family, except for Karyel and Iryella, and, of course, Charyn's mother, were dead.

When the six rode back into the rear courtyard just before third glass, a clearly relieved Faelln greeted Charyn. "I take it there was no trouble, Your Grace?"

"Not for us. There are a great number of houses and shops that have been damaged. It could be worse, but if the rain lets up, that might not happen." *Not in L'Excelsis, but what about farther downriver?*

Charyn just hoped the flooding didn't spread any further or turn out to be calamitous in some other fashion.

14

~~~~~

The rain stopped by midday on Solayi, although the sky remained cloudy and the air damp. Charyn tried not to dwell too much on the flooding, spending several glasses trying to improve his skills on the clavecin and working on learning and improving his technique with both the Pavane and Variations pieces.

He went back upstairs to his study and pored over the master ledgers, trying to see where he might squeeze out more golds . . . and then wondered how much the flood would set back Paersyt's work on his steam engine.

At fifth glass he entered the unmarked carriage for the ride to Imagisle, only to find himself looking from the carriage at the torrent that flowed under the bridge as he rode across the bridge to Imagisle. He also couldn't help but admire the skill and strength of the imaging done by the Collegium's founders, especially given the imposing stone river walls and the bridges, none of which bore any signs of age or damage after more than four hundred years, especially since the top of the river walls around the isle were still well above the torrent.

He even enjoyed walking through the rain with Aloryana to the anomen.

The thrust of Iskhar's homily was certainly timely, particularly one part where the chorister said, ". . . for most of the summer growers have been praying to the Nameless for rain. Now the rains have come, and people are praying that they will stop. A cynical man might say that it shows how people are never satisfied. Another might say that it shows the wisdom of moderation in prayer. But . . . a wiser man might ask whether the Nameless chooses to control the weather based on how many people pray for what. The idea that our prayers can induce the Nameless to behave in a way that fulfills our needs and desires is but another form of Naming . . . of believing or wanting to believe that we are greater than we are. We are not what we wish or believe ourselves to be. We are what we do. We are the sum total of those acts we do and those we choose not to do . . ."

As they walked back toward the Maitre's house, Aloryana looked to her brother. "You liked Iskhar's homily, didn't you?"

"How could you tell?"

"You listened, and you nodded."

"He had some good things to say, especially about how choosing not to do things is also important."

"He didn't say that. He said that we are what we do and what we don't do."

"It's the same thing. If we choose not to do something evil or unwise, isn't that also good?" *Especially for a Rex?*

"Maitre Gaellen," interjected Lystara, "says that's one of the most important parts of healing—not to do any harm."

"Something in common with Rexes," said Charyn dryly.

"Charyn," ventured Aloryana quietly, "did you like any of the women you invited to that dinner party?"

"I wouldn't have invited anyone I didn't like, unless she were someone Ferrand liked, and that wasn't the case." Charyn wondered exactly what his sister had in mind, because he only mentioned the dinner party in passing.

"You didn't answer my question."

"Yes. Why do you ask?"

"Because. That's why. You shouldn't be all alone in the Chateau."

"That's one reason why I'm here, to be with you."

"I'm glad you are, but I want to meet any woman you really like. Promise me that you'll let me meet anyone you're thinking about marrying *before* you ask her."

"Aloryana . . ."

"Promise me." Aloryana's voice was firm.

Charyn didn't know whether to laugh or sigh. Six months at Imagisle had definitely made Aloryana stronger, and she'd never been shy before. "I promise."

"Good. You've never broken your word to me."

"Was this your idea or someone else's?"

"It was mine." Aloryana smiled. "But I know some other people who'd agree with me."

So did Charyn.

15

~~~~~

Very early on Lundi morning, Charyn again rode out with a handful of guards to survey the flooded section of L'Excelsis. While the rain had subsided, the standing water had not, and the sky was still cloudy. When he rode out again on Mardi morning, the steamy fog rose off everything, but he was glad to see that the water had receded from most, but not all of the flooded areas. Unfortunately, the waters had also left behind mud, limbs, bushes, and occasional carcasses of various animals, but people were already out and beginning to clean up the mud and debris.

More than a few looked, at least in passing, at the six riders.

Once he returned to the Chateau, Charyn left word for Alucar to see him when he arrived, then began to read through Vaelln's latest report. He'd only gotten to the bottom of the first page when Alucar arrived.

"You wanted to see me, Your Grace?"

"I did. I've been surveying the damage caused by the flood . . ."

"The repairs that you paid for held."

"Which shifted the damage downstream. I feel that we should provide some aid to those whose homes and shops were damaged."

"There aren't enough golds in the treasury to recompense a fraction of the damage."

"I can't afford not to do something."

"Your Grace . . . you didn't cause the rains or the floods." After a pause, Alucar asked, "What about a notice that all factors and crafters in the flooded area, and only in the flooded area, will have any tariffs owed reduced by half, just for this year?"

"You're the one who said we're short of golds," Charyn pointed out.

"We are, but those are future golds, and many of them we would never see because they won't make enough to pay them in any event."

"A seemingly generous offer that isn't that generous."

"You can't afford a truly generous offer," countered Alucar.

"What about giving out food to some of the people? It wouldn't cost that much."

"The moment word gets out, people will swarm from everywhere."

Unfortunately, Charyn could see that happening. "Fine. Get me a bag of a hundred silvers."

Alucar frowned. "Your Grace?"

"Please just do it."

"As you wish, Your Grace."

Charyn could tell that Alucar was anything but pleased, but he knew he had to do something. After the Finance Minister left, Charyn picked up the latest copy of *Tableta,* reading the various articles before coming to one on the bottom of the first page.

Word is that our beloved Rex actually rode out in the rain on Solayi to look over the flooding when the river walls south of the west river piers collapsed. The Rex did pay for repairs to the pier walls earlier this year, to the benefit of factors and certain High Holders. Too bad he couldn't pay for more to strengthen the walls that failed and didn't protect flooded out crafters and others less fortunate. He also wasn't at services Solayi evening, at least not at the Anomen D'Rex. No one expects a Rex to hold back the storms, but you might expect that at least he'd pray for the afflicted.

Charyn wanted to shake his head. What had he done to merit that sort of personal attack?

But then, that was yet another reason why he needed to do something.

A quint later, Moencriff opened the door. He held a leather pouch. "Minister Alucar sent this. He said you'd asked for it."

"I did." Charyn rose from the desk and walked to the study door, where he took the pouch, hearing the sound of silvers against each other. "If you'd convey to Guard Captain Maertyl that I need to make another inspection ride in half a glass, I'd appreciate it."

"Yes, sir." Moencriff did not hide his puzzlement.

Charyn walked back to his desk and set the pouch on it, then turned toward the window and the sunlight beyond the glass, thinking how displeased Alucar had seemed. The fact that he hadn't delivered the silvers personally emphasized that.

He shook his head, then sat down at the desk and began to write his at-least-weekly letter to his mother. He needed to let her know about the flood, and what Aloryana had said on Solayi, among other things.

Three quints later, Charyn was once more riding south on L'Avenue D'Commercia. When he and the guards reached the intersection with the road to the Sud Bridge, where the ground sloped down into the flooded area, Charyn signaled them to halt. Then he studied the mud-covered streets and structures to the south, mentally mapping out where he wanted to begin, starting with the side street a block off the West River Road heading south. Most of the buildings fronting the West River Road belonged to factors or more successful crafters, and what he could afford to offer would mean little to them.

He gestured again and urged the chestnut forward, riding some fifty yards before turning south on the side street. The left side of the street consisted entirely of the rear sections of the larger buildings facing onto the West River Road. The right side held a mixture of small dwellings and shops.

The first building on the right looked as though it had been abandoned even before the flood, and Charyn rode past it toward the second, a narrow brick dwelling with just a door and single window facing the street. A man not much older than Charyn was sweeping the mud off the low stoop. Charyn rode up close to him and asked, "Is this your dwelling?"

The man looked up warily, as if to reply angrily, but he paused as he saw the mounted guards behind Charyn. "No one else'd be sweeping out all this swill . . . sir."

"I'm sorry that you have to," replied Charyn, leaning forward and extending a silver. "I wish I could do more, but I hope this will help. It's a token of my concern. Please keep word of this to yourself and your family for a few days. Otherwise, I won't be able to help others."

The man looked at the silver in his hand, then at Charyn, taking in the uniform greens, and his face screwed up in puzzlement.

"I won't keep you from what you need to do." Then Charyn urged the chestnut forward, moving toward the next building, where a gray-haired man and a boy were carrying buckets out of the shop, which looked to be a cooperage from the half barrel displayed above the double doors to the shop.

The man lowered the bucket and watched as Charyn approached.

"Is this your cooperage?"

"It is. It was, anyway. Why do you ask?"

Rather than answer directly, Charyn bent forward in the saddle and handed the cooper a silver. "A token of my concern. Also, your tariffs for this year will be half of last year's. Please keep this to yourself for a day or so."

As he moved on, Charyn could hear the boy ask his father, "Who was that man?"

He didn't hear the answer, if there was one.

Then next dwelling was vacant, or, at least, no one answered when one of the guards rapped on the door.

In front of the fourth building, a white-haired woman and a small boy were scraping mud off the stoop. A younger woman, if still old enough to be Charyn's mother, carried out a wooden bucket filled with muddy water and emptied it onto the mud-covered stone pavement, a pavement that had more broken stones than intact ones, at least it seemed that way to Charyn.

"What are you looking for, dandy-man?" snapped the old woman.

"For whoever's house this is," replied Charyn.

"It's mine," replied the woman with the bucket. "Leastwise, I'm the one paying the rent. What might you be wanting?"

Charyn eased the mount toward her. "To offer a token of my concern." He handed her the silver. "I wish it could be more, but there are so many who need assistance." He straightened in the saddle.

"Sir . . ." offered the woman, "Widow Baarlan lives in the next cot. She can't come to the door."

Charyn handed the woman a second silver. "I trust you will give this to her, then."

That was a gamble, Charyn knew, but he had the feeling that the woman would do what he hoped. *Sometimes, you can only hope.*

"That I will, Your Honor."

"Thank you."

The house beyond the widow's had been empty for a time, with no glass in the single window.

The next building had a basket over a narrow door, and a man and a woman were working hard at scrubbing the mud off the lower bricks. The walk and stoop were already clean, and the door was wide open. From what Charyn could see, the floor beyond the door was already clean.

The woman looked up at the riders, then gestured to the man. He turned, frowning.

Charyn beckoned for the man to approach, which the basketmaker did, if gingerly, then tendered the silver with the same words as before.

"You're right, sir. It's only a token. What do you expect in return, Your Grace?"

"I'm asking nothing. Do you pay yearly tariffs?"

"After this?"

"Your tariffs, if you owe anything, will be halved for this year. That's only for those factors and crafters who were flooded." Charyn nodded, then eased the chestnut toward the next dwelling.

He wasn't looking forward to the next few glasses.

Charyn's legs and back were aching when he rode back into the rear courtyard of the Chateau at a quint past fifth glass. He'd seen and smelled more than he'd thought, and he'd given out every single silver.

Will it do any good?

He had no idea, but he'd had to do something.

16

Charyn made another inspection ride out to the flood-affected area of L'Excelsis on Vendrei, and while the standing water had vanished, that part of the city reeked of moisture, drying mud, and an underlying scent of corruption under a blazing white harvest sun that seemed to be trying to return the land to a state of drought as quickly as possible.

When he returned to the Chateau and his study, he quickly read through both newssheets.

In addition to a detailed assessment of the flood damage, *Veritum* included a brief story on Charyn:

> The Rex, wearing no trappings of regiality, rode out for days to survey the flooded area of L'Excelsis south of the west river piers. On his last tour he handed out silvers to those there who were cleaning up their homes and shops, asking them to tell no one for a day or so. Many of those who received those coins from the hand of the Rex himself had no idea who the young man with the armed guards even was. He never identified himself, but this newssheet has confirmed that it was the Rex. The Rex admitted that the silvers were only a token, but since when has a ruler shown any concern for those afflicted by the ravages of nature?

On the other hand, the report from *Tableta* was anything but favorable.

> The Rex is definitely trying to earn the title of "beloved." His newest stratagem is handing out silvers to those who

suffered the ravages of the flood. Those silvers would have been better spent rebuilding the river walls. Then again, handing out a few silvers was far cheaper than spending golds to rebuild the walls . . .

Charyn shook his head. *It's not as though I have the tens of thousands of golds necessary to rebuild all the river walls in L'Excelsis.* He still had to wonder just why *Tableta* had such a dislike of him. He didn't recall anything like that before . . . except, he reminded himself, he'd never even known the newssheets existed before he became Rex. His father had banned them from the Chateau D'Rex.

He was still thinking that over when Moencriff opened the study door. "Several letters, Your Grace."

"Thank you." Charyn walked to the study door and took the missives. By the seal, one was from his mother, one from Paersyt, and another from Factor Elthyrd.

He decided to read those from Elthyrd and Paersyt first, beginning with the one from the Factor Councilor.

Your Grace—
As I may have suggested as a possibility when you were so kind as to see me last week, the attacks against imported wares and those produced by manufactorages have continued, and in one case, an entire factorage building was burned to the ground. Factor Eshmael's cotton and woolen fabrics in the building were destroyed, in addition to the factorage itself. There have also been attacks of this nature in Kherseilles and Cheva.

  In view of the meeting of the councils next week, I wanted you to be aware of the growing severity of the problem. Combined with the disruption of river shipping, this has many factors greatly concerned . . .

Charyn shook his head. The guilds and the artisans were

unhappy, and likely several of them were behind the destruction, and that was making the factors unhappy. And no one was happy about two floods in two seasons.

And right now, you don't have an answer that will make either group happy.

He set aside Elthyrd's letter and picked up the newssheets, going through them quickly once again . . . but there was no mention of a fire or any damage at a factorage. Yet the first attack on a shop had been mentioned. If there had been as many as Elthyrd had reported, why weren't they in the newssheets? *Especially when they can take time to report on where you ride.*

He dropped *Tableta* on top of *Veritum* and picked up the letter from Paersyt, wondering what problems it held. Had the flood damaged his factorage? He took a deep breath, then slit the envelope and extracted the single sheet.

Your Grace—
I am relieved to be able to report that the recent floods
largely missed my modest works, aside from a few digits
of water in one part of the work area. The damage to
the piers and the high and turbulent state of the river,
however, will require a delay in water trials of the
steam engine until the launching ramp beside the pier
is available and such time as the water is calmer and is
not crowded with debris. That may be as long as another
two weeks, if not longer.
In the meantime, I am working on some possible
improvements to the seals for the driveshaft to the water
screw . . .

This time Charyn nodded. He couldn't have expected anything else, and at least Paersyt hadn't had anything destroyed.

Once he finished reading what Paersyt had written, he decided to read his mother's letter, hoping there wasn't more bad news.

Dear Charyn—
The rain flooded some of the lowland and bottomland
fields. It struck harder south of Rivages. I only hope
that L'Excelsis isn't flooded again. As Rex, that's not
something that you need, although that's what you must
expect.

Aloryana just wrote me. I cannot tell you how pleased
she is that you're seeing her every Solayi. Since she has
to attend services, your being there makes it much better.
She reports that she is continuing to study with Palenya
and to practice, although it's more difficult to find time
to practice because there's really only the one clavecin
available . . .

Should you think about looking into getting another?
Charyn shook his head. Then, there'd still only be two for
the same number of student imagers, and that wouldn't do
much for Aloryana. He almost felt guilty for having a clavecin all to himself.

Bhayrn is getting somewhat better about learning what
it is to run a High Holding. He still gets frustrated when
I make him read ledgers and tell me what the figures
show about the holding. Karyel, on the other hand,
is most adept with such figures. He does tend to make
errors because he jumps to conclusions before reading
everything.

Iryella is more like Aloryana. She likes music and can
play the clavecin well for her age. She prefers the harp,
but that may be because she recalls her mother playing
it . . .

When he set down Chelia's letter, Charyn couldn't help
but think of the irony if Karyel and Iryella turned out in
a better fashion than Bhayrn. *But now who's jumping to*
conclusions?

17

~~~~~

Mardi morning found Charyn pacing back and forth in his study. The weekend had been mostly quiet, and he'd enjoyed the time with Aloryana at services and at the Maitre's house afterward, although Chorister Iskhar's homily about duty and false humility had grated on him for reasons he wasn't sure he could explain. Charyn certainly didn't think he was humble, and he thought he tried not to be arrogant . . . but there had been something about the homily . . . and then there was the fact that Palenya was coming to tune the clavecin. For the moment, he pushed that thought aside.

Lundi had been without incident. He hadn't even received any more letters from either his mother or from Factor Elthyrd—nor a response from Alyncya from his last letter.

The latest edition of *Veritum* had contained a very short story about an unexplained fire that had burned down one of Factor Eshmael's factorages and destroyed all its contents. The Civic Patrol had declared the fire had been deliberately set, but had not been able to determine who set the fire or why. There was no story about that fire or other damages to factors' goods or buildings in *Tableta*. All that puzzled Charyn, but he had no real idea why the newssheets published some stories and not others.

Since pacing solved nothing, he finally settled behind the table desk and went over the language of the proposed law on water return, then jotted a note to Sanafryt to have fifteen copies of the language made. That reminded him, again, that he really did need a personal secretary or at least a scrivener. That was another matter he'd put off, and shouldn't have. *But how can you find someone truly trustworthy?*

After a time, he nodded.

Then he turned to another petition, one about the inability of High Holders to punish known poachers who were not on a High Holder's own lands when an entire village knew who was poaching and when everyone in the village claimed not to know. Charyn set that one aside to discuss with Sanafryt.

He was halfway through the first page of a complaint by a High Holder Leomyk, which seemed to be about the location of a regial courier road with regard to a gristmill, when Moencriff knocked on the study door.

"A letter for you, sir." The guard tried not to smile when he handed the missive to Charyn.

As he took the letter and caught sight of the bold penmanship, he understood Moencriff's smile, even as he wondered if he'd been that transparent about his interest in Alyncya. *More transparent than you realize, obviously.* He walked back to the desk, slit open the envelope, and immediately began to read.

Your Grace—
I must apologize for the delay in replying to your kind letter of the fourth of Agostos, but I neglected to mention that I sent my previous correspondence to you just before we left on our journey to Vaestora. Although your letter was forwarded to me I did not receive it until late yesterday . . .

Charyn looked at the date—10 Agostos.

. . . You will likely receive this just before we arrive home because Father decided we should return with High Holder Calkoran and his wife. She would not normally accompany him every time he travels to L'Excelsis for the Council meetings, but she will this time. That is due to a certain invitation, I would guess, but I did not ask, and Lady Saelya has not volunteered her reason or reasons.

I look forward to that time when you play "Variations on a Khellan Melody" for me, but I will not press you on when that may be. You have many challenges before you and much that must take up your waking hours.

Our visit here in Vaestora has been pleasant, and Staenyla approved highly of your idea of her occasionally accompanying her father to L'Excelsis. So did High Holder Calkoran, although Staenyla will not be coming in Agostos, since she will be in charge of the hold house in the absence of her parents.

You posed an intriguing question about whether we should be judged more on intent because we have a choice in what we do. Do we in fact have a choice? We may in some matters, but not in others. Did your sister Aloryana have a choice in becoming an imager? For that matter, did you really have choice in becoming Rex? For if you had declined to accept the burden, would not it have fallen to your brother—without his choosing, either? Then, there are degrees of choice. How much choice do I have in whom I might wed? I am fortunate in that my father will not force a match upon me, no matter how well-endowed a suitor might be, but I cannot seek out a husband in quite the way that a High Holder or a Rex can seek a wife.

Charyn half-smiled, half-frowned at the pair of veiled messages in those lines. At least, he thought there were two messages there.

The other question of import is whether, in many cases, intent matters in the slightest. If I intend no evil, but an act of mine harms another, how does my intent make me less guilty? I may have wished for the best, but my information may have been lacking, or my judgment may have been poor, and the result even worse. Good intent may ease my guilt or conscience, but how can it reduce

*the harm? If a poor grower's child starves because his
crops fail, as do those of all his neighbors, is that loss
any less than if the child dies of the flux or is run down
by the horses of a careless teamster?*

*Should we then, perhaps, inquire into what lies
behind your question? Could it be that the attribution of
greater evil to maleficent "intent" implies that men have
the power to cause evil and that refraining from doing so
thereby elevates them, whereas nature is not considered
more elevated when there are not destructive droughts or
ruinous rains?*

*You see, Your Grace, that, as you noted about my sire,
I am also wont to reply in greater honesty than is often
appreciated.*

I remain, your interested correspondent.

Once more, her signature was her formal full name.

At least she's letting me know that she's still interested.
Charyn slipped the letter back into its envelope and then
placed the envelope in the cabinet behind his desk.

He thought about replying immediately, but decided
against it. He might have more of interest to say after the
Council meeting, and after talking with High Holder and
Lady Calkoran at the "family" dinner. And there was also
the fact that Alyncya had made it more than clear that she
had no interest in being rushed into anything . . . especially
with Charyn.

And . . . he wanted to see how he felt after he saw Palenya, something he'd avoided for months. *Did you really do
the right thing with her . . . for both of you?*

He was still thinking that over when Moencriff rapped on
the study door.

"Yes?"

"Sir," said Moencriff, "the musician is here to tune the
clavecin. You asked to be notified when she arrived."

"Thank you." Charyn took a deep breath and stood.

Then he walked to the study door and made his way down to the music room . . . and then inside.

Palenya had set a satchel beside the clavecin and was rising with a cloth of some sort in hand. She wore imager gray. As she saw Charyn, she stopped, and inclined her head. "Your Grace."

Charyn tried not to wince at the formality, but managed to return the greeting. "Musician Palenya."

"I wasn't sure if you'd be here."

"You mean, if I'd come to see you," Charyn said lightly. "How could I not?"

Palenya's face tightened. "Your Grace . . ."

Charyn shook his head. "You're the best musician and clavecin tuner I know. Even if it weren't . . . for what was . . . a good musician deserves respect. That's something you taught me. I'm well aware that I've avoided you, but that was not out of lack of respect, I hope you know."

"I know. I appreciate that kindness . . . all your kindnesses. But there are some things that are not meant to be. I've hoped that you've come to understand that." Her smile was sadly knowing.

"That's taken a little more time." He managed a smile. "I do have a favor to ask. One that I'll pay for."

"Oh?" Her tone was guarded.

"I'm trying to learn two new pieces. They're both likely beyond my unaided skill, but I've been working hard on both of them. I'd appreciate it if you would let me play through them and offer your skills in improving what I'm doing."

"I can do that."

"That's all I'm asking."

"Do you want to do it before or after I tune?"

"Before. Something might come up later. There are a few matters . . ." Charyn shook his head, then went to the music cabinet and retrieved both sets of sheet music.

After returning and sitting down at the clavecin, he began

with the Farray "Pavane in a Minor Key." When he finished, he looked up. "I don't play it as well as you do."

"You're still having problems with the way Farray uses ritards, and you're rushing the tempo at the end of long phrases. I have to say that you have gotten better."

"Surprisingly, I have more time to practice. There's no one else here in the Chateau most of the time."

Palenya dropped her eyes but for an instant before saying, "Now do the other piece."

Charyn set up the music for "Variations on a Khellan Melody," then waited as he saw Palenya studying the engraved notes.

She looked from the music to him. "I don't recognize the hand of the engraver, but it's done very well, someone likely taught by Heldryk. If I had to guess."

"You're right about that, I think," replied Charyn.

She continued to study the music. "It's a piece by Covaelyt that's seldom played and played in public even less. That's a shame, because it has a certain charm. Might I ask where you found this?"

"I didn't. Someone played it at an entertainment, and I asked what it was, and a week later, I received the music as a gift. It's harder than it seemed when I heard it played."

Palenya frowned. "It's more complex than it would sound. Why don't you play it for me? As well as you can. I won't say anything until you've played through it."

Charyn seated himself at the keyboard and began, hoping his rendition didn't contain too many misfingerings or errors. When he finished, he looked up.

"Your fingering in some of the transitions is adequate. It could be better. You have the tempo of the piece, but not the spirit. We'll need to work on the fingering. Also on consistency."

Charyn grinned. "You haven't changed."

"Why should I? You want to play better, and that means you need to know what's wrong. That doesn't change just because you're Rex." There was a lightness that tempered the last words.

More than a glass later, Charyn rose from the clavecin. "Thank you."

"Most of that you did yourself." She offered a smile of amusement. "I told you that you'd get better if you practiced more."

"You did, and I've followed that advice." *If not for the same reasons that you had in mind.*

She looked directly at him. "It wouldn't have worked, you know?"

"You told me that before."

"You really weren't listening then. I think you're listening now."

"Are you happy at the Collegium?"

Palenya nodded. "You were most generous, and everyone there has been welcoming. I don't think any musician could have asked for more."

Charyn smiled. "You aren't just any musician, and you never were." He paused, then said, "I told you that before, and you weren't listening to me then, either. Are you listening now?"

"Yes. But . . . I know I wasn't just any musician . . . to you. There are other musicians as good."

"Not many."

"I'll accept that."

"You do owe me one other thing."

She frowned, momentarily, before saying, "The composition . . . the nocturne, you mean."

"That's exactly what I mean."

"You'll have it when it's right. I have worked on it. I did hope you'd be here today."

It was Charyn's turn to be confused.

"I needed to see you to get the ending the way it should be. Music is more than just the notes and the melody."

"I can see that." Charyn took the golds from his wallet—

three of them. "I'm paying myself because these come from what I've earned off the lands that were mine before I was Rex." He couldn't have said why that was important, but it was. "And they're for the tuning and the lesson." He handed them to her.

"That's too much."

"No, it's not. Part of that is because you're among the very best, and part is because I can trust you, both with my life and to be honest in instructing me. I really can't buy that, but I can offer a token of my appreciation for it."

Palenya shook her head slowly. "Take very good care of yourself, Charyn. Solidar needs the ruler you can be."

"Whatever that is," he replied, not quite wryly, "I wouldn't be that without all you've given me."

"And I'd be a barren, bitchy, widowed musician with nothing if it weren't for you." She smiled. "I need to tune the clavecin, and you need to get back to ruling."

"Then I'll leave you to it." He offered a last smile, then turned and left the music room, forcing himself not to look back.

18

‿‿‿⁓

Just after seventh glass on Meredi morning, Charyn was seated behind the table desk in his study, going over the order in which he wanted to present matters at the meeting of the councils that afternoon. Except his mind drifted back to Mardi afternoon—and Palenya.

He'd thought over his time with Palenya the previous afternoon, and the lesson that had been a lesson . . . and not anything more. *Should it have been?*

That unspoken question almost hung in the air.

Then he shook his head. *Palenya was right.* Yet, as he was coming to realize, he could never repay her for all she had given him, although with the funds he had provided her and the stipend, she should always be comfortable, especially since she was also housed and paid by the Collegium. *And she's also safe there.*

At that point, Norstan appeared.

"Your Grace?"

"Yes?"

"Chorister Saerlet is here. He appears agitated. He thinks he should speak to you before the Council meeting."

"Bring him up. I'll see him now." Much as Charyn had doubts about Saerlet's probity with golds, if the chorister was agitated, it was likely for a good reason, if one Charyn likely would not like.

In what seemed moments, a slightly disheveled Saerlet entered the study, inclining his head and saying, "Your Grace," after which he made his way toward the table desk and then took the chair to which Charyn gestured.

"Something appears to have given you concern."

"Yes, Your Grace. Chorister Orlend has just arrived from Caluse. He had to flee his anomen there because men in white robes and hoods stormed it."

"The True Believers?" Charyn wasn't exactly pleased with the thought, especially given the two white belts that had been delivered to him.

"It would seem so, sir. The floods were even worse in Caluse. Thousands and thousands of hectares of croplands were flooded. The crops were largely destroyed. The True Believers were chanting that the Nameless was punishing those who turned from the True Faith and the teachings of Rholan . . ."

"Why didn't Chorister Orlend come with you?"

"He was exhausted. He is not a young man, Your Grace."

"Is he, perhaps, carrying more weight than he should?" Charyn was likely indulging his suspicions, but he was curious.

"Your Grace, he is old enough to be older than your father."

"Then he does carry considerable bulk, I take it?"

"That is not the question, Your Grace."

"What is the question?"

"An anomen has been attacked and profaned. The chorister had to flee for his life."

"That isn't good, I grant you, but what do you expect of me? I am Rex, but I'm not a chorister, nor should I be the one to tell choristers what to preach in their homilies or what not to preach. I also do not control the Civic Patrol of Caluse, or for that matter, the Civic Patrol of L'Excelsis. Have these True Believers actually struck or attacked Chorister Orlend?"

"They would have if he had not fled."

"Did he go to the Civic Patrol of Caluse?"

"The Civic Patrol said that matters of faith were not their concern."

Charyn was silent for several moments. *What can you do? Should you get involved in a dispute over beliefs? But what if there are more of these attacks on choristers? And who sent those white belts and why?*

"Don't you have a duty as Rex to protect your people?" pressed Saerlet, his voice fringing on indignation.

Charyn managed not to snap back, but took a deep breath before replying. "I have a duty to protect them against foreign enemies, as well as a duty to make sure that High Holders do not exceed their rights. I have the duty to set the laws of the land, but protecting people against lawbreakers within cities is usually the province of the Civic Patrol."

"The Civic Patrol did nothing. Surely, you can do something in such an instance."

Charyn took another slow breath and waited before replying. "Chorister Saerlet, the only thing within my immediate power would be to send a company of army troopers to Caluse. What do you think would happen, if, instead of sending assistance to ruined growers and crafters, I sent army troopers to Caluse to reclaim an anomen and to protect Chorister Orlend? Would that help either the chorister or me?"

"Then what will you do to stop such an outrage? I told you it wasn't the first. How long will you wait?"

That's unfortunately a very good question. "You raise some good questions. I'd like to discuss the matter with the Minister of Justice before rushing to a decision. Chorister Orlend is here and safe, is he not?"

"Yes. But the anomen . . . who knows what those . . . those unbelievers . . . have done?"

Another question occurred to Charyn, one he'd never considered. "Who owns the anomen? Any anomen?"

"You own the Anomen D'Rex."

"But it's the only one I own. Who owns the Anomen D'Excelsis? Or the Anomen D'Caluse?"

Saerlet did not answer for several moments. Then he finally said, "The congregation does. Each congregation entrusts their anomen to the chorister."

"So any damage to the anomen is a loss to the congregation?"

"I suppose it must be. As your chorister, I never thought of it that way."

"Let me talk this over with Minister Sanafryt. I'll get back to you and Chorister Orlend. A day or so won't make any difference, and my doing the wrong thing could make matters much worse. Also, I can bring up the problem to the councils so that they're aware of it as well."

"I suppose . . ." Saerlet looked dubious.

"Chorister, some of my predecessors made quick decisions on matters they didn't know enough about. They often weren't good decisions."

"When you put it that way, Your Grace . . ."

"I can assure you that I won't forget the matter." *There's no way I dare to, as widespread as it seems to be.* Charyn stood.

So did Saerlet. "Chorister Orlend and I thank you, Your Grace."

No sooner had Saerlet left than Moencriff ushered Elacia into the study.

She inclined her head to Charyn. "I have the responses for the dinner on the twenty-eighth. High Holder Plessan regretted, or rather his personal secretary did, since the High Holder and Lady Plessan D'Priora went to visit relatives near Ferravyl and a message to them would not arrive in time for them to return. High Holder Fyanyl will attend, but not Lady Fyanyl. She is in her confinement and a travel of some forty milles would be excessive at present. The others accepted." Elacia laid a sheet on the desk. "They're all listed. You will seat them in order of precedence, I assume."

"Of course." Charyn knew his aunt wasn't exactly questioning. "Except for you. You have Mother's precedence in her absence. And Ferrand will be seated by his holding's precedence, not by his relationship to the Rex."

"That is likely for the best." Elacia's voice was level, an indication of reluctant acceptance.

"What about this evening?"

"I'll be checking with the cooks shortly. Since this is a family dinner—on the other side of the family, so to speak—you won't need me to stay for the actual dinner, will you?"

"No. Once you're satisfied this afternoon, you can certainly leave."

As soon as Elacia left, Charyn picked up the list and glanced over the names, all High Holders bringing their wives—except for Fyanyl and, of course, Shendael, who would be accompanied by Alyncya.

Then he stood and walked to Sanafryt's study, entering and closing the door behind himself, motioning for Sanafryt to remain at his desk. "I just had a talk with Chorister Saerlet . . ." Charyn related the gist of what the two had discussed, then asked, "As Rex, do I have a legal obligation to protect a chorister from dissatisfied parishioners?"

"Not the way you put it. You have no obligation to provide affirmative protection, but you can require the local authorities to prosecute those who damage property or harm individuals."

"And if they don't?"

"You can bring the town or city authorities before the High Justicer for failure to enforce the law." Sanafryt smiled wryly. "That would mean I'd have to prove they knew who committed the crime and failed to charge them. That might be difficult. It would be impossible if they honestly don't know, and they could claim that, since those who threatened the chorister apparently all wore hoods."

"So it would be difficult to do anything with what Saerlet and Orlend know now?"

"More like impossible, Your Grace."

Charyn took a deep breath. "Has anything like this come up before?"

"Not since the time of Rholan, I don't believe."

"As Justice Minister, what would you suggest?"

"The only thing I can suggest is that you send a proclamation to the regional governors declaring that violence against any chorister or anomen is a criminal attack and should be treated as such by the Civic Patrols and other local authorities. That is the law, but some may not understand that it applies to religious practitioners and buildings."

"I think, for now, that's the most I should do. Would you please draft something to that effect?"

"I can do that, Your Grace."

"Oh . . . there's one other thing. Do you attend services at the Anomen D'Rex?"

"No, Your Grace, we live closer to the Anomen D'Ouest."

As he walked back to his own study, Charyn couldn't help thinking, *Why are all these things that haven't happened in centuries or never occurred before all happening when I'm Rex?*

Or had other things happened to his predecessors in the same fashion and he just hadn't known it? He had the feeling that it was probably the latter.

That realization wasn't that much help.

As had come to be normal, Maitre Alastar arrived at the study door early—this time more than a quint before first glass.

Charyn was the first to speak, as he stood to welcome Alastar. "Good afternoon . . . whether it will be or not."

"That sounds more like your father, except you say it so much more cheerfully."

"There are more than a few problems, as you know. By the way, while I didn't reply to your letter about Antiagon Fire, I support your decision and will be saying so when Chaeltar brings it up."

"You didn't tell him that?"

"I wrote him that I was considering the matter. I decided that, if I wrote him my decision, he'd just write everyone else about how I hadn't considered the matter."

"He will anyway, if he hasn't already."

"That's likely, but I want the other High Holders to get the impression that I've studied it and didn't react immediately. Also, I'd rather deal with it one less time." Charyn moved to the chairs at the side of the conference table and gestured, then sat down, as did Alastar.

"That's probably wise. Deferring a decision beyond the meeting wouldn't be."

Charyn understood the reference to his father's practice of not deciding until a decision was forced on him, but did not comment, instead saying, "Not all children of imagers grow up to be imagers, do they?"

"No. Quite a few don't. More than half, in fact."

"So they have to make their way elsewhere?"

"Some do. Many prefer to work at the Collegium. Why do you ask?"

"Do you have any children of imagers who are not imagers that might do a good job as my personal scrivener?"

The silver-haired Maitre frowned. "I'll have to think about that. I assume you're asking me because of the need for trustworthiness?"

"I've observed that imagers are very trustworthy, and I would think any child raised there would be as well."

"Not all imagers have been trustworthy. There have been a few that have been anything but that."

"I doubt that is so now," replied Charyn dryly.

Alastar chuckled. "You may be giving me too much credit."

"And you may not be taking enough credit," countered Charyn.

The Maitre only shook his head.

Less than half a quint before the glass, Moencriff ushered Marshal Vaelln into the study.

"Your Grace, Maitre Alastar . . ."

Charyn stood and moved more toward the window. "Are there any great surprises since your latest report?"

"One of our flotillas engaged the Jariolans just off the Abierto Isles. We lost five ships, mostly third-raters, but one second-rater. We sank twelve Jariolans. Only one first-rater of theirs escaped. Right now we control the seas around the Isles."

Charyn nodded. "I'll wait to hear the rest until the others are here, when you can fill in the details."

Promptly, as the chimes struck the glass, the factors entered the study, followed by the High Holders. Charyn waited until everyone was seated, then took his place at the head of the table and gestured. "Marshal Vaelln, if you would brief the councils on the Jariolan situation."

The Marshal stood, then cleared his throat. "Our position around the Abierto Isles is vastly stronger at present . . ." From there he detailed the battle between the two forces and the results. ". . . in the Southern Ocean, we still lack sufficient ships to protect all Solidaran merchanters. Since the last Council meeting, we have sunk four more Jariolan privateers and two warships in the waters off Otelyrn, but several Solidaran merchanters have also been lost."

"How long will this drag on?" asked Hisario.

"Until the Jariolans stop attacking our ships or until we sink all of theirs, whichever comes first," replied Vaelln evenly.

"I meant, how long will that take?"

"It will take two to four years for us to drive the Jariolans from the oceans, assuming that they don't start building ships faster than they are. I cannot say if or when they might decide to approach Rex Charyn with terms."

"They rebuffed our diplomatic efforts less than a year ago, you might recall," added Charyn.

Hisario nodded.

"There's another aspect to the Jariolan problem, and

that's what's happened to High Holder Ghasphar," declared
Chaeltar. "His ships are armed with guns that fire Antiagon
Fire shells. He lost his senior imager armorer. Without an
imager of skill, he cannot create the Antiagon Fire for those
shells, but Maitre Alastar has refused to send an imager to
help him. This I find unconscionable." Chaeltar turned and
looked at Alastar. "High Holder Ghasphar is the only merchant shipper who has armed his vessels and whose ships
have fought against the Jariolans, and you, as Maitre, are
refusing to support him? How in good conscience can you
do that?"

"As I have responded to you and to Rex Charyn, the Collegium has done nothing to forbid adult imagers from working for High Holder Ghasphar to make Antiagon Fire. We
have kept children from being used to make it because Antiagon Fire is dangerous, both to its makers and users. The
fact that the High Holder lost his experienced imagers, most
likely to those dangers, and the fact that others want nothing
to do with it, should tell you just how dangerous it is."

"All weapons are dangerous to some degree," returned
Chaeltar. "We are at war with the Jariolans. If you do
not help High Holder Ghasphar, then you are helping the
Jariolans."

"What you are saying is that you want me to order—to
force imagers—to do something that could kill them, so that
High Holder Ghasphar will make more golds, or lose fewer
ships. You're not talking about what will win this conflict
with Jariola, but how it will affect Ghasphar financially."

"What about the men on those ships?" countered Chaeltar. "Some of them could die."

"They could," agreed Alastar. "But every man on those
ships has a choice about whether to sail on that ship. Likewise, every grown imager has a choice about whether to
make Antiagon Fire, and none of them have shown that they
want to."

"It's not the same," said Chaeltar.

"Are you saying that sailors can choose, but imagers shouldn't be allowed to?"

"Antiagon Fire can't be that bad."

"Have you seen personally what Antiagon Fire can do?" asked Alastar.

"It destroys Jariolan ships," replied Chaeltar.

"Only in limited circumstances, and that's if the ship with such shells can get close to another ship. The *Diamond Thuyl* was sunk by long-range gunfire. The majority of Jariolan warships have that capability. During the last battle of the High Holder revolt, several rebel imagers created Antiagon Fire and launched it against the army and the imagers supporting the army. When confronted with two other imagers, the insurgents lost control of the Antiagon Fire. As a result, the Collegium lost a third of its most capable imagers and more than three thousand troopers died, all in an instant. Antiagon Fire is unstable and dangerous to its users, and especially to those who make it."

"And you were there?" Chaeltar's voice was scornful.

"He was," declared Charyn, his voice like ice. "I wasn't, but I've talked to a number of senior army officers who were, and every single one of them talked about that Antiagon Fire and about Maitre Alastar's leadership and personal courage. He went out there and fought. So did most of the capable imagers. A lot of them died, and none of them were rewarded with golds. On the other hand, I do know that High Holder Ghasphar has made a great number of golds over the years, and that gold was earned partly by the deaths of imagers and sailors. But I don't hear that he's sailing on those ships or making that Antiagon Fire himself. I don't see you out there, either. And no, I'm not there, either. But, unlike some, I'm not about to insult those who have risked their lives, or who still often do—and who've put their bodies between me and death." In the momentary silence that followed, Charyn said quietly, "I support the Maitre's decision, and I think we've heard more than enough about poor High Holder Ghasphar."

Chaeltar opened his mouth, but before he could speak, Fhaedyrk said firmly, "I think both the Rex and the Maitre have made the point clear. Ghasphar can take the risks faced by other shippers, or not, as he sees fit."

Even Hisario nodded, Charyn noticed.

After a moment of silence, Charyn spoke. "I'd like to bring several matters to the attention of the councils, although one is certainly known to most, that being the recent flood of the River Aluse. It's clear that repairs to the river walls in L'Excelsis will need to be undertaken. I'm having the Minister of Finance and the Minister of Administration look into how much can be accomplished this year with the funds available. Whether such repairs can be made will also depend if the water levels subside enough to make them practicable."

Calkoran immediately added, "There were also significant damages to the riverbanks and to piers south of Vaestora and north of L'Excelsis. There was even more damage around Caluse, according to High Holder Vorranyl."

"Lake Shaelyt overflowed and inundated the hamlet there," added Elthyrd, his voice raspy. When he finished even those few words, he had to cough into a handkerchief.

"Is there any possibility that you could provide more funds for river wall repairs in the future?" asked Calkoran. "The High Holders in my area have contributed to maintaining the riverbanks and walls, but there are few near the river on the reaches surrounding Talyon or Caluse. Vorranyl and Kurm are the only large High Holdings south of Aluse until you get close to Villerive, and there aren't that many there."

"We'll have to see what funds there are," replied Charyn. "There might be more golds available once we finish with the Jariolans."

"Might be?" asked Khunthan.

"If we don't get more flooding, if the Ferrans don't attack . . . if . . ." Charyn shrugged. "After being Rex for only six months or so, I can see that there's always something that needs to be fixed or funded that no one expected." After a brief hesitation, he said, "You might have noticed a sheet of paper in front of each of your places. It's a draft of a possible change to the Codex Legis. It's short. Please read it. Then we'll talk about it."

Fhaedyrk was the first to finish, and he looked up sharply at Charyn, but did not speak. Jhaliost was the next, and he looked anything but happy. Calkoran nodded, but in a way that could have meant anything.

When everyone was looking up and at Charyn, he said, "More and more manufactorages are being built, usually on streams and rivers. As some of you know, I've had a number of complaints about river and stream water being fouled so that downstream users cannot use the water in the way they used to . . . or sometimes not at all. I asked Minister Sanafryt what could be done to address the matter under existing law. The answer I received was that nothing could be done. He also pointed out that, in the current state of the treasury, I could not hire enough people to patrol the waters, even if a law existed to require keeping the water clean. Then I realized that, under current law, if one individual damages another's property, the damaged person can seek redress. The draft you have would create the presumption that damaging another's water is a form of damaging other's livelihood. What are your thoughts?"

"Why are you even raising this?" demanded Chaeltar.

"I'm not. I've received a number of petitions on the matter, from both High Holders and from factors. The problem is simple. Right now, the person farthest upstream has the cleanest water, and he can do anything with it. He could have a huge hog farm and dump hog waste in it so much so that a weaving mill downstream couldn't use the water. The water could be so bad that no one could drink it, or wash with it."

"Leave the law alone," suggested Basalyt. "Let people work it out."

"The Rex has a point," interjected Khunthan, much to Charyn's surprise. "There are parts of Khel where the only sources of water are a few streams and rivers. There aren't any laws, but the custom is much the same as what the Rex proposes. Most of the time, there is so much water in old Bovaria or Telaryn that no one has to worry, but if there are more people and more manufactorages . . ."

"Why is this our problem?" asked Fhaedyrk.

"It's not," replied Charyn. "But it will be, sooner than you think. Two of the petitions before me are asking that I do something about bad water being caused by an upstream user. In one instance, the upstream user is a factor, and the one damaged is a High Holder. In the other, the reverse is true. Whatever I do will upset someone. If I do nothing, the same thing will happen. I can't fairly rule just for High Holders or just for factors, can I?" Charyn looked around the table. Although no one spoke, he could see his question had dismayed all of the councilors. "Likewise, if I rule for the downstream users, both factors and High Holders will be upset, and the same will happen if I do nothing or if I rule for the upstream users."

"Then why are you bringing this before us?" asked Fhaedyrk.

"Because you all asked to have a greater role in deciding how Solidar is governed. That doesn't mean just the easy decisions. It also means hard decisions that will affect everyone." After a long pause, Charyn asked, "Or would you prefer that I just hand out decisions as I see fit so that you all can blame me?"

At that, Elthyrd laughed. Unhappily, the laugh turned into a long coughing fit.

Charyn waited.

Finally, Elthyrd said, slowly and carefully, "We did ask for a greater role, did we not?"

Fhaedyrk nodded. "This was not what we anticipated, however. Still . . ."

Charyn nodded. "I'm not asking for an immediate decision. I'd like each of you to take the draft with you and to consider it. Share it. Get the opinions of others. Then, next month, when we meet again, perhaps you will have better suggestions. This is not an overwhelming problem. Not yet, but the way manufactorages are growing . . . it will be."

Fhaedyrk looked to the other High Holders, then to Charyn. "That seems most reasonable."

"Now," declared Charyn, "there is one other matter I would hope all of you will keep your eyes and ears open for. Over the last month or so, I've received reports about an unusual set of occurrences . . ." From there he went on to describe the reports about the activities of the True Believers, ending with, "These reports have come from not only choristers, but from various senior officers, and from all over most of Solidar, with the possible exception of Khel. Given that every anomen is essentially independent, the rise of a militant united alternative version of the faith of the Nameless disturbs me."

Charyn watched as the councilors exchanged glances.

Finally, Harll spoke. "I've heard about the True Believers. I don't know any, but they had a big meeting last summer in a little town called Gahenyara. They built their own anomen there, and they said they were going to build another in Cloisonyt, maybe one in Montagne after that."

"Then it's just another faith," declared Basalyt dismissively.

Maitre Alastar cleared this throat, loudly.

"Yes, Maitre?" said Charyn.

"Any faith that begins by using force to run out choristers and take over anomens isn't just another faith. Fifty years ago, no one in Caenen had ever heard of the Duality, and most of Caenen worshipped the Nameless. Today the Priest-

Autarch of the Duality rules Caenen, and there are almost no living worshippers of the Nameless in Caenen . . . and no High Holders, either. The ancient Naedaran civilization here collapsed after the followers of Erion kept attacking them. Any faith that can gather adherents to commit violence is something to be watched."

"You sound like a most devout follower of the Nameless, Maitre," said Chaeltar. "I wouldn't have guessed."

"I'm scarcely that devout, but there's a great deal to be said for a faith that encourages thought over beliefs imposed by force."

"Belief is for those who have nothing else," suggested Jhaliost.

"And that is why a violent faith that appeals to such is the most dangerous," replied Alastar. "With nothing to lose, they're willing to believe almost anything."

"I'd also like to point out that, when properly trained," added Vaelln, "the best troopers are often from the poorest backgrounds. If these True Believers gather the poor and train them, that could result in another kind of revolt."

"All I'm asking," said Charyn, "is for all of you to be aware that these True Believers might be a problem and to inform me of anything that may occur with them."

"We can do that," agreed Fhaedyrk.

"Does anyone else wish to bring up anything?" Charyn studied those around the table. "Then we'll meet again on the eighteenth of Erntyn." He stood and stepped back, watching as everyone filed out, wondering as they did why Elthyrd hadn't brought up the problem with the damage to factors' warehouses and goods.

When the two stood alone in the study, Alastar said, "The True Believers may be a problem, but they're a result, not a cause."

"What do you think the cause is?"

"The same reason why the factors are having their stocks of manufactured goods destroyed."

"What do you know about that?" asked Charyn, curious because the matter hadn't come up at the meeting, and he hadn't discussed it with Alastar except in passing.

"There have been two reports in the newssheets, and more than a few instances beyond those."

"But Elthyrd didn't mention them when I asked if there were other matters for the councils."

"The factors may not want others to know the size of the problem," suggested Alastar.

"That would mean it's far larger than they're saying." After a pause, Charyn added, "You never did say what the cause of both might be."

"The growing dissatisfaction of crafters and poorer workers. The factors' interests are aligning more with those of the High Holders and against those of crafters and workers, and some of those workers and crafters believe that the choristers are supporting the factors and High Holders."

"I'd thought that some workers and crafters might be behind the destruction of goods, but attacking choristers?" Charyn had a good idea why some choristers might well be attacked, but he wanted Alastar's reaction. He thought about mentioning the white belts, but decided against it until he knew more.

"Some choristers are every bit as enamored of fine garments and food as High Holders and wealthy factors."

"Iskhar doesn't seem that way, but I could see that with Saerlet." Charyn wasn't so certain about Refaal.

"Iskhar isn't, but I'd concur with your thoughts about Saerlet." Alastar smiled. "I need to be going. We'll see you at fifth glass."

"I'm looking forward to it."

After seeing Alastar out of the Chateau, rather than return to his study, Charyn made his way to the music room, where he spent more than a glass at the clavecin, before heading back up the grand staircase to his study, where he read several more petitions, pausing more than once, as he hoped Alastar might come up with a recommendation for a personal scrivener.

A half a quint before fifth glass, he was in the receiving parlor near the main entrance. He assumed that Maitre Alastar and those from Imagisle would arrive first. Instead, the first coach to appear was not a gray and silver one from Imagisle, but a dark blue and silver one. Moments later, High Holder and Lady Calkoran stepped through the entry, where Charyn met them. He noticed that Saelya had the same slightly honey-colored complexion as her husband, one they shared with Alyna and Malyna. *Pharsi blood.*

"Your Grace, I hadn't expected . . ." began Calkoran.

"This isn't a formal dinner, but more of a family affair, if of an extended family." Charyn inclined his head to Calkoran's wife. "It's a pleasure to meet you, Lady Calkoran . . . but might I call you Saelya?"

A quick quizzical look flashed across the High Holder's face as his wife smiled and said, "Of course, Your Grace."

"Charyn, in private, and this is private."

"I have the feeling that you received a certain missive," continued Saelya, "since few know my given name, and since I haven't ever been in L'Excelsis before."

"I did indeed, and was most pleased that it arrived."

"I wondered . . ." offered Calkoran, with an amused expression.

At that moment, Aloryana hurried through the doors, then caught herself and advanced more decorously toward her brother.

"Aloryana, I'd like you to meet High Holder and Lady Calkoran." Charyn looked to the pair. "Aloryana is not only my lovely sister, but also an imager."

Saelya inclined her head. "I'm pleased to meet you, Aloryana. I've heard most favorably about you."

"Thank you. Whoever said that was likely being kind, but I appreciate it."

Behind Aloryana were Alastar, Alyna, Lystara, and Malyna.

Charyn gestured to them and said, "And I believe you know this group, at least by name."

"I haven't had the pleasure of meeting either Maitre Alastar or Lystara in person," said Saelya.

"Well . . . now you have," said Charyn. "I thought we'd repair to the anteroom adjoining the music room for a moment. I've been informed that Aloryana wishes to take Lystara on a quick tour of the Chateau. Anyone who wishes to accompany them certainly can. It's rather familiar to me, and I will remain in the anteroom with the refreshments while anyone who chooses to accompany Aloryana may do so." Charyn looked to his sister. "Anywhere in the Chateau proper except my study."

"Yes, Charyn."

No sooner had everyone reached the music anteroom than Charyn and Alastar were left by themselves.

"Dark lager?" asked Charyn.

"Please." Alastar smiled. "I've seen enough of the Chateau. It was kind of you to open it to the others."

Almost immediately, a server appeared with a beaker of dark lager and a goblet of the white Tacqueville for Charyn.

"Thank you," said Alastar.

Charyn nodded as he took the wine, then said, with a slight shrug, "Aloryana wanted to show Lystara, and I thought . . . Besides, the Chateau feels rather empty at present."

"Your brother isn't here?"

"He's spending most of Agostos at Ryel with Mother. I hope he's learning something about running a High Holding."

"He's your heir, right now, isn't he?"

For Alastar to ask that question told Charyn that the inquiry wasn't a question at all. "He will be for a time, I'm sure, since I'm not in a position to rush into finding a wife."

"Then perhaps he would prefer to be here."

"He doesn't seem happy when he's here, either," replied Charyn. "I thought he might be happier knowing he'd have his own holding when he came of age, but that didn't please him, either." Charyn shook his head. "Part of that might have been that I told him he needed to learn a bit more about running a holding before I'd be comfortable turning it over to him. I thought that might give him some incentive, since it's just a bit more than a year before he turns eighteen. That just made him mad."

"Hmmm . . . it doesn't seem as though he likes the position he's in."

Charyn understood that as well. "He doesn't. That's why he's at Ryel for now."

"That may be the best you can do. Your mother is quite a woman." Alastar looked toward the anteroom door, where Calkoran was entering. "You've seen enough?"

"The ladies indicated that my presence was less than welcome." Calkoran smiled genially.

"Wine, lager, or ale?" asked Charyn, gesturing toward the sideboard where a server waited.

"I'm of the same persuasion as the Maitre." Calkoran accepted a beaker of lager and turned to the other two. "I've never been here before. In fact, I think the first High Holder Calkoran was the only one to see the Chateau after the imagers rebuilt it. He was a Khellan marshal, you know, before he served under the first Maitre. That was when he was a commander before he became Maitre. That's the family legend, anyway."

"That much is true," said Alastar. "I read some of the early history when I first became Maitre."

"I read some of it as well," said Charyn. "That's how I found out that Alyna and Malyna are distant relatives, very distant cousins, I suppose."

"They are?" Calkoran raised his eyebrows. "So you weren't being humorous when you said it was a family gathering of sorts."

Alastar laughed softly. "He may have been being humorous, but there's truth behind the humor."

"A distant truth," admitted Charyn.

"Might I ask, before the ladies return, why you include the Factors' Council at these monthly meetings?"

"Because, as a group, they have as much power and wealth as the High Holders, and I don't want another conflict. The more they're included, the more both sides can see the problems, and, I hope, the more we can work together."

Calkoran looked to Alastar. "Was that your idea?"

"No. It was his from the start. So was the idea of including the Collegium."

Calkoran looked back to Charyn. "You're asking a lot of some of the older High Holders."

"I know. But the times are changing, and they're changing faster than ever before. If we don't change with the times, Solidar will fall apart."

"He's right, you know," said Alastar. "You wouldn't be a High Holder if the first Rex Regis hadn't changed things so those of a Pharsi heritage could be High Holders."

"There is that," replied Calkoran with a wry smile. "Zaerlyn leaned on me pretty hard to become a councilor. I'm beginning to see why." His eyes settled on Charyn again. "Why are you pushing that change to water law?"

"Because I'm already seeing a conflict building between High Holders and factors over using water. I want the joint councils to agree on a consistent law that's seen as fair for everyone, based on equal treatment. There are already a number of factors who have more wealth than many High Holders. There will be more, I suspect, but I don't know, that the number of High Holders is slowly declining, and the number of wealthy factors is rapidly growing."

Calkoran nodded. "It appears we are living in interesting times. Is that true of the Collegium as well, Maitre?"

"Equally so, I'd say. Some of the changes are welcome, of course. With thanks to Rex Charyn, the Collegium now has a marvelous clavecin that we've installed in a music room. We also have more imagers from High Holder families than previously, and, there's actually a factorage now on Imagisle . . ."

Charyn listened as Alastar talked, nodding occasionally, and wondering when Aloryana and the others would return.

Less than half a quint later, thankfully, Alyna led the four other women back into the anteroom, where they all had their choice of beverages.

After a time, Charyn made his way to Aloryana. "Are you going to play something for me?"

"Only if you play first."

Charyn raised his eyebrows.

"Please."

He grinned. "All right . . . if Malyna will also."

Aloryana looked to Malyna.

"Just one piece."

Alastar smiled and said, "I do believe we're going to hear a very short recital."

Charyn found himself leading the way into the music room, where he sat down at the clavecin and played Nocturne Number Three. When he finished, he gestured to Aloryana, who joined him for the duet. Then she played the Serkuyn prelude, while Malyna, who played last, played "Variations on a Scherzo," the piece she'd played months before, the last time Charyn had heard her perform.

As Malyna left the clavecin, she turned to Charyn. "You played well."

"You also played very well."

She smiled. "It's good to have a clavecin at the Collegium. Thank you."

"Do you play in public?" Calkoran asked Charyn.

"No. Only for family and close friends. It would seem frivolous otherwise, I fear."

"You're probably right."

Before all that long, Charyn sat at the head of the table

with Saelya on his left and Calkoran on the right. Beside Calkoran was Alyna, and beside Saelya was Alastar. Aloryana sat opposite Charyn, with Malyna between Aloryana and Alastar, and Lystara between Aloryana and Alyna.

Charyn looked to Aloryana. "If you'd offer a grace?"

Aloryana flushed for a moment, then said, "For the grace from above, for the bounty of the earth below, for Your justice, and for Your manifold and great mercies, we offer our thanks and gratitude, both now and ever more, in the spirit of that which cannot be named or imaged."

When she finished, and everyone was served wine, Charyn lifted his goblet. "To family and friends."

"To family and friends."

Moments later, the dark-haired Saelya looked to Charyn. "Your Grace, I had no idea you played clavecin . . . and so well."

"My repertoire is still limited," Charyn confessed, "but I'm working on expanding it. I never thought I'd find practicing and learning new music enjoyable and even relaxing, but it is." He smiled. "And I also find that I need something to take my mind off the rest of the day."

"Don't we all," said Calkoran cheerfully.

"Have you always enjoyed playing?" asked Saelya.

"No, I haven't. Only in the last year, and especially since I became Rex. Part of that is doubtless because all the assassination attempts forced me to look toward fewer outdoor activities."

"Surely, that's changed now, hasn't it . . . given who was behind those attempts?" asked Calkoran.

"It's much less likely," Charyn admitted, "and I've begun to resume more public appearances, if without fanfare or advance notice. I did tour the flood-damaged areas of L'Excelsis . . ."

"That's good. People need to see their ruler," Calkoran declared heartily.

"Do you know who the figures are on the stone frieze above the main entry?" asked Saelya.

"The one in the center of the group on the left, I understand, is the first Rex Regis. The others around him are his senior officers. The group on the right, I have no idea."

"The frieze doesn't look that old."

"It is. All the stonework in the Chateau is the same as when the first imagers restored it. The stone is much harder than normal stone. Bullets don't even chip it."

"Bullets?" asked Calkoran.

"There have been more than a few fired at the Chateau in the last fifteen years."

"I think it's remarkable that the frieze is still there. Do you think that the first Rex Regis really looked like that?"

"Since the frieze was likely imaged rather than stone-cut," interjected Alastar, "it's likely a fair representation."

"Just to think, after all those years," marveled Saelya.

Charyn nodded and took another swallow of the Tacqueville white. Perhaps he'd have a better chance to talk with Aloryana on Solayi evening after services.

19

Even by the time he reached his study on Jeudi morning, Charyn found himself feeling somewhat melancholy. Yet, the conversation the evening before had not been discouraging. The food had been good, and Charyn had definitely enjoyed playing the clavecin, although he wished he had learned his "newer" pieces well enough to play them before others. From what he'd observed, Aloryana and Lystara had enjoyed themselves while they'd been at the Chateau. Malyna had been slightly reserved, most likely because she was neither as young as Aloryana and Lystara nor as interested in what the older members of the party had discussed.

In the future, you need to keep that in mind.

As for the meeting of the councils, he'd gotten the councilors to look at the water problem, and he'd raised the issue of the True Believers. He was concerned that Alastar had linked them to the destruction that Elthyrd had brought to his attention, and he couldn't help but wonder how much Argentyl actually knew about that destruction.

Finally, he wrote out an invitation for Argentyl to meet with him on the following Lundi, at a time of Argentyl's convenience, and had Sturdyn arrange for it to be dispatched.

You should have done this sooner. Much sooner.

He looked down at the petition from a High Holder Laesheld. He'd only read the first page, enough to know that it dealt with yet another issue of water rights and usage.

After taking a deep breath, he stood and walked to the open window, where only a hint of a hot and damp breeze brushed past him. For a time, he just gazed blankly toward the north, thoughts drifting through his mind—the flood, the need for repairs, the lack of golds in the treasury, the brutal combination of drought and flood on crops and what the result was bound to be, the ongoing and undeclared war with Jariola, the conflict between the factors and the artisans and crafters, the growing problem of the True Believers, the issue of keeping the water in streams and rivers from being too contaminated, the problem with Bhayrn, his worries about Elthyrd's continuing illness . . . and, of course, Alyncya, and whether he was attracted to her because she had many of the talents that Palenya had . . . or largely because of her own attributes and personality.

Finally, since there was only one of those problems he could address at the moment, he returned to the table desk, took out paper, dipped the pen in the inkwell . . . and began to write.

After some time, he reread what he had set to paper.

Lady-heir Alyncya—
While your letter was indeed delayed by the circumstances of our geographical separation, I enjoyed it nonetheless, and your ruminations upon choice and intent, as well as the implications of your examples, were definitely thought-provoking.

Last night we had a pleasant gathering here, a dinner attended by what one might call extended family, since Maitre Alyna, Maitre Malyna, and Maitre Lystara are all distant blood relations, since Maitre Alyna is related through marriage to High Holder and Lady Calkoran, and since, of course, Aloryana is my sister, while Maitre Alastar is married to Maitre Alyna. All those master imagers in the Chateau gave me pause. I'm not certain there has ever been such a gathering here. I did persuade Aloryana to play for us, and the two of us played a duet. Maitre Malyna and I also each played one piece. I did not play "Variations on a Khellan Melody." My grasp of it is not yet barely competent, let alone acceptable for even extended family, but I certainly would have enjoyed the evening more had you been here and joined us in playing.

I do hope that none of your holdings were damaged by the recent floods. Thankfully, only a small part of L'Excelsis was inundated, and the water receded comparatively quickly, but it's obvious that I will need to fund repairs of the river walls in several places—once the water levels of the river drop enough so that work is practicable.

In your latest correspondence, you suggested that men find harm created through human intent more evil than harm caused by nature because, while they cannot change what nature does, they can make a choice and that the act of making a choice elevates them, at least in their own minds. That may well be so for some men. While nature has no choice but to follow its course, men and women often, but not always, have the ability to choose, and those who find ills caused by intent more evil may honestly believe that the ability to discern between good and evil is tarnished by choosing to do evil.

There is also the problem of defining "evil," for what one person may call evil, another may not. A factor may not pay his workers enough for them to buy enough food, and that worker will claim that is evil. The factor, in turn, will say that if he does pay more, then he and his family will suffer. Further, he may point out that the worker would have no job at all if the factorage costs more to operate than the coins its goods bring in. Yet each may think the other "evil" in intent.

Many men feel that whatever riches, power, or privilege that they have is theirs rightfully, and that anything that diminishes those riches, powers, or privileges is wrong, even evil, no matter how any of those were initially obtained, or, for that matter, how they may lose any part of what they have. In order to justify such blame, they often attribute evil to others, particularly those who have gained most, or those they believe have kept them from regaining what they have lost. When they attempt to take violent action, as did the rebelling High Holders, they claim that they had no choice. From the little of life that I have seen, often such a claim means that their violence was the only choice they found acceptable, not that there were no other choices.

There are indeed times when we have few meaningful choices, as you pointed out so eloquently, but there are also times when pride, stupidity, arrogance, or shortsightedness prevent us from seeing or choosing other possibilities, a shortcoming with which, upon occasion, I have become most painfully and personally aware.

In this regard, I will close, thanking you once more for your thoughtful correspondence and hoping for your reply.

Again, he signed with just his name, then sealed the missive and readied it for dispatch.

After several long moments, he looked at the petition on his desk. With a deep breath that was not quite a sigh, he picked it up and resumed reading, forcing himself through the words with the thought that undue delay would only make matters worse.

20

Just before fifth glass on Solayi, the unmarked coach carried Charyn from the rear courtyard of the Chateau down to the Ring Road and then onto the Boulevard D'Rex, heading toward Imagisle. As he passed the Anomen D'Rex, he studied it, but he saw no one at all around the structure. The Boulevard D'Rex was almost empty, but that was hardly surprising on Solayi evening.

When the coach came to a full stop outside the Maitre's dwelling, Lystara and Aloryana, as always in their imager grays, immediately hurried to the coach so that Charyn didn't even have to get out.

"How was your week, Ladies?" asked Charyn once they were settled. "Since the dinner on Meredi, of course."

"We're imagers," said Aloryana.

"You are, but you both merit the title of Lady as well."

Lystara frowned.

"Aloryana is still my sister, and you are an unmarried Imager Maitre, which merits the title of Lady, at least in speech." Charyn paused, then added, "But then, Aloryana is probably right, in the sense that most ladies don't earn their titles, while maitres do, especially your mother. She certainly deserves a title."

"She has one. She's Senior Imager."

"She deserves that." *And more.* "I still can't believe all the buildings that she created."

"She doesn't like anyone to talk about it. When Father brings it up, she says that buildings are easy compared to running the Collegium." Lystara grinned. "He still brings it up sometimes."

"And the rest of your week?" Charyn prompted Aloryana.

"I'm working on concealments. They're harder to do than shields, but I don't get as tired once I get it."

"It won't be long before it gets easier," said Lystara. "How long have you been able to hold one? Really hold one for as long as you want?"

"Two weeks."

"In another few weeks, it will be as easy as walking."

"Do you two still run every morning?"

"Except when it's raining hard," replied Aloryana. "Are you still exercising with the guards?"

"Most mornings. It's safer that way." He smiled sheepishly. "Also, I don't slack off."

"That's why Father has the younger guards lead the way on the morning run," said Lystara.

"He still runs with all of you?" asked Charyn.

"He does, but he runs with most of the others," said Lystara.

Charyn didn't know what she meant.

"Lystara, Malyna, and Maitre Alyna are in the fastest group," explained Aloryana. "I'm in the second group with Maitre Alastar, but I'm getting faster."

"What about your studies?"

"They're easy now, but I still have to work, especially in arithmetics and calculations. Maitre Alyna teaches those."

As the three got out of the coach, and walked toward the side door of the Anomen D'Rex, Charyn realized that not only had Aloryana grown several digits in the months she'd been at the Collegium, but that she resembled both Malyna and Lystara in her carriage and overall appearance. *She really is becoming an imager.*

The three, followed by a pair of guards in brown, had just stepped inside the anomen when Chorister Saerlet hurried up.

"Your Grace, it's so good to see you again. I was afraid you were forsaking the Nameless."

"That, I'm not doing, Chorister, but I am attending some services at Imagisle with Aloryana, at least for a while."

"I hope my homilies aren't keeping you away."

Charyn shook his head. "I'm looking forward to what you have to say this evening."

"Will I see you after services?"

"Most likely not. I'd prefer not to tempt fate. Have you heard any more about the True Believers?"

"We should talk later, Your Grace. I need to get ready." Saerlet almost fled.

"He doesn't seem happy," murmured Aloryana.

"No, he doesn't." Charyn looked to Lystara. "We should leave quickly, with the last word of the benediction."

Lystara nodded.

"If you're really worried, we could leave under a concealment," suggested Aloryana.

"We'll see," replied Charyn.

Once Charyn and the others were inside the roped-off regial area, Charyn glanced down the nave toward the main entrance. The anomen had never been full anytime that he'd attended services—except for the memorial service for his father—but it seemed to him that there were even fewer attending. *Perhaps because it's midharvest and hot?*

Still, just as the chimes struck the glass, Saerlet appeared in the middle of the dais and stood there while the choir offered the invocation, then intoned, "We are gathered here together this evening in the spirit of the Nameless and in affirmation of the quest for goodness and mercy in all that we do."

Charyn managed to murmur most of the words of the opening hymn, "Words Unspoken," as well as the confession, a ritual in which he had little faith. By the time Saerlet stepped to the pulpit, offering the usual "Good evening," Charyn just hoped that the chorister had something at least halfway inspirational to say.

"And it is a good evening, for under the Nameless all evenings are good, and we should offer thanks for that goodness." Saerlet paused for a long moment before continuing.

"All of us have heard of Rholan the Unnamer. His sayings about goodness, and what it is and what it is not, have been repeated over the years. Rholan, as some of you may know, was not terribly fond of righteous choristers, and in more ways than one alluded to the fact that what we say from the pulpit is not the only way to worship the Nameless or to live a goodly life . . ."

Charyn frowned as he heard what seemed to be chanting coming from the back of the anomen. He glanced in that direction.

At that moment, the main doors of the anomen flew open, and hooded white-covered figures poured into the nave.

Charyn could easily make out the long chant.

"Free Rholan from false faith! Drive out the cowardly choristers! Drive them out! Drive them out!"

For an instant, Charyn froze. He'd never expected anything like what he saw and heard. Then he turned to Lystara. "We'll need that concealment now. We're leaving by the side door."

"Yes, sir." After a slight hesitation, Lystara said, "We're concealed. Stay close to me."

The three turned and walked swiftly to the side door. The two guards scrambled to follow. Once the five were in the side hall, Charyn saw that two figures in white stood at the end in front of the door closest to the main doors . . . and to the coach.

Charyn looked behind them, then said quietly, "There must be a door back there." He turned, and Lystara turned with him. Dhuncan, the second guard, motioned for the others to precede him, but Dhuncan still stayed close to Lystara, just behind Charyn.

There was an outside door, some ten yards farther along the corridor, solidly barred, which was likely why the True Believers hadn't entered that way. Charyn unbarred it and opened it gingerly, one hand going to the pistol in his jacket. But the door opened onto a narrow stoop below which was the stone paving surrounding the anomen. No one was close by.

When everyone was out, Dhuncan closed the door, and Charyn looked for the unmarked coach. He didn't see it at first, but finally saw that it had been moved farther around the circle, and the driver stood on the seat looking one way and then the other.

"There's the coach," said Charyn. "There's no one close to it." He glanced back at the main entry to the anomen, where still a score of white-clad True Believers continued to chant.

"Not yet," said Lystara. "We need to run."

"Then we'll run," said Charyn.

The five began to run.

Charyn was glad that the chanting was loud enough that no one could hear the sound of boots on pavement. Once they neared the coach, Charyn said, "When we get within a few yards of the coach, drop the concealment so that Staavyl can see us, and he doesn't drive off."

"Tell me when," replied Lystara.

After several moments, Charyn said, "Now!" Then he called out, "Staavyl, get ready to start as soon as we're in the coach!"

"Yes, sir!" The driver dropped down into the seat.

"Move ahead, Parrtyn," said Dhuncan. "Get the coach door open quick, and then swing up back."

Parrtyn nodded, then rushed ahead and opened the coach door.

Then Charyn heard shots, one after another, and Lystara staggered.

"Get . . . in the coach," she gasped. "I'm all right. But hurry."

Another shot rang out, and Staavyl slumped in the driver's seat.

"Get inside!" snapped Dhuncan. "I'll drive." The guard scrambled up to the driver's seat.

"To Imagisle! It's closer and safer," said Charyn, as Parrtyn closed the door behind Lystara.

The coach began to move immediately.

Charyn looked to Lystara. "Are you all right?"

"I'm not hurt, but I'll have some bruises tomorrow, I think." She turned to Aloryana. "Are you shielding?"

"I am."

"Good."

"Just yourself," added Lystara.

Charyn looked at the anomen, but all he could see as he looked back was the group of True Believers around the doors of the anomen, still apparently chanting. *So who was shooting at you . . . and why?*

There hadn't been any overt threats, unlike the last attempts . . . unless the white belts had been a threat . . . or had they been a warning? Charyn had certainly gone out of his way not to offend anyone unnecessarily, including the True Believers. *But why were the True Believers there? Was that why Saerlet had been so discomfited?* And then there was the question of why the True Believers were so angry at Charyn. *What have you done to them? Besides be Rex?*

Charyn didn't have any answers to that.

He kept looking out the coach windows, but no one seemed to be following them, although Dhuncan had the coach moving at a rattling and almost bone-jarring speed, a speed that slowed once the coach was perhaps half a mille from the Anomen D'Rex and approaching the bridge to Imagisle.

It felt like a glass passed before Dhuncan brought the coach to an abrupt stop in front of the Maitre's dwelling. Charyn immediately got out and looked up to Dhuncan. "How is Staavyl?"

The burly guard shook his head. "He was dead before I reached him."

In moments, Alastar was hurrying from the dwelling to the coach, followed by Alyna.

"What happened?" asked Alastar, looking from Charyn to Lystara and then back to Charyn.

"The True Believers burst into the anomen in the middle of Saerlet's homily. Lystara shielded and concealed us and we ran to the coach. Someone, maybe more than one, shot at us. Lystara's shields kept most of us safe, except for Staavyl. He was the driver. I told Dhuncan, who took over, to come here. Here we are."

"How are you?" Alastar asked his daughter.

"I'm fine. I'll probably be a little sore tomorrow. I think seven or eight shots hit my shields."

Alastar winced, but said, "Two rifles then. Most of them have five-shot magazines."

"It looks like I won't be attending services for a while," said Charyn as dryly as he could manage. "I'll need to be unpredictable when I leave the Chateau."

"That might be for the best," replied Alastar. "You'll need two imagers to ride back to the Chateau with you. Whoever shot at you likely knows you came to Imagisle, and they might be waiting at the bridge. I'd suggest taking the east bridge from Imagisle and then the Nord Bridge over the Aluse. That's longer, but they likely won't have enough people to cover the east bridge." He looked back to Lystara. "Are you certain you're all right?"

"I had Aloryana look me over to make sure nothing got through the shields. I don't have any wounds or sharp pains."

"You're pale. Go inside and get something to eat." The Maitre looked to Aloryana. "Go with her and make sure she eats . . . and you do, too."

"Yes, sir."

Once the two had left, Alastar asked, "Do you have any idea . . . ?"

Charyn shook his head. "That I've been attending services was in the newssheets. That was why I tried to be unpredictable as to where I'd be. I guess I wasn't unpredictable enough." He paused. "But . . ." He didn't know what else to say. Then he added, "Over the past two weeks, I received two white belts. There was no message either time. Just the belt. I didn't know whether they were a threat or a warning."

Alastar frowned. "They sound more like a warning."

"But how would I know?"

"That's a good question. Could it be someone who wanted to claim they warned you . . . in case you weren't hurt?"

"I suppose so, but I don't know who that might be."

"Put that aside for now. Could the shooters or whoever was behind them be someone who was upset by what happened to Ryel?"

"It could be, but who? Outside of Karyel and Iryella, no one in that part of the family is left alive, and Uncle Ryentar's son . . . he's only something like eight. And it's seven months later."

"But it's only been in the last month that you've been that visible outside the Chateau." After a moment, Alastar asked, "What about Argentyl and the guilds?"

"I sent him a missive last week requesting he meet with me on Lundi. I haven't heard back."

"You may not."

"They'd shoot me over the artificers' standard?"

"Didn't Argentyl say that some wouldn't be happy? They've destroyed four warehouses and goods in almost ten other factorages."

"That many?" Even as he asked that, Charyn wondered how Alastar knew so much more than he did.

"Most likely even more. That number came from the Civic Patrol on Vendrei." Alastar turned to Alyna. "Are you up for a ride to the Chateau D'Rex?"

"You don't . . ." began Charyn.

"The last thing Solidar needs is another assassination," said Alastar. "For whatever reason. I'll also send a messenger to the Chateau immediately letting them know you're fine. We have to saddle up, but there's always a duty messenger."

"You and your guards need something to eat and drink also," added Alyna.

More than half a glass passed before the coach and the two imagers, riding guard, left Imagisle by the east bridge, taking the East River Road up to the Nord Bridge, and then, on the far side of the River Aluse, the Boulevard D'Ouest to the Ring Road and the Chateau D'Rex.

That ride was much longer and slower than the ride to Imagisle had been, and Charyn kept looking at Staavyl, his body wedged into the rear-facing seat.

How did that happen? And why Staavyl? Just to stop the coach so that they could get to you?

Yet, as he thought about it, he hadn't seen anyone with a rifle near the True Believers, and the True Believers hadn't even been looking in the direction of the coach. But that didn't mean that someone involved with them hadn't been hiding somewhere and firing at him. And it had to be someone who knew that he used the unmarked coach.

But there could be more than a score of people outside of the Chateau guards who know that.

Just after the coach crossed the Nord Bridge, Charyn began to smell smoke. He looked out the right window. He didn't see any sign of smoke there, but that might have been because of the dim twilight. He looked to the other side, but, again, saw nothing.

He was still pondering all that had happened when the coach headed up the drive to the rear courtyard of the Chateau.

Charyn was barely out of the coach when both Maertyl and Faelln appeared, a clear sign that the imager messenger had delivered word about what had happened at the Anomen D'Rex.

"Are you all right, sir?"

"I'm fine. Maitre Lystara saved all of us—except Staavyl. His body is in the coach. Maitre Alastar and Maitre Alyna were kind enough to accompany me back to assure my safety." Charyn turned and looked at the two riders. "Once again, I find myself in your debt, and especially in Lystara's debt. She handled herself . . . like an imager."

Alyna smiled. "She will be sore tomorrow. Taking that many bullets on a shield at once does leave bruises. But it also reminded her that accompanying you and Aloryana was anything but babysitting."

"I suspect it also gave Aloryana some more incentive to work on shields and concealments."

"That, too," added Alastar.

After the two imagers rode down the drive, Charyn turned toward the rear door to the Chateau. He still could smell a faint odor of smoke, but he'd seen no sign of fire on the rest of his ride.

21

Charyn was up very early on Lundi, early enough that Artiema was still star-accompanied. While the first thing he wanted to do was to talk to Guard Captain Maertyl, he didn't, realizing that Maertyl couldn't do what Charyn wanted until much later. So Charyn read Devoryn's *History of Solidar* for a time, then forced himself through exercises, cleaning up, and eating breakfast before cornering Maertyl in the tiny guard study.

"Yes, sir?" The captain was on his feet instantly.

"I need you to send a few guards to find Chorister Saerlet and bring him here. While they're there, whoever's the lead guard needs to see what damage there is to the anomen and report back to me on that. Would you also send a responsible and perceptive guard to request the immediate presence of Chorister Refaal of the Anomen D'Excelsis? Finally, report Staavyl's death to the Civic Patrol, if that hasn't been done, and find out what, if anything, the patrollers have done."

"On the last, sir," Maertyl said, "I reported it last night. There was only one patroller at headquarters. The others were either patrolling or searching for the men who set fires at two warehouses."

"So . . . no patrollers even looked into Staavyl's killing?"

"Your Grace . . . you own the anomen."

For a moment, Maertyl's words didn't seem to make sense. Then they did. "Finding the killer is up to the Chateau Guard, then?"

"Yes, sir." Maertyl sounded anything but happy.

"I suppose we could request assistance from Marshal

Vaelln, but I don't see what good that would do at the moment." Charyn paused. "Do you?"

"No, sir."

"Do you even know how he was shot?"

"Yes, sir. He was hit three times. We found one bullet. It's from a standard rifle, the kind we use, the kind the army uses, and . . ."

"The kind used by the rebel High Holders?"

Maertyl nodded, then said, "We're not missing any rifles, and every guard and rifle was accounted for at the time Staavyl was shot."

"So it's likely impossible that he was shot by a guard or a guard's rifle?"

"It appears that way, sir."

"When will the memorial be?"

"Late Meredi afternoon. At his anomen. That's where his wife wanted it."

Charyn nodded. "I'd like to attend."

"Your Grace . . . ?"

"I'll think about it. You'll have someone bring back Saerlet right away?"

"I'll send one of the lead guards with five men."

"Thank you."

After he left Maertyl, he stopped by Norstan's study.

The seneschal bolted to his feet. "Your Grace!"

"Have you heard any word from Argentyl?"

"No, sir."

"Let me know immediately if you do."

"I will indeed, sir."

As he made his way up to his own study, Charyn considered the fact that someone had been setting warehouse fires at the same time as the True Believers stormed the Anomen D'Rex. Had the protest been planned at a time when civic patrollers were elsewhere? Had those men who set the fires just felt that no one would be expecting an attack at the time when many people would be at evening services? Had the attempted assassination already been planned and had the protest just been a fortunate coincidence for the shooter? Or an unfortunate one because Staavyl had been forced to move the coach? *So many questions, and not a hint of an answer.*

When he approached the study door, Moencriff said, "Your Grace, I put a letter on your desk. A messenger just brought it from Factor Elthyrd."

"Thank you." Charyn had a very good idea about its contents. He wasn't surprised in the least as he sat at the table desk and read.

> *Your Grace—*
> *Word may not have yet reached you, but over the*
> *past several days, there has been more destruction of*
> *manufactured goods, and three warehouses have been*
> *set afire. If you already know of this, please accept my*
> *apologies for the repetition.*
>
> *This destructive behavior cannot be countenanced.*
> *Factors are losing their livelihood, and their workers are*
> *losing their positions and wages. The Civic Patrol seems*
> *unable to catch those who are involved in this despicable*
> *and treasonous destruction. Therefore, the Factors'*
> *Council is now offering substantial rewards, up to ten*
> *golds, for names and proof of action against factorages*
> *and warehouses.*
>
> *If this does not provide the necessary information*
> *to put a stop to these acts of willful destruction, the*
> *Factors' Council will be forced to take much stronger*
> *action, and the Factors' Council wanted you to be aware*
> *of our position.*

Charyn lowered the missive. He had a very good idea what measures the factors might take, given that at least some of them had their own armed guards. The Factors' Council had already decided on what they were going to do well before Elthyrd wrote. Charyn also had the feeling that the reward scheme had been Elthyrd's, in hopes of finding who was behind the fires and destruction. But since protecting their own property was certainly their right, until they did something more than that, there wasn't much he could do at the moment. *Which is exactly the problem.*

The fact that he could do so little immediately reminded him of Bhayrn, who always wanted to act strongly and immediately . . . and like their father, without considering the ramifications.

Rather than worry over what he couldn't do, or Bhayrn, he turned to a lesser worry, a letter from High Holder Fhaedyrk about the proposed law to reduce or at least limit the contamination of rivers and streams caused by manufactorages. Charyn read over the paragraph that was central to the High Holder's concern.

> . . . *understand fully the problem if every new factorage or use alongside a stream fills the water with waste, but the law, as proposed, makes no provision for existing and long-standing facilities . . .*

Charyn shook his head. Grandfathering existing facilities without any conditions would encourage those individuals to expand while placing higher costs on newer factorages. *What about allowing older facilities to exist for a time before complying? Maybe require a fee for them instead until they do?*

He was still mulling over the possibilities when Moencriff rapped on the door.

"You have a package from Factor Estafen, sir."

A package? Charyn frowned. What could Estafen be sending him? He thought for a moment. It had to be something concerning the ironworks.

It was indeed—a report from Engineer Ostraaw addressed to Factor Suyrien and forwarded by Estafen, the bulk of the small package being everything that surrounded the document, clearly to separate "Suyrien" from the Rex. Charyn read through the short report, his eyes taking in the key phrases.

> . . . *orders for more than two hundred rifles received on Vendrei from the Solidaran Factors' Council, accompanied by a deposit of two hundred golds, the balance of eight hundred and twenty golds to be paid in coin immediately upon delivery . . . delivery to be no later than Six Erntyn . . .*
>
> *Attached is a map of the property. As you requested, I have noted the two locations where a manufactorage might be placed without disturbing either the ironworks or the rifleworks . . .*

Charyn studied the small map. He could see advantages and disadvantages to each position, and that meant he'd need to talk to Ostraaw.

Less than a quint passed before Maertyl appeared in the study. "Chorister Saerlet has vanished, sir."

"Did the True Believers take him?"

"His valet doesn't think so."

Saerlet has a valet? What else does he have? Charyn stood. "We're going to the Anomen D'Rex. I need to look at Saerlet's personal quarters."

"Now, Your Grace?"

"Now. But not in the coach. I'll just ride with the guards in a guard's uniform. I haven't done that before."

"If that is what you wish, sir, I'd suggest that Undercaptain Faelln lead the men, to give the impression he's acting in your stead."

"That's a good idea. When can we leave?"

"In about a quint. You have a guard's jacket as I recall, do you not?"

"I do. I never returned those I obtained during and after the problems last winter. I'll meet Faelln in the rear courtyard in half a quint or so."

Once Maertyl left the study, Charyn walked to the window and looked down at the courtyard, thinking. What had Saerlet been hiding? Why had the chorister not wanted to tell him immediately whatever he'd thought he needed to impart to Charyn? Had Saerlet been threatened in some fashion by the True Believers?

He only hoped that there might be something in Saerlet's quarters that shed some light on what had happened on Solayi.

Slightly more than a quint later, Charyn rode beside Ashkar, one of the regular guards, and behind Faelln as they headed around the Ring Road to the Boulevard D'Rex. Charyn could see that almost everyone on the roads or on the sidewalks gave the riders only the most cursory of glances.

Saerlet's personal quarters consisted of a square dwelling set some thirty yards directly behind the southeast end of the anomen. As he dismounted, Charyn studied the two-story structure, constructed of solid gray stone blocks and roofed with split-slate tiles. The window trim and shutters were dark green, and there was a covered porch on the left side of the dwelling.

He and Faelln walked to the front door, where the undercaptain knocked firmly.

The two waited for some time before a graying man in a brown shirt and trousers opened the door and offered a puzzled look at Faelln.

"I'm Undercaptain Faelln of the Chateau Guard. This is Rex Charyn. He's not in finery, given what happened last night. Who might you be?"

"Mhassyn. I'm the chorister's personal assistant."

Saerlet has both a personal assistant and a valet? Charyn frowned.

"Good," said Faelln. "We need to look through the quarters."

"Undercaptain . . . Your Grace . . . these are Chorister Saerlet's private quarters."

"Quarters that the Rexes of Solidar have provided for generations," said Charyn. "Have you forgotten that?"

Mhassyn shrank back. "I beg your pardon, Your Grace."

"Where is the chorister?" asked Charyn as he stepped into the entry hall, a space some three yards square.

Faelln closed the door and glanced around, his hand on the hilt of his sabre.

"I don't know, sir. Ekillyt said he gathered several sets of garments for the chorister. The chorister left and said he'd be gone for a time. By the time I got back here, he'd already departed."

"Did he say where?"

"No, sir. Ekillyt said he didn't say."

"Is Ekillyt the chorister's valet?"

"Of course, Your Grace. With all the vestments and appearances . . . you know."

Another thought struck Charyn. "What about Chorister Orlend? Wasn't he staying here as well?"

"He left on Samedi, Your Grace. I don't know where."

"Thank you." Charyn eased past the assistant and looked into the chamber to the left of the entry hall, a sitting room with several settees and chairs, elegantly upholstered. The window hangings were a lavender velvet, trimmed with cream silk. He turned to the room on the other side of the hall, a study with floor-to-ceiling dark wooden bookshelves on the rear wall, and a door out to the covered porch on the outside wall. The matching dark wooden furniture glistened, and all the brass fittings had been recently polished.

The formal dining room had a long table that could have seated ten people, with two sideboards. Again, the well-polished wood of table, chairs, and sideboards all matched.

"Chorister Saerlet's personal chambers are upstairs?"

"Yes, Your Grace," replied Mhassyn glumly.

Once upstairs and as soon as he entered the dressing room,

Charyn saw the two large armoires. Between them was an elaborately framed full-length mirror on a stand. Charyn frowned. He walked to the nearest armoire and opened it. It was filled with shirts, most of them gray or green or white, but shirts in all sorts of fabrics, cotton, linen, silk, possibly even bamboo cloth. Then he walked to the second armoire and opened the doors. It held jackets and trousers, and ten pairs of polished boots in a rack across the bottom—black, light and dark brown, gray, beige, and one pair trimmed in silver.

He has ten times the clothes I do, and those cottons, woolens, and silks must have cost hundreds, if not thousands, of golds.

Charyn turned to Faelln. "I'm through."

"Yes, sir." Faelln's voice and expression were even.

While Charyn didn't agree with the tactics or likely even the religious fervor of the True Believers, when it came to the personal finances of Chorister Saerlet, and the apparent mingling of the anomen's coins and Saerlet's personal funds, it would appear that the men in white had a certain point.

That still left the question of why they had shot at Charyn, rather than the chorister.

Just because you're the Rex and presumed to be wealthy at the expense of the poor? Or because they believe you support corrupt choristers? Or perhaps both?

Charyn shook his head and turned toward the staircase. "We can go." He looked at Mhassyn. "If and when Chorister Saerlet returns, inform him that I wish to see him. Immediately."

"Yes, Your Grace." Mhassyn swallowed. "Will that . . . I mean . . . is there anything else?"

"No. I've seen quite enough." *Quite enough.*

Charyn said nothing until he and Faelln were outside the dwelling. "Rather an elaborate wardrobe, wouldn't you say, Undercaptain?"

"I'd rather not say anything, sir."

"You don't have to, but I'll have to do something about it. That's if Saerlet ever shows up."

"Do you think he will, sir?"

"If he finds out what I've seen, I wouldn't."

Faelln's only comment was a short barked laugh.

Charyn remounted and rode back with the guard detachment. Once again, no one paid more than passing attention to the mounted guards.

As soon as he reached the Chateau, he dismounted and turned to Faelln. "I have another unpleasant duty. Craftmaster Argentyl was supposed to see me today. He has not shown up. I need him found and brought here. He just might be connected to what happened yesterday. If he cannot be found, I need to know as much as you or your men can find out about where he might be." Charyn paused, thinking. "His shop is just a block north of the corner of where Fedre crosses Quierca, on the south side."

"We'll take care of it, sir."

Charyn had no doubt Faelln would do what was necessary. He also doubted that Argentyl would be anywhere to be found.

In the meantime, he went back to consider the river problem that Fhaedyrk had brought to his attention, among other things, including the problem of unseen poachers and silent villages.

A glass later, he'd set aside Fhaedyrk's question and was wondering if Alastar would be able to find someone suitable as a personal scrivener when Sturdyn, relieving Moencriff, announced, "Guard Captain Maertyl and Chorister Refaal."

"Have them come in."

Maertyl walked slightly behind Refaal, expressionless.

Refaal wore a jacket and trousers of dark green, and a shirt and chorister's scarf of light green. The look on his face was a combination of indignation and fear, but he stopped before the table desk and asked, "Why did you send guards for me without as much as a by-your-leave?"

"Your Grace," prompted Maertyl, his voice like cold iron.

"Your Grace," added Refaal, an edge to the words suggesting anger barely held in check.

"I summoned you because the True Believers stormed the Anomen D'Rex last night and attacked me and killed the guard driving my coach. Also because Chorister Saerlet has fled without a word of where he went, and I'm beginning to think that both of you know more than you told me, and I'm anything but happy about that."

Refaal froze. "The True Believers attacked you?"

"They shot at me and my sister and my guards. I don't think they were aiming at Aloryana or the guards. Also, Saerlet was upset before the service and said he'd tell me afterwards. Obviously, that didn't happen. Instead, he left right after the unfinished service. So . . . what did you and Saerlet fail to tell me?"

"Sir . . . when we were here, we told you everything we knew."

"What did you find out later that you didn't tell me?"

Refaal did not reply.

"Guard Captain . . ." began Charyn, his voice ominous.

"I got . . . a message . . . more of a note, really. It wasn't signed. It said that if I didn't start preaching homilies based on the true teachings of Rholan, I wouldn't be a chorister for long."

"When did you receive this note? Do you still have it?"

"Yes, Your Grace." Refaal lifted his hand rapidly. "Here—"

"Slowly!" snapped Maertyl. "Very slowly. There's a pistol at your back."

Refaal paled. His hand was trembling as he slowly extracted an envelope from his jacket and laid it on the table desk. "That's all I know. Oh . . . it was under the door to my quarters on Vendrei morning. I went to see Saerlet on Samedi. He said that he thought you were coming to services on Solayi and that he'd talk to you about it. He also said that I should preach a homily about Rholan, one that concentrated

on his well-known sayings, and that I should say something
to the effect that these have been passed down for so long
that they've been accepted as fact, but are they, and do they
mean what they meant then? He said I didn't have to answer
those questions, but leave it up to the congregation to think
about them for the week. He said that would buy time and
that we could come and talk to you this week."

"If you were going to come to talk to me, why did you
have to be forced to come?"

"I was afraid. When all the Chateau guards appeared and
insisted on my coming with them, why wouldn't I have been
afraid?"

"That's a fair question. I have one for you. Did you preach
the kind of homily Saerlet suggested?"

"I'm afraid I did."

"Was there any reaction after the service?"

"None that I could tell."

Charyn turned to Maertyl. "Captain, is there anything the
chorister hasn't said or that you think I should know?"

"He told his assistant to tell anyone who asked that he'd
been called to the Chateau D'Rex." Maertyl offered a grimly
amused smile.

"Do you have a valet?" asked Charyn.

Refaal looked totally bewildered. "A valet, sir? Why
would I need a valet? I only have a few sets of clothes, and
three sets of vestments."

Charyn turned in his chair and took a sheet of paper from
the cabinet, laying it on the side of the desk facing the standing chorister. Then he stood. "Sit down. Take the pen and
inkwell. You're going to write a sentence and sign it." At the
horrified look on Refaal's face, he added, "It's not a confession or anything like it." *Not if you're as innocent as I suspect.*

Refaal sat in the chair farthest from the window, on the
front edge, looking at Charyn warily.

"Just write these words. 'Preach a good homily about
Rholan and his sayings.' Then sign it."

As Refaal began to write, Charyn picked up the envelope. While it had been slit, there was no sign of a seal,
and the paper was the type, as he'd learned earlier, used by
merchants and artisans, but not usually by wealthy factors
and High Holders. As he suspected, however, the words on
the single sheet of paper were written in standard merchant
hand.

*Preach your homilies about the real Rholan. Don't keep
preaching about the false Rholan. If you go back to the
True Beliefs, you'll stay a chorister.*

That was all that was on the paper.

Charyn nodded. "Were you ever a clerk for a factor or
merchant?"

"No, Your Grace. I was trained as a boy at the old scholarium in Solis. That's where most choristers learn."

From a cursory look at what Refaal had written, Charyn
doubted the chorister could have written the note, but
then, he wouldn't have believed what his late aunt Doryana had written. He looked back at Refaal. "You can
go, but I want to know *immediately* anything you find out
about the True Believers or where Chorister Saerlet may
be. Is that clear?"

"Yes, Your Grace."

Charyn looked to Maertyl. "Thank you. If you'd have
someone ride back with the chorister so that he can bring
back the mount."

"Yes, sir."

When the two had left, Charyn just shook his head, not
quite certain what to make of all that seemed to be happening at once.

At the fourth glass of the afternoon, Faelln stepped into
the Rex's study . . . alone.

"I take it that Craftmaster Argentyl was nowhere to be
found?"

"Yes, Your Grace. His shop was closed, and no one was in the family quarters above the shop. It appeared that no one had been there for several days. Neighbors had not seen Argentyl since sometime on Vendrei. One neighbor said Argentyl helped load a wagon late that afternoon. His family has not been seen for more than a week."

"You think he sent his family off first?"

"It seems likely."

"Did you find out anything else?"

"Several of the crafters wanted to know why you weren't doing anything about the factors who are making cheap goods that take away the artisans' customers."

"Were they violent?"

"No, sir."

Faelln's tone suggested he wasn't saying something.

"But they weren't happy, and some of them could have been?"

"Several of them said that some of the factors who had large manufactorages were hiring boys for a copper a day and treating them worse than any High Holder ever did."

"They're probably right," said Charyn tiredly.

Faelln's tone softened. "Can you do anything about it, sir? It doesn't seem right that they're hiring boys cheap and putting grown men out of work."

"It's not right. What I can do is another question. Some of the factors will oppose any change, but the High Holders might stand behind me." *If for different reasons.* Charyn's voice turned wry as he went on. "Minister Sanafryt always makes the point that I have to be able to enforce any new law I make. He's right, and that's what makes changing things hard. That's why I'm working on ways to use the laws so that others help enforce them." He laughed. "Not that you need to hear that. Your job is hard enough without listening to me." A smile followed. "Thank you for finding out about Argentyl."

Once Faelln left, Charyn walked to the window, not really even looking out into the late afternoon. He wasn't so sure that Faelln hadn't understood what he'd said more than Bhayrn ever would. And that was sad, in another way.

22

After his morning routine on Mardi, but before he made his way up to his study, Charyn stopped to talk to Maertyl.

"I wanted to thank you for the way in which you dealt with Chorister Refaal, and for all the time you spent on Solayi evening. I do appreciate it."

"It is my duty, Your Grace, but thank you."

"Also, if you'd convey my appreciation to the guards who had to pull extra duty."

"I'll do that."

Charyn caught a hint of a smile and said, with a smile of his own, "If you haven't already."

"I did take that liberty, Your Grace. You were concerned about more immediate matters."

"Even so, I should have conveyed that earlier. Thank you for taking care of it." Feeling somewhat embarrassed, Charyn quickly asked, "What is your opinion of Chorister Refaal?"

"I only spent a glass or so with him, Your Grace."

"That's more time than I have. Does he strike you as honest, or mostly so?"

"Mostly so, sir. I don't see him in a white hood."

"I don't, either. Or Chorister Saerlet, either." Charyn paused. "I do see Saerlet as one of the reasons for the True Believers. Did Faelln tell you about his armoires?"

"Yes, sir." Maertyl shook his head. "That doesn't become a chorister."

"If I had garments like that, it wouldn't become a Rex, either. With what he spent on clothes, I could have paid for river wall repairs . . . well, some repairs . . ."

"I understand, Your Grace."

"Have you heard anything more about the True Believers?"

"I asked some friends in the Civic Patrol. They don't know any more than we do."

"Do they think that some of the True Believers might be behind the fires and destruction of factorages and warehouses?"

Maertyl frowned. "Might be more that some of those setting the fires are also True Believers, rather than the other way around."

Charyn could see that.

When he reached his study, the first thing he did was read the newssheets. Both *Veritum* and *Tableta* had stories about Solayi's events. Charyn began with *Veritum*.

An unknown assassin attempted to kill Rex Charyn as he was leaving the Anomen D'Rex on Solayi evening. The Rex departed before the conclusion of services when more than two-score white gowned and hooded protesters rushed into the anomen as Chorister Saerlet began his homily. The protesters chanted phrases such as, "Free Rholan from false faith! Drive out the cowardly choristers!"

The Rex left quickly by a side door and was unobserved until he and his party and guards had almost reached his coach. Shots rang out, and the Rex's coachman fell, fatally wounded. Another guard took over as driver, and the Rex and those with him escaped without further injury, according to reports from the Chateau Guard and the Civic Patrol. The reason for the attack is unknown, as is the attacker, who was never seen.

The protesters are members of a religious cult called the True Believers. They believe that choristers have moved away from the teachings of Rholan and are slaves to those of wealth and power, while enriching themselves.

There have been reports of scattered protests at other anomens across Solidar . . .

The story in *Tableta* was rather different.

Our beloved Rex must have a habit of making enemies.
On Solayi evening, someone shot at him as he was flee-
ing a True Believers protest during evening services at
the Anomen D'Rex on Solayi. The only casualty was his
coachman, who died on the spot. Once again, Rex Charyn
is fortunate enough that his enemies are poor shots. But
how long can his luck last? Luck is useful, but luck alone
will not solve the difficulties facing Solidar . . .

After Charyn finished reading *Tableta* and dropped it on
the desk, he walked to the window and looked out at what
promised to be another hot and hazy harvest day.

Momentarily, he debated shutting down *Tableta*. He supposed he could order the army to occupy the building, but,
as he recalled, the High Holder rebels had done that, and
within days, the newssheet had been printing again. So what
would shutting down the newssheets do besides give the impression that he was opposed to the True Believers and that
he was as high-handed and uncaring as they'd thought his
father had been? He opposed the Believers' methods, but
even before he'd become aware of them, he'd been skeptical
of both Saerlet and of Refaal's predecessor.

What Charyn had since learned about Saerlet and even
Refaal suggested that something needed to be done about
the way choristers handled their anomens—and the coins
that passed through them, all too many of which seemed
to have found their way into Saerlet's hands . . . and splendid garments. *But what can you do?* More important, what
should he do?

That reminded him about the fact that he hadn't seen a
draft of the proclamation he'd asked Sanafryt to draft about

the duty of Civic Patrols to protect anomens and choristers. So he walked to Sanafryt's study and asked about it.

"I'll have it to you this afternoon, sir."

"Once the wording is final, you'll also need to send a copy to the Civic Patrol in L'Excelsis and the rest of Bovaria, and to the regional governors."

Sanafryt nodded.

"Do you have any more thoughts on the poaching problem?"

"No, sir. As I told you earlier, there are laws against poaching, but if no one sees or knows who the poacher is—"

"Or no one is willing to say who it might be. But doesn't that suggest that something is wrong, if an entire hamlet is silent?" *Or that they're all short of food?*

"Those problems don't lie with the law, Your Grace."

Charyn had to admit that Sanafryt had a point there.

He smiled ruefully and headed back to his study.

A quint or so past eighth glass, Moencriff announced, "High Holder Delcoeur is here to see you, Your Grace."

"Have him come in."

Ferrand's words seemed to rush before him. "I just heard about what happened on Solayi. I can't believe it. Who could possibly . . ." Ferrand waved his hands, as if he couldn't find the words to finish his sentence.

"Who could possibly want to kill me? Apparently, there is someone. It could be a True Believer, or it could be a disgruntled crafter, or possibly an unhappy High Holder or heir . . . or someone who just doesn't like Rexes." Charyn kept his tone of voice dry.

"But how could anyone think that removing you as Rex would benefit anyone? There would just be another Rex, and he wouldn't be as good as you."

Considering Bhayrn, Charyn had to agree, but . . . "Ryel wasn't thinking about Solidar. Neither were the rebel High Holders. They were all thinking about what they wanted."

"In time, they still would have been worse off."

"That's what I think, but we'll never know for sure." Charyn barked a laugh. "And you'll pardon me if I say that I'd rather not have you find out."

"I'd agree with that." Ferrand paused. "Bhayrn's still in Rivages?"

"So far as I know, and Mother would have let me know if he'd left."

"He doesn't seem to like being in the Chateau."

"He may not, but part of that's my doing. Then I insisted he spend time in Rivages learning something about . . . I already told you that."

"You did. He'll do better there than carousing with Laamyst and his brother."

"He's never mentioned the brother. Well . . . perhaps in passing. He did mention that Laamyst liked to get away from his father whenever he could."

"Laastyrn's the heir. I've only met him once or twice. I wasn't impressed."

"I wouldn't know. Bhayrn's also made friends with Gherard D'Ghaermyn."

"The Ghaermyns . . . they're still as much factors as High Holders. Why would Bhayrn associate with them?"

"He met Gherard through Laamyst, I think."

"I've never met High Holder Laastyn or Laamyst."

"I'm about to meet Laastyn," replied Charyn. "He's among the High Holders who live close to L'Excelsis who are coming with you to dinner this Samedi."

"With all the balls, you've never met him?"

"His hold is thirty milles north of here, barely close enough to be considered local. Also, his daughters are much younger than Laamyst," said Charyn wryly. "It's more than enough work to learn about the High Holders with eligible daughters."

"Why did you even ask him, then?"

"Because Bhayrn spends time with Laamyst, and I probably should at least be familiar with Laastyn."

"That makes sense."

"I'd appreciate it if you'd spend some time with Laastyn, if you wouldn't mind?"

"I can certainly do that." Ferrand paused. "What about Alyncya D'Shendael?"

"We're exchanging letters. She spent several weeks in Vaestora."

Ferrand frowned.

"Calkoran's daughter is a close friend."

"Oh . . . I'll likely have to deal with that with my sisters . . ."

After another quint or two, Ferrand left.

As soon as he did, Moencriff, trying to keep his face impassive, handed Charyn a letter.

"Thank you." As soon as Charyn saw the handwriting, he understood, but he just nodded to Moencriff and walked toward the table desk, not slitting the envelope until the study door was closed.

He began to read immediately.

Your Grace—
While I have not had time to fully consider the matters
we have been discussing in our correspondence, when
I read about the attack upon you and your guards on
Solayi evening, I had to convey my concerns about
your well-being and my heartfelt wishes that you are
unharmed and in good health.

I very much look forward to seeing you at dinner on
Samedi evening.

Again, my concerns and warmest regards.

Warmest regards? Those words could mean anything, but the underlined "had" and the "very much" were definitely more hopeful.

While there were other matters stacked on one side of his table desk, Charyn decided to reply immediately, the immediacy hopefully conveying his appreciation as much as what he might write. After several failed attempts and the passage of more than a glass, he read over what he had written.

My dear Lady-heir—

Your concern for my well-being was most deeply appreciated, and I can assure you that I am unharmed and remain in good health. My spirits are sound, and certainly uplifted by your immediate correspondence and your warm words.

Although I am in good health, and much cheered by your letter, I am concerned about the various occurrences that have befallen both the people and the city of L'Excelsis in the past few weeks, particularly the violent events involving the Anomen D'Rex and the wanton destruction of factors' goods and property. Both reflect, in a differing fashion, a certain discontent with those who appear to have increased their golds to the disadvantage of those less fortunate.

This presents a problem to me as Rex, for a ruler cannot effectively, and should not morally, decree what each man should receive for his labor or for his skill and effectiveness in marshaling the labors of others in support of his lands or enterprises. Yet it seems less than right that the wages of one man should be arbitrarily depressed so that another may prosper more greatly than before. If a factor or a High Holder comes up with a new manner of improving goods or the manner of producing them and reaps rewards for such, should those who toil for him not also benefit? Is it untoward for a Rex to entertain such thoughts, do you think?

Perhaps I should not pose such questions, but you, as a most intelligent woman, think clearly and consider matters deeply, and is it not wiser to avail myself of your wisdom than to ignore your perception and intelligence?

*In closing more hurriedly than I would wish, I do
indeed look forward to seeing you at dinner on Samedi.*

He read it again. *It could be better.* But then, anything
could always be better. He signed his name, and then sealed
the letter.

23

Just before third glass on Meredi afternoon, Charyn approved Sanafryt's second draft of the legal proclamation declaring that violence against anomens and choristers was just as much a criminal offense as violence against any other persons or structures, and returned it to the Minister of Justice, with a request that copies be made and dispatched as soon as possible.

Immediately after that, Charyn donned a Chateau guard's dress uniform, along with the black mourning sash, checking to make sure his pistol was in place. Then he walked down to the rear courtyard, where Maertyl and half a squad of guards attired in the same fashion as he was were forming up. Several of the guards appeared surprised as they saw the Rex.

"I didn't tell anyone you were joining us," explained Maertyl. "I thought it was better that way."

"Much better," agreed Charyn.

Within a few moments, the group rode down the drive, with two guards leading the way, and with Maertyl and Charyn immediately behind them.

"Have you heard anything else about the True Believers or whoever's smashing factors' goods?" asked Charyn.

"No, sir, but it strikes me that it has to be artisans and crafters, not ruffians from the back alleys of the taudis. Those low-life toughs wouldn't know what to look for."

"I've gotten that feeling."

"It's not about machines or the like, Your Grace. It's about coins and respect . . . like . . . well . . ."

"Like it was with the Chateau guards?" asked Charyn dryly.

"I'd say so, sir."

"You're likely right about that as well."

The guards went from the Ring Road onto L'Avenue D'Commercia for roughly a half mille before turning left onto a street that didn't seem to be named. Three blocks later, they reined up outside a small single-story anomen—the Anomen D'Sud.

After they dismounted, leaving the mounts with two of the guards, Charyn handed a leather pouch to Maertyl. "This is in addition to the usual death golds."

Maertyl raised his eyebrows.

"It's not much, just five golds, but two didn't seem like enough for what happened."

Maertyl nodded slowly. "You don't want to give it to her?"

"Somehow . . ." Charyn paused. "Or do you think I should?"

"It might mean more."

"If you think so." Charyn raised his hand and took back the pouch.

Then he and Maertyl led the way into the anomen, taking a position along the wall on the left side of the nave, roughly halfway between the door and the low wooden dais. Standing beside Maertyl, Charyn studied the anomen, taking in the ceiling and the time-aged beams. The inside walls were whitewashed plaster over the stone outer walls, a plaster that was clean, but with an uneven finish that had doubtless resulted from decades of patching and repainting.

Small as the anomen was, even after a few more handfuls of mourners entered, by the time the chimes sounded fifth glass, less than two score stood waiting, not including Charyn and the Chateau guards.

"Emmalyn's the dark-haired one just below the pulpit, with the white-haired woman," murmured Maertyl.

"Thank you." Charyn couldn't see her clearly in the dim light, but he could tell that she didn't want to exchange glances with anyone, because she looked straight ahead without ever turning her head.

When the last chime sounded, a balding chorister in dark green vestments with a black and green chorister's scarf stepped up to the pulpit. "We are gathered here today in the spirit of the Nameless, in affirmation of the quest for goodness and mercy in all that we do, and in celebration of the life of Staavyl D'Guard."

The opening hymn was "The Glory of the Nameless," followed by the confession.

"We do not name You, for naming is a presumption, and we would not presume upon the Creator of all that was, is, and will be . . ."

When the confession was finished, the chorister offered the charge. "Life is a gift from the Nameless, for from the glory of the Nameless do we come; through the glory of the Nameless do we live, and to that glory do we return. Our lives can only reflect and enhance that glory, as did that of Staavyl, whom we honor, whom we remember, and who will live forever in our hearts and in the glory of the Nameless."

The hymn that followed was "In the Footsteps of the Nameless."

"When we walk the narrow way of what is always right,
when we follow all the precepts that foil the Namer's blight . . ."

Then the chorister said, "Now we will hear from Staaryn, speaking for the family."

The young man in faded blue stepped up on the low dais and turned to face the forty or so who had come to pay their respects to the family and to Staavyl. He swallowed several times before he finally spoke. "Staavyl was my brother. He was a good man and a good brother. When we didn't have enough to eat, he gave me half of what he had. He was like that with everyone . . ."

When Staaryn finished, barely able to utter his last words, the chorister stepped behind the pulpit once again. "At this time, and in the spirit of the Nameless, let us offer thanks for the spirit and the life of Staavyl and let us remember him as a child, a youth, a man, a husband, and a father, not merely as a name, but as a living breathing person whose spirit touched many. Let us set aside the gloom of mourning, and from this day forth, recall the glory of Staavyl's life and the warmth and joy he has left with us . . ."

With those words, all the women let the mourning scarves slip from their hair.

Then came the traditional closing hymn—"For the Glory."

> "For the glory, for the life,
> for the beauty and the strife,
> for all that is and ever shall be,
> all together, through forever,
> in eternal Nameless glory . . ."

As the last words of the hymn faded away, a few people at the back of the anomen began to depart, but most remained, moving forward toward Staavyl's widow. Charyn and the guards remained at the side of the anomen until most of those mourners slipped away. Then Maertyl and Charyn walked forward.

The widow saw the uniforms and stiffened.

"Emmalyn," began Maertyl, "you may recall me. I'm Maertyl, and I'm now guard captain. Not all the guards could be here, but the ones with me represent those who could not come." He turned. "This is Rex Charyn."

Charyn inclined his head. "I'm sorry for your loss. I wish it could have been otherwise. Staavyl was a good man." His words sounded trite, and Charyn knew they were. "There aren't words for a time like this. I know. My father was shot less than a year ago. I think I understand a little how you must feel."

The dark-haired woman's eyes were bloodshot, and she looked at Charyn, then asked, her voice slightly hoarse, "Why? Why did someone shoot my Staavyl? He was not a Rex. He was a man who drove for you."

"Because they wanted to stop him from driving me away, so that they could shoot me," replied Charyn evenly.

"Did you know someone was going to shoot at you?"

"I didn't know that. I used the unmarked coach just so that fewer people would know where I was. When we left for services, I had no idea someone was going to shoot at me. This is the only time ever that someone has shot a driver."

"Staavyl is still dead." Her voice was flat.

"He is. I cannot change that." Charyn lifted the leather pouch. "Nothing will bring him back, but I hope this will help you and your family."

"Coins are not life." She took the leather pouch gingerly.

"No, they are not, but no one can grant life. I can only express my concern and hope these will help make some of the other parts of life a little less difficult."

Emmalyn looked directly at Charyn. "At least you came. I thank you for that."

"In fairness to Staavyl and to you, I could do no less." Charyn inclined his head slightly, then stepped back.

The widow inclined her head, then turned.

Charyn nodded to Maertyl, and the two made their way from the anomen, followed by the other guards.

"You meant that about doing no less, didn't you?" said Maertyl quietly.

"I did. I try to be as truthful as I can be." *Which isn't always possible.*

But Charyn had lied about one thing. He'd put ten golds in the pouch, all out of his own personal funds.

24

Even by fourth glass on Samedi afternoon, Charyn knew little more than he had after attending Staavyl's memorial service—except that another factorage had been attacked late on Jeudi night and the looms smashed, while another warehouse that held imported porcelain had been set afire before dawn on Vendrei.

Charyn couldn't say that he was exactly looking forward to the dinner that evening with the "local" High Holders, but his father had avoided social interactions with all but a few High Holders, and, in the end, that had not served Lorien well, which might have been a contributing factor to why a number of High Holders had supported his young brother Ryentar during the High Holders' revolt. That, and the fact that Ryentar had apparently been both charming and in favor of restoring the powers of the High Holders.

Will more socializing with them serve you any better? He had no idea, but trying it might result in better results, and couldn't result in much worse.

When Charyn made his way down the grand staircase to the anteroom at slightly past fifth glass, both Ferrand and Elacia were there, Elacia also being Ferrand's dinner partner, since Ferrand couldn't bring an unrelated unwed woman unless they were officially affianced.

"The string players are here and setting up, Your Grace," Elacia announced.

"Thank you."

"Is Alyncya accompanying her father?" asked Ferrand.

"Their response indicated that," said Elacia.

"You're fortunate in that," said Ferrand.

"Not so fortunate as you think," replied Charyn.

"He can't make a single untoward move or a single suggestive comment, or even a single unguarded gaze," declared Elacia, her words clearly as much for Charyn as for Ferrand.

"And I couldn't exclude Shendael from a dinner for High Holders living around L'Excelsis." *For more than a few reasons.*

"I didn't think about that," admitted Ferrand.

"You should have, dear," said Elacia gently.

As Elacia headed for the archway into the music room, Ferrand said in a low voice, "I'm glad you're the one she's advising."

"I did tell you that you'd rather have your problems than mine."

"You might be right about that."

"Are you going to pursue Kayrolya D'Taelmyn? Or Marenna D'Almeida?" Charyn grinned.

"You arranged the seating at that little dinner, didn't you?"

"Only with your mother's assistance." After a pause, Charyn said, "Well?"

"They each have their charms." Ferrand smiled wryly and added, "And they're both younger daughters from good families with at least several siblings."

Meaning that Ferrand would be seen as a good match, rather than scorned for his father's financial problems.

Before that long the chimes were ringing sixth glass.

The first arrivals were High Holder and Lady Fhernon. Fhernon smiled broadly at Charyn. "Good evening, Your Grace. We appreciate the invitation."

"And I'd like to express my appreciation for your kindness to Ferron," added Lady Fhernon.

"How could I not be kind? He has demonstrated a quiet determination, honesty, and good taste."

"We still appreciate it."

The next arrivals were High Holder and Lady Laevoryn.

He was a young man perhaps five years older than Charyn, with sandy-blond hair and eyes of blue so dark that Charyn couldn't recall ever seeing that shade before. To Charyn, the blond and gray-eyed Lady Laevoryn scarcely looked that much older than Aloryana, although she must have been.

"It is indeed a pleasure to be here," offered Laevoryn. "Thank you for including Dercya and me."

Charyn thought he heard a hint of cold amusement in Laevoryn's voice, but replied warmly, "I became Rex rather suddenly, and I fear that I've lagged slightly in getting better acquainted with the High Holders in and around L'Excelsis. I am attempting to remedy that slowness. Welcome . . . and please enjoy yourself."

"Thank you. We certainly will."

Charyn managed not to frown as he turned to greet another High Holder—with his wife—he had not really met before—Ghaermyn, although he wanted to, given Bhayrn's friendship with Ghaermyn's eldest son. After that came High Holders and ladies, one after the other—Aishford, Taelmyn, Kastyl, Paellyt, Quensyl, and then Fyanyl, without his lady.

High Holder Shendael and Alyncya finally arrived.

"I'm so glad to see that you are healthy and well, Your Grace." Alyncya looked directly at Charyn.

For instant, he just looked back into her hazel eyes, before finally saying, "I am healthy and well, Lady-heir Alyncya, and I cannot tell you how much I appreciated your letter of inquiry and concern." And he certainly couldn't, not at that moment.

The faintest hint of a smile crossed her lips. "I'm very glad to hear that."

"As am I," added High Holder Shendael. "Are there no other family members attending this evening?"

"Only my aunt, Lady Delcoeur D'Priora, and my cousin, High Holder Delcoeur. My brother and mother have not returned from Rivages, and my sister is, of course, an imager."

"Of course. I had forgotten about your sister," replied Shendael. "She did attend one ball, as I recall."

"The Year-Turn Ball," replied Charyn, "just before she revealed she was an imager."

"She revealed?" asked Alyncya.

"She is apparently quite talented, according to Maitre Alastar. If she works hard, it's possible she might become a maitre in time."

"I had not realized that so many unrecognized talents lay in your line, Rex Charyn," said Shendael genially.

Not quite sure what to make of Shendael's observation, Charyn smiled and said, "Nor did I, but comparatively young as I am, I've come to realize that unrecognized abilities may lie undiscovered in many lines."

"Quite so. Quite so, but we must not keep you." Shendael eased his daughter away from Charyn and toward the far sideboard.

After High Holder and Lady Almeida arrived and Charyn spent several moments with them, the very last arrivals were High Holder and Lady Laastyn. Laastyn smiled pleasantly, with a hint of warmth, and said, "It's been quite a while since we've seen you, Your Grace. We see your brother quite often, so often that it feels like we should have seen you more recently."

"I'm glad to see you both, and I appreciate your kindness, and that of Laamyst, to Bhayrn. He's definitely enjoyed his times at your various properties."

"And we've enjoyed him. He's very direct and forthright, a welcome trait in a world that has come to be one where it's difficult to be certain whether what is said was really what was meant."

"Bhayrn often does say exactly what is on his mind."

"Would that more did. Being oh-so-polite and politic often keeps people from addressing the hard necessities in life."

"But it sometimes also keeps people from hatred and violence," suggested Charyn.

"At the cost of hypocrisies that fester and often lead to greater problems, and even less attention to necessities."

"Except one man's necessities are often irrelevant to another," replied Charyn.

"Do you find them so, Your Grace?" asked Salani, breaking her silence.

Charyn offered a short humorous laugh. "I can afford to find nothing irrelevant, even if I may not be able to do much about some matters."

"We all must prioritize, Your Grace."

"So we must." Charyn nodded, adding, "Please enjoy yourselves."

Once Laastyn and Salani, his largely silent lady, moved away, Charyn took a glass of Tacqueville white presented by a server, then started to move toward three couples—High Holder Taelmyn, High Holder Paellyt, and High Holder Quensyl, each with his lady. He had only taken two or three steps when High Holder Ghaermyn eased up to him.

"Your Grace, if I might have a word . . ."

"Certainly." Charyn wondered what Ghaermyn wanted, but suspected it must be urgent or important, because seldom was anything of import directly discussed at such functions, at least not openly. Either that, or Ghaermyn was attempting to take advantage of Charyn's relative inexperience.

"It is not widely known, but I am in a position similar to that of one of your relations . . ."

What relations? Most of Charyn's relations were either dead or too young to be anywhere similar to Ghaermyn. Except . . . "You refer to High Holder Zaerlyn?"

"I do. I have a number of manufactorages. These facilities build looming frames that are powered by waterwheels."

"Then has the drought made it so that fewer factors and others buy your frames?"

Ghaermyn shook his head. "Not yet, but the weavers and spinners are unhappy. I fear some of them may be among those destroying the frames and looms in the large manufactorages."

"But if the frames are being destroyed, would that not mean you can sell more?" Charyn had an idea of where the discussion was going, but he wanted Ghaermyn to lead it there.

"There have been several attacks on my main manufactorage. I have been required to hire a small army to protect it, and to spend golds on buying rifles to arm them. Even so, one small outbuilding was set afire and destroyed. These ruffians would bring down everything. If they are not stopped, Solidar will crumble and be forgotten like the Naedarans."

Charyn nodded, although he had his doubts about matters being that extreme. "There have been reports of a number of factors' manufactorages having such difficulties. I did not realize that High Holders were facing the same problem."

"It is not quite the same problem, Your Grace. I can guard my buildings because of where they are situated, but the cost of maintaining the guards will make it infeasible to continue producing frames. If I do not produce them, the factors will not be able to replace what they have lost. So we both will lose, if in a different fashion."

"It would seem that you have common cause."

"As do you, Your Grace. Is it not your responsibility to maintain the peace in Solidar?"

"I've thought about this, High Holder Ghaermyn. For me to guard all facilities and to track down these ruffians and malefactors will require either an expansion of the army or the expansion of the Civic Patrols in all cities and towns. That cannot be done, especially now, without increasing payments to the Civic Patrols or increasing tariffs, if not both."

"You're saying you can do nothing?"

"Everything costs coins. What would you suggest that I do?"

"Make a law against such destruction."

"That law already exists. The problem is catching the malefactors and proving that they caused such destruction. No one who knows seems to want to reveal anything. They need a reason." Charyn was trying to get Ghaermyn to suggest offering a reward.

"I can see that," replied Ghaermyn. "What about paying a bounty for such information?"

"I understand that the factors are already offering rewards up to ten golds."

"My son mentioned that."

"Gherard? How did he come by that?"

"You've met him?"

"No, but my brother has. That's how I knew his name. But how . . ."

"He's the one who handles the holding accounts at the exchange." Ghaermyn frowned. "Perhaps a greater reward would elicit greater information."

"It might," agreed Charyn. "If I did so, would that be something that High Holders and factors would support?"

"I don't see why not."

Charyn offered a wry smile. "When one asks for information and provides a reward for it, not all that is discovered may be favorable to everyone."

"I'll live with that."

"You've made an interesting suggestion. Thank you. It will definitely help."

"That won't be enough, Your Grace."

"You're right. It won't be, but it's a start." Charyn paused. "What do you think these men really want?"

"To destroy us."

"Do you think that?" Charyn frowned. "From what some guild craftmasters have told me, it's not the machines so much as the lower wages."

"I can't pay more than what others are paying. It wouldn't make sense."

"What if they had to pay what you did if you paid workers more?"

"You're talking as if the moons could become suns, Your Grace."

Charyn laughed gently. "You may be right, but there might be a way. I'll have to think about that."

"Thank you for listening, Your Grace." Ghaermyn eased away.

Charyn continued toward Taelmyn, Paellyt, and Quensyl and their wives, trying to catch a hint of what they were saying. He noted again that Paellyt and his wife were considerably younger than the other two.

". . . years since any High Holders invited . . . formal dinner . . ."

". . . don't worry . . . enjoy . . ."

Taelmyn turned as Charyn drew closer. "Your Grace, we were just talking about how long it had been since a Rex hosted a dinner for High Holders who weren't close friends or family."

"I've already done one of those, but the way my family and friends are vanishing, or removing themselves from L'Excelsis," replied Charyn lightly, "I will have no one with whom to dine. How long has it been since you or anyone of your lineage has dined here—not including balls?"

"I cannot remember."

"We'll have to make sure that doesn't happen again." Charyn addressed Paellyt. "And you?"

"I have no idea," replied the High Holder, likely only a few years older than Charyn. "My sire never mentioned it."

"How about you, High Holder Quensyl?"

"My grandsire dined here when I was a boy. He told me that there was music, and I'm delighted to hear the string quintet. Will there be a clavecin player? I'd heard that your father had a fine one, a woman, I believe? Good-looking as well, I heard."

"He did, indeed. Musician Palenya. Alas, I could not keep

her. She preferred to accompany my sister. Palenya is now the musician for the Collegium Imago."

"Must have been a loss for you," said Quensyl blandly.

"Oh . . ." murmured Lady Taelmyn.

Lady Paellyt frowned, but said nothing.

"The Chateau will miss her playing," said Charyn warmly. "She was a fine musician. She even managed to improve my playing, but at least now Aloryana can continue learning from Palenya, as can other imagers at the Collegium."

"Is it really true . . . about your sister?" asked Lady Quensyl.

"That she is an imager? It is true. She seems quite happy at the Collegium . . ."

After a short time that seemed interminable, Charyn moved on to a group that included Lady Almeida, High Holder and Lady Fhernon, High Holder Fyanyl, and Lady Ghaermyn.

"Your Grace," offered Lady Almeida, "the Tacqueville white is simply splendid."

"Thank you. It does happen to be my favorite."

Lady Almeida turned to Lady Ghaermyn. "Did you know that the Rex is an excellent clavecin player?"

"You're kind, but I'm merely competent, even for someone who isn't a professional musician. My distant cousin, Maitre Malyna, is better than I am, as is Lady-heir D'Shendael, and, before long, I suspect, my sister will be as well."

"Lady-heir Alyncya is quite good, I've heard. But . . . you have a cousin who is a maitre imager?"

"Two of them, actually. Very distant cousins. I didn't find that out until last year when I was researching the background of the Codex Legis. That was when I discovered that the sister of the first Rex Regis happened to be the ancestor of both Maitre Malyna and Maitre Alyna. Maitre Alyna is the Senior Imager at the Collegium and also Maitre Alastar's wife."

"Who would have thought it?" murmured Lady Ghaermyn.

"I've heard that Maitre Malyna is quite young for a maitre," said Lady Fhernon, "and quite good-looking."

"She's also a very strong imager. She was the one who saved my life, Bhayrn's, and Aloryana's the night my father was assassinated."

"Why was an imager besides the Maitre even at the Year-Turn Ball?" asked Fyanyl in a tone that verged on annoyance.

"As a favor to her father, High Holder Zaerlyn," replied Charyn cheerfully. "There are a number of imagers who come from High Holder families. In fact, the head of the Collegium in Westisle is a powerful imager who is the younger son of High Holder Calkoran."

After perhaps half a quint of pleasantly voiced, not entirely pleasant conversation, Charyn eased away and, still keeping a smile on his face, moved toward another group, this one that held Ferrand, Laevoryn and his wife Dercya, and Kastyl and his wife.

"Your Grace, it's been said that your sister is an imager," offered Laevoryn almost before Charyn joined the group.

"That's no secret. She is an imager, and she lives at the Collegium."

"You let her go there?" asked Dercya incredulously, her voice breathy.

"She chose to go. Where else could she be an imager?"

"But . . . how terrible," continued Dercya, "for a Rex's daughter to have to be an imager. To be . . . with people . . . who are not of her . . . background. And some of them, I've heard, are even Pharsis."

"She is living with Maitre Alastar and his wife Maitre Alyna, who is the daughter of a High Holder. Her brother is High Holder Zaerlyn."

"At least . . . that's more proper," breathed Dercya.

Charyn couldn't resist adding, "High Holder Zaerlyn comes from a Pharsi background, and so did the first Rex Regis."

"I'm curious," offered Laevoryn smoothly, before Dercya

could speak. "What do you think of Maitre Alastar? You have met him, haven't you?"

"I have. He attends the balls, and I met him when I accompanied Aloryana to the Collegium." Charyn was a little surprised that Laevoryn didn't seem to know that Alastar attended the Council meetings. *But then, that's never really been made much of publicly.* "Have you met him?"

"Several years ago."

Charyn noted a faint curl to Laevoryn's lips. "I take it you didn't get on."

"You might say that."

"He's not the most . . . solicitous of men," said Dercya in the breathy tone that was already annoying Charyn.

"As the Maitre of a group that has some imagers with great powers, he likely has to be rather decisive and effective," suggested Charyn.

"Effective for the imagers, no doubt," replied Laevoryn. "Aren't you concerned about that kind of power?"

"I have to be concerned about many different kinds of power, unhappily," said Charyn wryly. "High Holder Ghaermyn was telling me about ruffians who are trying to break loom frames and factorages."

"I'm most certain that any High Holder who needs to engage in commerce and any factor can take care of their own. It would be preferable that way, especially if those in commerce would at least show some deference to culture and tradition."

"What aspects of culture do you find most vital and important?" asked Charyn, partly curious and partly probing.

"The lasting traditions of society. The perpetuation of manners. Sculpture, because it lasts and reminds one of history. Personally, I also appreciate the customs of the hunt. A good hunt should be a work of culture. An appreciation of food and spirits." Laevoryn looked to Charyn, almost challengingly.

"I'm more interested in music and history," replied Charyn.

"Don't you think music is . . . so ephemeral?" asked Laevoryn, not quite dismissively. "It's so of the moment, and then it's gone."

"Like the morning mist," added Dercya breathily.

"I don't know about that," interjected Kastyl. "You can remember a good melody for a lifetime. We still listen to the works of composers like Covaelyt, and he's been dead more than four hundred years."

"Or Farray," added Lady Kastyl.

Ferrand nodded, but his eyes remained fixed on Laevoryn.

"How many people really know who Covaelyt was?" countered Laevoryn.

"How many people long remember who anyone was?" said Ferrand. "People hum or sing melodies without knowing who wrote them or why. Some music does last."

"Power is what lasts," declared Laevoryn. "Everyone in Solidar knows about the first Rex Regis."

"Everyone also knows who Rholan was," suggested Lady Kastyl, "and he had no power. He only had words."

Charyn nodded to Ferrand and moved away, wondering if Laevoryn was always as opinionated, and making a mental note to ask Alastar about Laevoryn on Solayi . . . among other things.

He made his way toward the last group of people with whom, as a group, he had not exchanged words since they arrived, one that included Shendael, Alyncya, Elacia, and High Holder Fhernon.

"You're making the rounds, I see," offered Shendael as Charyn approached.

"Isn't that what every thoughtful host should do?" Charyn smiled. "That, and try to make everyone feel at ease, at least as much as possible?"

"At least as much as possible," repeated Fhernon. "You've got that right. There are some who are never at ease . . . not if their host is the Rex."

"That does present a problem," replied Charyn. "If I try

too hard to make such people more at ease, then they'll worry that I'm trying to disarm them or deceive them. If I don't, they may think I'm callous or don't care."

"How much should a Rex care, Your Grace?" asked Alyncya.

"That's a question I've pondered, Lady-heir. The only way I can answer that is to say that a Rex should carry out his duties and responsibilities to his people and his land as well as he can, with the most care possible, but those cares should not outweigh his duty." Charyn laughed softly, adding, "Or as little as possible, because some cares always intrude." Before Alyncya, or anyone else, could reply, he went on. "And please don't ask me to say what I mean by 'as little as possible,' because I'm very new at being Rex, and I'll need more experience to answer that question."

Charyn thought he saw a hint of a smile in her eyes, but that might have just been what he hoped for.

"I don't know that any of us could answer that question fairly," said Shendael. "Tell me, how long do you think the problems with the Jariolans will last?"

"Until they stop attacking our ships or until we destroy their ability to do so, whichever comes first. They might decide to stop before we destroy all their ships, or they might not. Destroying all their ships will take years."

"I'm not sure that's an answer," said Fhernon.

Charyn smiled and said gently, "That means it's not the answer you wish to hear, but it's the best answer either Marshal Vaelln or I can give right now."

"Why do we have to fight at all?" asked Fhernon. "It seems like such a waste."

"We don't. That is, if we don't mind paying higher prices for tin, bronze, spices, and all manner of goods, if we don't mind having Solidaran ships sunk until we have no merchanters, and if we don't want our sailors turned into indentured slaves on Jariolan ships."

"You don't paint a rosy picture," said High Holder Aishford, who had drifted closer as Charyn had been talking.

"That's the best I can do," offered Charyn.

The soft sound of chimes filled the anteroom.

"I do believe it's time for dinner," said Elacia cheerfully.

"It is, indeed," agreed Charyn heartily, knowing that he had at least another two glasses of watching every word and every expression.

And that was exactly what he did for two glasses and a quint, until all the guests had left, except for Ferrand and Elacia, and the three of them stood in the main entry hall to the Chateau.

"That went very well," said Elacia. "Better than any such dinner here in years."

"In years?" asked Ferrand dubiously.

Elacia smiled sweetly. "This is the first such dinner for Charyn, and no one besides him has had one in at least four years."

What his aunt wasn't saying, Charyn knew, was that his father had been far more dour, even at his best.

"I'll be back in a moment," Elacia said, easing away from the two.

Charyn turned to Ferrand. "Did you find out anything interesting?"

"Outside of the lady-heir's quiet observation of you?"

"I think she was observing everyone."

"She was," said Ferrand cheerfully, "but you more than anyone."

That could be good or bad. "Anything else? Especially anything about Laastyn or Ghaermyn?"

"Ghaermyn didn't say much while I was around him. Laastyn was pleasant enough. He did mention something about several thousand hectares of timberland in Tilbor that he'd recently acquired."

"Nothing more?"

"Not really. The usual. Kastyl was complaining about how High Holders pay more tariffs than factors. His wife didn't say much at all. Oh . . . I forgot. At dinner, High Holder Laastyn was regaling a group about hunting boar on his lands in Talyon this summer."

"What about it?"

"I wasn't really listening that well," admitted Ferrand. "Just that he'd had to do it because his sons and their friends hadn't wanted to hunt boar, and there were too many for the land. He said something about your brother having an eye for a pretty woman."

Charyn frowned. That wasn't quite what Bhayrn had said. "What else did you hear? I was limited to what Almeida and Fhernon had to say, and Lady Almeida. She's willing to talk, even when she disagrees with her husband." Charyn grinned. "She likes you. She said you were extremely well-mannered."

"Did she mention Marenna?"

"Not a word, except that she wished Marenna took music as seriously as Alyncya."

"Did you hear anything about Kayrolya?"

"I couldn't hear what Taelmyn or his wife said at dinner. Earlier, Taelmyn was saying that it had been years and years since anyone in his family had been at the Chateau except for the seasonal balls. Quensyl made a veiled reference to Palenya, and I don't think Lady Taelmyn liked it."

"What did you do?"

"Turned the conversation to the fact that Palenya was musician for the Collegium and how it benefited Aloryana. I don't think, if you're interested, you'd have any trouble with either of the ladies, and given how strong-willed Lady Almeida is . . ."

"That's good to know." Ferrand paused. "I like both Marenna and Kayrolya, but . . ."

"But what?"

"I need to know them better. Either would be the same as far as dowers go, that is, there would be some, but nothing overwhelming." Ferrand smiled. "So I can get to know them better and see how things turn out."

"I told you that you'd rather have your problems."

They both laughed.

25

While Charyn slept somewhat later on Solayi morning, his sleep was anything but peaceful, given that he'd dreamed the same nightmare that had plagued him ever since his father's assassination, being shot by the faceless guard at the bottom of the grand staircase. He supposed such a recurrence shouldn't be unexpected after last Solayi's attempt by the True Believers, but it had still left him with a disturbed feeling.

Even so, he was in his study well before eighth glass, drafting a letter to Elthyrd. Even after two drafts, he wasn't totally pleased, but he read through it again.

Factor Elthyrd—
After your last letter, I have spent some considerable
time looking into ways that we could address the attacks
on factorages and factors' warehouses. In talking the
matter over with a number of individuals, I found one
High Holder who suggested that if I supplemented the
rewards offered by the Factors' Council, that additional
remuneration might induce those who know the
identities of perpetrators to reveal them.

As we have discussed, for me to employ the army,
at least initially, in this effort, would likely cause
more turmoil than results. I would, however, consider
providing additional funds to allow expansion of
the Civic Patrols in areas where violence continues,
provided some additional funds are also contributed
by the Factors' Council and provided some of those
joint funds are used to provide incentives for those

*patrollers who discover information that actually leads
to the discovery and punishment of those guilty of these
crimes.*

*The problem of violence will not be solved by punitive
measures alone, not when able-bodied men cannot earn
a living wage working in manufactorages and when, in
more than a few cases, the workers in mills and other
works are young children. I am considering amending
the Codex Legis to require all those who hire individuals
who are not relatives to pay a minimum level of pay for
a day's work. Such a requirement also would make the
hiring of young children less attractive. In this regard, I
would be interested to know what level of daily pay the
Factors' Council would recommend. I will, in time, also
be asking the same question of the artisans' guilds and
of the High Holders, but I thought the factors should
have the first words in this regard.*

*Of course, if the Factors' Council can offer another
approach to this problem, one that is both practicable
and within the resources of the Treasury, I would be
more than pleased to hear what that approach might be
and what it would entail to implement.*

As he signed it, and then sealed it, although it wouldn't
be dispatched until Lundi morning, Charyn doubted that either Elthyrd or the other factors would be pleased with his
proposal.

*Then let them make a better one—or keep getting their
factorages burned or destroyed.*

With that accomplished, he left the study and went down
to the music room, where he practiced for almost two glasses,
first working on "Pavane in a Minor Key" and then on the
Covaelyt "Variations," trying his best to recall what Palenya
had told him about each, particularly about his fingering.

Early in the afternoon, he took his pistol to the covered courtyard and practiced with it, not just aiming and

firing, but drawing it from his jacket and firing quickly, since that was likely the only time he'd need to use it. After a time, he shifted the holster and did the same with his left hand, not quite so accurately, but well enough to hit someone at close range. What was difficult for him was not to draw quickly, but to squeeze the trigger firmly and not jerk it right after the quick draw. Still, after practicing he felt better.

At fifth glass, wearing a Chateau guard's uniform, one of an undercaptain, he mounted the chestnut gelding and rode down the rear drive with three other guards. Instead of taking the Boulevard D'Rex, he led the way north to the Boulevard D'Ouest and took it to the West River Road, which led to the western bridges to Imagisle. From what he could tell, no one paid much attention to the four riders.

Still, he wondered how long before *Tableta* learned about that.

Alastar came out to meet him when he reined up outside the Maitre's residence. "You're probably safer riding as a guard than in even an unmarked coach."

"For now, anyway." Charyn handed the chestnut's reins to Dhuncan. "Thank you."

Alastar looked to the guards. "You can put the mounts in the stable. There are refreshments for you in the small tack room."

"I appreciate that," said Charyn.

"You're making the effort. Aloryana appreciates it more than you know, and we like seeing you."

"I don't know how long . . ." Charyn shook his head. "I still don't see why someone is shooting at me right now. Even if they killed me, it wouldn't change the situation between the True Believers and the choristers or the crafters and the factors . . . although I did learn on Samedi that some High Holders are also having problems . . ." As the two walked up to the covered porch, Charyn related the gist of what Ghaermyn had said.

"You might have somewhat better luck if the factors and High Holders agreed on something," offered Alastar.

"They've agreed in the past, on the issue of tariffs, when they didn't want to increase them. That sort of agreement wasn't exactly helpful."

"You changed that."

"True, but this is a bit different." Charyn didn't have a chance to say more as Aloryana hurried out to the porch.

She immediately hugged Charyn. "It's always good to see you."

"It's always good to see you, too."

Before that long, Charyn and Aloryana were walking down the cottage-lined lane toward the anomen, behind Alastar, Alyna, and Lystara.

When they entered the anomen with the Maitre and his family, there were several quick glances in their direction, but no one stared. Charyn suspected that the Maitre had had something to do with that.

Iskhar's homily at services did have one part that definitely caught Charyn's attention, so much that Charyn wondered if Iskhar had prepared it on the possibility that Charyn might be attending services.

". . . people ask why we live in such times of turmoil, as if this time of turmoil were unusual. Turmoil is not unusual. It is the human condition. We believe our turmoil is worse, because it is happening to us, as if we are more important than those who came before us and those who will follow us . . . that is nothing more than another form of Naming. It represents pride untamed by knowledge . . ."

Are all times always times of turmoil, or is life a mixture of more and less turmoil? Still, Charyn had to admit that the turmoil his father had faced was far worse than what he currently was encountering. *So far, anyway.*

He was still wondering about that as he and Aloryana walked back to the Maitre's house, accompanied by Lystara, the three of them following Alyna and Alastar.

"I didn't play anything new for you when we were at the Chateau," said Aloryana. "I've been working on some harder music with Palenya."

"You could have played one of those. I would have liked to hear it."

"Not for the first time with people who hadn't heard me play."

"I feel that way sometimes," replied Charyn.

"Is that why you didn't play any of your new pieces when we were at the Chateau?"

Charyn nodded.

"I'd like to hear one of them."

"They're hard, at least for me."

"Maybe you should ask Palenya for help."

"I did . . . when she came to tune the clavecin."

"You never told me that." Aloryana's tone was definitely accusatory.

"That's because it was a little . . ." Charyn couldn't find the right word. "Painful" wasn't totally true, not any longer, nor was "sad." "A little awkward."

"Because she was your mistress?"

"She was more than that."

"I know. She told me. She also said it was better that you find someone closer to your age who can have children."

"She told you that?"

"I asked her. I wanted to know some things." Aloryana didn't quite look at her brother.

"I didn't want her to leave."

"She told me that, too."

"That's why it was awkward."

"Charyn . . . you shouldn't avoid her just because you can't sleep with her."

For a moment, Charyn was stunned. "That isn't it at all. It isn't. And I didn't avoid her."

"Seeing her once in six months is the same as avoiding her. You're still avoiding her."

"I'm not. I just haven't made an extra effort to see her."

"For six months?"

"For some of that . . . well . . . it hurt to let go of her."

"Good," declared Aloryana. "It should have. It hurt for her, too."

"Did she tell you that, too?"

"No. She didn't have to."

Charyn didn't know what to say in return. So he said nothing, hoping Aloryana would volunteer more.

"You never said much about the women you had to that dinner."

"First, you're happy that my letting go of Palenya hurt, and now you're asking about other women."

"So you are interested in someone. Who is she?"

Charyn didn't know whether to sigh or laugh. "I am interested, but I don't know enough about her, and she's made it very clear that she doesn't know enough about me. She's also made it clear that her father will not agree to any match she opposes. In a way, he's made it clear as well."

"You still haven't told me who she is."

"You're going to insist, aren't you?"

"Charyn."

That name contained more exasperation than any single word should, Charyn felt. "If you'll keep her name to yourself—and Lystara."

"I won't tell," added the young maitre.

"So tell me," pressed Aloryana.

Charyn did sigh. "Alyncya D'Shendael-Alte."

"She's the heir? No wonder her father won't force her. But that's good. You need someone to stand up to you."

"Like you and Mother?"

"She'll have to be stronger. You're stubborn."

"And you're not?"

At that, Lystara laughed.

"Does she play well?"

"Better than I do. Better than Malyna. Not quite so well as Palenya."

"That's good. Have you asked her?"

"You said—"

"Are you thinking of asking her?"

"She's made it clear that she's interested. She's made it even clearer that I'm not to rush matters."

"She's very wise, then."

Charyn couldn't help but think Aloryana sounded more like their mother than his younger sister. "Why do you say that?"

"Because you're not quite over Palenya. Otherwise, you wouldn't be avoiding her."

Charyn glanced ahead. They were less than a hundred yards from the Maitre's dwelling. "You think so?"

"I do. But it's good you're interested in someone else. I'm glad she likes the clavecin. When will I get to meet her?"

"Ah . . . I hadn't thought about that . . . yet."

"You promised."

"I'm nowhere close to asking her anything."

"You're thinking about it. I can tell. I want to meet her."

Charyn offered a crooked smile. "So I should just tell her that my younger sister wants to meet her?"

"Why not?"

"I promised you that you could meet anyone I was considering seriously. Right now, it's not that serious."

"It's more serious than that. She just won't let it be, it sounds like."

"Perhaps I should just allow you to work matters out."

"Don't sound so stuffy, Charyn. I didn't like it when Father was stuffy. I don't like it when you are."

Charyn didn't recall their father as stuffy. Autocratic and seldom able to compromise, but not stuffy.

As Alastar reached the steps to the front porch, he turned back and looked at Charyn. "You're coming in, I hope."

"If you're inviting, I'm accepting."

"Excellent. I now have a keg of white wine. Not as fine as your Tacqueville, but reasonably good."

"You didn't have to do that."

"Working with you has been much more productive than with some of your predecessors, and certainly more pleasant, and we've enjoyed having Aloryana with us as well."

"Thank you." Charyn didn't need to say that working with the Maitre had been far easier than working with either factors or High Holders—or crafters and artisans.

In what seemed moments, the five were sitting in the parlor, Alastar and Alyna with dark lager, Lystara and Aloryana with pale ale, and Charyn with a white wine slightly drier than his Tacqueville white, but still very pleasant.

"Iskhar's homily was interesting," offered Charyn.

"Mostly true, I think," commented Alastar, "but there have been times when the turmoil has been greater than now."

"So far," replied Charyn. "But as I said earlier, I worry that the crafters' unhappiness could lead to even more violence."

"This had to come sooner or later," said Alyna. "Imagers could have made many goods better and for less cost than crafters. Alastar made sure we didn't, and that made matters more difficult for Imagisle. Now that factors are developing more machines, the crafters and artisans are going to have to find a way to live with the changes that are coming."

"I'm trying to find that way, but so far . . ." Charyn shook his head. ". . . I don't see anything that doesn't involve golds and force."

"You may have to use both, as long as the amounts of either aren't excessive," replied Alyna. "High Holders are certainly no strangers to using both."

"Speaking of High Holders," said Charyn, "I had some who live close to L'Excelsis for dinner last night. One of them was Laevoryn. He's not much older than I am. I don't think he's that fond of you. If he's not, that means I should be wary, but it would be good to know why."

Alastar smiled. "The way you phrased that doesn't give me much choice, I think."

"Charyn should know," said Alyna.

"The elder Laevoryn housed and supported a company of the brownshirt rebel troopers who killed a number of student imagers during the High Holder revolt. He tried to kill me and a few others when we cornered him in his hold house. The troopers with me shot him. His son was rather aggrieved when I suggested that, given his father's rebellion against the Rex, any action along those lines on the part of the younger Laevoryn could forfeit his lands and holding, especially since there was some suspicion that the young Laevoryn had been involved with the death of the nephew of a factor, although nothing was ever proved." Alastar paused. "He can't be that much older than you."

If Alastar mentioned something as not being proved, Charyn thought, the Maitre clearly believed that there was some connection, but likely wouldn't say more. "He looks a few years older, although his wife looks younger than Aloryana."

"No doubt she's quite . . . pliant," suggested the Maitre. "He didn't strike me as a young man who would brook any opposition to anything he wants or thinks."

"I got that impression as well," replied Charyn.

"Was High Holder Shendael there as well?" asked Aloryana, an innocent look upon her face.

"He was. He's widowed, and he brought his daughter Alyncya. Ferrand was there also, as was Aunt Elacia, and Ferron D'Fhernon's parents as well."

"Is Ferron still interested in Malyna?"

"Since he wasn't there, I couldn't ask him, and his parents didn't say anything about her or him."

"What about Ferrand? Is he interested in anyone?"

"You'd have to ask him. I'm not about to guess as to whether he is or to what extent."

"He talks to you. I know he does."

"He does, and that's between us," Charyn returned with

a smile. "Now, it's time to change the subject." He took a swallow of the wine before looking to Alastar. "Have you any recommendations for me for a personal scrivener or secretary?"

"I've given it some considerable thought, and there are two young men who might be suitable, but I need to talk to each of them again. I'll send you a written recommendation in a day or so."

"Thank you. I do appreciate it. There is one other matter. Have you noticed the rather sinister way in which the news-sheet *Tableta* refers to me?"

"I have observed that their stories reflect less than favorably on you."

"I'd thought about visiting their facility, with a few guards, and just asking them what they expect of me."

"They might tell you," replied Alastar, an amused tone in his voice. "But I don't know that a visit would serve you well until after you've taken some action to deal with the attacks of factors and warehouses. Then, if they complain about what you've done, your question might have more effect. Of course, it also might not have the effect you'd wish."

Charyn laughed. "You have a very polite way of telling me that it's a very bad idea."

"He got in that habit in dealing with your predecessors," said Alyna dryly.

Charyn noticed that Aloryana frowned at that, if only momentarily. "Father had trouble seeing things in different ways. I'm trying not to fall into that trap."

"We all have that tendency. The question is not whether we do," replied Alastar, "but what we do about it."

"As always, Maitre, you're very practical." Charyn took another swallow of the wine, knowing that he needed to be leaving before long.

26

The first thing Charyn did on Mardi morning when he entered his study was to read the newssheets. He was relieved to discover nothing printed about himself in *Veritum*, but far less happy about the long and detailed story about the continued destruction of factors' goods and warehouses, although heartened slightly by the observation that the damage was clearly created by "ruffians who apparently believe that such destruction will stop the building of manufactorages that provide goods at lower prices for the people of Solidar."

Tableta's view was, predictably, rather different.

. . . the Factors' Council is offering rewards for the names of those individuals who have tried to rid L'Excelsis and Solidar of poorly made imported wares and inferior cloth churned out by starving children. The factors of Solidar and even some High Holders insist that low wages and cheap goods bring prosperity. How can this be when able-bodied crafters and men are thrown out of work? How can cloth that shreds after a few wearings contribute to well-being . . .

The story went on from there.

In addition, there was a very short story on the Anomen D'Rex, just a few lines at the bottom of the first page.

Chorister Saerlet of the Anomen D'Rex has vanished, unsurprisingly, after a protest of True Believers revealed that the now-missing chorister had pocketed a large proportion of offerings and spent them on splendid personal raiment, rather than on food for the poor or other worthy causes. Services did continue on Solayi, with assistant chorister Faheel presiding. Our beloved Rex was nowhere to be seen. Could it be that he doesn't trust the Nameless to keep him safe?

Charyn was surprised that *Tableta* somehow didn't blame him for Saerlet's excesses. *That might come next week.* Even if most of what Saerlet had amassed had been during Charyn's father's reign.

Also waiting on the table desk was a reply from Factor Elthyrd that said that any funds Charyn wished to provide to the Factors' Council in support of efforts to bring the malefactors responsible for the destruction of wares and facilities would be gratefully accepted.

After reading that, Charyn walked from his study to Alucar's.

The Minister of Finance looked up from his desk as Charyn sat down across from him. "I'm almost finished with the calculations of the funds required to support the regional governors. Is that why you're here?"

"One of the reasons. Do you have an idea of the total cost and how much could be saved by shifting the functions to the High Command?"

"I do, but I'd recommend against trying to get savings that way."

"What could be worse than all these corrupt regional administrators?"

"A larger number of self-serving officers that you would have great difficulty removing. I grant that you have that authority, Your Grace, but putting that responsibility in the hands of military officers would give them total control of Solidar. Even if it did not work out that way, to remove one who was corrupt, you would have to take away some of the Marshal's authority over his officers."

"I have that authority now."

"Not in reality," replied Alucar. "You have authority to remove the officers of the High Command. That is as it should be. But you don't know who the good subcommanders, or majors, or captains really are."

Charyn sat there for several moments, thinking. Finally, he asked, "Then why did you work out the calculations? If what I suggested won't work, why didn't you just say that?"

"First, I was so surprised when you suggested it that I didn't know what to say. I had a feeling there was a problem, but I wanted to think about it. Second, you're right. There is a problem. By working out all the numbers, I could see that the differences in what regional governors spend were considerable, especially in areas that shouldn't be that different. That allowed me to come up with a recommended budget for each regional governor, by spending categories. The governors will be required to list their local tariff and import tariff receipts and expenditures by category. By comparing what a governor spends each season to previous seasons, you can see whether they're being excessive."

"They'll lie."

"Of course they will, but since they don't know what they've spent in the past by these categories, and we do, you'll have better control than you do now. And . . . if the figures are way out of line, I can send someone to find out what they've been doing."

"What if they just pocket some of the tariffs?"

"They do already. But this way, you have something against which you can measure what they're collecting, or say they're collecting, and what they're spending." Alucar paused. "This is just the first step."

Charyn raised his eyebrows.

"Once they start reporting this way, you can set up regional auditors to check their ledgers."

Charyn had his doubts about whether such a scheme would work, but . . . it couldn't hurt to try some of it. If nothing changed, then they could try something else. "Once you have all the details worked out, we should talk. There is one other matter." Charyn went on to explain about providing some limited funds to the Factors' Council.

"A hundred golds wouldn't be too great a burden."

"Then send a hundred to Elthyrd and say that it's to be used to gain information, and that if they want or need more, you'll need an accounting."

"I can do that. Do you think it will work?"

"It will get information. Whether that information will lead anywhere is another question, but we can't have unhappy crafters continuing to burn down warehouses and destroying goods. I'm trying to work out a way to make them less unhappy, perhaps by insisting on a minimum daily wage."

Alucar winced.

"Do you have a better suggestion?"

"Not at the moment, Your Grace."

"If you do, please let me know." Charyn stood. "I look forward to seeing your proposal for better control of regional governors' spending."

Even before Charyn reached the study door, Moencriff opened it and said, "There's another letter on your desk, sir. It's from Factor Paersyt."

"Thank you." Charyn entered the study and immediately opened and read the missive.

> *Your Grace—*
> *I am informing you, as requested, that we have*
> *installed the steam engine and have operated it with*
> *the boat docked at the piers. The engine operated most*
> *successfully. Unfortunately, the vibration from the*
> *screw was excessive. Had we continued, we would have*
> *damaged both the hull, the gearing, and the shaft and its*
> *support posts.*
> *I will be testing various screw designs as well as a*

more sturdy gearing system. Redesign of the positions
of the screw, the shaft, and the rudder may also be
required. As I explained earlier, these difficulties are
to be expected. The fact that the engine functioned as
expected is a very good indication that we can produce a
propulsion system that will be superior to that afforded
by the use of sails . . .

Charyn did not quite shake his head. Paersyt had indeed
explained that there might be many redesigns and much rebuilding, and that it might take as long as a year, if not longer, to get even the small engine and boat to work properly.
And after that . . . building a larger version for even a frigate
would take much more work.

At least the ironworks and the rifleworks were continuing
to make coins.

27

Slightly after midmorning on Jeudi, a letter from Alastar arrived by imager messenger. Charyn read it immediately. The Maitre's words were short and to the point, recommending one Wyllum D'Imagisle as a possible personal scrivener and saying that unless Charyn sent a message to the contrary Wyllum would present himself on Vendrei afternoon with a letter of recommendation. Since Charyn had no reason to object, he informed Norstan that he would see young Wyllum whenever he arrived. He also discussed the pay for a scrivener with the seneschal, which would be roughly that of an assistant ostler or a lead guard.

Charyn then went back to work studying the report that Alucar had compiled on the regional governors and that had been waiting on his desk for him when he entered the study. He hadn't finished working his way through it, but he was getting the feeling that his Finance Minister was far more thoughtful than he had initially believed, and certainly more astute financially than Charyn himself was.

But isn't that the way it's supposed to be? Except it hadn't been in the case of Aevidyr, and still wasn't.

"Captain Maertyl's here, sir."

"Have him come in."

Maertyl walked into the study, and Charyn gestured for him to sit down across the desk from him.

"I thought you'd like to know that the Civic Patrol caught two young men last night trying to set fire to a factor's warehouse. They had oils and rags and strikers. The patrollers waited until they started to light the rags."

Charyn looked to the somber-faced captain. "You don't look too happy. What else should I know?"

"One of the men was Keithell's son Weith."

Keithell? For a moment, Charyn didn't recognize the name. "The former stablemaster here? His son?"

Maertyl nodded.

"Weith told the patrollers that you'd discharged and flogged his father for no reason at all, and that he'd lost his job as a weaver's assistant because you aren't protecting the workers. I told my friends in the Patrol the whole story so that the patrollers know what really happened, but . . ."

"There's a possibility that what he said will get out."

"More than that. They'll hang Weith and the other man. Keithell will use it for all it's worth. He was always a nasty bastard, and no flogging could change that. Begging your pardon, sir, but it might have been better if you'd executed him."

With a wry expression, Charyn shook his head. "Then it would have come out that I killed the father, and my failure to work out a solution to the problem between the crafters and factors led to the son's death. One way or another, it wouldn't be good, but if I had executed Keithell, it would have been worse. I take it that the rewards are bringing in some information."

"Some."

"We'll have to see where they lead."

"They'll lead to more men being hanged, sir, and that won't be good."

"Given all the destruction they've caused, what else can the justicers do?"

"What about exiling the young ones, the ones that are only boys, to the Montagnes D'Glace?"

"That hasn't been done in hundreds of years."

"Or indenture them to the navy if they're under eighteen?"

"That *might* be possible. I'll have to check with Marshal Vaelln."

"That would be better for you and for them, Your Grace."

"I'll see what's possible, Maertyl."

"Thank you, sir."

Once the captain left, Charyn immediately wrote a letter to Vaelln inquiring about penal indenture through naval service, then had Moencriff arrange for it to be sent. After that he headed down to the main level to find Norstan, whom he located in the dry produce storeroom.

"Sir? You could have sent for me."

"I just had a question. Since I'm likely to be taking on a personal scrivener, as we discussed this morning, I forgot to ask if there is a decent room in the servants' quarters?"

"There are several in both men's and women's spaces."

"The scrivener will likely be a young man. There are several young people who come highly recommended by Maitre Alastar, but whichever one I choose will be one who doesn't have the imaging talent of his parents."

"You do need a scrivener, sir. Someone beholden to you and the Maitre would be good."

Charyn nodded. "I'll introduce you once I make a choice. Thank you."

"Yes, sir."

Later that afternoon, Charyn finally received the letter he'd been anticipating for some time. Again, he hoped his anticipation was warranted. He only waited long enough to be alone in his study before opening it and beginning to read.

Your Grace—

To begin with, I must thank you, on my own behalf and on behalf of my father, for the exquisite dinner you provided on Samedi. The refreshments and food were excellent, and you were indeed the perfect host, as even my father had to admit. I must offer my sincere regrets for the tardiness in expressing our appreciation, a tardiness that is especially unwarranted, given the grace and wit that you displayed throughout the evening and

*your graciously reserved, but quiet concerns for my
feelings and situation.*

*I must also apologize for my delay in replying to
the substance of your last two letters. I regret my lack
of punctuality, but that delay was occasioned by my
desire to consider fully the questions that you posed so
thoughtfully and eloquently . . .*

Most likely neither. Charyn smiled and kept reading.

*You have, perhaps in not so many words, suggested that
the word "evil" is often used to describe acts undertaken
with deliberate intent to cause harm, as opposed to those
acts undertaken for other purposes, even if such acts have
indeed caused great harm. You cite the worker and the
factor who each find the other's acts to be evil in intent,
because those acts have adverse impacts upon the other.
Whether one calls the act "evil" or not does not change
the result or remove the injury. That being so, what is the
purpose of calling an act or individual evil? In this regard,
I would be most interested in your further thoughts about
the use of the word "evil" as an appellation.*

*As for your observation about improvements in means
of production being shared between those who create
the improved means and those whose labor employs
those means, I would agree that such means should
not decrease the pay of those who labor, or worsen
their working conditions, but if all the cost and effort
of improving the means of production is borne by the
factor or High Holder, should not his share of those
rewards be greater than that of the laborer, who has
contributed no more than his previous efforts? In my
most humble opinion, the role of the Rex should be
limited to preventing harm, rather than ordering how
such rewards might be shared. For a Rex to order how
the revenues received from a factoring enterprise shall*

*be divided would take rights from the factor or High
Holder, and possibly even from the workers, and invest
them in the Rex. Yet the Rex has provided none of the
golds to pay and build improvements, nor any of the
labor required to utilize them.*

*From what you have pointed out in the example of
the Codex Legis imposed by the first Rex Regis, one of
the duties of the Rex is to protect the people of Solidar.
Thus, while there is an obligation to prevent harm to
both those who labor and those who factor, for what
reason should a Rex go beyond that duty?*

*As you, my most diligent correspondent, can see, I
fear that your efforts to draw out my thoughts may only
reveal my shortcomings in philosophy and law, whether
that law be natural or crafted by the minds of men, for
women are seldom involved in the formulation of legal
codes.*

*I <u>do</u> look forward to your thoughts in reply and
remain, with the warmest of regards,*

Her signature remained full and formal.

Charyn reread the last two sentences, pleased by the single
underlined word, yet wondering how many letters would be
ended with warm or warmest of regards.

Then he went back over the letter.

For what reason should a Rex go beyond that duty? The
clear implication was that he should not go beyond that duty,
but that he did have a duty to protect the crafters and workers
from practices that worsened their condition. Still . . . even
if the factors did provide the means to increase rewards,
they wouldn't be able to realize those rewards without their
workers, and that argued that at least a small portion of the
increased rewards should go to the workers.

After close to a glass of scrawling down thoughts and
ideas, he put those aside. She'd waited awhile to write him.
There was no sense in rushing a reply.

28

~~~~~

Charyn wasn't looking forward to reading the newssheets when he reached his study on Vendrei, and wanting to get the worst over first, he immediately picked up *Tableta*. The first part of the story on the capture of the two arsonists was reasonably factual and straightforward, but a later section bore out Maertyl's concerns.

> . . . the younger man, one Weith from the southwest river-side district, claimed he'd been forced into acting against "the selfish High Holders, factors, and Rex" because the Rex had flogged and fired his father for no reason at all except not wanting to pay him what he was worth and be-cause the factors had fired Weith so they could hire boys for half the wage . . .
>
> Does that sound like our caring factors and beloved Rex?

No, but it certainly sounds like Tableta. Charyn read through the rest of the scandal sheet, noting the story on the loss of another merchanter off the coast of Otelyrn, re-ported strictly factually, as was a report on the growing loss of crops in Antiago.

The *Veritum* report on the arson and apprehension was straightforward and factual, without any speculation, but Charyn wondered how many more acts against factor-ages would occur and whether those perpetrators would be caught . . . and how many others were occurring in other cities and towns.

Promptly at first glass, Sturdyn announced, "Wyllum D'Imagisle to see you."

The young man who entered was rail-thin, several digits taller than Charyn, with black hair and wide-spaced brown eyes. He looked to be a year or two older than Bhayrn and wore dark brown trousers and a matching jacket over a pale tan linen shirt. He immediately inclined his head. "Your Grace."

Charyn motioned to the chairs. "Please take a seat, Wyllum."

"Thank you, sir." As the young man approached the table desk, he handed a sealed envelope to Charyn. "Maitre Alastar requested that I give this to you."

"Thank you." As Wyllum seated himself, Charyn opened the letter, which briefly described Wyllum and noted that he had assisted Maitre Thelia and others in scrivening tasks, and that he had been a solid and careful worker. "Maitre Alastar recommended you as qualified to serve as my personal scrivener. Why do you think he did so?"

"He must believe that I can meet your standards, sir."

"Can you?"

"I don't know, sir. I don't know what your standards are. Maitre Alastar likely knows that far better than I do. I have a good hand. Maitre Thelia says that my hand is as good as that of any merchant clerk."

"Do you know standard merchant hand?"

"Yes, sir."

"What other styles?"

"The only other one that I've trained in is Collegium formal, sir. With a little practice, I could likely learn others."

Charyn turned and extracted several sheets of paper, then placed them on the desk in front of Wyllum, moving an inkwell and pen to where the young man could reach them. "If you would write a line in standard merchant hand and then write the same line in Collegium formal beneath it."

Wyllum took the pen, frowned slightly, but immediately and quickly wrote two lines, replacing the pen in the holder.

Charyn read the lines. Each read: "This is a test for Rex Charyn." The second line was similar to that used by the ministers and their clerks, if slightly more ornate. "Your hand is good, not that I would have expected otherwise. Why did you frown when you picked up the pen?"

"I would have cut the quill a little differently, sir. That was all."

"Can you make a pen?"

"Yes, sir."

"Besides being a scrivener for Maitre Thelia, what sort of work have you been doing at the Collegium?"

"I've acted as a duty messenger or runner. I can groom a horse, but if I stay around the stables too long, my eyes and nose get red and swollen, it's hard to see, and I sneeze a lot."

"Can you ride?"

"I can ride, but not well enough to be a courier. That was what Maitre Kaylet said."

Charyn talked to Wyllum for almost a glass, asking questions and listening, before he said, "As my personal scrivener, you'd be required to live in the Chateau. You'd have your own room, but it's not large. Would that be a problem?"

"No, sir. I have to share a chamber with Ashcryt now, and he snores."

"To begin with, if you decide to be my personal scrivener, you get your livery, a room, meals, and a silver and a copper a week."

"That seems fair, sir. More than a first, but less than a second."

"And you'll start on Lundi at seventh glass."

"You're really taking me on, Your Grace?"

"I am."

"Thank you, sir."

Charyn stood. "I'll take you down and introduce you to

Norstan the seneschal and to the guard captain. Norstan will take care of your room and livery."

Once Wyllum was in Norstan's hands and Charyn had returned to his study, he took a deep breath. Having a scrivener would definitely help, although it was likely to be almost more work for the first week or so, possibly longer, since it was clear that Wyllum didn't have the range of experience that Howal had possessed.

Still . . . it would make his life easier.

Just after third glass, he received a reply to his inquiry from Marshal Vaelln.

> *Your Grace—*
> *Thank you for your inquiry of yesterday.*
>   *The navy presently accepts some penal-indentured youths as sailor trainees, although most have come from coastal cities. Still, we do have supply barges that could transport such youths to Solis and would certainly accept youths receiving such sentences from justicers. Given the loss of sailors to the Jariolans, it would appear that such a punishment might well serve everyone's interests.*

Charyn took the letter, walked to Sanafryt's study, and handed it to him.

The Minister of Justice read it, nodded, and said, "This might help everyone."

"Then you'll make sure that all the youthful prisoners found guilty of destruction of factors' structures and goods receive such sentences in lieu of execution. If they're not guilty, however, I don't want this used as a means to create more sailors for Sea Marshal Tynan."

"I'll make that clear."

With that matter in Sanafryt's hands, Charyn decided to undertake drafting a response to Alyncya. That took a good glass before he was even halfway satisfied with what he had put to paper. He also wondered, absently, how differently Wyllum might cut the pens.

My dear Lady-heir Alyncya—
As always, your correspondence leaves me pondering questions that many would say are inquiries long-since settled by history, great philosophers, or even by the brute force of successful conquest. When questions involve living breathing people, each generation must find its own solutions while considering the accepted wisdom of the past and weighing it against the concerns and discoveries of the present.

You asked if there happened to be a special reason to call an act "evil," and I would reply that an act perpetrated for the specific purpose of inflicting pain and suffering deserves that appellation.

You also made the point that when a High Holder or factor improves the means of production through new devices or procedure that he pays the costs, and therefore should reap the rewards. I would also grant that when such happens the factor or High Holder also bears the risk, for not all changes work out. Even if he did provide the means to increase rewards, he would be still unable to realize those rewards without the workers, and, for that reason, I would submit that at least a small portion of the increased rewards should go to the workers. Yet it appears that, in practice, not only do the workers not receive small increases, but in many cases, those who are necessitated to work in such manufactorages because their former livelihoods have been destroyed now earn far, far less than before, while those owning such manufactorages have increased their earnings multifold.

The results of this disparity are now appearing with regularity, and I doubt that the strict application of existing laws will reduce such violence, that is, unless a veritable army of civic patrollers invests itself in every

area where large manufactorages exist. The cost of
such patrollers must fall upon someone, and since the
Treasury of Solidar has few reserves remaining at the
moment, any such army of enforcers of the law will, of
necessity, be paid by those with golds, either directly
or through their tariffs. If they choose not to pay, then
they will pay through continued events of destruction,
which will likely fall more greatly on smaller factorages
without the silvers to pay for adequate guards for their
facilities. Would it not be better, and likely less costly,
simply to pay workers slightly more?

Since I am neither factor nor High Holder, I may have
missed some crucial aspect of this situation, and, if I
have, I would honestly appreciate your enlightening me
in instances where my logic or facts are inadequate.

There is, however, one area upon which I may be
able to shed some light. According to the materials
in the rather capacious archive of the Rex, the Codex
Legis was written almost exclusively by two individuals,
Vaelora Chayardyr and Quaeryt Rytersyn, with close
to equal contributions to its content. What they created
was not amended or changed in the lifetimes of either
the first Rex Regis or his successor. Not only that, but
she was the sister of the first Rex Regis and served for a
number of years as his Minister of Administration. The
archives show that the Codex Legis still remains largely
as she and Quaeryt Rytersyn wrote it. He was an imager
who married her and became the first Maitre of the
Collegium Imago. Also interesting is the fact that Maitre
Alyna, one of the two most powerful imagers in Solidar,
and perhaps the world, is Vaelora's descendant.

With this historical note, I will close and await your
reply.

Finally, he signed and sealed it, then gave it to Moencriff
for dispatch.

29

On Solayi afternoon, Charyn, again attired as a guard undercaptain, rode to Imagisle with three guards, attended
services at the anomen there, enjoyed conversation and
refreshments at the Maitre's dwelling afterward, and then
rode back to the Chateau. It didn't appear that anyone even
gave him a second glance.

By Lundi morning, since he hadn't heard anything from
or about Chorister Saerlet, it also appeared that the chorister was still in hiding. *Or disregarding your order to come
to the Chateau.* Just to determine exactly which might be
the situation, Charyn asked Maertyl to send a few guards
to the Anomen D'Rex to see if Saerlet had returned or left
any word.

Wyllum appeared promptly at a quint before seventh
glass on Lundi morning. "What would you like me to do?"

"First, set yourself up at the end of the conference table
there. Then I'm going to give you several petitions to read,
just so you have a little understanding of what you'll be
copying. Once you've read through them, then I'll tell you
what to write." Charyn smiled. "Some of it will be rather
dull, I fear."

Charyn picked up the draft reply on the matter of the courier road bordering the property of High Holder Leomyk.
"This is what Minister Sanafryt drafted. Most of it is agreeable to me, with the exception of the third paragraph. I want
you to write down what I say, then I'll look at it, possibly
change it, and then you'll rewrite the reply with the change."

"Then what, sir?"

"Then it goes back to Minister Sanafryt so that he can

make sure that what I changed is in accord with the law as laid out in the Codex Legis. If it is, he returns it, and I sign and seal it, and you make another copy for the archives. That's so there's a record of decisions."

"Maitre Alastar does that, too."

"It makes sense." Even though Charyn wouldn't even have considered it two years earlier.

After spending a quint or so on that reply, Charyn then took Wyllum and introduced him to each of the three ministers, then returned to the study.

"For the moment, I'd like you to copy the lists on the corner of the desk. They're the people who've attended dinners here at the Chateau lately. The originals will go back to the files held by Lady Delcoeur D'Priora, who is also my aunt Elacia, and who is acting in place of my mother until she and my brother Bhayrn return from the Ryel holding in Rivages." Charyn quickly explained that situation and then added, "The reason I want copies is to be able to refresh my memory without disrupting either my aunt or my mother."

Once Wyllum was busy copying the lists, Charyn began to read Vaelln's latest report on the Jariolan situation, which remained essentially unchanged, and the completion of the shipyard buildings in Solis, two weeks ahead of schedule, although the keel on the first ship being built there would likely still not be laid until sometime in Feuillyt because the necessary amount of live oak timbers had not yet reached Solis.

At ninth glass, Maertyl entered the study. "Your Grace . . . about Chorister Saerlet. Assistant Chorister Faheel has heard nothing, nor has anyone else at the Anomen D'Rex."

"Thank you. I appreciate knowing that. Have you heard any more about either the True Believers or the attacks on the factorages?"

"No, sir."

"You might be interested to know that it is possible under the law to substitute penal naval indenture for execution for those under eighteen who have committed serious crimes, short of murder. Marshal Vaelln has agreed that the navy will accept such youthful offenders. I've told Minister Sanafryt to so instruct all justicers."

For a moment, Maertyl's face softened. "That's fairer for the young ones, I'd think."

"Not that they'll think any punishment is fair," returned Charyn, "but we can't accept burning buildings and destroying goods."

"No, sir."

"I'm still trying to work something out, but it's going to take time. That brings up something else. Would you have someone check to see if Argentyl has ever returned to L'Excelsis?"

"No one is likely to tell us anything, sir."

"You're right. Have someone ride by his shop to see if it's still closed up. If by chance he has returned, I'd like to see him."

"Yes, Your Grace. Is there anything else, sir?"

Charyn managed not to wince at Maertyl's even tone. "No. Thank you for letting me know about Saerlet."

Once the door to the study closed, Charyn turned to Wyllum. "There is one other thing . . ."

"Yes, sir?" Wyllum swallowed.

"What you hear in the Chateau stays in your head. Always. You may ask any questions you have of me when we're alone, but you may not speak to anyone else of what you hear. Is that clear?"

"Yes, sir."

"Good."

Wyllum resumed copying, and Charyn went back to reading the documents on his desk.

When the latest letter from his mother arrived, just after second glass, he immediately opened it.

Dear Charyn—
For a number of reasons, I have decided that we will
be leaving Ryel early on Jeudi, the fifth, several days
earlier than I had planned. With some good fortune, we
might arrive within a week, unless we linger at Vaestora,
although that is unlikely.

Bhayrn and I have talked over his situation, and
he feels you're being unjustly severe with him, given
the expertise of the regial landwarden at Lauckan.
Bhayrn has made some progress in his understandings
of the basics of a High Holding, enough that, under the
circumstances, perhaps you should consider removing
conditions for his assumption . . .

Charyn winced at those words, which essentially meant
that nothing either of them could do was going to change
Bhayrn.

I've had several delightful letters from Aloryana, who is
most pleased at your attentions and who has confirmed
what you told me about your efforts to become more
social. Elacia and I have exchanged several letters
about the invitations to the Autumn-Turn Ball, since
those need to be sent before I return to L'Excelsis. We've
gone over the invitation list and added a few young
ladies who should be invited by name, not only for you,
but for Ferrand, as well as a few suitable High Holder
heirs . . .

Why does that not surprise me? Part of that might well be
his mother's realization that adding more young women to
the specific list before Charyn made known any overt preference would also be a sound political move.

. . . I do believe it would be appropriate, and necessary,
for Palenya to be the clavecinist at the ball now that

she is firmly established as the Collegium musician.
That would also show a strengthened tie between the
Collegium and the Chateau D'Rex in another manner
besides the inclusion of Maitre Malyna and Maitre
Alastar and Maitre Alyna . . .

Charyn could also see both aspects of that, as well as the
veiled hint that he was going to continue to need the support
of the Collegium for more than the immediately foreseeable
future.

. . . would also suggest another dinner at the Chateau,
this one for all the members of the two councils, and
their wives, after the council meeting in Feuillyt,
and possibly one for the leading factors of L'Excelsis
sometime in Feuillyt as well. We can discuss these
when I return, but I think you should give the idea some
thought . . .

In short, it can't hurt, and it might well help. Charyn
smiled.

The smile faded as he considered the fact that his father
had never undertaken any such dinners.

30

Charyn rose slightly earlier on Mardi morning, not by intent, but because he worried that Maertyl was more withdrawn and seemed less and less pleased with what Charyn was doing, and after what had happened with the previous guard captain, all of the changes Charyn had made would be less effective, if not negated, with an unhappy head of the Chateau Guard.

Even so, he didn't want to jump to the wrong conclusions. So . . . once he was in his study, he sent for Maertyl and then dispatched Wyllum to Sanafryt's study with a note requesting that the minister explain the basics of law, in less than a glass, to the scrivener. The explanation wouldn't hurt Sanafryt and would certainly help Wyllum.

Then he waited for Maertyl. He didn't wait long.

The guard captain was, as always, prompt, entering with a slightly quizzical expression.

"You sent for me, Your Grace."

"I did." Charyn gestured to the chairs. "There are a few matters I'd like your thoughts about. It might take a while. First, thank you for finding out about Argentyl. I know it wasn't likely that he'd returned, but I did need to have you confirm that he is still hiding. That's another indication that matters won't get better soon." He looked to Maertyl. "Or am I mistaken?"

"No, sir, I don't think so."

"Do you have any more thoughts on who might have been behind the shooting that killed Staavyl?"

"I can't say that I do, sir."

"Maertyl," said Charyn with a calm he didn't feel, "the

imagers recommended you as guard captain. I agreed. You've been loyal. You've been hardworking. You've been effective, but something is bothering you. I suspect you're unhappy with either events that affect the Guard or the way in which I've handled matters . . . or in your view, the way I haven't handled things. I may be Rex, but I can't address a problem if all I know is that you're displeased or concerned, and you don't say anything."

"It's not my place—"

"It is your place," interrupted Charyn. "That's one of the unpleasant aspects of being guard captain. You're not here, but when I meet with the factors and the High Holders, I have to tell them things they don't want to hear, things like the fact that there aren't enough golds in the treasury to make all the repairs to the river walls that are necessary, or that we can't build ships faster to deal with the Jariolans, or that we have to reach an agreement on how factors and High Holders use stream and river water so that it's not unusable for whoever's downstream. That's part of what I have to do. Part of what you have to do is to let me know when there's a problem. Maybe I can change things. Maybe I can't, but I can explain why I can't, or maybe you have a better idea. I can't do any of that if you don't tell me what I don't know." Charyn kept his eyes fixed on Maertyl, but he managed a soft laugh, and added, "And we both know that there's much I don't know."

For several moments, Maertyl did not speak. Finally, he said, "You're the Rex, sir. You've tried hard to be better than . . . the others. You're fair. You work hard . . . there's not a man in the Guard that would gainsay that."

"But . . . ?" Charyn forced himself to wait.

"Some things, here in L'Excelsis . . ." Maertyl shrugged in a manner that suggested he was reluctant to say more.

"I understand. Times are changing. For some crafters and the workers, they seem to be getting worse, not better . . . and I get the sense you feel that, at times, maybe more often than that, I'm not doing enough . . . or that I should have done something else."

"It's not that, sir . . ."

Charyn nodded and waited.

". . . it's that . . . the men see their brothers or their cousins without much on their table. They see factors dressed in silvers and with golds in their wallets. They don't even see High Holders safe and well-fed behind their walls . . ."

"They see a Rex who can play a clavecin and have others for dinner, and who seems to do little for them . . . perhaps?"

Surprisingly, Maertyl shook his head. "No, sir. You take exercises. You try not to put others in danger. You do your best to take care of those here. It's not that . . ."

"It's that they don't see me doing enough for their brothers and cousins? Their sisters and their children?"

"You said, sir, about there not being enough golds . . . Is that really true?"

"Unhappily, it is. If you would like, I can have Minister Alucar explain to you why this is so—"

"Your word has always been good."

"I can tell you it is because neither the factors nor the High Holders wanted to pay more in tariffs. That was the reason for the High Holders' revolt. I did manage to get them and the factors to agree to pay more beginning this year, but I will not have those golds until close to the end of the year. The additional amount will not be that great, and most will have to go to building ships, because, without tin for bronze, spices, and other goods we will all be poorer . . ."

"I understand that, sir. What about wages for workers?"

"I'm trying to find a way to require factors and those who own manufactorages to pay at least a minimum daily wage. If it's high enough, then they won't use children—"

"You can change the law. You're the Rex."

"What happened when my sire tried to raise tariffs without getting some form of agreement? I recall when troopers loyal to the rebel High Holders attacked the Chateau. It wasn't that long ago. Both the crafters and workers and factors have problems. I'd prefer to work out something for both that doesn't lead to another revolt. The last time, the ones who suffered most weren't the High Holders. They weren't the factors. They were men like the guards. They were troopers."

"You make it sound impossible, sir."

"I don't think it is. It's just horribly difficult, and it takes time. With the help of Maitre Alastar, I did get them to agree to an increase in tariffs." He looked at Maertyl. "It only took the deaths of my father, much of my mother's family, and several guards, much less than the thousands who died in the revolt."

After another silence, Charyn said, "What do *you* think I should do?"

"Is that why you're entertaining High Holders and factors?"

"One of the reasons. Another is more personal. I do need to find a wife. Right now, the only even halfway reasonable heir to the Chateau is my brother. That's also a reason why I tend to be at least a little cautious about appearing in public. I doubt Bhayrn is ready to be Rex."

For an instant, Maertyl's face froze. Then he said, "I think many people haven't thought about that."

"Do you think," began Charyn, "that the greatest concern of the crafters and workers is pay?"

"Working conditions, too, sir."

"That will be harder to address."

"Might I ask, Your Grace . . . why you thought to talk to me? The real reason, that is?"

Charyn offered a wry smile. "Because I hate seeing that blank expression on your face that suggests that either I don't care or don't understand."

Charyn could see that the directness of his words had left Maertyl momentarily speechless.

"Ah . . . sir . . . I never meant . . . disrespect."

"Maertyl, it is a form of disrespect when you feel you

cannot tell me what you think. I understand that you don't want to correct me or tell me I've overlooked something in public. I don't want that, either. I'm still vain and sensitive about things like that. But all you have to say is something to the effect that you need a few moments with me or that you have some information I might find valuable."

"You really are trying to help the workers and crafters, aren't you?"

"I am, but I can't promise anything yet except that I'm trying. I'm also worried about the True Believers because they have a reason, at least in some cases, to be concerned about how their offerings are being spent." Charyn offered another rueful smile. "There are rather quite a few concerns that have been brought to my attention."

"I'm sorry, sir, that I've added—"

Charyn shook his head. "The problem is mine. I don't have the experience to see all that I should. I need you to let me know when I may have overlooked something. That's all I'm asking for."

Maertyl offered a smile in return. "I can do that, sir. Thank you."

"Since you're here," Charyn said, "why don't you give me a verbal report on how matters are going with the Guard, who's doing well, and what problems might come up, and what you think might be the best way to deal with them, should they occur . . ."

31

~~~~~~

Just before midmorning on Jeudi, Norstan peered into the study. "Your Grace?"

Charyn beckoned for the seneschal to continue.

"Factor Estafen is here to see you, sir. He says it's urgent."

"I'll always see him."

"I thought so," said the seneschal. "He's outside." He opened the door and stepped back.

The black-bearded banking factor stepped into the study. "I thought I'd best see you myself, Your Grace." Estafen glanced to Wyllum.

"If you'd go get something to eat in the kitchen, Wyllum."

"Yes, sir."

As soon as Wyllum was out the door, Charyn explained, "I've had to get a personal scrivener. There are just too many papers and documents. Now . . . you were saying . . ."

"It's Father. He was already ill, but last night, just as he was leaving the piers, he was attacked by several men. They beat him. They likely would have killed him, except that several of the unloading crew saw the attack and immediately ran to help him. The attackers fled. Between the flux and the beating, he's very ill. Maitre Alastar even sent Maitre Gaellen to tend to him, but . . . he's likely not going to last the week."

"Who beat him? Or who paid the men? Does he have any idea?"

"He said it could be other factors or workers, but . . ." Estafen paused. "I don't see that. Father's always paid his men better than the other factors do. He said they worked harder and better. The Civic Patrol is looking, but the attackers all wore something over their faces."

"Could they have attacked him because he's the chief factor on the Council?"

"That's always possible." Estafen's tone suggested neither agreement nor disagreement.

Charyn just stood there, silently, for a long moment. "I worried about him. The last few times I saw him, I asked him about that cough. He told me it was just a temporary consumption. I hoped it was. But to hear that he was attacked . . . that's something that I never expected."

"We didn't, either. He asked me to let you know."

"I've appreciated his advice and help more than I can say," said Charyn.

"He said you'd have made a good factor, Your Grace, that you were one, in fact." Estafen shook his head.

"Would it be untoward if I called on him immediately . . . or is he . . . ?"

Estafen smiled sadly. "He's still in his right mind, but he's so weak. If you . . ."

"I can go right now," declared Charyn.

"He'd like that, I think."

Less than half a quint later, the unmarked coach, with two guards in brown, rolled down the rear drive and followed Estafen's carriage along the Boulevard D'Ouest, across the Nord Bridge, and then east to where they turned west on Nordroad, before coming to a small mansion across from Hagahl Lane. There was enough space in the drive for both teams and coaches.

Charyn accompanied Estafen through the side entry and into a spacious hall.

A square-faced gray-haired woman dressed in pale blue frowned as the two approached.

"Mother, this is Rex Charyn. He's here to pay his respects to Father."

Charyn could see a definite jolt of surprise. "I owe him a great deal, and he should hear it from me."

"He spoke well of you, Your Grace. Your presence alone says why."

Charyn wasn't sure of that, but he wasn't about to argue.

"He's propped up in the sitting room. He says that if he can't die on his feet, he won't give the Namer the satisfaction of dying in bed. Maitre Gaellen is with him. Maitre Alastar left a little while ago."

The red-and-gray-haired Maitre Gaellen sat in the straight-backed chair set at a slight angle to the large arm-chair that held the ashen-faced factor, then rose as he saw Charyn. "Your Grace, I hadn't expected to see you here."

Charyn couldn't help but wonder how Gaellen knew who he was, and that must have showed on his face.

"I saw you at the Anomen D'Rex and asked Maitre Alyna."

Elthyrd looked to Estafen.

"You sent me to tell the Rex," said Estafen. "He insisted on returning with me."

A faint smile appeared on the old factor's bruised face. "A man . . . can't . . . do much better . . . than be . . ." A wrenching cough interrupted Elthyrd's words.

Charyn just waited.

". . . attended . . . by the Maitre . . . the Rex."

"Obviously," said Charyn, "I came as soon as I heard. I already worried about your consumption, but to hear you were attacked . . . I couldn't believe it."

"My health . . . wasn't what it should . . . have been. Tried to keep that . . . from others." Each word was accompanied by a labored wheezing. Elthyrd's eyes fixed on Estafen.

"Father's been worried that the High Holders will claim the factors have lost control of L'Excelsis and will demand that you use the army to stop the fires and destruction."

Elthyrd nodded assent to his son's words.

"I've already said that would be a bad idea." Charyn wasn't about to point out that executing all those who were found to be setting fires and destroying goods was also a bad idea. He didn't want to upset Elthyrd, not when he was deathly ill. "I'm trying to work out a better approach to stop the violence."

"Trust . . . Hisario . . . not Eshmael . . ."

Charyn looked to Estafen.

"Eshmael is most likely to be the one who will replace Father on the Factors' Council," explained the banking factor. "One of his manufactorages was burned. Just coincidentally, it was the oldest and least profitable, and its destruction will reduce Eshmael's tariffs."

Charyn recalled that Eshmael's name had been mentioned as losing a manufactorage to the destruction, but nothing about it being old and less profitable. He also recalled something that Alucar had explained. "Unlike the fact that the loss of a vessel won't, as I recall?"

Estafen looked slightly puzzled, but Elthyrd nodded.

"So Hisario doesn't trust Eshmael, either?" asked Charyn.

"He . . . doesn't," offered Elthyrd.

"Is there any other factor I should trust?"

"Cuipryn . . . he's a good man."

"Anyone else besides Eshmael I should beware of?"

"Noerbyn . . . too close to Eshmael . . ."

"I shouldn't be tariffing you with such," apologized Charyn. "I just came to offer my respects, and to tell you how much I've appreciated both your advice and your honesty. You've made my work as Rex much less difficult than it would have been otherwise."

"Helps that . . . you listen . . ."

Despite the effort it took Elthyrd to speak the words, they still held a wry tone.

"It would have been both discourteous and unwise for me not to listen." Charyn held up a hand. "You don't have to respond to everything I say. Your efforts made possible the compromise over tariffs, and that will allow us to build more warships to deal with the Jariolans, and that will benefit everyone in Solidar over time. You gave me early warning about the difficulty with the conflict over the artificers' standard and the pay of manufactorages' workers. And you kept confidences that allowed me to learn more about factoring than I believe any previous Rex has known. I appreciate all of that and more, and I wanted you to know that." *Too often we don't tell others what we appreciate when they're alive to hear it.* While Charyn's father had been anything but perfect, he had done his best, and he had loved his family, and with his sudden death, Charyn had never had that chance.

Elthyrd nodded slowly.

"I don't want to take any more of your time with Estafen and the rest of your family, but I did want to say a few words to you." Charyn inclined his head. "And, again, to thank you." He stepped back.

Estafen accompanied him out of the parlor.

Outside stood Elthyrd's wife. "You're leaving so soon, Your Grace?"

"Every word for him is an effort. Those words should be mostly for all of you. I did want to express my admiration and appreciation for all he's done, both for me as Rex and for Solidar."

"I thank you for coming."

"It's little enough for what he gave me. I wish I could do more for him."

"Do what you can for others. As he has done." She offered a faint smile before turning and entering the parlor.

Charyn took several steps down the hallway before asking Estafen, "How likely is Eshmael to replace your father as head of the Factors' Council?"

"Hisario will take over as the head of the Council. Whoever follows Father will represent the area of Bovaria. Most of the factors who've lost goods want Eshmael to take Father's place. The others favor Kathila."

"I didn't know there were women factors."

"She's one of the few, and she does a fair amount of business with the Imagisle factorage. Her daughter is also a maitre—Maitre Thelia."

It took Charyn a moment to recall exactly where he'd heard that name. "She handles the accounts for the Collegium, I think."

"That wouldn't surprise me," said Estafen.

"I am surprised that any factors would put her name forward." *Or any woman's, for that matter.*

"Only a few are. Others might, but none of them want to be seen as offering an alternative to Eshmael."

"Might I ask why?"

Estafen glanced around the seemingly empty hallway, then lowered his voice. "He holds grudges, and unfortunate occurrences have occurred to those who've opposed him." He offered a tight smile. "The same's true of Kathila, except those who had occurrences there, well, most folks thought they were deserved. People are wise not to cross either one, but I've never had any difficulties with Kathila. Neither has Maitre Alastar, I understand."

Unfortunately, that likely didn't mean as much for Charyn, since only a fool would play false with Alastar, and a woman who survived and prospered as a factor in L'Excelsis couldn't possibly be a fool. "Did your father mention that he might be crossing Eshmael?"

"He only said that Eshmael was cross with him for not pushing you to bring in the army immediately."

Would that be enough to try to kill or weaken Elthyrd? Charyn had no way of knowing.

Neither man spoke again until they were outside.

"Thank you again for coming," said Estafen as he stood by Charyn's coach.

"I wanted very much to come. Thank you for letting me know and giving me the opportunity."

"Father wanted you to know, and I can see why. Thank you, Your Grace."

Charyn could only incline his head in return.

As he rode back to the Chateau, he realized, again, just how much more difficult dealing with the joint council would be without Elthyrd's presence and strength of character. He also wondered who had been behind the factor's beating. Eshmael? Except that was so obvious. *But sometimes it is the obvious that's true.* As for who might replace Elthyrd . . . neither Eshmael nor Kathila sounded exactly ideal, at least not from Charyn's point of view.

32

Just after ninth glass on Solayi morning, Charyn had finished practicing "Variations on a Khellan Melody" and was leaving the music room when Undercaptain Faelln joined him as he walked toward the entry hall of the Chateau.

"Sir, a letter from Factor Estafen just arrived."

As he took the sealed letter, Charyn had a very good idea what was inside, given that it was Solayi. "You could have disturbed me. I was only practicing on the clavecin."

"It came a few moments ago. I waited for you to finish the piece, sir. It seemed a shame to disturb you over a few moments. I enjoyed hearing you finish it."

"If you're enjoying my practicing and misfingerings . . ." Charyn shook his head.

"Most of the guards and staff like to hear you play. There have been others whose playing they have not enjoyed."

Charyn knew who that was, but only said, "And one whose playing we all enjoyed."

"How is Musician Palenya faring, sir?"

"As you may recall, she is now the musician for the Collegium, and she is doing quite well. Aloryana is still taking lessons from her, as is Maitre Malyna. When Musician Palenya last tuned the clavecin, she spent some time improving my playing on my new pieces, and she will likely be playing with the players for the Autumn-Turn Ball." Charyn stopped and turned to face Faelln. "If this is what I think it is, we'll have to work out some way for me to attend the memorial service."

"You intend to go, sir?" Faelln's voice was without expression.

"Factor Elthyrd was of great assistance to me. He was also the head of the Factors' Council. We didn't always agree, but I respect him, and I believe I should show that respect."

"Then we'll manage, sir. If you would let us know of the time and place."

"I will. Thank you."

"My pleasure, sir."

Charyn had a thought, one he should have come up with earlier. "Oh . . . Faelln . . . there is one other matter. Have you or Captain Maertyl had someone watching the area around the Chateau to see if someone is keeping track of who is coming and going?"

"Yes, sir." Faelln paused. "The captain posted someone starting the morning after Staavyl was shot. There's always someone looking during the daylight glasses. We haven't seen anyone watching for any length of time, or different people watching from the same spot, or close to it. There are only certain places along the Ring Road where a watcher can see all who come and go. Well . . . except for the windows in some buildings."

"You'll let me know if you do start to see watchers like that?"

"Yes, sir."

"Thank you."

Charyn did not open the letter until he was alone in his study, since Wyllum did not work on Samedi afternoons or on Solayi. Estafen's short missive said exactly what he thought it would, with the exception of two lines which said that a memorial service would be on Meredi the eleventh of Erntyn and that Charyn was welcome to join the family at the Anomen D'Nord.

Leaving the letter on the table desk, Charyn walked to the window, from which a slight breeze issued. Outside, the sky was hazy with heat, but without clouds.

He was going to miss Elthyrd—and would have even without the problems created by the conflict generated by the growth of manufactorages, the ever-increasing number of wealthy factors, and the problems of too many poorly managed High Holdings. *One of which is likely to be that of your own brother before too long.*

At the same time, he was somewhat concerned about attending the memorial service, although Charyn *thought* that Faelln agreed with the necessity of his presence.

The other problem he faced was the need to do more entertaining after Autumn-Turn, when the more social time of year began. *Perhaps more than the small dinners for High Holders and the wealthier factors?* And a word to Maertyl about the necessity of those dinners wouldn't hurt.

What with one thing and another, it was slightly after fifth glass when Charyn rode out from the Chateau toward Imagisle, once more wearing a guard undercaptain's uniform, and accompanied by four other guards, one more than earlier, just in case. He again took the longer route, the one that did not pass the Anomen D'Rex, although he did wonder how former assistant chorister Faheel was doing in replacing Saerlet.

Most likely, just fine. Charyn just hoped he was trying to look a bit behind the myths about Rholan.

When he reached the Maitre's house, he didn't see anyone immediately. So he and the guards rode back to the stable and dismounted there; then he started to walk back to the house. He was halfway there when Aloryana appeared.

"I wasn't sure you'd be coming. You usually send a letter."

"I'm sorry, but last week I said I would be."

"I told you he'd be here," added Lystara as she joined Aloryana.

"You don't have to be sorry. I'm just glad you're here. You do look good in that uniform," said Aloryana.

"You look good in imager gray," returned Charyn. "How are you coming with your shields?"

"Better. A little stronger." She sighed. "I can't become a

third, though, not until they're strong enough to stop two bullets."

"You said you could stop one."

"I can, but stopping one tears my shields apart, and I can't get them back together fast enough." At Charyn's almost horrified expression, she went on. "The Maitres don't shoot at any of us. Not directly, I mean. I stand behind a stone barrier and extend my shield a little bit over a target. It still hurts, though."

"She's getting better at rebuilding them," said Lystara. "She's very good at concealments, though."

"Maybe you should also practice how fast you can create shields," offered Charyn. "That is, if Maitre Lystara or Maitre Alastar haven't already suggested that."

"They both have," said Aloryana, her voice almost woeful.

"It's not the same, I know," said Charyn, "but it's taken me almost a year to learn how to draw and fire a pistol accurately and quickly. I got very frustrated, even furious. What you're doing is much more difficult than that."

"Do you practice that?" asked Lystara. "Really shooting when you do?"

"Once a week, usually." He laughed softly. "I'm not an imager. I hope I don't ever have to use the pistol that way again, but being able to do that has saved my life twice. One of those times, though, I needed the help of an imager."

"Howal?" asked Aloryana.

Charyn nodded. "I'd likely be dead without him."

"He's in Estisle now," said Lystara.

Although Charyn recalled that, he just nodded, since Alastar and Alyna had left the Maitre's house and were walking toward them.

"You know about Elthyrd . . ." began Charyn.

Alastar nodded.

"Do you have any idea who might have been behind the attack?"

"The only ones I know of who might benefit immediately are his son Thyrand and Factor Eshmael. Thyrand isn't that sort, not in the slightest. Eshmael is, but I find it hard to believe that he'd be so obvious."

"But would most people think a beating is the same as an outright killing?" asked Charyn. "Maybe the point wasn't to kill him. Not outright, anyway."

"That's a good question. I hadn't thought of it quite that way." Alastar paused. "We can talk about this later." Then with a broad smile, Alastar gestured toward the anomen and began to walk, saying, "Your presence may flatter Iskhar too much."

"More likely worry him to death," countered Alyna. "Having the two of you listening would worry any sane chorister."

"Speaking of that . . ." began Alastar.

"Saerlet hasn't returned or sent word. I don't know anything more about the True Believers."

"Unfortunately, I do. There was a protest last Solayi in Villerive. The True Believers tied up the chorister and weighted him with stones before they threw him in the river. Then they vanished. The Civic Patrol there found a chest filled with silvers hidden in his quarters."

"I can't say that surprises me," replied Charyn. "I hadn't realized it was such a problem until I inspected Saerlet's wardrobe, and discovered he was paying both an assistant and a valet, and that was in addition to the assistant chorister. I always wondered about Saerlet, but I didn't do anything. Now . . ." He shrugged helplessly. "If I make a law about choristers, it will seem like I'm trying to take control of the anomens to get their golds, and if I don't, then people will say I don't care. If I merely say something, then I'll be attacked for only spouting words."

Alastar nodded. "You've thought about it, clearly. So have the True Believers. Of course, none of it would be happening if so many choristers hadn't gotten so greedy. But they obviously thought no one was watching or cared. Because anomens and choristers don't pay tariffs, not even the Rex knew what their offerings brought in."

"Tariffing them certainly wouldn't be a good idea," said Charyn.

"No," said Alastar agreeably, "it wouldn't."

Charyn laughed. "What are you suggesting that I'm obviously not understanding?"

"It's not the payment that counts here. It's that people didn't know."

"So I should enact a law that requires choristers to publish an accounting of their offerings and what they spend it on? That won't work unless there's some way . . ." Charyn broke off. "Fraud! If the accounts published to the congregation are fraudulent . . ."

"That might work. In any event, it might get people to think."

"Is that what Iskhar has to do?"

"He's responsible to the Maitre," said Alyna.

All of which brought home to Charyn that neither he nor his father had ever exercised such oversight—or if his father had, there was no record of it. *Another problem to address.* He managed not to sigh.

Not for the first time, he was beginning to wonder how Solidar had held together as long as it had . . . and, looking at the Maitre, he suspected he knew part of the reason. He also had the feeling that what had sufficed in the past might not work in a changing future.

He tried not to dwell on that as he and Aloryana entered the anomen.

As he took his place, standing beside the Maitre at the side of the anomen near the front, he realized that his presence seemed only to draw passing glances. *The Maitre's doing . . . or just acceptance?*

He wondered what Iskhar might say in his homily and then wished he hadn't, because Iskhar launched into a homily on a subject that already worried Charyn.

". . . reports from several places in Solidar that a people calling themselves the True Believers are attacking ano- mens and choristers because they feel those choristers are not teaching the true beliefs of the Nameless. Beliefs about the Nameless, or any Deity, by their nature, cannot be true or false. For something to be proved true or false, we must have physical evidence. We have no physical proof that the Nameless exists nor do we have proof that the Nameless does not exist. We have physical proof that Terahnar exists, and we have observed the moons long enough to know they exist . . . but we have no proof that the Nameless imaged them into being . . ."

From there Iskhar went on at more length than Charyn would have liked about beliefs often verging on childlike wish fulfillment, and he was glad when he and Aloryana walked out into the somewhat cooler early-evening air, heading back to the Maitre's house.

Charyn just listened as Aloryana told him about her week.

Abruptly, she asked, "When will Mother be back in L'Excelsis?"

"Sometime this week, she said in her last letter. I'd guess late on Mardi or Meredi, but no later than Jeudi."

"Good. Is Bhayrn coming, too?"

"She wrote that he was."

Aloryana nodded.

Less than a quint later, Charyn was enjoying a goblet of white wine in the Maitre's parlor when Alastar turned to him and said, "Maitre Gaellen told me that you paid your respects to Elthyrd last Jeudi. That was the last day he was alert. He never really woke up on Vendrei, according to Maitre Gaellen, just slept and got weaker."

"I didn't know that it would be quite that soon, but I feared I'd be too late if I waited."

"You were right. Are you planning to attend the memorial service?"

"I'd thought I would."

"In disguise, I presume?"

"How else?"

"I think you should go, in the formal mourning garb of the Rex." Alastar held up a hand. "Alyna and I would be more than glad to share our coach with you. The three of us together would make a stronger presence."

Charyn appreciated the indirect offer of protection. "Thank you. I'd be glad to accept."

Alyna smiled. "He wouldn't have offered if you hadn't decided to take the risk of going unshielded."

"I do owe Elthyrd more than I can ever afford to admit publicly."

"We both do," said Alastar dryly. "I fear we'll miss him too soon and too much."

Charyn nodded to that and took another swallow of the wine.

When Charyn left Imagisle, half a glass later, he and the guards used the east bridge, but so far as he could tell, no one noticed. He was relieved when he was back in the Chateau, he had to admit.

33

By Meredi morning, while Lundi and Mardi had been uneventful with no more violence by disgruntled crafters or
workers, or by the True Believers, Charyn wasn't terribly
optimistic that the calm would continue, especially since
Veritum had reported the capture of three more men accused
of setting fires.

Vaelln had sent another report to Charyn saying that it appeared more Jariolan warships were sailing toward the Abierto Isles in an effort to block the various ports on the Isles
to Solidaran shipping and that Sea Marshal Tynan had sent
two more first-rate ships of the line and several others to
bolster the Solidaran fleet already in the area. That was not
a surprise, but a large naval battle was bound to be costly,
even if Tynan's fleet was victorious. Yet given the continuing depredations by Jariolan privateers and warships on
Solidaran merchant shipping, Charyn didn't see that there
was any real choice.

Then there was the problem of the True Believers. Saerlet was still in hiding . . . or dead, although Charyn had the
feeling that Saerlet was too wily for the True Believers, unless the chorister had just been unfortunate. He'd also heard
nothing more from Paersyt, but all the refinements that the
engineering factor had mentioned would take far more time
than the less than two weeks since Paersyt's last report.

Elacia was in her study, working out details for dinners
later in Erntyn and in Feuillyt, with recommendation of who
should attend.

Sanafryt was working on language that would require

choristers to post the totals of offerings and expenditures in a place open to their congregants within a week after the end of each season and to make failure to post subject to a penalty for the first offense, a stronger penalty for the second offense, and possible imprisonment for a third, with significant financial discrepancies subject to charges of fraud. The Justice Minister had not been happy with Charyn's request, and even less pleased when Charyn had suggested that if he wasn't happy that he should come up with a better idea to deal with so many greedy choristers that they had inspired a religious uprising of sorts—which was scarcely helpful when Charyn was already trying to deal with the other problem of hungry workers and factors locked into keeping pay low because their competitors did.

On top of that, Charyn hadn't received any response to his last letter to Alyncya. Given the fact that he'd written and dispatched his last letter more than ten days earlier, the lack of a response was worrisome.

She could be traveling again. Except she'd never mentioned that. *She did suggest, more than once and in various ways, that you were rushing matters.* But Charyn hadn't even suggested courtship, only wanting to know more about her. *Isn't that courtship?*

He turned from the window, only half open because, for the first time in weeks, the sky held thin gray clouds, from which fell intermittently a desultory drizzle, walked back to the desk, and picked up Mardi's edition of *Veritum,* reading again the article on Elthyrd, factual and largely measured. Then he lowered that newssheet to the desk and picked up *Tableta,* his eyes picking out the comparatively mild jabs.

Elthyrd D'Factorius, noted timber and rope factor, and the head of the Factors' Council of Solidar, died on Solayi after a short illness that was worsened by a reported beating by unknown assailants last week . . . known to be one of the least unfair factors in what he paid workers and in providing adequate working conditions . . . considered honest by the standards of factors . . .

The accompanying story suggested why the writers of *Tableta* were comparatively restrained in their treatment of Elthyrd.

. . . no recent reports of attacks against factors and their manufactorages in the past few days . . . early word is that the Factors' Council is leaning toward the replacement of Elthyrd with Eshmael D'Factorius, one of the factors reported to demand the most out of his workers and to pay them the least . . . Eshmael's selection is likely to be condemned by all the crafting guilds . . . if Eshmael is confirmed this newssheet would not be surprised to see attacks against the most oppressive factors to redouble in the days and weeks ahead . . .

If that isn't a barely veiled threat, I've never seen one. And from what Charyn had seen of the factors, it was more likely, not less, to result in the Factors' Council picking Eshmael. That would only make Charyn's efforts more difficult.

At ninth glass Charyn made his way to the front entry of the Chateau D'Rex. He wore the same attire as he had for his father's memorial service, formal regial greens without insignia, and a black-trimmed green mourning sash.

Maertyl met him at the entry. "I'm glad you're going with Maitre Alastar, sir."

"That makes two of us."

"Do you think there will be violence at the memorial service?"

"At the service? I don't think so. Afterwards, it might be possible. If anyone wants to take a shot at me, I'd say that it would be then. Before a memorial service wouldn't help anyone's cause because it would be considered not only hurtful to the mourners but also a form of Naming. At least, I'd think so." Charyn shook his head. "But when people are hungry and angry, habits set by manners and tradition can vanish quickly."

"Even *Tableta* showed Factor Elthyrd some respect."

"They were easier on him than they've been on me or most factors."

"People don't realize . . . well . . . that even the Rex can't change things alone."

That, Charyn knew, was an apology, one best acknowledged indirectly. "You're right. Some do, but most don't. Part of the job of a Rex is to work things out so that everyone thinks he is working for everyone's good, and not just for the High Holders or the factors . . . or even just for the crafters. That's the hardest part. At least, it seems that way to me. That was one of the reasons I kept meeting with Craftmaster Argentyl. If I'd known earlier what I know now, I would have worked more with him much earlier. But it's so much easier to see where you should have gone once you've walked to the edge of a cliff with mountain cats creeping up around you."

At that moment, Charyn caught sight of the gray and silver coach. "If you have any thoughts about that, I'd like to hear them later. Either late today or in the morning."

"I'll think about it, Your Grace."

"Good. I look forward to hearing what you have to say." After a nod to Maertyl, Charyn made his way down the white stone steps to the waiting coach, which he entered.

"Good morning," offered Alastar.

"The same to you . . . and my thanks. You're going well out of your way to take me with you," said Charyn as he settled into the rear-facing seat in the gray and silver coach.

"It's not that far," replied Alastar.

"By that," replied Charyn with a wry smile, "I take it you mean it's a slight inconvenience compared to the difficulties of dealing with yet another Rex."

"That's almost exactly what he means." Alyna punctuated her words with an amused smile. "Especially since the only remaining trustworthy members of the regial family are a fourteen-year-old imager and the widow of the previous Rex."

"I didn't realize you had such a high opinion of my current heir," replied Charyn.

"Do you dispute that opinion?" returned Alyna, her voice amused, but scarcely cheerful.

"No, but I would be interested in knowing how you came to that opinion."

"By observation, by listening," said Alastar, "and by your brother's choice of friends."

"Which ones do you take exception to?" asked Charyn.

"I'm not aware of anything terribly prurient about any of them, but neither am I aware of any outstanding qualities in any of them."

"And their families?"

"The same of them. I do believe that Ghaermyn is as greedy as the most grasping of factors and that Laastyn may be extended more than is wise in his efforts to increase his lands, as Ghaermyn appeared to be a decade or so ago."

"Has Laastyn borrowed to do so?" asked Charyn, thinking about Ferrand's father, although the late High Holder Delcoeur had borrowed to enable his gambling, not to buy lands.

"Not that I'm aware, but taking on distressed lands, which are usually those available at an apparently reasonable price, often results in unforeseen costs."

Charyn had been aware that Laastyn had bought timberland in Tilbor, but not that he was buying lands continually, only that he seemed to have quite a number of holdings in different places. "I don't think I've said much, except that Bhayrn doesn't seem to want to learn about being a High Holder."

"That says a great deal in itself," replied Alyna. "If he

can't be bothered to learn that, can he be counted on to learn what a Rex needs to know?"

"Also," said Alastar, "Bhayrn has never sent Aloryana a single letter, nor ever visited, although she still writes him occasionally. You never failed to write her at least once a week. You visited frequently, and recently you've made much greater efforts. Character isn't just measured by large deeds. All deeds count."

Charyn had to nod at that, but he also felt guilty that he hadn't visited Aloryana as much as he should have in her first months at the Collegium.

As the coach crossed the Nord Bridge, Charyn glanced down at the River Aluse, noting that the water level had dropped considerably. *Possibly enough for repairs to the river walls?*

The Anomen D'Nord was roughly some five blocks north of Elthyrd's small mansion, and as the coach came to a stop, Charyn saw that there was almost a squad of civic patrollers spaced out in front of the building. All of them wore black mourning sashes.

With them were two mounted imagers in gray, one woman and one man.

"You sent maitres in case of problems?"

Alastar nodded. "Charlina and Belsior. They're Maitres D'Structure. They both have strong shields. Charlina has other strengths as well. It seemed like a good idea, and it also will give them some experience."

As Alastar reached to open the coach door, Charyn asked, "Are you expecting trouble here?"

"It's a possibility." Alastar opened the door, stepped out, and nodded to Alyna.

Charyn followed the pair from the coach to the stone wall leading to the anomen and from there inside the anomen, which possessed a nave perhaps two-thirds the size of the Anomen D'Rex. The small crowd parted for the two maitres, then even more as they saw Charyn.

Alastar moved to the left side of the nave, where he and
Alyna took a position with their backs to the wall. That
didn't surprise Charyn, who stood beside Alyna.

Both imagers surveyed the mourners, who numbered several hundred, even at close to half a quint before the glass.
Charyn did the same, not that he could have done much,
even if someone pointed a pistol at him, except to draw and
fire in return. *And run the risk of shooting someone else.* It
was far wiser to trust in Maitre Alyna's shields.

A small choir, located in a loft above the right side of the
nave, began the service with a sung invocation, followed by
a spoken one from a tall chorister with a powerful baritone
voice.

Charyn paid more attention to the mourners, finally locating Estafen, standing beside a dark-haired woman, likely his
wife, with his mother on his other side. Beyond Elthyrd's
wife was another couple, the man being most likely Thyrand, who would inherit the timber factorage, from what
Estafen had indicated.

When the time came for someone to speak for the family,
Estafen was the one who stepped forward and onto the dais.
For a moment, he just stood there. Then he began.

"My father did not inherit a High Holding. He did not
inherit a factorage. When he began, he started with a leaky
barge and a flatboat he'd built himself. He knew what working with his hands meant. That's why he paid anyone who
worked for him what they were worth. That's why he didn't
keep those who wouldn't work as hard as he did. He taught
each of us the value of work . . . and the worth of those who
worked with their hands. Every one of us spent years working as laborers on boats and docks or with timbering crews.
His honesty and his hard work earned him admiration, from
those who worked for him, with him, or against him. Yet
he liked people and was willing to help almost anyone who
honestly wanted his advice. He loved and took care of his
family and those who worked for him. To the last day of

his life he had friends who still worked with their hands, friends who had coins, and those who did not. He never forgot friends, and he treated them each the same. No one who truly knew him would be surprised by those with whom he shared time and confidences. Those who did not know would likely be astounded. He took people as they were, and they took him as he was. I'd be honored if anyone could say half that of me when my time comes . . ."

When Estafen stepped off the dais, the anomen was silent for several moments before the chorister stepped up to the pulpit and offered the closing thanks for the life and spirit of Elthyrd, at the end of which the women let the mourning scarves slip from their hair.

Charyn realized that Alyna had not worn a mourning scarf, but rather a mourning sash, as had Charyn and Alastar.

The closing hymn was traditional—"For the Glory"— and after the echoes of the last words faded away, Charyn looked to Alastar. The Maitre did not move. Neither did Alyna. So Charyn stayed put. Almost a quint passed before the majority of the mourners left, and then Estafen, his wife, and his mother eased toward the three standing by themselves on the left side of the nave.

"You honored him," said Estafen. Then he looked to Charyn in particular. "I was surprised to see you here, Your Grace."

"For all that he gave me," replied Charyn, "how could I not have come? Also, for what you have given me."

"We still appreciate all of your presences," said Elthyrd's wife. "Thank you."

"Oh . . ." said Estafen. "Might I introduce my wife Zairleya? Maitre Alastar, Maitre Alyna, and Rex Charyn."

Zairleya looked stunned at Charyn's name, murmuring, "You never said . . ."

"I'm sorry. I thought you knew."

Zairleya looked sideways at her husband and raised her eyebrows.

Estafen flushed. "I am sorry."

Charyn smiled at the dark-haired woman. "He didn't know I was coming. That was my fault, not his. Don't blame him for my failings."

For a moment, Zairleya smiled at her husband, even as she shook her head almost ruefully.

"We won't keep you," said Alastar, "but we did want a few words without intruding."

"You were anything but intrusive," said Estafen, "and we appreciate your thoughtfulness."

Alastar gestured for Estafen and his wife and mother to lead the way from the anomen, then moved after them, if walking more slowly than he usually did, so that the gap between the two groups widened. Charyn wondered about that, but only until he stepped out into the still-cloudy afternoon, although the drizzle had faded away.

As soon as the three stepped outside the anomen, the red-haired Maitre Charlina rode up and reined in her mount a yard or so from Alastar. "About fifty True Believers formed up a little after the service began. Belsior and I used shields and just herded them away from the anomen. One or two tried to go around us, but we held, and they finally gave up and went away."

Belsior, who had reined up behind Charlina, added, "Some of them ran when I said that they could either leave or get arrested by the civic patrollers."

"Were there any rifles?" asked Alastar.

"We didn't see any, and there weren't any shots."

"Good. Once we're in the coach, you two can return to Imagisle," declared Alastar. "Thank you for taking care of things."

"Our pleasure, Maitre," replied Charlina.

When the three were seated and the coach was headed toward the Nord Bridge, Charyn asked Alastar, "You expected the True Believers, didn't you?"

"At the memorial service of the most well-known and visible factor in L'Excelsis? It was very likely. I didn't want them to spoil the service for Elthyrd's family."

"Did you also expect someone to shoot at me?"

"I thought it possible. The fact that someone didn't suggests that either no one knew you were coming or that the shooter has nothing to do with the True Believers."

"That could be both, or neither," suggested Alyna.

Alastar laughed. "She keeps me from jumping to conclusions. She's more for reasoned logic than I am, but that could be her mathematical mind."

Once Charyn returned to the Chateau, after thanking the maitres and watching them leave for Imagisle, he immediately made his way to his study.

Waiting for him was the draft language from Sanafryt dealing with choristers. He began to read.

In the interests of reassuring congregants of any religion as to how their dues, tithes, contributions, and gifts have been employed by choristers, or other religious functionaries charged with the collection, use, and disbursement of such funds, or of any of those functions, it is hereby decreed that within fifteen days after the end of each season, the chorister, or other such functionary, shall post . . .

While the initial premise was what Charyn wanted, the sections that followed contained definitions and conditions, all of which Charyn understood were necessary to keep choristers from finding ways around the main provisions. *Which some of them will definitely try.* And some, he knew, would just post fraudulent numbers and get away with it. *But this will give people a tool, at least.*

"Your Grace," called Sturdyn from outside the study door, "Lady Chelia and Lord Bhayrn have returned, with Karyel and Iryella."

Charyn immediately left the study and hurried down the grand staircase to welcome everyone back to the Chateau, not that he was that enthused about most of the returnees.

No sooner had Bhayrn stepped inside the main foyer than he looked at Charyn and demanded, "Who died? Was it Maitre Alastar? You're wearing formal mourning clothes. One of the guards said you'd just come back in an imager coach—"

"Factor Elthyrd died. He was head of the Factors' Council. I went to his memorial service. Maitre Alastar offered his coach and his protection."

"For a mere factor? You lowered yourself to that?"

"For a factor who was head of the Factors' Council and who was one of the few levelheaded ones. Yes, I went. And I accepted Maitre Alastar's protection because, as I wrote Mother, the last time I went to services in my own coach, I nearly got shot, and would likely be dead if it hadn't been for Maitre Lystara . . ."

"You should have the guards shooting them, not being the one shot," said Bhayrn disgustedly.

"That's not a good idea when you don't know who's shooting or from where. You just kill innocent people and make even more people mad at you. The madder they get, the more of them there are likely to take shots." From the corner of his eye, he saw his mother, directing Karyel and Iryella up the grand staircase.

"Not if they get shot first. That will tell them not to do it again. I still don't see why you had to go to a mere factor's memorial service."

"Because he wasn't a mere factor, and because he was helpful in getting tariffs raised, for one thing. Besides, if I hadn't, it would only make dealing with the other factors harder."

"Don't deal with them. You're the Rex. Tell them what to do."

"Just where did that get Father and Grandfather?"

"You're simple and soft, Charyn."

Before Charyn could reply, Bhayrn turned and headed up the grand staircase.

Chelia looked at her older son with a wearily rueful expression. "I'm sorry to hear about Factor Elthyrd's death. That will make matters more difficult for you."

"I'm glad you understand that. Bhayrn certainly doesn't."

"He understands what he wishes to understand."

"It must have been a long trip back," said Charyn wryly.

"It's not too bad if we don't talk about factors or most High Holders."

"What does he think a Rex can actually do?" asked Charyn.

"What they used to do, years and years ago." Chelia sighed. "If you'll excuse me, dear, it has been a long trip, and I'd like to freshen up and rest a little before dinner."

"I'm sorry. I didn't mean to keep you."

"I know."

Charyn followed his mother up the stairs, then turned and made his way back to his study. He hoped Bhayrn would be in a better mood later, but wasn't counting on it.

34

After doing his exercises and other morning efforts, when Charyn reached the breakfast room on Jeudi morning, he was more than a little surprised to find Bhayrn already there, with a beaker of lager, particularly since Bhayrn had avoided dinner with Charyn and their mother and left the Chateau for a time the evening before. According to Maertyl, the two guards accompanying him had said that he'd gone to High Holder Laastyn's estate just north and west of the Nord Bridge and returned fairly early.

"Oh . . . good morning," Charyn offered warily.

"Charyn, I'm sorry that I was so short with you last night. It was a very long ride yesterday, especially with Karyel, but Mother really wanted to get home." Bhayrn took a swallow of lager. "And every time I hear about things like people shooting at you, or these worthless workers burning factorages, I get even more upset."

"I tend to get upset as well," replied Charyn as he settled into his chair, definitely wondering about Bhayrn's shift in attitude from the night before. "That was one reason I went to Elthyrd's memorial service. He'd been helpful when few were, and his death is likely going to make things harder."

"Why don't the factors patrol their factorages and warehouses?"

"Some of them do, and they've been offering rewards." Charyn turned to Therosa as she set a mug of tea before him. "Thank you." Then he turned back to Bhayrn. "The Civic Patrol is beginning to catch some of those responsible."

"They should shoot them all."

"The ones who are eighteen or younger will likely end up as indentured sailors for ten years on a navy warship."

"That's too easy," said Bhayrn as Therosa set one platter before him and another before Charyn.

"Perhaps," said Charyn, "but with all the ships lost to the Jariolans, it's a way to get more sailors, and it also means we're not executing seventeen-year-old boys. Executing men that young upsets people. This way—"

"The navy gets cannon fodder, and the Rex isn't attacked as much. That makes sense. I understand that. I don't understand why burning down manufactorages will help people who barely make enough as it is. Destroying places where they can work just means fewer of them can make enough to live. I also don't understand those True Believers. What difference does it make what Rholan said hundreds of years ago?"

"That's a good question," replied Charyn. "From what I can tell, they believe that the choristers are filling their own wallets, rather than helping the poor, and, at the same time, are preaching homilies that are telling the poorer workers that everything is all right." He took several mouthfuls of the cheesed eggs, then a bite of the fried ham slice.

"It was all right until everyone got greedy," said Bhayrn. "The rebel High Holders got greedy. The factors got greedy. Then the workers and crafters got greedy, and they all blamed Father, and now they're blaming you for everything they think has gone wrong." He turned to his breakfast and ate several mouthfuls before asking, "What are you going to do about it? It doesn't seem like anyone agrees with anyone else."

"They don't. It seems to me that, if the factors all paid workers just a little bit more, most of the workers wouldn't be so angry, and that everyone would be better off."

"Until the workers got greedy again."

"What do Laamyst and his family think?" asked Charyn.

"High Holder Laastyn thinks the factors should handle matters so that the workers and crafters don't cause trouble."

"Did he say how?"

Bhayrn shook his head. "I don't know. That was how Laamyst said his father felt. He said that they'd caused the problem, and they needed to fix it. The rest of Solidar shouldn't be dragged into it."

Charyn could definitely see High Holders feeling that way. "Unhappily, people want me to fix it."

"You could tell the factors that they caused it, and tell them to fix it."

Charyn laughed ruefully. "That wouldn't help matters, but . . . I could tell them that the workers and much of the country felt they'd caused it, and ask them what they intend to do about it."

"You ought to take a stronger position. Tell them to fix it."

"I'll think about it." Charyn wasn't about to demand anything. Not yet, anyway.

"You're meeting with the councils next Meredi?"

Charyn nodded.

Bhayrn started to say something, then stopped. After a long pause, he said, "Do think about it."

"I will." That Charyn could promise. He finished the last of the eggs and asked, "Are you glad to be back in L'Excelsis?"

"Very glad. Can I take the unmarked coach later? Laamyst and I were thinking of visiting Gherard."

"Gherard D'Ghaermyn? Has he talked to you about the factorages?"

"Why do you ask?"

"I had his father and several other local High Holders to a dinner two weeks ago. Ghaermyn has several manufactorages himself. I wondered if you knew how he felt about the problems with factorages?"

"I've never talked about that with Gherard. His sister . . ."

Bhayrn shook his head again. "She's much more my type than Laamyst's sisters and cousins."

"Has Mother given you—"

"The lecture on propriety? At least twice . . ."

When Charyn left the breakfast room, and in passing Karyel and Iryella, who were about to enter it, he still wondered what exactly had resulted in Bhayrn's total change of attitude. It had to be something his friends had said, since Bhayrn clearly wasn't listening to either Charyn or their mother. He also wondered why Bhayrn hadn't talked about the factoring problems with Gherard, when he clearly had with Laamyst. So he made his way to his mother's sitting room, suspecting, since she usually ate early, that she'd asked for breakfast in her rooms, rather than deal with Bhayrn, Karyel, and Iryella, especially after spending every moment traveling with them for roughly a week.

Chelia was sipping the last of her tea, it appeared, when Charyn entered and sat down across from her. She smiled. "How are you this morning?"

"Much better. Bhayrn and I actually had a pleasant conversation this morning. I couldn't believe he was the same person as yesterday afternoon."

"What changed him? Where did he go last night?"

"High Holder Laastyn's. I imagine it was to see Laamyst and tell him how stupid his brother the Rex was."

"It sounds like Laamyst talked some sense into him." Chelia smiled sardonically. "Apparently, that's something that neither of us is able to do. Bhayrn would rather hear sense—or nonsense—from friends than anything from family."

Charyn had his doubts about Laamyst changing Bhayrn. More likely Laamyst had suggested Bhayrn humor his brother as a means to get his own way . . . and to keep Charyn from withholding a High Holding. "Do you know much about High Holder Ghaermyn?"

"Outside of the name . . . very little. Your father and my brother thought he was a come-lately not worth knowing, a man whose forebears parlayed small factorages and ill-paid workers into enough coins to buy near-worthless lands. At times, they have struggled to hold on to everything, although it's said that the current High Holder is . . . shall we say, shrewd." Chelia offered another sardonic smile. "The family has only been High Holders for four generations. And Lady Ghaermyn is an Aishford."

Charyn raised his eyebrows.

"The Aishfords have been struggling for years to remain as High Holders."

"Hasn't that become a problem for more than a few families?"

"If you were a High Holder, you wouldn't have that problem. Unless Bhayrn changes, his children will . . . unless he marries very, very well."

"What about Karyel?"

"I suspect he'll do very well. So will Iryella. It's a good thing she's your close cousin, otherwise she'd be setting her eyes on you or Bhayrn."

"She just turned twelve."

"A wife eight years or so younger isn't unheard of." Chelia's tone was amused. "And she's already interested in power. Everyone in that family is."

"You're in that family," Charyn pointed out gently.

"I said everyone. I meant everyone," replied Chelia. "There were just some things I wouldn't do . . . unlike my father, brothers, and sister."

"You're the only one left alive, aren't you?"

"Of my generation or before. There's often a very high cost to seeking power by any means . . . or even to holding on to it that way. I drew a few lines. They drew none." She smiled. "I also sent word to Elacia that the two of us should meet on Lundi morning. You really won't be needing her quite as much, but she still could be helpful at times."

"I leave that in your most capable hands, Mother."

"I appreciate that. Is there anything else, Charyn?"

"There is one thing. My personal scrivener Wyllum. I was hoping that you could spend a glass or two going over some of the details of formal correspondence. He's very bright, but he was raised on Imagisle."

"I can certainly give him some of the basics."

"This morning for a glass or two?"

"Of course. I'll be here. I'm sure you have much to do."

"Then I'll see you later."

From Chelia's chambers, Charyn made his way to the guard duty room, where he found Maertyl.

The guard captain looked up. "Sir?"

"If you'd stop by the study sometime when it's convenient for you and there's nothing pressing."

"Yes, sir."

Charyn's next stop was at Norstan's study, where he told the seneschal to arrange for Choristers Refaal and Faheel to meet with Charyn on Lundi on a matter of importance to all choristers.

"Do they know what that matter is, Your Grace?"

"They know what the problem is. I'm trying to work out a solution, or part of one. That's all they need to know."

"I'll take care of it, sir."

Once Charyn was in the study, followed by Wyllum, who had been waiting outside, doubtless talking to Moencriff, he turned to the scrivener. "We'll start on several replies to personal letters. Later this morning when Guard Captain Maertyl comes, you're to go to Lady Chelia's study. She'll give you a few more pointers and basics about wording and phrases, those to be used, and those to be avoided. Now . . . the letter to High Holder Ghaermyn. All I want to do is to convey that his letter to follow on our conversation raised some good points, and matters that I will certainly be bringing to the attention of the joint councils next week . . ."

For close to a glass, Charyn worked with Wyllum, then sent him off to Chelia when Maertyl arrived.

Charyn gestured to the chairs in front of the goldenwood table desk. "We never finished our talk yesterday, and I'd be interested in any thoughts you have about the violence that seems to be aimed at manufactorages and choristers."

"Your Grace . . . I'm just an armsman fortunate enough to have worked my way up in the Chateau Guard."

"Maertyl, you're more than that. You were picked by some very capable imager maitres, and you've done a good job at making the Guard much better. You know more than you ever let on. My problem is that I can't easily leave the Chateau without a certain amount of risk. I might take that risk if I were my father's age and had a capable heir. Right now . . ." Charyn shrugged. Maertyl had to know Bhayrn's shortcomings.

After several long moments, Maertyl cleared his throat. "I do see . . . not often . . . I see some friends from where I grew up. They tell me things . . ."

"You believe what they said, but you don't know for sure? Go on . . ."

"Yes, sir. Well . . . one of them was working for a master weaver. Not a big place, maybe three old-style frames. He was making three, maybe four coppers a day. They were doing hose. Then High Holders and factors stopped wearing hose and doublets and started wearing trousers and jackets. The master weaver couldn't make enough cloth and the frames weren't right. He had to let Jaskyn go. Best Jaskyn could do was as a shuttleman at a manufactorage. A little less than two coppers a day for ten glasses every day. His wife has to take in laundry now. He's got no way to get his own boys into a craft or trade . . ."

"This is happening in more and more places across Solidar," said Charyn. "Do you know of others?"

"There's Baertyl. He was a gunsmith. Used to do real well. Now, he can barely get by, and that's only on special pistols and hunting weapons. That rifle factorage at the iron-works turns out good solid rifles for half what Baertyl used to get . . ."

Charyn managed not to wince. He kept listening for almost a quint, before asking, "How much would it help if the manufactorages had to pay workers more, say two coppers a day instead of one and a half?" Most guards only got four coppers, but they got fed and had their uniforms supplied.

"It'd be a start. Wouldn't help everyone, but men could at least feed their families. That's what bothers most of them."

"It doesn't give them a trade or craft to go into, either," said Charyn.

"No . . ." Maertyl stretched out the word. ". . . but if the factors did what you did, with the lead guards, and an undercaptain, then men would see that, if they were good, they could look forward to something."

"I don't think I can tell factors," said Charyn ruefully, "how to run their factorages. While some of them might do that, I doubt most do . . . or would listen to me."

"If men saw you were looking out for them . . ." Maertyl paused. "The guards saw that you were making things better for us. And your going to Staavyl's memorial, that said a lot, too. So does your riding as an undercaptain. We know you can't always do that, but when you take risks, and you're the Rex, well . . . they see."

"All I can say is that I'll see what I can do." Charyn paused. "What do you think about the True Believers and the choristers?"

"I can't say I care much for either, sir, especially Chorister Saerlet . . ."

That makes two of us.

". . . Chorister Oskaar isn't half bad, though."

"He's the one who did Staavyl's memorial?"

Maertyl nodded.

"It's almost as though the poorer the place where the anomen is the more honest the chorister."

"I wouldn't say that, sir. Most likely, but not always. Where I grew up, when I was maybe nine, there was one chorister . . . he'd find ways to get young girls, give 'em ale with spirits, so they didn't know what they were doing . . ."

"What happened to him?"

"One day he wasn't there. No one seemed to know what happened. Some of the older folks had a talk with the next chorister. He was fresh out of their scholarium. Good man, but couldn't give a homily with the Nameless on his shoulder coaching him." Maertyl smiled faintly.

"You think it might work better if choristers had to post what offerings they got and what they spent them on?"

Maertyl frowned, then said, "I'd have my doubts. Good ones wouldn't need that. Bad ones would just make up figures."

"But if making up those figures amounted to fraud . . . theft . . . ?"

The guard captain smiled. "That'd keep a few of them more in line . . ."

After another quint, Charyn said, "Thank you. We should keep having occasional talks like this."

"You ought to talk with Faelln, too."

"I'd thought of that, but I wanted to know what you thought."

"I'll be telling him about what you said, and he'd tell me the same. Not anyone else, though, for either of us."

"Then I'll do that, not immediately, but I will." Charyn stood. "Thank you, again."

Once Maertyl left and Wyllum slipped back into the study, Charyn and Wyllum went over some changes he wanted made to the responses Sanafryt had drafted to deal with two new High Holder petitions.

After that, Charyn turned his attention back to the problem of the manufactorages . . . and the secondary problem that might become more of a problem later. Paersyt had already pointed out that his steam engine—or a larger version of it—would be perfectly capable of powering a manufactorage. *If he's right, then there will be even more manufactorages because they won't need waterwheels to power them.* And that would make the wage problem even worse . . . but he didn't have to deal with that just yet.

At just after third glass, Wyllum brought in the latest editions of *Tableta* and *Veritum,* both of which carried stories that said it was likely only a matter of time before a decisive naval battle between Jariola and Solidar would take place near or around the Abierto Isles. That scarcely surprised Charyn, given the reports Vaelln had been sending him, although it did indicate that the newssheets had sources in High Command.

Both *Veritum* and *Tableta* carried stories about the Factors' Council appointing Eshmael as the factor from the Bovarian part of Solidar, something that had to have been decided even before Elthyrd's death, Charyn suspected, since it happened so quickly. The *Veritum* story was short, factual, and without opinion. The *Tableta* story was not, at least not in one part.

. . . hardly surprising that the factors appointed the factor known for the lowest wages and greatest opposition to better working conditions and pay, or the one who'd pay a boy a third what a man gets . . . and deny that some of those boys are maimed or killed because they lack a man's strength . . .

Tableta also had a short story on Elthyrd's memorial service, which concluded with a worrisome few lines.

. . . a number of those attending the memorial service of Elthyrd D'Factorius were doubtless surprised to see our beloved Rex Charyn among the mourners, and even more surprised that he arrived escorted by the two most powerful imagers in Solidar—Maitre Alastar and Senior Imager

Alyna. Is our Rex so worried about being assassinated that
he needs their protection whenever he leaves the Chateau
D'Rex, or does this mean that the Maitre is in fact the
power behind the Chateau D'Rex? Does it matter? . . .

By late afternoon, just after he'd dismissed Wyllum for
the day and while he was still pondering what, if anything,
he could do to mute the continued sneering attacks by
Tableta, Sturdyn brought in a single letter, with his name in-
scribed on the envelope in penmanship that he instantly recognized . . . and, in a way, almost dreaded, given the time
that had passed since his last letter to Alyncya. He opened
the letter, again preserving her seal, and began to read.

My dear Rex—
As usual, your most thoughtful correspondence raised
questions that went beyond theory into aspects of po-
litical practicality. A thoughtful response required a
certain amount of diligent deliberation on my part, for I
would not wish my words to be misconstrued or to give
you offense, while still giving you an honest opinion, for
honesty must always be with us both.

An obvious but gentle bit of guidance . . . with some iron
behind it . . . Charyn kept reading.

Your question about the distribution of rewards from
improvements in a means of production is indeed a
valid one, and I cannot gainsay your point that not all
of the increased revenues should go to the factor or
High Holder. The more practical questions are those of
allocation and implementation. Indeed, how much of
the increase should be allocated to the factor and how
much to the workers? By what means should this be
determined? Yet, while both are necessary, the resources
to build, maintain, and operate a factorage are harder

to come by than are workers. Likewise, should an enterprise fail, the factor loses not only the proceeds from the sales of the goods, but the golds required to build and operate the factorage, while the workers lose only their daily wage. The workers lose nothing beyond their daily work, and they may be able to find other work. To build another factorage, the factor must find and risk even more golds.

Yet, I must agree that the wages paid to workers should not be so low that they cannot maintain health and life. Not only is such cruel, but any factor who does offer such low wages will in time find that only the most desperate and least able will wish to work for him. The difficulty, as I am most certain that you have ascertained, is that in shorter periods of time, the factor who pays less may reap higher rewards. Thus, those other factors who compete with him will be reluctant to offer higher wages because their returns will be lower, and in some instances, may result in their losing coins. So none are likely to be the first to increase wages unless required to do so, and if you impose such a requirement, those factors who are either the most greedy or the least effective will complain the most. Since there are few in any field who are markedly superior, my most likely flawed opinion is that any decree on your part will create more opposition than support . . .

Gently cynical as she is, she's right about that.

. . . Only when it becomes clear that workers cannot accept such low wages will many factors accept the necessity for change, and I would suspect that such acceptance will be rancorous and grudging.

I can say unequivocally that I was delighted to read what you discovered in the archive of the Rex about Vaelora Chayardyr and her authoring of much of the

*Codex Legis. I was even more pleased that you gave
her the credit due her. Clearly, she was a remarkable
woman. I find it regrettable that her accomplishments
have been relegated to the dust of the archives, but
refreshing that you have not only read them but
recognized the scale of her abilities and linked them to
Maitre Alyna. I do hope that your sister Aloryana will be
able to follow and build on the legacy of Vaelora.*

*What I also found interesting was that her husband
was the first Maitre of the Collegium, yet outside of the
archives less than a handful of people even know about
either of them. I certainly had not heard of either until
you mentioned them. That brings up another question,
one that intrigues me, but could be intrusive. If it is,
please do not hesitate to let me know . . .*

Charyn frowned. *There's something implied there.* Then
he nodded. *She'll accept, at least sometimes, an unfavor-
able reply, but she doesn't like her questions being ignored.*
He almost laughed softly. Alyncya wasn't a woman to be
ignored, or one who would easily accept, or accept at all,
condescension.

*. . . I would be most interested in knowing if you believe
the present time is merely a repetition of past patterns of
history, a distorted reflection of the past, connected to
the past by only those now living . . . or if you have some
other view of what the present time represents in the
course of history.*

*A seemingly open question, any honest answer to which
will likely reveal to her more than most men would consider
wise to expose of themselves.*

*As I am most interested in continuing this enlightening
correspondence, and learning more about you and your*

views, in the future I will endeavor to be more prompt in responding.

I remain, as always, with the warmest of regards,

For a moment, when he read the signature, he didn't realize that she had only signed her first name. He couldn't help smiling, if but for a moment.

Charyn had thought to practice before dinner, but decided, especially with her closing lines and signature, to work on a reply while he was alone in the study and had time.

Almost a glass later, he slowly read over what he had written.

My dear Lady-heir Alyncya—
I do appreciate your latest missive, questions and all, and will attempt to address them in careful candor.

I would agree fully with the way in which you posed the difficulty in the allocation of increased rewards resulting from the improvement in the methods of manufactorage. Given that difficulty, a most modest improvement in worker wages might be the best initial approach. As you pointed out most perceptively, no factor or High Holder would likely make such a decision when his competitors would not follow that example. And if the Rex were to require such an increase by decree, that decree would be met initially with rancor and bitterness, but upon consideration, it might be possible that factors would see that the cost of increasing wages might be seen as less than the costs of continued destruction, and that the imposition of higher wages by a decree modifying the Codex Legis as merely a means to allow factors and High Holders to do so and to place the blame on the Rex.

Your second question requires a certain self-examination, and therefore my response may be colored by the degree in which I may think better of my self than

I should. Nevertheless, I will attempt an honest reply. I do not believe that events in Solidar, or in any land, merely repeat themselves generation after generation, with only the names and other appurtenances changing. Nor would I contend that the present time is a partial or distorted reflection of the past.

I do believe that the basic nature of man, and of woman, does not change, although the circumstances in which each generation finds itself do indeed change. Thus, we tend to react badly when we do not think, or do not think carefully, as did at least some of our ancestors. When we think matters through, we may also react in a similar fashion to those before us when they considered matters carefully. Yet each of us does differ from our forebears, and even events that seem to be similar to those in the past are only roughly so at best. Greed and pride will provoke similar responses in those susceptible to those passions, as they always have. So will a passion for thought and care. I cannot dispute that at times events of the past may resemble situations of the present, but I must wonder if such situations, particularly those in times of turmoil and trouble, reveal a failure to learn the lessons of the past, rather than an unchanging pattern of destiny. In summary, I believe while the past is a guide, and can offer lessons in what is beneficial and what is not, the present is not an immutable repetition or even a reflection of the past, except so far as it reveals the nature of man and of woman and their successes and failures.

In reflecting upon the recent past of the regial family, it has occurred to me that those Rexes who appear to have been most successful have been those who could recognize and accept wise counsel, no matter what the source of that counsel, even when it ran counter to their initial determinations on what might be the best course

*of action. From a reading of the archives, Vaelora
Chayardyr gave wise counsel, counsel that both the first
Rex Regis and the first Maitre of the Collegium heeded
and accepted. I would like to think that I could be so
wise, young as I am as a Rex, as to follow their example,
especially if I am fortunate enough to find a woman as
wise and as honest as Vaelora with whom to share the
years ahead.*

*I trust it will not be too long before we can pursue
conversations such as these in person as well as in ink,
but, as someone counseled me, if indirectly, I understand
that in some matters to press on rashly can be most
unwise.*

*With my warmest regards, I look forward to your
reply.*

Charyn read it again, then signed and sealed it, hoping
he was charting a path between being too forward and too
reserved.

Then he left the study and headed down to dinner, where
he found his mother, Karyel, and Iryella all waiting for him
in the family parlor.

"You're a bit later than usual," offered Chelia.

"I had some thinking to do about the manufactorage violence and how to present the problem to the councils next
week." Charyn frowned. "Isn't Bhayrn eating with us?"

"He said that Gherard had invited him and Laamyst to
dine with him."

"He didn't mention that to me at breakfast this morning."

"We don't even see Cousin Bhayrn at breakfast," said Iryella. "Not often. He eats later than we do."

Charyn wondered if that might not be for the best, then
stopped himself from shaking his head. "This morning he
ate early with me."

"That must not happen often," said Karyel dryly, before

smiling warmly. "I don't see how you can eat so early. You must work at getting up early."

"Rex Charyn exercises before breakfast," said Chelia. "Perhaps you should join him before long."

"With the guards?"

"With the guards," affirmed Chelia.

Iryella looked toward the door of the family dining room, almost plaintively. When she realized Charyn was looking at her, she dropped her eyes and smiled coyly.

"I think we should eat," Charyn declared cheerfully, barely hiding his amusement at Iryella as he recalled what his mother had said earlier.

35

Even before he was fully awake on Solayi morning, Charyn could smell harsh acrid smoke, and his eyes burned slightly. When he went to his bedchamber window, drew back the hangings, and looked out, he could see a smoky haze to the east of the Chateau, along the river, thick enough that it almost obscured Erion's small and gibbous shape, but he saw no plume of smoke rising anywhere. He couldn't help but wonder what factorage or warehouse had been burned. Even before he dressed, a light drizzle began to fall.

He didn't exercise, Solayi being the day he practiced with pistols, rather than exercising, after which he asked Faelln, as the duty officer of the guard, if he or any of the guards knew anything about any fires. The best Charyn could determine from them was that the fires had been well south of the river piers.

Later, he spent close to two glasses practicing and working on his newer pieces on the clavecin. As soon as he left the music room, Chelia herded Karyel and Iryella into it. Charyn tried not to wince as Karyel began to play—the correct notes, Charyn thought, but whatever Karyel was attempting couldn't have possibly be written in that tempo, something that Chelia obviously knew as well, because, after several moments, the notes were played in tempo. After that, Karyel played again, somewhat closer to the tempo Chelia had played.

At least he isn't as hard on the clavecin as Bhayrn is. Not that Charyn had seen Bhayrn on Solayi, since he'd spent the night with Laamyst at High Holder Laastyn's L'Excelsis estate.

Charyn went to his study and closed the door. There he turned to the Codex Legis, searching to see if there were any provisions that might bear more directly on choristers, but occasionally looking outside, at the drizzle that slowly faded over the afternoon.

Just after fifth glass, Charyn donned the guard undercaptain's uniform and then an oilskin jacket, in the event that the drizzle resumed, since there were still high clouds covering the sky, and made his way down to the rear courtyard. The four guards who were to accompany him were waiting. The five mounted and rode down the drive to the Ring Road, but took L'Avenue D'Commercia to the Sud Bridge and rode across it, then up the East River Road to the east bridge onto Imagisle.

No one even seemed to look twice at the five riders.

Charyn was still studying the clouds when he reined up in front of the Maitre's small stable, clearly for guests because he'd never seen any horses stabled there. The clouds were neither lighter nor darker, and he left the oilskin with his mount and the guards, who were already making themselves comfortable in the tack room by the time Charyn walked up to join Aloryana, Alastar, Alyna, and Lystara.

Alastar gestured for Charyn and Aloryana to lead the way to the anomen, and Alyna murmured something to Lystara, who remained between her parents. Charyn had the feeling that Lystara had been asked—or quietly told—to give Charyn and his sister some time alone.

"Palenya told me she'll be playing at the Autumn-Turn Ball," Aloryana said quietly.

"She will be. She's the best clavecin player, and it pays well." Charyn frowned. "She's not upset, is she?"

"Not yet."

"What is that supposed to mean?"

"Don't play stupid, Charyn."

After a moment, Charyn said, "I'm certainly not going

to announce that I'm getting married. I'm nowhere close to even asking anyone."

"Then Palenya won't be upset. Neither will I. You promised, remember?"

"I told you . . ." Even as he replied, Charyn wondered how much Palenya would have been upset. *Except she did care for you, and you . . .* Charyn swallowed. *Are you trying to find someone so that it will be easier to forget?* He kept walking without saying a word.

Aloryana didn't say anything, either, for a time, then asked, "Have you had Alyncya to the Chateau again?"

"Not since the dinner for the High Holders living near L'Excelsis. I told you about that. That was over three weeks ago."

"You're interested in her."

"Yes, I'm more interested in her than anyone else. But . . ."

"But what?"

"I don't want to rush into marrying someone because Solidar needs an heir." *Especially anyone who can't measure up to Palenya.* "Besides, in some ways I scarcely know her. Equally important, from her point of view, she scarcely knows me."

"If you aren't seeing her, how can you learn any more about her?"

"You were just telling me I shouldn't rush. Now you're saying I should know more about her."

"You should know more about anyone, maybe more about several women."

"We've been exchanging letters. I *think* she's interested, but she never replies immediately."

"That's to keep you interested."

"Partly, I'd judge. Partly, it's to give her time as well."

"She wants to make sure you're really interested. I need to meet her."

"I promised you . . ."

"Just remember that."

Charyn was glad they were nearing the anomen. He wasn't certain that he was ready for any more of Aloryana's questions. *And what does that tell you?*

He was so preoccupied with his sister's revelation about Palenya and her questions that, by the time they left the anomen to walk back to the Maitre's house, Charyn honestly had no idea what Iskhar's homily had been about, and he found himself walking beside Alastar, with Alyna accompanying Lystara and Aloryana.

"You know," said Alastar, breaking into Charyn's conflicting thoughts, "that more than four warehouses were burned last night?"

"I could smell the smoke. I had the feeling that was the case, but none of the guards or anyone else knew anything except the fires had occurred well south of the river piers."

"Eshmael lost a warehouse—a large one—and he'll want to know what you intend to do when he comes to the Council meeting."

"I'd be interested in what the factors intend to do."

"They have the Civic Patrol knocking on the door of every artisan and crafter who's ever said a word against the new manufactorages." Alastar paused. "So far, they're just knocking. If the fires and destruction continue, they'll likely stop merely questioning. Last night, one patroller was shot, and another one burned to death when part of a warehouse exploded. Also, Argentyl's shop was burned to the ground, along with the cobbler's shop in the adjoining building."

"What do you suggest?"

"I'd rather not suggest anything, but it appears that neither the crafters nor the factors are inclined to talk to each other, let alone listen."

Charyn smiled, if bitterly. "What you're saying is that they're only going to listen to force, and that you'll lose your effectiveness in this instance if the Collegium is the one to apply that force."

"That's not what I said, and it's not what I'm implying," returned Alastar evenly. "There are less than twenty imager maitres with shields strong enough to withstand continued rifle shots. There are scores of manufactorages just in L'Excelsis, and that doesn't count those in nearby towns and cities. There are likely scores of angry workers and crafters. It's not a question of power, but what kind of power is necessary and who has that power."

Charyn got the message. Only the army had the ability to apply force in scores of locations across Solidar, and it was definitely looking like he was going to have to deploy that force. "Then the question is whether the Collegium will stand behind whoever applies that kind of force."

"The Collegium has always stood behind the law as set forth in the Codex Legis."

"The next months are going to be very interesting," replied Charyn dryly.

"All months are interesting in some fashion or another." Alastar smiled. "I hope you'll stay for refreshments this evening. Jienna made a special pearapple pie."

"I wouldn't miss that." *And Aloryana would be disappointed if I left early.*

The pearapple pie was excellent, as was the conversation, if according to the Maitre's rules, which required no talk about matters such as what the Rex or the Collegium might do in the weeks ahead, but only about subjects such as books, music, history or people who weren't alive . . . or the studies and recent achievements of young imagers.

Even so, Charyn did leave slightly earlier than he might have, since the clouds thickened, and a light drizzle resumed. The rain didn't get heavier until Charyn and the three guards were almost at the Ring Road, for which he was most thankful.

When he finally walked up the grand staircase, still wearing his oilskin jacket, Bhayrn waited for him at the top of the stairs.

"Where have you been?"

"I went to services with Aloryana and stayed a little to have refreshments and talk with her."

"I thought I saw the unmarked carriage in the carriage house."

Just to be contrary, Charyn replied, "You must be mistaken. How else would I have gotten there, especially in the rain?"

"Don't tell me you took the regial coach?" Bhayrn shook his head. "That must have been a sight for all the imagers."

"They're used to me attending services with Aloryana." Charyn paused and then added, "They don't take shots at me."

"You've only been shot at that one time since you forced Uncle to kill himself."

"That was his choice, as you well know."

Bhayrn opened his mouth, then shut it, finally just shaking his head before finally saying, "I'd like to use the unmarked coach tomorrow if the rain continues."

"I don't plan to go anywhere tomorrow, but if I do, I'll make other arrangements. Do you know if anyone has attacked Ghaermyn's manufactorages?"

"Why do you want to know?"

"Because some were burned last night, and I wondered if any might be his."

"He was ready for that. A mob tried. His men shot five or six of them, and the ruffians fled. It would be better if you took care of it, you know? Then everyone would understand."

"What about Laastyn? He doesn't have any manufactorages, does he?"

Bhayrn shook his head. "He has mines and quarries, and thousands and thousands of hectares in timber. Most of the timber is around Asseroiles, Laamyst says."

Charyn managed not to frown. "He doesn't like having factorages?"

"Just ones large enough to take care of the needs of his

lands and properties. Coins come and go, but the lands remain. He's said that several times."

"Do you know if he's still expanding his holdings?"

"Why do you want to know? So you can tariff him more?"

"I was just curious, but would that be so bad? From what Alucar and I have been able to determine, a number of High Holders are undertariffed, and a few are overtariffed. I told you that months ago."

"It isn't fair to raise tariffs just on the High Holders you find out about and not on the others."

"I know that. I'm not doing it." *Not in most cases, anyway.* "That's why we're working to update the holding records. That can mean either raising or lowering tariffs. We've done both."

"I'm glad to hear that." Bhayrn nodded almost brusquely. "I'll see you tomorrow. It's been a long day."

"Sleep well," said Charyn, but his brother had already turned toward his rooms.

Charyn shook his head. The only question was exactly what Bhayrn's friends wanted from him, and Charyn worried about the least of those possibilities and hoped that he could steer Bhayrn away from the worst.

∼⌒∽

36

Slightly before eighth glass on Lundi morning, Charyn received a relatively brief report from Marshal Vaelln which noted that the Jariolan and Solidaran fleets had met off the Abierto Isles and that the results were stated in the attached report from Sea Marshal Tynan.

Charyn read through Tynan's detailed and lengthy report, but what it amounted to was that in the battle between the Jariolans and Solidarans, Tynan's fleet lost sixteen warships, including two first-rate ships of the line, and five other ships were damaged so badly that they had to return to Westisle. The confirmed Jariolan losses totaled twenty-seven ships sunk, including seven first-raters, and seven others even thought to be so badly damaged as to be out of service, some of which might possibly be lost on the return to Jariola. The battle broke the attempted Jariolan blockade, but the loss of ships meant that the Sea Marshal had no way to send any more ships to Otelyrn to deal with the Jariolan privateers there.

Vaelln's letter had one other disturbing paragraph.

> . . . Tynan also reported under separate cover more
> than fifteen incidents of violence against factorages
> and factors' warehouses in Ferravyl and Solis over
> the previous week. Ten men have been caught, and five
> executed, five sentenced to terms in the penal supply
> galleys, but the violence has continued . . .

Between what Charyn had seen and heard, what Alastar

had said, and what Vaelln had reported, Charyn didn't see
that he had much choice.

"Wyllum?"

"Yes, sir?"

"We need to draft a letter to Marshal Vaelln . . ." Charyn
went on to detail what he wanted, then turned his attention
to reading the draft provisions dealing with choristers while
Wyllum worked on the draft.

Less than half a glass later, Charyn read over the second
draft of the letter.

Marshal Vaelln—
The continued and growing violence against factors,
factorages, manufactorages, and factors' warehouses in
and around L'Excelsis and, as reported by Sea Marshal
Tynan, in Ferravyl and Solis is clearly beyond the ability
of the various Civic Patrols to control. This suggests that
it may be necessary to use units of the army to restore
a more normal order. Before considering such a step,
however, I would appreciate your insight, expertise,
and suggestions on the matter. For that reason, I would
appreciate your arriving a glass before the Council
meeting on Meredi so that we can discuss the matter.

After reading it, he signed and sealed it, and had Wyllum
arrange for its dispatch and delivery to the Marshal.

At a quint or so after ninth glass, a package arrived from
Estafen, which Charyn opened personally, suspecting what
might be inside. He was right. The package contained a
monthly report from Engineer Ostraaw, with a note that the
increased revenues resulted from more rifle sales—from two
hundred two in Juyn to five hundred ninety-one in Agostos.

Two hundred of the additional sales went to the Factors'
Council, but who bought the additional hundred and ninety?
Charyn really did need to make another trip to the ironworks.

Ostraaw finished the report with the observation that he was keeping the gates closed for protection against the crafter mobs, and that, if Suyrien had any influence, to ask that the Maitre of the Collegium request entrance if the imagers needed access to the ironworks.

At the last, Charyn frowned. He had no idea to what Ostraaw was referring, and he couldn't very well ask Alastar without revealing that he owned the ironworks as a factor, and that was something he didn't want to reveal directly. *Maybe an allusion?* He'd have to think about that.

Then he handed the draft language about choristers to Wyllum. "Please make two copies of this language. I want the choristers to look at it."

"Yes, sir."

Just after midday, Sturdyn carried in an envelope. "A messenger from Councilor Eshmael brought this."

"Thank you." Charyn didn't even want to imagine what Eshmael had to say, particularly since the cloth factor had already lost both a warehouse and a manufactorage, albeit his smallest and least profitable one. Still, once Sturdyn had left, Charyn opened the envelope and began to read.

Rex Charyn—
The amount of destruction and loss caused by selfish crafters and lazy workers is intolerable. The number of malefactors is beyond the ability of the Civic Patrol to control, and the destruction is increasing. The factors and even some High Holders of Solidar should not be punished for making improvements in the creation of cloth and other goods. Yet this is what is happening. I have now lost both a manufactorage and a warehouse to this senseless violence. I am far from the only factor thus burdened.
It is imperative that you as Rex take immediate action. I look forward to hearing what that action will be at the Council meeting on Meredi.

The signature was "Eshmael D'Factorius."

Charyn had no doubts that the Council meeting would be even more acrimonious than he had expected. After reading the letter a second time, he placed it in the cabinet behind him and took a deep breath.

Shortly before first glass, Charyn turned to Wyllum. "I want you to stay here for the meeting with the choristers. Just listen. Don't say a word."

"Yes, sir."

When the two choristers arrived, Refaal was the first to enter the study. He wore the same dark green jacket, shirt, and trousers, although his chorister's scarf was a lighter shade of green. His dark brown hair was slightly mussed, and his oval face looked gaunter than before. Faheel didn't look that much older than Charyn. While Charyn had half-expected the assistant chorister to have the dark hair and the honey-colored complexion that would have gone with a name that sounded vaguely Pharsi, Faheel was tall, green-eyed, blond, and thin. His eyes flicked all around the study as he walked to the chairs before the desk.

Charyn waited until both were seated. "Have either of you two heard anything more from the True Believers?"

"No, sir," offered Faheel quickly.

"And you, Refaal?"

"I received a note yesterday. Rather it was left for me. It was unsigned. Like the other one. I brought it with me." The chorister extended the envelope, which had been slit open, but which bore no sign of a seal.

Charyn took the envelope and extracted the single sheet. There wasn't much to read, set forth in standard merchant hand.

> *Just keep preaching about the real Rholan and*
> *about real people.*
> *The True Beliefs aren't about gold.*

Charyn shook his head. "I doubt that Rholan ever advocated burning the goods and buildings of factors, but I wouldn't preach that in a homily at the moment." He paused, then turned to Faheel. "Have you heard anything from Chorister Saerlet?"

"No, sir. No one at the anomen has. I don't know anyone who has."

Charyn looked to Refaal. "What about you?"

"Not a thing, sir."

"I didn't ask you both here just to find out whether you'd heard more, but for several reasons. First, I'd like each of you to tell me—honestly—why you think all of these incidents involving the True Believers are taking place."

The two choristers exchanged glances.

Then Refaal cleared his throat. "It's only a guess, really, Your Grace. When I became chorister at the Anomen D'Excelsis, I was a little surprised. As I've hinted, the anomen needs repairs, and there were only the minimal pieces of furniture, and really, no furnishings to speak of in the quarters, not even wall hangings. I asked the sexton about that. He told me that Chorister Lytaarl took all the hangings and all the furnishings he'd purchased over the years, then purchased very inexpensive chairs, and a table and bedstead and bed—and one armoire."

"I take it Lytaarl had more than one armoire?"

"Three, the sexton said. I've had to purchase lamps, linens, just everyday things . . ."

"And?" pressed Charyn, knowing that Refaal wanted Charyn to complete the picture. "What does this have to do with the True Believers?"

"I don't think that the luxuries with which some choristers have indulged themselves have gone unnoticed. I also think that people, especially workers and crafters, get angry when they see this. Especially now, when times are hard for many."

Charyn gestured to Faheel. "Your thoughts?"

"I would agree . . . except some of the factors are angry at both the True Believers and the crafters. Yesterday, I spoke about the need to share the good things in life. One factor came up after and told me that he didn't think he should have to share with those who were lazy. He'd worked hard all his life, and few of his workers ever worked that hard. Another one asked me what choristers ever did besides talk about what others should do. When I said that we helped the very poor with food and clothes we gathered, he told me to look at why they were poor."

"Do you have many factors in your congregation, Refaal?"

"A few handfuls, perhaps. Most are crafters."

"And most who go to the Anomen D'Rex are factors, aren't they?" Charyn asked Faheel.

"From their attire, I would say so."

The two answers made a sort of sense to Charyn, except that there was one part that didn't. *Why did the True Believers storm the Anomen D'Rex and not the Anomen D'Excelsis? Were those who stormed the Anomen D'Rex actually from somewhere else in the city?* And if they were, how did they know just how much of the offerings Saerlet had been spending on himself?

Those weren't questions Charyn could answer at the moment. So he proceeded. "I have already issued a decree that makes clear that violence against choristers and anomens is just as much of a crime as violence against other people or structures. What other ideas do either of you have as the best way to deal with the True Believers?"

Once more the two exchanged looks.

This time, Faheel was the one to speak first. "I don't know, sir. After all this, I don't know that some people will believe it when I say that I live modestly and only have a few jackets and trousers."

"People will talk if we dress poorly, and they'll talk if we dress well," added Refaal.

"Wyllum," said Charyn, "if you'd give each chorister a paper."

The scrivener immediately handed a copy of the draft language to each chorister, then returned to his seat at the end of the conference table.

"Just read through them. After you do, we'll talk." Charyn watched the two as they read. Faheel appeared interested and nodded once. Refaal frowned more than once.

When both of them looked up, Charyn said, "What you read is language drafted by the Minister of Justice for possible proclamation as law. Your thoughts, Faheel."

"I don't know if it will help. It might. I don't see that it can hurt. Most choristers should keep accounts like that."

"Do you know if Chorister Saerlet did?"

"He kept accounts. I saw the ledgers. He never allowed me to look at them. I cannot find them. I've taken the liberty of starting a new ledger because it's not clear whether the old ledgers will ever be found."

Charyn frowned. He didn't recall seeing any entries in the regial master ledgers for the Anomen D'Rex, but he needed to check with Alucar on that. "But you could comply with those requirements?"

"Yes, Your Grace. It would take a few glasses, every month, but . . . if it made things clearer to people."

Charyn turned to Refaal. "And you?"

"It might take more time than that. Also, some people wouldn't believe what was posted. We could be charged with fraud even if we did nothing wrong."

"Doesn't the language say 'significant discrepancies' and define significance? A discrepancy of half a gold certainly isn't insignificant. Also, the language requires proof. A statement that someone thinks your figures are wrong won't suffice."

"Then, Your Grace," said Faheel almost tentatively, "how will such a law help?"

"I suspect, if this becomes law, that you're going to be more careful about your figures. Also, those who are good with figures in your congregation will likely look at what you post. I doubt that anyone will quibble over a few coppers, perhaps not even over a few silvers, but . . ."

Faheel nodded.

Refaal tried not to frown, then said, "Such a requirement might dissuade some of ability from becoming choristers."

"Perhaps any who might be dissuaded should not be choristers." Charyn smiled. "There's another question raised by the True Believers. Just what did Rholan say or preach? Is there anything beyond *The Sayings of Rholan*?"

"I don't know of anything," said Refaal.

"Ah . . . there is one book . . ."

Refaal looked hard at Faheel, who ignored the sharp glance.

"What is it?"

"It's a very old book. It's short. It's called *Rholan and the Nameless*. There's no author listed. It's one of the rare books at the choristers' scholarium in Solis. It's supposedly a copy of a copy. The copy was documented as being presented to the Scholarium in the last years of the first Rex Regis by his sister, Vaelora Chayardyr. There's no doubt that she did that. How authentic the text is . . . no one can tell."

Vaelora . . . again. How could someone so integral to the past of Solidar have been so thoroughly forgotten? That was something Charyn wasn't certain he'd ever completely understand.

"Much of it's said to be apocryphal," said Refaal sourly.

"There's no proof of that, either," said Faheel. "We know the copy is almost four hundred years old."

"A copy in Solis . . . that's not useful," said Refaal.

Faheel smiled. "I spent much of a year copying it. I have a fair copy."

Refaal's mouth dropped open. "You wouldn't preach from that?"

"I already have . . . a little."

Charyn managed not to grin at Refaal's look of outrage and consternation. "That's very interesting. That sounds like something that all you choristers should get together and discuss, just so everyone knows the book exists, of course. Maybe you should all even come up with standards for choristers. That might also help . . ."

Another glass passed before Charyn ushered the two out and then made his way to Alucar's study.

The Finance Minister looked up. "I hear you were meeting with choristers. Is this going to require more golds?"

"Not that I know of. How much are we providing to the Anomen D'Rex?"

"We provide nothing in terms of a monthly or seasonal stipend. At times, we have paid for major repairs of the anomen. Not recently, although, as you know, Chorister Saerlet asked for funds to refurbish the anomen and the quarters."

"I know. I turned him down on that. Do you have any idea how much Saerlet was taking in offerings?"

"From what I saw, he had between two and three hundred families attending services. If they each give a few coppers, that would be something like twenty silvers a week. I suspect some of the factors give a silver or two each. So, say between twenty-five and thirty silvers a week. Half of the offerings are supposed to go to the poor in some fashion. Now, he had to pay himself, the assistant chorister and his personal assistant."

"And his valet," added Charyn dryly, "but I doubt they get more than a silver or two a week, except maybe for Faheel. That would still leave at least five to ten silvers for him."

Given that Maertyl, as the Chateau Guard captain, only got three silvers a week, plus other benefits, and felt himself fairly paid, Charyn could definitely see why Maertyl had been less than pleased in viewing Saerlet's quarters . . . and why the True Believers weren't all that happy with some choristers.

"Do you attend the Anomen D'Rex, Alucar?"

The Finance Minister shook his head. "It's a bit . . . rich

for our tastes. We go to the Anomen D'Sud. I think the only minister who attends the Anomen D'Rex is Aevidyr."

Somehow, the fact that Alucar went to the very modest Anomen D'Sud didn't surprise Charyn.

Later, as Charyn walked back to his study, he wondered just how many golds had vanished with Saerlet. He still wondered why Saerlet had fled so quickly and vanished . . . and exactly what the message was behind the white belts.

But at least both Faheel and Refaal seemed able to deal with the threats posed by the True Believers.

37

~~~~~

The first thing Charyn did on Mardi morning was read the newssheets, beginning with *Veritum* because he preferred the somewhat more balanced presentation before reading the more incendiary *Tableta*. Two articles in *Veritum* caught his attention. One was a short story noting that in the past month, some fifty men had been involved in attacks on factorages, manufactorages, and warehouses. Nine had been killed by either factors' guards or by the Civic Patrol when they attacked patrollers or guards. Twenty-eight had been found guilty and executed; eleven had been sentenced to hard labor in the workhouse for periods from two to five years; and two under the age of eighteen had been remanded to naval indentured custody for five years.

The second story was somewhat more personal. Charyn focused on one section.

. . . in the latest incident to come before the regional justicer, three men planned and carried out a warehouse burning. The warehouse contained ceramic goods formed and fired in a large manufactorage south of Rivages. The fire destroyed goods valued at more than two hundred golds. The regional justicer levied a sentence of execution on the three men. Two were potters, and the third was a potter's apprentice. The two potters claimed that the large manufactorage priced its goods below their costs just in order to drive them out of their shop. The three were executed on Lundi, despite pleas by several crafters' guilds that the sentences were excessive . . .

The *Tableta* story presented the matter in a different fashion.

> . . . yesterday, three men were executed because they attempted to strike back at the cruelty and uncaring nature of the large manufactorages that are springing up all over Solidar. They set fire to a warehouse filled with identical ceramic goods churned out by one such manufactorage and priced so low that no individual potter can match the cost. One of the three was a nineteen-year-old potter's apprentice from Talyon. Executing young apprentice Roebin was not justice, but murder sanctioned by the factors of L'Excelsis. Roebin accompanied his brother Toalyn and the other potter, one Eramont, when they set fire to a warehouse owned by Eshmael D'Factorius. Toalyn had been fired by Eshmael when he refused to make repairs to the molding mechanism unless his pay was raised to two coppers a day . . .

So Eshmael isn't just a mercer, but he also has an interest in ceramics . . . and he's lost a third building. Maybe there was a link to Elthyrd's beating.

Then Charyn frowned. *A large ceramic manufactorage?* Wasn't that what Maitre Malyna's father owned?

He set down the newssheet, thinking, wondering what the High Holder paid his workers.

In midafternoon, after leaving Alucar's study, where he'd asked for a clarification about shipbuilding costs, Charyn heard a number of voices coming from the main foyer, one of which was that of Bhayrn. Curious, he walked down the stairs.

Bhayrn turned. "We were just going to use the plaques room. Mother's group isn't playing today."

"That's fine." Charyn looked at the other three, recognizing Amascarl and Laamyst. The third young man was dark-haired and green-eyed, with a neatly trimmed but thick black beard, and someone Charyn was fairly certain he hadn't met. So he stepped forward and said, "I don't believe we've met."

"Oh, no, Your Grace, but I've heard much about you. I'm Gherard." The young man met Charyn's gaze easily, then inclined his head, before smiling pleasantly.

"I've met your father, but never had the pleasure of meeting you. He'd mentioned his factorages. Do you have that much to do with them?"

"Well . . . a little. Father would like us to know something about everything, but with the troubles he hasn't said much."

"He was telling me that he had to hire a small army to protect them."

"No more than a squad, if that. At least, that's what he said. He keeps details to himself."

"That's understandable." Charyn smiled. "I won't keep you all." Then he turned and headed back up the staircase, wondering about why Gherard had been slightly uneasy about saying anything about the factorages. Why had Gherard said that his father hadn't said much? Was it the sensitivity of a family not having that long a history as High Holders? Or something else?

Or just the unease about meeting the Rex unexpectedly?

Charyn frowned. There was no sure way of telling, and he needed to go over the details of the meeting tomorrow with the councils.

38

A quint before noon on Meredi, Charyn stood from behind the goldenwood table desk in his study and said to Wyllum, "Once Marshal Vaelln arrives, you're to leave the study. You can do what you wish within the Chateau until second glass, when you're to return and wait outside with the study guard." He smiled sardonically. "After the meeting is over, you may have much to write."

Less than half a quint later, Moencriff announced, "Marshal Vaelln."

Charyn turned from where he stood by the open window, nodded to Wyllum, and said, "Have the Marshal come in."

As soon as Vaelln stepped into the study, Wyllum eased past him and stepped out.

The Marshal offered an amused smile. "Are matters that bad, Your Grace?"

"Not yet." Charyn gestured to the chairs, then settled himself behind the desk. "Wyllum is my new scrivener, and I don't want him immediately overwhelmed." After a moment, he asked, "What are your thoughts about the continued unrest over the new manufactorages?"

"I don't like the idea of the army being used as civic patrollers, Your Grace. That's not the best use of troopers."

"I agree. But matters aren't getting any better. I discussed this with Maitre Alastar on Solayi. The outbreaks are in so many places that the Collegium cannot offer much assistance. There just aren't enough imagers."

Vaelln nodded slowly. "I can see that. I talked it over with Vice-Marshal Maurek. He was the field commander at the last battle of the revolt. The imagers lost more than a third of their best in that one battle. That included the Senior Imager of the Collegium."

Charyn hadn't known that, either.

"There is one aspect to this." Vaelln took a deep breath. "The outbreaks are limited to where there are new large manufactorages. At present, there are only a few cities and towns with them."

"L'Excelsis, Ferravyl, Solis . . . so far," said Charyn.

"Possibly Nacliano or Kherseilles, although I have my doubts about Kherseilles."

Charyn raised his eyebrows.

"The old Khellan lands . . . they're . . . it doesn't seem as likely there."

"Oh?"

"They still hold more to crafting, and they don't have as many rivers to power manufactorages."

Charyn nodded, although he hadn't heard that before. *Then there's a lot you haven't heard and should have.* "How soon can you put the army in position?"

"In a few days here in L'Excelsis." Vaelln cleared his throat. "That's not the problem. How long do you intend to need the troopers? Just putting troopers in the streets will stop most of the outbreaks, but it likely won't stop all of them. The longer they patrol the streets, the angrier people will get."

Charyn nodded. "I thought about that. I may need you to let the Council know that after I tell them that's what I intend."

"Can I ask what you have in mind?"

"I'm thinking of making a change to the Codex Legis that requires any factorage that employs people who are not immediate members of the family of the factor to pay a minimum daily wage. I was thinking two coppers a day, but I intend to have the Council discuss it. There are details that will have to be worked out. I was thinking that two coppers would make it less likely that they'd hire children."

"You still might want to declare that children under fourteen can't work in any manufactorage required to pay the minimum. You also need to specify the maximum number of glasses in a two-copper workday. Too many factors will do anything." Vaelln snorted.

"What do you think about the idea?"

"If you act quickly, it might work. It also might send a message to the factors that working folks need to be paid enough to live." The Marshal shrugged. "I could be seeing it that way because I don't like the idea of the army being used for a long time as civic patrollers."

"There's another problem," said Charyn. "The Factors' Council has ordered several hundred rifles from the rifle-works. Many haven't been delivered yet."

"I'd heard something like that from Subcommander Lu-erryn. I don't much care for untrained factors or their men running around with rifles."

"That makes two of us," said Charyn dryly.

Before that long, Moencriff announced, "Maitre Alastar."

Alastar entered the study, nodding to both Vaelln and Charyn.

"You're a bit early," said Charyn, gesturing to the vacant chair beside Vaelln.

"I thought it might be prudent to find out if you have any surprises planned." The white-and-silver-haired Mai-tre took the chair. "You've been known to do that . . . upon occasion."

"We've been talking about using the army to stop the attacks on manufactorages and warehouses before the out-breaks become any more widespread."

Alastar nodded. "And then what?"

Charyn smiled. "The Marshal raised the same point. I'm going to try to get the Council's support for a law setting a minimum daily wage for manufactorages . . ." Charyn went on to explain.

"None of the councilors will like that." Alastar's tone was matter-of-fact.

"I don't like it," returned Charyn. "That's not the question. The question is whether anyone else has a better idea that will actually work."

"They won't have a better idea, and some will say that your idea will not work," replied the Maitre.

"Do you think it might work?"

"I can't tell you that. I've never heard of either a city or a land requiring that."

"But . . . that's what the guilds did, in effect, until the factors started finding ways to make things cheaper."

"Don't you think that might be why the factors looked to find ways to make things more cheaply?"

"I'd wager that they could still pay two coppers a day or some such and still make those goods more cheaply."

"You might be wagering your being Rex on that."

Charyn paused. "And I might not stay Rex, except by using the army, if I don't find a way to stop the unrest. If I have to rely on the army for too long . . . I don't think that will be good, either."

Alastar looked to Vaelln. "What do you think about that?"

"The army isn't trained to occupy cities and towns. They're trained to shoot at a known enemy. I'd rather not guess. It might work out over time. It might not."

Since neither the Maitre nor the Marshal said another word, Charyn addressed Alastar. "By the way, I saw in the newssheets yesterday a reference to a large manufactorage of ceramics south of Rivages. Isn't Maitre Alyna's brother . . ."

"High Holder Zaerlyn only produces large ceramic items—stoves and other . . . household necessities."

"I'm glad to hear that. I also ran across something about you and the ironworks the other day."

"Oh?"

"Something about entry, during the time when my father was Rex?" That was a guess on Charyn's part.

"You don't know about that?"

Charyn shook his head.

"That was when Vaschet owned the ironworks and he'd just built the rifleworks. Someone used the rifles to kill young imagers. Vaschet closed off the ironworks and wouldn't answer inquiries. So we took down the gates. I ended up immobilizing him and making off with his account ledgers. That was the real beginning of our discovery of the High Holders' revolt." Alastar looked to Vaelln. "I'm sure you remember that."

"All too well. Ryel was buying rifles and arming the brownshirts."

Charyn managed not to let his mouth drop. "I never knew that part."

For a moment, Alastar looked puzzled. Then he nodded. "I suppose you wouldn't. Your father likely wouldn't have mentioned it. Vaelln wouldn't have had any reason to tell you, nor would I. How did you find out?"

"There was just a mention in some papers about the Maitre and entry to the ironworks."

Vaelln snorted. "Begging your pardon, Your Grace, but that sounds like your father. He never could be as direct as he should have been."

Alastar shook his head. "Rexes need to be both direct and indirect. A good ruler knows when to be which."

Charyn understood what Alastar was implying—that his father was often direct when he should have been indirect, and indirect when should have been direct. "I'm learning that's not as easy as it sounds."

"Nothing about ruling is, Your Grace," said Alastar gently.

Just before first glass, Charyn stood and walked over to the conference table, where he placed two sheets of paper on the table in front of each chair, facedown. After that he handed two sheets each to Alastar and Vaelln, then returned to stand by the head of the table, while Alastar and Vaelln rose and moved to the two chairs set to the side of the window end of the table.

"The councils, sir," announced Sturdyn, opening the study door.

As had become customary, the senior factor, who was Hisario, given the death of Elthyrd, led the factors. Thalmyn came next, then Harll, Jhaliost, and Eshmael. Having never met Eshmael, Charyn concentrated on him, taking in his broad, almost flat face, muddy brown eyes, and short-cut nondescript brown hair. The factors took their place, standing on the left side of the long table. Then the five High Holders entered, led by Chaeltar, followed by Calkoran, Basalyt, and Khunthan, with Fhaedyrk, as head of the High Council, entering last. As head of the Factors' Council, Hisario moved to the chair immediately to the left of Charyn, while Fhaedyrk, as chief High Councilor, stood across the table from Hisario.

"Welcome to the Chateau once more." After motioning for everyone to seat themselves, Charyn sat down, then let the silence draw out before speaking. "Marshal Vaelln will begin."

Vaelln spoke for less than half a quint, succinctly describing the massive battle off the Abierto Isles, then summarizing the results, after which he remained standing.

"Are you telling us," demanded Chaeltar, "that we will have no real protection of merchant ships sailing to Otelyrn for close to a year? That is intolerable! Absolutely intolerable." He looked to Alastar. "And you and the Collegium refuse to even help traders arm themselves against privateers."

"No," replied Alastar. "We have only opposed forcing imagers to engage in work that could kill them."

"But you'll let sailors die and shippers lose ships," snapped Chaeltar.

"We've discussed that previously," said Charyn firmly. "The shippers aren't forced to hazard their ships and crews, and the Collegium will not be forced to hazard its students' lives."

"It's still the navy's responsibility to protect Solidaran shipping," replied Chaeltar.

"It is, indeed, but any failures there are not the Marshal's fault," interjected Charyn. "That fault lies with the previous council and my predecessor, who could not agree on how to pay for the necessary warships. This council has agreed to such a plan, but it takes time to build ships and train their crews. I doubt your hold house was built in a matter of months, and likely not even in a year."

"We're talking about ships!"

"We are, and we've launched and outfitted how many in the last half year?" Charyn asked Vaelln.

"Five, and another six will be finished by year end. Next year, there will be more."

"But you just lost almost two years' worth of shipbuilding in that battle," said Chaeltar.

"And the Jariolans lost almost four years of building," replied Vaelln evenly. "If they don't come to terms, and if matters continue as they have, we will control the seas entirely in a few years."

"That's too many 'if's,'" snapped Chaeltar, lapsing into a sullen silence.

"Does anyone else have anything to add?" asked Charyn.

"Won't the Jariolans just build more ships, the way we are?" asked Hisario.

"We've captured a few officers over the last months," replied Vaelln. "They are building new ships, but only about half as many as we are. They're also having trouble crewing them. That's one of the reasons they've attacked our merchanters. They've captured sailors and impressed them to crew their warships."

"How can that be?" asked Basalyt.

"Solidar is more than three times the size of Jariola. Also, Jariola shares a border with Ferrum. That means they have to maintain a larger army than we do. They can't afford to spend more."

"Neither can we," muttered Basalyt.

"There are three other matters," said Charyn. "The first

is the matter of allowing downstream water users to make a claim against upstream users for verifiable losses caused by substances or liquids added to the water. What is your feeling about what I proposed last month?" He looked down the table.

"The language you proposed at the last meeting is in accord with current practices in Khel," offered Khunthan. "I have no problem with that."

No one else spoke for a moment. Then Eshmael said, "This means any factor could lose everything if a downstream user claimed damages."

"The burden of proof is on the downstream user," Charyn pointed out. "He has to prove and support that damage before a justicer."

"That's a very high barrier," added Fhaedyrk. "I've talked to several advocates and two former justicers. They all agree that only very high levels of damage would be worth making such a claim."

"Then how will it protect the downstream user?" asked Eshmael, apparently unaware of the contradiction with his first question.

"It won't," replied Fhaedyrk, "unless the damage is great. As the Rex pointed out at the previous Council meeting, there is no perfect solution under law. This will merely rein in the worst of excesses."

Hisario looked to Fhaedyrk and nodded.

Fhaedyrk turned to Charyn. "After consideration, it is the opinion of the High Councilors that your proposal should be promulgated."

"The factors agree," added Hisario.

Eshmael started to open his mouth, then closed it.

Charyn knew the change to the law wouldn't resolve all the problems, but it was a start. He had the feeling that more than a few matters would be resolved, if only temporarily, on that basis. The next two matters would be far more contentious. "The second problem is the burning of manufactorages and warehouses."

"That's more of a problem than the Jariolans," insisted Eshmael. "That's happening right here, not on the ocean thousands of milles from here."

"You wouldn't say that if you'd lost vessels and their cargoes worth more than your warehouses," countered Chaeltar.

"They're both problems," Charyn quickly declared. "Because I worried about the matter even before violence erupted, I brought the matter of the artificers' standard before the councils several times. All of you decided emphatically that such a change to the Codex Legis was not warranted and that it was unworkable. By their actions, at least some of the artisans, crafters, and workers have declared that your position is unworkable. Some of them are willing to die to make that point." He paused, then asked, "How do you feel now about considering changes to the law along the lines I suggested?"

"That's fixing prices," said Hisario. "It won't work. Not for long. You'll have smuggling increasing, and the tariffs from imports will go down. People will still mismark goods."

"I'd have to agree," added Fhaedyrk.

"Price-fixing won't work," added Chaeltar.

"Why not?" asked Khunthan in an amused tone. "You all sort of agree on price levels, anyway."

"There's no way to standardize the goods effectively," replied Hisario.

"In other words," drawled Khunthan, "you set prices between yourselves, but don't do anything about setting quality standards? Or don't want to?"

"That would reveal too much to others," returned Eshmael.

"Then what would work to stop the violence?" asked Charyn, almost conversationally, even while he was fighting an almost visceral reaction against Eshmael.

"Lock up or execute the troublemakers," declared Eshmael. "That's what the laws are for. To make Solidar safe."

"That doesn't seem to be working all that well," replied Charyn. "So far, from what I can determine, just in L'Excelsis almost forty men have been executed or killed and another ten sent to the workhouses, but the factorages continue to be burned, possibly more quickly than ever. The same thing is happening in Solis and Ferravyl and elsewhere."

"Then bring in the army and kill more of them until they stop," Eshmael replied.

"I think the Rex is making the point that just killing the men setting the fires doesn't seem to be working," Fhaedyrk said firmly, looking to Charyn and asking, "Do you have something in mind?"

"I do. You each have two sheets in front of you. Turn them over and read over the one entitled, 'On Uniform Compensation.' Do not object or raise your voices until after each of you has read your sheet and until I have explained the other part of the plan." He watched as expressions of dismay ran across the face of every factor except, interestingly enough, Hisario.

When everyone was looking, or glaring, at him, he said firmly, "Just putting troopers or more civic patrollers in the city or around manufactorages won't work. Not by itself. Crafters and workers are angry. It appears that they're desperate because they can't make enough to feed their families. That's why I'm suggesting a daily minimum pay. If any one of you tries to do that, you're at a disadvantage compared to other factors. If you all have to, you're on the same ground."

"You intend to *force* us to overpay lazy workers? I can't believe any Rex would be that . . ." Eshmael shook his head, as if unable to finish his sentence.

"No. You can still hire and fire as you wish. You can certainly fire lazy workers or those who can't do the work."

"How can you as Rex declare what the wages should be in each and every factorage or High Holding in Solidar? They're all different," declared Chaeltar.

"I'm not proposing to set wages. I'm proposing to set a minimum wage, and to say that you can't hire children for men's work."

"You're giving in to those bastardly ruffians," declared Eshmael. "That's what they want. They want to ruin honest factors."

"Until the violence broke out, you were making more silvers than you ever did," said Charyn. "What the change in the law would do is to give them less than many were making before. No . . . for a time you won't make quite as much as you did, but neither will they, and we won't have factorages and warehouses burning every week."

"When you execute all of the troublemakers, that will stop the fire for good," said Basalyt coldly.

"As I said just a few moments ago," replied Charyn, "that has done nothing to stop the attacks and fires. We've killed forty men, and there are more fires and more destruction."

"It will take some time, but they'll see," added Eshmael.

"How many hundred do you want killed?" asked Khunthan. "How many factorages destroyed?"

"As many as it takes," snapped Chaeltar.

"Enough!" said Charyn firmly. "I asked a question that no one here has yet answered. Does anyone have a better idea than either changing nothing or doing what I proposed?"

After several moments, Fhaedyrk cleared his throat. "I can't see that anyone here has a better idea than the Rex."

"We haven't had enough time," snapped Eshmael.

"There has to be a better way," insisted Basalyt.

"Some way that doesn't have the Rex meddling in our business," added Chaeltar sourly.

"Fine," replied Charyn. "You can have your time, but you'll have to handle the fires and lawbreakers with your own guards and the Civic Patrol."

"That's outrageous! You're supposed to protect us." Eshmael's voice was almost a shout.

"As Rex, I'm supposed to protect everyone, not just the factors. You have a problem with the crafters and the workers. You want me to bring in the troopers to kill unhappy crafters and workers so that you can continue to make silvers. Using the army to patrol L'Excelsis and other cities will cost more golds than the treasury can afford, especially when we're fighting a war with Jariola. You don't want me to raise tariffs, but you want me to spend golds for your profit." Charyn thought he caught a glimpse of a fleeting ironic smile on Alastar's face, but he wasn't certain.

"The Rex does have a point," observed Khunthan.

"Point or not . . ." began Eshmael.

"There is one other matter," Charyn said, cutting off the factor. "Please read the second sheet."

When everyone had clearly finished reading, Calkoran spoke. "Why are you bringing this before us? I may be mistaken, but I doubt that there's anything here that any of us would dispute. I admit I'm not certain I see the need for the posting of accounts by choristers, but . . ."

"I brought it to your attention because I wanted you to know that there have been a number of incidents all across Solidar where members of a group who call themselves the True Believers have stormed anomens and, in more than a few places, killed choristers. I've been looking into the matter and have discovered several cases where choristers have most clearly enriched themselves without their congregations knowing the amount of their offerings being diverted. This sort of behavior appears to be what inspired the True Believers. I'd like to remove some of the causes of that anger. At the same time, I don't think a Rex should be making decisions about where those offerings go. I do think that the congregations should know. I wanted you to know what I plan to do and why." Charyn smiled politely. "After all, I did promise to keep you informed and to make you all more a part of governing Solidar."

Fhaedyrk turned to Charyn. "You think these True Believers will make more trouble, don't you?"

"Yes, I do. That's why I'm doing something now."

"So why aren't you doing something about the burnings?" asked Eshmael.

"I offered you an alternative. You didn't like it, and you didn't have another plan that the treasury could afford."

"You have golds in reserve."

"Not that many, as the more experienced members of this council already know. Building the new shipyard required most of the reserves. I've had to spend some of what remained on the pier repairs, and there are more repairs required for the river walls. The damages to the harbors in Westisle and Liantiago were expensive, even with the help of the imagers, and that resulted in the collection of fewer import tariffs."

Eshmael looked around the table, taking in several nods, finally saying, "We'll see."

"Is there anything new?" asked Charyn. After several councilors had shaken their heads, he said, "Then the Council meeting is over. We will meet again on the eighteenth of Feuillyt, unless some extremely urgent matter comes up before then." With a pleasant smile, one that he didn't totally feel, he stood.

After everyone else had left the study, Alastar turned to Charyn. "You could have imposed your plan, you know."

"The situation isn't bad enough, yet," replied Charyn.

"That could be risky for you."

Charyn nodded. "It will be, but neither the factors nor the workers are ready to compromise. More crafters will have to die, more young men be executed or imprisoned, and more factorages be destroyed before I can act."

"Why do you think that?"

"Because the army troopers are trained to kill, and they will. Right now, such deaths will be laid at my door, rather than at the factors'."

"Some will blame you."

"That's another risk I'll have to take. If I act too soon, no one will accept my acts. If I act too late, more people will be shooting at me."

"I wasn't aware that workers and crafters were the ones who shot at you." Alastar's voice was dry.

"I'm likely overstating matters. That happens when people keep shooting at you or threatening to."

Alastar just shook his head.

"I'll see you on Solayi evening, if that's still acceptable," said Charyn.

"It is. We'll look forward to it."

Once Alastar left, Charyn walked to the open window. The air outside was so still that not a breath of air moved into the study. He just stood there for a time, thinking, until Wyllum rapped on the study door.

"Sir . . . do you need me?"

"Wyllum, you can come in."

Charyn turned toward the desk and the papers on it.

Some two glasses later, he left the study and headed downstairs to meet Chelia, Bhayrn, Karyel, and Iryella in the family parlor before dinner.

Bhayrn was waiting at the foot of the grand staircase.

"Are you going out?" Charyn didn't recall being asked about the coach.

"I am. Gherard is coming by in his coach, and Laamyst will be joining us at Gherard's for dinner." Before Charyn could reply, Bhayrn went on. "Did you and the Council actually do anything? Or did you defer to them again?"

"There was nothing to defer to. They don't like the unrest. They won't spend coins on more civic patrollers, and they want me to end the unrest. I made a proposal. They didn't like it. So I told them the problem was theirs. I'm not about to spend golds to protect the factors when they don't want to do anything about it."

"Why should they? You're the Rex."

"I can't spend golds I don't have."

"Just bring in the army."

"If I do that now, all the crafters and most of the High Holders will blame me for the deaths that will happen, and the factors will keep doing what they are, and that means the burnings will continue."

"They will be anyway."

"Did you see yesterday's newssheets?"

"I don't read the trash sheets."

"The regional justicer sentenced a nineteen-year-old to death because he was with his brother when the brother set fire to a factor's warehouse."

"Serves him right."

"I didn't even find out until he was dead. He should have spent a year or two in the workhouse."

"If he was stupid enough to go along with that, he deserved what he got."

"Bhayrn . . . something like forty men just in L'Excelsis have died in the last month because they set fires. They did that because they don't have jobs or aren't paid enough to feed their families. The factors aren't willing to pay more, even though they're making more golds than they ever did. The crafters and the workers know that, and they're furious. It's not just here in L'Excelsis—"

"Once you kill all the troublemakers, the burnings will stop." Bhayrn shook his head. "You can force your own uncle to kill himself, but you worry about worthless workers who are lazy and spoiled. You need to be Rex. That means ruling, not dithering." Bhayrn gestured toward the front entry. "I'll see you later." With that, he turned and walked away.

Are you dithering? Charyn didn't think so, not with what Vaelln had said about using the army, but he also had the feeling that many of the factors and High Holders would think so. *How long can you afford to wait before bringing in the army?*

He took a deep breath and walked to the parlor.

Chelia was there, but not Karyel and Iryella. "Bhayrn won't be joining us."

"I know. He told me. He's spending a lot of time with Laamyst and Gherard."

"You used to spend a great deal of time with Ferrand."

"I think it's different. I couldn't say why."

"Bhayrn's different from you. That's why." Chelia turned as Karyel and Iryella entered the parlor, her eyes inspecting the pair before returning to Charyn.

Once the four were seated in the family dining room and served, Karyel looked to Charyn. "Why do you meet all the time with the Factors' Council, sir?"

"Because the factors are becoming wealthier and more powerful, and they pay more in tariffs than they once did."

"They're factors, sir."

"I can name several High Holders whose ancestors were factors. Just as important, the factors have the power to destroy a number of High Holders."

Karyel's face screwed up in puzzlement. "You'd let them do that?"

"It's not a question of my letting them do that. Some High Holders borrowed large amounts of golds from banking factors and others. If the factors didn't lend to them, the High Holders would have to sell so much of their lands that they'd no longer be High Holders. If any Rex stopped that practice, most of the High Holders and the factors would be very unhappy. If I told the factors that they couldn't collect from the High Holders, then they wouldn't lend those golds."

"Any High Holder who borrows that much isn't very smart," said Iryella.

"Sometimes, even High Holders are unlucky," said Chelia gently. "Drought and heavy rains can ruin the harvest for several years. It's happened that way more than once. By borrowing, one of the smaller High Holders has a chance to keep his lands."

"He should have planned ahead," declared Karyel.

"Sometimes, we can't foresee everything that could happen," said Chelia. "And times change. These days, manufactorages often make more golds than do crops. High Holders whose sires started manufactorages are in a better position than those whose sires didn't. An heir is sometimes captive to the mistakes of his predecessor." Chelia fixed her eyes on Karyel.

"Like me?"

"Like you. That's why you need to know as much as you can about as many things as you can learn . . ."

Charyn nodded, thinking about the forces set in motion before he became Rex, forces that seemed to hold him captive.

39

Charyn was headed to exercise with the guards on Vendrei morning when Maertyl gestured to him. Charyn immediately wondered what had gone wrong and where. "Yes, Guard Captain?"

"It's nothing to do with the Guard, Your Grace. One of the Civic Patrol squad leaders I know stopped by just a little bit ago. Last night, some patrollers ran into some men starting a warehouse fire. The men shot the three patrollers. Two of them died, and then the warehouse exploded. The men got away. The Factors' Council started issuing rifles to the patrollers this morning."

"Do you know whose warehouse?"

"A factor named Saratyn. He deals in glassware. That's all I know."

"Thank you. I appreciate the information very much."

All through the exercises, Charyn wondered how Eshmael would react . . . and how quickly. He also worried about civic patrollers with rifles.

As was more often the case than not, after exercising, washing up, and dressing, he ate breakfast alone, then made his way to his study. Wyllum wasn't there yet, but he'd left the newssheets for Charyn, suggesting that he'd gotten them before his breakfast.

Veritum reported that the Rex and the councils had taken no additional action to address the acts of arson and destruction against manufactorages, leaving the responsibility completely with the Factors' Council and the Civic Patrol. The story also noted that the Patrol had discovered tools and flammable oils in an unused stable near several manufactorages on the west side of the river, but had not discovered who had placed the materials there.

Interestingly enough, there was no mention of the Council meeting in *Tableta,* but Charyn had no doubts that his absence from the pages of that newssheet would be temporary.

Just after Wyllum appeared, so did Sanafryt, carrying several sheets of paper. "Your Grace?"

"Yes? Is there a problem with proclaiming the change to the Codex Legis dealing with choristers?"

"Not that kind of problem, sir. I just received this from the regional minister of justice in Solis. It's a copy of a document that was nailed to the door of the Anomen D'Montagne some two weeks ago. Regional Minister Kafrayt sent it by courier as soon as he made the copy. It's purportedly from the True Believers."

Charyn managed not to sigh. "Let me read it. Just sit down."

The document was relatively short.

Rholan the Unnamer, as the interpreter for the Nameless, intended that the lives of believers should be a constant search for meaning through their acts and deeds in order to improve their lives and the lives of others.

1. Meaning cannot be purchased through coins, whether of copper, silver, or gold. That being so, offerings made to the Nameless are of value to the Nameless, and to the giver, only so far as they enable the chorister and those under him to accomplish acts of meaning.

2. An act of meaning is one that improves the health, life, or spirit of both the giver and the recipient.

3. An act of meaning must be undertaken with no thought of personal gain in wealth, position, or stature. Thus, an act is bereft of meaning if the gift redounds to the benefit of the giver or of the chorister who performs it.

4. An act of meaning performed in hopes of personal gain in any form is nothing less than the sin of Naming, as Rholan declared more than once. Such acts have been too often performed by Choristers of the Nameless.

5. An act of meaning is diminished if it is given in guilt and in an attempt at penance or to obtain some form of absolution for an act of evil.

6. A chorister who diverts offerings meant to enable acts of meaning to the acquisition of personal ornamentation, fine raiment, or rich foods and beverages defiles the Nameless and betrays the ideals and teachings of Rholan.

7. Such choristers are Namers of the worst kind, for they pose as servants and interpreters of the Nameless while embodying the practices of the Namer.

8. Therefore, we proclaim that all such choristers must be cast out from their anomens and replaced by those who carry out acts of meaning in the spirit of the Nameless and as demonstrated by the life of Rholan.

9. Copies of these theses have been sent throughout Solidar to all True Believers as inspiration for the cleansing and reformation of the faith of the Nameless, as set forth by Rholan.

"Does Regional Minister Kafrayt have any idea who posted these theses or how many of them were sent?"

"No, sir. The chorister of the Anomen D'Montagne fled upon reading them, but he was thoughtful enough to send them to Solis before he disappeared."

Charyn nodded. "Get the copies of our proclamation of the change in the Codex Legis finished and dispatched immediately. And don't mention this document to anyone until a day after you have."

Once Sanafryt left, Charyn walked to the window. He

would have preferred to have issued the proclamation before such theses were spread. *But you really didn't dither or delay on this.* At the same time, he was well aware that he could have pressed forward more quickly. *But only if you ignored the Council . . . and that works against what you are trying to do.*

There was a single rap on the door before Chelia opened it and stepped inside.

Charyn turned and moved to stand beside the table desk.

"You mentioned the need for dinners after Autumn-Turn and had Elacia begin planning. You wanted one for the more important factors and one for the High Holders."

Charyn nodded. "I think it's necessary."

"As do I. The dinner for factors might best be the first, since you will see some of the High Holders at the Autumn-Turn Ball. Perhaps the twenty-eighth of Erntyn for the factors, and the fourteenth of Feuillyt for the High Holders."

Since Chelia's words were not a question, Charyn smiled. "Those dates would be good, and Wyllum can write the invitations for you."

"And a dinner for the councilors and their wives on the twenty-first of Feuillyt?"

Charyn nodded, not that he was looking forward to that particular dinner.

"Good. We can start this afternoon, after you go over the lists I've proposed. Feel free to add or remove any names, especially on the factors' list. These are just suggestions based on what we discussed the other night." Chelia extended two sheets of paper. "Also, since you made no provision for entertainment, I would suggest that Palenya and the string quintet be employed for both events, especially the one for High Holders."

Charyn could tell that the entertainment provisions were neither a suggestion nor a question. "You think that would be for the best?"

"She's one of the best clavecinists, and she shouldn't be

punished for having been your lover. Also, you shouldn't do anything that would indicate that you feel embarrassed or show that you feel she's beneath you."

"I've never felt that way."

"I know that. She knows that. So should everyone else. That's why she'll be coming here to teach Karyel and Iryella later this afternoon."

Charyn couldn't say he was surprised. "What time would you like Wyllum to join you?"

Chelia turned to the young scrivener. "I'll see you at half past first glass."

"Yes, Lady." Wyllum did not quite gulp.

Chelia smiled at her son. "He can bring the amended guest lists then." Then she turned and left the study.

Charyn looked to the wide-eyed Wyllum, then said in a matter-of-fact tone, "She's usually right, you know. While you catch your breath, I'll go over the lists."

"Yes, sir."

Charyn began by reading the factors' list, which began with the five members of the Factors' Council. There was one name his mother had added, and that was of Kathila D'Factoria. Charyn had not heard of any women recognized as factors in their own right until Estafen had mentioned Kathila, and now, if his mother had added her, there was definitely a good reason to include her. After going over the list again, he added Saratyn and several other factors he knew or knew about. Next, he read over the local High Holders list, making certain both Laastyn and Ghaermyn were included, but crossing off Laevoryn—he'd seen and heard enough of him—and noted that Chelia had recommended not inviting either Aishford or Paellyt. Charyn wrote "don't invite" beside each name. Chelia had also suggested adding Quensyl, to which Charyn wrote, "Not at present. He was snide about Palenya."

When he finished with the lists, he handed them to Wyllum. "If you'd copy each list for me."

"Yes, sir."

Charyn returned to considering his limited options in dealing with the problems facing him. He was still struggling when, at a quint past second glass, Sturdyn brought in a letter addressed in a hand that he knew immediately to be that of Alyncya. As soon as the study door was closed, he opened it and began to read.

> My dear Rex—
> Thank you for your most considered responses to the questions that I posed. You have obviously thought through the difficulties and the ramifications of each course of action open to you as Rex. Yet, I have noticed that you have refrained from any of the courses of action you described, that is, if the accounts in the newssheets are accurate. It would appear that either you have decided not to act, that the time for any of the actions you previously discussed has not yet come, or that you are considering a course of action that you had not previously contemplated. Whatever may be the reason for your refraining from immediate action, I am hopeful that your decisions in the matter reflect that same thoughtful nature that you have displayed in your correspondence.
>
> I must confess that I enjoyed and greatly appreciated your observations on history and the possible repetition of actions by later generations of acts undertaken by previous generations. Some recent acts that I have observed, not of yours thus far, seem to repeat a lack of perception or understanding of the unfavorable consequences of those types of acts in the past history of Solidar.

Not of yours, thus far? That was a polite way of saying that Alyncya would be quite willing to tell him when she thought he was acting unwisely. *As if that's any surprise.*

*. . . and it would appear that candor in presenting
counsel, or even factual descriptions, is often less than
fully appreciated, especially when such observations or
suggestions are presented by a woman. In that regard,
I will be most interested in seeing how you address the
difficulties that have been set before you, as they are
trials not resulting from error or misstep on your part,
but which could lead to even greater difficulties if not
successfully resolved.*

At those words, Charyn smiled wryly.

*In our short correspondence, we have discussed weighty
issues, but little of less import, for example, whether you
read anything besides piles of documents and papers, or
whether you would rather be hunting or riding, or if you
ever play plaques or whist, or even what your favorite
sweet might be. Do the morning or the evening glasses
seem more attractive to you? Or do you intend to remain
a rex of mystery to me?*

Charyn looked at the last words, realizing that was indeed
where the letter ended, except, of course, for the closing—
the same as before.

I remain, as always, with the warmest of regards.

The signature was also the same—"Alyncya."
For a time, he just sat there, letter in hand. He *thought* that
the last questions were favorable, but were they?
He shook his head. The only way he'd find out was to an-
swer the questions . . . and to pose some of his own.
He reached for his writing paper.

40

~~~~~

When Charyn woke on Solayi morning the first thing he sensed was the acrid odor of smoke. He bolted up and went to the window, drawing back the hangings and looking out over the city. In the still air, a thin haze blanketed L'Excelsis in whatever direction he looked.

How many more buildings were burned last night? That was his first thought. His second was, *What can you do to show concern without committing to using the army too soon?*

He was still thinking about it as he washed and then dressed. *Possibly asking Factor Eshmael for a tour of all the damaged factorages, manufactorages, and warehouses?*

That might work, but would he need to make some gesture toward the crafters and guilds? He decided he needed to think that over. That could be seen as pandering to the mob and would alienate both the factors and the High Holders, and having both groups angry at him was the last thing he needed at the moment.

He was so preoccupied that he almost failed to realize that Bhayrn was already in the breakfast room. "Oh . . . good morning."

"You actually slept to a decent glass," replied Bhayrn. "I almost can't believe it."

Charyn decided to ignore the not-quite-brotherly jab as he sat down across the table from Bhayrn. "I've scarcely seen you in the last few days . . . How was your dinner with Gherard and Laamyst the other night?"

"Enjoyable. I didn't have to be polite to Karyel."

"He's gotten much more mannered."

"On the surface, anyway. Iryella is more to my liking. She's not too bad. Laamyst might like her."

"She's a little young for him," replied Charyn.

"He's in no hurry to get married, and seven or eight years' difference isn't that much. Mother would see that she got a decent dowry."

And Laamyst would be indebted to you. Charyn wasn't about to voice that thought. Instead, he picked up the mug of tea that Therosa had set before him and took a sip before asking, "Have your friends said much about the problems between the workers and the factors?"

"Most of them wonder why you haven't done more. Gherard says too many of the workers at his father's factorages are too lazy to be paid more. Why don't you just offer a big reward for anyone who captures that artisan?" asked Bhayrn. "You know the one. The silversmith who never showed up to meet with you."

"I don't know that he's done anything wrong. I just think he knows who did." Charyn smiled at Therosa after she set a platter of cheesed eggs, ham strips, and green melon slices before him, as well as a small loaf of dark bread. "Thank you."

The server nodded and slipped away.

"It doesn't matter," replied Bhayrn. "If he knows anyone who's burned anything, he's as guilty as the others."

"But I don't *know* that," Charyn pointed out. "Besides, someone already burned his shop and living quarters, and he's nowhere to be found."

"You're the Rex. That's what counts. For someone so calculating, you're letting too many things happen. I still don't see why you don't turn the army out the next time those True Believers show up."

"There's a small problem there. I don't know where or when they'll show up."

"Just post a company at every anomen around L'Excelsis. Sooner or later they'll turn up."

"It's more likely that they won't show up so long as the

army company's there. Besides, there are likely a good score of anomens in and around L'Excelsis."

"Well then, that will keep them from showing up."

"Bhayrn . . . a company at each anomen would take more troopers than there are at High Command."

"Then perhaps you and Father shouldn't have moved so many troopers from L'Excelsis."

"I didn't have anything to do with that, and I don't have the golds for more troopers, not and deal with the Jariolans."

"Raise tariffs on the factors and crafters, then."

Charyn managed not to give an exasperated sigh. "I've just gotten the factors and High Holders to agree to the last increase."

"I wasn't talking about the High Holders. They pay enough as it is."

"Do you want me to start a factors' revolt?"

"They're all cowards. All they think about is how they can get more golds."

"If the factors decide not to lend to High Holders, a fifth of all High Holders will lose their holds in less than two years." That was a guess on Charyn's part, but he knew a significant fraction were already deep in debt.

"That's what the army's for—to keep the factors in line."

"It might be better not to start another war," said Charyn dryly, taking a bite of the eggs before they got cold.

"You're the Rex. You're going to do what you're going to do." Bhayrn stood. "Are you coming to services tonight with Mother and her charges?"

"Are you?"

"Mother's suggested it would be wise for me to do so." Bhayrn paused. "You didn't say whether you'd be coming."

"I didn't, did I? Why don't you plan on taking the regial coach?"

Bhayrn frowned.

"All right. I'll use it. You and Mother take the unmarked one."

"Then you're going to services at Imagisle?"

"Most likely. Would you like to join us?"

"No . . . I'll pass on that. If Aloryana wants to see me, it'll have to be someplace besides Imagisle." With a nod, Bhayrn turned and left the breakfast room.

For a moment, Charyn just sat there, stunned. Then he began to finish his breakfast.

Once he did, he made his way up to his study, where he drafted a letter to Eshmael, suggesting that the factor might come to the Chateau on Mardi or Meredi and guide Charyn to see the damage wrought by those attacking factors' facilities. When he finished, he set it aside, for possible revision before he had Wyllum dispatch it on Lundi morning.

All that made him conscious of just how much he missed Elthyrd's steady hand . . . and that also made him wonder, again, who would have wanted to remove such a steadying influence?

Eshmael? Because he wanted to be a factor councilor or because he felt Elthyrd was too deferential to Charyn and the High Holders? Or could it be a High Holder who resented Elthyrd's influence on Charyn? Or a rival factor?

Charyn shook his head. He just didn't know enough.

Then he spent several glasses going over petitions, the flow of which had resumed during Erntyn, until he'd had enough of High Holder and factor complaints, at which time he repaired to the music room—except that someone was practicing, intermittently, and the notes appeared almost spiritless.

When the playing died away, and the room was quiet, Charyn entered, to find Iryella sitting at the clavecin, disconsolately, it appeared.

"What seems to be the matter?" asked Charyn.

"Aunt Chelia told me I wasn't practicing enough. She didn't say that to Karyel, and he practices less than I do."

For a moment, Charyn didn't know what to say, because

what Iryella said didn't sound like his mother. "Is that *exactly* what she said?"

Iryella looked away.

Charyn waited.

Finally, Iryella looked up. "She said I had to practice more than Karyel because it didn't come as easily to me. That's not fair."

"No, it's not," replied Charyn. "Life isn't always fair. What that means is that you have to practice more to get better than Karyel does. I had to practice more than some people. Maitre Malyna plays better than I do, but she had to work much harder at it than I did. That's why I practice more than I used to." *One of the reasons, anyway.*

"I've heard you play. You're better than Karyel."

"I've been practicing longer, I imagine. Especially in the last year."

"But you don't have to practice. You're the Rex."

"If I want to get better, it doesn't matter if I'm the Rex. The clavecin doesn't care."

"That's a funny way to put it."

"It's true, though."

Iryella frowned.

"Do you want to practice more?" asked Charyn.

"No, sir. Not now."

"Think about what I said. If you want to get better, you'll have to work harder, sometimes harder than other people. There are probably some things that you do more easily than Karyel. We're all different."

Iryella eased off the clavecin bench. "By your leave, Your Grace?"

Charyn smiled. "You can go. If your aunt asks, tell her I'm practicing, and that you'll practice more later. Then do it . . . so you'll be telling the truth."

"Yes, sir."

Once Iryella left, Charyn seated himself at the clavecin

and began to play, first with the pieces he knew well, then working his way up to the harder works. While he was still rough on "Pavane in a Minor Key," he had the feeling that the "Variations on a Khellan Melody" was almost to the point where he wouldn't be embarrassed to play it in front of others.

Before he knew it, it was time to get ready to go to Imagisle, since he'd decided to leave earlier than he usually did and to take the Sud Bridge. Despite what he'd implied to Bhayrn, he wasn't taking the regial coach, but riding with guards, wearing an undercaptain's uniform.

When he was riding on the east and west sides of the river, he saw close to half a score of recently burned buildings, and realized that the damage could have been much worse—except for the fact that most structures in L'Excelsis were either of brick or stone, with slate or tile roofs. Still . . . he had no doubts that there were a number of buildings burned by disgruntled workers that he hadn't seen.

When he and the guards rode up to the Maitre's dwelling less than two quints past fifth glass, there was no one in sight, not that he expected anyone to be waiting, given how early he had arrived.

As he let the chestnut walk slowly toward the stable, Aloryana hurried out, almost at a run, until she caught up with him. "You're here earlier."

"I rode a different way, over the Sud Bridge. It didn't take as long as I thought," Charyn said as he dismounted. He led the chestnut into the Maitre's stable, with Aloryana walking beside him.

"Guess what?"

Given the happiness in her voice, Charyn smiled. "I don't know, but I wager it's good."

"My shields are good enough that I made third."

"That is good! Didn't Maitre Alastar say that it might take you until the end of the year?"

"That's what they thought, but Lystara's been working a

lot more with me, and that helped. She's really nice. So's Malyna, but we don't see her as much." Aloryana paused. "I'm just barely a third."

"How can you be barely a third?" asked Charyn as he stalled the chestnut.

"My shields stopped everything, but I didn't have enough strength to hold them after that. The tests don't say anything about that, but Maitre Alyna said that I'd passed, but to try to avoid being shot at until I was stronger. I'm doing more exercises, now, like the older imagers. Lystara says that will help."

After closing the stall door, Charyn gestured toward the front of the stable. "I'll wait here until it's closer to time to leave for the anomen."

"I got a letter from Mother yesterday. She said that Palenya is teaching Karyel and Iryella in the late afternoon. I'm glad she is. I was afraid you wouldn't want to see her anymore."

"I still care for Palenya," replied Charyn. "It's just . . . you understand. But I did have a lesson with her a little while ago, and I did pay her."

"Good!"

Charyn couldn't help smiling. Then he saw Alastar walking toward them.

"We didn't expect you this early," said the Maitre, who then turned to the guards. "Make yourselves comfortable. There will be refreshments after services."

"Thank you," said Charyn. "I didn't expect to be this early. I rode over the long way. I saw a good half score of burned warehouses and manufactorages. I'd hoped that some of the violence might die down."

Alastar shook his head. "Not yet. Two more warehouses were burned last night. Some of those who were involved were caught. Two civic patrollers were shot. One died."

"I'm going to ask Eshmael to give me a tour of all the destroyed buildings. That way, he can't say that I don't understand. He can also tell the other factors he's made things clear to me."

"Do you think that will help?"

"I'm hoping it will buy time."

"To what end?"

"To get the factors and High Holders to understand that the lowest possible wages aren't necessarily the most profitable."

"That may prove difficult."

"I don't expect otherwise, but . . . if I step in too soon . . ."

Alastar nodded slowly, then said, "You realize that Iskhar's homilies have gotten much better since you've attended services here?"

For a moment, Charyn wondered at the abrupt change of subject, before realizing that was the Maitre's way of suggesting he had doubts about Charyn's decision. *As if you don't.*

"Oh? You give me too much credit."

"I don't think it's a coincidence." Alastar motioned in the direction of the front porch, and the three began to walk. At the front walk, they were joined by Lystara and Alyna, and the three adults led the way down the lane toward the anomen.

"I really must thank you for allowing Palenya to become the Collegium musician," said Alyna.

Charyn laughed softly. "I'm most happy it worked out, but, as I'm sure you must know, I had very little to do with that. My mother and Palenya arranged matters so that even a blind man could have seen where to go."

"That's not so," declared Aloryana. "Bhayrn didn't see it, and neither did I."

"All too often," said Alastar dryly, "it takes a perceptive man to see the obvious. Except in hindsight."

All of that suggested to Charyn that there was too much he wasn't seeing, but he decided against admitting that publicly. "Aloryana told me that she's a third."

"Barely a third," insisted his sister.

"Her shields are barely adequate for a third," said Alyna, "but her concealments are excellent, and her control is outstanding for someone her age. As she gets stronger, the shields shouldn't be a problem. She's about where Malyna was at the same time."

As he entered the anomen, Charyn noticed that, while a few of the imagers glanced in his direction, no one seemed to dwell on his presence. He wasn't sure if that happened to be bad or good, or if it mattered at all.

The service proceeded as the services on Imagisle always did, but Charyn did find that some of what Iskhar said in his homily caught his attention a bit more than usual.

". . . in recent weeks, groups of angry believers have been storming certain anomens across Solidar. They've declared that certain choristers have been keeping too much of the offerings for themselves and that they've become Namers. This isn't something new. Rholan was likely killed because he was outspoken. He wanted the faith of the Nameless to change into something better. Some people extol change, as if change is always better. Sometimes change is good, and sometimes it's not. What we have to ask as imagers is how we can change for the better. When Maitre Alastar came here, the Collegium had not changed in decades, and it was dying because Solidar had changed, and the Collegium had not adapted to deal with those changes.

"Making changes in the physical world doesn't mean that the values of the Nameless or those of the Collegium necessarily need to change. It does mean that old values and old ways do need to be examined . . ."

Isn't that what you're trying to do? And it doesn't seem like either the factors or the High Holders want much examination of anything that might cost them. Charyn smiled sardonically, thinking how the factors had wanted changes that benefited factors, and, incidentally, reduced the power of High Holders, and now, those same factors were balking at changes that might help the crafters and workers. *But what about the powers of the Rex?*

He was still mulling over those questions as he left the anomen.

"You're looking rather pensive," observed Alyna.

"I was thinking about change, and the fact that, whether what's happening in Solidar is good or not, we really don't have much choice about it, only about how we deal with it."

"That's something that neither of your immediate predecessors truly accepted, except when faced with overwhelming force."

"I fear I'm no different, except that I might be seeing those overwhelming forces before they become quite so obvious."

"Forces?" asked Alastar.

"The True Believers are another force as well. I could be mistaken, but we'll have to see. Whoever wrote those theses seems to have thought them out."

"Theses?" asked Alastar.

"You haven't heard? I would have thought . . . you seem to know most things before I do . . ." Charyn went on to explain.

The five had just about reached the Maitre's house before he finished, and Alastar said, "That's something we didn't know, and I'd have to agree with you. I appreciate your telling us."

"I would have told you earlier, but . . . I thought you already knew, especially after Iskhar's homily."

"We knew about the True Believers here in L'Excelsis, and that there were problems elsewhere, but not about the theses." The Maitre shook his head. "Enough of that now. We should enjoy the refreshments."

For the most part, Charyn did indeed enjoy the refreshments and lighter conversation, and, as usual, he didn't want to leave, hoping that nothing untoward had occurred at the Chateau in his absence.

That hope seemed to be dashed almost as soon as he dismounted in the rear courtyard, because Faelln immediately appeared.

"Your Grace?"

"I take it that there's a problem?"

"More like a concern, sir. You know, we've posted men to watch the Ring Road and the streets around the Chateau. One of them . . . I almost hesitate to mention it . . . but someone wearing guard greens walked out from the Chateau's east garden just before you left and handed an envelope to a private courier who immediately appeared and rode off. The guards only saw it at the last moment, and whoever it was vanished before they got to the garden."

"Could they tell who the guard was?"

"No, sir. All the duty guards were accounted for, but I asked everyone in the stables, and no one was missing. It might have been an off-duty guard, but . . ."

"There's no way to tell who it might have been," concluded Charyn.

"No, sir."

"It might not be anything, but . . ." Charyn sighed. "If you and Maertyl will keep an eye out for anything else that looks out of order."

"Yes, sir."

As Charyn headed up the grand staircase, he considered the incident. It could have just been someone sending a message to friends or family, except the part about the courier appearing and leaving quickly, as if it had been arranged in advance by someone who didn't want to be identified . . . and there was one very likely suspect. Charyn shook his head.

"Charyn?" Chelia asked as he neared the top of the staircase. "How is Aloryana?"

"She just made imager third. She's very pleased. Maitre Alyna said that her progress was excellent and that if she continued, she might well become a maitre herself in time." That wasn't quite what Alyna had said, but what she'd implied.

"You must come and tell me. She hasn't been writing quite as much in the past few weeks. I suppose that's to be expected, but . . ."

Charyn understood. "I'll tell you everything she said."

~~~~~

41

On Lundi and Mardi, Charyn scarcely saw Bhayrn, except at dinner on Lundi. He did hear both Karyel and Iryella dutifully practicing on the clavecin daily. On Meredi morning, the first thing he did when he got to the study was to read the newssheets, beginning with *Veritum,* which reported that three more buildings belonging to factors had been burned, and that two rioters and one patroller had been killed. There was no mention of Charyn. There was also a brief story on a group of True Believers who had surrounded the Anomen D'Este on Solayi, chanting slogans against the refurbishment of the chorister's house.

Tableta was, again, snidely targeting Charyn, at least in part.

. . . the True Believers have set forth nine theses outlining their grievances against greedy choristers. Interestingly enough, the Rex has also shown an interest in choristers. He has promulgated minor changes to the laws that will now hold choristers accountable to their congregations and made failure to do so a crime. He has also directed the Minister of Justice and the Regional Ministers of Justice to enforce the new laws. Why is our beloved Rex more concerned about a handful of religious dissenters than about the deaths and widespread violence caused by disgruntled weavers and crafters? While the Rex has been attending services regularly, if on Imagisle with his sister the Imager, for the first six months of his rule, he was found nowhere near an anomen . . .

Charyn wanted to shake his head. The questions were fair enough as far as he was concerned, but no one seemed to be asking similar questions of the factors and High Holders, whose predatory and often deceptive practices and low wages had at the very least contributed to, if not caused, the violence and deaths.

He'd barely set aside the newssheets when Moencriff brought in a message from Estafen, or rather Estafen's transmittal of Engineer Ostraaw's latest report. The transmittal letter was far more alarming than the financial report, particularly one section:

> . . . as we discussed, the ironworks has been getting its heavy coal from Factor Karl. Karl has raised the price of coal from five coppers per tonne to six coppers. The price change will take effect for any heavy coal delivered after the first of Feuillyt. Karl suggested that further price increases are likely. Under current conditions, the ironworks will barely break even if the coal price remains at six coppers. If Karl raises prices to seven coppers a tonne, you will be losing eight coppers a tonne on pig iron and more than twice that on bar iron, unless we raise our prices . . .

From what Charyn had learned from Estafen, significant price increases weren't feasible, given what the other ironworks in Bovaria charged, particularly what the one in Ferravyl charged, and with an output of thirty tonnes a day, Charyn could easily end up losing twenty golds a week, and far more if coal prices continued to rise.

> . . . in addition, since the Aluse freezes over for much of the winter, we will need to purchase enough to carry us through those months at the higher prices . . . suggest we might meet the next time you are in L'Excelsis . . .

Charyn smiled wryly. Purchasing the ironworks was definitely going to cost him, one way or another. He needed to meet with Ostraaw as soon as possible to see if the engineer knew of other sources of coal, just in case.

"Wyllum, I'll have a letter for you in a bit. I'll need for you to arrange for a private messenger to carry it to the ironworks south of L'Excelsis."

"Sir?"

"The ironworks owner doesn't want anyone to know that the reply came from the Chateau."

In less than a quint, Charyn wrote out a reply to Ostraaw, saying that, since he was currently in L'Excelsis, he would be able to meet early on Vendrei morning and would be arriving in a gray coach at seventh glass. He'd hurried his reply to Ostraaw, because he was expecting Eshmael before long, who had readily agreed to accompany Charyn on a tour of factors' properties damaged by unhappy crafters and workers. He sealed the envelope with the black wax he'd used earlier, with an unmarked imprint, then handed it to Wyllum.

"You didn't want me to write a final draft, sir?"

"There wasn't time. Now . . . you need to arrange for a private courier. Tell the courier that it contains papers for Engineer Ostraaw at the ironworks. Factor Estafen asked me to look them over and return them to Ostraaw, but I don't want Ostraaw knowing the papers came back from the Chateau." That much was certainly true.

Charyn handed Wyllum three silvers. "It shouldn't cost much more than a silver from here to the ironworks. In a quint or so, Factor Eshmael will be here, and I'll be taking a coach ride with him to survey the damage to factorages and warehouses. After you take care of the courier, make yourself available to Lady Chelia for any scriving she may require."

"Yes, sir."

Not even a quint had passed before Moencriff announced Eshmael's arrival.

Charyn hurried down to the entry hall to meet the factor.

"Your Grace," offered Eshmael, his voice cool, but not cold, his brown eyes hard as he inclined his head.

"Councilor." Charyn nodded in return. "I have an unmarked coach waiting in the rear courtyard. The guards who will accompany us wear plain brown jackets."

"Do you worry that much about being shot?"

"I prefer to observe without being noticed, at least not being seen as more than a wealthy factor or High Holder." Charyn turned and led the way to the courtyard.

When the two stood beside the unmarked coach, Charyn turned to the factor. "Where would you suggest we begin?"

"Start on the West River Road a mille south of the piers and come north to the Sud Bridge, then cross the river and take the East River Road south . . ."

Charyn gestured to the coach, glancing back at the two mounted guards who wore plain brown jackets, then entered the coach after Eshmael.

After nearly a glass, Charyn had seen just about enough charred stone walls that were the remnants of warehouses and manufactorages, although he had noticed that three were already in the process of being rebuilt. He also wondered if some of the buildings would ever be soon rebuilt . . . and whether certain opportunistic factors had set fires to collect on indemnity bonds. He did not voice any of those thoughts, but just listened as Eshmael talked.

"You've seen the damage that these ruffians have caused . . ."

". . . that was my prime warehouse . . . took three ships to carry those Abiertan ceramics here . . . more than a hundred golds in just them . . ."

"Noerbyn's manufactorage . . . barely had the frames installed . . ."

By the time the coach rolled back into the rear courtyard,

some three and a half glasses after leaving the Chateau, Charyn had definitely seen enough burned and damaged buildings, and certainly heard enough from Eshmael.

"Now, do you see why we're concerned? The Civic Patrol has caught almost a hundred men and still more of them appear with oils and rags and even gunpowder . . . It's about time you did something about this, Your Grace."

"What do you suggest, Councilor?"

"Bring in the army. What else?"

As one of the guards opened the coach door, Charyn replied, "Something like eighty men have been killed or executed. How will killing more of them stop anything? It's likely that every death angers two more men, if not more, and prompts them to attack another factor. Would you have me bring in the army and kill everyone? Then who would do the work, and who would buy your goods?"

"The ruffians only buy the least expensive goods."

Charyn stepped out of the coach and waited for Eshmael to join him before replying. "Even if that's true, how will factors who have lost as much as you have any silvers or golds left to buy such goods?"

"All the more reason for you to act now."

"I will give your recommendations every consideration, Factor Eshmael. I wouldn't have asked for you to guide me and spend much of a day looking at the destruction if I weren't concerned. I need to discuss what you've suggested with my ministers and possibly with Marshal Vaelln. If you'd come early on Samedi, we can talk over the matter then."

"I look forward to that." Eshmael's words were curt, almost dismissive as he added, "Do you think courting factors with a dinner will help you?"

"Courting factors wasn't ever the main purpose of the dinner. Getting to know all of you better is."

"To what end?"

"To find a way to get factors, crafters, and High Holders to work together."

"Words . . . mere words."

"You think so? Have I held lavish entertainments? Have I confiscated lands or wealth? Haven't I put factors and High Holders under the same laws with regard to water rights and the justicers?"

"That's little enough."

"Eshmael," Charyn said firmly, "I became Rex far earlier than I or anyone expected. I've been Rex for less than seven months, and as you must have seen at the last Council meeting, it's not exactly easy to obtain agreements between factors and High Holders in any swift fashion, and both of you would be angered greatly if I imposed any requirements with which you do not agree. If I cannot obtain agreements, and if matters worsen, I may indeed have to impose requirements, but I'd prefer not to. I'd much prefer to work out matters with all members of the Council. That usually means everyone gives a little, rather than one group getting all it wants and the others getting nothing."

"What are you giving?"

"Every bit of the reserve funds has gone to needs that the Council has wished. So far, what have you given? And don't mention the damage we just viewed. I've had nothing to do with that, and neither did my predecessors. If you're honest, you'll acknowledge that."

Eshmael frowned. "We . . . factors don't have the power to stop those ruffians. You do."

"Factor Councilor . . . there's more than one kind of power. I'd like you to think about that, and we can talk about it later. I understand the costs of the damages to factors' buildings. Believe me, I do. You might recall that last Finitas certain ruffians destroyed most of the grain held in the regial granaries near Tuuryl. The loss was near twelve thousand golds."

"Twelve thousand? That can't be."

"It was. You're welcome to go and talk to the landwarden there. Otherwise there would have been more golds in the treasury reserves." Not all twelve thousand, but Charyn wasn't about to get into those details.

"It's not the same."

"No . . . it's not. Everyone suffers losses, but the losses are different. A warehouse is important to a factor. A ship and cargo lost to the Jariolans is important to a trader. Losing a job because a new manufactorage can weave cloth more cheaply is important to a weaver. Each loss strikes each man as important to him. That's something that I'd like the councilors to consider."

"We're creating jobs with the manufactorages," declared Eshmael.

"You are. Cheaper cloth is better for many people, but there's a cost to others. If such costs are too high, people get upset. Some get angry. If the costs are too high, there can be rebellions and thousands of lives lost. We've seen that happen twice in my life. I'd rather it didn't happen again. I'd like to think you wouldn't, either. I'd like to think that other members of the Council would consider that as well." Charyn smiled as warmly as he could manage. "I appreciated the tour and hearing what you had to say." *Even if I didn't agree with some of what you said.* He gestured toward Eshmael's modest carriage, which had been brought to the rear courtyard, and began to walk toward it.

"Your words won't change anything, Your Grace."

Charyn looked directly at the factor. "You're absolutely right. Only acts change things. You can act or not. And how you and the other factors—and the High Holders—act will determine what I must do as Rex."

"What about the crafters and their ruffians?"

"They've already acted, haven't they? The question isn't about their acts, but about what will most effectively stop their acts without creating even more destruction and deaths. That's what the Council needs to address at the next meeting . . . and what we can talk over on Samedi, if you wish. Now . . . if you will excuse me . . ." Charyn stepped back a pace from the factor's carriage, since it was clear that Eshmael would always have a response . . . if Charyn gave him the opportunity.

Eshmael looked as if he wanted to say something, then paused. After several moments, he finally spoke. "It may be that, if you don't use the full regial power, you shouldn't have it."

"While some would take that as a threat, I won't." *Not yet.* "I would point out that someone has to make such decisions in everyone's interest, not just in one group's interest. If the Rex's interest is paramount, then everyone else will be angry . . . but the same would be true if the High Holders obtained more power. You should have seen where that could have led. Likewise, if the factors' interests are paramount, what will the High Holders do? Both the factors and the High Holders wanted a greater say in how Solidar is governed. I've provided that." *With the help of the Collegium.* "But so far each of you is far more interested in your interests than in everyone's interests. In fact, you all seem to totally ignore other interests. I could make a decision in what I see as everyone's best interests, but it might be better if, before I do, you all come to an agreement as to what your common best interests are."

"Perhaps we should." Eshmael's words were icy, almost a threat. "Perhaps we all should."

"Again . . . I look forward to seeing you on Samedi." Charyn managed to hold a pleasant smile until the small carriage was headed down the drive to the Ring Road. Then he took a deep breath before turning and heading up to his study.

When he reached the study door, Sturdyn said, "Good afternoon, Your Grace. Wyllum is doing some scriving for Lady Chelia. She said that if you needed him urgently just to send for him."

"Thank you."

"There's a dispatch from the Marshal on your desk." Sturdyn tried not to smile as he added, "And a letter."

"You obviously know the writer."

"It would be a guess, sir."

"Not much of one, I'd wager."

Charyn was still smiling as he walked to the desk. The smile became a puzzled frown as he realized that with the letter was a wrapped package about the size of a small and thin volume. He immediately picked up the envelope. The hand was definitely Alyncya's. Reluctantly, he set the letter and package aside and opened the dispatch.

Vaelln's report was not entirely unexpected. While Jariolan privateers were still operating in the seas off Otelyrn, the lack of support from Jariolan warships had reduced their effect, and the Marshal had only heard of one merchanter being lost in the last few weeks, but doubted that the weeks ahead would show so few losses. Harvest storms had reduced the encounters between Solidaran and Jariolan warships, but several had occurred off the Jariolan coast, with one Solidaran frigate lost, but two Jariolan third-raters being sunk. More disturbing was Vaelln's concern that to maintain the present levels of fighting in order to keep the Jariolans from rebuilding their fleets would require an additional five thousand golds, or a comparative reduction in expenses elsewhere, and that he would shortly send Charyn a detailed study on the options available.

Charyn nodded glumly, then added the report to those already in the chest that held all reports from High Command.

With a smile, he took the smaller desk knife that Howal had imaged for him months ago, slit the envelope from Alyncya, replaced the knife, extracted the letter, and began to read, not even sitting down.

My dear Rex—

I must admit that your charming response to the teasing final paragraph of my last letter caught me by surprise. For that reason alone, although I have others,

*I determined to reply more quickly than has been my
wont . . .*

Charming response? *You weren't trying to be charming . . . just honest, because that's what she asked for.*

*. . . I had surmised that you just might be a man more
at home with sunrises than with candles dying under
burnt wicks, although that was but a surmise until you
confirmed it. Nor was I surprised to learn that your
reading tastes run to histories, rather than poetry or
philosophy. Yet there is beauty and cadence in verse that
can inspire and clarify both thought and feeling. For this
reason, I have enclosed with this letter a small book of
my own that has accomplished that for me . . .*

A book of my own? Charyn couldn't help smiling once
more.

*. . . I would hope it would do the same for you, although
what well-chosen words may bring forth in another is
always a guess, often even a mystery.*
    *Your words state that you are an "indifferent" player
at whist. I cannot imagine you are indifferent at anything
to which you put your mind and energies, especially given
that you have recalled my exact words for months, only to
repeat them back to me. Nor will I accept your contention
that your love of music far outstrips your "poor abilities"
with the clavecin. I have watched and heard you play.
I would wager that you began the effort to master
"Variations on a Khellan Melody" shortly after receiving
my less than professional transcription of the music and
that I will not hear you perform it until you are satisfied
that you play it without error and as well as you possibly
can.*

Charyn shook his head, even as his smile turned wry.

You requested that I reply in kind to my own questions. That is a fair inquiry, and I will endeavor to respond honestly. I say endeavor because I am well aware of my tendencies not to reveal vulnerabilities or behaviors that are less than admirable.

My inclination is to prefer day to either extremely early rising or to burning candles into charred wicks. I abhor useless piles of papers and documents, or anything else, that have been written only for the purposes of self-justification. While I enjoy reading the occasional history and the very occasional philosopher, poetry and music are my favorites, as well as gently witty conversation. I find plaques and whist only so enjoyable as those with whom I play, and that is doubtless a weakness on my part, but to be confined to a table and to be required to be charming and civil to someone whose company one does not at least appreciate, if not enjoy, is a form of social torture.

Social torture . . . a very good phrase.

My favorite sweet is Pharsi baklava, the kind made with pistachio nuts and clover honey, but my second favorite sweet is simply the perfect Orundo cherry. I enjoy riding, but only in temperate times, and I find hunting abhorrent, because its sole purpose appears to be to gratify the ego of the hunter while rendering the game being pursued even less edible.

That sentence alone, if mentioned to many High Holders, would definitely turn heads, but Charyn couldn't dispute it.

For the most part, you have written in thoughtful and disciplined fashion, yet I have no idea how your life

*proceeds from day to day, only that it must be far
more complex than what the gossips and newssheets
portray.*

In short, tell me more before I make any decisions.

I remain, as always, with the warmest of regards.

The signature was also the same—"Alyncya."
Since Wyllum had not returned, and there was nothing
immediately pressing, Charyn took out pen and paper and
began.

*My dear Alyncya—
In response to your letter, I had not intended my words
to be taken as charming, for, to me at least, charm
embodies a certain amount of dishonesty, and that is the
last talent I would wish to display or employ in writing
or conversing with you.*

Now what can you say? Charyn took a deep breath and
again picked up the pen.

*Let me just say that while subterfuge is unfortunately
necessary for a Rex in dealing with the strong
personalities and apparently inflexible agendas
manifested in my dealings with the councils and
ministers, such indirectness, even masked by charm, is
the last behavior I would wish to bring into personal and
family life. That being said, neither should rudeness,
abruptness, nor crude words or behavior be excused
under the guise of honesty, and I would hope that my
words and acts follow that standard . . .*

From there, Charyn simply discussed some of the events
of the past week, including his attending services with Alo-

ryana, the general substance of a few of the more interesting petitions he had received, the possible problems with the True Believers and their nine theses, as well as his response, and his tour of damaged buildings with Eshmael.

> *In closing, I would very much thank you for the loan of your book, which I will begin to read this very evening so that we can discuss it when next we meet.*
> *With my greatest appreciation and warmest regards,*
> *Charyn*

As he sealed the envelope, he just hoped he'd struck the right balance. He looked at the small, green, leather-bound volume again.

Not now. He needed to read it when he was alone, when no one could interrupt him.

~~~

42

Sometime after third glass, Charyn heard the faint sounds of the clavecin drifting up from the first level of the Chateau. While he suspected that either Karyel or Iryella was practicing, there was something about the playing . . .

He opened the study door and walked to the grand staircase, and then halfway down. After less than half a quint, he nodded. The pattern of well-played notes, followed by a more hesitant version of the same piece, meant that Palenya was at the Chateau and giving one of his cousins a lesson, most likely Iryella, from the hesitancy that followed the first player, since Karyel, like Bhayrn, played wrong notes and tempos without hesitation. After several moments, Charyn made his way to the music room, where he eased inside and waited, listening.

". . . playing well is not just striking the correct keys one after the other . . ." Palenya looked up as she realized Charyn was in the music room. "Rex Charyn."

"Might I have a very quick word with you, Musician Palenya?"

"Of course." Palenya turned to Iryella. "One moment." Then she walked swiftly to meet Charyn.

"Might I prevail upon you in two fashions, both musical?"

"Musically, yes, Your Grace."

"First, would you spend a little time helping me with those two pieces this afternoon, before you depart for the Collegium? Second, if you could arrive a glass early on Samedi in order to give me a proper lesson. As always, you will be paid. Your expertise should never be unpaid."

Palenya's voice was barely above a murmur when she replied, "You have been more than generous."

Charyn replied in an equally low voice. "I have been as generous as the times and events have allowed. I can never fully repay you, but I can pay you fully for every moment you work as a musician. That is the least I can do." Then he raised his voice slightly. "If that is acceptable, have Iryella or Karyel let me know when you are finished with their lessons."

"I will do that."

"And feel free to tell them how much work it was to teach me in the beginning."

"I just might, Your Grace." Palenya smiled.

Charyn smiled in return, then stepped back. "I won't interrupt again, but I didn't know how long you'd be here." Then he turned and left the music room.

As he walked back up the grand staircase, he thought over the brief meeting with Palenya. She'd been friendly, but warmly reserved.

What else could you expect? So were you.

Since Wyllum was still gone, Charyn picked up the latest petition and Sanafryt's suggested response and began to read.

More than a glass later, Iryella knocked on the study door, then opened it and peered in. "Your Grace, our lessons are over."

"Thank you." Charyn stood and left the study.

Palenya was standing by the clavecin when he entered the music room. "If you wouldn't mind, Your Grace . . . keeping this a bit shorter. I don't want to keep the Collegium coach waiting too long."

"I should have thought about that. What if I play each piece through, and you give me your suggestions. That way, I'll know what to work on, or at least some things to work on, and you can give me a proper lesson on Samedi."

Palenya nodded.

Charyn seated himself at the clavecin and began with "Variations."

After he'd only played ten bars, she stopped him.

"Your Grace . . . your fingering is acceptable, but . . . the melody from which Covaelyt adapted it was a dance. You show some of that, but not nearly enough."

Charyn stood. "I don't know that dance. Could you please play just a few bars so I have an idea?"

Palenya did so.

Then Charyn did his best to use a hint of the same rhythm.

"Much better . . ."

Two quints later, Charyn rose from the clavecin, hoping he could remember all of Palenya's comments. "Thank you." He handed Palenya three silvers. "Two for you and one for the poor coachman."

"Two is too much."

Charyn shook his head. "One of the two was for reminding me about the coach. Since you left, I don't get as many reminders."

"You should be very careful, then, Your Grace, about whom you marry."

Charyn laughed softly. "That thought has occurred to me ever since you first suggested it. Often."

She inclined her head. "By your leave?"

"Of course. Until Samedi."

Charyn had thought about walking her to the coach, but that would have been outside the bounds they both had agreed upon, and unfair to her. Instead, he just said, "Do take care."

She smiled a smile of rueful amusement. "I should be saying that to you, Your Grace. No one shoots at a musician."

"Sometimes being a merely competent musician sounds very good . . . except . . ."

"No one will let you. Not now."

"You're right. Again."

As he watched her leave, he realized, again, that he had already made too many choices that could not be reversed, not if he wanted to be even a moderately competent and decent Rex.

And with the thought of Bhayrn being Rex . . . Charyn shuddered.

Before all that long, it was time for dinner, and, for the first time in days, everyone was seated around the table.

Immediately after the grace, offered by Iryella, as Charyn served his mother and then himself, Chelia looked to Karyel. "How were your lessons this afternoon?"

"They went well enough," he replied pleasantly. "Musician Palenya said that it was obvious that I'd been practicing more."

Iryella looked away from her brother.

"And you, Iryella?" asked Chelia gently.

"She said I was making progress. She also said I needed to work harder than Karyel." Iryella looked accusingly at Charyn.

"I never said a word to Musician Palenya about either of you."

"Why are you still taking lessons, Your Grace?" asked Karyel.

"Because I still want to play better. It's a skill that doesn't depend on what other people do, except for whoever tunes the clavecin. Besides, I enjoy playing, at least when I've worked on a piece to the point where I know I'm playing it at least competently." Charyn took a small swallow of the Tuuryl red wine, and then a bite of the game pie.

"But . . . most High Holders don't play."

"They should," interjected Chelia. "Mastering an instrument requires mastering yourself, and that's something lacking in too many High Holders."

"What about hunting?" asked Bhayrn. "That's a skill worth mastering."

"It's useful if you need to support yourself, or if you intend to be an officer in the army, or possibly a butcher," replied Chelia dryly. "It's also good for boasting rights."

"You're just saying that . . ." Bhayrn stopped short.

"Because I'm a woman, and women know nothing of arms and killing? Might I remind you that Maitre Malyna is far better than you with a blade and has killed far more men than you ever will. She's also better at the clavecin and other skills as well. By the time your sister is Malyna's age, she'll be able to do the same."

"But they're imagers."

"Imaging doesn't help with blade skills or playing the clavecin," Charyn said mildly, recalling all too well how easily Malyna had bested him when they'd sparred that one time . . . and how elegantly she had concealed that mastery.

"Why do the imagers let women use blades?" asked Karyel, in a tone of innocence that Charyn suspected was largely feigned.

"Because there are too few imagers for women to have the luxury of being protected," replied Chelia immediately.

That response surprised Charyn, and it must have showed, because Chelia went on, "I asked Malyna about a great number of things while she stayed here, especially after your sparring with her."

"Is that why you exercise with the guards, Your Grace?" asked Karyel, with the tone of innocence that was already beginning to grate on Charyn.

"No. It's because I saw how fit all the imagers were, and also because the other forms of exercise, such as riding through the hunting park, would be unwise at present." Charyn didn't want to get into the point that he'd started exercising before the latest assassination attempt.

"It's safer to be a High Holder," said Karyel, not quite smugly.

"A loyal High Holder," replied Chelia sweetly, looking at Karyel, "unlike your treacherous great-uncle Ryentar . . . or others."

Karyel swallowed.

Iryella hid a smile.

"You haven't touched the vegetable ragout, Iryella," said Chelia.

This time, Karyel almost managed to hide his satisfaction.

"They're soft, and they squish," declared Iryella dolefully.

"I've never cared much for the vegetable ragout," said Bhayrn, "but we need to eat vegetables."

Charyn managed not to choke on Bhayrn's falsely sanctimonious tone.

"By the way," said Bhayrn to Charyn, "why didn't you take the regial coach on Solayi? You said you were."

"I changed my mind." Charyn offered what he hoped was a clueless smile. "How was Chorister Faheel's homily?"

"Adequate, but less tariffing than Saerlet's," replied Chelia. "Bhayrn wouldn't know. He slept through most of it."

"I was tired, and it was boring, all about responsibility to the Nameless."

"That's because you never get any sleep anymore. You're up late glasses with Laamyst and Gherard," replied Charyn.

"At least they're not boring. More lectures on responsibility are boring."

"At times, enduring repetition is a price we all must pay," replied Chelia. "For some, repetition is the only way they learn. Then there are those who never learn because they find learning itself boring. They usually die either young or poor, if not both, especially if they're also not responsible."

"Responsible to whom?" asked Bhayrn sardonically. "The factors, the rabble, the Nameless who has never once proved to be interested in our welfare?"

"For better or worse, you're beyond my lectures on responsibility, Bhayrn," replied Chelia coolly. "I will say that responsibility begins with being responsible to yourself, to be the best you can be."

"I'll be responsible to and for myself. My brother the Rex has set an excellent example."

"That's enough about responsibility," Charyn declared firmly before turning to Iryella. "Which piece of music that you've played or heard do you like the best?"

"I like all of them, but differently . . ."

By the time dinner was over, Charyn was more than ready to escape to his sitting room and the green leather-bound volume that Alyncya had sent.

Sitting in his favorite armchair, in the light of the oil reading lamp on the side table, Charyn studied the book. There was no title on the spine or the outside cover. Noting that there was no frontispiece as he opened it to the title page, he studied the few words set there in a script that was neither formal nor standard merchant hand.

> ### VERSE FOR AN UNQUIET TIME
> Pyetryl D'Ecrivain
> L'Excelsis, Solidar
> Fevier 237 A.L.

He'd never heard of Pyetryl D'Ecrivain. He also wondered why his name wasn't Pyetryl D'Bard, or had the surname "Bard" been reserved back two hundred years only for those who practiced sung verse or music?

Charyn turned to the first page and the four lines set in the middle of the yellowed parchment.

> *Rhythms in thought complex and words in rhyme,*
> *Last, as they are, beyond their present time.*
> *May these rhymed lines carry meaning and care*
> *To those who think, those who love, those who dare.*

Almost a challenge to anyone who opens the book. Somehow, the verse introducing the volume seemed fitting for Alyncya, at least from what he'd seen so far.

He frowned, noting several thin strips of pale teal ribbon, almost the regial colors, protruding from the pages in several places. He turned to the first marker, noting that, in obvious extravagance, each poem was written only on the face page, the one on the right as the volume lay open.

A QUESTION

The moons rise, then they set, as does the sun,
Time enough for lust, never so for love.
The iris blooms when spring has just begun,
The apple full fruits late, harvest being done,
They know not love, nor of the Nameless above.
What matters that when life's short course is run?

He read the words twice, aloud the second time, just letting the words echo silently in his mind.

After a time, he turned to the second ribbon bookmark, wondering what verse might greet him.

FOR A FAST FRIEND

Of all the glorious mornings I have seen,
That flatter fair the woodlands and their vales
With golden light aflame on leafy green
And shimmers bright from brooks in silver trails,
Was there a single dawn I'd wish to greet,
A solitary day I'd hope to spend
In bookish chores or studies most discreet
Before your eyes showed me a better friend?

Although we may put trust in stars and sun.
And praise the hunting moon we once thought god,
Cold ice presides where rivers used to run.
For what we have and where we trod,
Will vanish starless in the coming years
Unless we still hold fast against fate's fears.

Is that a message or a hope . . . or either?

Slowly, he opened the book to the last marker, taking in the lines set there and reading them aloud.

"MOONSTRUCK
"Tell me not of hearts faithful to the end,
  Or minds entwined by brilliant word or thought.
  For we'll have neither time nor gold to spend
  With all the strifes of heart and mind we've fought.

"For Erion's the moon to whom you've pledged,
  And Artiema's gold what suffices me.
  This conflict so direct, yet unacknowledged,
  Wounds us both, yet never sets us free."

Charyn swallowed as he finished the last line, then saw the lightly penciled question mark set in the margin opposite the last two lines, a mark that appeared fresh.

At least, she's posed that as a question. The mark couldn't have been an accident, not with the care that Alyncya had taken with everything else.

But how can you answer those questions?

Abruptly he looked back at the book and smiled. He definitely had some more reading to do . . . careful reading.

Which is exactly what she hoped.

43

~~~

At sixth glass on Vendrei, Charyn was already in the un-marked coach, heading south on L'Avenue D'Commercia toward the Sud Bridge and then farther south to the ironworks. He wore his factor's garb, including the gold jacket lapel pin that signified he was a member of the exchange as well, and his belt wallet held sufficient golds and silvers for what he might require. The driver, footman, and guards all wore the brown jackets and trousers.

His thoughts, however, were on Alyncya. Reading *Verse for an Unquiet Time* was taking longer than Charyn had an-ticipated, especially since he had chosen to read it alone in the evenings . . . and picking three verses that would con-vey what he wanted was proving difficult. While he was expected, he felt, to return the book with three passages marked, he would have preferred to keep it.

Perhaps you should copy the poems you mark, as well as several others that might be suitable in some fashion or another. He nodded, then turned his attention to what he might say to Ostraaw.

When the coach drew up to the massive gates, a guard stepped forward.

"I'm here to see Engineer Ostraaw," Charyn called from the coach. "He's expecting me."

After several moments, the guard gestured, and the gates opened.

As the coach moved through the gates, Charyn was glad he hadn't had to mention his identity as Factor Suyrien. Sooner or later, word would get out, but the later, the better. Every few days he could keep the charade going would be helpful. He didn't even want to think what the newssheets might write, but he was resigned to it happening, sooner or later.

When the coach reached the small building south of the rifleworks and pulled up, Ostraaw stood outside waiting. Charyn immediately got out of the coach and walked over to the narrow-shouldered, wiry engineer. "Good morning."

"The same to you, Factor." Ostraaw looked at the guards and the carriage. "You travel like a man very well off. Or one with enemies."

"As I've observed before, Engineer Ostraaw, my family is more noted than I am, and members of it have been killed. That tends to make one cautious."

"Yet . . . while you are known at the exchange and by a handful of factors, very little else is known about you."

"For the moment, that is for the best. Now, since I am here, we have several matters to discuss. First, if we could survey the two locations you suggested for a heavy manufactorage . . ."

"How soon would you be considering building such a facility?"

"Not until next spring at the earliest. I did say it might be a while, but it will happen."

"What sort of—"

"A heavy machine of some complexity. I'd prefer not to say more."

"You know who might buy it?"

"I know of two buyers already . . . if it can be designed to their specifications. My personal engineer has built a half-scale working model." Charyn wasn't sure that was absolutely correct, since the steam engine required to propel a frigate might be three times the size of what Paersyt had tested, or perhaps two engines of lesser size might be preferable.

"Would I know this engineer?"

"I couldn't say, but you definitely will in time," replied

Charyn with a laugh. "Now . . . if you could show me the two locations. I worry that the one might be flooded with the spring waters, and that the other might not have enough water flow for power."

Ostraaw frowned, then nodded. "I had those concerns as well, but other locations have even greater possible difficulties . . ."

Charyn listened as the two walked toward the open stretch of land beyond the rifleworks.

"The lower site here," said Ostraaw as he gestured, "has the best access to the river. If you'll be shipping heavy machines, this might be the better one."

"That's a point to consider," replied Charyn. "Can we see the upper site?"

"This way."

The lower site on the point was definitely too vulnerable to flooding so far as Charyn was concerned, but as he studied the higher one, he realized something he should have thought of earlier—if Paersyt's steam engines worked as well as he hoped, he wouldn't need to rely on water power at all after they'd produced enough engines to power the manufactorage. *And if they don't, you won't be needing a manufactorage at all.*

"You're looking rather amused, Suyrien."

"The upper site will work better than the lower one for what I have in mind, more than I'd realized. Thank you for taking me through them. I wouldn't have thought it without seeing it. Now . . . about the coal."

"I've tried to talk Karl into a lower price. He'll have nothing to do with it."

"Are there any other factors or High Holders that might provide coal for the old price, or one lower than Karl is charging?"

"There's no one on the exchange who's willing to do so. I've heard that there may be some High Holders who have mines not selling on the exchange. No one seems to know

who they might be. If you can find out who they might be,
that would be helpful. Otherwise . . ." Ostraaw shook his
head.

"I have a few people who might know more, but it will be
a few days, perhaps longer, before I'll be able to talk with
them. Buy whatever coal you absolutely need for the next
month. I'll let you know in the next week or so if I can find a
better price or someone who might be able to do so."

The engineer grinned. "Estafen said there was more to
you than meets the eye."

Charyn grinned back. "Since there's not that much striking about what meets the eye, I certainly hope so."

Ostraaw offered a hearty laugh.

"There is one other matter, and that's about what we're
paying the workers."

"You aren't thinking about lowering wages?" Ostraaw
looked alarmed. "The men work hard, and it can be dangerous at times."

"No. Quite the contrary. I wanted to know if you think
they're being paid enough for that kind of work. I understood that Vaschet was using prisoners and paying them
almost nothing."

"Some of them were, but that ended when Factor Estafen
took over. There's not a man here who makes less than five
coppers for each two days he works."

"Would it be ruinous to increase wages a little?"

Ostraaw frowned. "A copper more a week right now
would be possible."

"Then do it, starting at the beginning of Feuillyt. And if
you'd let them know it was a decision by both you and me."

"I can do that, sir."

"Is there anything else we need to discuss?" asked
Charyn.

"It might be helpful to be able to reach you quicker."

"I'm working on that, but it may be a while."

"Other members of your . . . family?"

Charyn shook his head. "I can assure you that you do not wish to deal with them. They believe that factoring is far beneath them and would treat you badly."

"I thought as much. That's why you're engaged in something far from your family?"

Charyn nodded. In a different way, that was true. "It would not have been possible without Estafen. Now . . . I need to go."

"I won't keep you."

The two walked back to the coach.

Three quints after leaving the ironworks, Charyn was inside Paersyt's factorage, spreading out the plans for the newest frigate.

"These are the ship plans for the newest frigate to be built in Solis. I'd like you to take a look at them. I'd be interested in knowing if and how you could add your steam engine to the ship and whether it would work. Or if a pair of engines might work better."

"You're asking a great deal, Your Grace. We've done some tests with the *Steamwraith,* but we're still working out some problems."

"When can I see the ship tests?"

The engineering factor cocked his head, then frowned. "We should be ready for the next tests . . . this coming Jeudi, I'd say."

"Can you make it early in the morning . . . seventh glass?"

"We can do that. At our pier."

"Excellent. Now . . . about the frigate plans?"

Paersyt shook his head. "Be better if I used these plans as the basis for designing a steam frigate from scratch."

"You're the engineer, but you'll have to come up with something that the new shipyard in Solis can build."

"I wouldn't design anything a shipyard couldn't build. Whether they'll want to . . . Shipwrights are very leery of design changes. That's understandable, because captains and crews could die if they try something different and it doesn't work. At the least, they could lose considerable amounts."

"For a warship, I'm more interested in the speed, strength, and safety."

"If I can make it work for a warship, it'll work better for a merchanter. And if we can, you'll be even richer."

"No . . . we'll be richer," Charyn corrected the engineer. "How long will it take you to build the larger engine?"

"Might be spring . . . might be a year . . . might be two."

Charyn shook his head and handed the engineer twenty golds. "That's for now. Keep sending me reports."

It was almost ninth glass by the time Charyn made his way up the grand staircase to his study. He'd barely remembered to remove the exchange pin from his lapel before leaving the coach. While most in the Chateau likely wouldn't know what it signified, someone might ask, and he preferred not to lie outright.

"You might want to read the newssheets, Your Grace," said Wyllum as Charyn walked toward the goldenwood table desk.

"Oh?"

"*Tableta* wrote about your touring the damaged factorages and warehouses. So did *Veritum*."

Charyn decided to start with *Tableta*.

Our beloved Rex finally decided to view all the damage created by the factors' decision to starve workers . . . Needless to say he inspected the damage, carefully guided by the worst offender of all, Councilor Factor Eshmael. Doubtless, Eshmael laid all the blame for the carnage on workers who are only trying to obtain a living wage. Factors are prospering more than ever, yet they find it necessary to hire mere boys or pay starvation wages to workers . . .

The other story of interest in *Tableta* was one about another protest by the True Believers, this time at the Anomen

D'Sud. It only mentioned Charyn in passing, saying that his proposed reforms were clearly minor, since they didn't seem to be having much effect.

Similar stories were also in *Veritum,* but the one about the continuing fires noted that Charyn had suggested the possibility of the Rex setting a fair minimum wage, noting that the matter had only been discussed. The True Believer story didn't mention Charyn at all, except by implication, by saying that the matter really was between choristers and their congregations, and that the changes in law only clarified that and made the choristers more responsible.

Charyn set the newssheets aside and looked to Wyllum. "Has anyone been looking for me?"

"Minister Aevidyr said that he hoped to have a word with you."

"I need to speak with Alucar first, but I'll stop by Aevidyr's study after that. Is there a list of which factors will be attending dinner on Samedi?"

"Yes, sir. Should I leave it on your desk?"

"That will be fine. I hope I won't be long."

Wondering what Aevidyr wanted, and knowing it was likely something else irritating, Charyn found himself marching swiftly to Alucar's study, almost as if trying to escape. He slowed, then stopped and took a deep breath outside the study door, before opening it and entering.

Alucar looked up from his desk as Charyn stepped into the study. "Yes, Your Grace?"

Charyn closed the door, ignoring the chair before Alucar's desk and remaining standing. "Vaelln sent me a report yesterday afternoon. The level of naval action has depleted stores of powder and shells to the point that the navy won't be able to maintain operations against the Jariolans by the beginning of Finitas."

"I received a similar report from Sea Marshal Tynan." Alucar fingered his smooth-shaven chin. "We should be receiving tariffs by then, and we might be able to divert some."

"Vaelln said he'd be sending me details on where he might be able to cut spending. I got the feeling he wasn't too hopeful about that."

"You've had me cut expenses wherever possible . . . but the regional governors haven't been as helpful in that regard as they might have been."

"I've mentioned that," Charyn said dryly.

"And as I've replied, Your Grace, anyone with whom you replaced them would have similar faults."

"Do you still think restructuring the whole regional governing system is infeasible?"

"Not over time, but at present, yes."

"We can't afford not to support the navy. It will cost us even more in the next two years if we can't bring this undeclared war to a halt."

"I must agree with your assessment. Vaelln won't need as much in the way of supplies in Ianus and Fevier, not given that winter operations are harder in Jariola."

"Unless they just send all their ships south to Otelyrn," replied Charyn, "where they'll cost the factors more ships, for which I'll be blamed. And if Tynan sends some of his fleet after them, that will require even more supplies."

"There is some good news," said Alucar genially.

"Oh?"

"The way you restructured the Chateau staffing has cut monthly expenditures by some fifty golds."

"But we're paying the guards more, and some of the others."

"It appears that . . . various people were dipping into the till, so to speak."

"I found out about the stablemaster and Churwyl."

"They accounted for about half of that. There were 'supplemental funds' sent to several regional governors as well, with your father's approval."

"And Aevidyr hasn't requested any more?" asked Charyn wryly.

"He did once. I suggested that he should ask you. He decided against it at the time, and then after Voralch absconded with the funds from the regional accounts in Solis, he must have decided not to press."

"I can't imagine why."

"Also, Assistant Chorister Faheel came to see me. He needed help setting up new ledgers for the Anomen D'Rex. Apparently, the old ones vanished, along with most of the coins in the anomen strongbox. Faheel did keep records of the offerings and his stipend and expenditures. So constructing new ledgers wasn't that hard." Alucar's voice turned sardonic. "Given the offerings he's received in total, I suspect that Saerlet made off with quite a few golds."

That didn't surprise Charyn, but it was getting so that very little did. "Faheel seems to be more honest."

"Your changes to the law might help keep him that way. I did tell him that I would require a copy of that monthly statement."

"Thank you. That was a good idea. And . . . now I need to see Aevidyr. Let me know if you have any more suggestions for finding the additional funds for the navy."

Alucar nodded.

After leaving and closing the door, Charyn took another deep breath as he walked the short distance to Aevidyr's study, letting himself in and closing the door.

"You were looking for me?"

"Yes, Your Grace. Regional Governor Chaanyk has requested supplemental funds to deal with the damages to the port at Tilbora that were caused by the recent floods there."

"That's something that the factors and High Holders of Tilbor will have to fund, I'm afraid. That's unless they want me to increase their tariffs."

"Isn't there a reserve fund . . ."

"There was . . . until the Aluse flooded, Liantiago was devastated, and the Jariolans stepped up the undeclared war against Solidaran shipping. That reserve was already low because my predecessor was precluded from raising tariffs . . . and because of the granary destruction at Tuuryl."

"I had hoped to be able to convey better news."

Charyn offered a sad smile. "I'd like for that, too, but I can't send golds we don't have." He paused, then added, "And I don't expect to see reductions in tariff collections from Tilbor as a way to fund repairs. Such an unfortunate occurrence might result in Regional Governor Chaanyk spending a great deal of time in a small space, or something even worse. You might want to make that quite clear."

Aevidyr swallowed. "Yes, Your Grace."

"Is there anything else?"

"The regional governor appointments for Telaryn and Khel . . . sir?"

"What about Rikkard D'Niasaen?"

"He was a local justicer for a time."

"And?"

"The factors support him." Aevidyr's voice was flat.

"But even though he comes from a High Holder family, some well-connected High Holders have reservations?"

"Ah . . . yes, sir."

"Then offer him the appointment. We can always remove him."

"Sir . . ."

"You wanted a decision. I gave you one. Prepare the offering letter."

"Yes, sir."

"If that's all . . ."

"Yes, sir."

After he left the Minister of Administration, Charyn knew he'd been precipitous, but Aevidyr was right about the fact that the position had been left vacant for too long. He would have liked to have filled the corresponding position in Khel, but so far none of the candidates were remotely acceptable. *Would Maitre Alastar have any suggestions?*

It certainly couldn't hurt to ask about that . . . and whether the Maitre knew any High Holders who had coal for sale.

He took another deep breath as he approached Sturdyn and the door to his study.

44

When Charyn woke on Samedi morning, he again smelled
smoke, and more haze hung over the river to the southeast
of the Chateau. He didn't bother to shake his head. When
he finished his morning routine, including the exercises
with the guards, at which he was now becoming proficient,
and stronger, he felt, he made his way to his study. There
he found Wyllum—and a report from Marshal Vaelln—
waiting for him.

"There's been one change to those who are attending the
dinner this evening, sir."

"Oh?"

"Factor Haaltyn—his wife is gravely ill, and he sent a
messenger regretting."

Charyn paused for a moment, trying to recall who Haaltyn was and why he'd been invited. Then he remembered.
Haaltyn was one of the main backers and investors behind
the L'Excelsis exchange, and he'd been invited solely so that
Charyn could meet him. There was no risk of him discovering that Factor Suyrien was Charyn, because Charyn had
never seen Haaltyn, nor even been close to the older man.
"I'm sorry to hear that. Would you draft a letter of condo-
lence about his wife that also conveys my regrets on not being able to meet with them both?"

"Yes, sir."

Charyn settled behind the desk and picked up Vaelln's
two-page report. He read it through quickly to get the sense
of it, then more slowly a second time, paying close attention
to the numbers and the assumptions offered by Vaelln for
those numbers. In the end, the Marshal thought he could

find two thousand golds to shift into additional naval supplies ... but those funds would have to be replaced within a year and a half or several supply ships would be laid up for lack of maintenance and all military reserve provisions would be exhausted.

Charyn shook his head, then drafted a reply agreeing to Vaelln's proposal. After a number of corrections and scratching out and replacing, he handed the marked-up sheet to Wyllum for him to write what Charyn hoped would be a final draft.

Next came his revisions to the draft Aevidyr had left offering the position of regional governor of Telaryn to Rikkard D'Niasaen.

By the time he had finished with everything that had piled up, partly because he'd been involved with the ironworks and Paersyt on Vendrei, as well as with Alucar and the ledgers, it was almost the first glass of the afternoon when he dismissed Wyllum.

He walked to the open window, through which blew a light breeze, a touch cooler than those of previous weeks, not surprisingly, since autumn was only a week away. For a time, he just looked down on the rear courtyard, not really thinking before turning back to his desk.

Once he sat down, he took out Alyncya's last letter and *Verse for an Unquiet Time,* a title that seemed strangely appropriate, even though the poet had written it some two hundred years earlier. *Maybe, for rulers, all times are unquiet.*

He'd meant to write Alyncya sooner, but, with everything, he hadn't finished reading *Verse for an Unquiet Time,* nor choosing the poems to select, let alone copying them and a few others.

Slowly, he opened the small volume and continued reading. Some of the verses were slightly dated, and some could have been written the week before. After a good ten pages, his eyes stopped on one poem. After a moment, he read it through again.

To the Nameless

Those men who claim our fate is set in stars,
Are those who never felt a prison's bars,
Who claim we're played by gods that we must serve,
And state man's justice is what we all deserve.

Ill-starred I am, and may I always be,
For those who serve the stars will never see
That men play god o'er those far less in fame
All self-extolling, with no sense of shame.
No god, no deity of sense and grace
Would stoop to take a human name or face.

A little cynical, there. Yet there was certainly accuracy behind the words.

Charyn kept reading, taking scraps of paper and inserting them in places where he thought the verse *might* be appropriate for a reply.

Further into the book, he came across four lines that struck him, although not the rest of the lengthy poem.

Of those obsessed with locks so fair and curled,
And coins stacked neat in chests they've bound in stone,
Of them, who storms through life with sails unfurled
Or bares his soul imperfectly in song?

By the time he'd read through the rest of the poems, it was time for him to ready himself for the evening ahead as well as for his lesson with Palenya and the possible conversation with Factor Eshmael.

When he walked downstairs to the music room sometime later, he wore simple formal greens without a sash or any insignia or personal jewelry. Then he sat down at the clavecin and began to play.

Palenya arrived at two quints before fifth glass, entering the music room as Charyn was working on the last section of "Variations." She remained by the door and said nothing until he finished. Then she moved toward the clavecin. She wore black trousers and a black blouse and jacket, as would all the musicians playing for the dinner.

Too severe to show her at her best. "How was that?"

"Better than on Meredi, but you lost some of the feel in the part just before the ritard that precedes the ending."

"Let me try that part again." Charyn mentally moved to the notes before that section, then began to play.

"A sense of anger, there! You're too precise."

Charyn almost laughed, then lost his place and did laugh. He stopped playing totally and shook his head. "I'm sorry. I never thought you—or anyone—except maybe Bhayrn— would tell me I'm too precise."

After several breaths, he went back and tried again.

"That was much better. I'd like to hear it from the beginning."

"In a moment. I hope we'll have a full glass to work, but I may have an angry factor arriving before the dinner."

Palenya raised her eyebrows.

"Factor Councilor Eshmael. He wants to convince me to bring in the army to stop the fires."

"You don't agree?"

"Let's say I have my doubts about doing so at the moment."

"When will be the right moment?"

Charyn shrugged helplessly. "I don't know. But I feel that today or this week isn't that moment."

"Sometimes feelings are better than calculations."

"Sometimes, they're not, and it's hard to tell which time is which." He smiled. "Right now, I'd rather deal with music." With that he began to play "Variations" from the beginning.

At two quints past fifth glass, Norstan appeared at the door to the music room. "Factor Eshmael is arriving, sir."

"Thank you, Norstan. I'll meet him in the receiving parlor." Charyn rose from the clavecin, inclined his head to Palenya, and said, "Thank you."

"You're welcome. Are you doing this for yourself . . . or her?"

"Both, I hope. I was enjoying playing before I heard her play. How did you know?"

"Because the piece you're working on must have come from her, and she likely played it for you and then sent you a copy."

"She copied it herself."

Palenya frowned. "That might not be for the best."

Charyn smiled wryly. "She's also written letters containing sections questioning some of my decisions as Rex, if diplomatically."

"That sounds better." After a moment, Palenya asked, "Are you trying to outdo her?"

Charyn laughed. "More like trying not to be horribly outclassed, and I'm certain her repertoire is far greater than mine."

"That might be very good." She smiled. "I shouldn't be keeping you."

"I added the lesson to your fee for the evening."

She just shook her head.

Charyn hurried back to the entry hall and the parlor right off it.

Eshmael turned immediately from where he stood, looking at himself in the mirror over the side table. The factor wore a rich brown jacket and matching trousers over a cream silk shirt, with a cravat patterned in dark brown and gold. His brown boots glistened. "I'm here, as you suggested." His words were cool.

"And your wife?"

"She'll be arriving with Noerbyn and his wife."

"I'm glad she'll be here."

"She wouldn't have missed it for anything."

The way Eshmael spoke suggested that the factor might well have wished not to be present.

"Would you like some refreshments?"

"Not at the moment, Rex Charyn."

Charyn gestured to the pair of armchairs set at an angle to each other, but did not speak until both were seated. "Have you thought much about what I said on Meredi?"

"I'd be lying if I said I had."

"Then you came to see if I had considered taking another course?"

"I doubt that you have. Your family has always been stubborn to the point of stupidity. But there's always a chance."

"It's interesting. Elthyrd said the same thing about you." Charyn offered an amused smile. "So what would it take to get you to agree to a two-copper daily wage for a nine-glass day?"

"Why are you pressing for that?"

"Because, whether I bring in the army or not, the fires and damage will continue until the workers your manufactorages have thrown out of work are either all dead or the factors give them some hope of being able to support their families."

"Aren't you being cheerful."

"No. Realistic, I fear."

"Rather unrealistic, I'd say. Those ruffians have to know who's boss."

"Eshmael . . . they know the factors are in control of what gets made, and what will be made. So do I. Being in control doesn't mean making them slaves. Even at two coppers a day, you're going to make more coins than you ever did, and they're making less."

"You don't seem to show that you know who's in charge."

"Then why have my father and I fought the High Holders and put them down? It would have cost us far less to side with them . . . and my father might well be alive today, as would my uncle." Charyn didn't see any point in granting that over the long run it would have been worse. Eshmael, like too many factors, was only concentrating on golds earned in the present year or so.

"Why didn't you?"

"Because, without the factors, my children would be under Jariola's oligarchic thumb. But it would have been much easier for my father and me. The same thing is true of you. You can make more golds now if you keep wages at the starvation level, but that's going to make more and more workers madder and madder." Charyn shrugged. "I'm willing to suffer now, rather than suffer a whole lot more twenty years from now. The question is whether you are or not."

"You can't stay Rex if the fires continue."

"You think not? How many High Holders who opposed my father survived? How many who have opposed me?"

"That's a threat."

Charyn shook his head. "I had nothing at all to do with any of that. Circumstances created those situations. If you study what happened, you'll see that, no matter how wealthy or powerful anyone is, when they oppose great changes, they usually lose. At best, they only postpone the change . . . and then they lose. I'm not here to threaten or force you. I'm trying to give you an opportunity to avoid future trouble."

"That's insane. How can you believe that?"

"Think about it. If I enact a law requiring a two-copper-a-day wage, you can grumble and blame me. But all factors will be in the same boat, and who comes out ahead depends not on who can pay workers the least, but who can make his products the best and least expensive in other ways. You'll be the ones paying the men, and in time, they'll forget how they got that pay . . . and be grateful for it." *Or as grateful as people ever are.*

"They'll want more. They always do."

"Of course they will. But if they say that's not enough, that's when I bring in the army. Then I can point out that you all have agreed, and that I'm supporting your agreement."

"It won't work, and we'll be stuck paying more."

"That's always possible, but . . . why don't you talk it over with the other factors? Talking among yourselves can't possibly hurt."

"If I mention what you said, they'll all say what I just told you."

"Why don't you see?" Charyn smiled and stood. "We've talked enough. We should go and get some refreshments." Charyn could see that Eshmael wasn't about to change his views, and that meant other factors needed to . . . or that he had to come up with another way to stop the violence.

"Might as well."

As the two neared the reception room, Charyn could hear Palenya and the strings playing.

When they entered, Chelia stepped forward. "Factor Eshmael, I'm so glad to meet you."

Charyn knew exactly what those warm words really meant, and probably so did Eshmael.

"Lady Chelia, I presume?"

"Indeed. I take it that your wife will be joining us shortly."

"She will."

"Before she does, you must join me for refreshments, and perhaps you can tell me more about yourself."

Charyn eased away, suspecting his mother could do more with Eshmael than Charyn himself possibly could.

Not surprisingly, the first two couples to arrive were Estafen and Zairleya and Estafen's brother Thyrand and his wife, whom Charyn had only seen from a distance at Elthyrd's memorial service.

"Your Grace," replied Estafen, "you've met Zairleya before, but not Thyrand and Chelani."

"I'm glad to see all of you," offered Charyn. "Welcome to the Chateau, and my most comfortable semi-confinement."

Chelani and Thyrand both looked surprised.

"I have to be most careful when I leave the Chateau. So far, there have been a number of attempts on my life. If the archives are correct, no Rex has been attacked so many times ever." Charyn smiled guilelessly. At least, he hoped so. "And I haven't started any wars, haven't massacred any holders, crafters, factors, or even High Holders. But this evening is for lighter talk . . . refreshments and an excellent dinner." He gestured toward the sideboards.

Thyrand and Chelani immediately took up Charyn's invitation and moved toward the sideboard with the wine and a ready server.

Zairleya looked to Charyn. "Estafen has mentioned you often, but he never has said much about you."

"Since I've only been Rex for eight months, that's likely because there's little to say. I have no wife, and enough difficulties were left me that my duties consume a great portion of each day."

"Surely, you must have other interests . . ."

"I do exercise, and I enjoy playing the clavecin to divert myself. When I can, I visit my sister Aloryana. As you may have read, she's an imager and lives with Maitre Alastar and his family on Imagisle. I've been known to read histories and play plaques and whist, if only tolerably."

"I've always admired people who could play any instrument. It's a talent I don't have," replied Zairleya.

"But you are remarkable in how well you sketch and draw," declared Estafen fondly.

"My drawing can be described, dear, as the Rex has put it, as tolerable."

"Far better than that." Estafen looked to Charyn. "She is far too modest."

At that moment, another couple appeared—Factor Councilor Hisario and his wife Marthyla—and Charyn excused himself to greet them . . . and then the youngish Factor Roblen and his wife and after that Factor Saratyn . . . and those who followed, including the copper factor Cuipryn and Factor Walltyl, who had made one of the chaises that had been a favorite of Charyn's in his less disciplined days.

The last of the factors to arrive was Factoria Kathila, alone, not that Charyn had expected her to be escorted. Although he judged she was roughly the age of his mother, he hadn't expected her to be as attractive as she was—with striking silver-gray hair, light gray eyes, and a slender but feminine figure. She also wore a black jacket and trousers, trimmed with silver-gray that matched her blouse.

Charyn inclined his head. "Factoria Kathila."

"Your Grace."

"Welcome to the Chateau."

"Thank you. I appreciate the invitation. Few factors are ever invited here."

"And you are the first factoria invited in her own right, so far as I can tell."

"Might I ask why?"

"You are on the local factors' council, and you're successful. Need there be any other reason?"

"Usually, there ulterior motives as well."

"I do have a general ulterior motive, and that is to come to know more factors than just those on the Factors' Council of Solidar."

"That suggests that you are either less than satisfied or that you wish to have a broader acquaintance with the views of factors not on the Council."

"I had thought that might be helpful. Either I would learn that they are representative or that they are not . . . or that the feelings of most factors might be somewhere in the middle."

"As one of the few women factors, would I really be representative?" said Kathila in an amused tone.

"Most likely not, but you're also more likely to have a more objective view of the others."

She laughed softly. "You're not at all what I supposed. You must take much more after your mother."

"I couldn't speak to that, but I do greatly value her advice."

"Then you take after her. Was High Holder Ryel . . . ?"

Charyn did not answer immediately, then said, "The way things turned out were my doing."

"Would she agree?"

"Unfortunately, yes."

"Then the next few months will be very interesting."

"I fear so. They don't have to be, but they will."

"No, Your Grace. They will have to be interesting, or you will lose control of Solidar. That would be a pity."

"It's too soon for force."

"Even after force was used on poor Elthyrd?"

"There's a question of who was behind that force. Do you have any ideas?"

"Suspicions of several who might wish a change. Proof or even indications . . . no." She offered an enigmatic smile.

"I see it the same way. Another reason I'm reluctant to use force now."

"That's true. But a month from now, it will be too late. That's only my opinion, however."

"I appreciate your opinion. Would you care for some wine?" Charyn motioned toward the sideboard, slowly moving that way, and Kathila moved with him. "The Tacqueville white is my favorite, but my brother prefers the Tuuryl red."

"For that alone, I'll take the white."

At that moment, Chelia appeared. "Factoria Kathila, I'm so glad you came."

Charyn understood and slipped away, thinking over Kathila's remarks about who might have been behind the attack on Elthyrd. *Several who might wish a change.* That raised another question—not only who might wish a change, but *why* they might wish that change.

After making a mental note to consider that more when he had time, he eased toward Roblen and his wife Ghemena, standing alone and looking almost bewildered in a corner of the reception room. "We didn't have much of a chance to talk when you arrived."

"It's all very strange, Your Grace," said Ghemena. "Factors' wives don't often get invited here."

"I'm glad you're here," said Charyn.

"You're about the only one close to our age," she said.

"That's true enough. I didn't expect to be Rex at my age."

"I didn't expect to have the factorage and manufactorage at my age," replied Roblen dryly. "We can't always predict those things."

"You know my story," said Charyn, "but I don't know yours."

"I was the younger son, but my brother, Gherard, turned out to be an imager. He died at the Collegium doing something he wasn't supposed to do. Father never really got over it. He died a little over a year ago."

"I understand that can happen. My sister is an imager."

"She is?" asked Ghemena, her eyes widening. "She's at the Collegium?"

"That's where all imagers end up."

"But . . . she was the daughter of a Rex."

"She's far better off being an imager," said Charyn. "And she's happier there."

"As an imager?" questioned Roblen.

"She's freer there than at the Chateau. She can choose whom to marry, or not to marry, and she's with other imagers."

"I hadn't thought of it that way," mused Ghemena.

Roblen still looked puzzled. After a long pause, he looked around, almost furtively, then asked, "Did you really suggest that there should be a two-copper-a-day minimum wage?"

"I brought it up. Neither the Factors' Council nor the High Holders' Council wanted it to be law. Why do you ask?"

"I'm already doing that. We haven't had any trouble."

"Is it costing you?"

Roblen shrugged. "It's tighter than I'd like, but I don't have the golds to rebuild."

"Are there others like you?"

"Not many."

Ghemena looked hard at her husband.

"I don't know many. Ghemena thinks more factors are paying two coppers now, and not saying anything."

"As Rex, I'd be the last to know." Charyn smiled. "What do you think of the wine?"

"It's the best I've ever tasted," admitted Ghemena.

After a time of pleasant small talk, Charyn eased away and made his way to a group containing Saratyn and Hisario and their wives.

"Rex Charyn," asked Hisario, "is the white a Montagne?"

"No, it's from Tacqueville. It's my favorite."

"I told you so," said the thin-faced Saratyn, who then turned to Charyn. "The crystal . . . do you know where it was made?"

"That crystal is doubtless older than I am, and I have no idea who made it or where. The Chateau archives might say . . . but they might not."

"Well . . . if you need more, I can match any pattern you have . . . and for a good price," declared Saratyn heartily.

He doesn't exactly sound like a factor devastated by the loss of a warehouse. "I'll keep that in mind."

For the rest of the evening, Charyn tried to talk as little as possible and listen as much as he could. No one else even came close to mentioning the fires, workers, or two-copper wages. Nor had anyone mentioned Elthyrd's death, except Kathila. Several wives, including Eshmael's consort, did ask if Charyn had his eye on a possible wife.

He answered that it wasn't his eye that counted but their response.

By the time the last factor had departed, Charyn felt worn out, and he turned toward the base of the grand staircase, where Chelia stood waiting.

"I didn't learn much, but I didn't expect to. At least one factor is quietly paying two coppers a day to avoid trouble, and several women want to know when I'll get married. Did you discover anything? Especially from Eshmael?"

"Nothing you say is likely to change his mind. For that matter, nothing anyone says will."

"Anything else?"

"Besides that Factoria Kathila has a daughter who's a maitre imager?"

"I found that out the other day. I should have mentioned it."

"She also believes that you're a bit more ruthless than you seem?" Chelia raised her eyebrows.

"I didn't say a word."

"I didn't think you did."

"What else?"

"Some of the wives just wish their husbands would pay the workers. Of course, they're married to the ones least likely to."

"Like Eshmael?"

"You may well have to do something with him. Or find a way around him."

"I've gotten that impression. Elthyrd said he'd be difficult."

"I told several of them that you had viewed the damaged or destroyed buildings at length with Eshmael and met with him twice about the difficulties. Kathila said to offer you her condolences."

"That's promising. I think she has more influence than she claims."

"With a few factors, but not with Eshmael or the other members of the Council."

That made sense to Charyn. "I have the feeling that a few factors would accept my proposal, just to end the violence."

"That may be, but will they go against Eshmael?"

"Estafen might."

"You need better than 'might.'"

Charyn nodded. He definitely knew that.

"You've been exchanging more than a few letters with Alyncya D'Shendael."

"She doesn't want to rush into something."

"Do you mind if I talk to her next week?"

"Not at all."

"You say that with considerable certainty."

"I think she can hold her own. If she can't or prefers not to . . . then, in all likelihood, it wouldn't work out."

"You have great confidence in her, or too much concern about me."

Charyn laughed. "There's no answer to that. I do have confidence in her, but I also have confidence in you."

"Sometimes, you do have to choose, Charyn."

"Sometimes, as you have pointed out, Mother, you have to know when a choice is necessary and when it is not."

This time, Chelia smiled. "I'm looking forward to conversing with Alyncya."

"I'm certain you'll find her most interesting. She also is very good on the clavecin."

"Better than you?"

"Most likely. Her repertoire is far greater than mine."

"Good. You'd never be happy with someone who can't match you, or sometimes exceed you." After the slightest of pauses, she added, "I think the dinner accomplished some of what you wished. How much, you'll see in the next weeks. Good night. I'm not so young as you are." With that, she turned and headed up the grand staircase.

Charyn couldn't help but think about her remarks about Eshmael . . . and Kathila's. Charyn could see why Eshmael wanted to be a factor councilor, but the more he saw of the man, the more he doubted that Eshmael was the type to be indirect enough to hire bravos and restrained enough to keep it quiet. So the better question might be who would prefer Eshmael to be the factor councilor, rather than Elthyrd or Kathila . . . and why.

45

~~~~

With so many thoughts swirling through his head, one of which, Charyn had to admit, was how to best reply to Alyncya, he didn't get to sleep early, and, as a result, slept far later than he usually did, even on a Solayi. So he was much later getting down to the breakfast room, where Bhayrn looked to be finishing up.

"Good morning," Charyn offered as he sat down across from his brother.

"It's not bad. Except it's smoky, and that means another factorage was burned. When are you going to do something about those miserable ruffians?"

"I'm working on it. That was another reason for the dinner last night."

"Pandering to the factors won't do anything. You should be able to see that by now."

"Bringing in the army will only make matters worse unless the factors back off, and using the army against them won't help, either."

"Use it against them both. Oh, I forgot. You never moved more troopers back to L'Excelsis so you can't."

"That wouldn't do much. There are problems in Solis, Ferravyl, and Nacliano as well."

"How did you manage that?"

"They were coming on long before I became Rex," said Charyn, accepting the mug of tea from Therosa, and saying to her, "Cheesed eggs and ham strips."

"You have an answer for everything." Bhayrn paused, then asked, "Are you going to services at Imagisle again this evening?"

"I'd thought to. Aloryana enjoys it. Would you like to come?"

"I told you. I have no desire to ever set foot on Imagisle."

"Why do you have such an aversion to the imagers? Malyna saved both our lives."

"She's a High Holder as well as an imager. Also, as you discovered, she's a relative. That makes it different for her, I suppose for Maitre Alyna as well, and Aloryana. But the imagers were responsible for Grandsire's death. Father told me so. In a way, that also contributed to his own death."

"How can you believe that?" asked Charyn. "Uncle Ryel would still have tried to kill Father. Besides, everything imagers did kept father Rex far longer than would have otherwise been the case. Just remember, Uncle was a High Holder, not a factor, and he was the one who had Father assassinated."

"That was because Father turned against him by siding with the factors."

"How? By insisting Uncle become head of the High Council?"

"You don't understand, Charyn, and you never will. That's because you and Father listen too much to the imagers. Most of them are just factors with a few extra abilities."

"Why do you keep ignoring the fact that it was a High Holder who had Father assassinated?"

"You really don't understand, Charyn. You look for the causes everywhere but under your own nose. For someone who calculates so much, you really see so little." Shaking his head, Bhayrn stood. "Which coach will you take for your rewarding evening with the imagers?"

"You can have the unmarked one," Charyn replied.

"Thank you, honored elder brother." Bhayrn turned and left the breakfast room.

Only a few moments after Bhayrn had departed, Chelia entered, accompanied by Iryella.

As Iryella sat down, Chelia glanced back toward the door, raising her eyebrows.

"A mild difference of opinion," replied Charyn. "He suggested that imagers were merely factors with a few extra abilities, and that I should treat them as such."

"All of us are just people with varying abilities," replied Chelia after sitting down beside her niece. "It's what one does with background and those abilities that matters." She looked to Iryella. "You need to remember that, especially. It's not who finds it the easiest to play a clavecin at first, but who plays best in the end. Your cousin Charyn is a good example of that. I never thought he'd play as well as some musicians."

"Yes, Aunt Chelia."

Chelia turned to Charyn. "Musician Palenya said you had another lesson yesterday."

"I did. I needed some help on a new piece. It's an older Covaelyt work—'Variations on a Khellan Melody.' Some of the rhythms are dance-like, but since I didn't know the dances . . ." Charyn smiled ruefully.

"I saw the music in the cabinet the other day. I don't recall it."

"Alyncya D'Shendael played it. I remarked upon it, and she sent the copy she engraved herself."

"It looked like the work of an engraver."

"I thought so as well, but she apologized that it was hers."

"I'll definitely look forward to talking to her."

"Are you going to marry her, Your Grace?" asked Iryella, definitely not guilelessly, and with a smile that bordered on a smirk.

"I am interested in her, Iryella. Neither of us knows each other well enough to decide anything like that."

"Men get choices. Girls don't." Iryella sniffed.

"Actually, Lady-heir Alyncya does," said Charyn. "She's the oldest daughter. Her father's a widower, and she has no brothers."

"I'd never marry if I were the heir," declared Iryella firmly.

"There are advantages and disadvantages to that, Iryella," said Chelia firmly. "We'll discuss them later."

Iryella started to speak.

"Later, I said," declared Chelia even more firmly.

Iryella shut her mouth.

"The other day Elacia hinted that Ferrand might soon be asking a young lady. Do you know anything about that?"

"Only that he was interested in someone, but didn't want to say anything yet." That was largely true.

"Even to you?"

"He knows you're very good at finding out what I know."

"You're obviously getting better at not letting me know what you don't wish me to know."

Charyn grinned. "And who might have taught me that?"

Chelia smiled back good-naturedly.

After finishing breakfast, Charyn took his pistols and went to the covered courtyard to practice. Still seething after his conversation with Bhayrn, he thought about imagining one of the targets was his brother, but decided against that. Fratricide, even imagined fratricide, was not a good idea. Instead, he visualized that one of the targets was Eshmael. That helped, and, even angry, he managed to improve his aim, if only a little, but, surprisingly, more with his left hand.

After shooting for a time, he cleaned and reloaded the pistols, replaced his favorite in the special angled holster concealed by his tunic, then made his way to his study. There he sat down at his desk and opened Alyncya's book of verse, and began leafing through it, trying to decide which verses to mark before writing the letter to her.

Choosing the first poem was easy enough, and Charyn smiled as he read it aloud.

"A LOVER'S QUESTION
*"The beauty of your sweet beguiling voice
Has brought too oft my senses to a halt,*

> *Enraptured so I cannot make a choice.*
> *In loving haze, I hear nor see no fault.*
> *Will then you choose love chaste or fierce desire,*
> *The ice of purity or heat of my desire?"*

In the end, he chose two other verses, as well as six others that he'd decided to copy for himself, including one that he'd likely never send, but which just appealed to him.

THE STREETS OF GOLD

> *When Variana's streets were paved with gold,*
> *And the Pharsi of Naedar were still recalled*
> *In wistful tales of heroes now untold,*
> *I strove to make the world more appalled,*
> *With words begriming every sordid deed,*
> *And drawing children starving in the street.*
> *Each pasture neglected and left to weed,*
> *With no act depicted as right or meet.*

> *Words fell like spears on most receptive ears,*
> *So now I seldom see a cheerful face,*
> *Nor hear most others speak, except of fears.*
> *Oh, how I long for days of vanished grace.*

He would have liked to have kept the entire book, but the markers had been there for a purpose, and that purpose required returning the book. He could have had Wyllum copy the book, but that felt wrong as well. However the interactions between Alyncya and him played out, they had to be just between them. That was also just another feeling, but . . .

Next came drafting the letter, and that was harder than selecting the poems had been, although he knew it should not be so, yet the final version would have to be from his heart . . . and without too much contrivance. *Or too much apparent contrivance.*

Three drafts, and some considerable time later, he read over what he had written.

> *My dear Lady-heir Alyncya—*
> *Now that I have read the poems of Pyetryl D'Ecrivain*
> *that you most graciously sent for me to read, I could*
> *not wait until this coming Samedi to respond. While*
> *each and every poem has its appeal, just as you selected*
> *three, in return I have marked the three that seemed to*
> *offer my most honest response, in both heart and mind,*
> *to those you marked.*
>
> *I have taken the liberty of copying several of the*
> *poems that most appealed to me, so that I could read*
> *them again, but I could not bear the thought of retaining*
> *a volume clearly so close to your heart, although I*
> *earnestly hope that I may be able to read it time and*
> *again in the near future.*
>
> *With deep affection,*

Again, he signed simply with his name, then locked both the letter, in its sealed envelope, and the book of verse in the hidden compartment in the bookcase behind the table desk.

On one level, their correspondence might seem like a game, but how else could they communicate without Charyn compromising her position? Or without limiting her ability to make a truly free choice?

You can't put her in that situation. Once, even if it had not been entirely his doing, was once too many. But then, no one ever said learning was without regrets . . . or pain. And Charyn had already seen and felt enough of both. He also knew there would be more to come, which made mandatory for him the precluding of unnecessary suffering where possible.

He locked the study and made his way to the music room, where he practiced for more than a glass before repairing to his apartments, and his dressing room, where he donned his uniform as an undercaptain of the Chateau Guard, then settled into the armchair in his sitting room and resumed reading in Devoryn's *History of Solidar*. He smiled, recalling his mother's indirect condemnation of the Sanclere *History*. She'd never said it wasn't good, just that she was glad to see he was reading Devoryn and not Sanclere.

As Charyn came down the grand staircase, in uniform, just before fifth glass, he saw Bhayrn entering the foyer from the front entrance. "Visiting friends?"

"Oh . . . no. Gherard just stopped by to ask me to dinner next Vendrei."

"You will be at the Autumn-Turn Ball?"

"Mother wouldn't have it any other way." Bhayrn's eyes narrowed as he took in Charyn. "You're wearing that undercaptain's uniform again. What on Terahnar for?"

"I'm less of a target this way."

"In the coach?"

"I thought I'd ride over. The weather's nice, and I don't get to ride that much anymore."

"You talk about the need for me to protect myself. What about you?"

"I take a different route to and from Imagisle every Solayi, both ways. People don't know my face, and no one expects a young undercaptain to be anything else."

"You keep doing that, and someone will find out," predicted Bhayrn.

"They're going to shoot at every officer in uniform on the chance it might be me? At any distance, there's little difference between the army uniforms and those of Chateau guards."

"They just might."

"And they just might find a cannon and fire it at the coach," returned Charyn dryly. "Are you sure you don't want to come with me?"

"I think I made it very clear how I feel about Imagisle."

"Then I'll see you later."

"Most likely not until tomorrow. After services, Gherard's driving me up to Laamyst's place north of here."

"How many does he have near L'Excelsis? There's the High Holding at Charpen, the town mansion, the summer villa near Talyon, and the one north of here. Is there another one?"

Bhayrn grinned. "There's one on the east side of the river near Caluse, but we're going to the one north of here."

"Then enjoy yourself."

"I aim to."

Bhayrn walked around Charyn and headed up the staircase.

Charyn shook his head and made his way to the rear courtyard.

Just before he mounted, Undercaptain Faelln walked across the rear courtyard. "Your Grace?"

"Yes, Undercaptain?"

"One of the lookouts noticed several men seemingly working on a wagon just off the Ring Road. They had been there for more than a glass." Faelln smiled sardonically. "I sent some guards with a wheelwright to help them out. There was very little wrong with the wagon axle or wheels, and they got the wagon moving and away from the Chateau. You might consider not attending services."

"I've already promised, and I really need to talk to Maitre Alastar."

"Then I'd suggest you and your guards ride down the narrow walk beyond the south bailey door and circle to the north."

"Thank you. I appreciate that suggestion."

"Might I also suggest you skip services once in a while? Perhaps next week?"

"I'll keep that in mind, Faelln. I know you worry about my safety, but I'm trying not to be totally confined to the Chateau."

"I understand, sir."

"I think what you're not saying is that it's better to be restricted than dead," replied Charyn. "Ideally, I'd agree. But I can't always follow the ideal. I will try to be more cautious, though." With a nod to the undercaptain, Charyn checked the rifle in the saddle holder before mounting, not that he ever hoped to use it, especially since he was much better with the pistol inside his tunic.

Then, following Faelln's suggestion, he let the lead guard take the narrower way to the west and down the haulers' lane to the Ring Road, immediately crossing it and taking a side street west of the Ring Road to bring Charyn and the guards to the Boulevard D'Ouest, from there across the Nord Bridge and onto the East River Road down to Imagisle.

The imager in the watch box on the Imagisle side of the bridge nodded politely as Charyn rode past, heading to the Maitre's house. Charyn wondered about the armored watch boxes, although he knew they must have been created at the time of the attacks on student imagers some six years before.

Aloryana waved to Charyn when he reached the drive to the Maitre's house, then walked beside him after he dismounted and walked the gelding down to the stable, followed by the four guards.

"Why doesn't Bhayrn ever come with you?"

"It's not you." Charyn paused, then went on, deciding that Aloryana should know the reason. "He doesn't like Imagisle. He believes most imagers think like factors, and he has no love of factors."

"He could still write."

"I don't believe Bhayrn's ever written anyone."

Aloryana shook her head, then asked, "How do factors think any differently from High Holders?"

"I don't see much difference, but Bhayrn definitely does."

"That's because he spends too much time with Laamyst."

"Have you ever met Laamyst?"

"Just once. He ignored me." An annoyed expression crossed Aloryana's face.

Charyn nodded. He'd only seen Laamyst a few times, but he had the feeling that Laamyst could be dismissive, especially of younger sisters. "What about Gherard?"

"Gherard?"

"The son and heir of High Holder Ghaermyn."

"I don't know him. Bhayrn never mentioned him. The one I saw most was Amascarl."

"Bhayrn still sees him, I know."

"He at least smiles."

By the time Charyn had his mount taken care of, and he and Aloryana had returned to the front of the Maitre's house, Alastar was standing on the porch. He turned to Aloryana. "Will you see if Lystara's ready?"

"Yes, sir."

As Aloryana turned toward the door, Alastar said to Charyn, "You're early again."

"I took another longer way to get here. The guards thought there might be some men watching the Chateau too closely."

"You do need to be careful." Alastar nodded. "We have some time before we have to set out. I understand you had the Factors' Council for dinner on Samedi night. How did that turn out?"

Charyn didn't ask how Alastar knew. "I had a ride through Solidar with Eshmael on Meredi, looking at all the damage to factorages and warehouses, then met with him before the dinner. Unless matters change dramatically, he's not changing his mind. He wants to keep workers' wages low, and he wants me to bring in the army to stop the violence. Some of the other factors would be happy to pay two coppers a day to stop the fires. Some actually are, but won't admit it publicly."

"Do you think that small an increase will stop the fires? Most are paying a silver for a six-day week."

"At two coppers a day, they'd still get two more coppers a week. But no . . . I think I'd still have to bring in the army. It's just that if they're paying more . . ."

"Most people would see that as justified?"

Charyn shrugged. "That's my hope. I don't see the factors agreeing to more than two coppers a day, and I don't see the violence ending any time soon."

"I would point out one thing for you to consider. There are nearly a thousand manufactorages in or around L'Excelsis. So far as we can tell, possibly seventy have been destroyed or severely damaged, mostly mills dealing with cloth."

"I'm afraid I don't see the point. What you seem to be saying is that the factors, as a whole, aren't that much affected. That suggests that they'll never accede to a higher wage."

"No. It doesn't mean they won't. It does mean that they don't have to. Not now," replied Alastar. "On the other hand, most families can't live on less than a silver a week. In time, when it becomes obvious that the factors won't budge and you haven't done anything, you'll likely have a much bigger problem."

Charyn offered an exasperated sigh. "You're saying that the factors won't agree unless somehow forced, and that the unrest will continue and eventually get worse."

"Most likely by early winter."

"So I have a little time, but not much."

"If you change nothing."

"Then there's Elthyrd's death," offered Charyn. "Do you have any idea who might behind that?"

"Eshmael has more reasons, but I doubt he has the ability to keep it secret. Any number of other factors, and even some High Holders, might have a motive."

"Why the High Holders?"

"Elthyrd's reasoned approach strengthened the factors. Eshmael's outbursts weaken them and make the factors seem less reasonable, and some High Holders might well believe that strengthens their position. His outbursts also make it harder for you, and you're not exactly without enemies."

Charyn hadn't thought that Elthyrd might have been

beaten just to weaken Charyn's own position, but it made sense, unfortunately.

Alastar looked up as Alyna, Lystara, and Aloryana appeared. "We'd best start walking."

Aloryana joined Charyn. "Palenya told me that you're practicing more, and your playing is still getting better."

"That's likely because she's still helping me."

"Do you still like her?"

"I'll always like her. I also respect her."

"Are you going to ask Alyncya D'Shendael?"

"I'm interested, but . . . it's as much up to her as me."

"Good. You shouldn't insist on anyone marrying you who really doesn't want to. I said I wanted to meet her. When will that be?"

At the edge in Aloryana's voice, Charyn turned and stopped. "Maitre Alastar, do you have any objection to Aloryana attending the Autumn-Turn Ball?"

"No. Would you prefer to have her enter with the regial family or with Alyna and me?"

"With Alyna and you. She is an imager, and that separation, in public, needs to be maintained." Before anyone could interrupt, Charyn went on, "I know. My father broke that rule with Malyna, and so did I, but right now, I think it's better if she's seen on the imager side." He looked to Aloryana. "What do you think?"

"I think I should accompany Maitre Alastar and Maitre Alyna, but I shouldn't be announced."

"Is that acceptable to the Collegium?" asked Charyn.

"It is," replied Alastar.

"Some people will murmur and wonder what's behind it," offered Alyna with a smile that Charyn saw as mischievous. "That might be for the best."

"Now that's settled," said Alastar genially, "we should proceed."

"We should," agreed Charyn. He smiled ruefully, realizing that Alastar and Aloryana had arranged the entire conversation. *Or, more likely, Aloryana and Alyna.*

Iskhar's homily was anything but terribly uplifting, not with its message about the need to see others without inflicting a name on them. To Charyn, that seemed all too common. Everyone seemed to have a name for those they opposed.

On the way back from the anomen, Charyn broached the question of whether Alastar had any recommendations about High Holders' sons in Khel who might make decent regional governors.

"Have you ever thought of naming a woman as a regional governor?"

"A woman? I don't think that would set all that well."

"That's too bad. If not, you might consider one of the younger sons of High Holder Moeryn, then. I think the youngest is named Thealyt. Good family, and Moeryn was the High Councilor from Khel almost twenty years ago. Very solid and honest family. I've occasionally exchanged letters with Moeryn. I don't know that Thealyt would accept, but I'm certain he'd do well at it."

"I'll keep that in mind," replied Charyn. "I have another question. One a factor might ask."

"Oh?"

"Do you know any factors or High Holders who might offer decent prices for coal delivered to L'Excelsis, besides from a factor named Karl, that is?"

Alastar smiled. "Actually, I do. Alyna's brother, High Holder Zaerlyn, had to develop a coal mine because of problems with Karl several years ago. Now . . . whether his prices would be any better, that I can't tell you." Alastar paused. "Might I ask why you're interested?"

"I'm working on a project that might need a fair amount of coal."

"You? You mentioned that you had an account at the exchange . . ."

"At this point, I can't purchase through the exchange." That wasn't quite what Alastar had hinted at, but it was an answer that would suffice.

"There's no account there in your name."

"Not as Rex, no."

Alastar smiled. "I won't press, but if some High Holders or factors found out . . ."

"Some already know. It will come out, but not for a time. Besides, why shouldn't the Rex have access to the exchange?"

"Some would say you already have too many advantages."

"Some will always be critical," replied Charyn wryly.

Before long, the five were walking the last few yards to the Maitre's dwelling.

As Charyn paused at the steps, Aloryana eased close to her brother. "Thank you for understanding."

"You set it up, didn't you?"

"I only brought it up indirectly. You didn't have to ask about my attending the ball. You could have put me off or asked me to come later."

"Except it's easier for both of you at the ball, because any conversation can be ended with less awkwardness, if need be. Or simply postponed to a later date, if matters go well."

"I hoped you'd understand."

Charyn was just glad he'd managed to do the right thing. *You just hope it's the right thing.*

⌐⌐⌐

46

After going through his morning routine, and working even harder on the exercises with the guards, the first thing Charyn did on Lundi morning when he reached his study was to have Moencriff dispatch the package that contained both the letter and the book of poetry to Alyncya.

Next he sat down at the desk and wrote a short letter to Ostraaw giving him High Holder Zaerlyn's name and saying that the High Holder had recently developed a coal mine and might be receptive to selling, although whether the price would be better was uncertain. After signing and sealing it, again in black with a blank seal, Charyn handed it to Wyllum.

"Remember the last letter to the ironworks? Send this one the same way by public courier. Ostraaw shouldn't know it's coming from me."

"Didn't you sign it?" asked Wyllum.

"I did, but with a family name familiar to the engineer. It's mine, but it's a device that's used for various reasons. There's nothing in the letter that isn't strictly within the Codex Legis, but no one in the Chateau outside of me, you, and my mother knows that I'm using a family name. I'm trusting you to keep that entirely to yourself."

"Yes, sir, I will."

"Excellent. Here are the silvers you'll need."

Once Wyllum left, Charyn walked to the open window, through which blew a comparatively cool breeze, hopefully presaging the cooler days of autumn. He didn't smell a trace of smoke, and that was good, because he didn't need any more burning factorages . . . or Bhayrn bringing up the matter in a snide way. And, of course, on the present morning Bhayrn couldn't have, since he wasn't at breakfast, because he hadn't returned from Laamyst's until past midnight, according to the duty logbook that Charyn had glanced through.

I just hope he had a good evening and that he'll be in a better mood.

From there Charyn's thoughts turned to what Alastar had said the previous evening, especially the implication that there was something else Charyn could do to get the factors to raise workers' wages. Or was it something that Charyn could do to stop the fires without bringing in the army?

He'd thought about a tariff levied just on the factors, and immediately dismissed that, given the troubles he'd had there. Even an increased trade tariff on incoming goods would be seen as a violation of his pledge.

But what else was there that he could actually control?

After pacing back and forth in front of the windows for almost a quint, he decided to deal with Aevidyr on something he could accomplish. He hadn't walked to Aevidyr's study immediately, knowing that the Minister of Administration was seldom particularly early in his arrival at the Chateau, but with seventh glass past, he made his way there.

Aevidyr looked startled when Charyn entered the study. "Your Grace? I didn't know you were looking for me."

"I didn't leave word. So no one knew. What do you know about High Holder Moeryn?"

"Moeryn . . . Moeryn . . . Oh! He served one term as a High Councilor from Khel years ago. That was while I was still a regional minister in Tilbora. I can't say I ever knew him." Aevidyr frowned. "Is he still alive?"

"He is . . . or at least was a year or so ago, and I've not seen anything about his death. I'm considering offering the regional governorship to his youngest son Thealyt."

"I don't know anything about him. No one's recommended him, unlike Nuaraan D'Nualt."

"Someone has recommended him. Maitre Alastar did.

I've had much better fortune with his suggestions. Draft a letter offering him the position, if you would."

"Your Grace . . ."

"Yes? Were you going to tell me that High Holder Nualt would be most disappointed, or perhaps High Holder Nacryon?"

"Ah . . . yes, Your Grace."

"I'm certain they'll be able to contain their disappointment, and that they'll be pleased with the appointment of the son of a former distinguished High Councilor." Charyn paused. "Or would they rather that I appointed the son of a well-established factor?"

Aevidyr swallowed. "I'm certain that they will accept the son of a former High Councilor."

Charyn smiled. "I look forward to seeing the letter." Then he turned and left Aevidyr's study, stopping by his mother's study.

"How is your morning going?" asked Chelia.

"Not too badly, which means that it's likely to get worse. I have invited an additional guest to the Autumn-Turn Ball, but she's requested not to be announced."

"Oh?" Chelia didn't sound particularly surprised.

"Aloryana will accompany Maitres Alastar and Alyna."

Chelia nodded. "It's better that way. You are getting serious about Alyncya D'Shendael, aren't you?"

"Why do you say that?" Charyn knew very well why she'd said that, but wanted an admission.

"Because you promised Aloryana that she could meet the young woman, and meeting her at a ball is the easiest way. I assume you will make the introductions."

"I'd planned to, both for you and Aloryana."

"It might be best if I introduced myself to Alyncya. That is, unless you're determined to ask her to marry you immediately."

"You think that if I make both introductions . . . ?"

"I do. Young men, even Rexes, do introduce lady friends

to sisters without it being taken as a commitment or a potential commitment. However . . ."

"I see your point. Then I should introduce Alyncya to Aloryana early. I'd thought to ask Aloryana to the second dance, and after that . . ."

"No. That is a trifle obvious. You can ask your sister to dance two or three times. I'll wait."

As he left his mother, Charyn smiled wryly. As he'd suspected, Aloryana had written something to their mother.

When he returned to the study, Wyllum immediately said, "That package is on its way, sir. Also, while you were gone, an army courier brought a dispatch from Marshal Vaelln. It's on your desk."

"Thank you."

Charyn doubted that the news contained in the dispatch would be good. At best, it would show more progress against the Jariolans, but still more losses of merchant shipping. At worst, there would be lost warships and lost merchanters. He immediately opened the dispatch and began to read. There was good news. The Solidaran fleet off Jariola had destroyed three more Jariolan ships with no losses. The bad news was that two Jariolan privateers had sunk and taken the cargoes of seven merchanters bound to Solidar from Otelyrn. While the privateers were sunk, in turn, by a Solidaran third-rater, the cargoes and crews were lost.

Almost as an afterthought, Vaelln noted that construction had begun on the frigate in the new shipyard in Solis, several weeks ahead of schedule.

After rereading the dispatch more carefully and finding nothing he'd overlooked the first time, Charyn added the dispatch to the others now in the file chest that contained only material from the Marshal, a chest he'd been forced to add given the volume of what Vaelln had sent. *If this keeps up, you'll need another chest by year end.*

~~~~~~

47

Meredi morning found Charyn again reading the news-sheets, resigned to the fact that there would be little good news printed and hoping that the bad news wasn't terrible.

The *Veritum* story was relatively straightforward, just noting that the warehouse of one Arasanyt, a factor in wool-ens and linens, both imported and Solidaran, had been dam-aged by fire, but that the presence of a large water tank had enabled the factor to save stock in one wing of the building.

On the other hand, what appeared in *Tableta* was very dif-ferent.

> Despite the continuing fires of factorages and warehouses in L'Excelsis and throughout Solidar, fires set by workers desperate and unable to feed their families on the starva-tion wages offered by factors, neither those most respect-able factors nor our most beloved young Rex appear able or willing to address the cause of those fires. Men need decent wages to feed their families. Chief Factor Eshmael refuses to accept this basic fact. All he—and many other factors—cares about is how great his profits will be. Our beloved Rex is perfectly willing to fight an undeclared war with Jariola, one in which our mighty and growing navy seems unable even to stop scarcely armed privateers from sinking and pillaging our ships, but he is not willing to fight for the right of workers to a decent wage . . .

How do you fight for that . . . Charyn frowned. He really hadn't made any attempt to talk with the craftmasters or the guilds after Argentyl had vanished. Then he shook his head.

That wouldn't resolve anything. The workers only had the power to disrupt. *There has to be something to bring the factors around . . . or a way to give them what they want that does more than that . . .*

A quint later, he was striding along the upper corridor toward Alucar's study.

The Finance Minister looked up from his desk at Charyn's abrupt entrance.

"Your clerks have records of all the factorages in L'Excelsis, don't they?"

Alucar frowned. "We have records of all the factorages that pay tariffs, not just in L'Excelsis, but everywhere in Solidar. I'd estimate those records account for eight out of ten at best."

"Excellent."

"What do you have in mind, Your Grace?"

"Increasing tariff revenues and making factors and High Holders more accountable. Also bringing the army to bear. Let me explain. You've already pointed out that we aren't collecting all the tariffs we should. Isn't it true that we know, for the most part, all the High Holders? Whether they pay all the tariffs they should is another question, but they all pay something. Isn't that so?"

"There might be a handful who don't pay anything, but they'd be small High Holdings in very out-of-the-way places, like in the heart of the Montagnes D'Glace. There are still many High Holders who aren't paying what they should. That's why we've been working to update the information and records."

"That means that where we're missing the most in tariff collections is among the factors?"

"That's true, but I'd judge that half of those probably wouldn't contribute much."

"Do you have a clerk or two who can quickly read ledgers and compare names and locations to the tariff records to determine whether someone is paying tariffs? Not necessarily the correct amount, but whether they're paying them at all?"

"We could compare names to the tariff rolls . . . in most cases, anyway. But I doubt if many of those who aren't paying tariffs have decent ledgers . . . or any ledgers at all."

"But if they don't, and there's no record of their paying tariffs, we can come back and insist on tariffs. We'll also know who they are, and we can add them immediately to the tariff rolls for the future."

"That's true. It will take a considerable amount of work. Just what exactly do you have in mind, Your Grace?"

"Making things fair," replied Charyn with a smile. Then he went on to explain.

When he finished, Alucar shook his head slowly. "You're taking quite a risk there."

"Everything's a risk, but the High Holders will support it. They've always contended that the factors weren't paying their share. They'll also have less to complain about regarding our efforts to make their records and tariffs more accurate if we're doing something along the same lines with the factors. The factors can't complain . . . not too loudly, because the aim is to make sure that they're paying what they should, and the workers will like it because they'll see that I've decided that the factors need to be put in their place. I can also point out that I'm not increasing tariffs on those who pay them, and that those who don't pay them are taking an unfair advantage over those who do."

"They won't just open their doors to my clerks."

"No, they won't. But they will if there's a squad of troopers behind them. That's where the army comes in. Since the army will already have to be there to protect the factorages and warehouses . . . what better way to pay for what the army is doing than to put the costs on those factors who aren't paying?"

"That could generate another kind of revolt."

Charyn shook his head. "This time around, the clerks won't ask to see the ledgers of anyone who's on the tariff rolls. They'll just check off the fact that the factorage is on the tariff rolls, and perhaps offer an estimate to the factors, and take notes for the future. I'll leave the exact details to you, however, on how to get them on the tariff rolls with the least effort and conflict."

"That makes more sense than asking for everyone's ledgers. You'll still get resistance."

"As I recall, there are laws and penalties for not paying tariffs."

"They've only been enforced selectively."

"So . . . your clerks can simply tell them that, if they pay the tariffs due, no penalties will be assessed and no one will go to the workhouses. If they resist, however . . ."

"Some factors will protest."

"I'm certain that some of them will, but they're the ones who asked for the army to protect them. Now . . . what you need to do is to copy down the names and locations of all the factorages in L'Excelsis onto separate lists for your clerks. Wyllum can help do that. The lists need to be by district, and I realize that may take some time . . ."

"We can't do this overnight, Your Grace."

"How long will it take to get the names of the factorages along the river on the west bank, south from the Sud Bridge?"

"Two or three days."

"Then, when you're ready, we'll send out two clerks, each protected by the army. I'd think a squad for each clerk would be enough, but I'll need to talk to Vaelln about that. They'll go from factorage to factorage. Can your other clerks and Wyllum keep making up lists for other districts while the two clerks are checking factorages?"

"Yes, Your Grace."

"So we could start on the third or fourth of Feuillyt? That might be later, of course, if the army isn't ready."

"I could tell you more accurately tomorrow. I need to look into the tariff rolls."

"That would be fine. I'd also appreciate your keeping the reasons for what you're doing with the records to yourself until I've met with Marshal Vaelln and determined if it's possible to handle matters the way I think we can."

"I certainly will, sir."

Charyn paused. "At some point, you might check the tariff records of High Holder Laastyn. I understand he recently obtained several thousand hectares of timberland in Tilbor, and he has to have at least four or five other properties just around L'Excelsis, a lodge in Talyon, and lands near Asseroiles. Also, High Holder Ghaermyn has a number of factorages here in L'Excelsis. You can include the High Holders' factorages in L'Excelsis, can't you? We can't just look at the establishments of factors."

"I'd already thought that, Your Grace."

"Thank you." Charyn nodded and then left, walking back toward his own study more slowly.

Once he stepped inside, he looked to Wyllum and said, "If you'd draft a message to Marshal Vaelln, requesting his presence at first glass of the afternoon tomorrow. It needs to be drafted and sent immediately."

"Yes, sir." The scrivener looked questioningly at Charyn.

"It's not an emergency." *Not yet.* "But it's important. Once we've sent off the letter, I'll explain why and how you'll be involved."

Even though Charyn had finally come to a decision about what to do, he still worried. At the same time, he had to remind himself that his father's failing to come to decisions and to follow through on them had cost him dearly. *But so had bad decisions.*

What was unfortunately all too clear, from what several influential and knowledgeable individuals had all told him, was that he was almost out of time before matters would get worse—much worse. And Elthyrd's death might just be the first of more than a few.

He took a deep breath and waited for Wyllum to finish drafting the letter.

48

On Jeudi morning, Charyn took the unmarked coach, leaving the Chateau at a quint past sixth glass, early enough that it was unlikely to be noted, unless, of course, someone had decided to watch every single person who came and left the Chateau at every glass of day or night.

That could be possible, even likely. He shook his head. That kind of worrying could turn him into someone like his father or grandsire.

Even so, when the coach stopped at the shore end of the pier nearest to Paersyt's factorage, Charyn was relieved to see that no one but Paersyt and the men nearest him were on that pier, and that those men on the piers to the north paid no attention to the coach, or to Charyn and the two brown-coated guards who accompanied him as he walked out to the end of the pier.

The boat tied there didn't appear all that prepossessing, somewhere around twelve yards from stem to stern and possibly five yards abeam at the widest. A small pilothouse perched on the deck some four yards back from the bow, behind which was an open area some five yards long, containing the steam engine and, behind it, what appeared to be the gearing system that connected to the shaft leading to the water screw that presumably was located somewhere under the stern section of the boat. A thin trail of smoke rose from the top of a metal chimney—*smoke funnel*, Charyn recalled from the drawings Paersyt had sent him—that extended up from the firebox assembly. The last three yards of the boat were also decked with a ship's wheel mounted at the front of a slightly raised area just forward of the stern.

Paersyt stood beside the wheel. When he saw the riders and recognized Charyn, he jumped from the boat to the pier and walked to meet the Rex.

"How do you like the looks of the *Steamwraith*?"

"It looks different."

"She. Ships are always women."

Charyn looked at the river, the current flowing strongly, but not rushing. "Your boat can make headway against the current?"

"We've made three short trials with the engine in its current configuration. If we don't have problems, you'll see."

"How many times have you had problems?"

Paersyt shook his head. "You don't want to know. That's why we've had trials, almost a month of them."

Charyn nodded. "Go ahead." He wasn't about to say what he felt—that he worried about staying long in any one place.

"Yes, sir." With a smile Paersyt turned and reboarded the *Steamwraith,* where he gestured to the man standing by the firebox before taking his place at the wheel.

The fireman shoveled more coal into the firebox, and Charyn waited.

After a time, the trail of smoke from the funnel increased, but nothing seemed to happen. Charyn kept watching. Then, Paersyt gestured again, and the fireman pulled a long lever. With a hissing sound, the pistons began to move, slowly at first, then more swiftly, and the boat gradually moved farther away from the pier.

Charyn noticed the water being churned up behind the boat, leaving a wake as the small craft headed toward the center of the river, being carried downstream even as it moved away from the pier.

The thickness of the smoke increased, and once the *Steamwraith* was well clear of the pier and some twenty yards out into the river, Paersyt turned the boat into the current. Charyn found himself holding his breath, but the boat, amazingly to Charyn, began to move faster, even against the current, and before long was approaching the Sud Bridge.

When the craft turned downstream, it seemed almost to fly toward Charyn and the pier. He noticed that several men on the pier to the north had stopped loading and were watching the *Steamwraith* as she slowed and eased up to the pier.

Before that long, Paersyt was on the pier. "There was still a bit more vibration than I'd like. Over time, that could be a problem."

"Problem or not, that was amazing!" Charyn didn't have to feign enthusiasm. "Even the men on the other pier were watching."

"Most likely to see if the engine exploded."

"Can you build a bigger engine?" asked Charyn. "One able to power a boat twice this size with hundredweights of cargo and still be able to move against the current like the *Steamwraith*?"

"If you have the golds and patience. Building this one took almost seven months. Increasing the size and power . . . that will take work. And golds."

"Let me know how much. I want you to build it so that once we have a manufactorage in place, you can build scores of engines."

"Me?"

"You. Don't you want to be the engineer who changed Solidar? This engine can be used for many things, I think."

"I don't know who will buy them . . ."

"If no one else will, I will. The navy could even use engines like this one along the coast against smugglers."

"It won't be easy, Your Grace."

To that, Charyn just nodded. Nothing was easy, but seeing how the *Steamwraith* had moved and handled, he couldn't help but believe that Paersyt's engine was going to change Solidar . . . and, in time, all Terahnar. "Just let me know what you need. I may not be able to give you everything necessary immediately, not with the demands of the war, but we'll do the best we can."

"You've always kept your word, Your Grace."

"I need to be going," said Charyn. "But keep sending me reports."

"Yes, sir."

Charyn was back at the Chateau and in his study well before eighth glass, where Wyllum immediately said, "Minister Alucar was here earlier. He didn't say what he wanted, just that he needed to see you."

"We'll walk over there together."

Wyllum raised his eyebrows.

"As I told you the other day, Minister Alucar is going to need your skills and help. I wouldn't be surprised if that was what he was going to ask about."

"Just copying lists?"

"That's sometimes very important. His clerks can't afford to make mistakes. Actually, I can't afford to have them make mistakes." *Factors are going to be angry enough at me as it is.*

When they reached the study door, Charyn rapped, then opened it and stepped inside. "You were looking for me?"

"Yes, Your Grace. I was wondering . . ."

"Wyllum is ready to start work any time you need him, beginning this moment."

"Thank you, sir. You left the Chateau quite early . . ."

"I had a meeting with Factor Paersyt. Actually, I went to see the water trials of his engine."

"He has it working? Water trials?"

"It can be used for many things, it appears. We'll see." Charyn nodded to Wyllum. "I'll let Minister Alucar know if I have any urgent need for you. Otherwise, you'll be working for him for a time." Charyn looked to the older man.

"Likely a week. It might be less."

Just after Charyn stepped away from Alucar's study and was heading back to his own, Aevidyr appeared.

"Your Grace?"

"What is it, Aevidyr?"

"It's about the regional governorship of Khel, sir."

"What about it?"

"I've just received a letter from High Holder Nacryon. He indicates that he will be greatly disappointed if his brother-in-law—that's Nuaraan D'Nualt, you might recall—"

"If Nuaraan isn't appointed?"

"Yes, sir."

"Just write him back and tell him that a selection is finally in process. And, Aevidyr, if Nacryon or any other High Holder discovers anything before that choice has accepted or refused, I will expect your immediate departure. Is that clear?"

For a moment, the Minister of Administration was silent. "Yes, Your Grace."

"Good." Charyn smiled. "A number of High Holders may complain, but, in the end, most of them will be happier with my choices than theirs."

Once Charyn was back in his study, he read through the responses to petitions drafted by Sanafryt. With Wyllum now working for Alucar, Charyn had to write out the changes himself, not that he particularly minded.

Marshal Vaelln arrived half a quint before first glass.

Charyn gestured to the chairs and did not speak for several moments after Vaelln seated himself. "As you must be aware, Marshal, the violence in L'Excelsis hasn't subsided in the slightest. From the reports I read, it continues at about the same level, but the anger of both workers and factors continues to grow. I think it's now time to bring in the army to cool things down here in L'Excelsis. I may also have to bring in the army elsewhere, and I'd like you to inform Marshal Tynan of the possible need in Solis."

"I already have informed him of the possibility, Your Grace."

"I appreciate your forethought."

"We can prevent much of the violence and destruction, Your Grace. I doubt we can cool angry factors and workers by using force."

"Your presence will reduce the number of factorages and warehouses being destroyed, and that will cool down at least many of the factors. I doubt, as I suspect you do, that the army will be able to stop all the destruction."

"Then what, Your Grace?"

"Under martial law, I can exercise more authority . . ."

"You always could, without the pretext of martial law."

"That's true, but pretexts are sometimes useful. I'll use martial law to suspend all executions for those trying to fire or destroy factorages, unless, of course, they kill someone."

"Your Grace . . ."

"Instead, they'll spend five years in the navy galleys or in other service as you see fit. With more men and boys not getting executed, that might help. They'll at least get fed. Combined with what else I'm putting in place, that might cool down some of the workers."

Vaelln looked more intently at Charyn, but did not speak.

"The other support duty I'll need from you is several squads who will support Alucar's clerks in taking a census of manufactorages and factorages. It has become apparent that quite a number of factorages are not on the tariff rolls. It would seem fair to me, and it should seem fair to the factors, that if the army is to protect their property then all factors and factorages should be paying their tariffs . . ." Charyn could see the hint of a grim smile on Vaelln's face.

"I like the thought behind it, Your Grace. The factors won't."

"No . . . but if they complain too much, who will support them? The High Holders won't. They've insisted, with some justification, I've recently discovered, that there are a significant number of factorages and manufactorages not paying tariffs. The guilds and the crafters won't mind seeing the factors pay what they owe . . ."

"There is one difficulty. The army will have to be deployed mainly at night. That means two sets of duty rosters."

"Not so many as that. There are only likely to be two or three, possibly four clerks needing protection. Initially, wouldn't a squad be enough for each clerk?"

"Would you mind explaining the details of what you wish, Your Grace?"

"Of course. The problem is that many factorages aren't on the tariff rolls and others are only paying a fraction of what they owe . . ." From there Charyn went on to explain what he had in mind and how long it might take. Then he waited for Vaelln's response.

"Do you intend to maintain martial law for the weeks if not months this . . . census or these audits will take?"

"I don't think that will be necessary, but if it appears likely . . . well . . . if it appears likely, it may not be my problem."

"Do you think that's a possibility?"

"It's a possibility. Anything's possible. With the army in position, if necessary, I can also suggest that if the factors don't start treating workers better I may have to take other steps."

"We're already short of golds . . . and so are you," Vaelln pointed out.

"Minister Alucar's numbers suggest that as many as two in ten factorages and manufactorages aren't paying tariffs. That should bring in quite a few golds."

"You seem to have given this some thought."

"I've tried. How long before you could move army units into L'Excelsis?"

"We've already worked out the plans, just in case. Easily by next Meredi."

"The fourth?"

Vaelln nodded.

"And the squads to protect the clerks could be ready then?"

"Yes, sir. That part is the easiest."

"Then plan to begin the main army's duties on the evening of the fourth, and the squads supporting the clerks on the morning of the fifth. We should meet again late on the afternoon of the third to go over matters. Say . . . fourth glass?"

"Fourth glass."

"And you will inform me if we need to meet earlier in the event you discover some unforeseen problems?"

"Yes, Your Grace." Vaelln cleared his throat. "I might also suggest an extra company or at least a few extra squads be posted around the Chateau for a few days after you announce this."

"Surreptitiously, I think would be best."

Vaelln nodded, then asked, "Might I ask why you decided to involve the army now?"

"By realizing that there wasn't anything close to a perfect way out of this mess, only one that *might* be workable. I'm giving the factors what they asked for, but not quite in the way they demanded. They'll get protection. By assuring that fewer rioters get executed, I'll be seen perhaps as not quite so cruel, and by making sure the factors pay their fair share of tariffs, the High Holders won't be outraged."

"Aren't you letting the High Holders off more easily?"

Charyn shook his head. "For the last three months we've been quietly auditing High Holders and increasing or decreasing their tariffs. That process will take several years, but unlike the factors, we know almost all the High Holders are paying tariffs at some level."

"The next few weeks will still be interesting."

"I know. And Marshal, you and you wife do need to be at the Autumn-Turn Ball."

Vaelln offered an amused smile. "I hadn't thought otherwise, Your Grace."

"Then I will see you on Samedi." Charyn smiled and stood.

The smile faded once Vaelln left the study.

Charyn knew that his plan was anything but perfect. But he had to do something, and what he'd put together was the best he could come up with. The question was whether it would be enough. He was still worrying when he entered the family parlor before dinner, half surprised to see Bhayrn waiting there for him.

"Where were you this morning?" asked Bhayrn.

"I had some business with an engineer," replied Charyn. "It didn't take long."

"What sort of business?"

"About a naval matter."

"Shouldn't you be leaving that to the Marshal and his engineers?"

"As a matter of fact, I met with Marshal Vaelln just this afternoon."

"You still haven't done anything about stopping the burning of factorages."

"That's not quite true. There's something in progress."

"Not more proclamations and useless laws, I hope."

Chelia entered the family parlor at that moment. "What were you saying about useless laws, Bhayrn?"

"That we didn't need any more of them, and that we need action to deal with the ruffians who are destroying factorages."

"I didn't know you were such a partisan of the factors, dear," replied Chelia sweetly. "I was under the impression that you'd be happy to have them all reduced to penury. Or does the fact that Gherard's father has factorages have something to do with that?"

"The workers and the factors deserve each other," declared Bhayrn, "but the fact that they don't follow the laws is intolerable. That's why Charyn should just bring in the army and make them settle their differences right here and now."

"How do you propose I do that?" asked Charyn, half

wondering if Bhayrn actually had a new idea, and half ready to dismiss whatever his brother said.

"Just shoot every worker who tries to destroy something and tell the factors to stop causing trouble or you'll increase their tariffs."

"While we could use higher tariffs," agreed Charyn, "the factors would likely revolt if I imposed a blanket tariff increase on them."

"They're not paying their fair share as it is. Everyone knows that."

"Everyone . . . or only the High Holders?" asked Chelia.

"That's why they're getting richer and the High Holders are losing golds," said Bhayrn.

"That might be one of the reasons," said Charyn. "It's not the only one."

"How generous of you to condescend to accept my poor thoughts." Bhayrn's voice oozed sticky-sweet venom.

"That will be enough, Bhayrn," said Chelia. "Charyn said you had a point. Have the grace to accept it. Here come Karyel and Iryella. We will have a pleasant dinner."

"That we will," agreed Charyn.

"Of course," said Bhayrn almost cheerfully, with such an abrupt change of tone that Charyn had a good general idea of what his brother was thinking, not that saying it would do anything but make Bhayrn wary . . . and that was definitely something Charyn couldn't yet chance.

49

~~~~~

At just before seventh glass on Samedi evening, Charyn looked at the dressing room mirror, checking himself, even though he wore exactly what he'd worn to the last ball—regial formal greens, trimmed in silver, pale green shirt and black cravat, black trousers and boots, and, of course, the gold-edged deep green formal sash of the Rex. After a last glance, he left his dressing room and walked toward his mother's study, worried, he had to admit, about a great number of matters. He wouldn't have put it past Eshmael to create some sort of scene, or workers to storm the Chateau in protest of a ball when they felt they were underpaid, or use the evening to burn down more manufactorages. Then, he had hopes, but no idea how Alyncya's meetings with Aloryana and Chelia might turn out . . .

He pushed those thoughts aside as he rapped on the study door.

"You can come in, Charyn."

His mother stood by the window, looking out to the southeast, not quite toward the river nor exactly toward the hunting park beyond the Ring Road. She wore the same gown of regial green trimmed in black she had at the Spring-Turn Ball and would do so at balls until after the Year-Turn Ball. "As always, you look most regial."

"It's probably best that I do." He grinned, but only momentarily.

"You're about to do something important, aren't you? This coming week?"

"Why do you say that?"

"Because you've either decided or are about to. You always get a bit more reserved when something weighs on you. You're far better than your father, though, and we won't even speak of your grandsire." Before Charyn could comment, she went on. "Who do you plan to dance with in what order?"

"As I told you. The first dance with you, the second with Aloryana, the third with Maitre Alyna, and the fourth with Lady Fhaedyrk."

"The fifth should be with Factor Eshmael's wife."

Charyn nodded glumly, then said, "Alyncya after that, then Aloryana, so I can introduce her to Alyncya."

"While they're talking, find another young woman to dance with, one you could conceivably marry."

"So people will speculate that Alyncya is merely the most favored instead of the only choice?"

"Is she the only choice?"

"I'm not terribly interested in anyone else right now."

"You need to keep your options open as long as possible. That will also protect Alyncya."

Charyn, unfortunately, understood that as well. More than a few people in Solidaran history had tried to force their agendas on the Rex through his wife or intended. "Shall we go?"

Chelia nodded, and the two left the study and walked along the south corridor, across the landing at the top of the grand staircase, and then into the small sitting room that adjoined the grand ballroom.

Charyn couldn't help but think how empty the chamber felt, with just the two of them there. They really hadn't needed to arrive that early, but Charyn's father had always insisted. *Old habits die hard.* With that thought, Charyn smiled wryly, knowing that Bhayrn wouldn't have that much trouble breaking the habit.

His brother, in point of fact, had no problems transcending habit and past custom and, well past the half-glass, and the time when the players offered incidental music and guests began to arrive, the sitting room door opened, and Bhayrn entered, wearing greens nearly identical to those Charyn wore, but without a sash. "Am I presentable, Charyn, Mother, trussed up in greens for those young women who will have to settle for the younger brother and who can never hope to be more than the wife of a High Holder?"

"A very well-off High Holder," replied Chelia, "with absolutely no encumbrances on his holdings, unlike so many, like poor Ferrand."

"It wouldn't be so bad if I didn't know that I'll be inspected like a bargain bull."

"You need a better comparison," said Charyn dryly. "You've worn that one out."

"Pardon me for not having your gift with words."

"If I truly had a gift with words, you wouldn't be grousing at what I said." Charyn kept his tone light.

"At least, I only have two obligatory dances."

"No," replied Chelia with an amused smile, "you're obligated to dance most of the evening, but, besides me, Aloryana is the only woman with whom you must dance. With whomever else you dance is your choice."

Left unsaid, but still hanging in the air, was the suggestion that Bhayrn choose wisely.

As the chimes sounded eighth glass, the music from the players died away. Charyn nodded to Bhayrn, who led the way into the ballroom. Charyn and Chelia followed to the music of the "Processional of the Rex." As soon as Charyn took a position before the dais on which the musicians were seated, Charyn gestured, and a brief fanfare followed.

"Maitre Alastar D'Image, Maitre Alyna D'Image," announced the Chateau herald.

Charyn watched as the two, followed closely by Aloryana, approached him. Both nodded to Charyn, who inclined his head in return. Then the two maitres stopped and stood a yard or so to Chelia's left, with Aloryana a pace back.

Charyn could see several of the High Holders looking at

Aloryana and then to him. He kept a pleasant smile on his face as he watched the entry of the High Councilors, followed by the members of the Factors' Council of Solidar. Once the last of the factor councilors had been announced, followed by Marshal Vaelln and his wife, the orchestra began to play, and Charyn turned to his mother, took her hand, and began the dance. Behind them, Bhayrn danced with Aloryana.

"There were a few strained glances at Aloryana, but not many," said Charyn.

"More the fact that she wore a gown of imager gray, likely one from Alyna. The fact that she's here and that you and Bhayrn dance with her will convey a different message."

"That we don't reject imagers from our family or that the Chateau and the Collegium stand more closely together?"

"Isn't your goal to convey both?"

Charyn couldn't dispute that.

After the very short first dance ended, Charyn eased his mother to Bhayrn, then turned to Aloryana. "Might I have the next dance?"

"You don't exactly have to ask," replied his sister.

Charyn grinned. "It feels better to ask."

"Just remember that with Alyncya. When am I going to meet her?"

"In a while. I have three more obligatory dances."

"Maitre Alyna and who else?"

"Lady Fhaedyrk and Madame Eshmael."

"Be charming. Why is Bhayrn so gloomy? He didn't really want to talk at all. It's like we're strangers all of a sudden."

All of a sudden? He hasn't written or seen you in months.

"He never writes me back, either."

"He never was a letter-writer, and now, I think it's dawned on him that he's going to be just a High Holder, and he's not pleased."

"Just a High Holder?"

"I'm Rex, and you'll end up as an imager maitre. I suspect he sees either as better than being a High Holder and having to run a holding and worry about golds."

"You worry about golds all the time. So does Maitre Alastar."

"Bhayrn tends to forget that."

Aloryana shook her head.

As the music came to an end, she looked up at Charyn. "You won't make me chase you down, will you?"

"Absolutely not. I promised."

"Good."

Surprisingly, at least to Charyn, Ferrand appeared and asked Aloryana for the next dance, while Charyn gathered himself together and approached Alyna.

As they began to dance, Alyna said, with a hint of a quirky smile, "You asked me much earlier than at the last ball, Your Grace."

"I should have asked you earlier. I'm trying to remedy that."

"Are you being kind to an older woman?"

"No. I'm being careful with a friend and a powerful imager who likely holds at least part of my future in her hands."

"I'm glad you started with 'friend.'"

"You and Alastar are among the very few with whom I can be honest."

"You still have your secrets."

"As do you," he replied, smiling. "But I've never lied to either of you, nor, from what I can tell, have you to me."

"That makes you unique among recent rulers."

"It also remains to be seen whether that's effective or not."

"Deception never served your predecessors well."

"Sometimes," Charyn admitted, "I wonder if anything will serve well, between the High Holders and factors, and now, even the crafters."

"It doesn't have to work well. It only has to work." Then,

before Charyn could reply, she went on, "Aloryana seemed happy dancing with you."

"I think so. I certainly hope so. She worries about Bhayrn. So do I."

"The younger brothers of rulers are always a potential danger. Those of unwed rulers are both necessary and a worry."

"Even you seem to be suggesting I find a suitable lady."

"Charyn . . . merely suitable will not be enough for you . . . or for Solidar." Her words were delivered with a smile, but there was a firmness behind them.

"You and my mother agree on that."

"That doesn't surprise me in the least."

Charyn laughed softly. "So how is Aloryana really doing?"

"Better than she believes. She works very hard . . ."

Charyn mostly listened for the rest of the dance.

Lady Fhaedyrk looked slightly surprised when Charyn asked her to dance, but assented. Their conversation was pleasant, but hardly memorable.

Factor Eshmael looked anything but pleased when Charyn asked his wife.

Orlandya, on the other hand, smiled and said to Eshmael, "Don't deny me such a small pleasure."

Once the music resumed and they moved away from Eshmael, she said, "Am I an obligation or a diversion?"

"A diversion, I sincerely hope. That is, a diversion from having to be most formal and correct."

"I'm glad you explained. Is it true that the imager who entered with the Maitre is your sister?"

"It is indeed. She's been at the Collegium since Ianus, and she's an imager third. It's likely that in a few years she'll be a maitre, if she works hard."

"Have there been other imagers in the regial family?"

"Not for generations, so far as I know. Are there any in your family?"

Orlandya laughed. "We don't know of any." The smile faded. "Tell me, are you angry with Eshmael?"

"Angry? No. But I don't think he understands the depth of the anger and desperation felt by the displaced weavers and others. I suspect he believes that I don't appreciate the situation of the factors."

"Do you?"

"Probably not as much as he does. But I do understand the need to make silvers and not to lose them. I don't see that as generating as much rage and desperation as that experienced by men who work hard and still can't make enough to support their families."

"Have you ever actually been in business or run anything?"

"Actually, I have. I have some lands that I was in charge of for several years before I became Rex. I took an active role in managing them and was able to increase yields and production significantly."

"Is that . . . usual?" Orlandya offered a quizzical expression.

"I think I'm the first son in many years to do anything like that," admitted Charyn.

"Are you going to do something about the fires and destruction?"

"Yes."

"When?"

"Soon. As soon as a few details are worked out."

"Is that an empty promise, Your Grace?"

"I haven't exactly made any empty promises. Some that took some time to accomplish, but not empty ones. That's one reason why some factors and High Holders are less than pleased with me. I won't promise what I don't believe it's possible for me to accomplish." Charyn managed a pleasant smile. "What about you? Where do you come from?"

"From here in L'Excelsis, Your Grace. My father was also a factor. Vhadym. Did you know him?"

"I can't say that I did . . ."

Before long, Charyn returned Orlandya to Eshmael, with a smile and a nod, and then made his way around the floor, finally locating Alyncya, who happened to be talking to Ferrand, not exactly by chance on Ferrand's part, Charyn suspected.

With a nod and a wink, Ferrand eased away. Charyn couldn't help smiling as he neared Alyncya, who wore another peach gown, one somehow different from the last one, but how he couldn't have said.

"I wondered how long before you asked me."

"The first five dances are a formal requirement. You're getting the first dance where I can escape protocol."

"When you can . . . or when you choose to?" Alyncya's tone was amused, if with a slight undercurrent.

"I think you're also asking how tightly I'm committed to formality."

"I just might be."

As the music resumed, Charyn took Alyncya's hand, saying, "I'll have to let my actions tell you that. I hope you received my last letter . . . and your book."

"What if it was a gift?"

"I'd be happy to have it, but it seemed that we should share it. Sharing thoughts about the poems seemed . . . right." Charyn squeezed her hand, just slightly. "I tried to show you that by the three I picked out."

"I know. Did you pick them out to appeal to me . . . or to you?"

"To let you know how I feel."

"You're gently direct, Charyn. It's still unsettling."

"I'm not naturally given to subterfuge."

"Those words were very carefully chosen."

"I haven't exercised, at least I hope I haven't, any subterfuge with you. I've had to as Rex. I don't like it, but it's proved necessary."

"I can see that." She squeezed his hand gently.

"I was very glad for the faint question mark beside the third poem you marked."

"You read closely, don't you?"

When it means so much . . . yes. "I try."

"Why did you mark 'Choice'? It's . . ."

"Not thought to be a typical love poem? But it is. Listen . . .

> *"The chorister in surplice green*
>   *Invokes the deity unseen*
>   *With word and music most sublime*
>   *And ritual from ancient time.*
>
> *"Pray tell us now, and if you can*
>   *The worth of rites so born of man,*
>   *Or if the moons of hunt and love*
>   *Will lift us best to sky above."*

"You memorized it?"

"How could I not?"

Charyn thought that she shivered slightly, and he added, "I copied the ones I marked and several others."

"Just the love poems?"

He shook his head. "I liked some that weren't, like 'The Streets of Gold.' The image he sets of the past in the first lines . . . 'When Variana's streets were paved with gold / and the Pharsi of Naedar were still recalled . . .'"

Abruptly, she looked away for a moment, then back. "You really don't do much halfway, do you?"

How can you answer that? After a long moment, he finally said, "Not if it's important."

A faint smile appeared. "I think a better answer might be, not if you can help it."

Charyn just looked at her.

"Your Grace . . . I do believe the music is over."

Charyn flushed.

Alyncya smiled. "Thank you . . . so much. Will I see you later?"

"You will. I have a favor to ask. I promised to introduce someone to you. Would you mind?"

For an instant, Alyncya stiffened.

"No . . . it's not my mother," said Charyn with a smile. "If you wouldn't mind . . ."

"How could I mind?"

Ignoring the question, Charyn said conversationally, "I'm glad you met Ferrand, already. Besides being my cousin, he's also a friend." Then he turned toward Aloryana, who was talking to Alastar, and guided Alyncya toward his sister. As they approached, Alastar turned toward Chelia, asking her for the next dance.

"Aloryana, this is Lady-heir Alyncya D'Shendael. Alyncya, this is my sister, Imager Third Aloryana D'Imagisle. Aloryana wanted to meet you and asked if I would make an introduction."

"If you would excuse us, Charyn," said Aloryana pleasantly.

"I will see you both later," replied Charyn, stepping back and moving away, hoping that the two would get along.

"Thank you," said Aloryana, who turned to Alyncya. "Charyn has mentioned you often, but he's said very little . . ."

Although he desperately wanted to hear more, Charyn kept a pleasant smile on his face and moved away, looking for an unattached young woman. He saw Kayrolya D'Taelmyn talking with Ferron D'Fhernon, but decided against interrupting, for several reasons, including the fact that he saw Ferrand approaching.

Then he saw Bhayrn exchanging a few words with High Holder Laastyn. Bhayrn shook his head to whatever Laastyn said, then said several words before turning away.

At that moment, Charyn caught sight of Shaelyna D'Baeltyn, standing beside her parents. That made it easy, and he joined them. "Shaelyna, if I might have the next dance?"

"Of course, Your Grace." Her smile was poised and pleasant, as it always seemed to be. "I wondered if we might see you."

"How could you not?" Charyn smiled pleasantly as he took her hand and they began to dance.

"The young imager you danced with . . . that was your sister, wasn't it? I almost didn't recognize her in gray and green. I didn't realize she was an imager, but then, she wasn't at the Spring-Turn Ball, and she had been at the Year-Turn Ball."

"We discovered she was an imager right after that."

"That must have been quite a surprise."

"Very much so."

"Does she also play the clavecin?"

"She does. We even occasionally played a duet together."

"My parents were quite surprised at how well you played that evening you invited us to the Chateau. I was as well . . . and then to hear Lady-heir Alyncya play . . ."

"She plays very well. Well enough to be a musician. That was a surprise to me. Do you play?"

Shaelyna shook her head. "Nothing like either of you. Ferrand really is your cousin?"

"Oh, yes. Second cousins. We had the same great-grandparents. My grandmother was the sister of his grandfather."

"He's quite pleasant, and cheerful."

"I've always found him so."

After that dance, despite wanting to ask Alyncya to dance again, Charyn asked Faerlyna D'Kastel, and then Diasyra D'Taulyn, simply because she was sweet, intelligent, and a good dancer.

Then he went and found Aloryana and asked her to dance, not asking the obvious question until the music started and they were actually dancing.

"How did it go?"

"She's very intelligent. She might be smarter than you are."

"That wouldn't surprise me. She's also a better musician. Did you like her?"

"Charyn . . ."

"Well?"

"I do like her. She might be too good for you."

"What is that supposed to mean?"

"I think you attract her and scare her."

"I could say the same about her. I'm incredibly attracted to her and yet . . . well, I'm scared she'll reject me, and that would . . ." He shook his head.

"Don't look now," said Aloryana with a smile. "Mother is introducing herself."

Charyn swallowed.

"They're headed to the sitting room."

"Thank you so very much."

"You're very welcome." She smiled wickedly at him. "I like sometimes seeing you being unsettled."

"Wait until you like someone and have me and Mother interrogating them. Or perhaps Maitre Alastar and Maitre Alyna."

"I can wait."

"What else? About Alyncya."

"I told her I wouldn't tell you, and I won't. You need to ask her."

Charyn, unfortunately, could respect that.

After finishing the dance with Aloryana, and surrendering her to Ferron D'Fhernon, Charyn went to one of the sideboards and took a goblet of the Tacqueville white, looking around to see if he saw Ferrand. He did, but Ferrand was clearly enjoying a dance with Kayrolya D'Taelmyn. Charyn couldn't help but smile. Ferrand deserved someone like Kayrolya, and they seemed to go together well.

He glanced toward the other sideboard, where several

High Holders were gathered, but then he realized that there were two separate groups. One group consisted of the young High Holder Laevoryn, High Holder Ghaermyn, and someone else facing away from Charyn. The other three were High Holder Khunthan, High Holder Basalyt, and High Holder Plessan. Charyn wondered what the two High Councilors were discussing with the younger Plessan.

After another dance passed, Charyn eased his way around the dance floor to where Alyncya stood with her father.

"Good evening, High Holder Shendael."

"Good evening, Your Grace. I see your sister was present."

"She asked to be here. She asks very little, and there's little that I can give her now that she's an imager."

"Except all the important things," said Alyncya.

"I try to provide those as well."

"If you two will excuse me . . ." The High Holder eased away.

"Would you like to dance?"

"I'd rather not. I'm warm. Could we walk over to the window, the open one beyond the sideboard?"

"We certainly could."

In a few moments, the two stood at the window, looking westward into the evening sky. Charyn looked sideways at Alyncya, taking in her profile, her high forehead, straight strong nose, but not excessively so. Beyond her, he could see both moons, Artiema about to set, with Erion the hunter higher in the western sky, pursuing.

"It's a pleasant evening," he ventured, then added, "I've thought about you a great deal."

Without looking at him, she replied in a low voice, "And I, you."

Charyn waited, uncertain as to whether to speak, then forced himself to wait.

"When I came to the Year-Turn Ball, I never expected . . ."

"Nor did I."

"You were . . . attached." Alyncya's voice was even. "I knew that even before your mother told me. Do you think all men have mistresses?"

"From my life," replied Charyn, dreading where the question was leading, "I couldn't say. I know that my father, from the time that I can remember, never had a mistress. I understand that, while my grandsire turned to other women, that was after his wife had several lovers."

"You know where I'm headed. You've had a mistress." Alyncya's voice was cool.

"One. A tutor and a mistress. She was the one who truly taught me to play the clavecin. She also taught me a great deal about people."

"Usually, men have mistresses after they're married . . . when they tire of their wife."

"Or, occasionally, as I noted, when their wife tires of them," replied Charyn gently. "Strange as it may seem to you, I didn't seek out a mistress. My mother chose Palenya for me, and Palenya had to approve of me as well."

"Your mother? Was that because she feared your taste in women?"

"No. It was because she feared I'd turn out like all the other men in her life."

"All of them? She actually said that?"

Charyn nodded. "Word for word. You can ask her, if you wish."

"I just might."

"That might be for the best."

Alyncya looked into his eyes and offered a smile, an expression somehow rueful, amused, and sad all at once. "From your answer, I doubt I need to. But I will. Not this moment, but later."

"How was your conversation with Aloryana?"

"She's charming . . . and very protective."

"Would you care to—"

"Not at the moment. Not any time soon, in fact. I promised I wouldn't. It's up to Aloryana."

"Shall we dance?"

"Must we? I'd rather you kept talking to me."

"I'd rather you did some of the talking," said Charyn.

"She hasn't been in the Chateau for some time, has she? Palenya, not Aloryana."

"She left more than six months ago. She's now the musician for the Collegium."

"She's the one playing the clavecin, isn't she?"

"She is."

"She's not what I expected."

"She's the one who really taught me how to play the clavecin. She, and in a way, Aloryana."

"Your sister loves you a great deal."

"I love her."

"She said that she asked to meet me, and that you agreed."

"She did, and I did."

"I'm very glad of that." Alyncya finally turned to face him, her hand reaching for his.

For long moments, they just stood facing each other, holding hands.

Charyn felt strangely, totally exposed.

"I need to know you better."

"And I need that from you," he replied.

"This won't be easy . . . for either of us."

"No . . . it won't."

"I don't mean about your being Rex . . . or all the terrible problems you face."

"I know what you meant." He paused. "I think I do."

She smiled warmly. "That's one of the things I like about you." She glanced toward the musicians on the dais. "I do suppose we should dance." The hint of almost a grin appeared. "That way . . ."

Charyn found himself flushing, but that didn't stop him from taking her hand as the music began. He did hold her more tightly than he'd dared before, and when he looked at her, she smiled.

"Do you recall any other poems from the book?"

"There was one . . . 'To the Nameless.' The last two lines struck me in particular. 'No god, no deity of sense and grace / Would stoop to take a human name or face.'"

"You're not terribly religious, are you?"

"I think I'd prefer to say that I try not to be a slave to blind belief."

"I like that way of putting it."

Neither said much more as they danced, and Charyn enjoyed that, too.

As the music died away, and Charyn guided Alyncya toward where her father waited, he murmured, "We need another dance."

"I'm not going anywhere."

"Neither am I."

After returning her to her father, Charyn went to find Ferrand.

Ferrand just looked at him and offered a broad smile. "I never saw you look the way you did when you were dancing with Alyncya."

"You looked rather pleased when you were dancing with Kayrolya."

"I'll admit it. We get along well."

"My mother asked about you."

"That's likely because mine asked yours if she knew my intentions. What did you say?"

"That you had intentions, but that I didn't know what they were. That's because I don't . . . or didn't, but I imagine your mother saw what I did."

"Are you going to ask her?" Ferrand raised his eyebrows.

"In a way, I already have. And in a way, her answer was that she's very attracted, but wants to know me better."

"Don't you ever just plunge in, Charyn?"

"Actually, if you think about it, plunging in is really my

nature. I've had to work hard against it, because that doesn't work all that well for a Rex. At least, most of the time, it doesn't."

"Sometimes, it does," replied Ferrand. "It's one thing to rein in your nature. It's another to deny it." He grinned. "And I'm not going to deny mine. It's time for another dance."

"With Kayrolya?"

"Who else?" With that Ferrand was gone.

Except for another dance with Alyncya, Charyn really didn't remember much of the rest of the ball. He found himself almost surprised when everyone had left and he stood at the top of the grand staircase with his mother.

"Where's Bhayrn?"

"He left around ninth glass," replied Chelia. "He said he had a headache. He'd danced with several of the younger daughters, and he was cheerful about it. I didn't see much point in insisting he stay."

Charyn could definitely see that. "Did he say anything else?"

"Just that he'd had enough of the ball and that he'd see me tomorrow." Chelia began to walk toward the grand staircase.

As he walked with her, Charyn asked the question he'd been dreading asking. "How did your meeting with Alyncya D'Shendael go?"

"She seems intelligent and quietly delightful. I think I'll like her. Aloryana likes her very much. She said that, in some ways, Alyncya reminded her of Malyna and Maitre Alyna."

"Both strong women," said Charyn dryly.

"You need a strong woman. You and the Chateau would destroy a weak woman over time."

"Me?"

"You. Not in a crushing or controlling way, but because of your intensity. Why do you think both your aunt and uncle acted as they did?"

"They didn't have much choice if they wanted the holding to go to Karyel."

"No. Your intensity made it all too clear that there was no other choice." Chelia offered a low and sardonic laugh. "Blood will tell. You have both your father's stubbornness and the creative intensity of the Ryel lineage. With the right woman beside you—beside you and not behind you—it might be enough to save Solidar."

"Is Alyncya the right woman?"

"Only you can answer that question, Charyn. Don't rush to answer it, either. The wrong answer could be disaster . . . for all of us." She turned toward her apartments. "Good night, dear. It's been a very long evening."

"Good night." Charyn just stood there for several moments, then turned toward his own quarters.

Blood will tell . . . But what exactly would it tell?

That was something else Charyn wasn't certain he wanted to know.

50

Although he slept well, Charyn woke comparatively early on Solayi morning. He also rose in a cheerful mood, a feeling somewhat diminished when he realized that he was, again, smelling the acrid smoke of burning wood. Still, that couldn't completely dampen a certain elation as he cleaned up and dressed, thinking mostly about Alyncya.

He was the first in the breakfast room and was sipping his tea as he waited for breakfast when Bhayrn arrived and sat across the table from him. "Good morning. How was your evening?"

His brother frowned, then said, "Uneventful, but not unpleasant."

"I saw you talking to High Holder Laastyn."

"He saw you dancing with Alyncya. He wanted to know if you were going to make an announcement. I told him you hadn't calculated that out yet."

Charyn ignored the barb, old as that particular point was getting, and asked, "Did you meet any young women you fancied?"

"I enjoyed dancing with Cynthalya D'Nacryon. She's a year or so older, I think, but she was very pleasant. Wasn't her father a High Councilor at one time?"

"He was, but that was a while ago."

"You danced with the D'Shendael daughter a few times. She's attractive, but not a raving beauty. I take it you like the fact she's the heir."

"The first time I met her at a ball, she wasn't the heir."

"You certainly got more interested once she became the heir."

"Actually, what attracted me was her conversation."

"Do you expect me to believe that? You calculate out everything."

"Not everything," replied Charyn pleasantly. Looking to Therosa as she set the platter before him, he said, "Thank you."

"I'll have what he's having," said Bhayrn, "except I'll have dark ale instead of tea."

"Yes, sir." Therosa slipped away quickly.

Fearing that Bhayrn was in one of his moods, Charyn immediately began to eat, alternating the cheesed eggs, fried potatoes, and ham strips.

"Getting back to our conversation," said Bhayrn after a time, "just what don't you calculate?"

"Family, people, music."

"That would cheer Uncle Ryel greatly, if he were only present to hear it."

"He lived longer than he would have if I'd calculated, rather than felt. It should have been obvious long before I allowed myself to realize he was behind it." Charyn took a swallow of tea, and then a mouthful of bread.

"Oh . . . and what about Palenya? When she no longer suited you, you eased her off to the Collegium, and you justified it in a calculated fashion with golds and finding her a respected and permanent position."

"You're half right. She asked to leave. I allowed it and justified it."

"How graciously noble."

"What's the point of all this, Bhayrn?"

"Just to point out to you that you're no different from the rest of us, except that you're Rex."

"I don't think I ever claimed I was anything, let alone different."

"You could have fooled me."

Charyn decided he'd had enough to eat and took a last swallow of tea, then stood. "It appears to me that you're seeing what you want to see."

"And you're not?"

"We all see some of what we want. The question is how much. Enjoy your breakfast."

As Charyn left the breakfast room, he was shaking his head. *You shouldn't let him get to you so much.* But given that Charyn never knew whether Bhayrn was going to be pleasant, sulky, or confrontational, and that Charyn really didn't like unnecessary confrontation . . . *That's another weakness on your part. There are times when confrontation is necessary and shouldn't be avoided.*

He took a deep breath, then headed up the circular staircase to his apartments, where he reclaimed his pistols. From there he made his way to the covered courtyard. He spent a little more than a glass practicing, using both hands, after which he cleaned the weapons and reloaded them before making his way to his study.

When he opened the window closest to the table desk, the slight breeze seemed less smoky than the air had seemed earlier. At least, he hoped so.

You're going to have to confront the factors, not just with the army, but personally, immediately after Vaelln moves the army into L'Excelsis.

He sat down at the desk and began to write, trying to get his words in order so that he could effectively tell the Factors' Council that there was a price to pay for order, and that they would pay it.

By the time he needed to change into the undercaptain's uniform for services, he felt he had a better grip on himself and on the words and reasons he'd need to present to the factors when the time came.

Charyn couldn't say he was surprised when he came down the grand staircase to find Bhayrn waiting in the foyer.

"I thought you'd be along. You're very predictable, you know, Charyn. People who calculate often are. That's why, sooner or later, you're going to get shot. Don't say I didn't tell you. There are only so many ways to get to Imagisle."

"There are quite a number, I've discovered," said Charyn lightly.

"But there are only three bridges," replied Bhayrn. "Others can calculate, too."

"All that raises an interesting question, one I've been thinking about for a while. Why does someone want to shoot me? I can understand why Uncle did. I can understand why the High Holders wanted Grandsire dead, and even Father, but what sense does it make for any of them to want me dead at the moment?" Charyn had his own answers to the question, but wanted to hear what Bhayrn had to say.

"Some of them must resent how you maneuvered them into increased tariffs. The factors are angry that you didn't bring in the army immediately. Some don't like your being so close to the Collegium." Bhayrn shrugged. "I'm sure there are other reasons as well."

"Enough to risk getting caught?"

"You don't have the faintest idea who really shot at you at the Anomen D'Rex. If they'd killed you then, no one would have known. It could easily happen again, especially if you keep riding out, undercaptain's uniform or not." Bhayrn shrugged. "You probably won't listen to me, but that's what I think."

"Regardless of what you think, I do listen." *I don't always agree, but I listen.*

"Since you're not taking a coach . . ."

"Mother can choose which one she wants to take Karyel and Iryella to services."

"Is it all right if I go with them and then use the coach? I'll have it back before midnight."

Charyn nodded.

"Then I'll see you later."

More than a quint later, as Charyn rode along the Boulevard D'Ouest toward the Nord Bridge, he couldn't help but think about what Bhayrn had said. Much as he disliked his brother's attitude, Bhayrn was right. He needed to be more careful and less predictable.

Although he was much more alert and aware on the ride to Imagisle than he'd sometimes been before, he saw no sign of anything untoward. Nor did he see any True Believers anywhere, but then, he didn't pass close to any anomens on the route he took to Imagisle.

The duty imager nodded politely as Charyn and his four guards passed the east bridge sentry box, and a quint later, Charyn was stabling the chestnut in the Maitre's stable. From there he walked to the front porch, arriving there just as Aloryana came out.

"You're even earlier today."

"Bhayrn said I was too predictable. Since I'd already agreed to come, the only way I could be less predictable was to leave the Chateau earlier. Did you enjoy the ball?"

"I did. In some ways, more than the last time."

"That's good. You didn't say much about your conversation with Alyncya."

"What did she tell you?"

"Nothing. She said you'd have to be the one to tell me."

"Good."

"It appears that neither of you wishes to reveal that conversation. Am I that terrible?"

"Charyn . . . you're being stuffy again."

"Can you tell me what you told her?"

"I said you were stuffy, pompous, too smart for your own good, but, besides that, you were good-hearted when you were sensible enough to listen to your heart."

"You said *that*?"

"It's true enough," replied Aloryana. Her voice softened. "I might have said it in a kinder way."

Charyn kept walking for a time before he said, "You really did say something like that?"

"She needed to know. I also said that you want the best for everyone, especially the people you love, and that sometimes you hide that and sometimes you try too hard."

"That's something," Charyn replied sardonically.

"If she's serious about you, she needs to know. She'll give up a lot to marry you."

"Being an imager has changed you."

"No. It's allowed me to be me." Aloryana paused. "Maybe not what I should be yet, but I have the chance."

Charyn almost replied that Aloryana had always had that chance, but managed not to blurt out that reply, instead managing to nod, recalling what Malyna had said, and the fact that no one had even recognized who Malyna was, even as a High Holder's daughter, when she'd stayed at the Chateau.

Iskhar's homily was about how soon the bounties of harvest—and of life—were forgotten as the fall turned into winter, and how quickly people often squandered their harvests and then complained about winter and advancing age. Charyn understood the point. He'd seen it with the High Holders and some of the factors, but his thoughts kept going back to what Aloryana had said she'd told Alyncya.

Are you really that stuffy and pompous? Then he recalled his first real conversation with Alyncya and winced. *Sometimes* . . . But if he'd been that way, he couldn't have been totally insufferable, or she wouldn't have been as open and inviting. *Would she?*

But that led to another question, and whether he was coming off as too young and pompous to the factors and High Holders. *Where's the line between firmness and arrogant pomposity?*

Alastar stepped up beside Charyn as the five left the anomen to walk back to the Maitre's dwelling. "You've been uncharacteristically quiet today."

"I've had a lot to think about."

"Including the lady-heir you spent a noticeable amount of time with last night?"

"Partly. Mostly, I was thinking about Aloryana and how much she's already changed."

"That worries you?"

"Should it?" countered Charyn, not wanting to share his thoughts.

"That depends on whether you're more concerned about her or yourself."

Charyn managed not to wince at Alastar's matter-of-fact statement. "You do have a way of unsettling a man."

"You can't be unsettled if you're not already conflicted about something. Take Eshmael. You can offer him facts that disprove his position. That might make him angry, but it won't unsettle him. He believes to his core that he is right in what he believes. You wouldn't be who I believe you to be if you weren't conflicted about a number of things. You were raised in a tradition that you've come to realize has its flaws, and your power as Rex comes from that tradition. You're trying to change that tradition to fit the way Solidar is changing. Now your sister is changing into someone entirely outside that tradition, and you're interested in a lady-heir who can actually refuse you, which is also outside that tradition. On top of that, as Rex, you're facing a type of worker discontent that rejects certain aspects of traditional relationships, and you're at least open to thinking about it, I'd judge, from your suggestion about worker pay."

"I don't see you offering any solutions."

"Solutions aren't mine to offer, Charyn. You know exactly what your options are, in all of those areas. Despite what you think, you're still the most powerful man in Solidar. You can be conflicted in what you feel, but you can't afford to be conflicted in how you act, nor can your actions be perceived as indecisive." Alastar's voice softened slightly. "You also proved you know that not to do something, or to wait to do something, is not a lack of action . . . provided you address the problem in some fashion." He paused, then added, "And I've said enough."

"More than enough," murmured Alyna from where she walked behind them with Lystara and Aloryana.

Charyn thought he heard a smothered giggle from either

Aloryana or Lystara, but managed to say, "I appreciate your words. You and Aloryana have given me a bit to think about." *More than a bit.*

Preoccupied as he was, and also considering Bhayrn's remarks about predictability, Charyn didn't linger over refreshments at Maitre Alastar's. That way, he could say that he was returning earlier than he usually did, early enough that it was still twilight when he and the four guards left the Maitre's stable and headed toward the east bridge.

He had just ridden past the sentry box and was in the middle of the bridge when a group of figures in white charged onto the east end of the bridge, chanting, "The choristers must go. The Rex must know!"

True Believers here?

Then a series of shots rang out.

Charyn turned his mount and flattened himself against the gelding's neck so that his mount was largely shielding him from whoever was shooting. Before he could swing his right leg over the saddle, knives jabbed into his calf, but he managed to keep the gelding between him and the shooters. Another of those knives slashed into his right hand, the one that gripped the saddle pommel, and the gelding half-reared, then turned to the right. Yet Charyn knew he couldn't let go, and grasped the chestnut's mane with his left hand, even as his right spasmed and his fingers slid off the leather of the saddle.

More shots echoed across the bridge, some seemingly flying just above Charyn as the chestnut struggled to move away from the white-clad True Believers. Screams and shouts rose, and then faded away.

Abruptly, the shots stopped.

"Sir! Sir!"

Somehow, Charyn kept a hold on the chestnut's mane, not certain who was shouting.

Then another of the guards rode up beside. "They're all gone."

Charyn struggled to clear the foot on his unwounded leg from the stirrup, and then half-fell, half-slid off the gelding, teetering on his one good leg, still grasping the chestnut for balance with his left hand. He found himself looking back across the bridge to the east, but there was no one there, except two sprawled figures in white, and two imagers sprinting toward them.

"He's wounded!"

"Get him back to the Maitre's house!"

Then a figure in imager gray appeared, followed by another, and an authoritative voice ordered, "Get him to the infirmary. It's closer. Send for Maitre Gaellen. Lead the chestnut to Maitre Kaylet. The mount's wounded as well."

"The chestnut has to be hurt worse than me," Charyn insisted.

"Sir . . . I need to bind that leg. You're losing blood."

Charyn found himself being half-walked, half-carried past the sentry box and along a drive to a gray stone building. Before he knew it, he was stretched out on a pallet table and a slender older imager was working on his calf. He thought he recognized the imager, but couldn't put a name to the man, possibly because whatever the imager or healer was doing hurt so much that stars sparkled in front of Charyn's eyes for a moment.

"Your boot stopped the worst of that bullet. Otherwise, you'd have broken bones, but there was a lot of bleeding. Now . . . let's see that hand." His eyes narrowed, as his fingers gently felt over the hand.

Even the gentle touch sent jolts of fiery pain up Charyn's arm.

"You're right-handed, I take it?"

Charyn nodded.

"It's going to be a while before you'll get much use out of the two little fingers. And a time before you can use the hand more than just a little because of the splint and dressing."

"If ever?" asked Charyn.

"They won't be what they were. I need to work on that some." His eyes didn't quite meet Charyn's.

Charyn wasn't exactly in a haze of pain. He did lose some track of time before his hand and leg were dressed, but not enough track that he didn't see Maitre Alastar standing and watching just inside the door to the small chamber.

The imager healer finally turned to Alastar. "There's no sign of poison, and the wounds are cleaner than they might have been. I'd rather have him stay here or with you tonight, just in case."

"If he stays here, Gaellen, you're staying in the next room."

"Yes, sir."

Alastar looked at Charyn. "Apparently, you were right to worry about being shot." His voice was sardonically dry. He moved closer to Charyn. "How did you manage to escape with just leg and hand wounds?"

"I behaved like a coward," admitted Charyn. "I ducked and turned the gelding and used him as a shield."

"If you hadn't, you'd likely be dead, like the two guards who were on your right."

"They're dead?"

Alastar nodded. "Your two surviving guards and the duty imagers managed to capture several of the True Believers. The True Believers had no idea that someone would be shooting at you. Not the few that our imagers caught and questioned. They were told that the Rex was attending services on Imagisle so he didn't have to listen to True Believer protests about corrupt choristers."

"After everything I did?"

"People hear what they want to hear. Or so I've been told."

"Who told them I was here?"

"Some other True Believers. At least, whoever told them was also wearing those white garments and hoods."

"So it could have been anyone. Can you keep your imagers from saying much about it for at least a few days?"

"I've already put out that word. It might help reveal who knows what."

And it might not.

At that moment, Aloryana appeared almost beside Alastar. Charyn blinked. He could see that her cheeks were damp.

"Charyn!"

"I should survive," he managed. "I won't be playing the clavecin any time soon, not with both hands. Nor dancing."

"As you can also see," said Alastar with an almost helpless shrug, "your sister is quite good with concealments."

51

By midday on Lundi, Charyn was back at the Chateau, courtesy of Alastar and Alyna, and an imager escort. He had disliked being carried up the stairs to his own apartments, but at least he could walk a few steps, very slowly and painfully.

He could have walked farther with the help of a cane—except the pain and the broken bone in his right hand precluded that. Maitre Gaellen had also insisted that he sleep with his wounded leg elevated. He hadn't slept well at the infirmary, despite a healthy dose of willow bark tincture leavened with wine. Thinking about the two dead guards, and that the chestnut gelding hadn't survived, either, hadn't helped with sleeping.

He was sitting in an armchair in his sitting room, with his right leg elevated on a stool as he looked morosely at the bookcase opposite him, not really even seeing it, when Chelia stepped into the chamber.

"Are you feeling any better?"

"I don't think I'm feeling any worse." *Not that that's saying much.* "For what it's worth, Bhayrn was right. At least he didn't tell me so when I came in this morning."

"He was quite solicitous, I thought."

"As solicitous as he ever is."

"I did send word to Ferrand and Elacia."

"Thank you."

"Do you have any idea who might be behind this?" Chelia turned a chair to face her son and sat down.

"The problem isn't who might be behind it. There are too many people who could be." *The real question is just how deeply Bhayrn's involved.*

"Then, among those who don't like what you've done, who's not likely to be behind the latest shooting?"

"First, it's likely to be the same person who was behind the attempt at the Anomen D'Rex. Someone else might be copying that. It's possible, but I don't think so. Now . . . who likely isn't? I doubt that it's an unhappy crafter or worker. There was more than one shooter, this time, and probably the last time as well. They shot very accurately both times. I don't see crafters and workers having the time, the silvers, or the rifles. Because of *Tableta,* anyone who reads the news-sheets knows I've been attending services at Imagisle. But to organize two demonstrations or even influence them and carry the shootings out, that requires golds and contacts."

"You're saying it has to be a wealthy factor, a High Holder, or possibly a very senior High Command officer."

"I suppose an officer is possible, but I'm more inclined toward a factor or High Holder." Charyn's mouth twisted into a grimace. "There are enough of either who don't like what I've been doing."

"What about the True Believers?"

Charyn shrugged. "Most of them wouldn't have the re-sources, but there well might be an angry factor who's also a True Believer. That's certainly possible. But since they're all in white and hooded . . ."

"Why would factors want to kill you? Then they'd have to deal with Bhayrn."

"Bhayrn would have brought in the army weeks ago, and that's what they'd want. He's definitely more traditional."

"How many of them know that?" pressed Chelia.

Charyn nodded slowly. "That's a very good question." *And I'm very glad you asked what I already knew.* "I doubt that any of them know that."

Chelia smiled. "I'm glad to be of help. Is there anything else I can do for you right now?"

"Would you tell Maertyl and Faelln I'd like a few moments of their time?"

"They're not blaming . . ." Chelia paused, then said, "Or is that what you want to tell them?"

"That's exactly what I want to tell them . . . and a little bit more."

After Chelia left the sitting room, Charyn just sat there, thinking, and shaking his head . . . more than once. Then he eased the pistol out of the concealed holster, placed where he could use his left hand, studied it for a moment, and then replaced it.

Less than half a quint later, Maertyl and Faelln entered the sitting room, now guarded by Moencriff.

Charyn motioned the two officers to chairs, then said, "You both were worried, and you were right. Obviously, I will not be attending services anywhere anytime soon. I was also wrong for another reason. I thought my precautions would be adequate. They weren't. Because I was wrong, both Rykael and Ghasaen were killed. There's no way I can make it up to them or their families."

Maertyl nodded slowly, then said, "Your Grace, none of us fault you for what happened. You took the steps you thought would be the safest. You tried not to be too predictable. You avoided appearing in public in a way where people would notice you, and you avoided taking the very visible regial coach."

"Now, it appears," replied Charyn, "even those precautions were not enough."

"We need to think about what else might be possible and how to guard against it," said Faelln. "You don't plan to leave the Chateau any time soon, do you?"

"That depends on how well and how fast I heal, but it's safe to say I'm not going anywhere in the next week, possibly longer. I will need your help in another way. Because I can't leave the Chateau, I'll need Wyllum to go various places for me. What would be the safest way for him to travel?"

"I'd say for him to ride, with just a single guard," said Maertyl, "especially for the next few days. Whoever shot you knows, or will know, you're wounded. You wouldn't risk riding with just a single guard, and there would be signs that you're wounded."

"Have there been any more signs of people watching the Chateau?"

"Nothing obvious, sir," replied Faelln, "but there are buildings around the Ring Road where they could watch from their windows and we couldn't see them. They also might just have watched either the Anomen D'Rex or the Imagisle bridges."

"I think they were waiting for when you used the east bridge off Imagisle," said Maertyl.

"The west bridges are much more open. The imagers cut away many of the trees years ago after the High Holders used them as cover to shoot at student imagers."

"But they couldn't have gathered a mob of True Believers for every week, could they?"

"It's not likely, but . . . haven't you used the east bridge more often than the other bridges?" asked Maertyl deferentially.

Charyn had to think, mentally going back over the previous Solayis, before nodding, then saying, "They must have been watching for weeks." What it also told him was that someone had known for weeks, if not longer, that he'd been wearing a junior officer's uniform.

"It appears likely," Maertyl agreed.

Faelln nodded as well.

"I don't think I'll be making their memorial services," Charyn said.

"No, sir. That wouldn't be wise."

"You'll take care of the arrangements and let me know?"

"Yes, sir."

After the two had left, Charyn was mulling over what he knew, and not liking the implications, when Alucar appeared.

"Your Grace . . . I can't believe . . ."

"I don't think I really did, either."

"After all this, Your Grace, do you really think that you should proceed with the factors' tariff census?"

"After all this, it's even more important that we proceed. If I back off, that will show weakness." *Even more weakness.* "But I will need to reclaim Wyllum immediately for the rest of the day, and I may need him occasionally for a time." Charyn glanced down at the dressing and splint structure that immobilized more than half his right hand.

"Ah . . . I can see that, sir. I'll send Wyllum up right away."

"Make it in half a glass, and if you'd pass the word that I need to see Minister Sanafryt right away. Also, how many clerks can you spare for the tariff census?"

"Two for this week, and four beginning on the ninth."

"Starting slowly might be better anyway. I'll let you know if matters change."

Alucar nodded and left.

As soon as Sanafryt stepped into the sitting room, Charyn said, "I want a final draft of the law to impose a two-copper daily wage and a nine-glass day ready for me to read over by noon tomorrow. Oh, with no children under fourteen working in the covered factorages or manufactorages."

"I thought you were deferring that, Your Grace."

"It was deferred until the next Council meeting. That's only two weeks away, and you know how much I hate getting things at the last moment."

"Yes, Your Grace." Sanafryt sounded anything but pleased.

Charyn ignored the Justice Minister's barely concealed irritation. "Thank you."

A quint later, slowly, with Wyllum's help, Charyn limped to the study, where he sat behind the desk and looked to Wyllum. "The first letter is to Factor Estafen. You might recall that he's the head of the Banque D'Excelsis. The second one goes to Maitre Alastar. Now, for the first, I'd like a letter requesting that he and Engineer Ostraaw come to the Chateau tomorrow at the first glass of the afternoon. The second is to ask Maitre Alastar if he would be so kind as to attend me here tomorrow at second glass."

Wyllum settled himself at the end of the conference table and began to write.

When he finished, Charyn laboriously signed each one with his three half-working fingers and had Wyllum seal them. "Now, what I need you to do is to hand-carry each of these letters. You need to deliver the one to Estafen first. Then the one to Maitre Alastar. You're to wait for the Maitre's response, then return with it. Guard Captain Maertyl will provide you with an escort. Do you have any questions?"

"Am I likely to be shot at, sir?"

"I doubt it very much. Whoever shot me knows I'm wounded and that I'd have more than a single guard as an escort. Before you leave the Chateau, send Seneschal Norstan up here."

"Yes, sir."

Charyn didn't have to wait long for Norstan.

"You sent for me, sir?"

"I did. I need you to go see a Factoria Kathila. I'd like to see her sometime tomorrow afternoon after third glass, if she can do it then, or early on Mardi morning."

"You want me, sir?"

"Wyllum's on another task for me, and I need to see her. Obviously, I can't easily go to see her."

"Yes, sir."

Once Norstan left the study, Charyn took out the folder that held the poems he'd copied from Alyncya's small volume and began to read through them.

He hadn't even read the first one when Moencriff announced, "High Holder Delcoeur."

"Have him come in."

Ferrand's eyes fixed on Charyn the moment he set foot inside the study. "How do you feel?"

"I've felt better, but I've also felt worse."

Ferrand settled into the center chair across the golden-wood table desk from Charyn. "Your color's good. I didn't want to come too early. I stopped and asked your mother if you were well enough to see me. I didn't want to make things worse."

Charyn smiled. "Your being here is a tonic in itself."

"The word is that it was the True Believers again."

"They were just a convenient cover. The problem is that they could be a cover for anyone."

"Anyone?" asked Ferrand, raising his eyebrows.

"Not anyone. I doubt that a crafter or a worker is behind it, and probably not an unhappy chorister, given that the first time they tried was before I proclaimed the new laws for choristers. That still leaves enough factors and High Holders to fill half the ballroom."

"Not nearly that many. You know that as well as I do."

Charyn smiled sardonically. "That's what I'm saying. The numbers are far fewer, but there's no evidence pointing to anyone, none at all."

"Who knew you were riding out in a guard officer's uniform?"

"How did you know?"

"Your mother told me."

"Don't you read the newssheets?"

"Hardly ever. They're trash and gossip. No one of substance reads them."

"Trash and gossip notwithstanding, there have a been at least a half-score mentions of me wearing greens in *Tableta,* and almost as many about me attending services at either the Anomen D'Rex or the Anomen D'Imagisle."

"Factors are more likely to get their information from the newssheets."

"Uncle Ryel used the newssheets quite effectively."

Ferrand frowned. "He did, didn't he? I'd still say . . . but . . . even if only a few High Holders read them . . ."

"You see what I mean?"

"You know more than you're saying," declared Ferrand.

"I don't *know*. I suspect more than I'm saying or that I can afford to say, especially with all the difficulties I'm facing with the problems between the unhappy workers and the factors and some High Holders. I have to resolve those problems first."

"If you get yourself killed, then the factors and workers don't matter."

"They matter to Solidar, Ferrand. Some of the old-style High Holders would like nothing better than an armed confrontation between the factors and workers that would lead to the breakup of Solidar and the destruction of the government of the Rex, not to mention the destruction of the present Rex."

"What does that have to do with voicing your suspicions?"

"First, voicing them right now will only make it harder to prove anything. Second, both the High Holders and the factors—or many of them—will insist that I'm doing it to avoid taking action to stop the destruction of manufactorages and to distract people from the fact that I haven't stopped the loss of merchant ships to the Jariolans."

Ferrand cocked his head, then frowned again. "I hadn't thought about that. Then . . . why aren't you doing something about the manufactorage problem?"

"Just bear with me for the next few weeks . . . if you would."

"I can do that. You've always kept your word." After a silence, he said, "What does Bhayrn think about it all?"

"For the moment, he's been quite concerned and solicitous. Once he's convinced that I'm recovering, I'm quite certain that he'll be telling me to bring in the entire army and have the troopers shoot anyone who makes any trouble." Charyn chuckled. "For that reason alone, I plan to have dinner in my sitting room."

"You can't avoid your own brother forever."

"No . . . but I'd like to get a better night's sleep before talking with him at length."

"How is Aloryana taking it?"

"She was upset. She used concealments to get into the Collegium infirmary to see me as soon as she could."

"She can do concealments already?"

"She's already an imager third, and Maitre Alyna thinks she'll be a maitre in a few years . . ."

When Ferrand left a glass later, Charyn felt more cheerful, and he returned to the folder holding the poems he'd copied from Alyncya's book.

There was one he'd copied, not really knowing why, but which had struck him, somehow, as representative of High Holders . . . and, unhappily, of Bhayrn.

HONOR

The man who kills in honor's name,
Call him a coward all the same
For honor's but the face of blame,
Hypocrisy of fools who claim
That murder merits timeless fame,
And not the Namer's brutal shame.

After reading it again, he considered. In effect, the poet was saying that honor was a form of Naming, because the entire concept was based on not only acting in accord with justice and right conduct, but also defending to the death one's reputation for being honorable, to the point of killing someone over it. *Placing one's name above another's life.*

Killing in self-defense wasn't an honor killing, nor was killing to keep others from being killed. But what about killing to save a way of life . . . a way of doing things? Was that what motivated the man or men who sought Charyn's death? Or was it sheer self-interest? More likely some of each, but mostly the last, especially given his suspicions.

After a time, he resumed reading.

52

On Mardi morning, Charyn's hand hurt more, and his leg didn't feel any better, but neither seemed to have swollen. Since he didn't feel like going downstairs, he had breakfast alone in his sitting room, which meant the eggs were cool, and the ham strips not much better.

Washing up and shaving was more of a chore, as was dressing, given that he had to do all those common tasks left-handed, which made him wish that he had a valet . . . but he'd never seen the need before.

When he hobbled to the study, again helped by Wyllum, he wasn't in the best of moods. Once he was settled, he sent Wyllum back to work for Alucar.

Unhappily, reading the newssheets did little to improve his state of mind. *Veritum* offered a cautious article about what had happened.

Early Solayi evening, a group of True Believers formed up on the city end of the east bridge from Imagisle chanting slogans urging the Rex to remove all corrupt choristers. A group of uniformed riders appeared. Then several of the True Believers fired shots. Two of the riders were immediately killed, and a third, believed to be Rex Charyn, but not confirmed, was wounded, apparently not seriously . . .

Tableta was, as usual, more critical.

Solayi night, shortly after services at the Anomen D'Imagisle, a group of Chateau guards and a guard under-captain, who was actually Rex Charyn in disguise, rode toward a group of True Believers who were protesting corrupt choristers. Several people in the group raised rifles and fired, killing two guards and wounding our beloved Rex, who was struck by at least two bullets. Neither wound is believed to be that severe, but no one at the Chateau D'Rex has confirmed or denied that.

Is our Rex so afraid of his people that he has to slink around in disguise . . .

Charyn couldn't help shaking his head at the illogic of the *Tableta* story . . . and the underlying assumption that he'd done something wrong. *Except some people certainly think so . . . or they think someone else could do better.* Like Bhayrn? Who couldn't even be bothered to learn how to run a High Holding? Or Uncle Ryel, who was willing to kill off any of his relatives who got in his way? Or Uncle Ryentar, who'd tried to kill Charyn's father and then, after being forgiven, had been a leading figure in the second High Holders' revolt?

But then, Charyn knew, he himself wasn't exactly without blood on his hands.

But what else could you have done? And that, he also knew, had been the rationale of too many men and women with blood on their hands.

What made the current situation worse was that while he had a good idea of who was generally involved, he had no idea how far beyond them the conspiracy spread, or even if it was a conspiracy, and who was a player and who was being played. *Especially who might be being played.* There was also the problem of exactly what games were being played, and how all the endgames would affect Charyn . . . and Solidar. Given all those uncertainties, acting on feelings, with even less proof than he'd had in the case of his uncle, would likely destroy much of his ability to rule.

Sanafryt arrived in the study just before noon.

"Here is the final draft you requested, Your Grace."

"Thank you, Sanafryt. I do appreciate it."

"You realize, sir, that if you promulgate that law, many factors and High Holders will not obey it, even with the penalty clauses you insisted upon."

"If I do have to promulgate the law, and they don't comply, then we'll have additional sources of revenue." Charyn offered a sardonic smile. "I might even find that as Rex I'll end up owning some manufactorages."

Sanafryt swallowed.

"It shouldn't come to that, not if the High Holders and factors can see reason." After a pause, Charyn said, "There's one other thing I'll need from you today, and that's a draft of a proclamation of martial law in L'Excelsis, with a curfew from ninth glass in the evening to fourth glass in the morning, and a warning that anyone found on the streets during those glasses risks being shot."

"Sir?"

"I may yet have to call in the army to stop the burnings and destruction. The streets need to be clear so that too many innocents aren't shot. And if things get worse, I don't want to have to wait for you to draft the proclamation."

"Yes, sir. Today?"

"Before fourth glass."

"Yes, sir."

"That's all I need for now. Thank you."

Once the Justice Minister had left, Charyn read through the draft of the wage law, word by word, line by line, but the wording was just as he had requested.

Moencriff announced Estafen and Ostraaw at a half quint before first glass.

When the two walked into the study, Estafen inclined his head and said, "Your Grace."

Ostraaw just gaped for a moment before finally saying, "Your Grace."

"Yes, I'm also Factor Suyrien," offered Charyn as he gestured to the chairs before the table desk. "I'd rise to greet you, but at the moment, that's rather uncomfortable." Once the two were seated, he continued, "As Estafen will confirm, I bought the ironworks and the rifleworks in my own name, with my own coins from my personal account at the commodity exchange. I had intended to keep this quiet for a time, but my being wounded has forced a change in that plan."

"Sir . . . ?" asked Ostraaw.

"I can't very well visit the ironworks in disguise any longer, and also I need some information."

"Whatever I can provide, Your Grace."

"I'd like to know what High Holders have purchased rifles in the last seven months, and how many. If there are none, that's fine, too."

"Just High Holders?"

"You reported that the Factors' Council bought two hundred rifles, didn't you?"

Ostraaw nodded.

"Any factor could have gotten a rifle from the Council, and most likely more than a handful of factors did. If any individual factors bought rifles, that information would be welcome, of course. Marshal Vaelln told me that the newer rifles were more accurate, and I was shot under conditions that weren't the best. I'm guessing that there's a good chance they used our newer rifles. In any event, I'd very much like to know who might be stocking up on rifles."

"I can send that to you by tomorrow morning . . . ah . . ."

"'Factor Suyrien,' 'Your Grace,' or 'sir' . . . I seem to have ended up being all three."

"He was a factor before he was Rex," added Estafen.

"Might I ask why . . . an ironworks? Was it just for the rifleworks?" asked Ostraaw.

Charyn shook his head. "The rifleworks is likely to prove helpful in ways I hadn't anticipated, but I wanted the ironworks for the manufactorage I'm still planning."

Estafen's eyebrows rose, but he did not speak.

"It's likely to be a year or so, but I intend to manufacture something that will be of great interest . . . if it works as planned." Charyn shrugged. "It might not, but I'm hopeful."

"A Rex as a manufactor?" asked Estafen.

"Why not? Merely being a landholder is getting harder and harder and requires holding more and more land to get the same return . . . or spending much more time working with tenants and landwardens." Charyn looked to the engineer. "Have you told the men about the increase?"

"Yes, sir."

"Good. I would appreciate it if you'd not mention that Factor Suyrien and the Rex are the same person, at least not until *Veritum* or *Tableta* announces it."

"I can do that, sir."

"Do you have any other questions?"

"Can I send reports and papers to you here, directly?"

"From now on. But send them to me as Rex Charyn. Is there anything else?"

"No, sir."

"Then . . . if you wouldn't mind waiting outside for Factor Estafen, I have a few matters to discuss with him."

"Yes, Your Grace."

Once Ostraaw had left, Charyn straightened himself in his chair and looked directly at Estafen. "From what group do you think the person behind the attempts on my life comes? Workers, factors, or High Holders?"

"I strongly doubt that any workers would attempt an assassination, no matter how strongly they might feel."

"That suggests they have no great love of me, but see no point in risking their lives or families to strike against me."

"That would be a fair assessment, Your Grace."

"What about the factors?"

"A handful of them might risk it."

"What might be their characteristics?"

"Very well-off, but not so well-off as they believe they should be, possibly even in a precarious financial position, arrogant, and well-connected to certain less savory personages in L'Excelsis."

"Why not those factors with great wealth and high reputation?"

"Factors like that can endure any Rex, or so they believe."

"Then you would make a similar judgment about High Holders?"

"Wasn't your father's assassination undertaken by a High Holder who could have been described in that fashion?"

"That's true. Uncle did believe he should have been Rex." Charyn smiled. "Would you be willing to list any High Holders and factors located in or close to L'Excelsis who met your description? Especially those you believe to be in a precarious financial position."

"Your Grace . . ."

Charyn took a sheet of paper and eased it across the desk, then pushed the inkwell after it. "I need your advice. If you would write only the names and nothing else. There will be no record connecting that list to me or what I asked."

Once Estafen finished writing a list that filled the single sheet and returned it, Charyn looked at the list quickly, then smiled. "You wrote it in standard merchant hand."

"I thought it best that way, Your Grace."

"I should have suggested it."

Estafen frowned.

"You wouldn't know this, I don't believe, but all the threatening notes to my father and to me were written in standard merchant hand. The late Lady Ryel had once done the bookkeeping for the family shipping business in Solis."

"Have you received any notes since then?"

"No, I haven't."

"Most interesting," mused Estafen.

"I've thought so." After a pause, Charyn said, "Thank you for coming. I appreciate your assistance, your tact, and your knowledge."

"Is there anything else . . . ?"

Charyn shook his head. "As always, you've been most helpful. You'll pardon me if I don't stand . . ."

Estafen rose, then inclined his head. "I wish you well, Your Grace, personally . . . and politically. The last thing Solidar needs is a change of Rex at this time . . . or a civil war between factions and High Holders."

All of which are possible if you don't act quickly and carefully. But all Charyn said was, "I appreciate your help and your thoughts."

When he was again alone in the study, he looked over the names on the list again, which included more than a half-score High Holders, most of whose names were already familiar, such as Laevoryn, Aishford, Plessan, and Paellyt . . . and, of course, Ferrand, who was still busy paying off his father's considerable debts. The one name that was a surprise was that of Ghaermyn, but that might possibly have been because the High Holder had married an Aishford. Such a marriage would have suggested to Charyn that Ghaermyn had no concerns about a minimal dowry, but then, given his mother's comments about the Ghaermyns, maybe no other High Holder family had been interested in marrying into a commercial, come-lately High Holding. Interestingly enough, Laastyn was not on the list, which tended to confirm Bhayrn's comments about Laastyn being very conservative in his holdings.

He was still thinking over the implications of Estafen's last words when Maitre Alastar entered the study.

"You look somewhat better than the last time I saw you."

"Thank you, I think. How is Aloryana?"

"She's fine. She worries a great deal about you, you know. If she were a maitre I doubt that anyone could keep her from protecting you."

"Then it's good that she's not."

"Your letter was less than informative."

"That's because I had to have Wyllum write it, and I didn't know who might see it."

"Where is Wyllum, by the way?"

"He's working with Minister Alucar on the lists that we'll be using to make certain that all factors who qualify are paying tariffs . . ." Charyn went on to explain, ignoring Alastar's initially raised eyebrows. When he finished, he asked, "Is there anything else you would like to know?"

"Don't you think this is going to increase the danger to you?"

"I don't think the danger to me will change as a result of what the army and the Finance Minister will be doing. The factors want me to do something to reduce the violence against their facilities. This will do that. There's one other matter that you should know about, and there are two tasks for which I'd like your assistance."

"Oh?"

"The other matter is that on Jeudi morning, the morning after the army begins patrolling L'Excelsis at night, which will also require a curfew, most likely from ninth glass in the evening until fourth glass in the morning, I will promulgate a law requiring a two-copper-a-day, nine-glass working day for all workers who are not members of the immediate family of a factor or High Holder. The law will also forbid the hiring of children under fourteen, unless they are immediate relatives of the owner of the factorage. This will be effective beginning on Lundi, the ninth of Feuillyt."

"Many won't obey."

"If they don't, they'll pay a one-in-ten increase on their annual tariffs, and any worker who reports such a violation will receive a one-gold reward, and the Finance Ministry will not reveal the identity of such workers."

Alastar's eyes widened, slightly.

"It may take a little while, but it should work, and the High Holders won't back the factors on this. One aspect where you could be most helpful is to contact several members of the craftmasters of L'Excelsis. I'd like to meet with them late this week. If they're reluctant to come to the Chateau, I'll come to the Collegium."

"Might I ask why you need to meet with them?"

"Let us just say that they don't have a voice with the councils, and they should, just as the Collegium does."

"You're wording that very carefully."

"Wouldn't you, in my position?"

Alastar offered a wry smile. "What else are you asking?"

"I may have to make some public appearances, possibly in front of True Believers, or workers. If I do, would it be possible to have a strong and concealed imager nearby to shield me? I know it's neither wise nor practical to have an imager protecting me every moment, but . . ."

Alastar nodded. "We could do that, but if you feel that you need such protection in special circumstances—"

"If my judgment is anywhere close to accurate, I'm relatively safe here, at least for now. I believe that, if an imager appeared here, all L'Excelsis would know it before too long, and, at present, that would not be good."

"There are certain implications . . ."

"There are, but it will take a little longer to determine which implications are accurate and which are not."

"You're playing a dangerous game, Charyn."

"So long as there is a Rex as the head of government, the game will always have dangerous times. This is one of those times." Charyn laughed softly. "I imagine most Rexes have felt that way at one time or another. So have many Maitres, I'd guess."

A faint smile crossed Alastar's face. "I wouldn't dispute that. We can contact some of the craftmasters. Whether they will meet is up to them. I will encourage them to do so, and I'll let you know as soon as I can. The other request we'll be happy to accommodate."

"Thank you."

"Do you think what you're trying will work?"

"I do." Charyn smiled. "But whether it will work well enough . . . we'll just have to see."

Alastar stood. "I won't tariff you longer, and finding and talking to craftmasters is going to take some time."

Once Alastar left the study, Charyn called for Moencriff.

"Yes, sir?"

"Could you have someone get me a cool pale ale?"

"Yes, sir."

The ale arrived, and Charyn finished it and had some time to think over his next meeting before, exactly at third glass, Moencriff announced, "Factoria Kathila."

The elegant silver-haired factoria inclined her head as she neared the desk, then said, "Your Grace," and seated herself.

"Thank you for coming."

"How could I not answer a summons from the Rex?"

"You could, but it wouldn't be in either of our interests."

"Exactly. What is it that you'd like me to do?"

"First . . . tell me what factors might be upset enough to try to kill me. Then tell me if any of them have the intelligence and resources to try it."

"I can't do that, Your Grace. There are likely close to a thousand factors in and around L'Excelsis."

"And you know who every single one with significant resources happens to be. You also most likely know which ones are outspoken and which are dangerous."

"You give me more credit than is due, Your Grace."

"Less, I think. You're a woman. You've built a factorage wealthy and powerful enough to land you on the Factors' Council of L'Excelsis, and your name was raised as one of two to succeed Elthyrd." Charyn offered a pleasant smile and waited.

"You definitely take more after your mother's side of your family, at least in perception. Otherwise, you're far more direct."

"I'd prefer to be."

"There's such a thing as being too cautious."

"So I've been told. Now . . . who has the resources to attack me without it being known? Besides you, that is."

"Your Grace . . . that would be most foolhardy of me."

"Besides which, if you wanted me dead, I'd likely already have had a memorial service." Charyn just looked at her, again waiting.

"I can't answer that question directly. I will say that those factors I know who have such resources have no desire to see you dead, and those who have the desire to see you removed from rule have neither the resources nor the ability to carry out anything that would accomplish such a deed. I will also say that there may be factors with resources greater than I know or abilities unknown to me."

"I doubt there are many."

"It only takes one, Your Grace. That is why I must answer as I have."

"What about High Holders—those near L'Excelsis?"

"Half of them likely have resources enough. I don't see those who are largely landowners caring enough about workers' wages to risk what you could do to them if they were involved in such a plot. There are still at least a score of others who own manufactorages, but, I'm far less privy to knowledge about the finances of High Holders, except for the handful whose situations are so precarious that everyone knows."

"I'm young, and may not know them."

"You aren't that young. But . . . there's certainly little harm in naming those. Most precarious, until recently, was your friend the new High Holder Delcoeur. I've heard that he's repaid much of his sire's debt, possibly due to the counsel and aid of a friend."

"Mostly counsel. He's very sensible, as is his mother."

Kathila nodded. "Then there are High Holders Aishford, and Paellyt, and young Plessan. Also, Caarnyl and possibly Fyanyl. There may be others, but those are the ones bruited about for some time." She smiled pleasantly. "You knew most of them, didn't you?"

"The first four. I wondered about Plessan. I hadn't heard

about the last two." In fact, Charyn didn't even recall coming across Caarnyl's name at all.

"You're obviously contemplating action of some sort."

"As you told me at the dinner, acting too late would be the same as failing to act at all . . . or words to that effect."

"What else are you going to ask of me?"

"What else should I know that you believe either I should know or that would be valuable for keeping order in L'Excelsis and throughout Solidar?"

"A Rex has no friends, only allies. A few allies endure. Most don't. And the last people one suspects of betrayal are often the first you should suspect. Everyone in the end follows self-interest."

"You're very wise . . . and very cynical. That's also why you're successful." Charyn could see that she had said what she was going to say . . . and he understood that she'd answered his questions in a way that she could deny having said anything, while giving him very strong indications. "I won't ask more of you. Not for the present." He stood, very carefully.

"Thank you, Your Grace. The next month should be very interesting."

Charyn nodded. Her last words had not been an observation, but a suggestion.

Once Kathila left, Charyn again looked to the open window, then fingered the edge of the grip of the hidden pistol with his left hand. At the knock on the study door, he straightened.

"A letter for you, Your Grace," Sturdyn announced.

"If you'd bring it in . . ."

The guard immediately walked in and placed the letter on the desk, carefully not meeting Charyn's eyes before leaving.

As Charyn recognized the handwriting, he understood why Sturdyn had averted his gaze. *All the Chateau staff probably knows.* But he couldn't help smiling as he awkwardly managed to slit open the envelope and extract the single sheet.

My dear Rex—

You have my deepest concerns and affection, as well as my hopes for a quick and complete recovery from the untoward attack on you and your guards. While I would like to be able to say that such an assault is unthinkable, in these most interesting times, it is clearly anything but that.

I so enjoyed the Autumn-Turn Ball and the comparatively short time I spent with you that news of your being wounded came as a shock and a surprise. I greatly appreciated the chance to meet your sister and your mother, and that you have them to support you in a way that I currently cannot is a comfort to me, although I would that I could, and I hope their presence is a great benefit to you as well.

Once matters have settled down, perhaps it will be possible for my father and me to pay a call on you, but we will not press, knowing that you have much on your mind with your duties as rex.

> *With my deepest affection,*
> *Alyncya*

Charyn couldn't help smiling as he finished the letter. Guarded and carefully written as it was, there was no doubt that Alyncya was truly concerned . . . and cared more than she was about to put down in ink.

After rereading it, he eased it into the compartment in the bookcase behind him.

Barely a quint before fourth glass, Sanafryt returned and placed a single sheet on the desk before Charyn. "The proclamation of martial law, Your Grace."

"Thank you, Sanafryt."

"After what happened on Solayi, do you think it wise to implement this proclamation?"

"The circumstances will tell me whether it's necessary. If it is, I'll need it immediately. If not, no one need know I considered it."

"Do you really think . . . ?"

"I'll let you know if it's necessary. Thank you."

Sanafryt frowned for a moment, then inclined his head and left the study.

Vaelln arrived just as the chimes struck fourth glass. He carried a leather folder under his arm.

Charyn gestured for him to take a seat. "Thank you for coming."

"You've had a more difficult week than I have," replied the Marshal, his tone warmly ironic.

"If all goes well, you'll have a more difficult week to come," returned Charyn.

"You're rather cheerful about it." Vaelln's words weren't quite dour. "I assume you're saying that if we keep order that will be difficult, but it will be for the best."

"I was thinking, more like hoping, that no one will be perfectly happy with what I'm doing and your men will be enforcing, but the results will lead to reluctant acceptance by all groups, rather than violent outrage." He handed the proclamation of martial law to Vaelln. "What are your thoughts on this?"

The Marshal read through it, set it on the desk, and said, "The curfew is to make it easier for us and what else?"

"To remind people that the Rex has some power, and to make it harder for the worker troublemakers to create too many explosions and fires. Also, since I'm also going to promulgate a mandatory two-copper, nine-glass day for the manufactorages, and prohibit the hiring of young children in manufactorages, it should make the rebellious workers less popular."

"Isn't there a possibility you're trying to do too much at once?"

"There's a risk there, but the problem is, as I see it, that none of what needs to be done can be done one thing at a time because what one group needs, another hates. I'm trying to give something to each group all at once, at a time when the army is in position to damp down violence."

"You may set them all off at once."

"I think it's more likely that I'll set off small numbers of each group at once, small enough that the army and possibly the imagers can keep them under control."

"You've talked to Maitre Alastar?"

"He was here earlier. If I need to make public appearances, he'll provide protection for me. You may have to provide a squad or two to apprehend troublemakers."

"You think you'll need to do that immediately?"

"I'd be very surprised if I don't have to do it, but even more surprised if the need will be immediate, since more than a few people suspect I'll call in the army to keep order, but very few know what else I'm doing."

"You've talked about the wage law at the Council meetings."

"That's so they won't be too surprised," said Charyn dryly. "I've said nothing about martial law or curfews, and the factors have no idea about the tariff-roll census."

"That's one thing you didn't detail. Are you still planning on the same number of clerks?"

"This week, just two. Starting on Lundi the ninth, there will be four. The extra two clerks are needed to finish copying the tariff rolls to be used."

"There will be companies on standby," replied Vaelln. "We may need them."

"I'd appreciate it if you'd go over exactly what you've planned for this," said Charyn.

Vaelln opened the leather folder, from which he extended several sheets. "These are the patrol plans and command structure for L'Excelsis. I already sent a copy to Sea Marshal Tynan in the event he needs to implement similar city controls in Solis."

Charyn began to read.

Between the questions Charyn had and Vaelln's explanations, it was close to fifth glass before the Marshal left the study. Immediately, he asked Sturdyn to summon Maertyl.

When the guard captain entered, he inclined his head. "Your Grace?"

"I'm certain you must have gathered that something is about to happen, Maertyl."

"I have wondered, sir."

"I'm going to ask you to keep everything I tell you to yourself and to Faelln until I issue a proclamation tomorrow. You are especially not to reveal it to anyone else in the Chateau until then."

"Yes, sir." The guard captain frowned.

"I'll be proclaiming martial law over L'Excelsis tomorrow. Tomorrow afternoon, the army will begin to patrol the areas where factorages are located. I will also be promulgating a change to the Codex Legis that will require all factorages to pay their workers a minimum daily wage of two coppers for a nine-glass day, and that will prohibit the hiring or use of children under fourteen in manufactorages unless they are the immediate relatives of the owner. In addition, beginning on Jeudi morning clerks will begin to visit all factorages in L'Excelsis to make sure they are recorded on the tariff rolls. Those are the matters I just finished discussing with Marshal Vaelln. You are the second person to know what I am doing. Minister Sanafryt knows that I *might* declare martial law and impose the wage law at some time, but he does not know if and when that will be."

Maertyl just stood there, as if uncertain as to what he might say.

"I'm telling you because, first, you should know. Second, because what you have told me was helpful in my determination about how to proceed. Marshal Vaelln is holding some troops in reserve in case my actions prompt riots or other actions against the Chateau."

"Your Grace . . . I do not think there will be riots. Factors or High Holders may mount attacks, but I cannot see workers storming the Chateau after you have mandated better wages for them." A grim smile crossed Maertyl's face. "I would suggest that you allow us to search any factor or High Holder who wishes to see you."

"Anyone except Factor Estafen or High Holder Delcoeur . . . and perhaps one or two others." Charyn paused. "It is most important that no one else in the Chateau knows this, except Faelln, until it happens. Some individuals may have the best intentions and still reveal what is going to happen."

"Yes, Your Grace. I *do* understand." Maertyl inclined his head. "Thank you for informing me and trusting the two of us."

"You've earned that trust, and I cannot tell you how much I appreciate your trustworthiness."

"Is there anything else, sir?"

"Not at the moment." Charyn offered a wry smile. "At least, I hope not."

Maertyl hadn't been gone for more than a few moments before Chelia stepped into the chamber, closing the door quietly but firmly, then walking to the desk and sitting down facing Charyn.

"You've had quite a procession of visitors today. It would suggest that you're up to something."

"I am. I'm trying to narrow down the number of those I suspect who might be behind the attempts to shoot me. I was also discussing with Marshal Vaelln what would be necessary if I bring in the army to stop the burnings and destruction."

"If . . . or when?"

"It's looking more like when, but I'd prefer you keep that

to yourself. And don't tell Bhayrn. I'm not sure he could refrain from telling his friends, no matter what he promises."

"You're sounding like your father."

"That may be, but I trust your discretion. I trust Aloryana's. I trust Maitre Alastar and Maitre Alyna. I have my doubts about Bhayrn's ability to withstand his friends' desires to know. Am I wrong?"

Chelia shook her head. "He knows you don't trust him, though. That makes him even more unhappy with you."

"Does he ever talk to you about his friends? Aloryana said that he's mostly turned away from Amascarl."

"He never says much about them. About the only thing he's said is that they accept him for who he is, and they don't criticize him for what he's not."

Charyn winced. "I never criticized. I just told him he needed to learn how to run a High Holding."

"You should know that, for Bhayrn, such words are a criticism."

"Then he needs to grow up." After a moment, Charyn smiled ruefully. "I suppose you could have said the same thing about me when I was his age."

"Your father did. But he was pleased when you began to ask questions of the ministers and try to learn from them."

"He never said anything."

"Charyn. That wasn't who he was. Don't tell me you didn't know that."

"I knew. It would have been nice . . . the best I ever got were words to the effect that at least I'd learned something from going to the exchange."

"From him, that was a compliment."

"I know."

"Are you coming down for dinner?"

"I thought I would. It might take me a bit."

"Bhayrn will be at dinner. I'd appreciate it if you'd be very forbearing and quietly charming. You usually are, at dinner, but he seems a bit edgy."

Charyn understood the quiet implication that he be for-bearing at breakfast as well as dinner. "Thank you for let-ting me know." He stood, carefully and slowly. "I suppose I should begin the slow descent."

"I'll need to look at your leg and hand later."

Charyn laughed softly. "I'm certainly not going far."

By taking his time, Charyn made his way to the family dining room with Chelia, where they were almost immedi-ately joined by Karyel, Iryella, and Bhayrn.

After Iryella said the grace, and everyone was served, Bhayrn immediately poured the wine—red for himself and Karyel, white for the other three. Then he lifted his goblet. "To your quick healing."

After everyone drank, Charyn turned to his brother. "Thank you."

"You're welcome."

"How are you feeling, sir?" asked Karyel.

"My leg and hand are sore, and they likely will be for a time."

"How long before you can ride again?" asked Bhayrn.

"I think it's more of a question as to when I can ride safely again. I could ride now, but it wouldn't be a very good idea, as you pointed out. I should have taken your advice."

"You could have been shot in the coach, almost as easily," replied Bhayrn.

"You're kind, but there are metal plates in the coach body. Someone would have to get closer in order to fire through the windows."

"I have to say," Bhayrn commented, "I still don't know how you survived with so few wounds, especially when half your guards were killed."

Charyn took another swallow of the Tacqueville white before replying. "That's likely because they shielded me enough that I could duck and turn the chestnut to take some of the shots." He shook his head. "Maitre Alastar told me that they had to put him down. Two of the bullets went into his lungs. He didn't seem that badly hurt on the bridge."

"Better the gelding than you," said Bhayrn.

"If I'd listened to you," replied Charyn, "Rykael and Ghasaen and the gelding would all be alive, and I wouldn't be limping and effectively one-handed."

"I can't believe that those True Believers were so upset with you," said Bhayrn. "You went out of your way to address their concerns, and they still tried to kill you."

"It does seem strange," offered Charyn, taking his knife and using it to separate a chunk of fowl from the slice on his platter, a chunk that he then speared with the knife so that he could eat it one-handed.

"That's the problem with the rabble," Bhayrn went on. "You give them what they want, and they're still not grateful. Some of the factors aren't that much better. That Eshmael . . . from what the newssheets say, he's trying to tell you what to do, and he's only been on the Council . . . what? Less than a month?"

"Four weeks, I think."

"I still think you should have brought in the army the moment the rabble started burning and destroying."

"Maybe I was thinking that the factors and the workers deserved what they gave each other," said Charyn dryly. "Of course, I couldn't claim that publicly, but at least some of the factors seem to think starving their workers makes them work harder. And some of the workers think that burning their place of work will get them higher wages."

For several moments, Bhayrn was silent. "I thought you liked the factors."

"Factors are people. I like some of them. Elthyrd was a good man and a good factor. So are others. Some aren't, and right now, it seems like too many factors are listening to the ones who aren't thinking."

"That's why you should have brought in the army. The greedy ones don't think about anything except golds."

Rather than comment on Bhayrn's observation, Charyn continued to eat, if not as carefully as he would have liked, by continuing to use his knife to cut morsels one-handed and then spear them.

"How are your friends these days?" Chelia asked Bhayrn.

"They're fine. Laamyst and his family left this morning for Charpen."

"Charpen?" asked Iryella. "Where is that?"

"It's some thirty milles northwest of here," replied Bhayrn. "In the middle of nowhere. But the land there is good. That's what Laamyst says, anyway."

"I thought they'd left Solayi morning," said Chelia.

"Something came up, I suppose." Bhayrn shrugged. "It just might have been that everyone stayed too late at the ball. Anyway, they left this morning."

"What about Gherard?" asked Charyn.

"Oh . . . he and his family almost never leave L'Excelsis. By the way, I'll likely have dinner with him tomorrow night."

"I haven't seen Amascarl recently," said Chelia. "Is he all right?"

"I guess he's fine. We're not as close anymore. We don't see things quite the same way." Bhayrn shrugged again. "It happens." He looked to Charyn. "Do you still see Ferrand as much?"

"Not quite as much, but part of that is because he's interested in someone, and between learning more about his holding and her, whoever she is, that's taking more of his time, a great deal more."

"He hasn't told you?"

"Not yet. I have a good idea . . ."

"Who is she?" burst out Iryella.

"Since it's only a guess on my part," Charyn said gently, "it wouldn't be right for me to say."

"Well . . . you spent more time with a certain heiress than

with anyone else," said Bhayrn with an expression that was half smile, half smirk.

"That's possible," Charyn conceded genially.

"Possible?" Bhayrn shook his head.

Charyn just smiled. The rest of the dinner would be pleasant. It absolutely would be, not only because he'd promised his mother that, but for more than a few other reasons.

53

Once he was in his study on Meredi morning, Charyn quickly read through the few petitions and the draft responses Sanafryt had sent to him. Then he spent two glasses explaining to Sanafryt how he wanted them changed, also noting that he would have simply had Wyllum rewrite them, except for the fact that Wyllum was engaged in an urgent effort elsewhere.

Then, slowly and with extreme care, slow word by word, he wrote a short reply to Alyncya, sealed it, and had Moencriff dispatch it.

Then Moencriff brought in another letter. Charyn opened it, awkwardly, to discover that it was from Paersyt.

Your Grace—

I was shocked to learn of the attempt on your life. I'm not much with the pen, but I do want you to know I'll do anything you need done if it will help.

We did fix the vibration problem with the shaft, and now the Steamwraith is much smoother and even faster. As you instructed, I'm working on the plans for a much larger engine. I will keep you informed.

My very best wishes for your rapid return to full health.

Charyn smiled, an expression that faded slightly after a moment, since Paersyt's letter of good wishes was the only one he received, except for the one from Alyncya . . . and, of course, there had been Ferrand's immediate visit.

Just before the first glass of the afternoon on Meredi, Charyn called in Maertyl.

"Yes, Your Grace."

"From the moment you leave this study, Guard Captain, not a single person is to leave the Chateau without you or Faelln hearing it from my lips and only from my lips. I have just signed the declaration of martial law and the new wage law, and until those are copied and sent, no one is to leave the Chateau. Nor is anyone to enter, except Marshal Vaelln or Maitre Alastar. Nor is anyone to talk to anyone who comes, except those two. If there are questions, you or Faelln are to come to me and no one else. You are not to tell anyone but Faelln why, just that those are my orders."

Maertyl nodded. "That includes members of the regial family?"

"It includes everyone from the kitchen sculls to guards to ministers to the regial family."

"Very good, Your Grace."

From Maertyl's tone, Charyn could tell that the guard captain agreed.

Then, after waiting a good two quints, so that Maertyl would have time to inform all the guards, Charyn sent for Sanafryt again.

Sanafryt entered the study almost gingerly. "You summoned me, Your Grace?"

"I did. I've just signed and sealed the declaration of martial law and the new wage law."

Sanafryt swallowed. "Your Grace . . . ah . . . That is most unusual . . . the factors . . . the High Holders . . ."

"Before long, Marshal Vaelln will be moving troopers into L'Excelsis. You will make copies of both proclamations to send to all members of the councils, in addition for another five to be sent to any craftmasters that can be found, as well as copies for Marshal Vaelln and Maitre Alastar. Those copies are to be made and sent this afternoon."

"Your Grace . . ."

"This afternoon. You may request additional clerks from Minister Aevidyr, but only those located in the Chateau. You are not to leave the Chateau until those tasks are accomplished and you have reported to me personally that they are."

"This is most irregular, Your Grace . . ."

"Burning manufactorages and two assassination attempts on me are both irregular, Minister Sanafryt. Everyone has wanted action. Now all of them will have that action, all at once."

Slightly less than a glass later, Bhayrn burst into the study, followed by Sturdyn with a drawn sabre.

"Stop right there!" snapped Charyn, his left hand already around the grip of the still-holstered and concealed pistol. "That is, if you don't want Sturdyn to cut you down."

Bhayrn stopped, then saw the drawn sabre. His face paled. "You really would, wouldn't you? Your own brother."

"What the frig do you expect, Bhayrn? I'm in no shape to wrestle with you. I've been shot at twice and wounded once. Sturdyn doesn't know what you have in mind when you charge in like a mad bull."

"I can't believe you called in the army and didn't say anything. You didn't tell me. You didn't tell Mother. How could you possibly do that?"

"Then how did you find out?" asked Charyn.

"I was going to go to Gherard's, but Maertyl told me that you'd ordered the Chateau sealed off and that I couldn't leave."

"I never mentioned the army to Maertyl," Charyn lied.

"No . . . your precious guard captain wouldn't tell me. Neither Alucar nor Aevidyr could either. Sanafryt told me."

"You could have asked me," said Charyn. "If you'd asked I would have been happy to tell you."

"How was I to know that? You never tell me anything."

"I'm telling you now. The only way to deal with the factors, the workers, and the High Holders was to do several things at once. The timing is important. There's an old saying about one person being able to keep a secret, and two being able to keep it for a short time, and three being the same as shouting it from the rooftops. The only one who knew the exact timing was Marshal Vaelln. He had to, in order for the army to be ready." Charyn didn't like lying, but it was easier than telling Bhayrn that he couldn't trust him not to reveal it to his friends.

"You led me to believe you weren't going to call in the army. Your own brother."

Charyn shook his head. "I never said that. I told you that the factors wanted more silvers, but refused to give up a few coppers, and that I wasn't going to bring in the army under those conditions. When it became clear that neither the factors nor the workers would budge, I decided to give them each what they wanted, and put the army in place to keep the peace."

"Why did you give in to the workers? Why, for Terahnar's sake?"

"Because I don't like to see children starving, for one thing, and I don't like factors getting more golds by starving people."

"You're going to destroy Solidar."

"Solidar was about to destroy itself if I didn't do something. You said so yourself."

"You don't understand, Charyn. You never have. You never will. You calculate and never see what's right before you." Bhayrn half-turned, then stopped. "How long am I to be confined in the Chateau?"

"Until sometime after fifth glass, depending on events. I really wouldn't suggest going anywhere after that, but that's up to you."

"What am I supposed to tell Gherard?"

"Just tell him the truth—that I sealed off the Chateau and didn't tell you I was going to. I'm sure he'll believe you." *Given what you've likely said about your older brother.*

"The only people you told were commoners . . . not even your own family. I still can't believe it." Bhayrn sneered, then turned and walked past Sturdyn.

The guard looked to Charyn. "I'm sorry, sir. He walked up and politely asked if you were in. When I said you were, he charged past me."

"That's understandable, Sturdyn. Lord Bhayrn can be very unpredictable. I didn't realize he also might be violent. If you would pass that on to Moencriff so that both of you are aware of his . . . eccentricities."

"Yes, sir. Thank you, sir."

Once Sturdyn returned to his post outside the study door, Charyn took a deep breath, thinking over Sturdyn's description of Bhayrn's behavior. Then he shook his head.

At two quints past fourth glass, Sanafryt entered the study. "All the proclamations are copied and sealed and ready to dispatch, Your Grace. Guard Captain Maertyl won't let the couriers leave."

"Those were my orders." Charyn raised his voice. "Sturdyn . . . if you'd have Maertyl come up here for just a moment . . ."

"Yes, sir."

Within moments Maertyl was in the study. "Yes, Your Grace?"

"Guard Captain, you're to allow the dispatch riders to leave the Chateau with the proclamations, but no one else. A glass after the last dispatch rider leaves, then anyone else who desires to leave the Chateau may do so. That includes Lord Bhayrn."

"Yes, Your Grace."

"Thank you." Charyn tried to put both concern and thanks into his tone of voice.

Once Maertyl had left, Charyn turned to Sanafryt. "I do have a question for you. How did Lord Bhayrn find out about the declaration of martial law?"

"He burst into my study and wanted to know why he

couldn't leave the Chateau, Your Grace. I told him that I didn't know about that, but that you'd signed a declaration of martial law, and that was likely the reason. You didn't say that I couldn't tell anyone, and he is your brother."

"I didn't, that's true. I just wanted to know. Thank you."

As he sat alone in the study in the late afternoon, Charyn knew that all he could do at the moment was wait . . . and that it might be some time before he could—or should—do anything else.

54

~~~~~~

Charyn woke early on Jeudi morning, worrying about what might have happened—or not happened—the night before. Although he certainly didn't smell smoke, he was still concerned about the impact of his proclaiming martial law. He'd seen some of Vaelln's troopers as they had ridden and marched past the Chateau and into the factoring areas of L'Excelsis southeast of the Chateau late on Meredi afternoon.

Once he was fully awake, Charyn washed and dressed as quickly as he could and made his way down to the duty room.

Lead Guard Reynalt immediately addressed him. "Is there anything you need, Your Grace?"

"I just wondered if you'd heard anything—good or bad—about fires or destruction."

"No, sir. The local civic patrollers haven't heard of anything. We haven't heard any shots, but we likely wouldn't. There aren't any factorages near here. The closest ones are well over a mille away. A company of army troopers is here. Some are in the stables and some are stationed where it's not obvious in the gardens and other places."

"Thank you."

From the duty room, Charyn made his way to the breakfast room, since there was no way he was going to be exercising for a while. He wouldn't be seeing Bhayrn for breakfast, and possibly for quite some time, since Bhayrn had left the Chateau for Gherard's father's estate on the northeast side of L'Excelsis the previous evening—without saying a word to Charyn. Charyn only knew that much because Maertyl had refused to send guards with Bhayrn unless he knew where they were going.

Charyn could have refused his brother protection, but that would have been unwise on several counts.

Chelia arrived in the breakfast room—alone—just after Charyn began to sip his tea while he waited for cheesed eggs and ham strips, which he had often, simply because he liked them.

"You're walking a little better."

"A bit," Charyn conceded. "We won't have Bhayrn's company this morning."

"I've never seen him that angry before." Chelia absently picked up the mug of tea that Therosa had set before her, then took a small sip.

"Nor have I, but I didn't want to risk anyone knowing what I did until it was done."

"Doing all that at one time is a risk, especially the daily-wage law." Chelia's words were almost matter-of-fact.

"Not as much as not doing them." Charyn smiled sardonically. "Of course, I could be very wrong."

"What do you think will happen today?"

"I'd be very surprised if much happens this morning. By this afternoon, or no later than tomorrow morning, I'll have Eshmael writing or even appearing and demanding that I rescind the daily-wage law. The High Holders will say nothing, but at least some will agree that at least I did something. Then, by tomorrow, when Eshmael finds out that Alucar's clerks are beginning to check the factorages against the tariff rolls—"

"I don't believe you mentioned that, dear."

Charyn waited to answer until after Therosa had set his platter before him, along with a basket of biscuits. "Alucar believes that two in ten manufactorages aren't even on the rolls. Since we're already reviewing the tariffs of the High Holders, I thought it only fair to do that for the factors as well. After all, the factors who are paying shouldn't have to shoulder the costs of those who aren't."

"*Most* of the High Holders will definitely approve of that."

Charyn caught the slight emphasis on "most." "I do understand that there are a handful of High Holders who are most likely greatly undertariffed . . . but why should the others pay more on tariffs for a hectare of land than do they?"

"You had best hope that there are not too many whose tariffs will rise dramatically."

"Will those of the Ryel High Holding?"

"No. Doryana knew that they would be under scrutiny. All the holding's assets are listed correctly. She and brother dear were very scrupulous in that regard."

If not in a number of other ways. Charyn didn't have to say that. He stopped speaking when Therosa arrived with a platter for Chelia. After the server returned to the kitchen, he went on. "That's one matter that I'll have to be very careful about when I gift Lauckan to Bhayrn—to make sure all the assets are on the tariff rolls." Charyn began to eat some of the cheesed eggs.

"He won't appreciate such honesty." Chelia toyed with a biscuit before breaking it in half.

"He should be grateful, but he won't be. He'll get a High Holding. I doubt that his friend Laamyst will, for all of Laastyn's sweep of lands across Solidar. Gherard will, of course, but Ghaermyn's younger sons likely won't, no matter how many golds Ghaermyn has stacked up."

Chelia nodded. "There was some controversy about whether the great-grandsire even had the minimum in land to be a High Holder. Ghaermyn's father added more lands, but not enough to split off a High Holding for a second son. The only hope for one of Ghaermyn's younger sons or for Laamyst would be a grant of regial lands. That's rather far-fetched as matters now stand."

Charyn managed not to wince. "Thank you for the reminder for me to be more careful."

"Isn't that supposed to be part of being a mother?"

"It is, and for that, I'm grateful." *Unlike some.* "I just got a report on the harvest from Chaeryll. It's slightly better than I'd hoped. The Tuuryl lands . . . they don't look as good . . ."

The rest of the breakfast conversation was about crops and weather.

When Charyn arrived at his study, Moencriff immediately said, "Both the newssheets put out special editions this morning, Your Grace. Wyllum brought them up before he went back to work with Minister Alucar."

"Thank you." *Special editions?* When he thought about it, the Rex imposing martial law likely merited a special edition.

The *Veritum* story was factual and simple.

Yesterday evening, with the declaration of martial law by Rex Charyn, army troopers moved into the factoring areas of L'Excelsis in an effort to put an end to the weeks of sporadic violence and destruction aimed at factoring properties. The Rex also imposed a late-night curfew, from ninth glass in the evening to fourth glass in the morning . . .

The rest of the lengthy piece was largely a history of the issues and problems, with examples of the properties that had been destroyed or burned and the numbers of men caught and executed or sentenced to indenture or the workhouses.

Charyn wasn't quite sure what to make of the *Tableta* story.

While our beloved Rex Charyn is confined to his Chateau recovering from the wounds suffered in the attack by the religious zealots known as the True Believers, that has not stopped him from bringing in the army in an effort to stop the widespread violence against the greedy and heartless copper-pinching factors more interested in piling up golds

than in the survival of their workers . . . The only problem
is that he has done nothing to deal with the cause of the
violence, and his acts are likely to be too little too late . . .

Haven't they learned about the daily-wage law? That was
possible. Or were they holding off announcing it for other
reasons.

The rest of the stories were a more incendiary version of
what *Veritum* had reported.

Charyn shrugged. It could have been worse. *And if*
Tableta *can make it worse for you, it will.*

Just after eighth glass, a letter arrived from Ostraaw with
a listing of individuals who had bought rifles over the past
eight months. There were almost seventy individuals who had
bought one or two weapons, but only a handful who had
bought more. Those Ostraaw had thoughtfully listed together on an additional sheet:

High Holder Laevoryn	10 rifles	Fevier
High Holder Paellyt	6 rifles	Maris
High Holder Caarnyl	5 rifles	Maris
High Holder Calkoran	5 rifles	Avryl
High Holder Varranyl	15 rifles	Agostos
High Holder Kurm	15 rifles	Agostos
High Holder Ghaermyn	30 rifles	Agostos
Laamyst D'Laastyn	5 rifles	Agostos
Factor Cuipryn	5 rifles	Ianus
Factor Lythoryn	10 rifles	Fevier
Factor Saratyn	5 rifles	Agostos
Factor Noerbyn	5 rifles	Agostos

The first thing that struck him was the purchases of the
two High Holders from Caluse. Why would both of them
have purchased rifles in Agostos, when there weren't any
manufactorages there? Then . . . he remembered. The True

Believers had stormed the anomen there and chased out the chorister.

Would that be enough to prompt buying rifles? Perhaps, especially if they'd been surprised by the violence of the demonstration.

Charyn understood why Ghaermyn had bought thirty rifles in Agostos, since the High Holder had mentioned buying them and arming his men. He frowned. There was something about that number, though . . .

Try as he might, he couldn't recall what bothered him about that, and the fact that Laamyst had bought five rifles was also rather interesting. Why would he have bought them, when his father had already bought rifles, and why not the seneschal of the holding?

As for Calkoran . . . the only reason Charyn could guess for his buying rifles was that he'd taken the opportunity to do so when he'd come to L'Excelsis.

The short list of factors made a different sort of sense. Cuipryn forged cartridges for the rifleworks, and had likely bought the newer rifles to make certain that his cartridges fit. Lythoryn operated a mint and likely armed his guards. Besides that, his mint was near Rivages and nowhere close to L'Excelsis. Both Saratyn and Noerbyn had suffered from having warehouses or manufactorages being burned.

He didn't see the names of other factors on the lists, especially that of Eshmael, but then, given that two hundred rifles had been purchased in Agostos by the Factors' Council of Solidar, he hadn't expected Eshmael to purchase weapons if he could obtain them otherwise.

Even by noon, there was no word from Alastar about craftmasters, nor had Bhayrn returned to the Chateau. Charyn half-wondered if Bhayrn ever would, then shook his head.

Sooner or later . . . he'll have to.

55

Charyn was up again early on Vendrei, partly because his leg had bothered him, on and off, although the wound had seemed to be healing when Chelia had changed the dressing the night before, and partly because he wasn't looking forward to the reactions of both High Holders and factors, once they discovered the ongoing census of manufactorages and the daily-wage law. He was relieved, slightly, that he had not smelled or seen any smoke when he'd gone to the window and looked out toward the river and to the south, although he had seen a squad of army troopers posted by the gates of the rear drive.

Chelia was actually in the breakfast room when he entered. "How did you sleep?"

"Tolerably, mostly. How about you?"

"Let's say I've slept better."

"Bhayrn?"

She nodded. "At times, he seems pleasant and reasonable, and at other times . . ."

He seems like Father, except worse. Despite that thought, Charyn just nodded understandingly and took a slow and long sip of tea.

"It doesn't seem as though anything was burned last night," offered Chelia.

"That's one good thing. I'd hoped to be able to talk to some craftmasters, but I've heard nothing from Maitre Alastar."

"They may not want to talk even to him, or they may be in hiding."

"Or both."

When Charyn finished his breakfast, he made his way up

to the study. The fact that Wyllum wasn't there confirmed that he was still working on copying tariff lists for the clerks who were checking factorages against those lists, but copies of both newssheets were waiting on his desk.

Charyn read them quickly, but the stories in both centered on the declaration of martial law and the fact that, for the moment, the burning and destruction had stopped. *Veritum* offered the hope that everyone would see reason and that the army would not be long on the streets.

Tableta was less optimistic:

> . . . while the Rex has stopped the immediate destruction, he has done nothing to deal with the underlying problems, to wit, the boundless greed of factors and the miserably low wages paid by those factors . . .

Charyn frowned. "Moencriff! Would you tell Minister Sanafryt to join me?"

"Yes, sir."

As soon as Sanafryt entered the study, Charyn said, "I noted in the newssheets this morning that there was no mention of the wage law."

"I sent copies to everyone you requested, sir."

"Then, that means the factors and High Holders are keeping that news to themselves. Have two more copies made of the wage law and dispatch them to the newssheets."

"To those scandal rags, Your Grace?"

"To those very scandal rags. Immediately. We need the workers to know what the new law says. Otherwise, before long, we'll have a resumption of violence."

"Yes, Your Grace."

"Oh . . . you can tell Guard Captain Maertyl that your messenger or clerk should have two guards as escorts when he delivers those late this morning."

"Late this morning, sir?"

"Is that a problem?"

"No, sir."

"Excellent."

Shortly after Sanafryt had hurried off, Alucar appeared. "If I might have a moment, Your Grace?"

"Of course." Charyn gestured to the chairs. "Is there a problem with the clerks checking the tariff rolls?"

"Not so far. There is something else, though. I did have one of the clerks look over High Holder Laastyn's recorded holdings. The tariff records are . . . interesting."

"How interesting?"

"His High Holding at Charpen is registered, as are a hundred hectares and a large dwelling north of here. No lands are registered to him in Asseroiles. Nor are any in Tilbor, but we wouldn't have a record of that yet, not if the acquisition was recent."

"What about the lodge or place in Talyon? Or the town dwelling in L'Excelsis?"

"There's no record of any large structure or land listed for Laastyn anywhere near Talyon."

Charyn frowned. "Bhayrn stayed there, and Laastyn told Ferrand that he himself had been hunting boar there just over a month or so ago."

"I recalled you mentioned something about a lodge in Talyon. So I made inquiries."

"And?"

"Laastyn apparently owns it, but there are no records of it and the five hundred hectares around it ever being tariffed. Not in recent years, at least."

"How could that be?"

"The tariff rolls for Laastyn were updated some eight years ago. The older records are missing."

"Eight years ago. That was before you became Finance Minister."

"The changes appear to have been made when there was no Finance Minister. I wasn't appointed for more than a year after the death of Salucar."

"You weren't related . . . ?"

"Only distantly, if that. I never even met Salucar. I came from Extela, and he was, I believe, from Ferravyl."

"Then who was handling the Finance Ministry?"

"When it was being handled at all . . . Aevidyr was. I mentioned that, I believe, after Slaasyrn's death."

That alone told Charyn something he didn't want to hear . . . but didn't surprise him in the slightest. "What about the town dwelling?"

"That's actually listed as belonging to Laastyrn. It was deeded to him a year ago Juyn. Laastyn also deeded some two thousand hectares of land near Tacqueville to Laastyrn on the seventeenth of Agostos."

"Why would he do that?" asked Charyn. "Laastyrn's the heir, anyway, and he's not married so it's not a matter of providing for a wife or child if Laastyrn died before his father. I could see if the house and lands went to Laamyst . . . or even one of the daughters. Are there any other tariff records that were . . . updated . . . during that time period?"

"The clerks have been rather busy with the tariff rolls, but I did a quick look through the records. You asked about Ghaermyn. He's only listed as having a single manufactorage, in addition to various lands within sixty milles of L'Excelsis."

"Just one?"

"One, Your Grace. Those records were . . . updated about the same time, and the previous records are missing."

"Are all the entries made in the same fashion . . . something like standard merchant hand?"

An expression of modest and momentary surprise crossed Alucar's face. "Why . . . yes."

"Why did you look so surprised?"

"That's not a question I ever expected, Your Grace. I doubt your father even knew what standard merchant hand was."

Charyn stopped to think, then realized that, despite the

role that standard hand had played in his late uncle's plotting, Charyn himself had never mentioned it to any of his ministers. Howal wouldn't have, and mostly likely Wyllum wouldn't have, either. "So we have tariff records altered, in a hand that can't be traced, and Laastyn, Ghaermyn, and who knows who else haven't been paying all the tariffs they owe for something like eight years?"

"It appears that way, Your Grace."

"I see." After a moment, Charyn said, "You are not to mention this to anyone. Not yet. Write up a report on what you've found and how much in unpaid tariffs there may be."

"I can only estimate some of those numbers. We have no figures on the number of hectares or structures on some of those missing properties."

"Are there any other High Holders whose tariffs are that underpaid?"

"There may be, but I haven't discovered others. These two I found late yesterday."

"What are the penalties for failure to pay tariffs?"

"For small sums, factors or High Holders are required to make up the difference with a one-in-ten penalty. For sums of tariffs due and unpaid above a hundred golds, the property may be forfeited to the Rex as well."

"Has either ever happened?"

"There are a number of instances of factors repaying small sums. No High Holder has ever been prosecuted before a justicer or High Justicer for failure to pay tariffs. Most just paid tariffs due for the previous and present year, with penalties, and once, according to the records, for three years."

Charyn was so stunned he didn't even shake his head. "We need to revise and restructure the entire tariff system."

At that, Alucar placed a folder on the desk. "I suggested that to your father three years ago. He forbade me to talk about it. His written order to me is in the folder. I was going to bring it up, but then you requested that we begin to go over the High Holders' records, and I thought that we might learn more about how to revise the system after we'd studied some of the records."

"Why else were you reluctant to bring the matter up?"

"After all the difficulty you had in increasing tariffs . . . I thought an accurate restructuring of tariffs would create even more problems. First, it would require hiring more clerks all over Solidar, and second, I feared what you have just discovered—that there are great inequities in the tariff rolls. Those inequities often benefited High Holders who are either well-connected, exceptionally devious, or very powerful. It struck me that the immediate priority was what you had already ordered, to obtain proper assessment of tariffs. Without that, any restructuring would be largely useless."

"You're likely right, but it would have been better if you let me come to that conclusion." Charyn smiled wryly. "You've been rather successful in using numbers and logic to educate me. I prefer that to being kept in the dark."

"I apologize, Your Grace, but old habits are hard to break, especially when one's position has been less than completely secure."

"So what power did Aevidyr have that made you reluctant to act against him?"

"Sir?"

"There has to be some reason why you didn't press."

"Aevidyr has been here for some considerable time. Your father was very supportive of Aevidyr. He never told me why. Also, there was no real proof of who did what. What isn't there doesn't tell who removed it or why. As for you, Your Grace, I was reluctant to immediately call your attention to certain discrepancies involving Aevidyr because that would have seemed as though I had been waiting to act against him as soon as your father wasn't there . . . and, again, with absolutely no proof. Aevidyr is extremely careful about that, as you may have discovered."

All too many times already. Charyn managed to nod.

"For some reason, he also removed most of the references to the time he was acting Finance Minister. Slaasyrn saved several when he saw what Aevidyr was doing and gave them to me. I've kept them locked away."

"Why would he remove records with his name on them . . . unless he'd done something wrong?"

"Slaasyrn didn't know because all of them were from Rex Lorien, telling Aevidyr what to do as acting Finance Minister. None of them dealt with tariffs or assessments. That bothered me, too, and I went through all the old records. Outside of the letters and documents Slaasyrn gave me, there's nothing in the files that mentions that Aevidyr was acting as Finance Minister."

"That's very strange. Could I look at some of those letters?"

"I can bring them by shortly, Your Grace."

"In the meantime, for the reasons you just mentioned, we'll keep this between us for now, but I would appreciate knowing about any more circumstantial evidence of the same nature."

"Yes, Your Grace."

"And as soon as you have the factors' tariff rolls and all the clerks finish working on that, you need to give me that report and then start working on how you think we should restructure the tariff records and collections."

"Yes, sir."

"So that not even you could get around it," Charyn added.

"Yes, sir."

Once Alucar left, Charyn just sat there. Why in Terahnar had his father let Aevidyr do all that? And why had Aevidyr, if indeed it had been Aevidyr, only deleted properties belonging to Ghaermyn and Laastyn? Or were there more? And why hadn't Alucar been more assertive in dealing with either Charyn or his father?

Finally, Charyn walked slowly to his mother's sitting room. He thought his leg didn't hurt quite so much.

Chelia looked up from her table desk as he closed the door

and then sat down in the chair closest to the desk. "What is it, dear?"

"Why did Father choose Aevidyr as his Minister of Administration?"

"Why do you ask?"

"Because he's clearly a tool of the High Holders, and he clearly went around Father, and he's tried the same with me. I'm not so sure that he didn't warn Voralch that I was going to remove him and bring him here."

"So why haven't you removed him?"

"Because I can't prove it, and I'm not sure who would be better who knows anything."

"Do you think your father didn't face the same problem?"

"I can see that as far as removing him, but why did he pick him?"

"I don't know, dear. Your father didn't ask me about Aevidyr."

"That suggests he did about Sanafryt and Alucar."

"Alucar was the landwarden for the lands in Extela. His reports were clear and made sense. He also provided the greatest amount of golds per hectare, and there weren't any complaints. I suggested your father bring him here after he'd dithered for a year over a replacement for Salucar."

"So Alucar has no real allies among the High Holders? Is he even from a High Holder family?"

"He's a distant cousin to High Holder Thysor, as I recall."

"That makes sense," replied Charyn dryly. It also explained why Alucar had known who Thysor was when no one else had . . . and why Alucar was meticulous and also incredibly cautious.

"What about Sanafryt?"

"He was the regional justicer here in L'Excelsis. He will bend the law toward the High Holders, but your father said he never broke it. He does give honest answers, if you ask the right questions. At least, your father thought so."

Charyn realized, as had happened too often, that he was

asking questions that he should have asked far, far, earlier. But that still left the puzzle of Aevidyr. "Father never said anything revealing about Aevidyr?"

"He never said anything at all, except something to the effect that he hadn't really had much choice in picking Aevidyr. I asked him why, more than once, and he never answered the question."

"Who is he related to?"

"He was born on the wrong side of the blanket to the younger daughter of High Holder Fauxyn, but he inherited some five hundred hectares of land near Charpen. He was picked as the regional minister of administration in Liantiago by your grandsire a year before his death. He was quite young for the post."

"Did the lands come from Fauxyn?"

"Your father said not. He refused to say where they had come from." Chelia's voice was flat.

"Grandsire?"

"It's likely, but your father would never talk about it. I never have, either. Not until now."

"Does Aevidyr know?"

"I'd be greatly surprised if he doesn't, although I've never said a word about it to him."

What twisted webs families weave in trying to cover their pasts. That also suggested another reason why his mother had arranged for Palenya to be his tutor and more. "That explains a few more matters." Like the fact that Aevidyr was a half brother to Charyn's father and had been fobbed off initially with a few hundred hectares of land. "Who else might know Aevidyr's parentage?"

"Unless Aevidyr has let someone know, I doubt that there's anyone alive who knows besides the two of us. His mother died in childbirth, and Aevidyr's foster parents lived in Villerive."

Charyn nodded, then stood. "Thank you."

He walked slowly back to his study thinking how what he had just learned might put an entirely different perspective on his suspicions. In some fashion, Aevidyr had known or discovered his true parentage and leveraged it.

He was still musing over what he'd learned from his mother when Alucar returned and handed a modest folder to Charyn.

"These are what Slaasyrn gave me."

Charyn leafed through the stack of perhaps ten letters, mostly brief letters from Lorien to Aevidyr. He pulled out two, one a brief note to Aevidyr asking why Aevidyr couldn't increase the penalties for late payments of tariffs and another demanding that Aevidyr find the funds for repairs to the old regial palace in Solis. "I'd like to keep these two for a little."

"That might be for the best, Your Grace. Is there anything else?"

"Not beyond what we've already discussed."

As soon as Alucar left, Faelln entered the study.

"Are there difficulties . . . ?"

"Not in the city, so far as I know, Your Grace. Factors Hisario and Eshmael are here to see you." Faelln offered a hint of a smile. "I suggested that they wait in the main foyer."

"I'll see them . . . so long as they're not carrying weapons."

"We'll make sure of that, Your Grace." With a nod, and an expression that suggested Faelln was scarcely displeased with the order to search the factors, Faelln turned and departed.

A fraction of a quint later, the two factors strode into the study, with Eshmael leading the way.

"Your guards searched us. Us . . . members of the Council. That's insufferable! Absolutely insufferable!" Eshmael's voice was almost a shout.

Charyn said nothing, motioning for the two to sit and

letting the silence stretch out. Finally, when the two were seated, he said, "As insufferable as being the target of yet another assassination attempt, Eshmael?"

"It does show a certain lack of trust, Your Grace," said Hisario evenly.

"I'll admit that, Councilor Hisario. But then, who should I trust? I've taken measures to make choristers more accountable to their congregations . . . and I was apparently shot after I did so by the very people I helped. I work out a way to build more warships to protect Solidaran merchant ships, and I'm attacked for not doing more when no one wants to pay more. The factors complain about their losses, but everyone has conveniently forgotten that the regial granaries suffered larger losses than anyone. You asked for the army to stop the destruction, and I've given you the army, and for now the destruction has stopped." Charyn smiled coolly. "What exactly is your problem?"

"You know very well," declared Eshmael, his voice now lower. "You used the excuse of destruction and burning to promulgate the law requiring all large manufactorages to pay workers at least two coppers a day, and, on top of that, to limit their workday to nine glasses. Now, I hear that you have clerks checking to make certain all manufactorages are on the regial tariff rolls."

"I gave you what you asked for. I also gave the workers a little something, a minute portion more out of all the golds you're making, just enough for them to feed their families. Where is it written in the Codex Legis that laws should only benefit those with lands and golds? And why should honest factors worry about whether they're on the tariff rolls?"

"That's just the first step toward increasing tariffs," fumed Eshmael.

"No. It's the first step toward making certain I don't have to come before the Council, likely for several years, if not longer, and ask for an increase in tariffs to deal with the Jariolans."

"Why are you doing this to the factors? That's totally unfair. Why not the High Holders?" snapped Eshmael.

"Finance Minister Alucar, under my direction, started reviewing the tariffs of High Holders more than two months ago. Those reviews take longer because of the scattered nature of their lands and holdings, but, so far, roughly two in ten High Holders have had their tariffs revised, mostly increased because land or holding acquisitions were not recorded properly."

Eshmael had started to open his mouth, then shut it.

"How many have been reviewed so far?" asked Hisario.

"Around fifty." That was a guess on Charyn's part. "It will take a while."

"This tariff-roll counting for factors," asked Hisario, "is it just in L'Excelsis?"

"We're starting in L'Excelsis, but Minister Alucar is working out the details for all of Solidar."

"Why now?" demanded Eshmael.

"Because I discovered a number of irregularities, and it seemed much better to clean up the records and then work on better procedures."

"If I may say so," said Hisario, "it's long overdue. Thank you very much, Your Grace. By your leave . . ."

"Of course. Pardon me if I don't stand at the moment."

Eshmael was clearly confused as Hisario escorted him out.

Charyn thought that Hisario's reaction was a good sign . . . but it could also be very bad.

For a time, he sat and thought over what he had learned and what it might portend.

Much later, Charyn once more limped to Alucar's study.

"Your Grace . . . you could have summoned me."

"All properties over two hundred hectares are required to be recorded here, and not just with the regional governors, are they not?"

"They're required to be."

"You're saying that likely not all are. Are they recorded by the landowner's name, as they are with High Holders?"

"That is the requirement."

"What lands are recorded in Aevidyr's name?"

"I would have to look, Your Grace."

"Please do, and let me know. I'd appreciate very much your not informing Aevidyr."

"Yes, Your Grace."

As Charyn slowly walked back to his study, he saw Maertyl coming up the grand staircase. So he stopped and waited for the guard captain.

"Sir . . . the guards just returned from escorting Sanafryt's clerk."

"Was there a problem?"

"Not one for you, I think. I sent Dhuncan and Aastyl. They're both solid. Dhuncan had to escort the clerk inside to the workrooms of *Tableta*. When they were leaving, he heard someone saying that the 'frigging factors' tried to hush up the wage law." Maertyl smiled. "I thought you'd like to know. You might not be their target quite so soon again."

Charyn shook his head. "*Tableta* will write something like I took an inadequate step in the right direction and even that the greedy factors tried to hush up. If I'm fortunate, *Veritum* might be a little more charitable."

"The men are proud of you for doing it, Your Grace."

I'm glad someone is. "It's unhappily both the least and the most I can do."

Maertyl nodded. "Guards and troopers know all about that. So do the civic patrollers."

Charyn was quite sure they did.

56

On Samedi morning, Charyn woke slightly later than he had been doing. While his wounds still pained him, especially when he moved them, Maitre Gaellen had stopped by the Chateau late on Vendrei and used a touch of imaging to further clean both wounds, although Charyn had felt nothing. Then Gaellen had told Charyn that both wounds were healing well.

After rising carefully and going to the window for a quick look out and a breath of the morning air, Charyn was relieved that nothing significant had burned during the night, at least not near the Chateau and, hopefully, not anywhere else.

A bit later, when he entered the breakfast room, he was surprised to see Iryella sitting at the table with a mug of tea and a platter of egg toast and ham strips in front of her. "You're up early."

"I had a nightmare. I didn't want to wake anyone else up, and I knew you'd be here before long. If you weren't, then Aunt Chelia would be before much longer."

"Do you want to talk about it?"

"No. It was a silly nightmare, except it was scary when I was dreaming it."

Charyn smiled. "I've had nightmares like that. I think most people have."

"Do you still have nightmares?"

"Sometimes."

"Do you wake up scared?"

"A few times." That was certainly true, especially when Charyn had the recurring dream about coming down the grand staircase and getting shot by a faceless guard. Of course, being shot at every month or so likely didn't help dispel the dream.

"You're the Rex."

"Bad things can happen to anyone, even Rexes, and nightmares likely come from our fears that they will." Charyn took the mug of tea from Therosa. "Thank you." Then he turned back to Iryella. "Most things we're afraid of don't happen."

"I know that. But some do."

Charyn nodded.

"Do you think the Nameless cares when terrible things happen to people?"

"I have no idea if the Nameless cares," replied Charyn. "I don't think we have any way of knowing."

"Neither do I. Karyel says the Nameless allows evil to happen."

"That would be hard to prove," mused Charyn. "If the Nameless stops some evil from happening, we'd never know, because it didn't happen. Perhaps people do more evil than the Nameless can stop, or perhaps the Nameless leaves us to our own devices, for good or evil." He caught the momentary look of surprise on Therosa's face as she set the platter with egg toast and ham strips before him, but simply offered a smile.

Iryella didn't seem to notice Therosa's reaction and replied, "Then whether there's more good or evil depends on who's stronger, the good people or the evil people."

"Or who chooses to act," suggested Charyn. "And how." *And when.*

At that moment, Chelia and Karyel entered the breakfast room.

"Not a word," said Chelia to Karyel before turning to Charyn. "We'll need to talk later."

"I'll be in my study."

Since Chelia's entrance and mood had effectively disrupted the conversation between Iryella and Charyn, Charyn finished his breakfast quickly, but without gulping it down, and then made his way up to the study. It was still early enough that only Sturdyn was there, but less than two quints later, an army courier delivered a report from Marshal Vaelln that Charyn immediately read.

There had been no attempts to burn or damage property on either Meredi night or Jeudi night. On Vendrei night troopers surrounded five men who carried oil jugs. One of the men fired at the troopers with a rifle. The troopers returned fire and killed the man. The others tried to flee. One escaped by diving into the river. One was wounded, and the other two were captured. All the jugs contained highly flammable nut oil. There had been no problems with the two clerks, who had made a total of forty-six visits to factorages or manufactorages on Jeudi and Vendrei.

Charyn nodded, then went to read the second page, which summarized the latest events in the undeclared naval war with Jariola. Little had changed. Two more new warships had joined the fleet, one first-rater and one frigate. Three Jariolan warships had been sunk, with the loss of one Solidaran frigate, and two more Solidaran merchanters had been lost off Otelyrn.

As he filed Vaelln's report with the others, Charyn had the feeling that he just might be making more progress in the war against Jariola than he was in dealing with the struggles between workers, factors, and High Holders.

He also couldn't help but wonder exactly what Karyel had done to displease Chelia, but breakfast hadn't been the place to ask.

He was still thinking about Karyel when Chelia entered the study and closed the door behind her.

"You weren't exactly pleased this morning," he said evenly.

"Karyel takes after his misbegotten grandsire. He tried to coerce one of the new chambermaids into his bed. When she wouldn't cooperate, he threatened her and her family. The last thing we need is another fifteen-year-old spoiled man-child having his way with an unwilling woman and another child born on the wrong side of the blanket, especially now."

Another spoiled man-child and another ill-gotten child? Charyn wasn't about to pursue either, especially not with his mother in the mood she was clearly in. "You told him that, obviously. What else?"

"I also told him that he has his High Holding on sufferance and good behavior."

"I was having a good conversation with Iryella when you two came in. She's a bit manipulative, but seems to have more common sense."

"She's *very* manipulative, but, as you've observed, she does have a head on her shoulders."

"You think I should have a talk with Karyel."

Chelia shook her head. "Not unless he misbehaves again."

"Do we need to look for a very proper and intelligent suitable match for Iryella?"

"If Karyel continues this way . . . it's possible. Finding him a suitable bed partner may be difficult, but better that than where he was headed."

"But necessary . . . as it was for—"

"You needed Palenya for other reasons, and I never worried about your being threatening or violent."

"Just not having an illegitimate heir to complicate matters."

Chelia nodded.

"And what about Bhayrn?"

"I just told him that he'd have to pay any claims out of whatever holding you bestowed on him. He understood."

He understood, but he likely wasn't happy about that, either. Charyn nodded.

"Just be cold and very formal with Karyel for the next week or so."

"I can do that." Easily, given that Charyn didn't even like Karyel.

With a rueful smile, Chelia turned and left the study.

Just after eighth glass, Alucar appeared.

"I thought you should know about what the clerks discovered on Jeudi and Vendrei. They visited forty-six factorages or manufactorages. Six were not on the tariff rolls. Of the six, five would be liable for the lowest possible tariffs, likely just over a gold each. The sixth was a larger manufactorage owned by a Factor Smeadyl that employed at least fifteen workers and might pay as much as ten golds."

Charyn had never heard of Factor Smeadyl, but he suspected he'd be seeing or hearing quite a few names he'd never heard before. "That's one in nine factorages not paying tariffs, a little lower than what you'd predicted, but still close."

"That number will likely increase, Your Grace. The area where the clerks began has more of the smaller factorages."

"Have you found out any more about Aevidyr?"

"He has some four thousand hectares of property on the tariff rolls. Outside of some five hundred hectares here in Bovaria, most of the other properties are in Antiago. One property consists of five hundred hectares of oil nut trees. The annual tariffs are almost fifty golds . . ."

"That means what?"

"That the income is close to a thousand golds a year."

And he's still staying on as Minister of Administration at two hundred golds a year? But Charyn only asked, "And the others?"

"They're lands that produce various crops. The tariffs on the rest run to not quite sixty golds." Alucar laid a folder on the desk. "You should look through this yourself."

Charyn took the folder and set it to the side. "Does it say how he got them?"

"The transfers say from whom and use the standard language—ten golds and other considerations of value.

They also list the size of the parcel and the tariffs paid for the previous five years."

"Thank you. I appreciate your digging that up." After a momentary pause, Charyn asked, "What properties do you have, Alucar?"

"A small house on twenty hectares just outside of Extela where my sister and her husband live. Ten hectares are in vineyards, and I pay, or they pay for me, four and a half golds a year, since a vineyard is, for tariff purposes, a factorage. Over the years, I've also bought a hundred hectares of regrowth timberlands near Vaestora, and, of course, the house where my wife and I live in L'Excelsis."

"And you've been Minster of Finance some six years?"

"Not quite seven."

"You're obviously good with coins, and in some years as a landwarden and then seven years as Finance Minister, you've managed to buy a modest house, I assume, and a hundred hectares of land."

"We've been very careful, sir. Neither Hesphya nor I have wealthy immediate relatives."

"And without familial and other . . . alliances . . . care has been necessary."

"Yes, Your Grace. Most necessary."

"I'm young, Alucar, but it seems to me that lack of care eventually catches up to almost everyone . . . in some fashion or another."

"There are some who believe that will not happen to them."

"Sometimes . . . it just takes longer," replied Charyn, offering a sardonic smile.

"At times, sir, it's seemed to me that depends on those who have the power to see that such occurs."

"I think it just takes longer when those in power don't notice or act. And sometimes, it only seems that they don't act."

"Unless someone perceptive is watching closely, Your Grace."

"I'm working on being perceptive. When you're young, there's more to learn. Every week, it seems I discover something I wish I'd known earlier."

"I think that's true at any age, Your Grace . . . if one is willing to look."

"Very good point, Alucar . . . and thank you, again, for the information."

"My pleasure, sir."

Honest as Alucar seemed and had so far proven, Charyn was quite certain that the Finance Minister had been pleased to provide that information.

Once Alucar left, Charyn read through the folder on Aevidyr slowly and carefully, checking each property. The oil nut lands had been purchased for "ten golds and other considerations" from Nualt D'Alte, of Barna, Antiago, some ten years previously. Two parcels of land, each of two hundred fifty hectares and apparently adjoining, had been purchased eight and nine years previously, each for ten golds and other considerations, from Laastyn D'Alte. Another parcel of five hundred hectares had been purchased from Basalyt D'Alte, but the documentation indicated that Basalyt had only held the property a year and that it had been previously held by Laastyn D'Alte.

Yet another property of a thousand hectares had come from one Chaastar D'Alte of Suemyron, while one of two hundred fifty hectares had come from Kaelsyn D'Alte of Hassyl. The most mysterious was one of two thousand hectares from a Factorius Lubarun of Lucayl. The name sounded familiar to Charyn, but he couldn't place it, yet he knew he'd seen it somewhere in the papers and petitions that had crossed his desk.

He finally set down the folder.

There was no doubt in his mind that Aevidyr had been

using his position both as a regional minister and as Minister of Administration to give High Holders and others advantages, most likely in the case of Laastyn to remove properties from the tariff rolls. And the way the tariff system had been operated in the past, Laastyn would only have been liable for two years' back tariffs, while, if the property dates were correct, he would have avoided tariffs for at least eight years. Given the worth of the "grants" to Aevidyr, the "exempted" properties had to be large indeed, particularly given what Aevidyr had apparently received in return.

Charyn's problem was simple. While the "exemption" of properties was established, if by their omission from the tariff records, there was absolutely no proof of who had accomplished the exemption. There was also no record of what Aevidyr had actually paid for the properties he had acquired, nor of anything resembling an asking price.

Was there any possibility that there were "exempted" properties held by the other High Holders who had "sold" Aevidyr lands? Even if there were such properties, it would take weeks if not months or years to track those down, and the few "exempted" properties that Alucar discovered wouldn't be enough to prove anything before a justicer. And while Charyn could certainly dismiss Aevidyr, any punishment that would be adequate for Aevidyr's deeds would be seen by many High Holders as cruel and capricious, especially following on the death of Uncle Ryel and Aunt Doryana.

And that means you'd better not do anything, at least for a few days, until and unless you can tie Aevidyr to certain High Holders.

And, at the moment, Charyn had absolutely no idea of how to do that.

After pondering and stewing for another glass, he left the study and limped down to the music room. There, he played the clavecin one-handed for a few moments, then shook his head. It just wasn't the same.

57

Charyn was finishing his breakfast on Solayi morning, and enjoying a second mug of tea, which was more than welcome, given the grayness of the day and the drizzle that enveloped the Chateau.

At that moment, Bhayrn appeared and eased into the chair across the table from his brother. "How are your leg and hand?"

"They're both still sore."

"But they're better, aren't they?"

"Maitre Gaellen says that they're healing well. The leg will heal faster than the hand because the bullet in the leg missed the bones and major blood vessels."

"That sounds like the Nameless was looking out for you."

"The Nameless perhaps, but definitely Rykael, Ghasaen, and the chestnut. They all took bullets meant for me."

Therosa almost tiptoed in, then set a tall mug of dark lager in front of Bhayrn.

"Thank you, Therosa. I'll have whatever's convenient."

"Yes, Lord Bhayrn."

Thank you and whatever's convenient. To Charyn, those phrases, especially after the apparently sincere concern about Charyn's health, didn't sound like the Bhayrn of recent weeks.

"However it happened, I'm glad you're still around," Bhayrn said. "And I have to say, even if I don't agree, combining the daily-wage law with the army seems to have put an end to the unrest. Do you think that will last?"

"I don't think it will please the angriest of the factors or the angriest of the workers, but if it eliminates most of the conflict, I'll consider it successful." Charyn shrugged. "But who knows? Someone could do something crazy and set everything off again."

"You even did something for the True Believers, but that didn't stop one or more of them from shooting at you. Do you think they'll settle down as well?"

Charyn thought about the question, and especially why Bhayrn had asked it, before replying. "That's hard to say. If they're acting on what they believe, and not on some hidden agenda, their complaint shouldn't be against me any longer. I've given them the power to take control of their choristers. But . . . some of them clearly want more from me."

"What more could you give them?"

Charyn fingered his chin, thinking and trying to word what he had in mind carefully. "They might want me to change the Codex Legis more, perhaps to place limits on the amount or share of the offerings that a chorister might appropriate for personal use."

"There aren't any limits now, are there?" Bhayrn turned his head and nodded to Therosa as she set the platter in front of him.

"No." Charyn paused, then said, hoping he was using the words that would obtain the right effect, "The Rex shouldn't do that. It would set a precedent that would allow the Rex to use law to control worship."

"But some of the choristers . . ."

"You're right. But the law I proclaimed gives the congregants a way to remove greedy choristers. It will take longer, but they can do it without breaking other laws."

"Do you think the True Believers will see it that way?"

"They should."

"Isn't that saying they should see it your way?"

"The law is designed to keep the Rex out of the affairs of every anomen. That's not seeing it my way."

"The most violent among them might not see it that way."

"They might not," Charyn agreed. "But it's not good for me to do something that will lead to greater problems in the future."

Bhayrn nodded, then said, "I do hope you're not thinking of attending services this evening."

"I promised Maertyl and Faelln both that I wouldn't leave the Chateau for at least a week, and I'll definitely be keeping that promise."

"Good. I know you want to see Aloryana, but why couldn't she come here?"

"I'd like that," admitted Charyn, "but I haven't asked her."

"It might be best if Mother wrote Aloryana and suggested it. I'll talk to her later." Bhayrn smiled. "I'd like to see her, too, but not on Imagisle."

Not wanting to disrupt Bhayrn's pleasant mood, Charyn just nodded, then asked, "How are things going for you?"

"I spent the last few days with Laamyst. We didn't do much, except talk and play some plaques. The Yellow Rose is closed because of the curfew."

"I didn't know you liked risqué theatre."

Bhayrn offered a crooked smile. "It's not my favorite, but Laamyst likes it, and every so often it's not bad."

"What about Gherard?"

"He'd prefer to game at Alamara's or Tydaal's, but he's not like Uncle Delcoeur was. He usually wins. He knows the odds for every hand. He got that from his father, but Ghaermyn stopped gaming when he became the High Holder. Gherard will, too." Bhayrn shook his head. "I don't go with them when they want to game for real silvers. That wouldn't be wise. Odds and mathematics aren't my talents."

"Half of success is knowing what your talents are and sticking to them," replied Charyn.

"You do that well."

"I try, but sometimes, as you pointed out, things don't quite work out that way."

After a moment of silence, Bhayrn spoke again, conversationally. "You know that someone's impersonating you? Either that, or you're doing something you shouldn't be."

"Impersonating me?" Charyn offered an incredulous look. "So that they can get shot instead of me?"

"Not that you. You know Gherard is at the exchange a lot for his father. He told me that the ironworks and the rifleworks were sold several months ago to a Factor Suyrien D'Chaeryll. The Chaeryll lands are yours. That means someone is impersonating you."

Charyn debated, then shook his head. "No one is impersonating me. I'm also a factor and a member of the commodity exchange under that name. I have been since well before I became Rex."

"You? You're Factor Suyrien?"

Charyn wasn't certain, but he thought that Bhayrn paled. "It took a little doing, but I need the ironworks for a project I've been working on."

"But that means you also own the rifleworks."

"I didn't even think about that part, but it's been useful as well."

"People won't like it that you're the one selling rifles to the army."

"Almost all of those were sold before I bought the ironworks."

"But in the future . . . ?"

"Anything I do that's constructive someone won't like. In fact, anything I do will make someone unhappy." Charyn smiled wryly. "That's one thing I've discovered."

"I suppose that's so. When do you think you'll be able to play the clavecin again?"

"Even badly, most likely several months."

"It must be awful not to be able to use your right hand."

"I can write a little, and use the good fingers to hold something in place. That's about it."

After another quint of pleasant, if innocuous, conversation, Charyn and Bhayrn left the breakfast room, and Charyn went to his study, while Bhayrn went to the main entry to wait for Gherard, after promising that he'd be back no later than eighth glass, possibly earlier, since Gherard didn't want to use his coach much later than that because of the curfew.

Once in his study, Charyn sat behind the goldenwood table desk, thinking. He would have preferred to pace back and forth in front of the windows, but they were closed against the rain that had followed the drizzle, and too much walking still hurt his leg. In fact, any walking hurt, but the pain was worse if he kept walking.

Bhayrn had been almost effusive, and Charyn feared he knew exactly why. Unfortunately, a good part of Charyn's problem with Bhayrn lay in his grandsire's and his father's reputation for being arbitrary and unreasonable. Even in dealing with the factor/worker conflict, at least some of the factors, particularly Eshmael, thought Charyn was being unreasonable. Given what Charyn wanted to accomplish and the balancing act required to keep matters under control, anything Charyn did to rein in or neutralize Bhayrn had to be seen as fair and rational, particularly by the High Holders.

He took a deep breath.

After a time, he thought about trying to write Alyncya a letter, then shook his head. Even the short response he had penned had been a tiresome struggle, as was even signing his name, and his signature definitely looked strange. And he certainly didn't want to dictate a letter to Alyncya.

Instead, he took out the folder with her letters and the poems he'd copied and read through the letters, then began to reread the poems. Recalling what he hadn't said to Bhayrn about the Nameless—that he had his doubts about whether there was a Nameless—he smiled as he reread one he had not marked for Alyncya.

UNHOLY FIRE

More brightly glows the greater moon's soft golden globe,
Pursued through space by fleeter hunter's striving speed,
Deities most ancient, oft praised in holy fire,
Signs long viewed on bright vestments and the priestly robe,
Stories justifying each arbitrary deed,
As if justice ever trumped man's hot desire.

Has the progression of deities always trailed the development of people . . . acting like an anchor . . . or does belief reinforce moral values so that progress can occur?

Probably both.

He was still pondering over that when there was a knock on the study door. Charyn frowned. "Yes?"

Chelia opened the door. "I didn't want to disturb you, but I wanted you to meet someone who came to visit me. If you wouldn't mind coming to my sitting room . . . it would be a pleasant surprise."

Charyn immediately stood. His mother seldom requested anything of that nature. Over the years, she'd occasionally suggested he meet various women of her acquaintance. Still, he wondered if the visitor was one of the High Holders' wives with whom she played plaques, or some distant relative, although there were few enough of those after the events of the last decade or so.

Chelia led the way to the sitting room, walking somewhat more slowly than her usual brisk pace to accommodate Charyn. Once there, she opened the door.

Charyn's mouth dropped open when he saw Alyncya standing beside one of the armchairs. Then he shook his head and glanced ruefully to his mother and then back to Alyncya. "I never even guessed."

"You weren't supposed to, dear," replied Chelia, seating herself in her chair.

Charyn continued to look at Alyncya, who wore a light

brown jacket and matching trousers, with a high-necked cream blouse.

"It hasn't been that long, Charyn," she said in an amused tone.

"For me, it has. I was just bemoaning the fact that I couldn't write you a letter. So I was rereading yours."

She raised her eyebrows.

"They're still lying on my desk. You can go look if you want."

"He was reading something that looked suspiciously like a letter," confirmed Chelia, smiling, then adding, "You need to sit down, both of you."

Charyn took the straight-backed chair and turned it, left-handed, so that he could easily look at both his mother and Alyncya, then seated himself.

"Alyncya's been here for almost a glass, and we've had a lovely talk."

"And who . . . ?"

"It was my idea," said Alyncya. "I did write your mother and asked if I could call on her. She was gracious enough to say that today would be a good day to do so."

"Scarcely gracious. I wanted more time to talk to the woman my son wants to marry."

Charyn tried not to flush. He wasn't certain he succeeded. "Have you had enough time?"

"I'm certain, Charyn, that I will have more than enough time in the years ahead, that is, if you don't do something insanely inane." Chelia rose from her chair. "I'm going to stretch my legs. I won't eavesdrop, and I'll knock so that I won't overhear what you don't want overheard. Letters are all well and good, but talking is better, and since Alyncya was calling on me, no one will know otherwise."

When the sitting room door closed, Alyncya said, "I didn't expect that."

"My mother can be very direct." *When necessary and it suits her.*

"You look tired and worn, but better than I'd expected from the newssheets and your reply."

"I had to struggle to write that, and I still have trouble even signing my name."

"Your signature was definitely wobbly."

Charyn looked directly into Alyncya's hazel eyes. "I can't tell you how much it means that you came here."

"You didn't know?"

Charyn shook his head. "I had no idea. None."

"You're the Rex."

"If my mother told the guards she was expecting a caller, they'd log you in when you arrived. I'd find out after the fact, but not before. I would find out in advance about anyone questionable visiting anyone else, except my brother." Charyn grinned. "Besides, I suspect some of the guards already knew your name. There have been a few messages sent to you by courier."

After a moment of silence, Alyncya said, "I had a very interesting meeting on Jeudi."

Charyn frowned. "You just spent time with Mother. Aloryana?"

"Well, I suppose I had two meetings. They were both at Imagisle."

"Aloryana and Palenya, then?" Charyn managed not to wince.

"I did tell you that I'd ask about her."

"You did. Should I be worried about how you feel now?"

Alyncya smiled. "I like your question."

That surprised Charyn.

"You're surprised? What you asked says a great deal about you, dear. You've hidden nothing. Neither did Palenya. But you're worried about how I might feel. You were right to worry. I worried. That was another reason I asked to call on your mother. I told you I'd ask her. I did."

"And?"

Alyncya's first response was an amused and ironic smile.

"She said, if somewhat less directly, exactly what you told me. That was also what Palenya said. Even Aloryana said that Palenya had been good for you. So . . . you've been incredibly honest with me . . . or both women are so fond of you that they'll say anything. And Aloryana is a bit like me, in some ways."

"I can't deny they're all fond of me, at this point, all in a mothering way, even Aloryana. I also doubt that any of them would say anything they didn't believe to be true. Just as I believe you wouldn't."

"You'd like to trust me, but I can't believe you're that certain."

"I'm certain you're attracted to me, as I am to you. I'm not certain that's enough for you. I am certain that your character is such that you're not given to willful deception."

"You read me fairly well."

Charyn shook his head. "You've allowed me to read you well. I don't see into people anywhere as deeply as I should. That's one of the reasons why I set out to learn as much as I could about people's actions, because too many people want to conceal what they want from a Rex. It seems to me . . ." Charyn wasn't quite sure how to say what he felt, and the last thing he wanted to do was to say anything that would push Alyncya away.

"It seems to you . . ." prompted Alyncya.

". . . that you . . . are uncertain about . . . that you don't know . . . about marrying a Rex."

"I'm very uncertain about what being a Rex does to men. I don't deny that, by the second time you asked me to dance, I wanted to know you better . . . much better. By now, if you were a High Holder, I'd have proposed to you." She smiled. "Lady-heirs can do that, you know? It's frowned upon, but not unheard of."

"But because I'm Rex . . . ?"

"From what I've seen and read, being a Rex can change a man, not for the better."

"I've seen that as well." Charyn paused, then went on. "That's one of the reasons I'm trying to change things. I've already created what amounts to a joint council of both factors and High Holders."

"I know. And I thought that the law that requires choristers to reveal what happens to their offerings was good. The daily-wage law . . . I can see that it was necessary . . ."

"Remember . . . it's only the *minimum* wage, and it doesn't stop factors or High Holders from firing bad workers or paying good workers more."

"Why are you trying to change things?"

"Because I don't like what I've seen. The Rex has both too much power and too little power, and that makes governing close to impossible. But to give him more would lead to rebellion and disaster and to take away any more would make him ineffective."

A slight frown creased Alyncya's brow. "How can you change that? Should you?"

"I could be wrong, but I think it's necessary. Two revolts in the last twenty years, and a Rex being assassinated, and now we've had manufactorages being burned and our merchant ships being plundered. Something's not right."

"It just could be the last few Rexes."

"When there's been no trouble like this for three hundred years? Somehow, I can't believe that it's just the Rexes, not by themselves."

"How would you change things? Could you?"

"Give the Council more power and more responsibility. If the councilors have a part in changing things . . ." Charyn shrugged. "Some of that is just a feeling . . ."

"But you'd still be Rex . . . Would they trust you?"

"It will take time, but I've made a point of only promising what I know I can do, and keeping those promises. Before long, we'll need a craftmaster or two on the Council."

"Neither the factors nor the High Holders will like that."

"It's not a question of liking. It's a question of listening. In just six months, I've gotten the factors and the High Holders to listen to each other. Sometimes, they even agree."

"What does that have to do with us?" she asked.

"Everything."

Surprisingly, to Charyn, she smiled again.

He waited.

"Now, let me ask you a question."

Charyn tried not to tense up. "Go ahead."

"Are you ready to hear about my past indiscretions? The reasons why I'm still unwed, especially since I'm actually older than you are."

"I wouldn't have known that."

"Not that much, just five months, but that makes me a spinster among the daughters of High Holders." Another amused smile crossed Alyncya's lips. "Are you avoiding the issue of past indiscretions?"

"No. I doubt that whatever they may be will change my feelings for you."

"What if I told you that I'd done something truly horrible?"

"That's rather hypothetical. So, hypothetically, I'd say that, if you did, you must have had a very good reason. Besides, as a very practical matter, I've already done two horrible deeds, neither of which is exactly secret. So who am I to judge?"

"You? Having a mistress isn't horrible. Worrisome to your possible wife, but not horrible."

"My uncle and aunt both committed suicide. I forced them to it by declaring that, if they were found guilty of treason, the holding would be forfeit to the Rex under the law. They were guilty. They were behind the assassins who killed my father. But I wanted them to kill themselves so I wouldn't have to seize the lands—"

"Why?"

"If I didn't take the lands, I'd be seen as favoring my mother's family and as weak. If I did, then I'd be punishing a fourteen-year-old heir who had nothing to do with it. If I seized the lands and then gave them back, the seizure would be seen as a charade."

"That is horrible," said Alyncya evenly. "But not doing it that way would have been even more horrible."

"Now . . . about your despicable deeds?"

Alyncya offered a sad smile. "What's despicable is that I have none. Everyone who has lived life sooner or later does something despicable . . . or at least disreputable. I've been very respectable and very careful . . . and that means I've done little."

"I can help you with that," said Charyn. "Marry me. Then you can counsel me, and we can share deeds of all sorts. Some are bound to be at least dubious."

"No." Alyncya stood and walked over before Charyn.

"Why not?"

"Because I want to do something my way. You know why." Her eyes fixed on him. "As Lady-heir D'Shendael, I'm asking. Will you marry me?"

"I will." Charyn eased himself to his feet.

Before he could put his arms around her, hers were around him.

Another quint passed before Chelia knocked on the door, then entered to see the two sitting side by side on the love seat. "I take it that you two have decided."

"She asked me to marry her, and I said yes."

"You understand what that means?" asked Chelia.

"The High Holding remains hers and is hers to bequeath."

"That's definitely for the best, especially if you have a daughter. Now . . . the wedding ceremony shouldn't be too soon."

"What about a small ceremony just before the Year-Turn Ball, on the thirty-fifth of Finitas?" asked Charyn. "Or would that be too painful?"

"Avoiding appropriate dates for those less meaningful is an exercise in futility," replied Chelia, almost tartly. "Also, it elevates meaningless tragedy. I would suggest that we keep the announcement and date within the families until you can announce it at the next Council meeting. Until Alyncya announces it, that is."

"That wouldn't be a problem, would it?" asked Charyn, looking to Alyncya. "That's only ten days from now."

"Not so long as I can make the announcement," she replied.

"A formal announcement in a setting that no one can refute in order to make sure that your position as lady-heir is maintained?"

Alyncya nodded.

Charyn smiled. So did Chelia.

58

Lundi morning, well before dawn, Charyn woke, soaked in sweat, half-pinned in his sheets, still feeling that the bullet from the faceless guard had slammed into his skull. He shuddered, then blotted his face with a corner of the sheet, even before untangling it, and finally sat up in his bed.

Why that nightmare now . . . a week after the shooting and right after Alyncya had turned down his proposal and offered her own? Her proposal amused him, as much as it told him that she certainly wouldn't be a submissive wife. *As if you ever wanted that.*

Was something deep inside his thoughts trying to tell him something? That he was in more danger since he and Alyncya had accepted each other? And why was the guard in the nightmare always faceless? *Because you don't really know who's trying to kill you? Or because what you suspect may not be correct?*

After he cooled down and dried off, he propped himself up against the comparatively simple goldenwood headboard that he had chosen as part of the redecoration to replace the more ornate one used by his father. All his pondering over the next glass or so led to the same conclusion—that, while he knew a great many of the pieces to the puzzle, he had only a general and vague idea of how they fitted together, almost like trying to figure out the last tricks of a whist hand when he had no idea what tricks had been played before—an almost impossible endgame because there were so many variations. *And if you play it wrong . . .* not only could Charyn himself be killed, but Solidar could easily come apart with all the tensions and forces in play, forces that Bhayrn not only didn't understand, but didn't even see, forces that could easily pit crafters against factors, and factors against High Holders, while the True Believers fractured the worship of the Nameless.

And yet . . . there was also so much promise . . . *if you can not only figure it out, but play the right endgame . . . and thwart all the other endgames . . .*

Because he was awake early, he washed and dressed and had breakfast alone, hardly surprising, given that he was earlier than usual and Bhayrn never seemed to wake early.

After that, he made his way to the study, where he was a bit chagrined to discover that Alyncya's letters and poems remained on the desk where he had left them. The secrecy wasn't nearly as important now that they were engaged, although some might quibble that it wasn't formal until it was announced publicly. Still he replaced them in the folder and slipped the folder back into the hidden compartment.

He knew he'd be rereading the contents more than a few times, since he wouldn't have that many opportunities, if any, to be with Alyncya until the announcement at the Council meeting. Both his mother and Alyncya had made that very clear.

Then he began to think about how he could resolve the problem with Aevidyr in a way that would work to his advantage and not to Aevidyr's. He was still thinking when Alucar arrived.

"Good morning, Your Grace."

"Good morning, Alucar. Are all four clerks on their way with army troopers?"

"They are, sir, and Wyllum will likely finish the last of his copying this morning or early this afternoon."

"Excellent. Now . . . I went through that folder, rather thoroughly, and I've been thinking over the properties that weren't on the tariff rolls. Would any of the clerks recall when or if changes were made?"

"Most likely not that far back. Slaasyrn would have been the most likely, but now . . ."

"He died right after I asked you to start updating the

High Holders' tariff records . . ." Charyn stopped speaking. Slaasyrn had died suddenly, supposedly because his heart failed—just after Alucar had begun the reassessment of High Holder properties. *And Slaasyrn would have been the only one who could possibly have discovered sooner or later that the records had been altered, and he would have known exactly what had happened.* But . . . three months later . . . how was there any way to prove that?

Then Charyn looked at Alucar.

The Finance Minister swallowed. "I didn't even think . . ."

"Don't say a word to anyone. Not yet. Not until I tell you." After several moments, Charyn asked, "Did Slaasyrn keep notes, or any kind of a journal?"

"Not that I know of, Your Grace."

"Don't mention anything about a journal or notes. If there is one, we don't want it to disappear. I would appreciate your looking into that . . . immediately, but only you. Keep it to yourself."

"Yes, sir."

"I also have another question. How are reassessments documented? That is, when a property owner buys or sells lands or factorages or whatever."

"A copy of the bill of sale is attached to the tariff assessment, and a copy of the notice of the change in tariffs due is also attached."

"Is there a separate record for the property, or only for the property owner?"

"They're the same record, sir. The documents go to the tariff file of the new owner. I suggested going to a system of dual entries . . ."

"But my father refused?"

"Yes, sir."

"So that means, if lands are missing from the owner's tariff file, there's no way to find them?"

"If we know about the property, we can reassess it, the way you're planning to do with the unrecorded factorages.

Or, if we know the previous owner, the bill of sale and the tariff readjustment notice on his tariffs could be used."

"But you'd have to know one or the other?"

"Yes, sir. That's why—"

"You wanted to change things, but, as you pointed out, it would take an army of clerks to accomplish that."

"Yes, sir. And with the tariff problem, and the hostility of the High Holders, it wasn't something that your father wanted to confront."

Charyn could, unfortunately, understand that. "See if you can think up a way to do that over time with fewer clerks."

"Yes, Your Grace."

"For the moment, that's all that I have."

Once Alucar had left the study, Charyn just considered the problem. Would there be any record of old readjustments anywhere? Then he nodded. It was worth a try. He opened one of the hidden compartments in the bookcase and extracted a set of keys, which he set on the left side of the table desk.

Given the timing of Slaasyrn's death, and everything else Charyn had recently discovered, Aevidyr was definitely looking even sleazier than Charyn had already believed, and what he believed hadn't been that favorable to begin with.

Since he couldn't do much at that moment, he turned his attention to the petitions on the desk and to Sanafryt's suggested responses to each, putting the ones he approved of in one pile and the few he did not in another, much smaller, stack, which he'd go over with Wyllum.

After a time, once it was well past seventh glass, he asked Sturdyn to request Aevidyr's presence.

The Minister of Administration arrived almost immediately.

"Have you heard back from Rikkard D'Niasaen?"

"Yes, sir." Aevidyr's smile was pleasant. "I was just going to tell you that he accepted the position and is on his way to Solis. If you'd like to see his letter of acceptance . . . ?"

"I would, thank you. And what about Thealyt D'Moeryn?"

"A courier just delivered something from Khelgror."

"See if it's from him and bring it and the D'Niasaen acceptance here. I'll wait."

Less than half a quint passed before Aevidyr returned.

The acceptance letter from Rikkard D'Niasaen was very much a polite and mannered response, except for the next to the last paragraph. Charyn read those words twice.

> *In accepting and carrying out the duties of Regional Governor, I will do so not only in full accord with the Codex Legis, but will treat all personages with equal gravity, graciousness, and courtesy under law, and I offer my deep appreciation for both the honor and the responsibility entailed by that honor.*

In short, he's going to treat factors and High Holders the same . . . and possibly even crafters. Charyn smiled wryly. That was going to be interesting. *He needs a little support for that.* "Aevidyr . . . I like Rikkard D'Niasaen's reply. I think I'll respond to it personally."

"With your hand, Your Grace . . . I could draft one for you."

"Wyllum's almost finished with his duties for Alucar. So it won't be a problem. Now . . . the response from Thealyt D'Moeryn?"

Aevidyr handed over the sealed missive.

Charyn studied the envelope for a moment. "I don't think we've had a courier yet today."

"It must have come in late on Samedi, then, after midday," said Aevidyr pleasantly. "It was waiting for me."

"Well . . . it's not as though either of us could have done anything on Samedi." Charyn managed to slit the envelope left-handed and withdrew the letter. He read through the very pleasant but formal acceptance, then nodded. "You can draft a response to this one for my signature." He handed the letter back.

"I could do both."

"I need to be very careful about what I reply to Rikkard D'Niasaen, don't you think?"

"There was that line about equal weight under law . . ."

"Exactly."

Once Aevidyr had left, Charyn wondered whether Aevidyr had delayed giving Thealyt D'Moeryn's response to him deliberately or whether Aevidyr had just left the Chateau early on Samedi. *But why would he want to delay it over a Solayi? Then again, are you seeing more than is there?* Charyn had his doubts, but he also knew that too many of his forebears had seen plots when there were none. *But Father didn't see the most obvious one of all. Your problem is that too much is obvious.*

While he waited for Wyllum, Charyn returned to reading petitions and replies. He was more than thankful to stop doing that, although he'd have to finish them later, when Wyllum arrived just after the chimes rang the ten glasses of noon.

"Minister Alucar says he doesn't need me anymore. All the duplicate tariff lists are done, sir."

"That's excellent. I need to dictate a letter to you. Once it's completed, sealed, and sent, we'll be heading down to the archives on the lower level. You've seen them, haven't you?"

"Norstan showed me where they were, but we barely looked into them."

"This time, you're going to get much better acquainted with them." *And so am I.*

"Have you looked into them often, sir?"

"I spent quite a bit of time perusing them last autumn. There's more there than most people realize. They can tell you a great deal if you know what to look for. Now . . . get your pen and inkwell. This letter will be to Rikkard D'Niasaen, regional governor of Telaryn."

"He's accepted the post, sir?"

"He has, and I'm hopeful that he'll be far better than his predecessor." But then, that was a rather low bar, given how much Voralch had stolen from the old palace and the regional accounts.

Drafting and redrafting the letter took longer than Charyn had anticipated, and it was almost two quints past the first glass of the afternoon when Charyn and Wyllum left the study.

Charyn turned to Sturdyn. "Wyllum and I will be searching for some records in the archives this afternoon, and we're not to be disturbed unless the matter is absolutely urgent."

"Yes, Your Grace."

"I suspect it will take much of the afternoon."

Less than half a quint later, Charyn unlocked the door to the archives. From his previous searches of the archives, the ones dealing with the early history of Solidar in the times of the first Rex Regis, Charyn had a general idea of which parts of the long storeroom held what, separated as they were by ministry, but not anything close to what file chest held exactly what, since each minister had apparently had a slightly different way of filing papers no longer deemed immediately relevant.

"We're looking for records from the Finance Ministry, not really old ones, but those going back eight to ten years, particularly papers dealing with adjustments to the tariffs of High Holders. You're to start at that end and look into each chest. Don't change the order of papers, but look at the dates. If the dates are well before 390 A.L., just close the chest and move on. If any of the dates are from 390 A.L. or later pull that chest out and then move on to the next chest."

"Yes, sir."

Charyn moved to the other end of the row, where he opened the first file chest. Dust puffed up in a cloud. He sneezed several times before he could begin to see the papers stacked inside. Then he leafed through them, discovering that the dates varied, from roughly 229 A.L. to 238 A.L. He was tempted to read more closely, to see if he could find any references to Pyetryl D'Ecrivain, but decided anything like that could wait, especially given the number of file chests.

The next chest also opened with a cloud of dust, although there was no dust on top of the chests, suggesting that Norstan had someone dusting the outsides of the chests, but not what was within, and that was the way it should be. The dates were ten years earlier than those in the first chest.

Almost a glass passed before Wyllum called out, "Your Grace . . . this chest has papers in it from 388 A.L."

"I'll be right there." Charyn finished a quick look at papers dating from around 267 A.L., then closed that chest and moved to where Wyllum stood.

"This chest, sir."

"Good. You keep looking. There should be at least one other chest with records near those dates. I'm going to see if there are any of the records or papers I need in this chest."

"Yes, sir."

Charyn began to look through the records carefully, a sheet at a time. He half-hoped that Aevidyr had slipped the tariff records for the "exempted" properties into the archival files, rather than destroying them, but doubted that was the case, which was why he'd likely need to also go through the more recent records from the Ministry of Administration.

Slowly, he plowed through the documents, pulling out several that held Salucar's name and dealt with reassessments of older properties, but found nothing of direct use, not exactly a surprise since papers with dates of 397 A.L. and a few years later were more likely to show such evidence.

Another quint passed before Wyllum found a chest of records for the year 394 A.L. The first thing Charyn noticed was that there was less dust in that chest. Part of that might have been because the records placed there had to be less than ten years old, and possibly might only have been shifted to the archives in the last few years. The second thing he noticed was that the papers were precisely in date order. *Meaning that their placement in the archives dated from when the very orderly Alucar became Finance Minister.*

While there was absolutely nothing in that chest bearing on

any of the individuals with properties illegally "exempted" from tariffs or for properties owned by Aevidyr, Charyn did remove a number of documents for his use.

"Might I ask what we're looking for, Your Grace?"

"You know you had to copy tariff records so that the clerks could go out and check to see if all the factorages were on the tariff rolls? Well, Minister Alucar has a similar effort ongoing with High Holders. There's a possibility that some of them aren't paying tariffs on certain properties. It's not likely that there will be records that got overlooked here, but it is possible, and those are what I'm looking for." *Among other things.* "Some of those properties may have once been owned by someone else and then never recorded when they changed hands, but the reduction in tariffs owed by the previous owner might be." Charyn knew those records would also exist in the records of the regional governors—except for the lands in Bovaria, since all of those records were in the Chateau—but he doubted he had the time to have those searched out, or if the regional governors in Tilbor and Antiago, Antiago especially, would be inclined to find them.

Over the next glass, Charyn and Wyllum found two more chests, and the results were the same . . . and Charyn added more documents to his short stack. There was also not a single scrap of paper in the archives covering the last fifteen years dealing with any properties belonging to Ghaermyn, Laastyn, or Aevidyr. That meant the only records were the incomplete ones in Alucar's current files.

"Now we need to find some records from the Administration section . . ."

What Charyn really wanted there wasn't so much records but records containing Aevidyr's signature, and those would likely be on reports, rather than letters, since the copies of outgoing letters wouldn't be signed, but only sealed, with the notation that the original was signed.

In less than a glass, Charyn had what he hoped would be

sufficient . . . if he could work out the details . . . and obtain some additional information from Alucar.

By the time the two trudged back up to the study, brushing dust off their garments, and with Charyn still occasionally sneezing, it was past fifth glass.

As he and Wyllum neared the study, Bhayrn appeared.

"Sturdyn said you were in the archives. Whatever for?"

"Trying to track down . . ." Charyn paused, then said, ". . . some missing lands, and some that aren't paying tariffs."

"Did you have any luck in the dust and dirt?" Bhayrn offered an amused smile.

"Some . . . but not enough." Charyn looked down at the stack of papers that Wyllum held. "Not yet." He sneezed. He could have held it, but he didn't want to say more. "I think I need to wash up a bit so I don't keep sneezing. We can talk later." He fumbled out a cloth and covered his nose and mouth for a moment. "You can go, Wyllum. Just leave those on the desk."

"Yes, sir."

"I'll leave you to clean up," said Bhayrn. "I won't be here for dinner."

"Laamyst or Gherard?"

"Neither. Amascarl. We've been out of touch. That's something I need to remedy." Bhayrn smiled again, warmly, then turned and walked toward the grand staircase.

Charyn managed to keep a pleasant expression on his face, even as he wondered what—or who—had changed Bhayrn's apparent attitude over the past few days. *And why now?* As he began to walk toward his apartments to clean up before dinner, he was afraid that he knew the answer to the last question.

59

~~~~~

The first thing Charyn did upon reaching his study on Mardi, after greeting Moencriff and Wyllum, was to read the newssheets, beginning with *Veritum*.

Late on Vendrei, *Veritum* discovered that in addition to proclaiming martial law and bringing in army units to stop the violence and burning of manufactorages, Rex Charyn had also proclaimed in law a requirement that all large factorages and manufactorages pay workers two coppers a day for no more than nine glasses of work. The law took effect yesterday, on nine Feuillyt, much to the consternation of the Factors' Council of Solidar . . .

Although copies of the law were sent to the Factors' Council and the High Council it took the Rex sending copies to the newssheets for this to become public knowledge. The Rex did this. He might have done more, but the Factors' Council did nothing . . .

The story in *Tableta* surprised Charyn, since it was as close to being fair to him as he'd ever read, and he wondered just how vicious the next one would be for the newssheet to compensate.

The Rex's failure to circulate widely his proclamation of a two-copper workday, and his belated dispatch to the newssheets, was only exceeded in lack of competence by the efforts of the Factors' Council to ignore totally the new law, even though they were notified immediately. Because the Rex issued the law on such short notice, factors elsewhere in Solidar will have to pay back wages once the word of the law reaches them . . .

At least, and at last, our beloved Rex has shown some faint interest in bettering the lot of the hardworking men of Solidar . . . we are not holding our breath until the next time he does . . . nor do we doubt that this was the most he dared do, given the violent opposition of not only much of the Factors' Council, but also that of some of the High Council . . .

They did get that right, if not for the reasons they think. He glanced down the newssheet to another story, one about the True Believers protesting in front of the Anomen D'Rex, and his eyes centered on a few lines:

. . . the protestors claim that the Rex's law is a step in the right direction, but that the Rex must do more than merely pass a law and replace his own corrupt chorister . . . protestors claimed that they did not protest Chorister Faheel, but that they surrounded the Anomen D'Rex . . . said they will keep showing up at the anomen until the Rex comes to meet with them . . . and that if he does not . . . then he does not deserve to be Rex . . . An army company rode up and the True Believers all fled before the troopers could get close enough to apprehend any of them.

For a time, Charyn considered the article, wondering if he'd missed something entirely. Obviously, the True Believers had timed their protest early enough that the army troopers were not out in force.

Finally, he set down the newssheet.

"*Veritum* was mostly fair, wasn't it?" asked Wyllum.

"They were right. I should have sent copies to both newsletters when the others went out. I should have known that Eshmael would sit on the two-copper wage law." Charyn shook his head. Times had changed and were continuing to do so, as evidenced by his having even to consider the news-sheets or that factors would try to ignore a proclaimed law. "But we did what we could." He picked up the newssheet again.

He almost missed the story in the bottom left-hand corner.

> Some months ago, a Factor Suyrien D'Chaeryll purchased the ironworks south of L'Excelsis, as well as the rifle-works within the ironworks. It has come to our attention that until a year ago, no one had ever heard of Suyrien D'Chaeryll, until he purchased a membership in the Commodity Exchange with a considerable stock of golds. It has also come to our attention that the D'Chaeryll lands were held by one Charyn D'Lorien. Presumably, that would suggest that our beloved Rex purchased ironworks for some purpose of his own that he does not wish known . . .

"Frig . . ." Charyn murmured as he set down the news-sheet.

"I saw the story about the ironworks, sir. I didn't tell any-one." Wyllum's voice was hesitant. "No one. Not a soul."

"I know. I know who did, and it wasn't you." The only real question was whether Bhayrn or one of Laastyn's sons had been the ones to tell the newssheet. Charyn took a deep breath. "Now we need to get back to the dull routine of making changes to several of Sanafryt's replies to petitions."

A glass or so later, when Charyn had finished dictating his changes and Wyllum was busy rewriting several of the re-sponses, Charyn turned his attention back to the documents he'd pulled from the archives. He didn't get very far in try-ing to assemble them into something that would work for his purposes before an army courier delivered another report from Marshal Vaelln, one which Charyn read immediately.

The latest developments were much like the last. The shipyard in Tilbor had launched another ship, this one a first-rate ship of the line, one that would be battle-ready by the end of Feuillyt. Three Jariolan rated warships had been destroyed off the Jariolan coast with no Solidaran vessels lost, but another Solidaran merchanter had been lost to Jariolan privateers in the waters off Otelyrn.

Progress ... but not enough to satisfy Chaeltar and the factors ... But then, it sometimes seemed like nothing was enough to satisfy some of them.

Vaelln also reported that while the army patrols had stopped a number of men breaking the curfew, there had only been one incident involving actual lawbreakers. In that instance, they had been forced to shoot, wounding two men and killing two others. The four had been found to carry several crude gunpowder bombs and jugs of oil.

Which means some of the workers are still angry and unsatisfied or that someone wanted to use the anger against factors as a cover for something else.

He placed that report with the others and turned to Wyllum. "When you're finished with those letters, and we've signed and sealed them, you can return them to Minister Sanafryt. After that, if you'd go tell Minister Alucar that I'd like to see him, and then make yourself useful to Lady Chelia. Oh ... one more thing. Would you tell Guard Captain Maertyl or Undercaptain Faelln that I need to talk to Chorister Faheel this afternoon."

"Yes, Your Grace."

Two quints later, Wyllum departed, and Charyn sat behind the desk, the fingers of his left hand fingering the two-shot pistol in its concealed holster, still thinking about how all the pieces didn't quite fit together ... unless ... *But why ... why would he ... how could he think ... and how could any High Holder believe ...*

Charyn shook his head.

Shortly thereafter, Alucar entered the study.

"Have you found out any more about Laastyn's timberlands near Asseroiles ... and in Tilbor?"

Alucar inclined his head. "By careful reading of the records, I did find that there is a hunting lodge near Asseroiles, set on five hundred hectares, but there is no current mention of the timberlands. I did discover the previous owner, the grandsire of the present High Holder Paellyt. Working backwards from the tariffs Paellyt paid, Laastyn has to own close to four thousand hectares. Paellyt did report the sale to Laastyn and there is a deed for forty-five hundred hectares. But the only reason those are in the records was because Paellyt paid fewer tariffs, and I had sent an inquiry. He sent copies of the bill of sale and the deed he delivered to Laastyn. This was just after I became Finance Minister, and I should have then cross-checked against Laastyn, but I failed to do so. Part of that was because so many papers had accumulated in the year that there was no Finance Minister, and part because the ministry was short two clerks because Aevidyr felt that the positions should be filled by the next minister. As a result," Alucar's voice turned ironic, "the four thousand hectares of timberlands aren't on the tariff records, and I'm as much at fault as anyone."

"And the Talyon estate?"

"There is no record of it in the tariff rolls. And so far, I cannot find any documentation of what might be a corresponding reduction in tariffs of another High Holder, or substantial small holder."

"Perhaps you should prepare a notice of immediate reassessment for those two properties . . . and since we don't know the exact size of the Talyon estate, estimate it at, say, five thousand hectares. He can challenge that, can't he?"

"With a deed of sale, certainly. That would show us the land size and the seller."

"Prepare it, but don't send it . . . Oh . . . and add in another ten thousand hectares in Tilbor."

"I can't do that. We don't even know where it is."

"Then draft a request that he forward the information on the property, which you understand to be well in excess of two thousand hectares, so that it may be properly assessed for tariff purposes. Once you have the drafts, I'd like to see them."

"Yes, sir."

After Alucar left the study, Charyn sent for Sanafryt.

Sanafryt arrived promptly. "Thank you, Your Grace, for addressing those petitions and signing and sealing them."

"I signed. Wyllum sealed. Signing is difficult enough at the moment. I have another question of law . . ."

"Yes, Your Grace?"

"Is there any criminal penalty for failure by a property owner to record property requiring payment of tariffs?"

Sanafryt looked scandalized. "Who would dare to do that?"

"About one in ten factors, for one thing, and several High Holders."

"But that's the responsibility of the Finance Minister. How could that happen?"

"He can't collect tariffs if the property isn't recorded. And there are several ways I know of that it can happen. If a small family factorage grows and doesn't report it . . . or if someone gathers together small plots of land . . ." Charyn offered a sardonic smile. "I'd be surprised if you couldn't think of some."

"It must have happened . . ." Sanafryt's forehead creased into a frown. Then he nodded. "You're right, Your Grace. There is a penalty for knowingly defrauding the Rex. Knowledgeably defrauding the Rex in amounts in excess of one hundred golds is considered a high crime, one that can be punishable by death, if the amount is grievous enough." Sanafryt barked a laugh. "That is why anyone who is discovered to underpay tariffs immediately repays the deficit while proclaiming loudly that it was unintentional and some sort of mistake. And since, in such cases, it is difficult to prove that the lack was intentional or permanent defrauding, the most that has ever happened, so far as I am aware, is a repayment of back tariffs with a penalty of at least one part in ten and where the deficit has been egregious, a doubling of the tariff for the current and previous year. I'm not aware of anyone egregiously underpaying tariffs for more than two years, although Minister Alucar might know of such an instance."

"Would not paying a tariff for a number of years be considered egregious?"

"That would depend on the case. If a High Holder failed to pay tariffs on a few hundred hectares out of ten thousand, and it was an out-of-the-way parcel with no records . . . I don't think any justicer would consider that egregious even if the tariffs hadn't been paid in a decade. They would have to pay the back tariffs and the one-in-ten penalty. On a substantial parcel . . . that would likely be another matter." Sanafryt frowned again. "Might I ask why you're interested?"

"Because we've discovered quite a number of factors that should have paid tariffs for some time, and possibly even some High Holders."

"If they can prove lack of knowledge, you can still insist on the back tariffs, and penalties, which will likely ruin most factors, but it would be difficult to prove egregious intent. For a High Holder with far-flung holdings, intent might be difficult to prove as well."

Charyn nodded. He wasn't exactly surprised. "Thank you. Minister Alucar thought that the law ran along those lines, but felt you would know the particulars." That wasn't quite true, but Charyn didn't think it conflicted with what Alucar had said. "If you have further thoughts on that, please let me know."

When Sanafryt left, Charyn returned to studying and organizing the papers he'd taken from the archives, and he was still pondering how best to use them when a courier delivered a missive from Factor Eshmael.

Even before he opened it, Charyn had a general idea of the contents, but he read it word for word anyway.

Rex Charyn—
As a member of the Factors' Council of Solidar I
would like to express my concern about your acts
in: (1) promulgating a law with an effective date less
than a week after the date of promulgation and (2)
compounding the difficulty by sending a copy of a legal
proclamation to the newssheets. These acts have made
it a practical impossibility for factors any distance from
L'Excelsis to comply in a timely fashion . . .

There was more, but all of that was either rhetoric or an elaboration on the difficulties, much of it almost fanciful, or so it seemed to Charyn.

As soon as Wyllum returned, Charyn dictated a reply to Eshmael, then had the scrivener revise it twice more before he was satisfied. Then he read over his reply again.

Factor Eshmael—
As the text of the daily-wage law states, the effective date
is either the ninth of Feuillyt in the year 405 A.L., or the
first Lundi of the week after the law is published by the
Rex or by appropriate local authority acting for the Rex,
but on no account later than the twenty-third of Feuillyt.
That means, in simple terms, that the ninth of Feuillyt
applies to factorages and manufactorages in and around
L'Excelsis, and that for most of the rest of Solidar, the
effective date will either be the sixteenth or the twenty-
third. It would appear that your decision not to circulate
the provisions to the factors of L'Excelsis merely added
to the difficulties of factors in L'Excelsis.
    The reason for the effective date was to assist in
quelling the unrest of workers who felt that the Factors'

*Council had failed to recognize their inability to sustain
life on a lower daily wage. This was part of an overall
plan to provide support for both factors and workers,
since the Factors' Council has proved unable to deal
with that unrest through the use of its own resources
and the Rex judged that to apply the force of the army
without some corresponding benefit to the workers
would further exacerbate the violence. Throughout
this difficult period, I repeatedly requested that, if
the joint council did not like my plan, the councilors
should propose another. In over a month, there were
no constructive proposals, only objections to the regial
proposal. Thus, as the violence continued to escalate, I
was required to act.*

*As the head of government in Solidar, my
responsibility is not just to the factors, nor to just the
High Holders, nor to just the crafters, nor to just the
working man, but to work out something that is practical
for all. This means it will be ideal for no group, but is an
attempt to address the welfare of all.*

*I trust you understand this, and I look forward
to further discussing the matter at the next Council
meeting. As always, I remain open to practical and
constructive proposals.*

Then Charyn signed the letter and had Wyllum seal it. He
also had Wyllum make three copies and send one to Hisario
and one to Fhaedyrk, with the remaining copy for Charyn
himself.

Eshmael wouldn't like it, but if he persisted in an intemp-
erate way, perhaps his correspondence might find its way
to *Tableta*. The newssheet might even publish it.

*Except that would really infuriate all the factors, and
that's the last thing you need to do at the moment, especially since some of them will be infuriated by your buying
the ironworks secretly.*

Charyn smiled. At least, sending Eshmael's letter to *Tableta* was an amusing thought, even if he wasn't about to do it. *Not yet, anyway.*

Chorister Faheel arrived just after the first glass of the afternoon, while Wyllum was helping Chelia.

"Your Grace, I thought you might not have wanted to meet with me. Thank you for seeing me."

Charyn was momentarily taken aback. "I summoned you."

"Your Grace, I sent a message to you on Solayi evening."

"You did?"

"Yes, sir. It was because of the True Believers. They gathered around the anomen that evening. They didn't try to enter the anomen, though, and they didn't start chanting until after services were over."

"What were they chanting?"

"'Show us the Rex,' time after time. Then one of them came up to the anomen door and said that they needed to speak to the Rex. I told them that you weren't in the anomen and that the last two times you had been near True Believers you'd been shot at one time and wounded another. Whoever it was said that they didn't do it, and they needed to speak to you."

"Why didn't they come to the Chateau and ask to meet me?"

"They're afraid that they'll be imprisoned or executed for something they didn't do. Then the army came, and they all ran."

"How did you send the message?"

"I walked here and came up to the front entry and handed the message to the guard. I told him it was a message from your chorister at the Anomen D'Rex."

"When was that?"

"It was well after seventh glass on Solayi evening. I didn't want to wait, but it took me a little while to make sure the anomen was closed up, and then I had to go to my quarters and write it up. I didn't expect to get an immediate answer, not at that late a glass, but I didn't want to put it off."

"I appreciate that." Charyn fingered the hilt of the miniature letter opener that Howal had imaged for him. "I'll have to see what happened to that, but I'm glad you're here. You've answered some of my questions. I have a few more. Does High Holder Ghaermyn attend services at the Anomen D'Rex?"

"I wouldn't know, Your Grace. His name isn't in the anomen records."

"What about Gherard D'Ghaermyn?"

"That name doesn't sound familiar, sir, but I'd have to check."

"Laastyn D'Alte or Laamyst D'Laastyn?"

"No, sir."

"What about Factor Eshmael or Factor Noerbyn?"

"I believe Factor Noerbyn is a congregant, Your Grace."

Charyn frowned. Who else? Then he recalled what Alucar had said. "Isn't Minister Aevidyr a congregant?"

"He is, sir. He's the only person in the Chateau I knew before you summoned me the first time."

"How did you come to know him?"

"Chorister Saerlet introduced me to him when I first came here two years ago. He and the minister were friends."

Charyn barely managed to nod. "I suppose that's not surprising. Aevidyr has been here quite some time. Have you ever talked to him?"

"Only a few words in passing, Your Grace. He's very polite, but very reserved, at least with me. From what I saw, he was much less so with Chorister Saerlet, but then they were much closer in age."

"Is there anything else I should know about the True Believers?"

"No, sir . . . well, there is one thing. The group that was there this last Solayi was very well-behaved. Their chants were even musical and they sang a hymn about Rholan. I didn't get all the words. But it was something like 'Rholan's words of inspiration, ringing from the halls of time, are for us the proclamation, with a meaning all sublime.' I think that was it. They really did not seem violent."

"They were before."

"I know, sir, but this group wasn't."

"Nothing else?"

"Nothing that I can recall, Your Grace."

"Thank you for coming, and I apologize for whatever delayed your message."

"You've been through a great deal, Your Grace. I imagine those around you are . . . rather protective."

"That may well be." Charyn did stand to dismiss the young chorister.

After the study door closed behind Faheel, Charyn finally shook his head. Aevidyr and Saerlet had been close, yet neither Saerlet nor Aevidyr had ever mentioned that, although Saerlet had said he had family in Antiago—where Aevidyr had been the regional minister of administration. And Saerlet had kept pressing for Charyn to attend services . . . and then, after the attack at the anomen, Saerlet had fled . . . most likely for his life.

Would there be a white gown and hood in Aevidyr's house? *Hardly, he's too cunning for anything that obvious.*

But perhaps he could track down what happened to Faheel's message . . . or find out if there had even been a message, although he was inclined to believe that there had been one.

"Moencriff, could you send word that I need a moment with either Guard Captain Maertyl or Undercaptain Faelln?"

"Yes, sir."

While Charyn was waiting, he thought about something else Faheel had said, about the reserved deportment of that group of True Believers. It was almost as if there were two separate groups, or perhaps a handful of True Believers that were more than just True Believers . . . with a very different agenda.

Less than a quint later, Faelln appeared. "Yes, Your Grace?"

"Chorister Faheel was just here. He told me, and I'm inclined to believe it, that he hand-carried a letter message here to the Chateau on Solayi evening sometime after seventh glass, possibly closer to eighth glass. For some reason, if there was a message, I never received it. I know your guards are very conscientious, but something might have happened. Or perhaps there was no message. Either way, I need to know."

Faelln nodded. "Given that it was Chorister Faheel, we both need to know."

"Thank you."

Faelln returned in less than half a quint.

"What did you find out?"

"The guard did take a message from a young man, with blond hair and wearing a chorister's vestments. He had just logged it in when Lord Bhayrn appeared and insisted on taking it up to you. The duty guard was thoughtful enough to log that as well, and he told Maertyl."

Under those circumstances, Charyn wasn't about to question the guard. "Then Bhayrn must have misplaced it, or forgotten to give it to me." Charyn shook his head. "He can be very forgetful. Could you and Maertyl make sure that messages are delivered directly either to the recipient, or to me—that is, if there's a question—and to no one else?"

"We'll explain it in just that way, sir, if you don't mind."

"You might also tell them that they can say that those are my orders, and that they're not allowed to make exceptions, and that if anyone has any questions, they can come to me."

"Thank you, sir."

"No . . . thank you. I realize it might be uncomfortable at times, but it needs to be this way, at least until a number of matters are resolved." Charyn paused. "That may take several weeks." Charyn had the feeling that, one way or another, matters would come to a head much sooner. He just wished he knew more clearly how to bring them to the end he desired . . . and in the way he desired. Direct action would stop matters, but the costs would be high, possibly too high, especially since he'd been forced to take direct action to deal with the impasse between the former crafters and the factors.

He also needed to hear what Bhayrn had to say.

When Wyllum returned, Charyn dictated a letter to Alastar, asking if he would be free to meet with Charyn early on Meredi afternoon to discuss matters of mutual benefit to Solidar and the Collegium, since a certain lead time would be necessary to implement them.

After that Charyn went back to work, organizing the papers he'd taken from the archives. What he had might work . . . if he couldn't find another way.

At half past fifth glass, he made his way to the family parlor, where he found Bhayrn. "You're not off anywhere tonight?"

"If I do go, it will be later. I'm not sure yet."

"Chorister Faheel came to see me today . . ."

"Faheel? Oh, him."

"He sent me a letter. I had Faelln check on it. Apparently, you were going to deliver it to me. Do you still have it?"

Bhayrn shook his head. "I tore it up. When I saw it was from that chorister and that it dealt with True Believers wanting to meet with you, what else could I do? How could they possibly believe that you'd want to meet with them after what happened? Twice! Not once, but twice. I couldn't believe the chorister had the nerve to put that in writing."

"It would have been nice to know that it happened."

"Charyn," said Bhayrn almost gently, "you too often believe the best in people, even when they've shown twice that they can't be trusted. If you let them, these True Believers will be the death of you. You can't give them a chance to get close to you. I was just trying to protect you."

Charyn paused for a moment before he spoke, so that his words would be right. "Bhayrn, I understand what you're trying to do, but if I don't know what's happening, all the caring in Terahnar won't be enough." And every word of that sentence was true.

"I was just trying to do the right thing."

"I understand. Believe me, I do. If there is a next time, and you're that concerned, you can tell me your thoughts about why I should or shouldn't do something."

"Well . . . for one thing, I don't think you should leave the Chateau for at least another week."

"I appreciate that. I certainly have no plans to do so." *Not yet, anyway.*

"No plans for what?" asked Chelia as she entered the family parlor.

"Taking outings away from the Chateau," replied Charyn. "Not until I'm much better and with great care."

"That sounds very sensible," said Chelia, "but no more talk of unpleasant things at dinner, if you don't mind."

"Excellent idea," said Charyn, since that was more than fine with him, and he needed time to think over what he'd learned over the day and consider if there might be a better way to accomplish the necessary.

60

Although neither his hand nor his leg pained him that much, at least so long as Charyn didn't bump into something with either, he didn't sleep all that well and woke up thinking about his recent conversations with Bhayrn. His brother's explanation for tearing up Faheel's letter verged on the absurd. Yet Bhayrn was capable of the absurd, as Charyn well knew, but he was also self-centered and certainly not stupid. And he had to have known that Charyn would have discovered that the letter was missing. And why was Bhayrn so insistent that Charyn not leave the Chateau for a while? If he wanted Charyn dead, that was almost contrary to such an aim, unless . . .

Unless what? That he's playing for time? Time to do what . . . and more important . . . how? And who is orchestrating it? Aevidyr? Ghaermyn? Laastyn? Bhayrn himself? Or someone else you haven't even thought of?

Charyn's problem was that it could be any or all of them, or, less conceivably, but also possibly, none of them. After eating early and alone and then going to his study, he sat behind the goldenwood table desk, pondering those questions, what he could do to determine who was doing what and who wasn't, and then . . . occasionally looking to the open window and the gray sky beyond.

He was startled out of his contemplative mood by Alucar's arrival.

The Finance Minister walked to the other side of the desk and set two sheets of paper on the polished wooden surface. "Your Grace, here is the proposed notice to send to High Holder Laastyn."

Charyn motioned for Alucar to sit down, then took the documents and began to read them, looking for any possible flaws or concerns. He didn't see any. He handed them back to Alucar. "What about High Holder Ghaermyn?"

"The clerks have not visited his factorages yet. They're farther south on the east side of the river."

"Have one clerk visit them all tomorrow and document how many he has. Then draft a letter of inquiry, asking why he hasn't paid tariffs on the ones that aren't on the rolls."

"Yes, Your Grace. What do you want me to do with the notice to High Holder Laastyn?"

"Send it in the usual manner."

Once Alucar had left, Charyn wondered what Laastyn's reaction would be. To ignore the notice for a time, to reply in a manner that constituted stalling, to have Bhayrn bring up the matter with Charyn, or to pay the back tariffs on the untariffed property and provide the information on the recently acquired timberlands? The reaction, or the lack of it, might reveal something. *And then it might not.*

At that moment, Wyllum hurried in and seated himself at the end of the conference table. "Unless you have something else for me, sir, I thought I'd continue making that copy of your father's biography for the family archive."

"Thank you. I should have done that earlier." *Like more than a few things.*

Wyllum settled himself at the end of the conference table and resumed work on the copy.

Roughly a quint later, Sturdyn announced, "Lord Bhayrn to see you."

"Have him come in."

Bhayrn hurried in and closed the door, but stopped just inside the study. "Is it all right if Laamyst, Gherard, and I use the plaques room this afternoon from a bit after first glass for a while? Likely no longer than to fourth glass. I've asked Mother, and she isn't using it, but said I should ask you to make sure."

"You can use it. I appreciate your asking."

"Thank you." With that Bhayrn was gone, almost as if he didn't want to talk to Charyn.

Charyn wondered about that, since Bhayrn had been much more effusive lately. Was his brother going to revert to being confrontational again?

When Alastar arrived at second glass, Charyn sent Wyllum to see if he could help Chelia with recopying the invitation list to the Year-Turn Ball, something that his mother had asked if Wyllum could do when Charyn did not need him. Then Charyn waited until Alastar was seated, letting Alastar open the conversation.

"Your request to meet was worded in an unusual circumlocution. Matters of mutual benefit?"

"That was one way of putting it. The problem is that there are too many possible conspirators, or combinations of conspirators."

"Oh?"

"I've found out about High Holders who've managed creative ways to avoid paying their full tariffs for almost a decade, but there's no evidence to connect them to those who might have arranged it. Chorister Saerlyt was enriching himself, then fled in what appeared to be terror right after the first shooting. And now, Bhayrn has been most conciliatory and friendly in the past week or so. He's gone very much out of his way, and he's refrained from making statements that would antagonize me. In the past, he's acted in almost the opposite fashion."

"Perhaps the last assassination attempt?"

"Perhaps . . . except the first three or four didn't seem to have much effect." Charyn paused. "What do you know about Minister Aevidyr?"

"Absolutely nothing except that he's been the Minister of Administration for well over ten years and that he's had nothing at all to do with the Collegium. Why?"

"He's managed to acquire a significant amount of property

during that time, in a way that suggests the property was sold to him for a nominal cost in return for various favors, but in a way where the evidence is at best circumstantial and at worse nonexistent. There's also no sign of gifts from wealthy relatives." Charyn wasn't counting the initial "bequest."

"That has been known to happen with high officials without . . . careful supervision."

Charyn did not speak for a time. Since Alastar did not break the silence, Charyn finally did. "Who would gain by having the True Believers blamed for the shootings, or if they'd been successful, my death?"

"Just about anyone well-known who would otherwise be a suspect, as I'm certain you've already determined."

"I fear I'm going to need your help. The problem is that I don't know when because this . . . plot . . . if it's even that . . ."

"Do you trust the Chateau staff?"

"Now . . . far more than anyone else in the Chateau, except my mother and Aloryana, and probably Minister Alucar."

"Why do you trust him?"

"He hasn't enriched himself, and he's never hesitated to tell me what I didn't want to hear. Also, he's very cautious, and he documented every time my father blocked his recommendations for improvements. Also, he has the most to lose if something happens to me."

"Why do you say that?"

"Beyond what I've told you, I have to admit that it's the way I feel." Charyn shrugged. "I know I could be wrong, but if Alucar is scheming he's doing it in a way that has so far benefited me and Solidar and not individual High Holders or factors."

"That's the most effective way to scheme."

"So . . . I should be wary of him as well?"

"As Rex, there's no one you shouldn't be wary of. How

wary depends on the individual." Alastar pursed his lips. "You seem to know all of those who may be involved. Why don't you just act against them? You have the power to do that. Why aren't you?"

"Because I don't know who else might be involved."

"Is that the only reason?"

"No." Charyn paused. "I hate the idea of being arbitrary and acting on what almost seems to be suspicion."

"Even if it means your own death?"

Charyn winced at Alastar's blunt question.

"Even if it means chaos and a Rex under the thumb of the High Holders?" added Alastar. "You want power more broadly distributed, and you're clearly working toward that. You're not there yet, and it will take you years, if not longer. No one else but a Rex can do that. Could your brother? Could the next in line after him? That's High Holder Regial, and he's not even of age yet. He's also from a very traditional lineage, and possibly one not even legitimate, to put it mildly."

"So . . . I've dithered too long, just like my father?"

An almost embarrassed smile appeared on the Maitre's face. "I wouldn't put it quite that way, and he never would have been able to ask a question like that."

"Then I'm about to ask for another favor. I'm going to escort you to the study door, where I'll tell you good-bye and then ask Sturdyn to fetch my brother—immediately. As soon as Sturdyn heads off, and isn't looking at you, I'd like you to return to the study under a concealment and sit over there by the table as a hidden witness."

"What are you hoping for?"

"That he'll lose his temper and reveal something when I really press him."

"And if he doesn't?"

"Then that will tell me something else." *Something much worse, most likely.*

"There's quite a risk to this, you understand?"

"Any greater risk than getting shot again, which is bound to happen if I don't do something?"

Alastar's first response was a sardonic smile. "What if your brother is as clever as you are?"

"Then that will confirm what I suspect."

"I presume you want me to shield you."

"Only if it appears necessary."

"You trust my judgment?"

"If I can't trust you, then I've already effectively lost."

"You do know how to make a point."

Charyn stood. "Shall we?"

Alastar just nodded and rose from the chair.

The two walked to the study door, Charyn slightly in the lead. He opened the door wide and stepped out into the corridor, then turned to the Maitre. "Thank you for coming, Maitre. I appreciate your doing this on short notice."

"The Collegium likes to help where it can, Your Grace."

Charyn turned to Sturdyn, but before he could say anything, the guard spoke. "Your Grace . . . Lord Bhayrn asked if he could bring his friends to see you once Maitre Alastar left."

For an instant, Charyn didn't know what to say. "I need to see Bhayrn by himself first. Immediately. He said he'd be down in the plaques room. His friends can stay there while I talk to him. In fact, they should definitely stay there. So you'd best check with either a guard officer or the lead guard before you ask Bhayrn to join me."

Sturdyn's face turned impassive. "Yes, Your Grace."

"I'll be fine here," said Charyn firmly, stepping back into the study, but not closing the door.

"Yes, sir."

Alastar took a step toward the grand stair, then said to Sturdyn, "Go ahead. You're younger and faster."

"Thank you, Maitre."

Charyn noticed that Sturdyn did not look back. He smiled

wryly, then waited until Sturdyn neared the grand staircase. By then Alastar had vanished.

"I'm behind you," the unseen Maitre declared.

Charyn closed the study door.

"This could prove interesting," murmured Alastar.

"Too interesting." Charyn settled himself behind the desk, but slightly back, so that he could move easily if necessary.

Almost a quint passed before Maertyl announced, "Lord Bhayrn," and stepped inside with Bhayrn. "Would you like me to stay, sir?" The words were not a question.

"I'd appreciate it, Guard Captain, if you'd wait outside for a bit. I need a brotherly talk with Bhayrn."

"Are you sure, sir?"

"I'll be fine," said Charyn. "But the Chateau might have visitors."

"Undercaptain Faelln is seeing to that, sir."

"Thank you."

As soon as the study door closed, Bhayrn glanced at the open window, then took three steps toward Charyn and stopped. "What the frig are you doing, Charyn? Have you gone out of your mind? I'm your brother. I've been looking out for you when you haven't been looking out for yourself."

"I've noticed the way you've been looking out for me. Always inquiring as to the way I rode to Imagisle . . . being surprised, almost disappointed, when I did something different from what you thought I'd do."

"I was just concerned." Bhayrn offered a sneer. "Not that you ever cared."

"I cared a great deal. I wanted you to be a successful High Holder. I even picked out the very best of the regial lands for you. You wouldn't even make more than a token effort at learning enough to handle a holding—and then you got angry about it and stomped off to Rivages like a spoiled brat."

"And I'm supposed to be grateful for the crumbs you dole out?"

"One of the best holdings in Solidar is more than crumbs."

"You don't understand. You don't understand *anything*. You never will."

"You mean how I don't understand how you've been played by your so-called friends, who've been playing you, even as they've been played by someone else."

For just an instant, a hint of puzzlement crossed Bhayrn's face. "You're the one being played. You're being played by the Collegium and the High Holders, and you don't even see it."

Charyn laughed. "You have a strange definition of being played. You're the one who'd end up being played by Laastyn and Ghaermyn. You're already being played, with all of them flattering your ego and telling you how they need a more traditional Rex and how unfortunate it is that your foolish older brother is Rex. Do you really think they even give a copper about you? All they want is an obedient Rex who won't question them, one who won't look into how they're defrauding the Rex on their tariffs or how they've bought off most of the justicers in Solidar, or how they've pushed younger sons into regional governorships so those younger sons can loot the treasury. Or even how they likely arranged for Elthyrd's beating so that the most intransigent factor would succeed him on the Council. You're blind to that, but then, you're blind to most things you don't want to see."

"Look who's talking."

"Did you really think that I'd buy that phony story about why you tore up Chorister Faheel's letter? Concern about me? Hardly. The concern was that I just might have gone over to the anomen and realized that your friends had created their own group of True Believers, with rifles. And if you became Rex, the way you all schemed, you'd have used the army against those True Believers and claimed everything was their fault. Wasn't that the reason for the white belts? Another touch to make sure Maertyl knew it had been the True Believers all along." Charyn well knew that the

True Believers were anything but blameless, but the moment wasn't right for rhetorical fairness.

For a moment, Bhayrn gaped, as if he knew nothing about the belts, then immediately retorted, "They killed people, and they shot at you, and you don't see that?"

"What I see is that Ghaermyn and Laastyn and a few others infiltrated the movement to use it to get rid of me and replace me with a puppet Rex easily manipulated by flattery. You've been used, Bhayrn, and you're too full of yourself and too stupid to see it. Everything's always someone else's fault. It's never your fault. Even Aloryana worried about that, and Mother's been worried about your self-centered willfulness for years."

"Keep them out of it."

"Why? They're part of the family. They see the same things I do. But you never listen to anyone who tells you what you don't want to hear. You just get mad, or you smile and pretend to listen. I don't know which is worse. So I'll make it very simple. You're not going to be Rex . . . ever. In fact, once everything comes out about your friends . . ."

"I may not be Rex, but neither will you!"

Bhayrn only had the pistol half out when Charyn shot him full in the chest. His mouth opened. "Your hand . . ."

"I saw more than you ever thought. You saw less. I practiced left-handed as well." Charyn shot him a second time, just as the study door opened.

Maertyl gaped for a moment as he saw Bhayrn sprawled face-first on the carpet, the unfired pistol not that far from his outstretched hand. "Are you all right, Your Grace?"

"I'm fine . . . except . . ." *for being betrayed by my own brother.* "You'd best lock up Bhayrn's friends. If they so much as raise a hand, shoot them."

"They're already disarmed, Your Grace."

"Good. Leave some guards here, but go restrain Minister Aevidyr. He's not to leave the Chateau."

"Yes, sir."

Charyn turned to the corner. "Maitre."

Alastar appeared.

A grim smile crossed Maertyl's face. "You were protected."

"I didn't need to shield him, Guard Captain," said Alastar. "He took care of the problem himself."

"You'd better go, Maertyl. I wouldn't be surprised if there isn't a squad of brownshirts wearing white hoods outside already."

"We sealed the doors when Sturdyn came down. They'll hold against cannon, and the company Marshal Vaelln had standing by is in place in and around the Chateau."

"Excellent. Once everything's calm . . . we'll need to take care of . . . Bhayrn."

"Yes, sir. We'll deal with it."

Once Maertyl had left the study, Alastar stood and walked over to the desk. "You could have let him shoot at you."

"No," replied Charyn sadly. "I couldn't. If anyone asks, I'll say I reacted without thinking. That will be a lie. The last time a younger son who plotted rebellion was allowed to live, thousands died. You were right." His smile was lopsided. "I have to be seen as both fair and cold. You need to stay around for my meeting with Aevidyr. But now . . . I need to see Mother."

Charyn stood slowly, setting the pistol on the desk. He'd almost forgotten he still held it.

"It might be best if I accompanied you at least to her door," suggested Alastar.

"You're right. Thank you."

Sturdyn fell in behind the two men as Charyn walked to the door of Chelia's sitting room.

Charyn knocked, then opened the door, and stepped inside.

Chelia stood, looking out the window. Charyn's eyes followed hers. Several bodies, clad in white gowns and hoods, lay sprawled on the drive and on the garden paths beyond.

Chelia's face was pale as her cold blue eyes met his.

"Bhayrn tried to shoot me. He never realized that I'd practiced left-handed. I'm sorry. I truly am." *Not so much about Bhayrn, but for you.* And that was something he really couldn't say. Not at the moment, perhaps not ever.

"You didn't have any choice. Not after what happened with your uncle Ryentar."

"I tried to show him . . ." *But not well enough.*

"Charyn . . . I understand. More than you may ever know."

Charyn did understand that.

"There will be no memorial service. I don't ever want to talk about it again. Ever."

Charyn wanted to say more, so much more, except . . . what was there to say? He'd tried. They'd all tried. Even Aloryana had tried . . . yet Bhayrn had refused to go see her or return her letters.

"Just go." Her voice softened a trace. "You have things to do. Do them."

Charyn did have more to say, but now was not the time. "Take care of yourself. We will talk later."

"I'll be here."

"Thank you."

"Charyn . . . you need to go."

Charyn nodded, then turned. Alastar was waiting outside, as was Sturdyn.

"We need to find Maertyl."

"He's in the main entry, sir," declared Sturdyn.

The three headed down the grand staircase. Charyn glanced toward the bottom, but there were no guards posted right at the base, although Maertyl stood several yards away, clearly waiting for them. He took a deep breath and looked to one side and then the other. When he reached the main floor he moved quickly away from the grand staircase and stopped just short of the guard captain. "Is everything under control?"

"Yes, sir. The army companies are in position and they killed or captured all the True Believers. There weren't that many." Maertyl's smile was cold as he added, "Minister Aevidyr is most displeased."

"He's not to go anywhere. Are Laamyst and Gherard still in the plaques room?"

"Yes, Your Grace. They were not cooperative. We had to . . . restrain them."

"They're tied up?"

"They are."

"Good. We need to see what they brought with them."

"We checked them for weapons. Except for belt knives, they weren't carrying any."

"I'm looking for something else." Charyn nodded in the direction of the plaques room.

Sturdyn led the way, followed by Charyn and Alastar.

Once inside the plaques room, Charyn surveyed it quickly. Laamyst and Gherard were bound hand and foot and tied to straight-backed plaques chairs. Two guards stood watching them. Interestingly enough, two of the plaques room windows were open. Charyn looked at them, wondering why, then abruptly nodded. Bhayrn had looked at the open window in the study.

"We didn't do anything, Your Grace," insisted Laamyst.

Gherard was silent, his eyes coldly surveying Charyn, Alastar, and Maertyl.

"No . . . I'm sure you didn't." After a pause, Charyn added, "But that was just because you didn't have the chance." He turned to Dhuncan. "What did they have with them?"

"Just what they wore, sir, and some cloaks. The cloaks are on the plaques table."

Charyn walked over to the table, noticing that there were three cloaks laid out side by side, seemingly identical. He frowned as he picked up the top one, which seemed unusually heavy, more like a winter cloak. Then he studied the lining. On one side the stitching of the lining looked loose. He turned to Sturdyn. "I can't do this easily one-handed. Cut that inside stitching a bit." He handed the cloak over, then pointed.

Although the guard frowned, he took his belt knife and cut several stitches. Then, with a pull on the threads, that side of the lining of the cloak unraveled, revealing something very white within.

Sturdyn's mouth opened.

Charyn nodded. "I think we'll find white gowns and hoods inside all three cloaks, but we won't open the other two until Marshal Vaelln arrives."

"How much of this did you know?" asked Alastar.

Maertyl leaned forward.

"Not enough. But I did know that someone wanted to pin my death on the True Believers. What I couldn't figure out was how they planned that after I decided to stay put, especially since Bhayrn was the one insisting that I not leave the Chateau because the True Believers were determined to kill me—even though I'd taken steps to address their concerns. Then, when Chorister Faheel told me about the True Believers last Solayi at the Anomen D'Rex, and I found out that Bhayrn had torn up the note, claiming that he'd done it to protect me, I started thinking along a different line, asking why he didn't want me near the True Believers. Then he was tense and trying not to show it earlier today when he asked me if he, Gherard, and Laamyst could use the plaques room this afternoon because Lady Chelia hadn't given him permission but told him to ask me. Why did Bhayrn want his friends in the Chateau when he was always trying to leave the Chateau?"

Charyn turned to Alastar. "I felt it wouldn't be long before another attempt would be made. I'd originally thought it would likely be on Solayi, having something to do with Aloryana, because Bhayrn had talked about having Aloryana come here then. But he hasn't written her or seen her in months, as you pointed out. That was what I'd thought we were going to talk about this afternoon, but when Bhayrn asked me about the plaques room, I got uneasy . . . and more uneasy . . . and I decided to confront him."

"So he thought you'd discovered the details of the plot when you had your guards bring him in?" asked Alastar.

"I don't see what else it could have been. I was just trying to get him off-balance to see what he'd reveal." That wasn't totally true, but close enough.

"Did you know he was armed?"

"I thought he might be, simply because he has access to his own pistols and rifles. There was also the possibility that he could have armed Laamyst and Gherard, but I honestly didn't think about that until afterwards."

A guard hurried up—Laanart, Charyn realized after a moment—and said, "Marshal Vaelln's just arrived."

"We'll meet him in the welcoming parlor." Charyn turned.

Maertyl and Alastar followed, with Sturdyn bringing up the rear.

The four reached the parlor only a few moments before Vaelln entered.

"Your Grace, I'm happy to see you healthy, or at least more healthy."

"I'm happy about that as well," replied Charyn dryly, his voice getting warmer as he went on. "I very much appreciate the rapid and effective efforts of your troopers."

"They had surprisingly little trouble."

"That's because the attackers were meant to fail. They didn't know that. They were likely ordered to attack and then withdraw. If there are any survivors, see if you can confirm that."

Vaelln looked at Charyn. "Why do you think they were supposed to fail? I'd prefer not to guess, Your Grace. What do you know that I don't?"

"They were a distraction and a cover for what was going to happen in the Chateau. Under some pretext, Bhayrn would have lured me down to the plaques room, either to play a few hands of whist, since they didn't have a fourth . . . something. Then he would have shot me. The shots were the signal for the false True Believers."

"Inside the Chateau?"

Charyn smiled. "Just before Bhayrn tried to shoot me, he looked to see if my study window was open. Two of the windows in the plaques room were open. Both sets of windows are on the back side of the Chateau. Then, after Bhayrn shot me, the three of them would have donned the white gowns and hoods and run through the lower part of the Chateau before quickly discarding the whites. Then the True Believers would have been blamed. Instead, when I shot Bhayrn first, I inadvertently signaled for the attack."

Vaelln shook his head. "Was anyone else in your study?"

"I was," said Alastar. "Rex Charyn asked me to witness the meeting while I was concealed. I was sitting beside the conference table when Bhayrn pulled out his pistol and tried to shoot the Rex."

Vaelln looked pointedly at Charyn's half-bound and splinted right hand.

"I've been practicing with both left and right hands for the past four months . . . well, until the last week or so."

"At least once a week," confirmed Maertyl. "Most of the guards know that."

"After the earlier attempts, I thought that might be a useful precaution." Charyn took a deep breath. "I just . . . didn't think . . . who the assassin might be."

"Where did the white gowns come from? And three of them?"

"Oh . . . I forgot to mention that. They were hidden inside the cloaks that Laamyst and Gherard—Laamyst D'Laastyn and Gherard D'Ghaermyn—brought into the Chateau. It is a gray and cloudy day, although I imagine they would have brought them in any event."

"Who else might be involved in this?"

"Minister Aevidyr," replied Charyn, "as well as High Holders Laastyn and Ghaermyn. I wouldn't be surprised if they were behind Elthyrd's beating or that some of the rifles were bought recently from the rifleworks. That won't be hard to determine, one way or another."

"Then the story in *Tableta* was true?" asked Alastar.

Charyn nodded. "I need the ironworks to build Paersyt's next steam engine. Now . . . I think it's time to talk to Minister Aevidyr."

"I'll have the guards bring him down here, if you'd like," offered Maertyl.

"Thank you." Charyn turned to Vaelln. "I'd appreciate your taking custody of the survivors of the plot as well as using your men to bring in High Holder Laastyn and High Holder Ghaermyn. Even if L'Excelsis were not under martial law, I believe being part of a plot to kill the Rex would still qualify as a high crime."

"Might I ask why a High Holder would risk that?"

"To cover up a past crime that would cost them their lands," replied Charyn. "This all started when I asked Minister Alucar to make sure that both High Holders and factors were paying the necessary tariffs . . ." Charyn went on to give a quick summary of what Aevidyr had done.

When Charyn had finished, Vaelln said, "Past failures to pay tariffs haven't been punished that severely, have they?"

"So far as we can tell, past failures didn't go back for ten years. Even if I didn't charge them with defrauding the Rex, and just assessed the normal penalties, the amount they owed would likely destroy them, and they knew I wouldn't forgive the debt. Under the present conditions facing Solidar, how could I? Should everyone else have to pay more to save cheating High Holders?"

"Why did they do it?"

"You'd have to ask them. I'd guess that they were having troubles, and my father was very forgiving. Then they discovered that no one even noticed what they weren't paying . . . and they got greedy." Charyn shrugged.

"Until you looked into it, and they got very worried."

"That's my guess. Laamyst and Gherard started to get very friendly with Bhayrn just about the time that I asked Minister Alucar to start looking at all the tariff records of the High Holders, and Bhayrn turned more toward them and away from his previous friends. I suspect that Aevidyr told them there might be trouble and the three of them hatched his plot."

"Just for golds? From High Holders?"

"Not exactly. Laastyn and Ghaermyn could have paid the tariffs, but it would have cost them enough in lands that they'd have lost their High Holdings." Charyn didn't have the exact numbers on that, but that was the only thing that made sense. "And Laastyn is most likely land-poor while Ghaermyn barely has enough lands to qualify as a High Holder."

Charyn also suspected that Laevoryn might have been aware of the plot, but doubted that there would be any evidence at all, even circumstantial, to connect him to the others, and there might even be other conspirators.

"And Elthyrd?" asked Alastar.

"He likely would have just been the first. Hisario would have been next, and he would have been replaced by another hothead. Then, as Rex, Bhayrn would have used the army to crush the crafters and workers. It wouldn't have worked, but that was likely what was planned."

"Unhappily," said Alastar, "I could see that happening."

"Your Grace," said Maertyl from the parlor door. "Minister Aevidyr."

Two guards escorted Aevidyr into the parlor, then stepped back and positioned themselves on each side of the door.

Aevidyr looked at Charyn. "Why have I been restrained?"

"We'll get to that," replied Charyn. "What did your father promise you?"

Aevidyr looked at Charyn scornfully. "My father was a factor in Villerive. He had nothing to promise."

"I meant your real father, not your foster father. My grandsire, if you will. He's the one who appointed you as a regional minister of administration in Liantiago." Charyn had the feeling that was a surprise to Alastar, and especially to Vaelln, but he kept his eyes on Aevidyr.

"He promised nothing."

"But there was the implied promise, wasn't there?"

"I haven't the faintest idea what you're talking about, Your Grace."

"You were very young for the post of a regional minister, but that wasn't enough for you, and you pressed my father for the ministerial position here, but he didn't grant you any lands, and you hadn't been able to gather enough through 'favors' you did for various High Holders in order for him to make you a High Holder." Charyn left out the approval of the High Council and went on. "So you decided to approach it in your own way, didn't you? You thought you deserved at least the same amount of lands that a younger child of a Rex received, and you used your position to do even more favors in return for lands and properties."

"This is all mere conjecture, Your Grace. You've invented this for your own designs, though I don't see what purpose any of it will serve."

"What I didn't invent, Aevidyr, is the fact that you became a regional minister in Liantiago, with nothing to your name but five hundred hectares of Bovarian cropland. You've never been paid more than two hundred golds a year, and you now have properties that return you around fifteen hundred golds a year, all of them purchased for ten golds and other considerations of value. Many of them were sold, if you can call it that, to you by High Holders, who subsequently had records of other of their properties vanish from the tariff rolls, at a time when you were also acting as Finance Minister."

"That is again entirely conjecture. Certain High Holders' records were erroneously entered or were not entered. That was certainly not their fault. Nor could it be mine, for I was not Minister of Finance."

"You were acting as Finance Minister . . ."

"You'll find no record of that. The responsibility was that of head clerk Slaasyrn. The late head clerk Slaasyrn."

"Ah, yes, poor Slaasyrn, who died suddenly right after I announced that the tariff records of all High Holders would be reviewed. Slaasyrn, who would have known, in reviewing those records, exactly who did what."

"That is merely conjecture on your part, a conjecture with absolutely no basis in fact."

"Regardless, it happened while you were acting Finance Minister."

"There's nothing to prove that."

Charyn smiled, coldly. "Actually, there is. I have two letters from Rex Lorien to you. One tells you, as acting Finance Minister, to find the funds for repairs to the former regial palace in Solis. The other asks why you cannot, again, as acting Finance Minister, increase the penalties for late payment of tariffs, and there is even a sealed copy of your reply. There are also other letters, which you couldn't destroy, and most of those properties removed from the tariff rolls dated to the time when you were acting Finance Minister. That means that all those transgressions, which amount to high crimes against the Rex, were your responsibility. I doubt that the High Justicer will absolve you of that responsibility, and since the amount by which your manipulations defrauded the Rex far exceeds one hundred golds . . ."

"You little scheming bastard of a Rex . . . I've as much regial blood as you do . . ."

"Take him away," said Charyn tiredly. "Keep him safe . . . and well locked up, along with the others."

"Do you require anything more of me, Your Grace?" Vaelln looked decidedly shaken.

"Not at the moment, Marshal. I'm hopeful that we'll be

able to lift martial law shortly, but the next few days will determine that."

"Yes, sir."

Within a few moments, Alastar and Charyn were alone in the parlor. Charyn sank into one of the armchairs. He discovered that his legs were shaking.

Alastar sat in the chair facing Charyn, looking directly at him. "Why did you decide to handle Bhayrn as you did? You could have let him shoot at you and then had him sentenced to death."

"Then there would have been countless claims that I fabricated the assassination attempt and sentenced him to death to keep the High Holders from reclaiming their rightful privileges. Either way his death was on my hands. There won't be as much uproar about a wounded Rex defending himself as one using the law to disenfranchise his poor younger brother. And I couldn't pardon him because of who he was. The High Holders and even some of the factors don't want Solidar to change. It already has, and it will change more. Those who oppose that change would have continued to seek Bhayrn out. Because he also believed in the old way of doing things, so long as he was alive, I'd be facing threats to my life as Solidar slowly fell apart."

"Don't you think that's rather dire?"

"With two revolts that already occurred centered around Uncle Ryentar? The younger brother of the Rex? And this one enabled by the bastard son of my grandsire because he felt disenfranchised?"

"Is all that a rationalization for consolidating your power as Rex?"

"When I'm trying to get the joint council to be a part of governing Solidar? When I'm trying to govern under the laws?"

"What do you really hope for, Charyn?"

"That I'll die a long time from now, and peacefully, as the last Rex of Solidar."

"Do you think that's realistic?"

"Perhaps not, but it's worth the effort. I don't think most people would have thought that the first Rex Regis could have unified Solidar. He couldn't have, without the imagers, and I won't succeed without you, either." Charyn looked hard at Alastar. "The imagers can remove me at any time if I become a tyrant. I'm well aware of that. The question is whether you'll help me or just remove me."

"So long as you keep trying to rule as fairly as possible, the Collegium will do what it can."

"That's all I'm asking. That, and the fact that you never mention what my goal is."

Alastar nodded slowly. "We can do that, provided you keep your word."

"I don't have any choice." *Not with all the blood on your hands and in your mind.*

"Did you ever?" Alastar's words were gently sardonic . . . and held a trace of sadness.

As Charyn slowly stood, he wondered what nightmares would now torment him . . . and for how long.

61

On Jeudi morning, Charyn rose well before dawn, this time for a sad and solemn purpose. Instead of wearing regial greens trimmed in black, he wore black entirely, except for the mourning sash, regial green edged in black. The blacks didn't fit his frame exactly, since they had been borrowed from the choir vestments of the Anomen D'Rex, but Charyn doubted anyone would care that much. He didn't feel like eating, and he only drank half of the mug of tea Therosa brought up to his apartments. Then he walked down to the family parlor, where he sat down and waited in the deep gray light before dawn.

Shortly, Chelia joined him. She studied what he wore, but said nothing.

"Black, in mourning and disgrace. Mourning for Bhayrn, disgrace for me. I should have seen it much sooner."

"Then what would you have done? Given him Lauckan and exiled him there, the way your father did his brother? So that you'd have to put down another revolt and kill him later . . . or fail to put it down and be killed? Once Bhayrn decided he was more fit to rule than you, only one of you would survive. Like all of the Ryel lineage, and you share it, like it or not, you did what you had to do. Your father did not. Treacherous relatives are the lot of all who rule."

Yet another reason to work to end the Rexes in a way that doesn't destroy Solidar. "Rather a sad commentary on monarchial rule, isn't it?"

"It's far better than what preceded it. Do you really want hundreds of squabbling High Holders, with weak regional rulers?"

Charyn couldn't dispute that, and the fact that he couldn't didn't much help.

At that moment, Faelln appeared at the parlor door. "The Collegium coach is arriving, Your Grace, Lady Chelia."

"Thank you."

Charyn stood, as did his mother. They walked out to the foyer and waited.

Wearing imager grays and a black and green mourning scarf, Aloryana was the first up the unmarked white stone steps and through the doors. She hurried to Charyn and put her arms around him. "I'm so sorry, Charyn."

Charyn just held her, his eyes burning.

"He didn't give you any choice. Not a real one." Her next words shook him. "That was his choice, not yours."

She's already grown up, an imager third who will be a maitre. Then the tears oozed from his eyes.

After a time, he started to let go of Aloryana.

"He wouldn't have wept for you," she murmured before releasing him.

I was weeping for you and me, not Bhayrn. But he didn't say that, not to Aloryana. He would, in time, but not yet.

Alastar and Alyna stepped forward. Both wore imager gray tunics and trousers, and mourning sashes. Both inclined their heads.

"Thank you for coming," Charyn said.

"We appreciate your thinking of us," said Alyna.

Charyn understood exactly what she meant—that Aloryana was living with her and Alastar and that it was helpful to everyone that they be at the small family farewell. "I appreciate your being here. None of this has been easy." *And you never expected it to turn out this way . . . which just might be why it did.* And that thought depressed him even more.

Chelia looked toward the rear of the Chateau.

Charyn nodded, then took his sister's arm. The two walked to the rear door, which a guard opened for them, and down the stone steps in the gray light that seemed to press in on Charyn. He turned to the left and walked past the stables toward the corner of the walled courtyard.

The pyre stood in the far corner. Bhayrn's body, covered in black canvas, rested on a bier in the center. Four guards flanked the pyre, two on each side. One of them was Dhuncan, and he held a burning torch.

The five mourners moved into position, in a line less than two yards from the pyre, with Charyn in the center, and Chelia to his immediate left, and Aloryana beside her. On Charyn's right was Alastar, flanked by Alyna. No chorister, not even Faheel D'Anomen, was present, because his presence would have made the farewell a memorial. Karyel and Iryella watched, as Charyn had ordered, from the study window.

After several moments of silence, Charyn took one step forward, then nodded to Dhuncan. The guard stepped forward and handed the torch to Charyn.

Charyn took the torch and stepped forward, raising it and saying, "For Bhayrn, son and brother, in sadness and regret that he could not come to terms with both himself and what bounties life and the Nameless offered him. Farewell."

Then he touched the torch in turn to each of the three reservoirs of oil before placing it on the pyre and stepping back in line with the others. The flames raced from the oil reservoirs, then slowed as they gnawed at the wood of the pyre.

Charyn stood, watching, thinking, remembering . . . as the flames rose around what remained of Bhayrn and his dreams of what never could have been.

62

~~~~~~~~

Much later on Jeudi, well after second glass, Charyn sat alone in his study.

He'd already taken care of the one absolutely pressing duty, that of requesting Sanafryt to draft the decrees charging Aevidyr, Laastyn, Ghaermyn, Laamyst, and Gherard with high crimes against the Rex and people of Solidar.

For perhaps the third time, he picked up the latest edition of *Veritum*. His eyes half-read, half-remembered the words.

> . . . men clad in white gowns and hoods attempted to storm the Chateau D'Rex. According to Marshal of the Army Vaelln, the attackers were not True Believers, but used the white garments to cast the blame on the religious dissidents in order to provide cover for an attempted assassination of Rex Charyn. The Rex foiled the assassination attempt by shooting the purported assassin himself, despite an injured right hand, the result of an earlier assassination attempt . . .
>
> One of the Rex's ministers and three High Holders, as well as some members of those families, have been taken into custody by the army. Marshal Vaelln has not disclosed whether others were involved in the plot, but he did indicate that, of the main conspirators, only the assassin was killed, and that all the conspirators would appear before the High Justicer . . .

Charyn set down that newssheet and picked up the other. The *Tableta* article wasn't as bad as it could have been.

A plot to assassinate Rex Charyn exploded into gunshots and death at the Chateau D'Rex on Meredi afternoon when Lord Bhayrn, the younger brother of the Rex, tried to shoot Rex Charyn, but found himself the victim of the Rex's left-handed shot. Also slain or wounded were a number of men wearing the white gowns and hoods of the True Believers. By this stratagem, the plotters attempted to place blame for the would-be assassination on the True Believers, whose recent record of violence against choristers would have made the charge plausible. The fact that the Rex is the only non-chorister attacked by the True Believers lends substance to the possibility that the earlier attacks on the Rex may have also be the work of the plotters. Those seized and gaoled by the army, under the provisions of martial law, include Minister of Administration Aevidyr, High Holder Laastyn and one of his sons, and High Holder Ghaermyn and his heir, Gherard D'Ghaermyn . . .

No memorial service will be held for Lord Bhayrn. One can scarcely blame our beloved Rex . . .

Not for that . . . but for not really seeing, until it was far too late, what Bhayrn had become. But then, would anything have changed matters? *You offered him the best of all the regial holdings that could be given . . . if only he had tried . . .*

"Is there anything I can do for you, Your Grace?" asked Wyllum, from his seat at the conference table.

"No, thank you." Charyn looked to the open window, wondering if open windows would always remind him of Bhayrn and those last fateful, terrible, and inexorably necessary moments. He looked back to the few papers on his desk, well aware that, beyond the window, the late-afternoon sky was clear, and white sunlight bathed L'Excelsis.

There were two draft responses from Sanafryt, in reply to petitions from High Holders Charyn had never met, or even heard of. After having read the petitions twice, he still didn't remember the issues.

He found himself looking nowhere when there was a rap on the study door.

"Your Grace . . . you have a visitor."

"I asked not to see anyone, except if it was urgent." Charyn didn't even look up.

The door opened. "I think it's very urgent . . ." began a feminine voice.

Charyn turned toward the door, where Alyncya stood. Stunned, he said nothing.

"Wyllum," said Alyncya firmly, "if you'd leave us."

Wyllum looked to Charyn.

"You can go, Wyllum."

"Yes, sir."

Alyncya walked to the chairs opposite the desk and looked directly at Charyn. "I need to be here. You need me here."

Charyn didn't dispute that. "Why did you come, after what I did?"

"I sat and watched my sister die. I could do nothing. It was terrible. I didn't have to do what you did."

"I shot my brother. Twice. I didn't do it because I was scared. I did it for reasons that not many people would understand."

"Try me." Her voice was gently firm.

"What I did was absolutely wrong. I killed my only brother because I feared that, if I didn't, Solidar would face another revolt and thousands more would die. Would that have happened?" Charyn shrugged tiredly. "I think so. But I don't know. Bhayrn was ready to follow anyone who would tell him he'd be a better Rex . . . and he didn't even want to learn the first thing about running a High Holding . . . After Aevidyr and Laastyn and Ghaermyn . . . there would have been someone else. And how could I execute those who were behind it . . . and let him go?"

"You felt you had to shoot him?"

"I'd have been a coward to let anyone else do it. That's not right. Alastar was there and would have shielded me. So, after a fashion, I was a coward anyway. But I had to be the one, not out of pride . . . but so that I can't forget. Does that make sense?"

"More than you know, dear one. More than you know."

"And then there's Aevidyr. I know that he schemed to enrich himself because he felt entitled to more. And he'll have to die as well, and he's my bastard uncle . . ."

"Aevidyr's your uncle?"

"Grandsire's son from a High Holder's daughter who died in childbirth. I didn't find out that until this week. I think it was this week. Grandsire made him a regional minister. Father made him Minister of Administration. I discovered he used his position to remove some properties from the tariff rolls of certain High Holders, in exchange for lands and other properties. When he discovered Alucar and I were reviewing all the tariffs of High Holders, he likely poisoned the chief clerk and then must have told Laastyn and Ghaermyn, and they came up with the idea of tempting Bhayrn into thinking he should be Rex. And Bhayrn wanted to kill me at the end."

"They owed enough to lose their High Holdings?"

Charyn nodded. "With all the weather damage and the war, Solidar needs those tariffs, and how could I just let them get away with it?"

"No fair Rex could or should."

"My uncle Ryel had my father killed and tried to kill the rest of us. My uncle Ryentar was seduced into supporting the High Holders' revolt because he thought it would make him Rex. My bastard uncle conspired to get my brother to kill me. I keep asking where will it ever end, and it won't, not so long as a Rex rules Solidar."

"After all this . . . you're not thinking of stepping down?"

Charyn shook his head. "No. There's no one to replace

me." His short laugh was bitter. "And likely that's the same thing every Rex has thought at one time or another." He paused. "But a man shouldn't be forced to kill his brother, or to face death if he doesn't, generation after generation. That's why I'd like to be the last Rex Regis of Solidar." He looked to Alyncya. "Do you still want to marry a man who killed his brother?"

"I'd only think of marrying you if you'll keep your word on being the last Rex of Solidar. I'd never want anyone else to face what you did. Especially our children."

Especially our children. The warmth and meaning of those words washed over him. After several long moments, he said, "This isn't something we can exactly tell anyone else . . . except I did tell Maitre Alastar that was my dream."

"Will you share that dream with me?" Alyncya stood and walked around the desk. "And the grief?"

"How could I not?" Charyn stood as she took his hands in hers.

63

On Vendrei morning, Charyn sat down at the table in the breakfast room, early and alone, as he suspected would be usual for some time. He had just taken a mouthful of tea when Iryella appeared.

"Might I join you, sir?"

"Of course." Charyn wondered what she wanted or if she just couldn't sleep. "What brings you down so early?"

"I woke up early. Why did you want us to watch the pyre yesterday, but you wouldn't let us join you and Aunt Chelia?"

"Why do you think?"

"Lord Bhayrn tried to kill you. That was wrong, but why couldn't we say farewell?"

"Immediate family has to be there, both to remind us that even those we have loved can turn from the right path and to show we care. Any others would be a sign of respect, and what Bhayrn did was not worthy of respect. I wanted you to see that."

"But the maitres were there, and they're not immediate family."

"They're acting as Aloryana's immediate family until she is of age."

"Because she's an imager?"

Charyn nodded, then waited as Therosa set the platter of ham strips and cheesed eggs before him, along with a small loaf of dark bread. "What would you like, Iryella?"

"Could I please have the eggs scrambled without cheese and ham and tea?"

"It will be a few moments for the eggs," replied Therosa. "I'll bring your tea right out."

Once Therosa left, Iryella looked to Charyn. "Why did he do it, sir?"

"Bhayrn, you mean? It's always difficult to know what someone else really thinks, even your own brother. We have to go by what they say and what they do. From what Bhayrn said and what he did, I believe that he didn't agree with the decisions I made as Rex and he thought he would be a better Rex." Charyn took a bite of the eggs, then realized he didn't feel like eating. He took another small bite before having some more of his tea.

"Why did he think that?"

"There were many reasons, I think, but the difference between us was that he wanted things to stay as they had always been, and I think that when times change, the Rex has to change, usually to keep the change from getting out of hand while allowing those things that cannot be stopped to take place in an orderly fashion. I'd say change is like a flooding river. You can't stop it for long. All you can do is to channel it away from where it will do too much damage and to allow it to flood where it won't."

"Is that why you declared martial law but ordered the factors to pay the workers more?" Iryella's voice held what Charyn thought was honest curiosity.

"That was my hope. We'll see how well that works."

"It will work, Your Grace," murmured Therosa, as she set the mug of tea before Iryella.

"Why do you think that, Therosa?" asked Charyn.

"No Rex ever listened to the little people before. You did two things for them. The two-copper law and the law to make choristers be more honest."

"Will it be enough?"

"We all hope so, Your Grace." Therosa slipped away before Charyn could say another word.

Charyn smiled wryly. "That also means that I can't stop listening."

"Lord Bhayrn only listened to his friends, didn't he?"

"I'm afraid so."

"Karyel's like that sometimes. Is that another reason why you wanted us to watch?"

"I hoped you might remember it in times to come and understand what happens when you see only what you want to see. We all like to see what we want to see, and we need to try to see what others see. They're often not the same."

Iryella nodded.

Charyn could see that she'd had enough of serious talk. "Are you going to keep practicing harder on the clavecin?"

"Until I'm better than either you or Karyel."

Charyn laughed softly. "You're likely better than I am right now."

"You'll get better again."

Charyn certainly hoped so.

After breakfast, most of which he left, Charyn talked briefly with Maertyl, then made his way to the study, where Wyllum was already waiting.

Alucar had left early, accompanied by two squads of troopers, to visit Ghaermyn's holding in order to determine how many properties weren't on the tariff rolls. He'd have to do that with Laastyn's properties as well, which would take longer, possibly much longer, Charyn suspected.

Just before eighth glass, Sanafryt entered the study. He set five documents on the desk before Charyn. "Here are the decrees."

"Thank you." Charyn read over each decree of high crimes committed against the Rex and the people of Solidar, then signed and sealed it, before handing it back to Sanafryt. "High Justicer Sullivyr is expecting this?"

"I already informed him that he would have the decree for his review before noon. It's more of a formality in cases like this. They've each so exceeded the law in so many ways."

Charyn nodded, even as he thought that the exercise of law by regial fiat would need to be changed, in time, to exercise only by consent of the Council. *You need to make a list of what needs to be changed, and why and when . . . a written list so that you don't conveniently forget in the months and years to come.* "When you return to the Chateau, I'll need you to work on a listing of the crimes for which a worker, a crafter, or a factor can be put to death. I'd also like some numbers on how many have been executed for those crimes. I'll need to know whatever you can find by midday tomorrow."

The Minister of Justice frowned.

"I'm certain that at least some High Holders will protest the forfeiture of most of the lands of High Holder Laastyn."

"I did inform you that, while you are within the scope of the Codex Legis—"

"I know, but just because there's no hard proof that Laastyrn was involved," *or even more than the flimsiest circumstantial evidence,* "doesn't mean that two generations weren't involved. Besides, Laastyrn gets to keep property and his life, just not the High Holding. He should count himself fortunate."

"What will you do with the lands, Your Grace?"

"Sell them off over time and put the golds in treasury reserves so that we're not caught the way we have been the last two years when unexpected expenses came up. The last thing this Rex needs is more lands." *A manufactorage or two, but no more lands.* "Ghaermyn's heirs can keep the main manufactorage."

"What about Aevidyr's lands? You took that out of the decree."

"He's not a High Holder. His life is payment enough. The lands will go to his wife and their children."

Sanafryt frowned.

"My grandsire didn't do right by Aevidyr. It didn't justify high crimes and treason, but I'd rather not punish any innocents."

Sanafryt nodded slowly. "I'd heard something . . ."

"I'd appreciate it if you kept it to yourself, for their sake, not mine."

"I can do that, Your Grace." He stepped back. "I need to get these to the High Justicer."

Not more than two quints later, Moencriff stepped into the study. "Maitre Alastar is here with two craftmasters, Your Grace. He said you wished to meet with them."

"I said that some time ago, but I would like to meet with them and the Maitre."

"Yes, sir." Moencriff opened the study door and gestured.

Alastar led the way, but stopped once the three were several yards from the desk. "I believe you've met with Argentyl before," said the Maitre, nodding to the dark-haired man on his right, "and Gassel said he'd come because someone had to look out for the interests of the stonemasons."

Charyn very much appreciated Alastar's deft introductions and gestured to the chairs in front of the desk. "Please sit down." Then he turned to Argentyl. "I'm glad to see you survived your . . . disappearance. I do wish we'd been able to talk sooner."

"It didn't seem useful then, Your Grace. Didn't seem safe to stay in the city, either." He paused to seat himself, then said, "The Maitre said you wanted to see us. Why now?"

"If you're willing, I'd like for you two to attend Council meetings every month, starting in Finitas. If either of you don't wish to undertake that task, I'd hope you could recommend two other craftmasters who would."

"What would be the point?" demanded Argentyl.

"There's no one on the Council to speak for the crafts and workers. I've noticed that the High Holders became a bit more flexible and open to making things better," *only a bit, but we have to start somewhere,* "when they have to express themselves in front of factors and when they heard what the factors' concerns were. I'd like the same thing to happen over time for crafters as well." After a pause, Charyn asked, "What do you have to lose?"

Argentyl looked to Gassel.

The stonemason cleared his throat, then said, "They've never listened before, Your Grace."

"They haven't had to listen with the Rex sitting at the end of the table," Charyn pointed out. "Or the Maitre of the Collegium."

Alastar nodded very slightly.

"You did impose the two-copper law," said Gassel slowly. "It's not much, Your Grace, but no Rex has done anything before. I'd be willing to give it a try."

"Why not this month?" asked Argentyl.

"Because the Council meets on the eighteenth. That's only five days away, and I need a little more time than that for the Council to realize that they don't have a choice and that they'll have to accept hearing how what they want to do, or not do, will affect crafters and workers." After another pause, Charyn added, "You'll also get to hear what problems they have, and, just like you, they have problems, and you might be able to give them a different view."

"What's in it for you, Your Grace?" pressed Argentyl.

"If the Council can work out things, then I'm less likely to do something that will make everyone angry, or someone so angry that they'll shoot at me again or try to shoot someone else . . . or burn down something. When that happens, everyone loses." Charyn smiled wryly. "Especially me."

The faintest smile creased Gassel's face, but vanished immediately.

"I won't press you more than I have," Charyn said, "but I think your presence would help. I don't say it will be easy, but you would help."

"I'll try it," said Gassel.

Argentyl nodded, then said, "Can't hurt to try."

"The meeting is always at the first glass of the afternoon

on the eighteenth of the month." Charyn nodded toward the table. "Over there."

"Begging your pardon, Your Grace," said Gassel deferentially, "is it true what the newssheets said, that you shot your brother left-handed?"

"Yes, it is. He pulled out his pistol and tried to kill me. I was a little faster."

"Do you always carry a pistol?"

"I've found it necessary. I wish it weren't." Charyn managed a pleasant smile. "Do either of you have any other questions?"

"Not right now, Your Grace," replied Gassel. "Might think of a few right after we leave."

"You can always ask me later. Thank you for coming and being willing to be at the Council meetings." Charyn stood.

The others did as well.

"Will we see you on Solayi?" asked Alastar.

"If you're willing to walk slowly to the anomen," replied Charyn with a smile.

"We can manage that."

After the three had left the study, Charyn waited a quint, then made his way down to the small guard duty room, hoping Maertyl or Faelln was somewhere near.

Maertyl was. "Yes, Your Grace?"

"Your couriers have delivered a few letters to the L'Excelsis estate of Lady-heir D'Shendael. I'm afraid I have no idea where that might be, but I'd like to take the unmarked coach there at around third glass."

Maertyl smiled. "I have several guards who know where it is. I think four guards will be sufficient now."

"Thank you."

A glass later, Charyn was in the unmarked regial coach as it headed along the Boulevard D'Ouest toward the Nord Bridge. He watched as the coach crossed the Nord Bridge, then immediately turned north on the East River Road, which shortly curved away from the river. After several hundred yards, Dhuncan turned the coach left down a narrower road. Ahead on the left was a three-story structure a mere thirty-five yards across, behind a walled front garden and before equally walled rear grounds. On the south side of the property was an open gate, with a sentry box for a single guard. Beyond the gate was a drive that led to a covered portico.

The guard stepped out of the box, clearly surprised.

"Rex Charyn is here to see Lady-heir Alyncya D'Shendael," announced Dhuncan.

"Ah . . . she didn't say anything . . ."

Charyn leaned out the coach window. "She surprised me the last time. Turnabout is fair play."

"Yes, Your Grace. I'll announce you." The guard did not quite run up the stone-paved drive.

Dhuncan eased the coach through the gate and up the stone-paved drive to the covered portico. By the time Charyn stepped out of the coach, High Holder Shendael was standing just outside the portico door, smiling.

"Welcome, Your Grace. I do believe you have completely surprised my daughter. If you'd join me in the parlor, she should be with us shortly." His eyes dropped to Charyn's splinted and half-bound right hand. "How is your hand?"

"The worst of the soreness is gone . . . unless I bump something."

Shendael led the way to the parlor, then gestured for Charyn to enter.

The parlor walls and ceiling were a blue so pale that it was almost white, offset by cream chair rails and crown moldings, while the parquet floor was largely concealed by a carpet several shades of blue darker than the walls with a border design of scallops. The two love seats and four armchairs were of simple goldenwood and upholstered in blue and cream silk. The side tables were of matching goldenwood.

"Tastefully simple and quite beautiful," observed Charyn.

"Thank you. Alyncya had it redone several years ago. The colors and design were all her idea." Shendael took one of the armchairs. "She runs the holdings as much as I do, maybe more these days."

Somehow, that didn't surprise Charyn. He settled into another armchair. "It's elegant, but also restful." *How could it not be elegant if she designed it?*

"I must say that you two surprised me," offered the High Holder.

"Oh?"

"As you have discovered, Alyncya is very quietly strong-willed, and, from what I've observed, few men of position and power are naturally attracted to such women."

"I was instantly attracted to her the second time I danced with her."

"And that's one of the reasons why I asked him to marry me," interjected Alyncya as she entered the parlor. "You'll notice, Father, that he said he was instantly attracted the *second* time."

For a long moment, Charyn just looked at her, taking in her face, eyes, and the smile she offered, as well as the tailored blue jacket and trousers, and the cream blouse. "But I remembered what you wore the first time."

"With a little help, as I recall." She settled herself into the vacant armchair closest to Charyn.

Charyn offered a sheepish smile. "That's true, but I was struck enough to write down what you wore."

"What other young ladies received such notes?" teased Alyncya.

"You were the only one whose dress and eyes I noted."

"At the third ball, he remembered every word I'd said at the second." Her lips quirked in rueful amusement.

"That's quite a compliment, dear," returned Shendael. "You've told me that most men don't recall what women say after a glass."

"It was a frightening compliment," admitted Alyncya, "and I told him so."

Shendael looked up to the liveried man who stood in the parlor doorway. "Could we interest you in a little refreshment, Your Grace? You're partial to white wine, as I recall."

"That would be wonderful," admitted Charyn. "Until now, it's been a long day . . . and a long week."

"Two white and one red, then." Shendael nodded to the server, who turned and left the parlor. "Might I ask what will happen to those involved in the plot?"

"Those directly involved will be executed. The High Holdings, but not all properties, of Laastyn and Ghaermyn are forfeit. They likely wouldn't have been able to hold them anyway, given how much in tariffs and penalties they owed." That was a guess on Charyn's part, since Alucar was still trying to discover all the properties not on the tariff rolls that should have been.

Shendael shook his head. "We've always been conservative. Something like that makes me grateful for that heritage."

"That conservatism is why you'd never need to be in that sort of position," Alyncya pointed out.

"Stripping a family of its High Holding won't set well with some of the High Holders," said Shendael.

"Trying to assassinate the Rex and cheating on tariffs for a decade doesn't set well with me," replied Charyn pleasantly.

"I imagine they weren't the only ones."

"No, they weren't. That's why the Finance Minister is revising property and tariff records. Interestingly enough, the factors aren't any better, and their records are also being updated."

"You're likely to have everyone unhappy with you."

Charyn shook his head. "Not if people think it through. I might not have had to increase tariffs if there hadn't been so many cheating. The honest High Holders and factors were supporting the dishonest ones."

Shendael laughed, a low almost growling sound. "I'd be wary of putting the word 'honest' close to most High Holders or factors."

"Perhaps I should say 'law-abiding'?"

"It's more likely closer to the truth."

At that moment, the server returned with three goblets of wine, presenting the tray to Charyn first. He took one of the whites and waited until the others had their goblets before lifting his slightly. "Thank you."

When Charyn took a small swallow of the wine, he found he really didn't feel like drinking it, but he took another very small swallow anyway.

"It's our honor," replied Shendael. "I never thought I'd see the Rex in my parlor, let alone find him affianced to my daughter." He smiled and looked fondly at Alyncya. "That is the proper way of saying it for your purposes, is it not?"

"It is, and thank you."

"Do you two think you can wait until Year-Turn?"

"Considering that, at one point, she said she didn't want to have another conversation with me until then, I'm more than happy with the present and much improved situation."

This time, Alyncya was the one to blush. "I told you he has a very good memory."

"You did indeed."

After less than a quint of light conversation, Shendael rose. "I'll leave the parlor to you two, at least for a time."

"Thank you, Father."

Once Shendael had left, Alyncya turned to Charyn. "You see. He's not so bad once he knows you."

"Once he knows that I'm most serious about you."

She smiled. "There is that." The smile faded. "You still hurt, don't you? I saw how you walked."

There's some hurt that's not physical. Charyn managed a smile. "I can see that there's still very little that escapes you. It's not as bad as it was . . ."

"You also barely drank the wine. Are you eating much?"

"I haven't been that hungry . . ."

"Bhayrn's death . . . or your having to shoot him . . . that's been hard on you, hasn't it?"

"What else could I have done? It would have gone on and on. Bhayrn never saw . . . never . . . understood . . ." Charyn shook his head. "If it hadn't been Laamyst and Gherard, it would have been someone else . . ."

"Charyn . . . that's part of being Rex. You have to make the decisions."

He gave a bitter smile. "My father didn't. He left it to Maitre Alastar to take care of Uncle Ryentar."

"Is that why you couldn't?"

He nodded.

Almost a glass later, with the two seated side by side on one of the love seats, Charyn said, "I really shouldn't overstay my welcome, especially since I came unexpected and unannounced. I can't tell you how much . . ."

She put a finger to his lips. "You have already." Then she said, "Unannounced, but . . . not totally unexpected. Earlier, though. I thought you might stop by tomorrow. But you've always been a little ahead of me."

"Would you attend services with me on Solayi evening? At the Anomen D'Imagisle?"

"As I've suggested before, you don't strike me as a very religious man."

"I'm not. Some of the principles offered by some choristers are good guidance, but . . . if I go to services there, I can see Aloryana and have refreshments after services at the dwelling of Maitre Alastar, because Aloryana lives with Maitre Alastar and Maitre Alyna and their daughter Lystara. Lystara, by the way, saved me and Aloryana from the assassination attempt on me. I think you should meet them all, since, except for Mother, they're largely the family I have left . . ." Charyn grinned. "At least until we're married."

"I'm also not that religious, but I'd very much like to attend services with you."

"Then, I will arrive here with the coach at a quint past fifth glass on Solayi." Smiling widely, Charyn stood.

So did Alyncya, turning in to him and drawing him to her, her lips on his.

After a very long embrace, she stepped back. "Solayi, just after fifth glass." Before he could reply, she added, playfully, "And not too early, either."

Charyn smiled ruefully, then nodded.

~~~~~

64

Charyn returned to the Chateau early enough for dinner on Vendrei evening, a dinner that included only himself, Karyel, and Iryella, since Chelia had left word that she was indisposed, as she had also been on Jeudi evening. Charyn had checked with Therosa to make certain his mother was in fact eating, and Therosa confirmed that Chelia was eating some of what was brought up to her, but not much.

That was something Charyn could definitely understand. He still didn't feel all that hungry.

After they sat down at the table and when Iryella said the grace, Karyel immediately asked, "How long will Aunt Chelia stay to herself?"

"Until she doesn't," replied Charyn. "That's up to her. This week has been incredibly difficult for her." *And that's understating it.* But there was no way Karyel would understand. Charyn knew that even he couldn't feel all that his mother felt, not after losing her husband and knowing that her elder son had shot her younger son—all in less than a year.

"Seems silly to me—"

"Karyel!" snapped Iryella. "You cried for days when Mother and Father died."

"I don't remember."

"Enough," said Charyn firmly.

The rest of dinner was largely silent, and Charyn made no effort to be cheerful. He did wish Alyncya had been there, but that would have been unfair to her. She'd already listened to him long enough.

After dinner, he retired to his sitting room. He tried to

read Devoryn's *History of Solidar,* but his eyes refused to focus on the words. Finally, he just sat there, thinking, wondering what he could have done otherwise . . . and if it would have made a difference.

Predictably, he didn't sleep that well. When he got up on Samedi, again early, he wondered why Bhayrn's death— *murder*—gnawed at him more than it had in the days right after he'd fired the shots.

Because you were numb . . . or just didn't realize fully what you'd done?

He finally went down to the breakfast room once he knew the cooks and Therosa would be there.

Therosa immediately appeared. "Yes, Your Grace?"

"Just tea, please, Therosa."

"Just tea, sir?"

Charyn nodded and sat down at the table.

Two quints later, he began a second mug of tea. After a single sip, he looked up as his mother walked into the breakfast room.

"Iryella said that you're not eating much," said Chelia.

"Therosa told me the same about you," he replied. "I asked."

"I haven't been very hungry." She sat across the table from Charyn.

"Neither have I."

"You were braver than your father, Charyn."

"Or crueler," he replied. "I just didn't see it ever ending."

"It wouldn't have. It didn't with your father and his brother, not until Maitre Alastar ended it."

"I can't imagine . . . you . . ." He broke off the words.

"You might well face the same problems if you and Alyncya have sons, each believing they're better fitted to be Rex."

"If I live long enough," replied Charyn, "there won't be another Rex."

"I assume you're not planning to let Solidar fall apart."

"Nothing like that. In the meantime, I'm going to gently force the Council to take more responsibility for changing things."

"Can you count on things going as you plan?"

"Some things won't work, but it's like getting the tariffs fixed. That took over a year for one little change. Or maybe it's like Paersyt's steam-powered boat. It's taken him years to get it to work, but that means we have an engine that can propel ships, maybe even carts of some sort. If we just keep working . . ."

Chelia offered a gentle laugh. "Your father never would have believed this."

"Neither would I," replied Charyn ruefully. "Nor the cost . . . in so many ways . . . and I've been Rex only eight months."

"Everything has a cost, Charyn. Especially change."

There was little Charyn could say to refute that, and to agree was trite. He just nodded.

"I saw Maitre Alastar with two men I didn't recognize. They weren't attired in the manner of factors or High Holders. All three were leaving your study. What do they have to do with your plans?"

"They were craftmasters. They'll be at Council meetings beginning in Finitas."

"A year ago, I would have said it wouldn't work," said Chelia. "Now . . ."

"It will take years, but I want the Council to consider matters as to how they affect not only High Holders and factors, but crafters and workers."

"Is that why you didn't impose martial law immediately?"

"That was a feeling. I couldn't prove it, but I wanted both the High Holders and the factors to see how strongly people felt, but I also didn't want matters to get out of hand. I listened to Maitre Alyna and Alyncya as well as to the Council."

Chelia frowned. "I knew you and Alyncya exchanged quite a few letters, but you didn't spend much time together until the past week or so."

"Those letters were sometimes very long. She asked a number of questions, many about factors, High Holders, and power."

"Just about those?"

Charyn blushed. "Poetry and likes and dislikes as well."

"That doesn't sound like the usual courtship, but neither of you two is quite the usual. Keep listening to her."

How could I not? "I intend to."

"I wish your father had listened more . . ."

Charyn just sat there, listening as she talked.

65

~~~~~

Something was nagging at Charyn as he left his apartments on Solayi morning. Although he thought he'd slept late, the light was leaden gray, and the air was cool. Not only that, but the Chateau was eerily quiet as he made his way to the grand staircase and started down the polished marble risers. His boots did not echo. In fact, they made no sound at all, as if the heavy air had absorbed their usual echoes.

He found he was breathing hard, and sweat dripped from his brow, despite the coolness of the air. Had an autumn storm blown in, dark and gray, but with heavy damp air?

As he took the last steps down to the polished marble tiles of the main foyer, he saw that neither of the two guards posted there moved, but stood motionless, like the painted statues of the ancient Naedarans. How could they not be breathing heavily in the oppressive and damp air? He tried to stop, but he kept walking toward the statue-like guards, as if his legs were being ordered to carry him onward, at another's command.

Before he knew it, he was on the last riser, and then on the polished white marble tiles of the foyer, even with the two guards.

The guard on the right turned, with brutal swiftness.

Charyn gaped, because above the guard's formal greens, there was Bhayrn's face, twisted in anger, and the overlarge pistol in his hand was aimed right at Charyn's forehead.

"Did you calculate it all along, Brother? Did you push me to the edge to make it easier to kill me? Did you ever think about what I wanted, or what I felt?"

Charyn could not answer, but stood there frozen, numb.

"Did you calculate leaving Palenya or the value of Alyn-cya? What good are your calculations now?"

With the last words, Bhayrn pulled the trigger, and the bullet emerged from the barrel of the pistol, moving inexorably and slowly toward Charyn's forehead.

Charyn tried to throw himself to the side, to jerk his head away, but his body was frozen in place, even as sweat poured down his forehead, and his eyes fixed on the grayish-black bullet that oozed through the silent air toward him as he fought to move. The bullet expanded into a black shroud . . .

"No!"

His own voice echoed across the bedchamber as he struggled to free himself from the shroud that enveloped him.

Abruptly, he was awake, and real sweat poured from him, even as he began to shiver, although the early-autumn air was barely cool.

He sat up in the bed and tried to swallow, but could barely manage it, so dry was his throat. After a few moments, he eased his feet onto the carpet and just sat there on the edge of the bed for a time, blotting his face and body with the corner of the sheet that had felt like a shroud.

66

~~~~~

By later Solayi morning, Charyn was feeling less washed out. He ate a small breakfast, with two mugs of tea, and then made arrangements with Faelln for the coach and guards to pick up Alyncya and take them both to services on Imagisle. After that, he spent time in his study, looking over the petitions he hadn't even realized were there.

He also read through some of the poems he'd copied, including "The Streets of Gold."

Although the subject matter differed from what he'd done, he read the last line aloud, because, in a way, it expressed what he felt when he thought of Bhayrn. "And how I long for days of vanished grace."

But how much of your vanished grace is just the destruction of innocence by necessity? And how much of that innocence was just naïveté?

He smiled ironically as he read the last poem he'd copied.

GLORY'S PRICE
Some glory in their might, some in their birth.
Some in their words, and others in their graces,
Yet our moons shine sightless on rock and earth
And ashen traces of the fairest faces.

Oh, hunter of the endless void and veil,
And golden goddess of the aching heart,
Can conscience and forbearance yet prevail
O'er endless strife that rends these selves apart?

Charyn wasn't quite sure where the remainder of the afternoon went, but even before fifth glass he was dressed in regial greens and down in the rear courtyard, where duty ostlers readied the unmarked coach. He did not wear a mourning sash, not after saying farewell to Bhayrn and especially not in public. Nor was he carrying his pistol.

By the time the coach reached the portico of the Shendael mansion, Alyncya stood there waiting. She wore a golden-brown dress with a matching jacket. Charyn smiled as he noticed the peach scarf that complemented the brown and brought out her eyes, and he kept smiling as he stepped out and helped her into the coach.

"This is a tasteful but unornamented coach. One would scarcely note it belonged to the Rex . . . except for the guards flanking it."

"It's the same one I arrived in on Vendrei."

"I was rather preoccupied in getting myself presentable for a very unannounced visitor."

"And I was only returning the favor. Your arrival on Jeudi was definitely a favor, if not a rescue." Charyn leaned over and kissed her cheek, a kiss slightly misplaced as the coach began to move.

"You were distraught and trying not to show it."

"I kept knowing it was going to happen and hoping that it wouldn't. But . . . I didn't really try to dissuade Bhayrn, not when he reacted so badly to everything I said . . . and now I ask myself if I should have. But, obviously, it's far too late."

"From what you've said, and from what I've heard from a few people, it was too late months ago."

"You're kind."

"Not at the expense of honesty. I couldn't even tell my sister that she would get better. I could only say that I was there with her and for her."

"I hope I never have to hear those words," said Charyn wryly.

"I hope not as well, but I won't say them." She smiled. "I

might say something else." After a moment, she added, "If it comes to that, don't lie to me, either."

Charyn winced. "We aren't even married yet."

"That's why it's a good time to make sure we're honest with each other."

"Gently honest," suggested Charyn.

"So long as the gentleness doesn't destroy the honesty."

"That's fair."

"Good." She took his hand. "What can you tell me about Maitre Alastar and Maitre Alyna that I should know?"

"Besides the fact that they're the most powerful imagers in generations, or that they've saved my family more times than they should have?" Charyn paused. "They're both very wise and sensible, but often you have to listen to what they don't say. They know far more about L'Excelsis than I do, possibly than you do . . ."

For the rest of the ride to Imagisle, Charyn recounted what he could, including how the two had welcomed him into their house and how they had made Imagisle a comfortable place for him when not many places had been.

Aloryana was waiting just outside the Maitre's dwelling when the coach came to a stop.

"I hope you don't mind that I brought someone with me," said Charyn, as he stepped down from the coach, then turned and helped Alyncya out.

"You brought Alyncya! I hoped you would. No one here has really met her." Aloryana turned to Lystara, who had just joined her. "Lystara, this is Lady-heir Alyncya D'Shendael, and . . . she's special."

Coming down the steps from the Maitre's house right behind Lystara were Alastar and Alyna, the latter with a faint but knowing smile on her lips.

"I think everyone here can keep it to themselves for the next few days," said Charyn with a smile. "Alyncya has asked me to marry her. I accepted."

"That's so she can keep her High Holding," added Alory-ana quickly. "She has to ask."

"Very few men agree to that," Alyna said in a tone that conveyed approval.

"When?" asked Aloryana immediately.

"Sometime around Year-Turn, possibly the Samedi of the ball," said Charyn.

Lystara frowned.

"Since I'm the one who was asked," replied Charyn, "isn't it my mother who gets to set the date?"

Alyna laughed.

"Now I need to be more serious," said Charyn. "Alyncya, might I present you to Maitre Alyna, Maitre Alastar, and Maitre Lystara, the only time I believe that an entire family has been composed of imager maitres."

Alyncya inclined her head. "I'm pleased to meet you all. Charyn, I know, regards you all as family. I'm honored."

"We're the ones who are honored," replied Alyna, "by your grace and Charyn's trust."

"Trusting you," said Charyn, "has been what has saved me and my family more times than not, and for that, I'm most grateful."

"And I'd be slightly grateful," said Alastar, not quite acer-bically, "if we could begin the walk to the anomen so that Charyn doesn't have to hurry."

Charyn just shook his head.

Not by coincidence, he found himself accompanied by Aloryana and Alastar, while Alyna and Lystara talked to Alyncya.

"How are matters with those behind the plot?" asked Ala-star. "If I might inquire?"

"I've signed the decrees finding them guilty of high crimes and sent them to the High Justicer."

"Then their execution is assured."

"Under the present law."

"That suggests . . . ?"

"It does, but it will take a little time. The first thing is to hope that no more violence occurs so that I can lift martial law, and the second is to revise and improve the finance and tariff system. The third is to begin to strengthen the Council—"

"You've already begun that. I'm curious about the ironworks. That was quite a surprise. Might I ask why?"

"Because I need it to build steam engines . . ." By the time Charyn had explained what he had in mind and why, they were approaching the anomen.

"If those engines do what you think, that will change all Solidar . . . and the world."

"If they work the way I think, we can truly control the oceans and trade, and there will be many more manufactorages. That was why I needed to push through the minimum-wage law before that happens."

"I think the next years will be quietly interesting," replied Alastar.

Several imagers stepped aside as Charyn and the Maitre and the others approached the doors. Once inside, Charyn took Alyncya's hand and guided her behind the two maitres to the left side of the anomen near the front.

Charyn did notice that there were a few more glances in his direction than there had been before, but he suspected those glances were far more to take in Alyncya than for another look at him.

He tried to concentrate on Iskhar's homily, which focused on greed as a manifestation of naming, in that trying to obtain anything—power, land, golds, or even reputation—no matter what the cost was a form of self-arrogation, and thus naming. Much more than that, Charyn really didn't recall, aware as he was of Alyncya standing so closely beside him.

On the walk back to the Maitre's house, which he could tell would take longer, he found himself flanked by Alyna and Lystara.

"Your leg still hurts, doesn't it?" asked Lystara.

"When I'm on it for a while."

"It's only been two weeks, Lystara," said Alyna.

"It seems longer than that."

Charyn nodded. "Much longer than that."

"You're very fortunate with Alyncya," Alyna observed.

"Better than I deserve, most likely."

"False modesty doesn't become you, Charyn," replied Alyna firmly, but without raising her voice. "It appears that you deserve each other, and that's good."

"I like her," added Lystara.

"She's very perceptive, and she's also very good with the clavecin."

"It will take both of you to hold Solidar together," Alyna went on.

"And the Collegium," said Charyn.

"How is your mother taking it?"

"As a devastating, brutal, and inevitable necessity."

"And you?"

"Pretty much the same. I keep looking back, though, but I can't see where I could have done much differently." Charyn snorted ruefully. "But then, that's one of my shortcomings. I tend to see what should be, or what I think should be, and proceed from there. That's why I need Alyncya, and you and Maitre Alastar . . . and the Council."

"Just keep that in mind, and you'll find a way." Alyna smiled. "There's a special cake waiting at the house. Aloryana had the feeling that, sooner or later, you'd bring Alyncya. She'd hoped it would be this evening."

"I needed to bring her." *As much for me as for anyone else.*

Before that long the six were back in the parlor at the Maitre's house, where Charyn sank gratefully into one of the armchairs.

Alyncya moved one of the straight-backed chairs next to him, and they both had white wine, cheeses, biscuits, and then cake . . . as well as cheerful conversation that never neared the events of the two previous weeks.

More than two glasses later, as the unmarked regial coach pulled up to the portico of Alyncya's mansion, she turned in the seat and kissed Charyn warmly and gently, then said, "I don't think I've ever had quite so lovely a time in going to services and afterward."

"Neither have I, but there will be more."

"Sometimes, first times are special."

"And sometimes," Charyn grinned, thinking of a Year-Turn Ball, "second times are."

67

On Lundi morning, Charyn couldn't help feeling guilty because he'd enjoyed Solayi evening so much, particularly when he stepped into the breakfast room, where his mother was already seated.

"Good morning," he offered, trying to sound pleasant, but not ebullient, while feeling worried about how she felt.

"You don't have to sound like you're tiptoeing in," replied Chelia sardonically.

"Even if I was? I've worried about you."

"I appreciate it. I understand you took Alyncya to services and to meet with Alastar and Alyna. How did that go?"

"Very, very well. Alyna did tell me, in no uncertain terms, to listen to Alyncya and you."

While Alyna hadn't actually mentioned Chelia, Charyn suspected she would have agreed with what Charyn said.

"Are you humoring me, Charyn?"

"Only a little." He smiled as he sat down across from her.

"A little is helpful. I understand you had a talk with Iryella the other morning."

"I did. She had some questions. I did my best to answer her without going into excessive detail."

"You made an impression. She asked me why Karyel couldn't be more like you."

Charyn winced.

"I told her that you and I were trying, but that some of that was up to Karyel. She seemed to accept that."

"You can't disinherit him for Iryella," Charyn said.

"But you can. It's not often done, but it has been."

"We'll see if it comes to that."

"We will."

And that was his mother, Charyn realized once more, feeling, but, in the end, very practical.

After a pleasant breakfast, Charyn made his usual trek up to the study, and, moments after he arrived, so did Alucar.

"I don't have every last calculation of the back tariffs due, but that's because it will take weeks to discover what unrecorded properties Laastyn has in Tilbor, Telaryn, and Antiago."

"Khel's not a problem?"

Alucar shook his head. "The Khellans are very proper. They maintain dual registries, and send a complete annual updated copy of each to the Chateau. With your permission, I'd like to use their system in the other regions . . . that is, once we get the more obvious discrepancies resolved."

"And once we replace a few more regional governors," added Charyn.

"Ghaermyn's lands and manufactorages, so far as I can determine, have always been in and around L'Excelsis. He owes eight thousand golds in back tariffs, but that's without penalties. Just the one-in-ten penalty each year over eight years would increase that to sixteen thousand golds."

"Is there a single manufactorage that is separate or that could be separated?"

"There are two."

"Pick the best, and transfer it to Lady Ghaermyn. As I recall, her given name is Elyssana."

"So it would go to Elyssana D'Ghaermyn? And the rest revert to you?"

"To the treasury. You'll have to arrange for their sale . . . and not cheaply. What do you have so far on what Laastyn owes?"

"At present, it's close to twenty-eight thousand golds. I'm guessing there's another five to ten thousand in unpaid tariffs. All of that to the treasury for future sale as well?"

"Not everything. Let Lady Laastyn—Salani D'Laastyn—

keep the river estate north of here and a thousand hectares of cropland . . . and whatever golds they have. They might last her the rest of her life."

"And Aevidyr's wife keeps his properties? All of them?"

"All of them," Charyn affirmed. Aevidyr at least had had a legitimate grievance against Charyn's grandsire Ryen, who had fobbed off his own son, his own child even if born on the wrong side of the blanket, with a few hundred hectares and no recognition and, eventually, a position as a regional minister. That seemed unfair and cold, especially considering what had happened to Charyn's uncle Ryentar, who had schemed to kill Charyn's father and had been forgiven—and then given a lavish and prosperous High Holding. Yet Ryentar had still thrown in with the rebel High Holders and tried to unseat and kill Charyn's father.

Surprisingly, Alucar nodded and said, "While it is your decision, those who know all the facts would likely agree that is fair."

"Is there anything else?" asked Charyn.

"Not at the moment, sir."

After Alucar left, Charyn just looked at the open window . . . and shook his head.

Then he dictated a letter of thanks to Alastar and Alyna for their graciousness and hospitality on Solayi evening, signed and sealed it, and had Wyllum arrange for its dispatch.

By the time Wyllum returned, Charyn had received and was reading the weekly report from Marshal Vaelln.

The Marshal reported that, likely because of stormy weather, there were no reports of naval encounters near Jariola. In the waters off the Abierto Isles, Jariolan warships had withdrawn rather than engage Solidaran ships, but another Solidaran merchanter had been lost to a privateer off Otelyrn. The troopers patrolling L'Excelsis had only dealt with minor curfew infractions. In closing, Vaelln suggested withdrawing the troopers if the situation remained calm for another few days.

Charyn nodded at that.

The next message was from Paersyt. Charyn read it immediately.

Your Grace—
I am very pleased to announce that the latest changes to the driveshaft have proved eminently successful as has the new water screw. The Steamwraith *is now faster and moves through even choppy water quite easily.*

I believe that a larger engine can now be built and that two of them should be sufficient to power a small frigate with twin water screws. I am now engaged in working on the plans for building such an engine, after which I will be revising my earlier rough plans for such a frigate . . .

Charyn was smiling when he finished reading what Paersyt had sent, and since the engineer wouldn't need more golds for a time, that was also good.

Slightly before noon, Sturdyn announced, "Chief High Councilor Fhaedyrk is here and wishes to speak to you, Your Grace."

"I'll see him." Charyn turned to Wyllum. "Now would be a good time for you to see if Lady Chelia has need of your skills."

"Yes, sir."

Wyllum left the study, and Fhaedyrk entered, taking the middle seat of the three chairs across from Charyn.

"What's on your mind, Fhaedyrk?"

"A number of High Holders have contacted me, Your Grace."

"About the sentences imposed on Aevidyr, Laastyn, and Ghaermyn . . . perhaps?"

"Ah . . . not so much about those three. The law and precedent are quite clear on that, particularly for a minister who is involved in high crimes."

"But . . . ?" Charyn had a good idea what the next concern would be.

"Young Laamyst was not even the heir. To seize all the lands of the High Holder . . . for the crimes of a younger son."

"Fhaedyrk," said Charyn calmly, "that is a technicality that ignores reality. Laastyn arranged to avoid paying tariffs and colluded with Aevidyr to assassinate me. Laamyst and Laastyrn spent a great deal of time with my brother, most of it after I began to investigate the irregularities in tariff payments and records. Are you and these High Holders contending that Laastyrn was totally unaware of what his father and brother were plotting when Laastyn and his younger son were both deeply involved? I'll grant that there's no direct evidence implicating Laastyrn, but the evidence against the High Holder and Laamyst is incontestable. Laastyn owes most likely more than forty thousand golds in unpaid back tariffs. That's without penalties. He also transferred a substantial town house and several thousand hectares to Laastyrn in late Agostos, just a few days before the first attack by the false True Believers took place. That strongly suggests that the High Holder was worried. Now . . . those properties were properly deeded and transferred, and I see no point in trying to prove the unprovable, even if I know, and you should know, that Laastyrn knew very well what was happening."

Fhaedyrk frowned. "You *knew* that and did nothing?"

"I only found out about the transfers less than two weeks ago. They looked strange to me then, and I said so to Minister Alucar, but until the entire scope of the plot unfolded, the transfers didn't make sense."

"The fact remains—"

"The fact remains that there are likely several other

High Holders who have failed to pay full tariffs over the past years because Aevidyr removed them from the tariff rolls. I'm willing to let those High Holders settle with the treasury—with full payment of unpaid tariffs and standard penalties—if . . ." Charyn didn't finish the sentence, but then said, "Under the Codex Legis, willful nonpayment of tariffs in excess of one hundred golds is a high crime. Now, I don't have all the figures I'd like, but over summer and harvest more than a hundred men were executed for causing fires and destruction to factorages. Likely half of them caused less than a hundred golds of damage. I do wonder what the newssheets would make of High Holders committing crimes of far greater financial consequence and not even serving in a workhouse, let alone not being executed."

"Your Grace . . . financial indiscretions and violence aren't the same thing."

"So it's all right for a factor or High Holder to pay a man so little that his family slowly starves . . . and if he gets violent about it, he can be executed, while a High Holder can defraud the treasury of tens of thousands of golds, plot and attempt the assassination of a Rex, and pass on most of his lands to a son who knew it all, but didn't get caught?"

Fhaedyrk took a deep breath. "I feared you might feel this way."

"Let's look at it another way. You and the factors didn't want tariffs to increase, but there weren't enough golds to repair river walls and harbor walls and to build the ships necessary to protect Solidaran merchanters. How many ships were lost because we didn't have the golds to build more ships? How many sailors died just because Laastyn and Ghaermyn—and possibly others—didn't pay their full tariffs?"

"I cannot answer that, Your Grace."

"It will take weeks if not months even before I know, but I do know already that what Laastyn and Ghaermyn owe in back tariffs would have paid to rebuild all the river walls in

L'Excelsis and to have built and fitted at least a half-score first-rate ships of the line. And the tariffs from those factors who aren't on the tariff rolls likely could have accounted for a few more ships."

"You're presenting your efforts as fair to both factors and High Holders, but some High Holders feel that you're slowly trying to destroy all the High Holders. Are you?"

"Fhaedyrk, that's the last thing on my mind. I have every reason to want to keep the High Holders around—the honest ones, that is. I don't think it's unreasonable for me to want to remove those that have shown that two successive generations have wanted to cheat Solidar and assassinate the Rex. I'm not sentencing Laastyrn to death or even taking any property that was in his name. Nor am I casting any of his sisters or his mother out into the street. Those who remain of that lineage will certainly still be comfortable, but they won't be High Holders. As far as Ghaermyn is concerned, there's no doubt there."

"No . . . that is . . . unfortunately . . . clear."

Charyn smiled coldly. "As for High Holders who discover they inadvertently didn't pay full tariffs, I might just consider waiving penalties, most of them, anyway, if *all* the back tariffs are immediately and voluntarily paid. And, over the next year or so, there will be a total revision of the tariff rolls, with complete property registration cross-indexed against the tariff rolls themselves so that such inadvertent omissions will be unlikely in the future. That should make matters much fairer, don't you think?"

Fhaedyrk swallowed. After a long pause, he said, "You've been very much a man of your word, Your Grace. Difficult as some may find it, there is a certain refreshing honesty in that, and most High Holders will appreciate it when they have thought over the matter. Those who cannot appreciate that stern fairness will accept it."

"Given that the alternative is worse?"

Fhaedyrk smiled wryly.

"Some High Holders don't seem to see that the times are changing," added Charyn, "and that if they don't change, they will lose their holdings. I did nothing to cause the times, and they have no one to blame but themselves for not changing with the times. For some, it's more convenient to blame others, whether it's the factors, the workers, or the Rex."

"It's clear you're committed to changing with the times, Your Grace. Will it be enough?"

"Not unless the Council changes as well. That's why I've tried to consult with and work with all of you."

"By imposing martial law?"

"I imposed it at the request of many members of the Council, and I did other things at the same time so that, as best I could, I offered something to each part of Solidar. If the Council has better ideas as how to govern for the best interests of all, I'm more than willing to listen. I'm not terribly interested in doing things that benefit one group at the expense of everyone else."

Fhaedyrk nodded slowly. "I will convey those thoughts to the others on the High Council."

"Oh . . . and one other thing. From here on out, there won't be a High Council. Or a Factors' Council. There will just be a Council. We're all in this together."

"There's always been a High Council."

Charyn shook his head. "There wasn't one at the time of the first Rex Regis and, frankly, the record of the High Council in the last few decades has been anything but exemplary. Or would you contest that?"

"Unlike your predecessors, Your Grace, you are most well-read in history and other matters. I will also convey to the other High Holders on the Council that you are willing to work with us. I'd prefer not to directly agree to the abolition of the High Council."

"So long as you don't meet officially or try to press a direct agenda for just High Holders, I won't officially abolish the High Council."

"Then we agree on that."

"On the terms I laid out. High Holders can still select five members of the Council, one from each region, by whatever method you all agree upon."

"We can work with that." Fhaedyrk's smile was pleasant, with perhaps a hint of warmth. "Did I tell you that you are most unlike any of your more recent predecessors?"

"I hope so. Matters didn't work out so well for them . . . or Solidar." Charyn stood. "I appreciate your forthrightness. We will work things out, although we may not always agree exactly."

"Thank you, again, for seeing me." Fhaedyrk inclined his head, then rose and left the study.

Not until the study door closed did Charyn take a long deep breath. He wasn't looking forward to Meredi's Council meeting, at least not to the part that would follow Alyncya's announcement.

"High Holder Delcoeur has been waiting to see you, Your Grace."

Ferrand? Charyn hadn't known he was coming. "Have him come in."

Ferrand entered the study with a wide smile. "Good afternoon. I think it's afternoon, now."

"I didn't know you were waiting."

"I don't mind. I came totally unannounced. I knew I might have to wait. You're the Rex, and a great deal's happened to you and around you. Was that High Holder Fhaedyrk who just left? He looked somewhat concerned."

"He likely did. I let him know that I'm treating High Holders the same way as factors and workers under the law. I wasn't quite that blunt, but I'm certain he got the message. Ostensibly, it was an appeal for me not to take away Ghaermyn's and Laastyn's High Holdings from their heirs. Laastyn's, really. Fhaedyrk could have cared less about Ghaermyn, I suspect."

"After all they did?"

"You don't know the half of it. Aevidyr schemed to get some of their properties off the tariff rolls something like ten years ago. So they also owed enormous back tariffs . . . and willful and protracted failure to pay tariffs, especially by a High Holder, is a high crime. But you didn't come to hear me talk about that. You look very happy. Kayrolya?"

"I asked last night, and she and her family accepted."

"Congratulations!" Charyn didn't have to feign enthusiasm. "I'm happy for the two of you. I thought it might be coming when I saw you two at the Autumn-Turn Ball. I hope your mother's pleased."

"She is. She likes Kayrolya." Ferrand grinned. "Now she can worry about Lacyara and Vaernya."

"Lacyara's only fifteen."

"That gives her plenty of time to worry. What about you and the Lady-heir Alyncya?"

"She asked me. I accepted. If you'd keep that to yourself until Meredi. That's when she'll announce it to the Council."

"She asked you?"

"Actually, I asked her. She refused me. Then she asked me, and I accepted."

For a moment, Ferrand looked puzzled. Then he nodded. "So she can keep the holding herself?"

"In case we have a daughter, especially."

"But you're the Rex. Do you need—"

"You never know, Ferrand. You never know how long Solidar will need a Rex. Now . . . I think we should go and have some refreshments and celebrate our good fortune." *Or what good fortune there is.*

68

Well before dawn on Mardi morning, Charyn donned formal greens and then made his way down to the official regial coach and the four mounted guards that would accompany him on his way to Army High Command headquarters. In moments, the coach was headed down the lane on the drive to army headquarters some three milles northwest of the Chateau D'Rex.

Some four quints later, the coach approached the guardhouse at the gates in the low wall surrounding what had been a High Holding in the time of the first Rex Regis. Two guards presented arms as the coach slowed to make its way through the gates before heading toward the main building with its sections of lighter-colored stones and masonry in the walls, replacements for damages caused by explosions during the High Holders' revolt.

The coach halted outside the headquarters building, where the Marshal and Subcommander Luerryn stood waiting in the gray before sunrise.

Charyn stepped out. "Marshal." He wasn't about to offer "Good morning" as a greeting.

"Your Grace." Vaelln inclined his head.

"Is it far?"

"Behind the headquarters. No more than fifty yards."

"Then we should go."

"You know, Your Grace, as I wrote you, it isn't necessary . . ." began Vaelln.

"High crimes aren't necessary, either, but since I ordered their death, it's almost the same as though I were the one carrying out the execution. That's why I'm here."

Vaelln paused, as if he might contest that, then asked, "Do you wish to speak to the condemned?"

"They cost me my brother and caused the deaths of other innocents. They would have destroyed Solidar had they been successful. I have nothing to say to them. Nor, as I wrote you, do I wish them to be able to say anything. That also may not be customary, but it is my command."

"That has been arranged as you instructed."

Neither of the officers spoke as the three walked across the stone pavement alongside the building, followed by Dhuncan and another Chateau guard, whose name Charyn couldn't recall at the moment. Ahead of them, a full squad of troopers, all the men wearing black uniforms, was formed up ten feet from the courtyard wall.

Vaelln stopped slightly back and to the left of the squad, as did Luerryn, Charyn, and the two guards. At that moment, Charyn finally recalled the name of the second guard—Dulaak.

The five stood there silently.

Charyn's eyes went to the eastern sky, slowly brightening.

A drumroll began, echoing off the stone wall, and to his right, Charyn could see more troopers in black, a pair escorting each of the condemned men, each prisoner gagged with his hands tied behind him, followed by a single drummer who stopped well short of the squad of troopers. As the drumroll continued, the troopers lined up the five a yard from the section of the wall faced head-high with bales of hay. Laastyn stood at one end, flanked by Laamyst, then Aevidyr, Gherard, and Ghaermyn.

None of the five seemed to notice either the Marshal or the Rex, their eyes on the troopers with rifles.

As the first rays of sun flashed from the eastern horizon, Luerryn called out, "Ready arms!"

Twenty rifles moved into position instantly and precisely. The drumroll stopped.

"Fire!"

In a moment, five men staggered, sagging, then collapsing and toppling to the stone pavement.

Dulaak swayed slightly on his feet.

A short, final drumroll echoed from the wall.

Charyn couldn't say that he felt anything, except that he'd seen it through to the end. *Except it likely won't be the end since the survivors from those families, some of them, anyway, will harbor bitterness and anger.* He just hoped that the example kept that anger in check, as the slaughter at the end of the High Holders' revolt had done.

"Order! Arms!" commanded Luerryn. "To quarters!"

As the firing squad marched away, Charyn saw a cart approaching, one that would take the five bodies to a single pyre, where only a fire tender would watch.

Vaelln turned to Charyn.

"Thank you, Marshal. I hope never to have to do this again." *But you will, if necessary.*

"We all hope that, Your Grace. Your firmness with High Holders may help in other matters."

Charyn just nodded.

The five walked back to the regial coach without further words.

Once there, Charyn turned to Luerryn. "I'd like to thank you as well, Subcommander."

"Your Grace." Luerryn inclined his head.

Charyn returned the gesture, then nodded to Vaelln. "Tomorrow, Marshal."

"Yes, Your Grace."

With that, Charyn stepped up into the coach.

On the ride back, he thought about the five traitors, the five he'd ordered killed . . . and the sixth, the one he'd killed personally. Deaths that were both necessary . . . and senseless.

He wondered how many more High Holders would behave as if the laws didn't apply to them. *Have you set enough of an example?*

He could only hope so.

Three quints later, when Charyn entered the Chateau, he made his way to the breakfast room. He wasn't certain he was even hungry, but he did want some tea.

Karyel and Iryella were seated at the table, finishing their breakfasts.

"Where did you go this morning, sir?" asked Iryella.

"To army headquarters to witness the execution of the traitors," replied Charyn as he sat at the head of the table.

"Why did you go?" asked Karyel. "Didn't you trust the army?"

Iryella rolled her eyes.

Charyn looked squarely at the Ryel heir. "Because I made the decision that these men should die, I should be there to see that decision executed. Too many men order the deaths of others without seeing the results." *Unhappily, some men glory in causing death.* "Too many High Holders think it can't happen to them. So long as I am Rex, there won't be two standards of law, one for those with wealth and power, and another for those with neither." Even as he said the words, he wondered if he were promising too much. *But you have to try.*

Karyel swallowed and looked away.

Therosa appeared and placed a mug of tea before Charyn. "What else would you like, Your Grace."

"Just bread and a small portion of cheesed eggs, thank you."

He sipped the tea.

He thought he could finish the breakfast.

69

When Charyn reached his study on Meredi morning, he discovered that both newssheets had put out special editions covering the executions on Mardi. As he almost always did, Charyn reached for *Veritum* first, reading the lead story warily.

> At sunrise on Mardi morning, five men were executed by firing squad at army headquarters. The five were behind the attempted assassination of Rex Charyn, and included High Holder Laastyn and his younger son Laamyst, High Holder Ghaermyn and his heir Gherard, and the Rex's Minister of Administration, Aevidyr. The other main plotter was the Rex's younger brother Bhayrn, who was killed in the attempted assassination . . .
>
> The regial decree finding the five guilty was reviewed and approved by High Justicer Sullivyr. The decree also revealed that the five had altered tariff records to substantially reduce the tariffs paid by the guilty High Holders . . . and possibly others. The amount of unpaid tariffs go back over eight years, and a fraction of what is owed would have merited the death sentence, although it has been more than a century since anyone has been executed for that crime alone . . .

The *Tableta* story was similar, except for a few lines, which Charyn read with bitter amusement.

> . . . by his decrees of execution, our beloved Rex has at last and at least allowed the hand of Regial justice to fall

almost as heavily on the privileged as it has for so many years on the less fortunate . . . a pity it took almost a year of attempted assassinations to encourage such a result . . .

"The newssheets weren't too bad, were they, sir?" asked Wyllum.

"They're close to what I expected. *Tableta* wasn't quite as hard on me as it has been at times."

"Why do you think they're so hard on you?"

"They're obviously not fond of people of position and wealth and power. As Rex, I have all three, if not as much of any of those as most people think."

Wyllum looked slightly puzzled. "Why do you say that?"

"My wealth and power are in fact limited. Position—that I obviously have. But the fact that it took three years for my father and then me to get a very small increase in tariffs suggests that the power of the factors and the High Holders does restrict what I can do. Also, the attempts on my life point out that I'm anything but invulnerable. The wealth is limited because some of the income from the lands goes to the treasury, and these days, there are more demands on the treasury than available funds."

"I didn't quite think of it that way."

"It's something I have to keep in mind. Speaking of that, do you have the copies of the new tariff appeal process for the councilors?"

"Yes, sir. They're in the folder at the head of the conference table."

"Thank you." Charyn set aside the newssheets and looked again at Vaelln's report. He had barely finished when Alucar arrived.

The Finance Minister placed several sheets on the desk. "Here are the figures on the number of factorages visited and how many of those factorages should have been on the tariff rolls and were not. The figures below are those factorages owned by High Holders. All the High Holder factorages and manufactorages are on the tariff rolls, but the first group shows those that appear to be paying appropriate tariffs, while the second grouping contains those whose tariffs are likely understated. Now . . . all of these are just those in or near L'Excelsis."

"I understand. Would it be your opinion that elsewhere there would be more under-reporting?"

"It would . . . except in Khel. That's for the same reasons I told you the other day."

Charyn read through the figures quickly, and then again, more carefully, before finally saying, "You don't offer any estimates on what additional tariffs will result from more accurate tariff rolls."

"No, sir. Without more information, it would be difficult to be accurate, other than to say that there will likely be some increased tariffs."

"In short, you don't want me to offer some estimated number that may not be accurate because it will reflect badly on you?"

"I don't believe in counting golds until they're in the strong room, Your Grace."

Charyn laughed softly. "And you certainly don't want me doing that."

"No, sir. Another Rex wouldn't value accuracy nearly so much as you do."

The double message of Alucar's words almost brought a smile to Charyn's face. "Then all I'll say is that more accurate tariff records are bound to increase the amount collected in years to come, but by how much remains to be seen. That's safe enough. Is there anything else?"

"Not at the moment."

"Then we'll talk later."

When Alucar left, Charyn turned his attention to studying the material the Finance Minister had left. When he finished he leaned back in his chair, fingering the exchange pin in his pocket. He'd put it there when he dressed, thinking it might be helpful at the Council meeting, although he couldn't have said why.

Almost exactly as the chimes began to ring out the ten bells of noon, Moencriff announced, "Lady-heir D'Shendael, Your Grace."

"Do you wish me to leave?" asked Wyllum.

"Not yet." Charyn then called out, "Have her come in."

Almost before he finished speaking, the door opened, and Alyncya entered in a pale teal jacket, with matching trousers and scarf, and also wearing, as she often did, Charyn suspected, a cream blouse. Her dress boots were also teal.

Charyn nodded as he stood from behind the table desk. *Perfect!*

Alyncya looked to the scrivener. "It's good to see you again, Wyllum."

"You'll be seeing more of each other. In time, you will also likely need his services."

Wyllum's eyes widened.

"It hasn't been formally announced," added Charyn, "but that will happen this afternoon. Do you think you can keep it to yourself until then?"

"Yes, sir . . . Lady-heir."

"Good. Now . . . if you wouldn't mind telling Lady Chelia that Alyncya is here, and that you're at my mother's service until after the Council meeting."

"Yes, sir."

Alyncya smiled. "And . . . Wyllum, you can talk about the announcement with Lady Chelia. She already knows."

"Thank you, Lady-heir." Wyllum grinned, then turned and hurried off.

"He's sweet, isn't he?" asked Alyncya after the study door closed.

"He works hard, always tries to do better, and is very dependable."

"How did you find him?"

"I didn't. I asked Maitre Alastar for someone from Imagisle who wasn't an imager who could be my personal scrivener."

"You've relied on him and Alyna a great deal."

"They're more likely to have my best interests, and those of Solidar, at heart than anyone but you, Mother, and Aloryana."

"They will so long as your interests are those of Solidar."

"That's true enough, but I don't see me surviving as Rex if my interests aren't close to what's best for Solidar." Charyn paused, then added, "And if I don't survive as Rex, then one of our children will have to be Rex, rather than a very well-off High Holder."

"You're very serious about that."

"Only with you. It will take much longer with others." *Decades, and that's if you survive that long, which didn't happen with either Father or Grandsire.*

"Then we'd better make sure everyone knows your interests are those of all Solidar," said Alyncya solemnly, except with the last word, she started to giggle, then shook her head.

"Obviously," said Charyn dryly, "I'm taking myself far too seriously."

"A little, perhaps."

Charyn shook his head, then said, "You are staying for dinner."

"You've told me that twice."

"Alyna, Alastar, and Mother will be joining us."

"You didn't mention Alyna."

"That was Mother's idea." It had been Charyn's as well, but he didn't see any reason to mention that. "So Alastar and I will be outnumbered."

"I doubt you two will ever be outnumbered." Alyncya smiled sweetly.

A quint before first glass, Alastar arrived, followed shortly by Vaelln, who looked momentarily surprised to see Alyncya.

"Lady-heir Alyncya D'Shendael will be making a brief announcement to open the Council meeting," said Charyn. "It's a requirement for a lady-heir who wishes to hold her bloodright to bequeath as she wishes."

"It's also rather rare," added Alastar. "So we'll all be part of something historic."

"Then we'll move on to the more usual matters for a council to consider," said Charyn, "beginning with your briefing the Council on the situation with Jariola. Have there been any surprises since the report I received on Lundi?"

"There was a severe storm off Jariola a little more than a week ago. One second-rater and one frigate suffered severe damage to their rigging and are proceeding to the Abierto Isles for refitting. The repairs may cost as much as a thousand golds and will take more than a month."

Charyn winced. *Just as you think things are getting better.*

"We're also having trouble in obtaining enough rope of quality for lines. We used to get some from Stakanar, but rope isn't that high-value a cargo, and with the privateers . . ."

"The price of rope is going up?" asked Charyn.

Vaelln nodded. "Marshal Tynan is doing what he can, but there's a limit."

"Are the costs of oak or fir going up as well?"

"Some factors think they might. There's word that some High Holders have been buying prime timberlands where they can obtain them cheaply."

Charyn could have said more, but just nodded. "Mention the storm, but not the rope problem. If it gets worse, we'll take that up at the next meeting." There were going to be enough contentious matters for the day's meeting as it was.

"The councilors are all here," declared Moencriff.

"Have them come in." Charyn moved to stand beside the head of the conference table, with Alyncya beside him, while Alastar and Vaelln stood before their chairs as the council filed in.

Every single councilor immediately looked to Alyncya, then to Charyn. Hisario smothered a smile. The others were either impassive, or, in the case of Eshmael, clearly puzzled.

Charyn and Alyncya remained standing as the others seated themselves.

"The first matter before the Council is an announcement by Lady-heir Alyncya D'Shendael." Charyn nodded to her.

"As a matter of public record," Alyncya said firmly and distinctly, "I'm pleased to announce that I asked Charyn D'Rex to be my husband and that he accepted my proposal."

"I very gladly accepted," said Charyn. "And because what has just happened is very rare, I will explain. For a lady-heir to be absolutely certain of retaining the rights to her inheritance, she must be the one to propose and announcement of that proposal must be made before the Rex or, if she proposes to the Rex, before the High Council."

"The High Council is pleased to witness the announcement," declared Fhaedyrk, "and we wish you both the very best."

Both Charyn and Alyncya inclined their heads to those at the table, and then Charyn escorted her to the door, glad that she would be staying at the Chateau for a time after the Council meeting. When he returned, he seated himself at the head of the table.

"That was something all of you should remember," said Fhaedyrk. "It has happened only a handful of times in Solidaran history, only once with the regial heir, and never with the Rex."

A wry smile followed. "We are certain to see more memorable moments in the months and years ahead, some perhaps not so joyful."

"Now, we'll hear from Marshal Vaelln," announced Charyn.

As soon as Vaelln finished his brief report, Chaeltar spoke up. "With all the bad weather around Jariola, why can't you move more warships to protect our ships trading with the countries of Otelyrn?"

"That would allow more Jariolan warships to leave their ports and also sail to Otelyrn," replied Vaelln patiently. "That would cost us even more merchanters. We have much of their fleet blocked in their own ports because they know that every time they engage us, they lose more ships than we do."

"So our merchanters have to pay the price?" snorted Chaeltar.

"I believe what the Marshal said, High Holder," replied Hisario, "was that if he removes the ships around Jariola our merchanters will pay twice the price they are now. As one of those shippers, I prefer the lower of two costs."

Charyn managed not to smile at the slight hint of condescension in Hisario's voice. "Are there any other questions about Jariola for Marshal Vaelln?" He looked down the table.

"Not about Jariola," snapped Eshmael, "but about when you're going to lift martial law and when the army is going to stop supporting the harassment of factors and even High Holders by the clerks of the Finance Minister."

"Marshal Vaelln and I have discussed the lifting of martial law within a short time. If the streets continue without trouble, I'd like to suggest that Solayi the twenty-second be the last night of army patrols." Charyn looked to the Marshal.

"That would seem reasonable if matters remain calm."

"Fine!" declared Eshmael, his voice loud and penetrating as he continued. "What about the harassment? When will that stop?"

"You mean," drawled High Holder Khunthan, "that you factors don't like the idea of paying your fair share of tariffs now that the Rex has discovered that many of you aren't paying any at all?"

Charyn refrained from smiling as he silently thanked Khunthan.

"And you High Holders are any better?" sneered Eshmael.

"Would any of your factors like to pay the same price that High Holder Laastyn and High Holder Ghaermyn did?" asked Charyn. "I'm not even asking the untariffed factors to pay penalties, only to start paying the tariffs High Holders and other factors do. What you're suggesting would let them continue not to pay tariffs. Besides being against the law, is that fair?"

"I don't like the way you went about it," replied Eshmael sullenly.

"There wasn't any other way to do it. For the information of all councilors, as of last night, over the last ten days, the clerks of the Finance Ministry, accompanied by army troopers, have visited three hundred and sixty-seven factorages in and around L'Excelsis. Initial indications are that fifty-five were paying less in tariffs than they should be paying, and forty-one were paying no tariffs at all. Tell me, Factor Eshmael, what does that say about factors?"

"What do you mean that there were indications? That could mean anything at all."

"Forty-one factorages were of the size that requires tariffs and were not on the tariff rolls. Fifty-five were of a size that normally pays more than the minimum, but were only paying the minimum. The troopers didn't break down doors," said Charyn. "All they did was to make sure that the clerks could check to see if a factorage was on the list, and if it wasn't, to ask the factor either to present proof of paying tariffs, in case there were mistakes. They estimated the tariffs that might be due, and presented the estimates to the factor, requesting that, if the estimates were incorrect, to provide proof that they should be lower. The army troopers were there so that the clerks didn't get hurt. We may reduce the number of troopers accompanying the clerks, that is, if you factors can assure us of the clerks' safety." Charyn looked first to Eshmael, then to Hisario.

Eshmael was silent.

Hisario cleared his throat. "I would suggest that you maintain the same number of troopers for the next week or so to allow the factors to spread the word . . . and to point out that, compared to what punishment the Rex levied on the High Holders, he is being eminently reasonable."

"At the suggestion of the Council," added Charyn, "so that Solidar may adopt a fairer and more equitable tariff system over the next few years."

Several puzzled looks followed Charyn's words, but before he had a chance to explain Chaeltar spoke out loudly.

"You see! We've contended all along that the factors were underpaying."

"As the investigation into Laastyn and Ghaermyn indicated, there are also likely a number of High Holders underpaying, but at least they're all paying something."

"How do you know that?" demanded Eshmael.

"Most of the High Holds are known and have been known for years. We have years of tariff records. Factorages and manufactorages are cropping up every week."

"If you're going to audit factorages," said Hisario mildly . . .

"*After* we deal with the gross negligence on the part of factorages, then we'll be looking at everyone's underpayments." Charyn smiled. "Minister Alucar is setting up a permanent part of the Finance Ministry that will continue audits. They'll also investigate complaints about either factors or High Holders not paying tariffs. Some of the better-qualified army units will become tariff police."

"That's not fair . . ." protested Basalyt.

"Both High Holders and factors have taken advantage of past regial sloppiness, but once the initial round of audits is complete, which will likely take two years, and even while that round of audits is taking place, any complaint about the audits can be brought before this Council. It must be brought personally by the High Holder or the factor, and I will abide by the Council's majority decision about the amount of tariff due." Charyn knew that was a slight risk, but the Council needed some voice, especially with what he eventually had in mind.

Hisario frowned. "Will you put that in writing?"

"I already have." Charyn took the sheets from the folder and handed half to Fhaedyrk and half to Hisario. "If you'd hand this out so that everyone can read them."

The first to speak was Thalmyn. "Isn't this just an excuse for higher tariffs?"

"No," replied Charyn. "Those already paying tariffs will see no increase in the rate, and it's likely that there won't be a need to increase tariffs for a much longer time. Also, I've already stipulated that the lands and properties reverted to the Rex by the decrees involving the traitors will not become part of the regial holdings, but will be held by the treasury and sold as soon as practicable without significant loss to their value. The golds received will go into the treasury reserves. That will allow us to have the ability to pay for things like repairing the river and harbor walls and roads and bridges damaged by floods."

"You didn't take everything, did you?" asked Basalyt querulously.

"Laastyn had already transferred significant property to his heir. I exempted the large river estate and some lands to provide for the former Lady Laastyn. I left one large manufactorage for the Ghaermyn family. Aevidyr had comparatively less property, and I left enough to provide for his wife and children."

"But you took the High Holders' positions," rejoined Basalyt.

"They seduced my brother into getting himself killed, and they cost Solidar something like forty thousand golds.

Had they succeeded in killing me, it's likely that there would have been far greater losses to everyone."

"There likely would have been an attempt to restore all ancient privileges to High Holders," said Alastar quietly, but firmly. "That would have created great unrest, most likely a civil war of some sort."

"They planned that?" asked Harll, the usually silent stone factor from Liantiago.

"That would have been the aim," said Calkoran. "Laastyn was quite vocal about putting factors back in their place, as he put it. He and Ghaermyn have been quite close lately."

"If you'd finish reading the sheets," suggested Charyn once more.

Chaeltar was the first to finish reading and respond. "This effectively makes Maitre Alastar a part of the Council."

"I said that I wouldn't be a part of audit decisions. If the five factors vote one way, and the five High Holders vote the other way, who else would you have make the decision?"

After looking up and down the table, Chaeltar finally said, "He'd likely back you."

"If you look at what's happened over the last fifteen years, the Collegium has opposed the Rex more often than it's supported him."

Surprisingly, both Hisario and Fhaedyrk nodded, and Khunthan said, "The Rex is correct about that. The Collegium has also likely acted against the Rex on a few occasions."

"I suppose that's the best we can hope for," said Chaeltar.

"The Rex has said this before," replied Alastar, "but he has been trying to provide the High Holders and the factors a greater role in government. With this provision," Alastar lifted the sheet, "he's given you a tool to oppose any unfair or exorbitant tariffing of either a factor or a High Holder. If I'm not mistaken, that's a solid step toward increasing your role in governing Solidar."

"He's still Rex," muttered Chaeltar.

"Useful change comes slowly," said Fhaedyrk. "Rapid change brings chaos and violence."

"There's still this business about the ironworks," said Eshmael sourly. "How do you expect us to take your buying an ironworks?"

Basalyt and Chaeltar both frowned. Calkoran smiled faintly.

"I bought the ironworks with funds raised from lands personally gifted to me before I became Rex. I also became a member of the commodity exchange at that time as Factor Suyrien D'Chaeryll."

A faint smile crossed Alastar's face.

"The reason for this was so that I could continue supporting the work of Engineer Paersyt, who has recently completed testing of a steam-powered boat propelled by a new steam engine and a unique water screw. The engine looks to be very promising as both a way to propel ships in addition to sail or even without sails and possibly even to power manufactorages without the need to locate them near water."

"The engine has actually been tested?" asked Hisario.

"A number of times. I saw it travel from the west river piers upstream to the Sud Bridge and back to the piers. He has since improved it and is working on creating a version large enough to power a frigate."

For several moments, the councilors were silent.

Then Hisario spoke. "I can't speak for anyone else, but for years I've heard nothing but complaints about Rexes who never listened and never did anything. We now have one who clearly listens. He's obviously trying to be fair to everyone, and he's giving us a voice. He's even paying out of his own pocket to produce something that will benefit all of us . . . yet he's been the target of more assassination attempts in less time than any Rex in history. They've all been by people who didn't want change. Whether we like it or not, we've got to deal with change, and we have a Rex who's willing to work with us, if we'll work with him. I'm not saying we'll always agree on everything, but we have a chance to work things out without another uprising or another revolt. We ought to try that for once. That's my view, anyway."

"You were really a member of the exchange?" asked Eshmael.

Charyn fumbled for a moment, then extracted the exchange pin and held it up.

Eshmael just shook his head.

"You've got a Rex who's a factor, Eshmael," declared Chaeltar. "Isn't that enough for now?"

"Practically speaking," said Alastar, "Charyn is both a High Holder and a factor, and with a sister who's an imager, I can't imagine a Rex better suited to work with everyone."

"On behalf of the High Council," added Fhaedyrk, "I can't imagine that we'll ever see a Rex better qualified to get us through the changes ahead."

"I agree," added Hisario, "especially if you'll sign and seal that paper you just passed around."

"I can do that right now," agreed Charyn, standing and walking back to his desk, where he sat down, and signed, awkwardly, the copy he had, then sealed it. He walked back to the conference table and laid the sealed declaration faceup on the polished wood, knowing that he'd taken the first irrevocable step toward reducing his own power.

70

Charyn stood at the sitting-room window and looked through the ice-rimmed pane out at the cold twilight sky of the last evening of a very long year. His eyes moved from the golden orb of Artiema well above L'Excelsis to the east to the small disc of Erion barely above the eastern horizon. *The hunter still pursuing the goddess of life and love.*

He turned and waited, wearing the close-fitting jacket of regial green, trimmed in silver, with silver buckles, the pale green shirt and black cravat, and black trousers. Using a right hand with several fingers still stiffer than he would have liked, he adjusted the gold-edged deep green formal sash that signified he was the Rex Regis of Solidar—the same sash he'd worn to the Year-Turn Ball a year earlier, and, earlier in the day, to a special and very private ceremony for family and the closest of friends.

He smiled as Alyncya stepped out from the dressing room, wearing a gown of regial green, but one trimmed in Shendael blue, edged with the slimmest of cream piping.

"How do you feel about this Year-Turn Ball?" asked Charyn mischievously.

"Less concerned than the last one. I've already told you that I was worried that you would ask me to dance and even more afraid that you wouldn't."

"I know, but I like to hear it."

"You don't have to take notes anymore."

"I won't have to pose questions either, like . . .

> *'Will then you choose love chaste or fierce desire,*
> *The ice of purity or heat of my desire?'"*

"But I like it when you do."

"Now," he answered with a smile.

"Even then. You just had to look for the answer."

He took her hand. "We should go and meet Mother. You look lovely, and every High Holder will want to dance with you."

"Most of my dances are saved for a Factor Suyrien D'Chaeryll."

And that was fine with Charyn.

EPILOGUE

Yesterday, at the Anomen D'Rex and throughout Solidar, thousands mourned the death of the last Rex of Solidar, Charyn, Rex Regis. In doing so, they also celebrated the life of a remarkable man and ruler, who began, at an age when most rulers strive to amass power, to reduce the power of the Chateau D'Rex and to transfer power gradually to the Council, eliminating the position of Rex at his death, and transferring what powers remained to the head of the Council. He also paid to develop the Paersyt steam engines that have become the backbone of the Solidaran navy and merchant fleets.

Young as he was then, some fifty-two years ago Rex Charyn began by forcing the factors to create a Solidaran Council of Factors and later by merging that Council with the High Council under his leadership, adding in craftmasters, the Maitre of the Collegium Imago, and the Marshal of the Army as councilors . . .

Rex Charyn and his late wife, Alyncya, former High Holder D'Shendael in her own right, are survived by their son, Suyrien D'Alte, and by their daughter, Loryancya, Shendael D'Alte. Rex Charyn's sister, Aloryana, who served as Senior Imager of the Collegium Imago, preceded him in death by only a month.

Tableta
16 Avryl 458 A.L.

Turn the page for a preview of

L. E. Modesitt, Jr.'s

THE MONGREL MAGE

THE SAGA OF RECLUCE

1

As Beltur walked along the stone walk on the south side of the causeway extending from the gates to the city, he glanced down at young Scanlon, walking beside him, half wishing he hadn't needed to bring the boy with him, but there was no help for that, not if he wanted to keep the burnet he was seeking from spoiling too soon. Satisfied that the ten-year-old was having no trouble keeping pace, Beltur studied the low-lying fields that stretched almost a kay eastward from the main gates of Fenard before reaching the outer walls. Supposedly, the water gates in the outer walls and levees could be opened to allow the river, such as it was, to flood the fields, making them impassable to an armed force.

The only problem, reflected Beltur, was that much of the time, the Anard River was little more than a stream, unlike the River Gallos, into which it flowed all too many kays to the northeast. He'd never quite understood how a cubit or two of water over the paved causeway and the fields would be much of a deterrent to a determined army, but then no one had asked him, and it was unlikely anyone who mattered would, or that they'd listen to a third-rate mage.

In the meantime, he needed to see if he could find enough burnet—just because Salcer hadn't gathered enough before he'd left, and there was no one else to gather it. *Not that the great white mage Kaerylt could be bothered, nor even Sydon.* Beltur swallowed his resentment, if he dared to do otherwise, especially given that Kaerylt was not only a powerful mage, but also his uncle and the only one standing between Beltur and his possible conscription as a battle mage for the Prefect's army. The very fact that the Prefect needed so much burnet meant trouble, since his principal use for it was as the main ingredient in a balm used to stop blood loss, and stockpiling the ingredients for that balm was a good indication that someone anticipated significant losses of blood.

As for Kaerylt getting the burnet himself, well, if Beltur were to be fair, he had to admit that it wouldn't have been the best idea to let his uncle or even Sydon anywhere near herbs, given that they both carried so much chaos that their touch would wilt the herbs largely to uselessness. *But then, while yours has much less chaos, you still carry enough to spoil the herbs.* It would just take longer, Beltur knew. Which was why Scanlon was accompanying him to the old herbalist's gardens.

Beltur took a deep breath and kept walking, thinking of the old rhyme.

> *Blood from the blade, screams in the night,*
> *Bind him with burnet, in dark or in light,*
> *So blood doesn't flow*
> *And order won't go.*

Although it was early morning, with the sun barely above the low rolling hills farther to the east, Beltur had not only to squint against the light, but to blot his forehead. The summer day was going to be hot, as were most of the days leading to harvest, and the stillness of the air made it seem even warmer than it was. He had no doubt that he'd be soaked through with sweat by the time he and Scanlon returned, since Arylla's cottage and gardens were more than a kay from the nearest gate in the outer walls.

"Why couldn't we have hired a cart, ser?" asked Scanlon.

"Carts and horses cost silvers. Walking doesn't. If you want your coppers, don't complain."

"Yes, ser." Scanlon shifted the empty cloth bag from one shoulder to the other.

Roughly a half glass later, after walking from the outer gates along the wall, Beltur rapped on the weathered door of the small cottage, whose gardens spread behind it under the old outer wall of Fenard. The gardens contained no trees. By edict of the Prefect, no trees were permitted within half a kay of the wall, despite the fact that all that lay between the outer walls and the city walls were fields and pastures.

The door opened, and a wiry woman stood there, wearing brown trousers and a patched brown tunic. Beneath short brown hair strewn with occasional gray, black eyes focused skeptically on Beltur, looking up at him just slightly, not exactly a surprise because Beltur was somewhat on the short side, and more than a head shorter than his uncle.

"Good morning, Arylla," offered Beltur with a cheer he did not entirely feel.

Arylla looked sourly at Beltur, then at Scanlon. She shook her head. "Brinn or burnet?"

"Burnet."

"Makes no sense to me why Prefect Denardre put a white mage in charge of making balms."

"You know as well as I do, Arylla." *Because the few healers in Fenard wouldn't.* "You won't do it, either."

"I could, but knowing why he wants it, I wouldn't sleep for days." She stepped back and motioned for the two to enter the cottage, then closed the door behind them, turning and walking toward a narrow doorway at the rear of the cottage.

"That doesn't make sense to me," Beltur replied. "You aren't even a healer. Besides, how can making something that can save a man's life be chaotic?"

Arylla stopped, her hand on the latch to the rear door. "War is chaos, especially if you don't have to fight. It's not like the Marshal or the Tyrant are ever going to attack Gallos. Or even the Viscount for all his talk. As for those traders from Spidlar, they hate war. Bad for trade, they say. Anyway, I've only got enough left for one bag."

"You have more than that," pressed Beltur.

"I do. You take that, and there won't be any come next summer."

He could sense the truth of her words, and that meant Kaerylt wouldn't be happy. But then, his uncle was seldom happy, and when he was, it wasn't for long, or so it seemed to Beltur.

"You have a bag for me to put the leaves in?"

"Scanlon, give her the bag."

"You haven't touched the bag, have you, Beltur?"

"No, and it hasn't been near Kaerylt, either."

"That'd be some small help. Wait here." She paused after opening the door. "And I'd thank you not to touch anything." Then she stepped outside, leaving the door half open.

As he waited, Beltur was glad they were inside, because the cottage was cooler than outside, if not by much, and they were out of the sun.

"She never lets us go with her," said Scanlon.

"No. Herbalists are like that." Except Beltur knew that Arylla had no problem with Scanlon, just with Beltur. She was protective of her plants and bushes. He couldn't blame her.

"Brinn costs more, doesn't it?"

"Usually."

"Why doesn't Mage Kaerylt want more of it?"

"It's not what he wants. It's what the Prefect wants." And burnet was easier to grow or find than brinn, and a great deal less expensive. "The Prefect most likely has all the brinn he needs." *Enough for his officers, at least.*

Scanlon did not ask any more questions.

Beltur waited and watched as Arylla cut the burnet, easing the long leaves with their ragged-looking edges into the bag. Despite her deft movements, the wait seemed to stretch into what seemed to be almost a glass, but was undoubtedly only a fraction of that, before Beltur could see Arylla returning. He stood back as the herbalist reentered the cottage and closed the rear door.

She handed the bag, seemingly slightly more than half full, to Scanlon, then looked to Beltur. "Half a silver, and a bargain at that. You got more than half a bag."

Beltur extended the five coppers. "Thank you."

"Still doesn't make any sense to me," murmured the herbalist, shaking her head, then adding in a louder voice, "You'd best be on your way. It won't get any cooler if you wait."

In moments, Beltur and Scanlon were walking back along the dusty road that paralleled the outer wall, puffs of dust rising from the mage's white boots with each step he took. He was careful to keep enough distance from Scanlon so that he wouldn't inadvertently brush the bag of burnet. The last thing he wanted was for anything to happen to the burnet, because his uncle would immediately blame him.

When the two of them reached the open gates of the outer wall, one of the guards in the black uniform and leathers of Gallos looked at Beltur. "What's in the bag, Mage?"

"Burnet. It's an herb for healing." When the guard looked skeptical, Beltur said to Scanlon, "Open the bag a little and show the guard."

"Don't bother."

The other guard frowned. "Why the boy? The bag's not that heavy."

"Chaos wilts the herbs, and they won't stop the bleeding as well."

The second guard waved them through.

The causeway was even hotter than the road outside the walls had been, and Beltur blotted his forehead again. He hated to think what the city proper would be like by late afternoon.

Unlike the guards at the outer gates, neither of the two at the inner gates gave more than a glance to Beltur and Scanlon, perhaps because they were more interested in a peddler and his cart, and the young woman with him. Once inside the walls, Beltur glanced up at the clear greenish-blue sky, then dropped his eyes to the ancient stones of the old city wall, a wall that supposedly dated back to the time of Fenardre the Great. Certainly, he could sense the age, with the random chaos that coated the old ordered stone blocks of the wall.

With a small sigh, he turned his steps toward the Great Square, well beyond which was the stone dwelling he shared with his uncle and Sydon, Kaerylt's main assistant, and also a much stronger mage than Beltur. Then he adjusted his heavy off-white tunic, almost wishing that he didn't have to wear it, because of the early heat of the day, and because it led people to think that he was a more powerful mage than he really was, as opposed to the weak white wizard he was. *Who can sense and use a small amount of order as well.* Then again, the white tunic did mean that he was less likely to be the victim of a cutpurse or other less savory types.

From somewhere drifted the acridness of burning wood and the more enticing aroma of fowl roasting. For a moment, he thought that it was too early for that . . . except it was already midmorning, and whoever was roasting the bird or birds wanted to have them ready by noon.

Beltur could feel his entire body tightening, the way he felt when there was a concentration of chaos somewhere nearby. He kept walking, slowly looking across the Great Square, taking in the various peddlers and their carts and stalls. His eyes paused at a stall that featured all manner of blades, mainly knives, but he realized that was because one of the older blades, an ancient cupridium shortsword of some sort, seemed to contain chaos. *For use against ordermages?* Pushing that thought aside, he kept searching, both with his eyes and senses, past a vendor with a rack of scarves, whose voice carried across the square.

"The finest in Hamorian shimmersilk scarves, all the way from Cigoerne . . . the very finest!"

"Perhaps the finest since the vanished silks of Cyad, if that," murmured Beltur to himself, as he continued to seek out the source of chaos, his eyes going beyond the silks peddler to a heavyset man with a cart piled high with melons of at least two types, who was so ordered that he couldn't possibly be the source of the chaos. Nor would a mage with that much chaos be comfortable for long near the grower.

Beltur glanced back over his shoulder and saw no one, but he could definitely sense the chaos several yards behind him, which meant that the mage was holding a concealment. The unseen mage was also fairly close. Wondering whether the mage was just moving across the square without wanting to be seen, or if he just might possibly be following them, although Beltur couldn't imagine why anyone that powerful would follow him, he said to Scanlon, "This way," and then turned to his right, away from the scarf vendor and between the stall with the knives and another stall where a wizened woman in gray was setting out cloth bags that looked to be herbal or fragrance sachets, not that Beltur could smell the fragrances amid the heavier odors of fowl and bodies.

Scanlon glared at Beltur for a moment, but kept pace with the mage.

After passing several rows of vendors, Beltur changed direction again, back toward the north side of the square and the side street that would lead to the old stone dwelling where he studied and lived under Kaerylt's sufferance—and largely did his uncle's bidding. Unhappily, the concealed chaos mage remained behind him, if slighter farther back, but still fairly close. That wasn't surprising, given that Beltur was a weak white who didn't hold that much free chaos near him, and most whites sought out chaos in sensing, possibly because many strong whites were practically order-blind. Given the power and the amount of chaos Beltur sensed around the other, there really wasn't too much else that he could do except continue on . . . and raise his feeble shields if it appeared that the mage following them was going to attack.

Still worrying, Beltur and Scanlon turned onto the street that led home, or the only place Beltur could have called home in the ten years since his father's death, since Beltur had no other relatives. He tried to stay on the east side, where there was still some shade. The street had no real name, but everyone called it Nothing Lane, because unlike Joiners Lane, Coopersgate, Baggersway, or Silver Street, there was no particular shop or occupation represented along its narrow way, among them a small inn with a sign proclaiming it was the Brass Bowl, even though most regulars called the public room the "yellow bucket," a cloth merchant, a fuller's shop, and a number of narrow dwellings including that of Kaerylt, although his could have been said to be on Middle Street as well, since it was on the corner of Middle and Nothing.

Kaerylt hadn't been pleased the one time that Beltur had referred to its location as "half-nothing."

Strangely, after Beltur and Scanlon had gone two blocks toward Middle, still two blocks from home, the other mage had stopped, then turned back toward the Great Square. Beltur wasn't sure what that meant, but he was glad the man hadn't kept following them. He blotted his forehead again. Even so, sweat was still running down the side of his narrow face and into his eyes. He took a slow deep breath and kept walking.

As the two neared the end of the second block, Beltur found he wasn't sweating as heavily. He was sure the shade helped, but he had been worried about the mage who had been seemingly trailing him. When he reached the heavy oak door, just one step above the uneven bricks of the sidewalk, he paused, then took out the heavy brass key and unlocked the door. The lock was heavy and crude, but it kept out casual thieves. Even Beltur could muster enough chaos to take care of those who were less casual, and Kaerylt never left traces—except ash—of those who were foolish enough to enter.

Once inside, he just slid the lock bolt, and blotted his forehead again. At least the stone house was cooler than outside, and would remain so until late afternoon, perhaps even longer. He motioned for Scanlon to lead the way to the storeroom, then followed, stopping outside the locked outer door. He used a touch of order to shift the stored chaos from the lock to the sealed cupridium box fastened to the rear of the door, then unlocked the door and opened it, stepping back and turning to the boy. "You know what to do."

"Yes, ser." Scanlon stepped forward and opened the second door, revealing the thin sheet of iron attached to the back side, moved forward.

Beltur watched from the hallway as Scanlon put the bag on the second shelf, beside several others there, then stepped back and closed the inner door on the small storeroom, the one place in the house that neither Beltur nor Kaerylt ever entered, unlike the larger storeroom and work spaces farther back in the house. Although the larger storeroom was also locked in the same fashion, a double door was not required.

After Beltur closed and locked the outer door to the small storeroom, replacing the chaos, Scanlon looked to Beltur, with a trace of a grin. "Do I get my coppers, now?"

"When we get to your house. Not until. The same as always."

"Mother will take them." Scanlon offered a mournful expression. "She always does."

"We'll see." Beltur hid a smile.

The two made their way from the building that was both dwelling and workplace back out onto Nothing Lane, crossing Middle Street, and hurrying slightly to avoid a dray being driven too fast by a young-looking teamster, before entering the fourth door on the east side of the lane, over which was a signboard of sorts that displayed two baskets, rather the halves of two baskets, because displaying a complete basket would have been an invitation to theft as soon as it was completely dark.

In the small room behind the door stood a sturdy dark-haired woman with a worried face, concentrating on weaving osier shoots into a small basket. She looked up.

"We're back, Therala."

Therala looked to her son. "Were you good?"

"He was quite good." Beltur nodded, then extracted the three coppers from his wallet and handed two of them to Scanlon, keeping the third hidden.

In turn, Therala held out her hand.

With a grimace and a sigh, Scanlon handed the coins to his mother.

"Your father needs help with the osier shoots."

"I'll go with him," said Beltur. "I need to ask Zandyl about a basket-weave belt."

"He doesn't like to make those." Therala shrugged. "Talk to him if you want."

"It can't hurt." Beltur managed a rueful smile, then turned to follow Scanlon, who trudged toward the rear workroom. Just before they reached the archway into the workroom, Beltur slipped the last copper into Scanlon's hand, murmuring, "Not a word."

The boy managed not to grin, then said to the man at the workbench, "Ma said you needed me."

"About—" Zandyl broke off his words as he looked up and saw Beltur. "Didn't know you were here, Mage."

"Therala said you weren't too keen on doing woven belts."

"Basket-weave anything for the right price."

"I thought a woven belt might last longer than a leather one."

"It true that you mages are hard on garments?"

"Some are harder than others. How much might a belt cost?"

"Half a silver."

Beltur nodded. "I'll have to think about it."

"Think too long, and it might cost more."

Beltur grinned. "Can't say that surprises me." He looked to Scanlon. "Thank you, again."

Then he turned and headed back toward the front room. Therala barely looked up as he let himself out and began to walk back home.

He still couldn't help but wonder why a powerful white mage had been holding a concealment in the Great Square . . . and why the man had followed him and Scanlon for two blocks from the square before turning away.

Did he think you were someone else?

Why else would anyone follow a third-rate white mage?

Beltur certainly couldn't think of any other reason.

In the meantime, he intended to clean up the main workroom, something that Sydon and Kaerylt felt was beneath them.

TOR BOOKS BY L. E. MODESITT, Jr.

THE ECOLITAN MATTER

Empire & Ecolitan
(comprising *The Ecolitan Operation* and
The Ecologic Secession)

Ecolitan Prime
(comprising *The Ecologic Envoy* and
The Ecolitan Enigma)

THE GHOST BOOKS

Of Tangible Ghosts

The Ghost of the Revelator

Ghost of the White Nights

Ghosts of Columbia
(comprising *Of Tangible Ghosts* and
The Ghost of the Revelator)

OTHER WORKS

The Forever Hero
(comprising *Dawn for a Distant Earth,*
The Silent Warrior, and *In Endless Twilight*)

Timegods' World
(comprising *Timediver's Dawn* and *The Timegod*)

The Hammer of Darkness	*Flash*
The Green Progression	*The Eternity Artifact*
The Parafaith War	*The Elysium Commission*
Adiamante	*Viewpoints Critical*
Gravity Dreams	*Haze*
The Octagonal Raven	*Empress of Eternity*
Archform: Beauty	*The One-Eyed Man*
The Ethos Effect	*Solar Express*